PELICAN

THE NEW PELICAN GUIDE TO ENGLISH LITERATURE

I

PART ONE

# MEDIEVAL LITERATURE: CHAUCER
# AND THE ALLITERATIVE TRADITION

## THE EDITOR

Boris Ford read English at Cambridge before the war. He then spent six years in the Army Education Corps, being finally in command of a residential School of Artistic Studies. On leaving the Army, he joined the staff of the newly formed Bureau of Current Affairs and graduated to be its Chief Editor and in the end its Director. When the Bureau closed down at the end of 1951, he joined the Secretariat of the United Nations in New York and Geneva. On returning to England in the autumn of 1953, he was appointed Secretary of a national inquiry into the problem of providing a humane liberal education for people undergoing technical and professional training.

Boris Ford then became Editor of the *Journal of Education*, until it ceased publication in 1958, and also the first Head of School Broadcasting with independent television. From 1958 he was Education Secretary at the Cambridge University Press, and then in 1960 he was appointed Professor of Education and Director of the Institute of Education at Sheffield University. He moved to the new University of Sussex in 1963 as Dean of Cultural and Community Studies, and later became Chairman of Education. Since 1973 he has been Professor of Education at the University of Bristol. Boris Ford has been editor of *Universities Quarterly* since 1955. He also edited *Young Writers, Young Readers*.

# Medieval Literature: Chaucer and the Alliterative Tradition

VOLUME

I

PART ONE
OF THE NEW PELICAN GUIDE TO ENGLISH
LITERATURE

EDITED BY BORIS FORD

*With an Anthology of Medieval
Poems and Drama*

PENGUIN BOOKS

Penguin Books Ltd, Harmondsworth, Middlesex, England
Penguin Books, 625 Madison Avenue, New York, New York 10022, U.S.A.
Penguin Books Australia Ltd, Ringwood, Victoria, Australia
Penguin Books Canada Ltd, 2801 John Street, Markham, Ontario, Canada L3R 1B4
Penguin Books (N.Z.) Ltd, 182–190 Wairau Road, Auckland 10, New Zealand

First published in *The Pelican Guide to English Literature* 1954
Reprinted fifteen times
This revised and expanded edition published 1982

Illustrations by Albany Wiseman, pp. 293, 295, 299, 301, 302, 305, 307, 311

Made and printed in Great Britain by
Cox and Wyman, Reading
Filmset in 'Monophoto' Bembo
by Northumberland Press Ltd, Gateshead, Tyne and Wear

# CONTENTS

# PART III

# PART IV

## CONTENTS

## PART V

# GENERAL INTRODUCTION

The publication of this *New Pelican Guide to English Literature* in many volumes might seem an odd phenomenon at a time when, in the words of the novelist L. H. Myers, a 'deep-seated spiritual vulgarity ... lies at the heart of our civilization', a time more typically characterized by the Headline and the Digest, by the Magazine and the Tabloid, by Pulp Literature and the Month's Masterpiece. Yet the continuing success of the *Guide* seems to confirm that literature – both yesterday's literature and today's – has a real and not merely a nominal existence among a large number of people; and its main aim has been to help validate as firmly as possible this feeling for a living literature and for the values it embodies.

The *Guide* is partly designed for the committed student of literature. But it has also been written for those many readers who accept with genuine respect what is known as 'our literary heritage', but for whom this often amounts, in memory, to an unattractive amalgam of set texts and school prizes; as a result they may have come to read only today's books – fiction and biography and travel. Though they are probably familiar with such names as Pope, George Eliot, Langland, Marvell, Yeats, Dr Johnson, Hopkins, the Brontës, they might hesitate to describe their work intimately or to fit them into any larger pattern of growth and achievement. If this account is a fair one, it seems probable that very many people would be glad of guidance that would help them respond to what is living and contemporary in literature, for, like the other arts, it has the power to enrich the imagination and to clarify thought and feeling.

The *Guide* does not set out to compete with the standard Histories of Literature, which inevitably tend to have a lofty, take-it-or-leave-it attitude about them. This is not a Bradshaw or a *Whitaker's Almanack* of English literature. Nor is it a digest or potted version, nor again a portrait gallery of the great. Works such as these already abound and there is no need to add to their number. What it sets out to offer, by contrast, is a guide to the history and traditions of English literature, a contour map of the literary scene. It attempts, that is, to draw up an ordered account of literature as a direct encouragement to people to read widely in an informed way and with enjoy-ment. In this respect the *Guide* acknowledges a considerable debt to those twentieth-century writers and critics who have made a deter-mined effort to elicit from literature what is of living value to us today: to establish a sense of literary tradition and to define the standards that this tradition embodies.

The *New Pelican Guide to English Literature* consists of nine volumes:

1,    Part One. *Medieval Literature: Chaucer and the Alliterative Tradition* (with an anthology)
1,    Part Two; *Medieval Literature: The European Inheritance* (with an anthology)
2.    *The Age of Shakespeare*
3.    *From Donne to Marvell*
4.    *From Dryden to Johnson*
5.    *From Blake to Byron*
6.    *From Dickens to Hardy*
7.    *From James to Eliot*
8.    *The Present*

Each separate volume, with the exception of the last and the European volume, has been named after those writers who dominate or stand conveniently at either end of the period, and who also indicate between them the strength of the age in literature. Of course the boundaries between the separate volumes cannot be sharply drawn.

Though the *Guide* has been designed as a single work, in the sense that it attempts to provide a coherent and developing account of the tradition of English literature, each volume exists in its own right and sets out to provide the reader with four kinds of related material:

(i) *A survey of the social context of literature* in each period, pro-viding an account of contemporary society at its points of contact with literature.

(ii) *A literary survey* of the period, describing the general charac-teristics of the period's literature in such a way as to enable the reader to trace its growth and to keep his or her bearings. The aim of this section is to answer such questions as 'What *kind* of literature was written in this period?', 'Which authors matter most?', 'Where does the strength of the period lie?'.

(iii) *Detailed studies* of some of the chief writers and works in the period. Coming after the two general surveys, the aim of this section is to convey a sense of what it means to read closely and with perception; and also to suggest how the literature of a given period is most profitably read, i.e. with what assumptions and with what kind of attention. This section also includes an account of whichever one of the other arts (here the visual arts) particularly flourished at the time, as perhaps throwing a helpful if indirect light on the literature itself.

(iv) *An appendix of essential facts for reference purposes*, such as authors' biographies (in miniature), bibliographies, books for further study, and so on.

In this first volume, and also in the closely linked volume on medieval European literature, there is included an anthology. The anthology in *Medieval Literature: Chaucer and the Alliterative Tradition* is made up of a selection of less familiar and less accessible poems, for example *Pearl*, which are discussed in the earlier chapters.

Thus each volume of the *Guide* has been planned as a whole, and the contributors' approach to literature is based on broadly common assumptions; for it was essential that the *Guide* should have cohesion and should reveal some collaborative agreements (though inevitably, and quite rightly, it reveals disagreements as well). They agree on the need for rigorous standards and have felt it essential not to take reputations for granted, but rather to examine once again, and often in close detail, the strengths and weaknesses of our literary heritage.

BORIS FORD

# NOTES

Notes designated by an asterisk or glosses by a
letter are given at the foot of each
page. Numbered notes are given at
the end of each chapter.

# PART I

# THE SOCIAL CONTEXT OF
# MEDIEVAL ENGLISH LITERATURE

DEREK BREWER

## Change and Continuity

Before the Norman Conquest of 1066 the English people were a loosely-knit unity based on the earlier Anglo-Saxon kingdoms, which had combined with the more Scandinavian-dominated elements of the old Danelaw in the North, Midlands, and East. Winchester, the old 'capital' of Wessex, was the centre. Celtic tribes occupied Cornwall, Wales, Strathclyde and the north of Scotland in a state of uneasy tension with the English. The English enjoyed the most advanced peaceful culture in Europe. There was no European people so rich in writings in their own tongue – indeed vernacular culture barely existed elsewhere.

The Norman Conquest built on this unity, allowing much fundamental continuity, yet also creating change. At first glance, indeed, there seems, especially from the point of view of literature, devastating change. Effective composition in English almost ceases soon after the Conquest. Although the Anglo-Saxon Chronicle took nearly a hundred years finally to dwindle away, French immediately became the language of the royal court. English landowners were often displaced from their positions of leadership and influence, while English bishops and abbots, if not immediately displaced, were replaced by Normans when they died. By William's death in 1087 there was only one English bishop, Wulfstan, responsible for the immense western diocese of Worcester, and he died in 1095.

The west of the country naturally felt the effects of the invasion from the South-east less, or less quickly, and it is in the western parts that the long-term continuities of English culture in the Middle Ages are more readily seen. For under the many changes was a fundamental continuity. That English is still the language of the English people is the obvious example. Five thousand Norman knights could not change that. William the Conqueror had neither prejudice nor policy about language. He intended to be king of the English, and was crowned in the ancient coronation ceremony which used both English and Latin, but not French. We may deduce from the tiny scraps of evidence left to us that often, perhaps usually, the children of his knights who settled in England must have acquired English as their mother tongue either from their English mothers (who may well have been the widows or daughters of the dispossessed English nobles), or from English nurses. The learned Latin historian Ordericus Vitalis, born near Shrewsbury about 1070, son of a Norman knight, tells us that he knew no French when he was sent, at the age of ten, to the abbey in Normandy where he spent the rest of his life, though he had already been taught Latin by Sigward, his presumably English parish priest. As the years went by, there was considerable intermingling between noble families, English, Norman and even Breton. They would all have known some English. By the twelfth century there were a number of the nobility and bishops and abbots who had English names, and it is hard to believe that they were ignorant of English. Meanwhile, ordinary people everywhere in England continued to speak English.

Nevertheless, the status of the language changed. The English language was deprived of the stabilizing effect of a written standard, such as it had enjoyed before the Conquest, and it was no longer the principal instrument of the official culture, that is, of those who had the greatest political, economic, social, intellectual and spiritual prestige. The social implications of this were very considerable.

## Towards a Unified Nation

In these earlier medieval centuries the general state of the country was very unstable. Local war-lords, brigands, and dispossessed men of all kinds were continually erupting into violence that could only occasionally be dignified as rebellion. During William's reign some of the instability was due to the Conquest, but much of it was the natural situation, common to all early cultures, and which is to be found in other lands even in the world today. It was more tolerable then (in terms of general survival) because weapons were so primitive. Nevertheless, the medieval history of England, as of Europe generally, is a story of progress, however halting, towards an organized national community with some real peace and good order, in which towns flourished, wealth was created, education and especially literacy developed, and a high culture was created in the mother tongue of the people. In England this great achievement took place between the Conquest and the end of the sixteenth century, after which an entirely new world-view, reflected in the scientific revolution of the seventeenth century, began to develop. Of course, internal peace and order had not been completely secured even then, but in terms of English society, culture and language, the natural climax of the long and successful struggle of the medieval centuries to produce a unified nation is found in the firm government of the later Tudors, and the possession in the common tongue of the Book of Common Prayer and the works of Shakespeare.

## The General Medieval Outlook

The general basis of this national culture was an agricultural society with a very primitive technology in the northern temperate zone. Much flows from this. Nature was neither lush nor intolerably harsh. Society was closely bound to the returning cycle of the seasons, with a narrow or non-existent margin of the production of food over consumption, so that a bad summer might mean death in winter. Hunger, as Langland says, is a great discipline for idleness and improvidence. Yet a primitive technology may sustain a general culture in which very complex ideas, perceptions and feelings can flourish. By the twelfth century in England there was a long cultural tradition arising both out of natural circumstances and the civilizing effect of Christianity. Summer and winter imposed a pattern of feast and fast, tied to the cycles of life and death. Food and drink meant survival, community, festivity. They were embodiments of social and religious triumph over the endemic suffering of life, experience for which we no longer have adequate symbols.

In such circumstances, Nature appeared both glorious and dangerous. In the Middle Ages all experience, reinforced by the teachings of Christianity, taught that Nature was ambivalent. Life was precarious: up to the nineteenth century in England, as in Europe generally, it is virtually certain that four out of five children born died in early childhood. Women were regarded as the weaker sex because so many young wives died as the result of constant child-bearing. Even apart from such hazards, the natural disasters of famine and plague, of accident, crime and endemic war, spared neither sex nor age. Death was the visible instead of, as now, the invisible companion to life. In that pre-scientific world-view the idea of death was different from ours. We may too easily read morbidity into the frequency of the references to death in much medieval literature, especially religious literature. Medieval people had a richer (though not necessarily truer) set of non-materialist concepts than we have of the nature of existence. For them, super-nature both completed and denied Nature, and the idea of death was more creative than negative: it was associated with ideas of judgement and everlasting joy and sorrow. Out of death, it was felt, came true life. Death threw a blazing light, ominous or joyous, on the activities of everyday life. All existence was significant because each individual soul was acting out his or her part in a cosmic drama. Seen in this light even the flattest of medieval lyrics, the most morbid of sermons, the most pedestrian miracle play may shine with previously unexpected significance. At the centre was the paradox of the suffering creator whose love for mankind had overcome death for himself and for all who had eyes to see and ears to hear. The young artisan-teacher who had suffered a criminal's death was celebrated as God himself by a series of monuments of surpassing artistic glory which show how, for example in the Gothic cathedral, primitive technology may be resplendently self-transcendent. God had originally made nature good: man had spoiled it: by suffering God had redeemed it.

*The Setting*

The medieval period was one of constant change and, on the whole, of improvement in the quality of life, notwithstanding some fearful setbacks. The population of England at the time of the Conquest was probably a million or a little more. By the middle of the fourteenth century it had risen to about three million. Then that particularly fearful epidemic of the bubonic plague termed the Black Death struck in 1348-9 and killed perhaps a quarter or more of the population. Yet one must not exaggerate its effects. It was an intensification of endemic misery. It seems not to have much affected, for example, building programmes, slow as they always were. The consequent shortage of labour improved the lot of the peasants by making their work more valuable, giving them more bargaining power. There may even have been a sort of economic mini-boom in the later fourteenth century, despite further severe epidemics. By amazing chance three English poets, by any standards amongst the greatest English poets, Chaucer, Langland and the *Gawain*-poet, survived the Black Death and later plagues, and they, with other writers, make the second half of the fourteenth century one of the most glorious in the whole of English literature. The population seems slowly to have increased in the fifteenth century, and despite the Wars of the Roses and the long reign of the weak king Henry VI the general state of the country by 1500 was more populous, peaceful, united, educated and prosperous than ever before.

The physical basis of life changed slowly but quite significantly. William the Conqueror devastated the north in quelling insurrection so that it took a generation to recover, but most place-names in England are from the pre-Conquest period and the full 'colonization' of the country was complete by the mid thirteenth century. Roads were unpaved green (or mud) tracks and communications on foot or horseback slow, but apart from moors and uplands the population was well distributed and there seems to have been a plentiful traffic.

The characteristic bonds and obligations felt by people were hierarchical, in the family, in the social system, and in the Church. The hierarchical pattern was so deep as to be taken entirely for granted and built into all social and literary expression, religious and secular. The king was supreme in his realm, as was seen when the boy king Richard II successfully called on the rebellious peasants to disperse on the occasion of the murder of their leader Wat Tyler in London in the Peasants' Revolt of 1381. A father was equally supreme in his family. God was thought of as both king and father of all. The essential bond was loyalty to one's superior, the worst sin was treachery. 'To serve' the appropriate superior was a noble act. Even in romantic love the beloved lady was thought of as superior, who could only be asked to give 'mercy' to her knight. 'To serve' becomes a synonym for 'to love'. On the religious plane Mary, mother of God, was Queen of Heaven, even though the actual status of women in ordinary life was inferior to men of the equivalent social status.

In secular life most people lived in the country in little villages or scattered houses built of wood, or of wattle and daub. A poor man would live with family and live-stock in a frail one- or two-roomed hovel like the 'sooty bower' of the old woman in Chaucer's *Nun's Priest's Tale*. Even the more substantial houses, with more rooms, of merchants and lords had little of comfort or privacy, though there was considerable improvement throughout the period. The open halls of Anglo-Saxon kings, with their benches and central fires, in which the whole court ate and drank and slept (images, for the Old English poet, of his warm and noisy heaven), had become elaborate castles by the fourteenth century, like that built for John of Gaunt, son of Edward III, at Kenilworth in Warwickshire, which Chaucer must have walked in. Even its ruins still allow us to recreate in imagination a crowded and varied court life. The grand hall with great windows in the Decorated style must have been a beautiful sight when filled with colourfully-dressed courtiers. The store-rooms and kitchens are impressive: but there are also smaller rooms with fireplaces where the privileged might retire for more intimate talk, where ladies might sew and have books read to them. At a less grand level the picturesquely fortified manor-house Stokesay Castle in Shropshire shows a thirteenth-century hall, which later centuries used as a barn, with the later development of withdrawing rooms. Langland complains in the late fourteenth century that lord and lady were withdrawing from the noisy communal hall to greater privacy – a social movement which reflects the increasing privacy of reading literature. Haddon Hall in Derbyshire retains a fine fourteenth-century hall of exactly the kind the *Gawain*-poet must have imagined that King Arthur held his feast in. A horseman could ride in through the door. Opposite the hall are the kitchens (as still in some Oxford and Cambridge colleges with similar halls). In Haddon Hall again are withdrawing rooms to which the lord's family might retire. It is in some such room, with lord and lady, their children, accompanied by a knight or squire, that a chaplain might read the poems of the *Gawain*-poet, or other romances, and songs would be sung to that fourteenth-century equivalent of a guitar, a psaltery. London had more great houses, especially along the Strand. John of Gaunt's house, the Savoy, must have approached the magnificence of small European palaces, and was full of artistic treasures. (It was burnt by the London mob in 1381.) We may imagine Criseyde living in a substantial house, built at least partly in stone, for Chaucer's Troy is thought of very much in terms of Chaucer's London. She could sit sewing in a paved room with her ladies, while one of them read aloud the story of the siege of Thebes. The garden at the back had sanded alleys between hedges. Pandarus had a similar house with a sizeable hall, a bedroom leading off, and a little room by the entrance where Troilus could hide. Merchants had similar houses, with shops in front; work and living were a much more unified activity in the Middle Ages than now. Men, such as priests, living on their own, would have single rooms, bed-sitters in modern terms, though a good deal less comfortable, with a chest for clothes, and a desk which might hold as many as the sixty books which Chaucer's Clerk of Oxford had at 'his bed's head' in his college room. Chaucer had what we would think of as a flat or apartment in the building above the gate at Aldgate.

## Reading, Writing and Individualism

The significance of such better homes, still a tiny minority, was that they allowed for private reading not only by day but at night, in the warm if dim light of a candle (which Chaucer says left his eyes bleary). Private reading to oneself is very different from hearing songs and stories in hall. Silent reading demands an individual, not a group, response, more solitary but more thoughtful. In the fourteenth and fifteenth centuries even works meant for the private reader, like Chaucer's *Canterbury Tales*, imitated the style of 'oral' literature, songs and stories told to a group, and *The Canterbury Tales* is ostensibly itself the record of an episode of group-storytelling. The movement from the group as audience to the individual reader is one of the most interesting and important in the literature of the medieval period. The group remains half-consciously the ideal audience for literature. But the more individualistic act of private communication based on the written word, on the manuscript, which is read to oneself in solitude, or at least in disregard of others, begins to take the place of the actual or implicit group performance. At first, reading or writing was accompanied by mumbling to oneself, but Chaucer refers to himself in the *House of Fame* (about 1375) as reading 'dumb as any stone' and so fixes a landmark in the development of the internalization of literary communication. The work designed for a solitary reader cannot rely on the warmth of a communal occasion as part of the total literary effect. The style has to do a different kind of work, must become more concise, develop a story and characters that are consistent, for the reader, unlike the hearer, can turn the pages back and check his impressions. The reader is more independent and can interrupt and resume his reading according to his own needs, not others'. The work is less bound to its original context, freer, far more individualistic, but also has to supply more in the way of literary effect, which in turn requires more effort, more education, on the part of the receiver, the reader. The style in the written book has to carry some of the weight which in a performance is carried by the personality of the reciter, by the presence of companions, by the significance of the occasion. There is both gain and loss in this development. It means that some medieval literature, like much folk literature, may seem flat to us until by imagination and knowledge we recreate for ourselves something of the feeling of the original occasion. A primarily oral style differs from a primarily written style, using somewhat different effects, through repetition with variation, word-play, hyperbole, the evocation of traditional feelings and ideas. It is direct and not naturally ironic. The *Gawain*-poet is a very good example of the fullest use of a traditional, basically oral style, though one enriched by knowledge that comes from reading, and tightened in style by writing. Langland is particularly notable for his word-play, especially puns, derived from an oral style, but elaborated by the possibility given by reading of building in several layers of meaning. Chaucer, too, is remarkable for the way in which, though he deliberately recreates the sense of group participation, he also exploits the ambiguities open to the writer who can distance himself from the reader, play with the relationship between himself and the reader, and so develop, exceptionally, a remarkable vein of irony. Writing allows him to load every rift with ore, to make himself remarkably elusive, while apparently maintaining the simplicity and directness of oral delivery.

In the early part of the medieval period everything was written on the cured skins of cattle or sheep (vellum or parchment). A great folio volume would require a flock of three or four hundred sheep. In the fifteenth century paper came to be used quite extensively, although it was still expensive. Books remained precious, but became much more common, often made up of a variety of items, as poems, histories, religious instruction, medical treatises, like the manuscript now at Lincoln Cathedral compiled by a Yorkshire country gentleman, Robert Thornton, in the first third of the fifteenth century. *The Canterbury Tales* is such a manuscript miscellany (lacking only the medical treatise), except that it is the almost miraculous product of a single yet amazingly various mind.

In the twelfth century only clerics could read and write – that was what made them 'clerks'. But the Church, because of its mission, had also to be an educational institution. In all Europe education had a primarily sacred inspiration and purpose. But in the thirteenth century in parts of Europe, and by the late fourteenth in England, education began to develop a more secular and everyday aspect. There was a small commercial school in Oxford in the late fourteenth century, for example. As the Thornton manuscript shows, manuscripts came to be written by laymen and cherished by their families for recreation and study. Large-scale official documentation in Latin, in which England is uniquely rich for the medieval period, had begun about 1200, though secular literature in English only slowly came to be thought worthy of record in the fourteenth century. Ability to write also became more general, and script changed from the beautiful, rounded twelfth-century Romanesque style to the more elaborate pointed Gothic of the thirteenth to fifteenth centuries, more mannered, and because more widely practised often less skilful. Before the Conquest books retained a 'sacred' aura, which the Bible never quite lost, but secularization followed familiarity as the period progressed. Probably more than half the population could read, though not necessarily also write, by 1500. In the fifteenth century we find increasing numbers of private letters in English, practically unknown before 1400, of which the most famous form the great Paston collection. This contains the family correspondence of several generations of a family of wealthy Norfolk landowners who lived near the village of that name. The letters are a fascinating miscellany of information about the Paston estates, struggles, misfortunes, marriages, and occasionally about their thoughts and feelings, which brings us close to everyday fifteenth-century life, albeit of a rather exceptional family. In general, the literate layman is a well-established figure by the fifteenth century, and there is much secular writing, both practical and literary.

At the very end of our period printing reinforces the effects of writing. Caxton set up his press in Westminster in 1477. His genius was to fulfil the natural requirements of the *vernacular* culture, leaving the learned Latin to others and concentrating on the great miscellany of religious and secular writings in English for which there was such a hunger at many levels of English life. Print carries the stabilizing, individualizing, internalizing effects of writing even further, so that the manner of communication itself affects what is said – the medium, as Marshall McLuhan declared, ultimately affects the message. But that was a slow process which would take us beyond our period. It is enough to notice here that the Book of Common Prayer and Shakespeare's plays deploy both the stylistic characteristics of communal participation, using repetition with variation, word-play, hyperbole, traditional wisdom, yet also the logical consistency called for by script and print, in a way entirely characteristic of late medieval English literature.

The status and quality of poets and storytellers reflect the same individualism developing from a communal base. We know the names of no poets in the English vernacular in the twelfth and thirteenth centuries. There must always have been persons in small communities, as in remote communities in Scotland and Ireland within living memory, who had a talent for singing songs and telling stories, and these communities existed at all levels. Most we can only guess at, from, for example, passing references to the minstrels and storytellers who called at castles, manor-houses and abbeys and were paid for entertainment. Langland gives a memorable picture of party-games, jests, and tales of Robin Hood in a London pub when he describes how Glutton was seduced from going to confession (*Piers Plowman*, B Text, Passus V). The Priory at Worcester held regular feasts with the citizens at the end of the fifteenth century where 'caroles' (of which modern Christmas carols are partial descendants, limited in theme and to one part of the year) were sung. At the high literary level of the court, esquires were required to entertain visitors with chronicles and poetry. Chaucer even shows us a reading party for ladies in Book II of *Troilus*. Thus literacy and individualism were built upon the group experience of song and story. The great river of popular traditional song and story in the mother tongue at first left little more than splashes, as it were, on the margins of manuscripts whose precious parchment was designed for more serious matters like rent-rolls and theology, but more and more story and song, secular as well as pious, came to be noted down. Some popular stories and songs are fortunately not lost to us because all levels of society enjoyed the same kind of entertainment, and secular 'writers' (the name is significant) as they developed drew from the general popular flow.

Chaucer, like Boccaccio in Italy, tells many folktales. Only in the seventeenth century did such literature come to be regarded as 'low'. And even style, however enriched it might be by writing or by a learned poet, was of the same sort at high and low levels. Even the elaborations of medieval rhetoric were no more, and no less, than a rationalization of traditional style, with word-play (e.g. puns), exaggeration, sententiousness (e.g. proverbs), and repetition with variation. Such is the basis of the style of medieval romance and lyric, of the great fourteenth-century poets, of the Book of Common Prayer and Shakespeare, and of much folk literature even today. Even learned poets had something of the minstrel in them. Tradition told that both Alfred and Hereward, when waging their respective guerilla wars two centuries apart in time, penetrated the enemy camp disguised as minstrels. The minstrel had free entry everywhere, and in earlier times had a whole repertoire of sometimes crude tricks and displays, beside song and story. By the fifteenth century most minstrels were professional musicians under the patronage of some great man, though they often moved about the country. They remind us of the close, if variable, relationship between song and story.

Then by the late fourteenth and fifteenth century we come to know the names of various authors and they themselves show signs of greater self-awareness. Chaucer is, as in other respects, *avant-garde* here, while the *Gawain*-poet is characteristically traditional in not revealing his own name. Langland does not quite like to indulge in 'mere' poetry, but reveals his name in puns, while Gower in his usual modest, quiet, efficient way let his name be known and organized his own scriptorium for the accurate copying of his texts. Malory, writing about 1470, is ready enough to tell us he is a 'knight prisoner', though he tells us no more, and several other authors tell us that they wrote in prison.

*Development of Town and Court*

Towns were also developing, the great instrument of civilization, freedom, order and peace, based on the prosperity which only trade and industry can bring. They were centres for many miracle-play cycles, now lost, which flourished because gildsmen organized and acted in them. The miracle-plays were probably written by clerics, in part with an educational purpose, and towns had also a festive cycle in the warmer part of the year, as we know Coventry had, which provided many occasions for communal celebration, for games, songs and stories. But London was the only city which developed an urban culture in any way comparable with that of the great continental cities. Many of the most creative developments of the Middle Ages, such as the new individualism, new feelings for personal identity and social freedom, a new capacity to regulate life objectively, as time by clocks, space by precise measurement, value by money, are centred on the growth of towns, though Chaucer is the principal English author to reflect this new social orientation.

Yet, as Chaucer's life and work also show, the town and the commerce it developed, with its consequent wealth and increased power, also supported in England the development of a much more archaic institution – the King's court – which was the centre of the political, social and legal power of the kingdom. The court bene-fited from the generally accepted belief in the divinity of kingship but was itself potentially more secular. Here, enabled by their wealth and the activities of international and national trade to enjoy luxury and refinement of life, courtiers found time for reflection, refinement and secular play. The peak of this development is Richard II's court at the end of the fourteenth century, which found its supreme literary achievement in Chaucer's writing. All his work is written for a courtly audience ranging in personality from knights and ladies, who were hardly more than boys and girls, to middle-aged warrior-administrators, moralists and lawyers, like Chaucer's friend and disciple, the Lollard knight, John Clanvowe, his friend the poet Gower, and his other friend the university-trained Strode (of whom the last two are addressed at the end of *Troilus*). Richard's court in its own way allowed that cultivation of secular personal relation-ships, and in particular love, which came to be seen as the supreme aim of secular life. As a European phenomenon this concept of romantic love greatly influenced much of later western literature.

The idea of the court in the fourteenth century was paradoxically built upon that ancient institution, the group of tried and loyal fighting men surrounding the person of the king, seen particularly as the war-leader of society. Long before, the classical Latin historian Tacitus had noted that this was how the Germanic tribes were organized; and indeed it was a pattern which the very nature of William's Conquest, with his personal domination over his knights, both reinforced and modified. However refined courts might become, knighthood and bravery were their founding sentiments. The circumstances of modern warfare have made it extraordinarily difficult nowadays to imagine the honour and glory that could appropriately be attached to war. In all previous ages it has been the case, as Dr Johnson remarked, that 'every man thinks the worse of himself for not having been a soldier'. Even nowadays we can recognize that courage, self-sacrifice, comradeship, loyalty, physical endurance, the sense of adventure, are still fundamental virtues; the excitement of fighting for a cause is still all too readily evoked in the modern world even for unworthy causes. Even the Church evoked militant imagery, and the good Christian must think of himself as Christ's faithful servant and soldier. The concept of the 'crusade', detestable as it may now seem to us for the cruelty and hypocrisy with which many held it, was nevertheless in essence a not ignoble ideal. Chaucer's knight, for example, is portrayed as the ideal Christian frontiersman, having fought against the heathen (though sometimes, oddly enough, in other heathens' service) on all the borders of Christendom. The only expression of Christian pacifism that we find was amongst the Lollards, the dissident late fourteenth-century sect which was inspired by Wycliffe and was an ancestor of the Reformation. But the devout layman and poet John Gower pleaded constantly for peace.

## The Church, Churches, and the Gothic Style

The Christian message of peace to all men, the existence of monasteries and of clergy who were not supposed to fight, paradoxically combined with militancy of various kinds, is an index of the almost total penetration of society by the Church in the Middle Ages. It presents us with an extraordinarily complex variety, of which only

a much simplified sketch can be given here. There is nothing like
it in our modern secularized society, yet we have similar feelings,
and much of what we now feel and express is the result of far-
reaching changes which were begun in the latter Middle Ages.

At the beginning of our period there was a sharp divide between
religious and lay life, though the division was 'vertical' rather than
'horizontal'. Religious and lay life were equally hierarchical, and
bishops and abbots corresponded in power and authority to great
lords. Churchmen were distinguished at least in theory from laymen
by three major characteristics: they were virgin, non-combatant and
educated in Latin. During the Middle Ages there was a fascinating
interplay between religious and lay life in which each side was
modified to produce that unified national Christian culture which is
represented by the Reformation and which only collapsed in the
latter part of the twentieth century, with so much else of traditional
English life.

First, a word or two about the physical and social structures which
characterized the medieval English church, always with an eye to
the vernacular literary culture. The Norman influence led to more
stone-built parish churches in the style characterized by the rounded
arch, still sometimes called 'Norman', though better called by the
name of the general European style of which it is part, Romanesque.
One of the earliest and greatest examples is the cathedral at Durham,
which had been a holy place for centuries before. The most interesting example in England of a Romanesque parish church, still with
magnificent sculptures, is Kilpeck, near Hereford; and the work of
the Herefordshire school, with many fine churches, is to be associated
with the kind of devout, educated society that produced the superb
devotional works, the *Ancrene Riwle* and the Katherine Group of
manuscripts, in the early thirteenth century.

The dark, constrained, earthy power of Romanesque flowered in
the styles of Early English (late thirteenth century), Decorated
(fourteenth), and Perpendicular (late fourteenth to early sixteenth),
all marked by the pointed arch, by elaborate stonework, and eventually by the height of the windows, and again part of an international style, the Gothic. The Gothic style is characterized by the
image the churches give of aspiring to the brightness of Heaven,
with their large bright windows and general sense of upward move-

28

ment. One of the latest and perhaps the supreme example among many superb cathedrals and parish churches is King's College Chapel, Cambridge. It is reasonable to see an analogy between the general Gothic style of architecture, manuscript painting, script, sculpture, and the style of late medieval literature. Gothic works, whether in the visual or literary arts, tend to create brightness and openness. They reveal a delight in Nature, yet a desire for the ideal; a certain tension of moral aspiration combined with a complementary pleasure in the comic, grotesque and ugly. Their richness of decoration may not be closely related to structural necessity – see, for example, the proliferation of woodcarving, not always decent, in the stalls of that great lantern of glass and stone, Lavenham church in Suffolk. Such decoration may be compared with the long descriptions in romances which are there for the pleasure that they offer in themselves and are certainly both elaborate and traditional.

The chief religious emblem of the Gothic juxtaposition of idealism and realism, with its accompanying emotional disturbance, is the way Christ came to be represented on the Cross. In Anglo-Saxon and Romanesque art he is shown crowned, with his body straight, his arms stiffly spread and his feet side by side nailed with two nails. It is a noble, unmoved figure. The crucifixion is his triumph. By contrast the Gothic Christ is shown twisted into the characteristic Gothic S-shape, hanging tormented, dying or dead, with bowed head, far more realistically portrayed body, and one foot placed above the other, both pierced by a single nail. This last characteristic is the significant marker of the Gothic Christ. The first reference to the single nail is late twelfth century in England, but the style rapidly spread all over Europe. It looks realistic but is anatomically impossible. The effect is to invite the beholder to pity and to suffer with the pathetic Christ who is nevertheless recognized as God, creator of the world which makes him suffer – a typically Gothic paradox.

Cathedrals, parish churches, monasteries, and chapels were scattered throughout the land, calling attention constantly to other dimensions of life than that of the visible everyday, claiming that suffering could be transcended and death overcome. Such buildings were as typical of medieval culture as the office block or the factory is of ours. Light was within them. Their walls were painted, their window-glass often brilliantly pictorial. Bells rang from them. And like most human institutions they multiplied themselves and their own activities to such an extent that their self-elaboration, artistic, ritualistic and verbal, became intolerable, obscuring their own ultimate purposes. The Church in general became corrupt and self-regarding, so that it defeated its own purposes, and much of the wild proliferation of late medieval religious fantasy in picture and writing that spread like some colourful cancer within the religious life was swept away by the wave of iconoclasm represented by the Reformation. As happened with many excessively elaborated services, many richly decorative works of art, so huge numbers of emotional religious poems and of ever more improbably elaborated saints' legends were also swept away in the Reformation, out of the consciousness of the English people. Yet before that happened the ideal and often the practice had been noble, as well as practical. The Church was the great originator and carrier of the culture of England within Christendom.

## The Social Structure of the Church

The main outline of the social structure of the Church was as follows. The country was divided into dioceses, with cathedrals as headquarters, under a bishop, and the dioceses were divided into parishes served by priests. Parish churches and cathedrals were served by secular clergy, who were celibate and educated, and responsible for the care of the souls of their flock. Their ideal is immortalized by Chaucer's poor Parson. Parsons lived in houses near the church and visited throughout the parish. Bishops lived in palaces with many servants, in the style of great lords. Although many bishops and priests failed to live up to the ideal, and there was much anti-clerical satire, the great developments in religious feeling and in education throughout the medieval period were largely their work.

Monasteries, on the other hand, were served by monks who were supposed always to remain enclosed in the one building. The greater monasteries were called abbeys and were governed by an abbot and a series of other officers. In the abbeys, beside the church where much time was spent in services, there was a refectory for communal eating (from the regulations of which originated many of the ideas of courtesy which spread to lay life) and kitchens, store-rooms, etc., with their accompanying servants. There had also to be a dormitory where the monks slept, a cloister where they might wash and even read, as well as exercise. There was a chapter-house for meetings and usually a library. While some monasteries were always poor and small, others, like Bury St Edmunds, developed into clusters of buildings of great extent like a small town. Pious patrons often bequeathed lands to abbeys and some of them became very large and rich. The monks in consequence came to be called 'possessioners' who were attacked on that ground by the ostensibly poor orders of friars. Wealth might indeed, in an institution like the Church, produce internal contradictions since monks were supposed to live penitential lives of chastity, poverty and 'stability', that is, staying in one place. They were to live lives of prayer and lamentation for the sins of the whole world and to work for their meagre sustenance with their hands. Surely many holy lives were thus lived lost to the world. On the other hand, the need for proper administration of a large organization with wealth and extensive lands inevitably led many monastic orders to develop what others felt was an undue interest in the world. The monks of the abbey might have to be sent out to manage the property and once again Chaucer gives us the classic example of the medieval equivalent, in monasteries, of a land agent, in his portrait of the Monk who is so keen on hunting and who travels so freely about the country.

Nevertheless, Chaucer refers with knowledge only to those monks who were outside the cloister. Within the cloister there is little doubt that, always taking into account human fallibility, most monks lived a life of reasonable dutifulness. They developed a form of meditative spirituality, 'chewing over' the Holy text of the Bible, called *lectio divina*, 'divine reading'. Apart from the undiscoverable influence it must have had over many religious lives it influenced such a great fourteenth-century woman mystic as Julian of Norwich and probably even Langland. Some abbeys became centres of learning with monks trained to write in well-equipped writing rooms. Such a room was called a *scriptorium*. The great twelfth-century Latin chroniclers must have used such *scriptoria* associated with libraries. The *Ancrene Riwle* and the Katherine Group of manuscripts in English probably proceeded from such a scriptorium unusually well-organized for the vernacular tongue, in Herefordshire. John Lydgate, the monk of Bury St Edmunds, must have benefited from its well-stocked library and its efficient scriptorium. Some monastic scribes compiled immense books which might include amongst their contents, for example, a copy of Langland's *Piers Plowman*, a text of Mandeville's improbable *Travels* (which curiously enough often accompanies Langland's work), one or two religious romances in English as well as a chronicle and devotional works in Latin. Occasionally Chaucer's *Parson's Tale* found itself in similar company. Such books of great value might be read from by a reader during the monks' meals, which were supposed to be conducted in silence, or they might be lent out to individual monks for private reading in their cells.

The monks also studied in the universities, where they played some part in Latin learning and controversy, but not in vernacular literature. Pious vernacular literature was sometimes copied in monasteries but the only monk who made a notable contribution to vernacular literature was the staggeringly prolific but mostly pedestrian Lydgate, of Bury St Edmunds. Very different were the friars. Whereas monks were enclosed, or should have been, friars had freedom of movement. The Franciscan Order (sometimes called the Order of Friars Minor and popularly known as Grey Friars, from their dress) was founded by St Francis in 1209. The order insisted on poverty but was so successful that bequests were continually making friaries prosperous. The order in consequence suffered a series of spiritual crises and sectarian splits as the more zealous members successively tried to reassert the ideals of the founder. The Franciscans specialized in popular preaching which required them to be both learned and pious, implying the use of both Latin and the vernacular of the country they were working in. They first arrived in England in 1224, settling in Canterbury, London and Oxford, and flourished greatly. At Oxford they produced such notable scholastic philosophers as Duns Scotus and William of Ockham, but Franciscans may also have been the authors of many of the pious, emotional English lyrics and carols. Several of them are known by name, for example, the prolific James Ryman. St Francis himself was the first person to receive famously the *stigmata*, that is, the image on his own hands, feet and side, of the wounds of Christ on the Cross. His kind of fervent devotion is exactly that represented by the Gothic crucified Christ. St Francis also originated the devotion to the infant child Christ at the Christmas crib. He wanted his friars to be 'minstrels of God'. Much of the popular religious feeling of the later Middle Ages with its warmth, expressiveness and intense idealism seems to reflect Franciscan attitudes.

There was another major order. The Dominican Order (*Ordo Praedicatorum* 'Order of Preachers', known as Black Friars, from their dress) was established by St Dominic in 1220–21 and from the first the Dominicans were especially devoted to teaching and study, though they also followed the Franciscans in intending to practise poverty. The Dominicans made the greatest intellectual contribution to the medieval church in Europe generally, and the greatest scholastic philosopher of all, the Italian St Thomas Aquinas, and his almost equally great master the German St Albert the Great, were both Dominicans. The Order was particularly helpful in the preaching of crusades and the hunting out of heresy; the Inquisition was mainly its responsibility. Dominicans arrived in England soon after the Franciscans and also established themselves at Oxford. Their contribution to general religious feeling and to vernacular literature seems to have been less marked than that of the Franciscans.

Although the Black and Grey Friars were dominant, there were other orders. In general friars were licensed to wander and beg within a particular area and they also preached and heard confessions. Since it was less embarrassing to confess to a visitor, and as the friars acquired the reputation for giving easy penances if they were well paid, they were popular with the people and unpopular with parish priests, moralists and intellectuals. Some major vernacular writers satirized them savagely, and Chaucer's picture of the Friar in his *General Prologue* is a fair example. Langland is positively obsessive about the iniquities of the friars.

Apart from the friars, another religious order, less organized and famous, was probably even more significant for the production of religious vernacular literature. This was the order which came to be called Augustinian Canons, or Canons Regular or Black Canons (from their dress). They were a kind of mixture of secular clergy, monks and friars. They lived in small communities as groups of priests serving such a substantial church as that at Southwell (with the wonderful stone carvings of leaves) under a rule attributed to St Augustine. Although they had no central directing authority, and were neither enclosed like monks nor a begging order like the friars, they were possibly the most numerous of all orders. They practised some religious austerities but were less extreme than the monks, allowing themselves, for example, to wear linen next to the skin instead of wool, and favouring more frequent washing. The author of the *Ancrene Riwle* was probably an Augustinian canon living near Wigmore in Herefordshire, though he had been to Rome and had probably studied at the University of Paris. The influential sermon-writer of the late fourteenth century, John Myrc, was an Augustinian canon, as was the notable contemporary writer on mysticism, the devout, yet sensible Walter Hilton. Probably many now anonymous devotional pieces in verse and prose were written by Augustinian canons.

Least organized of all the religious, but significant in the glories of English devotional life and literature, were the various recluses; men and women who withdrew from the world and even from organized religion, to live in relative solitude, to watch and pray, fast and meditate, and who produced or were the cause of the production of some of the most notable religious works in English. An early example is the saintly and influential recluse Christina of Markyate who is the subject of an extraordinarily interesting and realistic biography, written in Latin, which gives a vivid glimpse of twelfth-century upper class English people mingling with great intimacy with the Normans. She had a tremendous battle with her family in order to fulfil her vocation of chastity and religious suffering. She was a woman of remarkable character who eventually became famous not only for her devotion but also in connection with the celebrated type of embroidery known as *opus anglicanum*, and with one of the great twelfth-century illuminated manuscripts now known as the Albani Psalter. Another twelfth-century recluse was Godric of Finchale, near Durham, who after becoming as a very young man a successful merchant and seafarer, felt the call to a religious life and lived for sixty years a recluse in a cave, wearing out three suits of armour in his conflicts with the devil. To him is attributed one of the earliest lyrics in the English language, an affecting prayer to Mary. The *Ancrene Riwle* was written for three rich young sisters who took on the harsh austerities of the life of religious recluses about 1200. The extremely influential mystic Richard Rolle (d. 1348) who wrote richly emotive devotional works in English as well as Latin was also a recluse, after dropping out from the university of Oxford. Greatest of all was Julian of Norwich (c. 1342–c. 1413) whose *Revelations of Divine Love* are the product of profound religious meditation.

The margins of the Church where it interacted most significantly with other aspects of life, and where the influence of Latin and ecclesiastical organization were present yet not dominant, were the fruitful grounds for vernacular religious literature. This may be one of the reasons why women, who were in general less likely to know Latin, were so significant for religious writing in English. The more private and emotional nature of women's lives in those times also led naturally to a more private internalized form of devotion. From this, perhaps, arises the fact that the first autobiographical memoir in English was written by a woman who knew Julian of Norwich. Julian's own *Revelations* have an autobiographical base, since they concern her visions in May 1373, when she was apparently on the point of death. But the account that her slightly younger contemporary, Margery Kemp, gives of herself, though it still has a religious basis, is much more fully autobiographical. Margery was more of a religious hysteric than a mystic. But she gives a vibrant account of her life as a woman to whom religion and weeping were as attractive as sex was to the Wife of Bath. Margery was a secular woman, daughter of a rich merchant of Lynn. She was married and had fourteen children. In a sense she illustrates how effective had been the church's programme of religious education.

Margery, like the Wife of Bath, took part in many pilgrimages, where she plagued the other pilgrims by her lachrymatory and wailing devoutness. The pilgrimage is the underlying image of the two great works of the fourteenth century, Chaucer's *Canterbury Tales* and Langland's *Piers Plowman*. It illustrates something of the social flux and the curious mixture of secular and religious motivation, in other words the fruitful overlap of margins of experience, which are so characteristic of the fourteenth century. Both Langland and Chaucer refer in their works to themselves, thus reflecting the developing internalized autobiographical interest of the times. Langland tells us a little about himself in his poem and allows us to deduce more. He knew Latin and it may be guessed that he attended the university, probably Oxford, for a year or more without taking a degree, as many clerics did. He came from the Malvern hills in Worcestershire (another marginal area) but lived mostly in Cornhill, a poor quarter of London in those days, choosing to earn a miserable living for himself, his wife and daughter, by praying for the dead as a 'beadsman', receiving charitable payment for this. Thus he could meditate on and write and rewrite his great English poem. There are many manuscripts of *Piers Plowman* and it must have appealed to many sober, sensible men who lived partly clerical, partly secular lives as clerks, administrators, chaplains, even parsons, though the poem also appealed to monastic clergy. Chaucer's *Canterbury Tales*, on the other hand, illustrates a much more secular type of interest, although it has many religious elements and concludes with a religious condemnation of all the secular works that Chaucer had written. It was designed for an audience of courtiers and gentry. But one must remember that that circle included many merchants and other well-to-do town-dwellers of the type from whose families Chaucer also derived. The pilgrimage was a traditional religious image (used for example in the *Ancrene Riwle*) which underlay and suited extremely well much of medieval social life, not least in the way that it allowed the various classes to mingle with a common aim of Holy Day and holiday.

In the late fourteenth and particularly in the fifteenth century there was a tremendous increase of general religious literature, including lyrics, sermons, even treatises (like Chaucer's *Parson's Tale*), all in English. They all witnessed to the success of the Church in its educational mission. The Lateran Council of 1215 urged a great missionary effort upon the church, two aspects of which particularly concern us here. One was the new insistence on personal confession which promoted throughout Europe that new self-consciousness, capacity for self-analysis, sense of individual identity and moral responsibility which grew throughout the period and is so important. The other was an insistence on teaching the faith. The faith needs literacy. The ultimate aim of teaching was intellectual and spiritual advance through Latin, which is not our concern here, though it has always to be remembered as the central core of theological and scientific advance in medieval intellectual culture as a whole. English writing, however, indirectly benefited, both from the teaching which was necessarily at first in the vernacular, and also from the development of Latin learning which nourished writing in English by example and subject matter.

Finally, the universities which were the core of Latin learning need to be briefly mentioned, though mainly to dismiss them as significant contributors to English vernacular literary culture in the Middle Ages. There were two universities in England, at Oxford and at Cambridge, which were joined in the fifteenth century by the Scottish universities. All who attended them were by definition clerics and they naturally are central to the total intellectual history of the period. But their concern was specialized work in theology (including philosophy and science), law and medicine, all in Latin. Here little can be said about them, except to note that Chaucer, Langland and the later Scottish poets, Henryson and Dunbar do indirectly reflect in various ways by their learning and attitudes the influence of universities. It was not until the sixteenth century that universities became, under Humanist influence, more interested in the kind of liberal education which promoted vernacular literature.

## The Relationship of Church and Secular Society

The Church penetrated secular society in myriad ways, and Church, state and society became more closely and consciously linked in the later Middle Ages. Literacy was what made a cleric, and all clerical operations, even of secular administration, were carried out by men who could claim 'benefit of clergy' which was subjection to the law of the Church, less severe than secular law. Yet clerics performed many secular functions. On the other side, many lay organizations such as town guilds, which were organizations of senior craftsmen and tradesmen, adopted a religious basis and paid for a chaplain to pray for them. At the level of the gentry, chivalry was brought into the orbit of religion, and the creation of a knight was often turned into a religious service. Religion was a substantial social force, even if it, for that very reason, sometimes lacked spirituality and even became unduly secular in temper itself.

The Church's teaching of English in order to teach religion was of major significance (as discussed elsewhere, pp. 125ff.). By the end of the fourteenth century the effort had been so successful that there was a major demand by lay people for the Bible in English. It is characteristic of a complex situation that this demand was spear-headed by the contentious Oxford don, John Wycliffe, who wrote almost all, if not quite all, his works in Latin. But his arguments expressed the desire of a much greater number than those in univer-sities, and those lay people who felt it most fiercely came to be called Lollards. In the late fourteenth century a number of courtiers, many of them friends of Chaucer, who were hardened warriors become in middle age administrators and courtiers, were associated with Lollardry. But it also appealed to many people lower down the social scale.

Such people high and low may be said to have taken the Church's teaching literally, and they thus became, in a way familiar even in modern times, a radical anti-establishmentarian dissident group, paradoxically so much at odds with the Church that in the fifteenth century they were cruelly persecuted. Yet they show the penetration of Christian teaching even when they argued, as they did, against that doctrine of transubstantiation of the bread and wine into the real body of Christ which was first expounded by the Lateran Council of 1215. They were just as dissident and just as Christian when they denied the value of the priesthood or wished to disperse the wealth of the Church, and particularly when they called for the Bible in the mother tongue. Not unnaturally the Church repudiated this rebellious offspring which had taken the Church's teaching so seriously.

But though there may have been conflict there was also, for this very reason, less of a gap than there had been at the beginning of the period between lay and clerical. There is other evidence beside Lollardry of the closing of the gap. A good example of a successful battle fought by the Church itself to bring closer together religious and secular life was its achievement in obtaining the sanctification of marriage. Early in the medieval period it was possible for a man and woman to marry quite legally, even without witnesses, by simply clasping hands, explicitly saying they were marrying, and then going to bed together. This was known as clandestine marriage and al-though it is not the subject of Chaucer's *Troilus and Criseyde* its possibility in the background gives some plausibility to the way in which Troilus clearly feels that he is as good as married. Criseyde does not, of course, feel the same way and often enough after a clandestine marriage one or other of the partners reneged. Thus there arose many difficulties and lawsuits. By the middle of the sixteenth century, however, the Church in England had brought it about that all marriages had to be performed by a priest in public in order to be legally as well as theologically valid. To take another example, all the English vernacular secular romances accept implicitly that the *hero* should be chaste, as well as the traditionally chaste heroine. Once again Chaucer's Troilus is an example, in contrast with his Italian prototype, Troilo, in the poem by Boccaccio on which Chaucer based his own poem. The poem *Sir Gawain and the Green Knight* makes the hero's chastity the essential point of the poem. Gawain is also extremely devout, especially in the service of the Blessed Virgin. Yet he is equally certainly a secular courtier. No doubt the behaviour of knights in real life was often different but the point is that the ideals of secular life and religious life were coming close together from both sides. The ability to read and consequently to draw conclusions from the Bible would have brought them closer together still, though not necessarily in agreement. The late medieval church was thus untrue to its own nature in trying to preserve its own educationally and socially privileged position which it had quite rightly undermined by its own activities. Nevertheless, vernacular piety increased throughout the fifteenth century, genuine if often morbid and sentimental. The many pious and orthodox poems, sermons, saints' lives and other treatises in English all bear witness to the growth of religion, even apart from the substantial number of illicit Lollard Bibles and treatises which also circulated. The final achievement of a national church using for all purposes the mother tongue in a national state, needed a whole set of most extraordinary circumstances, including a wilful king and the new learning of Humanism, to bring it about, and is outside our present period.

That achievement of a fully unified national culture in the mother tongue was, however, inherent in most of the developments, economic, social, intellectual, and religious which took place during the Middle Ages, even though it also destroyed some things that were themselves essentially medieval. The triumphs of the sixteenth century in English culture may reasonably be regarded as the natural climax of that remarkable period of growth and improvement which followed the Conquest and which overcame such devastating disadvantages and disasters. Yet the medieval period is not to be regarded merely as a set of stages on the way to the sixteenth century. Leaving aside how far the sixteenth century may properly be regarded as intrinsically medieval, the earlier medieval centuries have their characteristic achievements, fascinating in themselves as well as of fundamental influence on later English history.

## NOTE

No single book, or small group of books, covers the whole period. A beginning may be made with Derek Brewer, *Chaucer and His World* (London, 1978), and books referred to therein. For the general developments associated with writing and print see, for example, M. McLuhan, *The Gutenberg Galaxy* (London, 1962), and (more technical) M. T. Clanchy, *From Memory to Written Record, England 1066–1307* (London, 1979).

# PART II

# A SURVEY OF MEDIEVAL VERSE
# AND DRAMA

JOHN SPEIRS

Anyone interested to read English medieval literature, for its own sake and as a preliminary to a fuller enjoyment of modern English literature, will first ask himself a number of questions. There is the question of what to read, and in what order to read it; and then there is the question of how to read each particular work of literature. These questions turn out to be anything but simple.

The question of what to read, of course, is not the same as the question of what exists to be read. The works that constitute English medieval literature, or the fragment of it that has chanced to be preserved, are still sufficiently numerous to involve a problem of judicious selection. We must wish to know what is *best* to read. Life is too short for reading much more than what Arnold once called 'the best that is known and thought in the world'. What needs to be recognized is that there *is* a task of selection to be performed; that there *are* works which are of more value than others; and that among these there are certain works which might indeed be a serious loss for any reader of English to have missed. The task is specifically one for literary criticism. Moreover, at a time when the function of evaluative criticism is neither widely respected nor always competently performed, the individual reader himself has to be unusually critical or, in other words, an uncommonly good reader. That means that one should not approach the reading of medieval English literature with confidence unless one is already fairly experienced in the reading of more modern English literature. Such reading involves a kind of active and intelligent collaboration on the part of the reader in recreating each unique work of literary art from the words on the page. It follows that generalizations about how to read are of little use and may be positively obstructive. Each work of literature requires to be individually re-made (or 'realized') by the reader for himself; but the more experience the reader has previously had in reading literature and the more experience of life the better, even if it has only taught him always to expect something different, to expect the unexpected.

There is no doubt about Chaucer. At least since Dryden he has been established, for our assent or dissent, as the first great classic of English literature. Of course, there is a solid body of academic opinion which holds that we are not competent to read the poetry of Chaucer and his contemporaries until we have acquired what is often called 'background'. But there is no end to the acquisition of 'background'. Such of Chaucer's 'background' as is relevant to his poetry is, after all, implied and indicated in the poetry itself, and the most relevant way to that background is surely through the reading of the poetry. The best preparation for reading the poetry of Chaucer and his contemporaries is experience in reading poetry.

It may perhaps be assumed from the start that English medieval literature is a part of English literature as a whole and, at the same time, part of European medieval literature. The idea that English readers should approach it by way of previous readings in European medieval literature rather than from experience in reading modern English literature is one of those ideas that turn out to be the less satisfactory the more they are examined. Until a reader has made himself proficient in reading literature – poetry, drama, novels – in his own language, he is unlikely to make much of literature in a language other than his own. The English reader who aspires to read European medieval literature will do well to begin by steeping himself in English medieval literature, and to approach the troubadours and trouvères through the poetry of Chaucer, rather than attempt to approach Chaucer through the poetry of the troubadours and trouvères. As he extends and deepens his reading of English medieval literature, he may, indeed, find that it will of itself lead him outward to the European literature of which it is a part – and not only to the French and Italian and medieval Latin literature, but also to the Old Norse and German and Celtic literatures. Thus with a certain inevitability he will be led to appreciate that throughout the Middle Ages there must have been the liveliest inter-connection and interplay between these diverse written and oral literatures. In the meanwhile, he will gradually have come to recognize that in reading English medieval literature he is at the beginning of modern English literature and that his understanding and enjoyment of modern literature will have been enriched by his medieval reading. He would recognize, for example, what was new in what Chaucer did as distinct from what was medieval. As Matthew Arnold recognized in 'The Study of Poetry':

> If we ask ourselves wherein consists the immense superiority of Chaucer's poetry over the romance-poetry, [we shall find that it] is given by his large, free, simple, clear yet kindly view of human life – so unlike the total want, in the romance-poets, of all intelligent command of it. Chaucer has not their helplessness; he has gained the power to survey the world from a central, a truly human point of view.

## Chaucer's Art

Chaucer (c. 1340–1400) is by general concurrence the greatest English medieval author, the centre of English medieval literature, as it seems to exist for us.

Furthermore, for readers accustomed to modern literature – not only non-dramatic poetry, but dramatic poetry and novels – Chaucer is the medieval author who is likely to appear most familiar and congenial. What was new and unfamiliar in Chaucer for his contemporary audience is probably just what seems most familiar to us. It is therefore not so easy for us to recognize that Chaucer was a very remarkable innovator. He adapted certain modes, themes, and conventions of French and Italian medieval poetry to English poetry for the first time. But he was a still more remarkable innovator than that might suggest. He developed the art of literature itself beyond anything to be found in French or Italian or any other medieval literature. (This is not, of course, to deny that he necessarily lost certain qualities in the process.) In *Troilus and Criseyde* he gave the world what is virtually the first modern novel. In the *Canterbury Tales* he developed his art of poetry still further towards drama and towards the art of the novel.

It should not be surprising, therefore, that Chaucer has seemed to many readers to stand at the beginning of modern English literature – as Homer has seemed to stand at the beginning of Greek, indeed of European, literature – almost as if he had founded or invented it. But it should equally be observed that the practice of the art of poetry had been continuous and widespread throughout the Middle Ages and that Chaucer comes towards the end of that whole period. Implicit in his art are centuries of both oral and written poetic practice and development in several European languages, including English itself, though Chaucer *does* consciously borrow very much from French and Italian poetry. Any idea that, because (from our viewpoint) Chaucer is an 'early' English poet, he is 'primitive' or 'naïve' should be impossible to anyone who responds to his poetry. The civilized delicacy of Chaucer's poetic art cannot be dissociated from that of his mind and spirit. Consider the witty urbanity of the opening of the Prologue to the *Legend of Good Women*, its delicate poise between polite scepticism and modest (perhaps essentially religious) recognition of the limits of human reason and experience; the polite ease of its conversational tone and manner is itself an aspect of the art:

> A thousand tymes have I herd men telle,
> That ther is joye in heven, and peyne in helle;
> And I accorde wel that hit is so;
> But natheless, yit wot*ᵃ* I wel also,
> That ther nis noon dwelling in this contree,
> That either hath in heven or helle y-be,
> Ne may of hit non other weyes witen,
> But as he hath herd seyd, or founde hit writen;
> For by assay ther may no man hit preve.
> But god forbede but men shulde leve*ᵇ*
> Wel more thing then men han seen with ye!
> Men shal nat wenen*ᶜ* every-thing a lye
> But-if him-self hit seeth, or elles dooth;
> For, god wot, thing is never the lasse sooth,
> Thogh every wight ne may hit nat y-see.
> Bernard the monk ne saugh nat al, parde!
>
> (1–16)

Chaucer's mastery of his art – which is at the same time a mastery of life – is rooted deep in past poetic practice and in a civilization already centuries old. On the other hand, his originality marks a new beginning. It would indeed be misleading to place the emphasis finally on Chaucer's urbanity rather than on the wealth and depth of his humanity and the fertility of his inventiveness. His genius owes more perhaps to the English language of which he is a master, the English that was *spoken* around him, than to the French and Italian poets from whom he consciously borrowed and to whom he certainly owes much.

*a* know, *b* believe, *c* consider.

Chaucer begins as a trouvère in English. It is very likely that his earliest work has not been preserved. But, in his poetry as we have it, he begins as a translator of *Le Roman de la Rose*. Thereafter, throughout his work, we see that he has continued to borrow and adapt from French and Italian poets even when he is most 'English'. The art of Chaucer, therefore, implies and includes the art – the conventions and themes – of the trouvères and of his French and Italian contemporaries. But the language of Chaucer's poetry is English; and, if we consider the colloquial character of Chaucer's English, even in such of his poetry as is not dialogue or monologue, it is unmistakably the English spoken by the community to which he belonged. English was, of course, the language of a people who were largely country folk, though there was already a middle class becoming wealthy, independent and important. Chaucer's poetry gained immensely in the vividness and variety of its imagery and its idioms from being in the spoken language of the medieval English people. But the language of Chaucer's poetry is unmistakably that English further shaped, refined, and pointed in the conversation of cultivated and witty courtly folk. If Chaucer's audience – though a portion of it may have been bilingual – was not English-speaking as well as courtly, why are his poems English and courtly? 'All art is a collaboration.' Chaucer's English poetry cannot be felt to be over-sophisticated, over-refined, or artificial. It is anything but superficial in that sense. There is nothing exclusive about it. It implies a whole varied community and a single civilization. There are implied in Chaucer's English not only the courtly folk, but the country folk and the new bourgeoisie, who figure also as characters in his human comedy; and for all its diversity, the community implied in Chaucer's English – in Chaucer's poetry – strikes us as a remarkably harmonious whole.

No amount of background knowledge is likely by itself to assist a reader in apprehending more sensitively and intelligently such essential aspects of Chaucer's poetry as its rhythm and imagery or, indeed, its whole structure, effect, and import. On the other hand, many of the subtleties and delicacies of his poems – the finer shades and subtler points of his irony and wit, for example – must at first be uncertain to a modern reader, before he has read his way alertly into a certain inwardness with Chaucer's idiom and mode of speaking. It is only by coming across particular words (such as 'curteisye', 'gentilesse', 'vileinye', 'fantasye', 'semblaunce', 'maistrye', 'kinde', 'vertu', 'corage', 'usage') again and again in the various living and changing contexts of Chaucer's poetry that the reader begins to acquire a feeling for their specifically Chaucerian shades of meaning and implications, a feeling more delicate and exact than he would get by providing himself with modern equivalents from a glossary or notes. Words acquire their *exact* meaning in Chaucer's, as in any other, poetry from the way in which they are used, from their interplay in particular arrangements or structures of words. The poetry itself shows that it was composed in the first instance not only for an intelligent, lively, and cultivated audience, but also for a circle of people who had common standards and who very well understood each other. We modern readers of Chaucer are, in that respect, comparatively outsiders. Nevertheless, if we ask why we are justified in saying that Chaucer, like Shakespeare, is for all time, one partial answer is perhaps that the greatness of his poetry – particularly as a presentation of the human comedy – depends on an inexhaustible 'source' in the life and speech of a whole varied community.

Chaucer's poetry appears to have been intended to be read aloud, as for centuries previous to Chaucer poems had been recited to companies of listeners. Though Chaucer was in some ways a new kind of poet in English, the art of poetry was to Chaucer still a social art, intended for the entertainment or instruction of a company. All poetry should be listened to, at least with the inner ear, and in the case of Chaucer that means listening to a kind of talking, even when it is the poet himself who seems to be talking familiarly to the company he is entertaining. But, above all in the *Canterbury Tales*, we are listening much of the time to the talking of *characters*, listening not merely to 'vowel music' but to full-bodied conversation implying in its movement and rhythm the accents, inflections, and even the bodily gestures of live speakers.

Chaucer's verse was not only spoken, but spoken differently from our own; it is therefore probably best to try to accustom ourselves to pronouncing it as nearly as possible in the way it is supposed to have been pronounced, yet to do this only in so far as it can be done easily and without becoming a distracting preoccupation. The spelling, which must surely have been intended by the scribes to be phonetic, is the principal guide. It is the vowels which have chiefly to be attended to. Moreover, it is essential to read Chaucer's verse metrically if we are not to fall into the error of supposing it to have merely what Dryden called 'the rude sweetness of a Scotch tune'. Thus the -e ending of so many of the words was generally pronounced (except when the succeeding word begins with a vowel). The surest guide as to when or when not to pronounce the -e is the metre itself, once the reader has instinctively fallen into it. Gradually his feeling for the variety and flexibility, the subtle and dramatic changes in conversational movement within the strict metrical formality, will grow from reading the poetry itself.

## Chaucer's Poems and Medieval Genres

Chaucer's greatest achievement, the *Canterbury Tales* (*c*. 1386–1400\*), is what the modern reader will probably read first. It will also be what he is most likely to return to again and again. For depth of interest, for the wealth of its impressions of the human comedy, and for its mature wisdom, it is unrivalled among Chaucer's works. *Troilus and Criseyde* (*c*. 1380–85) is its greatest predecessor among these. In this poem the modern reader will discover, emerging out of a medieval romance, what is virtually a great novel – the first modern novel. The more conventional elements in the poem, which were probably the most familiar to the original fourteenth-century audience, will be the least familiar to the modern reader. But he will make their acquaintance in this poem in the way that should be the most intelligible to a modern mind; even the medieval convention of courtly love, for instance, is handled critically in the poem. This criticism of conventions is, of course, part of the poem's 'criticism of life' in the Arnoldian sense of the endeavour to see life as it is; it is not abstract, but is presented, as by a great novelist, in terms of contrasts between flesh-and-blood persons – Pandarus, Criseyde, Troilus – and of live and developing human relationships. Thus Pandarus, the first great comic creation in English, contrasts with Troilus, the courtly lover of trouvère poetry; Criseyde, so various, so alive, seems to fluctuate between the two, though she is always a vivid and complex individual, the first complete character of a woman in English literature. The poem is both comedy and tragedy.

---

\* The chronological order of the poems is fairly well established, but their dates can only be conjectured.

It is comedy in its searching, though infinitely charitable, contemplation of human frailties, in the setting of the social scene; and it is tragedy in its recognition of the impermanence of human relationships and, finally, in the disastrous conclusion of the loves of Troilus and Criseyde and the defeat of the worldly wisdom of Pandarus.

Chaucer's first major poem is his *Romaunt of the Rose* (before 1373). In starting with this the reader will encounter a delightful new English poem and at the same time the nearest thing in English to the original *Roman de la Rose*. The English reader could have no more intimate introduction to the medieval French romances and allegories of courtly love, to the poetry of the trouvères, and, ultimately, of the troubadours. At the same time the poem may well come to seem to him the embryo out of which all Chaucer's poetry grows, although it is clear that the 'sources' which at different stages nourish the varied growth of Chaucer's poetry are many and diverse and are not all 'literary'. Chaucer's principal 'source' may surely be said to be the English that was spoken around him and out of which he made his poetry, drawing on it abundantly in his later poetry to express his direct observation and knowledge of the life around him. But the *Roman de la Rose*, his original *literary* source or model (in his poetry as we have it), may be observed to underlie not only the succession of dream-vision poems, but even, in some measure, the *Canterbury Tales*. Thus, right through Chaucer's poetry, the personifications of the *Romaunt of the Rose* may be observed in process of growing into the persons of the *Canterbury Tales*; and thus, out of the allegory of courtly love, comes *Troilus and Criseyde*.

The two parts of the *Roman de la Rose* are in effect two quite different poems.* The original courtly love allegory of Guillaume de Lorris (thirteenth century) is continued in a very different key by the sceptical Jean de Meung (*c.* 1250–1305). Both poets were of considerable importance for Chaucer. A reading of the first part of the Chaucerian *Romaunt of the Rose* will introduce the modern English reader in the most direct way possible for him to medieval courtliness and courtly love, to a poetry that was intimately associated with the spring festivals when both peasant and courtly folk danced and celebrated the annual triumph of summer over winter. This spring

* See the parallel medieval volume, *The European Inheritance*.

note continues right through Chaucer's poetry. Not least, the first part of the poem will introduce the reader to medieval allegory and its setting within a dream-vision. Although Chaucer's poetry not only grows out of but away from allegory towards a larger, freer realism, allegory still underlies even the *Canterbury Tales*.

Allegory was the way the medieval mind characteristically worked. It was a mode of seeing; by its means what was dimly thought or felt was made visible, the abstract made concrete, the barely intelligible made imaginable and so more clearly intelligible. The power of visualization is controlled, concentrated in allegory until it attains the order and lucidity of vision. The medieval allegorical habit modified the language itself. The English of our medieval literature is full of personifications or of words and phrases that are on the point of becoming so; and personifications are a feature of allegory. As in Dante, so in Chaucer frequent similes promote the distinct visualization which is an essential aspect of allegory and is still an aspect of the 'realism' of the *Canterbury Tales*.

In his part of *Le Roman de la Rose* Jean de Meung contributes a sceptical tone and attitude which, as we can observe in Chaucer's poetry, had a share in promoting the growth and maturity of Chaucer's much larger, more humane wisdom. The mocking spirit of Jean de Meung is by no means discordant with that of the *fabliaux*, those ribald and anti-clerical tales which appear to have been particularly popular among the new, increasingly independent bourgeoisie of both France and England. The *fabliaux* provide Chaucer with a contrast of attitude to the poetry of courtly love, as well as a disrespect for clerics, which he made the basis of a more profound comic criticism. Certainly it cannot be accidental that in the *Canterbury Tales* Chaucer has turned to the *fabliaux* as a source of several of his best tales. Chaucer's *fabliau* tales must, of course, be distinguished from the rudimentary tales that the *fabliaux*, as they existed orally, must in general have been. In Chaucer's hands they have been shaped with masterly comic art.

The poem which the reader will come to next after the *Romaunt of the Rose* – because it appears to be the nearest to it both in composition and in its form and nature – will be the *Book of the Duchess* (*c.* 1369). Though the poem is an elegy, the lady who is dead is seen in recollection as when alive, the lady of the poetry of courtly love and something more, the first Chaucerian impression of a lady. This is still a somewhat immature poem. In the *Parliament of Fowls* (*c.* 1380), a delightful poem in celebration of St Valentine's Day, the garden has borrowed – or Chaucer has borrowed from the poetry of Boccaccio – something of the quality of early Renaissance Italy. But the liveliest passages of the poem are the very dramatic dialogues between the assembled birds.

This poem, apart from its unique value as a poem, introduces one of the most popular genres of medieval literature, the Bird and Beast Fable. These tales of talking birds and beasts were certainly not invented in the Middle Ages, though they were then added to and elaborated upon – when folks in the villages and small towns still lived familiarly with animals. (It has been argued that this species of tales may have originated in the impersonating of animals and birds by humans dressed in skins or feathers in the dramatic rituals of the ancient communities. In the same way there might well have originated the innumerable tales of metamorphoses, humans changed into animals or animals changed back again into humans; and thus might also have originated the tales of talking animals.) The possibility of a rich human comedy, playing upon the absurd resemblances between humans and animals, was realized from these tales by various medieval poets and above all by Chaucer himself in his masterpiece, the *Nun's Priest's Tale* of Chauntecleer and Pertelote.

In the clash between the 'gentils' and the 'cherles' in the bird-debate of the *Parliament of Fowls* we can also see emerging one of the *social* comedy themes of Chaucer's later poetry. Their *flyting* – exchange of satiric abuse – introduces yet another of the recurrent features of medieval poetry. It is again a feature which has a long ancestry, for it has been traced back to the flyting-match that was a regular preliminary to, or substitute for, the combat between the two antagonists – Summer and Winter, the Old Year and the New, the Old Divine King or God and the New – in ancient dramatic rituals. It is said to have been the origin of the boastings and abuse exchanged by heroes in epic poems and, indeed, in tragedies. In its humorous or satiric aspect it is more evidently a feature of comedies, and it has been convincingly claimed as the origin of satiric poetry itself.

From the *Parliament of Fowls* the reader will pass on to the *House of Fame* (*c.* 1380), which – at least in the second and third books – is a masterpiece of comic fantasy, with a graver undertone of contemplation of the vanity of human wishes. Out of his reading of Dante, and also of Ovid, Chaucer has made something entirely his own – informal, easy, familiar, conversational in tone. Thus, by way of these delightful poems, the reader will find himself back with *Troilus and Criseyde* and will better appreciate its magnitude and significance. Between *Troilus and Criseyde* and the *Canterbury Tales* comes the *Legend of Good Women* (*c.* 1385), whose Prologue is, perhaps, the loveliest of Chaucer's May vision poems. The God of Love and the Lady clothed in green, whom he conducts as his Queen at the head of a long procession of women across a meadow, are surely a happy reminiscence of the King and Queen of the May festivals, and this is not incompatible with their particular significance in the poem. The tales – the Legends themselves – appear to have come mostly or ultimately from Ovid. But they show already that poetic-dramatic genius in presenting scenes and persons which is one of the characteristics of the far greater *Canterbury Tales*, the great human comedy of the literature of the Middle Ages.

The *Canterbury Tales* should be read as a whole poem and not simply as a collection of tales from among which one may pick self-contained masterpieces. The unity of the *Canterbury Tales* as it stands is not altered by the fact that the whole poem as planned remained incomplete and that several of the individual tales appear not yet to have been arranged in any final order when the poet died. In what we do have, there are indeed more than the beginnings of a formal arrangement: certain groupings of the tales have been made, sequences have been established, deliberate contrasts between tales are apparent. Nevertheless, there had been no final arrangement, and it seems superfluous for modern editors to attempt to do more in that way than Chaucer himself had already done. It is superfluous principally because the tales themselves seem to have the power to combine, in more or less any order in which one reads them, into a unity that builds up out of contrasts, an orderly impression of the rich disorder of life. The reader, therefore, should not allow what he happens to know of the uncompleted scheme to interfere with his feeling for the organic completeness of the poem as it stands and for its inclusiveness as an impression of the diversity of human life.

It follows from this that while each tale has its own individuality and can be enjoyed in and for itself, in relation to the other tales it has a far richer significance. The *Clerk's Tale* of Patient Griselda, for example, so often studied out of its context, is a deliberate contrast with the Wife of Bath's Monologue and with the tale of the disillusioned Merchant, whose own wife has proved no Patient Griselda at all. A tale unusually solemn in itself – and too good to be true, so to speak – thus becomes part of the comedy.

But each tale has still further significance not only in relation to other tales but also in relation to the great *Prologue*, to the interludes between the tales, to the character of its own teller, and to the characters of the other Canterbury pilgrims who tell the other tales and who are imagined to make up the audience – indeed, in relation to the whole movement and animation of the larger dramatic poem which the *Canterbury Tales* virtually is. In its total impression, the Canterbury Pilgrimage of the poem is the procession of the human comedy itself. The diversity of the tales fulfils the promise of that initial diversity of pilgrims presented in the *Prologue*, 'characters' who are individuals and at the same time are morally and socially representative. In the interludes between the tales these 'characters' are set in action, talking, disputing, and the tales themselves are a livelier extension of their talk. These tales are the entertainment the pilgrims provide for each other and at the same time they are a fuller revelation of themselves, their interests, attitudes, and antagonisms. For example, the *Friar's Tale* is directed against the Somnour: he tells how a rascal somnour falls in with a fellow-traveller, a forester clad in green who turns out to be a fiend and carries the somnour off to hell; the *Somnour's Tale* is at the expense of a friar and is his reply to the *Friar's Tale*. Thus the two rascals mutually expose one another in their tales.

Most of the tales appear, with regard to their sources, to be old traditional tales that were told in this age of story-telling when there were rich oral as well as written traditions to draw on. In making his Canterbury Tales Chaucer appears to have drawn much more freely than in his earlier poems on less narrowly 'literary' sources. Some of the tales are based on old romances or 'Breton lays', others on *fabliaux* or 'merry tales'. But of almost every one he makes a work of the maturest and wisest art. Yet where the art seems most mature, the traditional roots are also the deepest. The Wife of Bath's great dramatic monologue is a brilliant new invention of sophisticated art. But it grows out of ancient roots, partly the traditional flytings between man and wife, contentions for the 'maistrye' such as that between Noah and his wife in the Miracle Plays. The Wife of Bath herself is a new type – the bourgeois woman, one might call her – yet in essentials she is as old as humanity.

In reading and re-reading, one will necessarily exercise one's judgement as to which are the outstanding masterpieces among the tales. I would myself mention the *Nun's Priest's Tale* and the *Pardoner's Prologue* and *Tale*, the *Wife of Bath's Monologue* and *Tale*, the *Merchant's Tale* of January and May, the *Canon's Yeoman's Prologue* and *Tale*, the *Franklin's Tale*, and the tales of the Miller and Reve and of that other quarrelling pair, the Friar and the Somnour. I am not overlooking the *Knight's Tale* or the *Clerk's Tale* or the *Prioress's Tale*, but simply emphasizing that in Chaucer's hands the comic becomes a work of art. The *Miller's Tale* is not only Chaucer's comic art at its maturest but – and this is only another way of saying the same thing – it is his poetry at its richest. Consider the fertility of the imagery out of which Alisoun, the rich old carpenter's young wife, is created. The tales are poetry – the *fabliaux* tales no less than the others – poetry that in its creation of characters, scenes, episodes and dialogues is of the nature of dramatic poetry.

The *Canterbury Tales* is one of the two greatest achievements in English medieval literature, the other being a poem of a very different kind, the alliterative *Sir Gawain and the Green Knight*. The contrast between some of Chaucer's tales is sufficiently striking. But the contrast which these two masterpieces make with each other is even more striking, and their creative diversity is a remarkable testimony to the flourishing condition of English poetry in the fourteenth century.

### The Alliterative Poems and 'Sir Gawain and the Green Knight'

The alliterative poems of the West Midlands and the North-west are very unlike Chaucer's poetry in important respects and, indeed, make a most stimulating and interesting contrast with it. These alliterative poems show by comparison in what respects Chaucer was an innovator in English – the extent to which he brought English poetry into accord with the poetry of France and Italy, and also what he did that was new not only in English but in European literature. At the same time, the comparison with the alliterative poems is not all to Chaucer's advantage. While he has gained in witty urbanity and courtly ease and smoothness of versification, he has sacrificed extra-rational and pre-Christian elements and a certain massive native strength, all of which are found in the alliterative poems. Moreover, the latter are just as much works of art, in their different traditional kind, as are Chaucer's poems, and they imply as noble and as cultivated audiences – though these were evidently located in the provinces and were naturally conservative in their tastes.

The masterpiece among the alliterative poems which have survived from the fourteenth century is undoubtedly *Sir Gawain and the Green Knight*, which I will discuss at some length, as it deserves. But there are others which in their nature may properly be grouped with that poem, and which are scarcely less masterly; these include *Winner and Waster*,★ *The Parliament of the Three Ages*, *The Awntyrs of Arthur at the Tarn Wadling*, the alliterative *Morte Arthur*, and *The Destruction of Troy* (this and Lydgate's *Troy Book* are the two principal English medieval Troy books). It is a remarkable fact that *Sir Gawain and the Green Knight* itself and most of the other alliterative poems which we may associate with it are virtually accidental survivors from the Middle Ages. Had it not been for the chance preservation of a single MS – the only MS in which the poem is preserved to us – we should have known nothing of this masterpiece. The same is true of most of the poems which constitute the so-called alliterative 'revival' of the fourteenth century. (*Piers Plowman*, which has been preserved on forty-seven MSS, is a very special case.)

Now, since these poems have been preserved virtually by accident, we may surely conclude that there must have been others; that, magnificent poems as several of them are, they are the accidental survivors of what – judging from these poems alone – must still have been a widespread and flourishing tradition of alliterative poetry in the West Midlands and the North-west of England. Not one of these poems reads like a self-conscious attempt by an isolated poet to 'revive' a disused and archaic mode. The reason why the pre-

---

★ This poem is included in the anthology in this volume.

decessors of these poems in the same living tradition have not been preserved to us must either be that these predecessors were never written down or, if they were, the MSS have been lost. Whichever explanation is the right one (and I am inclined to the former), these poems seem to me unmistakably the final poems we have in English of the great oral tradition of Northern European alliterative poetry, oral in the sense that they could have been originally composed and remembered and recited without the intermediary of writing and reading. In such a tradition, their art, much more even than Chaucer's, must have been the product of a collaboration between the poet and his audiences as well as between the poet and his predecessors. For although Chaucer's art is still largely social, he is much more the new kind of individual artist than his contemporaries of the West Midlands and North-west.

*Sir Gawain and the Green Knight* (latter fourteenth century) is a great poem, and the strength and vividness of its poetry depends on the very wealth of its vocabulary. The poem must be read aloud to enable the masterly rhythm to come into play, and it will then be realized how little this alliterative verse is awkward or uncouth. The poem has the unity of a very completed, very deliberately constructed and finished work of art. But the unity is more than a construction; it has the character of an organic unity, a unity of growth.

The poem is clearly a midwinter festival poem. The seasonal theme is the poem's underlying, indeed pervasive theme. The Green Knight, whose head is chopped off at his own request and who is yet as miraculously or magically alive as ever, bears an unmistakable relation to the Green Man – the Jack in the Green* or the Wild Man of the village festivals of England and Europe. The episode (the First Fit of the poem) in which the Green Knight rides into the hall of Arthur's castle among the courtly company at the Christmas feast and demands to have his head chopped off is exactly a Christmas pageant play or interlude – a castle version of the village folk play – become real. The subject of our poem is a kind of contest – not the orthodox kind of knightly contest but a kind of ritual contest in which the two antagonists are Gawain and the Green Knight.

* It can scarcely be accidental that so many village pubs in England are called The Green Man.

Further, Gawain must engage in a quest, and must pass certain tests; thus the whole has very much the character of a story of an initiation.

*Sir Gawain and the Green Knight* is of course a Christian poem But it is Christian rather as some of the medieval Christmas carols are, as Christmas itself is; Christian in harmony with pre-Christian nature belief and ritual, a Christian re-interpretation of these. It is Christian to about the same depth as it is a courtly romance. The whole poem is, in its very texture – its imagery and rhythm – an assertion of belief in *life* as opposed to winter deprivation and death; and it seems finally to discover, within the antagonism between man and nature, between the human and the other-than-human, a hidden harmony, expressed in the kind of humorous understanding that develops between the Green Knight and Gawain.

The poem begins with a superb impression of the Christmas and New Year festivals at Arthur's castle. But the ceremonial banquet has hardly commenced, the first course brought in with 'crakkyng of trumpes', when

> Ther hales in at the halle dor an aghlich*ᵃ* mayster

He is no mummer disguised as a Green Knight who rides into the hall; he is the Green Knight.

The huge impression, larger than life – the Green Knight on the green horse – is massively built up. He is not only faery but robustly substantial and a fiercely humorous character. The emphasis on his glittering array – the jewel-like greenness of his green colour and that of his horse, the glittering green jewellery, the rich embroidery of multiplied 'bryddes and flyghes' – is unmistakably significant of life resurgent. It is as though the summer has entered. A 'salvage' intruder, he 'breaks the good feast', disturbs the ceremonious courtly order with his presence and his challenge; the contrast is, at one level, between 'nature' and 'sophistication'. He evokes a half-amused, half-horrified fascination. If he is life, he is wild, uncouth, raw life. His demeanour and his behaviour in this castle of courtesy are outrageously discourteous. In essence he is the *other* – the other than human.

The challenge, to who will, to chop off his head on condition

*ᵃ* terrifying.

that he who dares to do so will submit to have his own head chopped off on New Year's Day a year hence by the survivor, is accepted by Gawain, Arthur's sister's son, the pattern of courtesy. The dismembering act is gruesome enough. Yet the chopping off of his own head is to this amazing fellow but a 'Crystemas gomen'. With a savage yell ('a runisch rout') he flings out of the hall, fire struck from the flints by his horse's hooves.

The opening paragraphs of the Second Fit, superbly conveying an impression of the changing seasons, the revolving year, are not mere decoration. We are not just told that a year has passed; we experience the year changing, the alternating pattern of the seasons; everything is in movement, and we live through the year. The day approaches when Gawain must set off on his quest for the Green Chapel to keep his tryst with the Green Knight on New Year's Day and take the return blow. The concluding emphasis is on the waning of the year. The year's revolution has, however, again brought round the Christmas–New Year season. The poem is thus maintained right through as a Christmas and New Year festival poem.

The winter landscape through which Gawain now rides on his quest for the Green Chapel is not mere decorative background to a romance; it is the northern European Waste Land, the Utgard of Norse mythology. That is to say, it is actual winter as it may be experienced among the mountains of North Wales after a blizzard. The geography of Gawain's search for the Green Chapel is, and is intended to be, significant. The actuality of the experience of desolation – Gawain's experience of being a stranger in a mountainous frozen region – depends upon the actuality of this winter landscape. The experience is distinct because the landscape is distinct (in contrast to the indefinite dream landscapes of the *Faerie Queene*). It is a landscape from which God (originally perhaps the god) appears to have withdrawn. The actuality of this ice-bound universe is itself dependent upon distinctness and accuracy of sensation, on the sharpness or piercingness of the sensory impressions and the subtlety with which these are distinguished and differentiated:

> Ner slayn wyth the slete he sleped in his yrnes
> Mo nyghtes then innoghe in naked rokkes,
> Ther as claterande fro the crest the colde borne rennes,
> And henged hegh over his hede in hard iisse-ikkles.

As if in answer to his prayer Gawain is confronted with the miracle of a castle, seen first as like the sun shining through the trees –

It shemered and schone through the brode okes.

The lord of this castle (Sir Bercilak de la Hautdesert – the surname is perhaps significant) will, in the Fourth Fit, turn out to be the Green Knight. As a guest Gawain is restored by the warmth of hospitality and to the folk in the castle he is the pattern of courtesy.

The events of the three days before New Year's Day – the day of Gawain's tryst at the Green Chapel – are the subject of the Third Fit. They are days of apparent rest for Gawain but really of most perilous testing. During each of these three days the lord of the castle proposes to be abroad hunting. Each evening Gawain will exchange whatever he may have won during the day in the castle for whatever his host may have won in the chase. On his success or failure in these days of testing by the gay, youthful lady, his distractingly lovely hostess, will depend, though he does not guess it, his success or failure, indeed his life, at the Green Chapel.

The three episodes of the testing of Gawain by the lady who each morning steals into his chamber are interwoven with the three hunts. These slow-motion, gay but slyly perilous bedchamber scenes contrast with the vital activity and rush of these realistic hunts. The hunts are also symbolic parallels to the encounters in the castle between the lady and Gawain. The shy deer, the ferocious yet courageous boar, the cunning fox are the qualities of the natural man which Courtesy has to vanquish or, at least, civilize. Gawain's first natural reaction when the lady enters his chamber – like a huntress, 'with naked fote, stalking in my chamber' – is to pretend to be asleep and evade the issue (the deer); but he overcomes his shyness and is victorious by changing it into the exercise of a beautiful tact, a skilful and adroit courtesy. At her second visit she seeks to provoke his 'corage', the fierceness of his instincts (the boar); he is victorious by the *moral* courage with which he opposes his almost irresistible beautiful opponent without falling into discourtesy. But on the third occasion Gawain in ignorance partially identifies himself with the cunning (the fox) of the proffer of the Green Girdle – which later he recognizes as having been a snare – by accepting and concealing it.

The complex rhythm or pattern in this Fit is composed by the rotation of each day, slow – dangerously slow – in the castle in Gawain's chamber, swift in the hunt; each day opens with its dawn scene and closes with its evening feast after the day's hunt. Gawain's success each day synchronizes in the poem with the death of the hunted beast for which he faithfully exchanges the lady's kisses; there is one kiss to be exchanged on the first day, two on the second, three on the third. The humanity of the scenes distinguishes them from the 'temptation' scenes of the *Faerie Queene*; the gay laughing lady has more affinity with some of Chaucer's wives. The Third Fit draws to a close with the New Year's Eve Feast.

Gawain's journey through winter in quest of the Green Chapel is resumed in the Fourth (and last) Fit. The sense of time passing is again conveyed – on this occasion the passing of Old Year's Night into the wintry dawn of the New Year. The Green Chapel turns out to be not a chapel at all; it is 'nobot an olde cave', possibly a tumulus or barrow. Possibly in the wilder regions of Britain (as J. L. Weston thinks in *From Ritual to Romance*) such ancient shrines of an earlier worship were still places of worship – certainly of veneration or fear – as late as the fourteenth century. The experience that immediately follows is of a sudden, overwhelming release of life-energies, as of some sudden thaw in which the pent-up, gigantic life beneath the frozen earth bursts free or as of thunder among the mountains; suggestions of rushing water and wind powerfully contribute to the exhilaration of the experience. It is the Green Man sharpening his axe. The chief actors in the poem – essentially the hero and the god, man and nature – now again, as in the First Fit, confront each other.

The final test is executed by the Green Man with grim humour – two feints and a blow that merely grazes the skin, shedding a few symbolic drops of blood on the snow. For the Green Man turns out not to be such a bad fellow after all. The graze is for Gawain's fault in accepting and concealing the Green Girdle, from the lady. There follows immediately an impression as of a rebirth.

> And when the burne segh the blode blenk on the snawe,
> He sprit forth spenne-fote[a] more than a spere lenthe,
> Hent heterly[b] his helme, and on his hed cast,

*a* i.e. he sprang from his kneeling position, kicking out with his feet, *b* seized vigorously.

Schot with his schulderes his fayre schelde under,
Braydes out a bryght sworde, and bremely he spekes –
Never syn that he was burne borne of his moder
Was he never in this worlde wyghe half so blythe.

What is achieved seems to be a kind of adjustment, if not reconciliation, between man and nature, between the human and the other than human. In a more limited sense, the courtly order has been put to the test of nature. As a consequence Gawain recognizes his own nature, knows himself.

Once we begin to realize how closely worked is the art of the poem, how complex the poem is in its significance as a work of art, it should be possible to avoid the error of regarding it simply as a recorded myth, the record of the story of a ritual. A conscious artist, the poet *begins* from a myth; he *ends* with the poem we have.

The poem – the work of a highly conscious and sophisticated artist – implies also a conscious and sophisticated audience. If we required evidence that there existed in England in the fourteenth century not only a vivid local life but – in what we regard as a remote locality – a high degree of *civilization*, we need only point to this poem. Thoroughly *local* as the poem is there is nothing provincial in a limiting sense about it; it is, in the best sense, sophisticated. It implies, as Shakespeare does, a highly refined and complex literary art, which engages at all levels.

From *Sir Gawain and the Green Knight* the reader might well pass to the other associated poems of the Gawain Cycle, such as *The Awntyrs of Arthur* and *The Avowing of Arthur*. Alternatively, he might turn to *Winner and Waster* or *The Parliament of the Three Ages*. These latter vivid, satiric, and weighty poems are, in structure, flytingmatches and the nearest thing to a kind of ritualistic dramatic poem. The fact that the dramatis personae (the Three Ages, incidentally, are Youth, Middle Age, and Old Age) appear in a vision in alliterative poems of this nature should make us hesitate to derive the dreamvision convention in English medieval poetry solely from *Le Roman de la Rose*. The vision had also been a feature of the poetry of the North of Europe, where the poet was, perhaps, longer regarded as having the sacred character of a prophet than in the South.

Langland's (b. *c.* 1331) *Piers Plowman* is generally approached from

Chaucer's *Canterbury Tales*, and, indeed, it provides a usefully sharp and decisive contrast. But if we approach it from the reading of the other fourteenth-century alliterative poems – particularly *Winner and Waster*, its immediate predecessor in the tradition in which it belongs – we shall perhaps be in a better position to estimate its individual value as one among a number of alliterative poems. It is difficult to judge the poem as a whole because of the vastness of its bulk. The poetry has not, throughout the whole work, the density and richness of texture and significance of *Sir Gawain and the Green Knight* and *Winner and Waster* and *The Parliament of the Three Ages*; nor has it, at a first impression, the organic completeness of these masterpieces of art. Passages stand out from it very strikingly, and it may be that the new reader would be well advised to begin by appreciating them first, before attempting to grasp the work as a whole. These individual passages usually turn out to be those in which the poet is most 'traditional' – as in the presentations of the Seven Deadly Sins and the episode of the Harrowing of Hell.* The Seven Deadly Sins appear to have been creations (or re-creations from some older mythological or ritual figures) of the folk imagination as it took possession of the vernacular preachers. Through the vernacular sermons the Seven Deadly Sins evidently passed into the poetry and drama of the Middle Ages. These monstrous caricature figures – radically simplified or selected aspects of human nature, magnified and distorted, yet not less real than ordinary human life, though imbued with a fearful intensity – are early expressions of a large and important element in what became the English comic tradition, notably in Ben Jonson, and still present as an element in the kindlier comedy of Dickens. The Harrowing of Hell was an episode in the annually performed Miracle Cycle, and the moving rendering of it in *Piers Plowman* may well have been inspired by actual performances witnessed by the poet. Indeed, it is remarkable how much of the imagery in *Piers Plowman* could have come from seeing Miracle Plays.

The poem has been much investigated as a social document rather than as poetry. It contains – even as an allegorical vision poem – a large element of realistic social and moral satire. But the innermost

---

*Passus XX from the C Text, which contains the Harrowing, is included in the anthology in this volume.

core of its significance is certainly a mystical one. Its central symbol is that of Piers the Plowman as Christ.

Another poem which should be distinguished, for very different reasons, from the main group of fourteenth-century alliterative poems is *Pearl*.★ This poem has been preserved on the same manuscript as *Sir Gawain and the Green Knight* and is in the same dialect: it has thus come to be associated with it. But *Pearl* is a very different kind of poem. It is much more personal and private, less social in that it could not be described as being of the nature of 'oral' poetry or intended for the entertainment, or even enlightenment, of the convivial company in the great hall. It is made up of 101 elaborately rhymed and alliterated stanzas arranged into twenty sequences, the stanzas of each of these sequences being knit together by a final line refrain rather as in a ballade. The landscape of the dream-vision, the Earthly Paradise, is opulently decorative and brilliantly coloured in effect like a MS illumination or stained glass.

Nevertheless it would be grievously unjust to the poem to suggest that its interest and value are purely 'aesthetic' in the narrower sense. It has, of course, a mystical and theological significance, and is related to a public occasion – a high feast of the Church:

> In Auguste in a high sesoun
> When corne is corven with crokes kene.

Harvest is here associated not only with fruition but with cruel death. The poet has lost a 'pearl of price' which has slipped through the grass (the usual interpretation is that the loss was that of the poet's infant daughter). In a dream-vision he finds himself wandering in what seems to be the Earthly Paradise. It is distinguished from the garden of the Rose by its 'chrystal cliffs' and generally from all mundane gardens by the suggestion of its eternal, unfading jewel-like quality, and by its quality of light. On the opposite bank of a river which he cannot at present cross (the water of life is crossed only at death), he sees his Pearl transformed and transfigured now to a 'Heavenly Pearl', a maid decked in pearls as a Queen of Heaven, his daughter lost and restored, but still separated from him. The grain sown in the earth has flowered in heaven; the Rose that fades in nature has been eternalized as an unfading jewel – 'gathered into

---

★ *Pearl* is included in the anthology in this volume.

the artifice of eternity'. The child (cf. Beatrice) now instructs the man in heavenly wisdom and sacred theology and shows him finally a vision of Heaven. The poem appears to be in the nature of a religious exercise, the elaborate craftsmanship being itself a part of the disciplining perhaps of a rebellious personal grief. A detailed analysis of this poem would, I think, bring out the essential differences, rather than resemblances, between it and the other alliterative poems.

## The Metrical Romances

There are about sixty English medieval metrical romances extant. These, though they should all be studied in relation to each other, are of varying quality and require to be sorted out judiciously. But a few of them have some distinction and deserve to be known and valued by the general reader. Workers in the field of the origins of literature[1] have shown in great and convincing detail that the medieval romances are at the end of a process of evolution from myth or ritual to romance. The reader ignores their findings at some risk of an impoverished reading of the romance. Once the Arthurian romances – and other romances that may be associated with them – are recognized as being rooted in mythology, they at once begin to show themselves full of meaning and the more interesting as poetry.

The extant English metrical romances appear to belong to stages in the transition – during the thirteenth, fourteenth, and fifteenth centuries – from oral poetry to written composition. *King Horn* (c. 1225), which is perhaps the earliest, and *Havelok the Dane* (c. 1275) are explicitly minstrels' lays; and even those that come at the very end of this phase of minstrelsy (which was virtually over by the fifteenth century) cannot be dissociated from the recital, though some of them may have been written compositions and not merely written down. Many, in the form in which we have them, are evidently English redactions of earlier French romances. The tales which form the substance of these poems, and of the French romances on which many of them seem to be based, must have existed earlier and been transmitted and continually reshaped orally. Many of these tales, particularly those which form the substance of the Arthurian romances and of the Breton lays, have been regarded as Celtic, and their principal channel of development into French and English and German as the Breton story-tellers who were bilingual.[2] (As Bretons these *conteurs* would have had access to the rich storehouse of Celtic tales that had their origin in ancient Celtic myth and ritual. The richest original source may have been Irish; but Brittany and Wales, Cornwall and the West of Scotland shared much the same ancient culture. As professional story-tellers at the courts of kings and nobles in early medieval France and England, the Bretons told their tales in French.) Thus what may have been originally Celtic tales were made into French romances, influenced in greater or less degree by the spirit of courtliness and chivalry, the spirit of the troubadours and the trouvères. From French they passed into German and English. So the gods of ancient mythology became, on the one hand, medieval knights and, on the other, their monstrous or other-world antagonists; the spring or earth goddesses became courtly ladies or queens or, retaining their other-world character, fays.

If we compare the extant romances we should quickly recognize that a number of themes or motifs keep recurring in them, though always as variations. The impression grows that these themes are – or were at one time – related. There is, for example, the theme of the union of a mortal with an other-world being. Sometimes a mortal queen meets a splendid other-world stranger, or she is abducted by the King of the Other World. Or a mortal man – a knight – may meet in a forest a lady, surpassingly lovely, who is clearly a fay and who woos him. The knight may dwell in the other world with his faery mistress for, perhaps, seven years until he breaks some taboo which deprives him of her, to his inconsolable grief. Sometimes a knight may pursue through the forest a hart which turns out to be a faery messenger or guide. Often, indeed, the faery cavalcade are seen by a solitary mortal as they ride, in splendid attire, hunting through a forest or hawking by a river.

In one or two romances which have evidently come under ecclesiastical influence, such unions with an other-worldly being are regarded as unions with the devil, and the offspring may show demonic tendencies or be possessed of the devil (*Sir Gowther*, *Richard Coeur de Lion*). But in most of the romances there is no such sinister interpretation. Instead, we have the theme of the marvellous child, born of a union between a mortal and an other-world being, who is exposed or lost, and then found. This is the theme of the boy born to be king, exposed or exiled, who grows up in a poor man's hut perhaps or in some menial station in some other king's court, and in the end returns to claim his kingdom and be recognized as the true king. In several of the romances a similar cycle of separation and restoration is undergone by a wife or queen. Indeed, the theme of the child or wife lost and eventually found again is one of the most recurrent in the romances.

In many romances the theme is of a succession of tests – a kind of initiation – which a knight must undergo to prove his manhood; of a contest between a knight and some other than human or other-world character. This contest may be prolonged and may take many forms other than that of a direct combat. But a combat – often of an unusual kind – is frequently the climax, perhaps with the owner of what may be an other-world castle.

There can be no doubt that these themes are fragments of what was originally a mythology or several. R. S. Loomis and J. L. Weston in particular have gone far in an endeavour to reconstruct the mythology; and they regard it as (in relation to the Arthurian and associated romances) specifically Celtic. Thus the antagonists – the knight and the keeper of the other-world castle – were originally different phases of one and the same god, perhaps the old and the young sky-god, or the old and the new year, winter and summer. They are opposites and yet one and the same. The young god slays and supplants the old; yet he *is* the old renewed, become young again. In the original ritual – for a myth is the story of a ritual, the story the ritual enacts – the old divine king and the young king who supplanted him evidently impersonated one and the same god.

After the ritual combat follows the ritual marriage. The victor marries the goddess or queen. This goddess, the spring or earth goddess, has become in the medieval romances the faery lady or queen. She may correspond, in the Celtic mythology, to Proserpine. The loathly lady and the lovely lady of the romances are also essentially one and the same, as can be seen in those tales in which the former, disenchanted by the embrace of a courteous knight, changes back again into her original lovely and youthful self (e.g. Chaucer's *Wife of Bath's Tale*).

Least influenced by French romances and perhaps nearest to the Old Irish tales (perhaps combined with Norse), are the poems of the Gawain cycle which comes from the North-west of England – these include, besides *Sir Gawain and the Green Knight* itself, *The Avowing of Arthur* and *The Awntyrs of Arthur*, already mentioned. One of the most interesting of the northern English romances that may be associated with these is *Sir Perceval of Galles* (fourteenth-century MS). Perceval is brought up in the woods by his mother – evidently a water-sprite – as a 'wild man' and has the task of revenging his slain father, like Orestes or Hamlet. Among the first of the romances to be read might well be the charming group that are based on the Breton lays – *Sir Launfal*,★ *Sir Degare*, *Le Freine*, and perhaps *Sir Orfeo* (all in MSS of the fourteenth century). These are not specifically Arthurian, but they unmistakably belong with the Breton lays. In the lay of *Sir Orfeo* we meet the legend of Orpheus and Eurydice taken (at some time) possibly from the *Metamorphoses* of Ovid, but, having become associated with medieval traditional tales in the stream of oral tradition, it has been itself completely transformed into the nature of a Breton lay. The first of the other romances to be read should, perhaps, be those that have been regarded as peculiarly English or Scandinavian – *King Horn*, *Havelok the Dane*. But even those tales, from quite other sources and places, which form the substance of romances other than the Arthurian romances and the Breton lays, appear to have been modified by the influence of the latter and shaped according to the familiar traditional pattern. Even the latest of the 'new' compositions are combinations of the old.

Some of the English medieval romances appear to have passed through a process of remaking – or at least of rehandling – for successive recitals, until each was given the shape it had when written down on the MS on which it has been preserved. We must not assume that this process was always, or even usually in later tradition, one of improvement. On the contrary, many of the romances (such as those interesting ones preserved in the Percy Folio MS *c.* 1650) look like poems which have deteriorated in the process. It may be that some of them were originally works of individual genius, comparable even to *Sir Gawain and the Green Knight*, and have fallen into their present confusion in later tradition.

The process was, we know, complicated for medieval English

★ This poem is included in the anthology in this volume.

poetry by the fact that there was undoubtedly in early medieval England a phase of bilingualism – a phase when many people were both French- and English-speaking. During this phase, we may guess, the redactions from French into English were made. We have no right to assume, however, that such redactions were necessarily what we think of as translations, involving the intervention of reading and writing. As poems were made and shaped orally by minstrels, the redactions could be (and possibly often were, up to the fourteenth century) made orally. Poems were made to be heard, not read; and by the makers themselves, we may assume, the poems were heard as they were composed, rather than composed in writing. There was, of course, a long phase of both oral and written traditions, existing side by side. These traditions were certainly not isolated from one another; on the contrary, they drew freely from each other's repertory. Thus tales that were told were made into written tradition and later taken back again into the stream of oral recital and re-shaping.

It seems certain that many of the ballads that were collected in the seventeenth, eighteenth, and nineteenth centuries originated from the medieval minstrels' lays, though many were modified also (judging from their formal structures) by the medieval dance-songs. The ballads must have been flourishing among the unlettered people earlier than the centuries in which they were collected. The balladists (like the Elizabethan dramatists, in their different way) must have been successors of the minstrels of the early Middle Ages and of still earlier communities – no longer honoured and listened to by kings and nobles, but now occupying a humbler station among the people. Ballad recital and composition were still, to some extent, a collaborative activity. It is possible to see in the ballads – the ballads as they were sung or recited dramatically – a social and popular dramatic art that still flourished among the people, particularly in Scotland, up to the eighteenth century. Moreover, the themes of many of them are recognizably those of medieval romances. Thus, the minstrel's lay of *King Horn* is of the thirteenth century: the ballad of *Hind Horn* was there to be collected 600 years later (*c.* 1825).[3]

### Malory's 'Morte D'Arthur'

Though this chapter is primarily a survey of poetry (medieval prose being left to the next chapter), there are some advantages in including at this point Malory's prose *Morte D'Arthur* (printed by Caxton 1485). For it is best approached after a reading of the English Arthurian verse romances which preceded it, rather than from the poetry of Tennyson and other poets who have since used it as a source. As Professor Vinaver has shown in his edition of the works of Malory, what is really a succession of separate prose romances has been given an appearance of unity, of being one 'book', by the way they were edited and printed by Caxton (under the misleading title of *Morte D'Arthur*). There could be no greater contrast than that between Malory's exceedingly 'literary' fifteenth-century prose romances and the English verse romances or lays of the thirteenth and fourteenth centuries. Malory's prose, with all its seeming simplicity – it is a stylization of earlier medieval prose – is in some respects the nearest thing in medieval English to the prose of Walter Pater. There is a tone of *fin de siècle* about Malory's book.

At the end of the Middle Ages and the end of the long efflorescence of medieval romance in many languages, Malory endeavoured to digest the Arthurian romances into English prose, using as his source chiefly an assortment of French Arthurian prose romances. But this traditional material has not been organized so as to convey any coherent significance either as a whole or, for the most part, even locally. Malory persistently misses the meaning of his wonderful material. (This may have been partly because apparently he had no access to the earlier and better sources – if we except the fourteenth-century English alliterative *Morte Arthur* – and was dependent, or chose to be dependent, on his French prose romances.) The comparison with *Sir Gawain and the Green Knight* is in this respect – as, indeed, in nearly all respects – fatally damaging to Malory's *Morte D'Arthur*. The modern reader does best to accept the book as essentially episodic, a book to be dipped into rather than read through. Once we have fallen under the spell of such an episode as that of the Maid of Astalot, it is to it that we shall return.

What is it, then, that constitutes the charm of the book, that draws readers back to parts of it again? Partly it is the 'magic' of its style – those lovely elegiac cadences of the prose, that diffused tone of wistful regret for a past age of chivalry, that vague sense of the vanity of earthly things. Yet the charm of the prose is a remote charm; the imagery is without immediacy; there is a lifelessness, listlessness, and fadedness about this prose for all its (in a limited sense) loveliness. There is also the fascination of the traditional Arthurian material itself, even though we feel it is not profoundly understood. The material fascinates the reader in spite of Malory's 'magical' style, which seems to shadow and obscure rather than illuminate it. Malory's Grail books, for example, include some of the most fascinating of his traditional material. We find here once again the Waste Land, the Grail Castle, the Chapel Perilous, the Wounded King, and so on, but reduced to little more than a succession of sensations and thrills. The recurrent appearance of the corpse or corpse-like figure on a barge and the weeping women – fragments of an ancient mythology though they are – become in Malory merely tedious after a number of repetitions, and the final effect is one of a somewhat morbid sensationalism.

Some qualification of these strictures should be made on behalf of the last four books of Caxton's Malory, which may be felt to have an impressive kind of unity of their own. The lawless loves of Lancelot and Guinevere, the break-up of the fellowship of the Round Table through treachery and disloyalty, the self-destruction of Arthur's knights and kingdom in a great civil war, the last battle and death of Arthur, and the deaths of Lancelot and Guinevere have, as they are described, a gloomy power, and are all felt as in some degree related events. This set of events appears to have been deeply felt by Malory, partly as a reflection of the anarchy and confusion of the contemporary England of the Wars of the Roses.

## Medieval Lyrics and Carols

About the English poetry of the end of the fourteenth century it is still possible to make two broad distinctions. There is what may by then be called the old-fashioned kind of poetry; this is represented by the alliterative poems of the West and North Midlands which appear to come at the end of the oral tradition of Northern European poetry. On the other hand, there is the new-fashioned kind of poetry that is captivating the Court, London, and the South; this poetry, though English, is recognizably related to the traditions of the troubadours and the trouvères. Chaucer is the great poet of this new kind of poetry in English, though he went on to do things that were newer still. This newer kind of English poetry shows itself already in the century before Chaucer, in some of the features of the English songs and lyrics that have chanced to survive in about half-a-dozen MSS, and of an early thirteenth-century debate-poem or flyting called *The Owl and the Nightingale*.

The character of many of the thirteenth-century lyrics itself suggests clearly enough that they are words intended to be sung. Furthermore, the earliest of the English lyrics that have survived are anything but simple in the sense of being rudimentary or primitive, first awkward attempts. On the contrary, their genuine simplicity and spontaneity of effect are those of a complex and subtle art or craft of song-making. The word-structures of the songs were probably evolved in association with the music-structures which they were intended to fit. Moreover, the basic or original structure both of the music and of the words was evidently often determined by the dance – particularly by the ring dances. Thus several of the medieval songs, for example four short pieces preserved together on a fourteenth-century MS, 'The Irish Dancer', 'The Hawthorn Tree', 'All Night by the Rose', 'Maiden of the Moor', appear to belong with the sacred dances of the old Nature religion, and may have been evolved for special festival occasions, such as the May Day rites.

The division between secular and religious (Christian) lyrics appears to be somewhat artificial, or at least superficial. If one considers their imagery, versification, and indeed total textures, no radical division is observable. Moreover, the Christian lyrics are just as much rooted in pre-Christian myth and ritual, in the rites and ceremonies of the old Nature festivals, as are the so-called secular lyrics. Many of the Christmas songs were evidently associated with the ceremonies, games, and plays of the Christmas feast, and are explicitly songs for the boar-feast or ale-feast as the Christmas feast still largely was. With the more convivial of the Christmas carols we may associate the body of songs and lyrics which express the jollity of the medieval English folk on festive occasions.

As distinguished from the more boisterous jollity there is a note of 'mirth' (a word used then with a fuller and richer meaning than today) in many of the lovely hymns to Mary. Some of these are lyrics of courtly love transformed or transmuted. But also, in several of the most beautiful of them, Mary has something of the significance still of the tree goddess, the flower goddess, or the spring goddess.

In such carols as 'There is a floure sprung of a tree', 'Of a rose, a lovely rose', 'There is no rose of swich vertu', she is either herself the Rose or she is the tree out of which the Rose, who is Christ, springs. In other lyrics Mary is the tragic mother whose child is slain. The unusual, original beauty of the Corpus Christi Carol depends largely on the medieval association of the Crucifixion with the Grail myth.

While very many of the best lyrics are either spring songs or songs for Christmas, it would be giving a one-sided impression not to refer also to the lyrics on the decline of the year, the onset of winter, melancholy utterances or meditations on the uncertainty of the human lot, such as 'Wynter wakeneth al my care'.

In the fifteenth century many more of the lyrics seem 'literary', though there are still nearly as many of the 'traditional' kind. Towards the end of the fourteenth century already, Chaucer and Charles d'Orleans (in his English lyrics) are composing ballades and roundels modelled on the French with deliberate literary craftsmanship. But the old close association between words and music was never quite broken and continues and leads up to the songs of the glorious Elizabethan song-books.*

### 'The Owl and the Nightingale'

There is one English poem of about 1200 (the earlier of the two MSS is c. 1220), *The Owl and the Nightingale*, which, though not a song but a debate-poem of considerable length, may properly be associated with the thirteenth-century English lyrics and read along with them. Moreover, it provides a contrast with a contemporary alliterative work, Layamon's *Brut* (also c. 1200) which is much more the kind of thing one might have expected. If one were attempting to plot a history of early medieval English literature on the evidence of the scanty number of stray texts that have been preserved, *The Owl and the Nightingale* would have a place out of all proportion to its intrinsic merits, though these are not inconsiderable. There seems to have been nothing like it in English before, though it is improbable that so accomplished an English poem of its particular kind could in fact have been an isolated work. As it now stands among

---

* A selection of lyrics is included in the anthology in this volume.

what has survived, a poem earlier perhaps than the earliest surviving group of medieval English lyrics, it seems to represent all by itself an immense modification of the English sensibility, indeed to be almost the first evidence of an English sensibility as we have come to recognize it in English medieval poetry as distinct from Anglo-Saxon poetry. The English language, accustomed to move in the traditional alliterative kind of verse, is here discovered moving easily in rhymed verse (octosyllabic couplets) as to the manner born, as if this kind of verse had long been natural to English. This new kind of verse has certainly been adapted from French and medieval Latin. Yet the English of the poem still instinctively, as it seems, forms itself into frequent alliterative phrases. This poem also may well have been the work of a poet who was bilingual or trilingual, familiar with the contemporary French and Latin poetry, including debate-poems, and perhaps capable himself of composing in these languages. But, if so, he has in this English poem let the genius of his English language have full scope.

The greater part of *The Owl and the Nightingale* is a dialogue between the two birds, and it is thus very near to being a dramatic poem. The rest of the poem sets the scene and provides a spectator's impressions of the quarrelling birds. The opposition is not merely one of ideas but of persons; it is no impersonal academic debate on a set subject. It is essentially a flyting match in which the two birds are the antagonists. As such, it has an ancient ancestry, for the ceremonial flyting match is a phenomenon much older than the Middle Ages and seems to have been almost universal.

The nightingale starts the flyting match by abusing the owl. Her vivid description of the owl, head bigger than all the rest of him, accurate in relation to the bird, is of course a caricature if he is thought of as human. The effect on the owl is vividly seen; he is all swollen and bulged with inarticulate rage as though he had swallowed a frog. The debate thus begins dramatically as an exchange of abuse. Instead of fighting, however, the hostile birds agree to argue. The arguments are full of sense as well as being lively and satiric, and thus the poem is substantial and yet never dull. Nor, at the end, is either bird felt to have decisively the upper hand; the two are well matched, judiciously balanced against each other by the poet. The satiric flyting match and the seriously thoughtful debate – for the poem delightfully combines both these aspects – are sustained to a well-managed dramatic climax. For a critical moment there is a threat of actual battle. But the tiny wren intervenes as peace-maker, and the birds agree to fly off to seek judgement from a certain Master Nicholas of Guildford (perhaps the poet's friend or even, it has been suggested, the poet himself). We are not told what the judgement is. The balance is held, judgement suspended to the end.

The poet's greatest asset is his English vernacular. In listening to his disputing birds, we are listening to English as it must then have been talked in the poet's particular locality. With the conversational language, the contemporary life of the people has entered the poem – and the wild life of the countryside as it was familiar to the people. The satiric humour of the disputants is often of a savage kind, but one becomes aware that the violence of the disputing birds is comprehended within an understanding humour and humanity on the part of the poet as comic observer of life. The final impression of this familiar-talking poem is paradoxically not one of quarrelsomeness, but rather of friendliness, intimacy, and sociability. The colloquial English of the poem is saturated with the traditional wisdom of the people as it has been stored up in proverbial phrases. The wisdom of the poem as a whole is not so much a clerkly wisdom (though the poet may have been a clerk), as of a broad human experience.

## The Miracle Cycles

Four versions of the complete English Mystery (or Miracle) Cycle have been preserved – the York, Chester, 'Towneley MS' (probably Wakefield), and 'N-town' (probably East Anglian) Cycles. These have evidently been fashioned and shaped for the annual performances by the work of many hands. Though they have been preserved in MSS of the fifteenth century and later, it is probable that they had assumed or been given much the form in which we find them in the MSS by the end of the fourteenth century or the beginning of the fifteenth. Certain of these plays will seem to stand out from the rest of the Cycle as being more what we think of as plays – comedy or tragedy – presented to an audience. But even these should be viewed in their places in the Cycle – the larger play – in which they are episodes.

The Cycle as a whole appears to be still essentially at the stage of ritual drama. Probably those present at the annual performances should be regarded as worshippers and therefore, to a greater or less extent, participants. The actors or more active participants were probably, for most of the Cycle, not yet actors performing for the entertainment or edification of an audience, but rather impersonators in a ritual. We should probably not think of there being a marked division into spectators and actors as yet, although a few of the plays are beginning to imply an audience and therefore the beginnings of such a division. From our viewpoint, of course, we see the Mystery Cycle as in process of becoming what we may call, for the sake of suggesting the distinction, *art* drama. The few outstanding plays have, indeed, already become so. But even these are dramatic poems, the fullness of whose meaning depends on their still being rooted in ritual and ritual drama. The annual performance was, it would seem, nothing less than the great occasion of the year in the town-community life of the Middle Ages. The townspeople, as organized and incorporated in their Craft Guilds, performed it as an intrinsic part of the Corpus Christi procession at the height of the year (June). It was clearly what gave significance to the life of each year for both the individual and the community in which he belonged. Indeed, this Cycle of events and participation in it each year was probably felt to be more important to the townspeople than what we now look back to as the historical events of that year.

The Mystery Cycle represents or reproduces what might perhaps be called a history of the world – of mankind in relation to God – from the Creation to the Last Judgement. But, if so, it is a history different in kind from what we recognize as history today. The frequent anachronisms are not blunders. Past and future co-exist in the immediate present of each performance. Thus the whole Cycle itself concludes with what we should think of as a future event, the Last Judgement. The purpose or effect of the annual performance was evidently that of a ritual, namely to give significance or meaning to life for that year. The significant past had to be, and therefore was, annually recreated in order to make, and make fortunate, the future for that year, fortunate for the community as a whole and for each individual member of it. Between the Creation and the Judgement the central mystical events – central for everyone concerned – are the birth, death, and resurrection of Christ. The Old Testament episodes between the Creation and the birth of Christ are no more than a preparation for this great central sequence. The whole corresponds, of course, to the cycle of the Christian year.

The historical origins of the plays that have come to form the Mystery Cycle can, we know, be traced back to the embryo Latin plays which appeared first as intrinsic parts of the Church services at Easter and at Christmas. The first of these formal liturgical plays seems to have been the representation of the Resurrection. But corresponding to this little play – almost exactly parallel to it even in the phrasing – there appeared at almost the same time also a Nativity Play. Thus, the Sepulchre approached by priests impersonating the three Marys was the central object in the Easter Play: the cradle approached by priests impersonating the Three Shepherds was the central object in the Christmas Play. Yet the size and nature of what by the end of the fourteenth century had become the English Mystery Cycle cannot be entirely accounted for as a straight development or expansion from these priestly performances. The Mystery Cycle is a truly communal or national drama. There are things in the plays of which the Church became more than doubtful and, indeed, the whole Cycle became, from the Church's point of view, something which had got entirely out of hand. Was it merely the tendency in unregenerate human nature to turn sacred things to buffoonery and farce which was responsible for the transformation? There is surely a profounder explanation. It is clear that for the people the Mystery Cycle was profoundly important and not merely an opportunity for releases of rowdiness.

The explanation almost certainly is that there always had been – among the Scandinavian, Teutonic, and Celtic peoples as still earlier among the Greeks – a ritual drama since before Christianity. Everywhere among the people in the Middle Ages there were fragments of this older, pre-Christian dramatic ritual – ceremonies, dances, games – still being practised. They were being practised in some cases almost desperately, in defiance of the prohibitions of the Church, because they were still obscurely felt to be sacred and fundamental to life. Certain of these survived almost to our own day among the folk, as the Mummers' Play, the Wooing (or Plough) Play, the Morris Dance, and the Sword Dance. It is now generally agreed that these are not the blundering efforts of the folk at spontaneous dramatic creation, but are the degenerate and confused remnants of the dramatic ritual of an ancient Nature religion that had survived among the folk. We have come to think of the Miracle Play as standing alone, as virtually the only thing in the nature of drama in the Middle Ages (apart from the Morality Plays which the ecclesiastical authorities tried to offer as a substitute in the fifteenth century and which by the early sixteenth century had begun to be secularized). But that is because we too easily assume that only what has been recorded existed. There was, on the contrary, a great deal in the nature of dramatic ritual outside the Church with which the new Christian drama could become at least partially associated; and what we do in fact find in the Mystery Cycle itself is a profound union of the new and the old – such as the priestly class could not by itself have accomplished, even supposing it had wanted to do so.

The classical Greek drama was developed, we know, out of earlier dramatic rituals. The evolution of the English drama – the drama, above all, of Shakespeare – is perhaps more complex. It is necessary in its case to take account of the influence of Classical models at the Renaissance. Nevertheless, the only truly national or English drama before the Shakespearean is the Mystery Cycle – and that is certainly already the outcome of a union, a unique combination, of the dramatic rituals of the old religion and the new. Thus the Herod and the Pilate of the Mystery Cycle bear an unmistakable resemblance to the Turkish Knight of the Mummers' Play. But do we not also see them again on the Elizabethan stage itself as the prototypes of some of the villains and of the clowns (or at least farcical characters)? The Elizabethan dramatists did not need to borrow the stage type of the ranter or the boaster from Latin comedy or the Senecan tragedy – though the more scholarly were quick to find a classical sanction for their own creations. These types were vividly there already in the English dramatic tradition itself as Herod and Pilate, and generally as the antagonists in the flyting matches that so frequently enliven the Mystery Cycle. The association of buffoonery with death, which is another feature of the plays of the Mystery Cycle, has again its counterpart later in the mixture of comedy and tragedy which is so characteristic of Elizabethan drama and which so distressed neo-classic critics. Furthermore, certain of the themes and symbolisms which are to be found in Shakespearean drama – such as some of the symbolical significance of storms and disorders, both social and natural, the themes of winter and spring, of youth and age, of death and birth, of the lost one and the found one, and of disguises and metamorphoses, recognitions and restorations – are already present in the English Mystery Cycle and, more universally, in the dramatic rituals with which the Cycle had undoubtedly become associated and upon which it drew.

These plays yield their full meaning only when they are recognized as poetic drama rooted in ritual drama. They should be responded to fully as poems. The formula that drama is 'character in action' will only tend to inhibit this complete response, just as it does in regard to Shakespeare. In these plays it is of no use always to be looking for something in one of the characters to account for what happens. The dramatis personae can be vivid persons or presences, created in the poetry of the dialogues and monologues; but what happens can never be explained simply in terms of character or motive. Impersonal forces, forces outside and often greater than personality, have as much or more to do with the shaping of events; and the impersonal elements and conditions are what the poetry makes us apprehend as much, at least, as it makes us apprehend the persons involved.

Many of the best individual small plays are to be found in the Towneley Cycle. The fact that several of these are so similar in texture has produced the hypothesis of a single dramatic poet of genius – the so-called Wakefield Master – as having been their maker. They include the Noah Plays, the two Shepherds' Plays,* and the dialogues between devils (or demons) which form the bulk of the Play of the Last Judgement. The devils are grimly humorous characters who have every appearance of being descendants of the earth demons or demons of darkness of some earlier mythology. The Abraham and Isaac Play, both in the Towneley version and in the versions in the other Cycles, will also be found especially interesting as having the elements, to some extent realized, of a tragic situation, a family tragedy (not unlike some of those to be found in the Sagas), the tragedy of a father under an overriding obligation or doom to slay his son. Nearness of kinship between the slayer and the slain (though in this case, after pro-

* The Towneley Second Shepherds' Play is included in the anthology in this volume.

longed suspense, the slaying is prevented just in time) is, as the Greeks knew, particularly tragic. In the Crucifixion sequence the slain god of ancient ritual and myth is Christ; but the new Christian significance is developed, in the dramatic presentation of it, largely in terms of the older symbolism. Two of the most impressive of the York plays, in addition to the York *Crucifixion*,★ are the *Fall of Lucifer* and the *Harrowing of Hell* (the Towneley *Harrowing of Hell* appears to have been borrowed from the York Play). The *Harrowing* is conceived largely in terms of the triumph of light over darkness, and it seems to bear a relation to the first breaking of light on Easter Morning. It is immediately succeeded in the Mystery Cycle by the *Play of the Resurrection*.

## Gower and Mannyng

After the wide sweep of reading through the poems of the thirteenth and fourteenth centuries – the alliterative poems, the minstrels' lays or verse romances, the songs, the plays – we shall perhaps be in a better position to see the new, fashionable, more purely 'literary' poetry in true perspective. After Chaucer, the 'literary' poetry – at least the English (as distinct from the Scottish) poetry of the fifteenth century – is very derivative from his work, and from his earlier poems in the French dream-vision mode rather than from the *Canterbury Tales*. But the freshness has quite faded.

The poet who is perhaps nearest to Chaucer – in so far as it is possible to be near to Chaucer without having anything of the Chaucerian genius – is Gower. Gower's verse (he was Chaucer's contemporary and friend) certainly implies the same social and cultural milieu as Chaucer's. In Gower's English book, *Confessio Amantis*† (1390–93) – it is notable that of the three books he composed, one is in Latin, one in French, one in English – we recognize again the well-bred, easy conversational tone and manner that we are familiar with in Chaucer, and the smooth-flowing – perhaps in Gower's work, too smooth-flowing – verse. Yet *Confessio Amantis*, for all its great length and considerable achievement in workmanship, is a pale shadow compared not only with the *Canterbury Tales* but also with the other poems of Chaucer.

★ This play is included in the anthology in this volume.

† A tale from *Confessio Amantis* is included in the anthology.

Here, more than 300 years before the eighteenth century, is a kind of poetry which has the prose virtues, which is, in fact, more prosaic than a great deal of prose. What we are given by Gower is seldom more than simply the adequate statement. His modesty or sobriety of style must be allowed its due; his is the middle way of style. But it is hard to be sure whether, in Gower's case, the middle way is not simply the way of mediocrity. Gower's very lack of emphasis, whether studied or not, becomes in time monotonous.

If we compare *Confessio Amantis* with a somewhat earlier collection of plainly told tales in verse, Robert Mannyng of Brunne's *Handlyng Synne* (early fourteenth century), the comparison is not in every way to the advantage of Gower. The octosyllabic couplets of *Handlyng Synne* may lack Gower's smoothness, but several of the tales, if cruder, are more vigorous and vivid than most of Gower's. *Handlyng Synne* has a plain practical moral intention, though this does not interfere with the traditional tales themselves; and the tales are retold as *exempla*, as it was the custom to introduce tales into sermons as *exempla*. 'The Dancers of Colbek' is an interesting case of such a rehandling of a traditional tale. As it stands in *Handlyng Synne*, it purports to be a warning to people of what might happen to them if they dance in church. But it appears to have been originally a tale warning of the dangers of interfering with sacred or magical dancers. The Christian priest who curses the dancers gets the worst of it in the end; he and his daughter both die. The dancers who cannot stop dancing appear, on the other hand, in an ecstasy or trance, to be dancing in paradise or fairyland, because at one point it is said of them that they feel neither snow nor hail.

In *Confessio Amantis* – otherwise a typical medieval collection of tales within a framework – Gower is less single-minded than Manning and manages, indeed, to combine the roles of a courtly-love poet and a Christian moralist; the courtly lover must learn to be a good and virtuous man. Following Gower – in the dream-vision of the fifteenth century – moralizing heavily invades the poetry of courtly love; whereas in the literature preceding Gower, the allegory of courtly love and moral allegory – the allegory of the Seven Deadly Sins – had been fairly distinct, though the Sins do appear marginally even in Guillaume's part of *Le Roman de la Rose*. The tales in each book of *Confessio Amantis* purport to exemplify one of the Seven Sins.

But the principal interest of *Confessio Amantis* is as a collection of tales. Many of them appear to have come originally from Ovid, and all appear to be among the innumerable tales which were in circulation in this great age of tale-telling and had become part of medieval tradition, both oral and written. A few are found also in Chaucer, in the *Legend of Good Women* and in the *Canterbury Tales*; the tale of Constance is rendered both by Gower and by Chaucer (the *Man of Law's Tale*), and Gower's tale of the Knight Florent is Chaucer's *Wife of Bath's Tale*. Even the tales from Ovid have been modified by their association in medieval tradition with those numerous other tales that had been made into romances. Among the best of the renderings in *Confessio Amantis* is that of the tale of Ceix and Alceone from the *Metamorphoses*. The impression of the distraught Alceone rushing into the waves to take her drowned husband in her arms has, indeed, some power and is one of the very few moments in which Gower merits comparison with Chaucer himself. Another of Gower's best tales is that of Rosiphele, and particularly the passage in which the faery company is seen riding by, as in so many medieval romances. The impression of Medea as a witch (in Gower's tale of Medea) gathering herbs by moonlight to renew old Aeson, is become characteristically medieval in quality; it is another passage of unusual interest as compared with *Confessio Amantis* as a whole.

## The Scots Poets

The most living poetry in the fifteenth century and early sixteenth century until we come to Wyatt was composed in Scotland, for it is unlikely that even the Skelton enthusiasts would claim that he is the equal of the Scots poet, Dunbar.

The poet of *The Kingis Quair* (attributed to James I of Scotland, 1394–1437, though the attribution has been disputed and the poem certainly seems to belong with a group of poems of the *latter* half of the fifteenth century) may properly be called a Chaucerian, though in a very limited sense. The poem purports to be autobiographical, and this may account for its fresher quality as compared with other poems derived from Chaucer. This kind of poetry may also have been still something of a novelty in the North, something fairly recently transplanted; Chaucer's poems were perhaps being read more freshly by Northerners. *The Kingis Quair* is full of Chaucerian echoes and reminiscences – often closely verbal. The poet is evidently thoroughly familiar with the Chaucer of the earlier poems and of the *Knight's Tale*, rather than of the *Tales* as a whole.

The poem begins and ends with the medieval conception of human life as within a fixed frame, our fortunes determined by the stars. Throughout the poem there is an interplay on the Boethian themes of necessity and free will, fortune and freedom. The man (unlike the birds whose spontaneous joy he wonders at) has not yet experienced love – whose service is freedom – until he looks down from the tower in which he is imprisoned and sees for the first time his lady in the garden below. This lady is very unlike the flower-like and spring-like Emily of the *Knight's Tale*, her prototype, in that she is a heavily ornamented princess dressed rather as if she were going to a fashionable ball, though again it is a May morning. Suddenly the lady is no longer there; her departure is felt as a desolating loss, and the prisoner's day is turned to night. He lays his head on a stone and has a vision. He ascends to the palace of Venus, who refers him to Minerva for good advice. Minerva, indeed, fills the poem with too much 'sentence'. But the poetry recovers freshness when the poet finds himself in a meadow by a river – surely not only the garden of *Le Roman de la Rose* but the meadow of numerous medieval romances. When the dreamer awakes, a turtle-dove comes to his prison window (like the dove to Noah's Ark), bearing a message of hope from his lady, a bunch of flowers.

The most stimulating transition from Chaucer to the great Scots poets would be by a reading of the *Testament of Cresseid* by Henryson (before 1450–before 1508). We at once draw breath in a harsher air. *The Testament of Cresseid* is a Lent poem, a poem for the season of repentance, a wintry season in the North; it is a winter night's tale. The poem opens with a huge impression of a cold wintry night and the ageing clerk among his books in a very human domestic scene. Himself past love, the book he takes to shorten the night is Chaucer's *Troilus and Criseyde*. He wonders what could have happened to Cresseid in the end, and the *Testament* describes what he imagines to have been her end. He sees her as the cast-off mistress of a great lord, Diomede. There is little of the 'courtesye' of Chaucer here; the *Testament* is altogether grimmer, though this poet, too, has 'pitie' for Cresseid. She returns to her old father, who takes her back compassionately. Praying in the temple of Venus, Cresseid bitterly accuses Cupid and Venus for her unhappy fate. She is rebellious, not yet recognizing her fault in deserting Troilus. Then a tremendous event seems to happen (in a dream-vision). As if the universe is moved, the divinities of the Seven Planets descend to judge Cresseid for her rebellion against the nature of things.

As Cresseid awakes, there comes the moment of recognition when she looks in a glass and sees her face disfigured with leprosy. There is no such grim moment in Chaucer. Though the primitive notion of pollution seems to have something to do with it, the leprosy seems, partly at least, to represent (in a grim form) the transformation or metamorphosis from youth to age, the withering of the flesh; it is the work of the moon and of Saturn, who is Elde and Winter. The suddenness comes partly from the recognition that this subtle, silent, gradual change has, in her own case, occurred. It is the common fate of humankind, man or woman, sinful or innocent. The leprosy – in the Middle Ages an ever-present threat to the reader himself – enormously intensifies the horror.

Cresseid can never again belong to the human community, the normal social round, represented by the boy who comes in cheerfully to call her to supper. Her aged father delivers her in at the 'spital-house' at the town's end, and we pity both father and daughter. From melancholy recollection of her vanished youth, gay and beautiful, she is recalled by a leper woman to the actuality of her present condition, recalled to the bleak, dreary round, the mechanical monotony of a leper's begging existence – 'Go leir to clap thy clapper to and fro'.

One of the great moments in literature – once read, unforgettable – is towards the end of the poem when Troilus himself rides past the group of lepers, among whom is Cresseid. The episode recalls to the reader of Chaucer the other and so different occasion when Troilus rode in triumph down the street past Criseyde's house. Though neither knows the other, there is a half-conscious recognition on Troilus's part; it seems to him that he has seen that face somewhere before and he flings to Cresseid his purse. When she learns who it was who has passed by, then at last she recognizes and acknowledges her fault. She dies, and a leper man takes from her dead finger the ring that Troilus had once given her. The poem ends with an epitaph which sums up her life and death in brief contrasts.

Henryson is no moralist, in the narrower sense of the word. His background is not simply the Abbey School of Dunfermline (where he is reputed to have been a schoolmaster), but the surrounding Scottish countryside and community to which he belonged. His wisdom – and his poems are very wise about life – evidently came from his having lived long and profoundly as a member of that whole Scottish community. We may come into direct touch with this wisdom by reading his *Fables*,★ where it is dramatically and humorously presented through the talk and adventures of his beasts and birds. They are essentially Scottish peasant folk talking and acting, the country folk Henryson knows and whose shrewd and humorous knowledge of life, particularly of human weaknesses, he shares. The wisdom of each tale is not in the added *moralitas*, but is conveyed concretely and dramatically in the tale itself. Several of the best are tales of the fox; others are of mice, diminutive creatures whose troubles and perplexities are sympathetically imagined. The fable of the Swallow and the Other Birds is one of the wisest. The poet's interest and pleasure in the work going on in the fields as he takes his walks in spring, and at a later stage in summer, can be felt in the descriptions. Through his intimate connection with the local life, with the life and labour going on around him and changing with the seasons, the poet seems to establish a sense of the whole life of the earth.

In Henryson's *Orpheus and Eurydice*, particularly Orpheus's journey through Hell in quest of his lost Eurydice, the myth from Ovid has again come to have a perceptible affinity with the medieval traditional tales. The landscape of Hell, through which Orpheus makes his way, is so real because it is Henryson's own. Among Henryson's shorter pieces, *The Garment of Gude Ladies* – a poem with a very taking metrical movement – describes the dress the poet would have his lady wear; she should be dressed in virtues and heavenly graces. A charming portrait of a lady is revealed, and here Henryson is a very tender moralist.

It will not do to describe Dunbar (*c.* 1460–*c.* 1515) as a Chaucerian. He certainly inherits the Chaucerian modes and themes, as he inherits

★ The Fable, *The Lion and the Mouse*, is included in the anthology.

others which, though medieval, are not specifically Chaucerian. Thus in several of his poems he seems rather one of the last of the goliards, the *clerici vagantes* of the earlier Middle Ages, in this respect more like his near contemporary Villon. But even when Dunbar borrows from Chaucer, it is always the difference from Chaucer that is most striking. He is, among other things, a 'court man', as Henryson is not, perhaps even something of a 'malcontent'.

Dunbar comes very late, at the culmination of medieval poetic practice. Perhaps because he is more of a fashionable poet than Henryson, this 'lateness' is more apparent in his work. He has at his command – and is well aware that he has – a variety of alternative modes in which he can choose to work. His technical skill and versatility are what may first strike the reader. It may be that Dunbar's poetry appears to be more various than it really is. There is a great variety of modes and forms, but perhaps not a corresponding variety of experience. It may be said, further, that he is technically brilliant without being really very new. He made new formal combinations, but he is not essentially an innovator. He does not invent anything really new as Chaucer, for example, virtually invents the English novel in *Troilus and Criseyde*. By Dunbar's time among the poets there was, it seems, a dying or decaying of the finer inventive spirit of the Middle Ages.

There are several fairly distinct varieties of language in Dunbar. Thus he draws upon the medieval Latin and French vocabularies to aggrandize his Scots in forming the poetic diction – the 'aureate diction' – in which a number of his show-pieces are composed; and he frequently interpolates Latin lines or phrases effectively. On the other hand, the largest proportion of his poems is colloquial Scots in character, evidently based on the language that was actually spoken by the people in Dunbar's part of Scotland. Dunbar, then, draws for his different kinds of poems on different vocabularies. His show-pieces and ceremonial poems – corresponding, we may imagine, to the pageants and processions of public or royal occasions – are those in which he uses lavishly the 'aureate diction'. These heavily ornate poems, with their bejewelled and formal landscapes, dazzle one, but except here and there life has largely escaped from them. It seems that poems at a remove from spoken language must necessarily lose touch with life. There is little that is spontaneous about Dunbar's two principal show-pieces, *The Goldyn Targe* and *The Thrissill and the Rois*. *The Thrissill and the Rois* celebrates, with its assembly of heraldic beasts and emblematic flowers, the marriage of James IV of Scotland with Margaret Tudor, daughter of Henry VII. The shorter poem, *To Aberdeen*, also seems to correspond to what it describes, the formal processions, pageants, plays, and dances on the occasion of a royal visit to the Scottish town.

Though, among such a bewildering variety of modes, it may be difficult at first to find the living core of Dunbar's poetry, it is undoubtedly to be found among the poems in colloquial Scots. It is here that the sap flows vigorously. These familiar, realistic poems are mostly comic or satiric, though a number are gloomy or morose; indeed, many of the comic or satiric poems also have something of a sardonic or morose tinge, and even Dunbar's mirth is often of a violent or desperate character. The wealth and vitality of Dunbar's colloquial Scots is indeed remarkable, and his vocabulary of scurrility and abuse is particularly rich; the old flytings renew themselves in many of his poems.

It is once again the differences between Dunbar's alliterative poem, *Tua Mariit Wemen and the Wedo*, and Chaucer's *Wife of Bath's Prologue*, rather than the resemblances, that are most striking. Dunbar's wives are much less complete human beings than the Wife of Bath. In them, human nature is reduced to its animal elements, and they contrast with the profound and rich humanity of Chaucer's Wife. Though outwardly they are noblewomen, splendidly arrayed, gay courtly ladies, they expose themselves in their private gossip as merciless, primitive creatures, at the level of instinct and appetite. They tear at their men 'with murderous paws'. The poem is very strong meat, and presents the brutal obverse side to the poetry of courtly love. The descriptions of the midsummer night, which draw upon the 'aureate diction' and contrast effectively with the colloquial Scots of the monologues, produce an effect of midsummer opulence, rococo June with its festoons of flowers and leaves and its singing birds, and contrast sharply with the horrors exposed.

Another of Dunbar's most striking poems is his *Dance of the Seven Deadly Sins*. It is to be remarked that it is a *dance* of the Sins. The characters of the satanic pageant are imagined as caught up in a dance frenzy, communicated in the rhythm of the poem. (The relation of this episode to the witch cult might be worth investigating. Similarly, the scene in Alloway Kirk in Burns' *Tam o' Shanter* is probably not purely the invention of the poet.) For all their weirdness, Dunbar's Seven Deadly Sins are local characters, rooted in a particular locality. The poem ends with a wild dance of Highlanders whom the Devil smothers – Dunbar being a Lowlander. Indeed, the whole poem seems to go to the pipes or the fiddle.

Among Dunbar's many flyting poems there is one on a considerable scale, *The Flyting of Dunbar and Kennedy*. In this poem the two poets abuse each other like two fish-wives. But, of course, it is a game – a game which (most readers would agree) Dunbar wins. In Dunbar's comic-satiric poem, *To the Merchants of Edinburgh*, the reader gets to know the character of the town, what it is like to live in, its noises and its smells. The impression is of a lively place, the habitat of a boisterous and vigorous community living among high houses which shut out the sun from each other and from the streets.

Two of the most individual of Dunbar's gloomier poems are *Meditation in Winter* and the famous *Lament for the Makars*. In the former, it is not only winter that oppresses his spirits, but his own morbid moods. He turns with anxiety to summer, as he has turned to song, dances, plays, wine, and some 'lady's beautie', turning away from his oppressive fears of old age and death. In the *Lament for the Makars*, the procession of life is dominated by Death. The Latin phrase, *timor mortis conturbat me*, is impressively used, lending a liturgical solemnity to the contrasting familiar Scots, like a funeral bell tolling. But what makes Dunbar's poem speak directly to us is its homely, personal note – the makar's concern about his friends and about himself.

Spiritually as well as technically, Dunbar's poetry is late: it has a disenchanted and distrustful sardonic air. The poet's temperament appears to have been peculiarly sensitive to the gloomy, indeed often morbid, spirit of the end of the Middle Ages. There could be no greater contrast than between this tone of Dunbar's poetry and Chaucer's spring-like gaiety. It is with certain of the Jacobeans – notably Ben Jonson – not with the earlier Elizabethans, that Dunbar may be felt to have some affinities of mood, though his forms and modes are still those of medieval poetry.

Lastly, the reader should not miss Gavin Douglas's (1475?–1522) Scots translation of the *Aeneid*. It is the first version of the complete poem in any branch of English, and in the opinion of some critics, the greatest. Ezra Pound said (I think rightly) that Douglas gets more poetry out of the *Aeneid* than any other translator. But it is a different poetry from that of the *Aeneid*. As a poem in its own right it is the culmination of the medieval Scots poetry and in the succession from Henryson and Dunbar. Its characteristics are those of medieval Scots poetry; the differences between Douglas's Scots *Aeneid* and the original *Aeneid* are the differences between the Scots and Latin sensibilities.

In Douglas's Prologues to different books of his *Aeneid*, his indebtedness to his Scots predecessors is even more evident than in the translation itself. He renders again, but with a new particularity of observation, the seasonal theme of so much medieval poetry. His winter, as might be expected from the nature both of his Scots language and his experience, is the most real of his seasons and may be compared with the winter in *Sir Gawain and the Green Knight*.

## The Morality Plays

The Morality Plays are a species of allegorical plays or dramatic allegories, presenting a somewhat drastic simplification of life. There is no use assuming that the few specimens we have (from the fifteenth and early sixteenth centuries) are intrinsically very remarkable or interesting. But the *kind* of thing they are may be interesting to us for special reasons. They may be interesting to us not only because Morality art is one of the elements in the more complex Elizabethan dramatic art, but also because they are a species of drama that is different both from the modern naturalistic drama and also, on the whole, from Elizabethan poetic drama.

The kind of allegory which, as a Morality Play, is set upon the stage is *moral* allegory. The germ of it may, perhaps, be traced back to the medieval sermons and to the kind of thing that is found in *Piers Plowman*. Such a play is a theatrical projection of the moral consciousness, the knowledge of good and evil. A man – any or each or every man – is imagined as faced with two alternative sets of choices, sharply distinguished as good and evil, right and wrong. These are visualized as two sets of persons and, indeed (when the moral allegory is made into a Morality Play), impersonated by actors together with Everyman himself. The idea of two sets of alternatives gives rise to the idea of a conflict between them for possession of the soul of each man. Where there is conflict there is certainly the potentiality of drama.

The difficulty is that the moral conflict in general is not – or is not primarily – a conflict between persons. It has its centre in the mind of a man. To attempt to project the moral conflict on to a stage is to attempt to externalize an inner drama. Allegory was the established medieval method of visualizing or imagining the inner workings of the mind; it had been very much developed in the earlier literature of the Middle Ages. The new problem was how to set it upon a stage.

The characters proper to allegory are personifications; they are impulses, moods, attitudes and states of mind, qualities, virtues and vices, physical (and mental) conditions such as old age and youth personified. In a typical Morality Play these personifications, as separate figures impersonated by separate actors, are grouped round a central figure who is a man. This man is not a particular but a representative man, Everyman or *Humanun Genus*. It is for possession of his soul that these personified impulses and forces contend. Though the contention is for a human soul, and is focused in that human soul, the characters in a Morality Play are mostly not themselves human. I say *mostly* because we do have, for instance, Everyman's Friend and his Relations among the *dramatis personae*. But even they are generalized (as Everyman himself is); they are the Friend and any Relations of anybody.

Further, in a typical Morality Play there are, in addition to the straight personifications, other important *dramatis personae* who are not human. They are the metaphysical or supranatural beings or powers of medieval theology or mythology – Angels and Devils. These Good and Bad Angels (or Devils) imply a metaphysical or supranatural universe, Heaven and Hell – what E. M. Forster calls 'the huge scenic background' which in the ages of faith lent dignity and significance to human life. The moral conflict is thus conceived as not merely of concern to the man in whose mind it takes place. Powers from the outside – supranatural powers – meet in his mind and contend for his soul. (Indeed, it is very unlikely that the majority of the audience at a Morality Play, or even the authors of these plays, conceived these supranatural or magical powers as non-material. Certainly, if we take into account the contemporary witch cult, they were popularly believed capable of assuming material shapes and liable to intrude physically upon human life as they were seen to do in the plays. This popular belief would undoubtedly be of assistance to a dramatist.) But the presence of the Angels and the Devils – in so far as they could be freed from popular beliefs or superstition – implies that the moral law is not merely man-made, that the necessity or obligation of moral choices is not merely a human idiosyncrasy, but that it has a universal or absolute validity. Behind the forces of evil, as they concentrate in the mind of a man for possession of his soul, is Hell; behind the forces of good, as they concentrate for his protection, is Heaven.

The conventions of Morality art – the art of dramatic moral allegory – should be of special interest to us who have experienced for so long a narrow and rigid naturalistic drama which seeks to confine the dramatist to the superficies, to what people *say* to each other, whereas what they do *not* say may be much more significant. Here, in the Morality Plays, is almost the opposite extreme from our naturalistic drama, a drastically non-naturalistic mode. Of course, there is a certain amount of realism in the Moralities as there is in *Piers Plowman*, and these realistic passages are often the more lively passages; but the whole conception and framework of a Morality Play is non-naturalistic. There could be no easy confusion between Morality art and everyday life or surface appearances.

We have to admit that this non-naturalistic drama, as represented by the Morality Plays still extant, was on the whole a failure. But it did not, I think, fail because of the nature of the form itself, as has been generally argued. The causes of the failure were, no doubt, sociological rather than purely literary. The conditions of civilization in England in the fifteenth century, when the Morality Play should have developed, appear to have been unfavourable to the development of poetry as a whole. If the 'types' in the Moralities had been as vividly recreated as those in Bunyan's *Pilgrim's Progress* (e.g. Mr Worldly Wiseman), or if the Seven Deadly Sins as they appear in the Moralities had even been as real as they are in *Piers Plowman*, they would have been effective dramatic characters. That they have not this degree of reality is not the fault of the form itself. But there is no Chaucer among the authors of the Morality Plays, no dramatist capable of writing dialogue as dramatic as that of the *Canterbury Tales*.

The earliest extant Morality Play is *The Castell of Perseverance* (*c*. 1405). One of the latest, and probably the best, is *Everyman*, extant in a printed edition of the beginning of the sixteenth century, a play which is still very moving. The note of unexpected parting – a parting that has the aspect of a desertion – is peculiarly poignant in this play. To the careless Everyman comes a messenger – the moment of recognition that he must die. The world, everything, and everyone, that Everyman has loved forsake him. He is deserted by Fellowship, his Kindred, his Goods, and, at the very end, also by Strength, Beauty, even Knowledge. Only his Good Deed is entirely faithful. Though the play is the play of the Salvation of Everyman, it has the late medieval awareness of mortality; shadowing it, as shadowing the Moralities in general, is the *Danse Macabre*. The play has a simple elegiac style and dignity and is certainly impressive in its grave ecclesiastical way.

Among the more interesting of the Early Tudor or early sixteenth-century Moralities are Skelton's *Magnificence* and Sir David Lyndsay's *Satire of the Three Estates*. Whether these are strictly speaking Morality Plays, might, however, be disputed. They are more concerned perhaps with social and political satire than with the salvation of the soul. They are, however, in themselves nonetheless interesting; they may even be found more interesting. The later Moralities in general have lost the wholeness or single-mindedness of the medieval Catholic moral vision; they attempt less to deal with the human moral situation as a whole. They are more fragmentary in that sense, but they contain a farcical element which becomes interesting for its own sake. Indeed, we find in the Tudor Moralities the morality and the farce falling apart. Several of the best survivors of the Early Tudor dramatic pieces appear to be the work of members of Sir Thomas More's household, and of these the farcical Interludes attributed to the John Heywood who married More's niece are still entertaining reading. These are essentially farces and, as such, should be dissociated in one's mind from the Morality proper. They are not just broken-down Moralities, but a distinct *genre*. They go to a jigging, dancing movement, and their themes are similar to those of the old *fabliaux*.

The Interlude has sometimes been explained as an entertainment devised to fill a gap in an evening, but it may be that the word carries the idea of a play (*ludus*) performed by or between (*inter*) two or more players to entertain the company after dinner in the hall. There is a fragment of an English Interlude preserved from as early as the thirteenth century, *The Clerk and the Maiden*. There may have been many such, having nothing to do with the Morality Plays.

## From Medieval to Elizabethan

One of the benefits the reader may expect to obtain from an acquaintance with medieval English literature is a sharpened appreciation both of the ways in which Elizabethan literature still has deep-rooted affinities with that earlier literature out of which it has grown, and also of the ways in which it is different and new and sometimes more complex. The resemblances are implicit in the fact that the Elizabethans are using the same English language at a not so very much later stage of development, and often in much the same ways as their not so distant predecessors. The age of Shakespeare is much closer, not only in time but in other respects, to the age both of Chaucer and of the minstrels than it is to ours. The traditional order which Elizabethan and Jacobean England inherited from the Middle Ages appears, throughout the country as a whole, not to have been radically changed from what it had been. As ever, the Court circle appears to have been the most susceptible to the new fashions from the Continent – now principally the new fashions from Renaissance Italy. But if the court of Elizabeth was, at least to some extent, a Renaissance court, England as a whole appears to have been still to a great extent medieval.

This survey cannot attempt to retrace the history of the emergence of the 'new' drama in the sixteenth century in relation to the 'old'. The traditional art which shows itself at intervals throughout the Miracle Plays has had, perhaps, less acknowledgement as an element in the Elizabethan drama than has (at any rate recently) Morality art. Yet, when taken together with the dramatic games, ceremonies, and dances widespread among the people, it may be even more deep-rooted, subtler in its shaping influence, and certainly not less important. The Morality element is now beginning to be recognized as at least as important as the more famous Senecan or Classical influence, important though the latter was stylistically and in other ways. Together with the traditional morality itself, the Elizabethans did not fail to inherit and make use of some of the forms in which it had been expressed.

Broadly speaking, Shakespeare and his fellow dramatic poets may be regarded as the Elizabethan successors of the minstrels of the former age. The plays performed in the London theatres by companies of actors have taken the place of the near-dramatic recitals by single minstrels in the great halls. The audience in the great hall must have been comparable in its diversity to the audience in an Elizabethan theatre: all ranks and stations from the nobles downward were assembled in the former, and from the courtly and scholarly folk downward in the latter. Thus in both places one finds the conditions for an intimate relationship and critical collaboration between entertainer and audience. What must have altered unfavourably the conditions of minstrel art – apart from the increase in the habit of private reading, resulting from the accumulation of MSS and, later, printed books – was the withdrawal of lord and lady to private apartments in the manor-houses in and about the fifteenth century. Though in Tudor times Interludes appear to have been performed in great households for (and by) the assembled family, these performances had become something in the nature of private family entertainments. But the Elizabethan drama was a truly national drama. As has been well said, the Elizabethan theatre held a cross-section of the English nation. Consequently the Elizabethan drama appealed at various levels, and is both popular and sophisticated art. It grew out of the traditional civilization of England as a whole and was at the same time in touch with the new Renaissance culture of the scholarly and courtly poets, sensitive to Classical and Italian influences and models, but not subservient to them.

The advantages which the dramatic poets enjoyed are apparent if we compare them with Spenser (1552–99), the greatest genius among the non-dramatic poets before Donne – and Donne is peculiarly close to the dramatic poets. The comparative rootlessness of Spenser is implied in his curiously rootless language, so far removed from the current speech of his own or any time. Spenser became, of course, an exile from the Court and from the courtly and scholarly circle with whom he felt he belonged and to whom he aspired to return. But his exile from the courtly circle did not plant him any more deeply in the English people. It merely removed him still farther away from them (into Ireland). The *Faerie Queene* (*c.* 1590), brilliant as it is with a remote moon-like brilliance, is indeed a poem of exile. The landscapes of the poem through which the knights wander are wildernesses which surely bear some relation to the wild country of Ireland, inhabited by 'savages', as Spenser must have viewed it from his castle window. The *Faerie Queene* is the work of a poet of genius who has the grave disadvantage of really belonging to no particular country. Medieval romance and allegory float in the poem together with elements of Renaissance Italy and Classical mythology, mingle vaguely as in a dream-pageant, and this they can do because, despite the glowing colours and the music, all are insubstantial and remote. Spenser is, of course, as different as can possibly be from Chaucer, though he drew upon some of the decorative aspects of Chaucer's poetry and also upon Chaucer's vocabulary for some of his archaisms: but they were not archaisms in Chaucer. Spenser is also essentially different from his own contemporary Elizabethan dramatic poets (though Marlowe learned what Eliot has called 'melody' from him). The dramatic poets are rooted in a past traditional England that was still immediately present around them, and yet they are at the same time alive and alert to all that was new.

Of all the English – as distinct from Scottish – poets of the fifteenth and sixteenth centuries, the one who occupies a central and connecting position between Chaucer and the Elizabethans is Sir Thomas Wyatt (1503–42). His verse (composed in the reign of Henry VIII) both relates back to medieval English verse, including the alliterative verse, and points forward to Elizabethan and Jacobean verse. He is as much a precursor of Donne in some of his poems as, in others, of the Elizabethan lyric poets; for while certain of his smoother musician's poems (under the influence of Italian and French models) come somewhere between the medieval lyrics and the conventional Elizabethan songs and lyrics, others, notably the Satires, because of their more dramatic, colloquial, or introspective character, point forward to Donne as well as backward to Chaucer.[4]

# NOTES

This chapter includes a version of John Speirs' account of *Sir Gawain and the Green Knight* taken from his book *Medieval English Poetry* (London, 1957), and is reproduced by permission of the publisher.

1. See particularly R. S. Loomis, *Celtic Myth and Arthurian Romance*, and J. L. Weston, *From Ritual to Romance*. But see also C. B. Lewis, *Classical Mythology and Arthurian Romance*.

2. On the other hand, C. B. Lewis in his *Classical Mythology and Arthurian Romance* argues with considerable weight of reason and evidence that the Arthurian romances are only superficially Celtic and that the tales out of which they were made were a residue of Classical myths and accounts of ritual performances circulating as tales, oral and written, throughout the West in the early Middle Ages. May we not perhaps conclude, very tentatively, that in this age of tale-telling there was a great flowing-together of tales from many and diverse sources, combining and coalescing, to form the rich repertory of the medieval *conteurs*?

3. The ballad-romance of *Thomas of Ercildoune and the Quene of Elf-Land* (fifteenth-century MSS) is one of the finest of the medieval romances and deserves to be at least as well known as its folk-ballad successor, *Thomas the Rhymer*.

4. See H. A. Mason's distinguished book *Humanism and Poetry in the Early Tudor Period*.

# POSTSCRIPT: CHANGING PERSPECTIVES

DEREK PEARSALL

The essay that precedes is one that John Speirs wrote over a quarter of a century ago (it remains virtually unrevised because of his sudden death), at a time when the study of medieval English literature at British universities was beginning to emerge as a predominantly literary rather than a predominantly philological discipline. It would not be too much to say that Speirs' essay, along with his book on medieval poetry, was an important factor in that change. The student or would-be reader of medieval poetry who looked around in the early 1950s for up-to-date critical writing on any poetry but that of Chaucer would have found the prospect remarkably barren. There was much on language and phonology, authorship and date, sources and analogues, 'backgrounds' (Speirs' assault on 'the acquisition of background' is characteristically to the point), but little evidence of criticism that concerned itself with enhancing enjoyment of the reading of the poetry as poetry. *Sir Gawain and the Green Knight* was still submerged under its analogues, the Plays still seen as an episode in the inevitable progress towards Shakespeare; *Pearl* was being haggled over by the 'autobiographical' and the 'allegorical' interpreters, and *Piers Plowman* a scene of carnage in the midst of a long-running and vituperative scholarly debate concerning multiple or single authorship. The student beginning his undergraduate study of Middle English literature could have been forgiven a sigh as he faced the prospect of still more on loan-words and philological cruces.

The situation I have described is now history, and so much has happened since the early 1950s that it now appears to be very ancient history indeed. The study of Middle English poetry has blossomed in so many new ways, under the influence of new critical ideas and new ways of reading, and under the pressure of an unprecedented expansion in the number of people dedicated to it as a professional pursuit, that it might be said now to be threatened, if anything, by an excessive luxuriance of critical interpretation. Some of the stages in this process, this shifting and multiplying of perspectives, are worth tracing.

The single most important influence at work in this process, the yeast that has stirred the ferment of ideas, has been the advent of the New Criticism, particularly in the work of Charles Muscatine. There had been effective 'close reading' of medieval poetry before, especially by such brilliant, intuitive critics as C. S. Lewis, but no one before had shown the relevance to medieval poetry of the full range of modern techniques of interpretative analysis, particularly the concentration of attention on form and structure, and on local details of style, imagery and vocabulary. Muscatine, in his analysis of the interplay of the 'courtly' and 'bourgeois' styles in Chaucer, provided a dialectical model which seemed to release important meanings that had hitherto lain obscured. He discovered complex patterns of opposition, tensions, ambiguities, paradoxes, all of them embodied in what might broadly be considered the 'style' of the poetry. Such ideas were none the less convincing for being particularly appealing to modern taste. At his best, in his analysis of the more sophisticated of the *Canterbury Tales*, such as the *Merchant's Tale* and the *Nun's Priest's Tale*, Muscatine seemed to open completely new horizons in the understanding of a poet who was seen as deeply serious, deeply committed to a vision of life in which the contingent and the transcendental, the ridiculous and sublime, the human and the non-human, warred irreconcilably but could be harmonized momentarily in the artifice of style.

Muscatine supplied a model too for the activity of the artist in relation to what he called the 'crisis' of the late fourteenth century. For him it was an age of collapsing values, of flux and change, when traditional ideas of social hierarchy, chivalric idealism and religious faith were being subjected to increasing pressure and fragmentation. Langland's reaction to this crisis was different from Chaucer's, but for both it was the shaping spirit of the age. Muscatine also saw – and here he was at his most suggestive and influential – a relation between this age of crisis and the development of late Gothic art. Here, too, he recognized a war of styles, a tension, a duality, expressed in ever more fragmentary and feverish compositions, in which traditional ways of shaping the visual world were invaded by a restless naturalism.

Many writers have taken up these challenging and provocative sociological and art historical analogies, but the more central concern has been with the development of interpretations of Chaucer and other medieval writers which lay stress on the tensions and ambiguities of their poetry as a reflection of a complex and many-faceted view of life. Donaldson, for instance, has taken the idea of the fallible narrator in Chaucer and refined it into an instrument of great subtlety for revealing the layers of ironic significance in the *Canterbury Tales* and *Troilus and Criseyde*, as well as in the earlier dream-vision poems. The extension of his arguments by less sensitive critics, particularly in the supposedly dramatized narrations of the *Canterbury Tales*, has produced more confusion than insight. Dream-poems such as *Pearl* and *Piers Plowman* have also lent themselves to interpretation in terms of an ironically conceived dreamer-narrator and Lawlor's study of the latter poem makes the dramatic role of the dreamer central to the poem's exploratory techniques.

Other techniques too have been used for detecting and elucidating ironic and ambiguous patterns of meaning. One important technique is to isolate areas of disturbance in the language, style and structure of a poem, and to recognize in these the manifestation of deeper ironies or conflicts at work in the poet's view of life. John Burrow, in the standard and most influential reading of *Sir Gawain and the Green Knight*, sees an ambiguity in the author's view of Gawain which reflects some decline in the valuation of chivalric idealism. In his more extended study of late fourteenth-century poetry, he develops this notion of a pragmatic, unheroic, realistic, domesticated vision of life in relation to Chaucer, Gower and Langland, as well as the *Gawain*-poet. Burrow assumes that these writers knew what they were doing in embodying a more complex and ambiguous view of life in their poetry, but Elizabeth Salter, in her extremely influential study of the *Knight's Tale* and the *Clerk's Tale*, takes a more radical view. For her, the clashes of style and inconsistencies of narrative technique in Chaucer are evidence of unreconciled conflicts in Chaucer's own mind, doubts and ambiguities in his interpretation of the matter of experience as well as struggles in the manipulation of the poetic medium.

This persistent consciousness of the poetic medium has been an important legacy of the New Criticism. Elizabeth Salter herself demonstrates it at its most effective and illuminating in her study of *Piers Plowman* (which also makes it very clear that the mystical writings of Langland's contemporaries are no mere 'background' to his poem). The more obvious poetic self-consciousness of poems like *Pearl* and *Sir Gawain* has inspired important studies by Kean, Borroff, Spearing and Benson. Chaucer is less obvious, especially as his verse seems so often a transparent medium, and the real subtlety here has been discovered in the artifices of narrative technique. Chaucer's manipulation of point of view, his shifting perspectives, his withdrawal from all the traditional positions of narrative authority, has led some recent critics, such as Lanham and Burlin, to see in the play of artistic illusion against representational realism the central strategy of Chaucer's narrative art.

All this is to some extent adumbrated in Muscatine, but there is another approach to medieval poetry which stands at some removes from his in both ideological assumptions and critical method, and which has achieved an equal if not equally creditable dominance in the criticism of the last twenty-five years. D. W. Robertson's *A Preface to Chaucer* consolidated in a single monumental study an approach to medieval poetry which had been developing and gaining adherents over the previous fifteen years. 'Historical criticism', as this approach calls itself, takes as its axiom that medieval poetry must be read according to the dominant ideological assumptions and recommended literary techniques of its day. It is assumed therefore to be pervasively Christian (and specifically Augustinian) in its meaning and systematically allegorical in its techniques. *Piers Plowman* is not a tortured and idiosyncratic quest for spiritual enlightenment, but a systematic exposition of the dogmas of the Christian faith, as those dogmas are found in the Bible and patristic commentary; *Troilus and Criseyde* is not a complex and subtle and compassionate exploration of the beauty and sadness of human love, but a consistent demonstration of the blasphemous and idolatrous nature of sexual passion; all touches of humanity clinging to the Wife of Bath are merely vivifying details in an iconographic portrait of the heresy of the flesh. Robertson's own scholarship and magisterial tone gives weight to all his utterances, and much of what he says is manifestly true, especially where it has to do with explicitly didactic works (his exposition of the genre of Robert Mannyng's *Handlyng Synne*, for instance, is more authentic than Speirs' old-fashioned view of it), or with explicit biblical allusions in secular works. He has also provided some important clues for the study of literary works in his handling of certain iconographic motifs in the visual arts.

In the hands of his disciples, however, his methods have become a mere key to unlock an arsenal of scholarly footnotes, and the hunting-out of patristic allegories has become a threadbare exercise. At the same time, the model that Robertson provided of a serious commitment to the literature of the Christian Latin Middle Ages has contributed to advances in critical understanding as significant as those of the New Criticism. It is not 'background' that one is speaking of here, certainly not, at least, in the form of providing inert bodies of information as a substitute for the challenging business of actually reading the poetry; it is rather the recognition that medieval poetry exists within a context of assumptions and attitudes and ideas, particularly religious ones, which we have to absorb into our own understanding if we are to read aright. It is quite clear, for instance, that *Piers Plowman* needs this context of understanding, as Frank and Bloomfield have shown, as well as the sensitive response to the poetic and dramatic mode. Chaucer, too, has profited from the bringing to bear of a well-informed and imaginatively sensitive scholarship. But the most striking advances have been towards a truly historical and truly critical understanding of such distinctive forms as the medieval religious lyric and the medieval religious drama. The study of these two areas of poetic creativity has been transformed out of all recognition since Speirs wrote. For the former, Rosemary Woolf has shown how the true nature of these poems, and their part in a true grandeur, can only be understood if they are seen in their Latin context, and as expressions of devotional, meditative and didactic needs which are simply different from all that the modern reader expects of 'lyrics'. For the drama, the pioneering work of Kolve and Woolf gives us an opportunity to see the intrinsic quality of the plays in relation to their informing religious purposes, and to recognize that they have dramatic powers of their own which are, again, simply different from those we are familiar with.

All that Speirs had to offer on such poetry was the familiar but vague and unsubstantiated suggestion that their strength lay in their roots 'in pre-Christian myth and ritual' (p. 72, of the religious lyrics), 'in ritual and ritual drama' (p. 77, of the mystery plays). Even here, however, he may have had his finger on something, for Axton has shown, of the plays at least, that they had an important debt to lost folk-plays. There is also an increasing fashion for seeing the Middle English romances as forms of psychic myth, as well as for interpreting them in terms of a modified structuralism.

The reader of Middle English poetry is now, therefore, faced by an alarmingly rich array of contending persuasions. This can be nothing but healthy provided they recognize the twin needs of close reading and a sense of context. For the former, the slowly evolving *Middle English Dictionary* is an important ally, while the recent *Chaucer Glossary* is invaluable in its particular field. As for context, there is increasing recognition of the importance of Middle English prose, of Anglo-Norman and Latin writing in England, and indeed of the whole European literary tradition, in the understanding of Middle English poetry. At the same time, John Speirs must be given his due, and it must be recognized equally that a sense of context is a part, albeit an essential part, of the activity of mind of the intelligent, alert and sensitive reader, and not a substitute for that activity.

# MIDDLE ENGLISH PROSE

T. P. DOLAN AND V. J. SCATTERGOOD

It is not easy to make any absolute distinction between prose and poetry. Poetry is often characterized by rhyme, regular rhythm and unusual lexical and syntactic choices; but any or all these characteristics may be lacking in what is clearly a poem, yet strikingly present in what is clearly prose. They are present, for example, in the celebrated closing lines of *A Tale of Two Cities*: 'It is a far, far better thing that I do, than I have ever done; it is a far, far better rest that I go to, than I have ever known.' Had Dickens regarded this passage as poetry he would no doubt have arranged for its proper lineation; but since it is prose the lineation was left to the printer's compositor. In other words, with poetry the length of the lines is determined by the author; with prose only by the width of the page.[1]

Even such a limited distinction can be made with greater confidence after the development of the printed book than before. It is true that in most manuscripts dating from between 1100 and 1500 poetry is written out so that the lines on the page correspond to the author's lineation, whereas prose is written across the full width of the page, so that it is easy to tell what is meant to be poetry from what is meant to be prose. But there are factors which blur even this distinction.

One is that copyists of manuscripts did not always keep to the poet's lineation, and so writing which reads like poetry looks on the page like prose.[2] Another factor is that some medieval authors writing in the one medium drew on material written in the other.[3] Usually a poem serves as source for a piece of prose: perhaps the best known example is that section of Malory which draws on the alliterative *Morte Arthur*. In the following passage from the fight with the giant on St Michael's Mount, Malory's prose preserves some of the poetic characteristics of its source and at times its detailed wording:

Than[a] the gloton gloored and grevid full foule. He had teeth lyke a gray-
hounde, he was the foulyst wyghte[b] that ever man sye,[c] and there was never
suche one fourmed[d] on erthe, for there was never devil in helle more
horryblyer made: for he was fro the hede to the foote[e] fyve fadom longe and
large,[f] And therewith sturdely he sterte uppon his leggis and caughte a clubbe
in his honde all of clene[g] iron . . .[4]

Even if the source were no longer extant, one could reasonably
deduce from the passage itself that it derived from something written
in alliterative long lines.

Though there may be no absolute distinction between poetry and
prose there are, nevertheless, certain broad generalizations to be made
about the separate functions of these two modes of discourse. Prose
tends to conform more closely to the structures of articulate speech
than poetry does. In its need for cohesion prose spells out, formalizes
and deliberately limits the scope of what it means, whereas poetry
may more readily suggest and hint. Therefore, prose is better
equipped than poetry for carrying information which can be assimilated by the reader, since the syntax must include the necessary signposts of speech (prepositions, conjunctions and so forth). Here may
be another distinction between prose and poetry: the actual wording
of prose is usually less significant, and less memorable, than the underlying meaning; whereas the actual wording is as essential a part of the
poem as its meaning, which may in any case be ambiguous or uncertain.

A great deal of Middle English prose is extant though much of it
is not yet published in modern editions, and it is hard to make useful generalizations about it. Before 1500 English culture was de-
centralized and diversified: prose texts survive in various dialects; the
range of subject matter is wide (saints' lives, sermons and homilies,
doctrinal treatises, controversial tracts, scientific or quasi-scientific
manuals, chronicles, romances, and letters both official and personal
are all in evidence), and the literary manner varies from the simple
and demotic to the highly artificial and ornate. To some considerable
extent the availability of the various styles of prose depended on
historical factors and it is proper that some initial consideration be
given to these.

a the glutton stared and became very horribly annoyed, b creature, c saw, d created,
e thirty feet tall and broad, f and with that he violently leapt to his feet and seized,
g pure.

Already, in the Old English period, prose was a highly developed, sophisticated, flexible medium. Those who needed to do such things as formulate laws, or draw up charters, or set down medical recipes, or record events, used a simple (though sometimes necessarily technical) vocabulary, uncomplicated sentence patterns and few or no decorative devices. Those, such as Aelfric or Wulfstan, who needed to heighten their basic prose in order to persuade or move their audiences used a variety of devices – lexical and syntactic repetition, rhyme, and particularly alliteration.[5] But in the eleventh century the literary culture of England was badly disrupted by the Norman Conquest. The incoming French aristocracy and higher clergy spoke and wrote their own language, with Latin as the written medium for the highly educated. Spoken English was confined largely to the populace and the lower clergy, so not much English was written. Some literary continuity[6] is apparent, nevertheless: the *Chronicle* continued to be written in English prose at Peterborough until 1154; and the works of Aelfric and Wulfstan continued to be copied and used at places such as Worcester until well into the twelfth century. And the various types of Old English prose were imitated in works composed after the Conquest. The alliterative manner, for example, survived in the homiletic texts of the 'Katherine Group' (see below) and the 'Wooing Group', composed in the West Midlands early in the thirteenth century; it reappeared occasionally in the writings of the late fourteenth-century Yorkshire hermit Richard Rolle and his followers; and it was still in evidence in controversial tracts such as *Jack Upland*, dating perhaps from the early fifteenth century.

By the time Rolle was writing, however, three centuries of French cultural dominance had left their mark on English prose; not only were works in French (or more properly Anglo-Norman) written in England, but Englishmen had also acquired the habit of looking to France as a country of higher and more sophisticated civilization, and of imitating or translating works written there. Friar Lorens d'Orléans's *Somme Le Roi* was thrice translated, and the influence of French on English prose[7] is plain in the following passage on purgatory from one of these translations, *The Book of Vices and Virtues* (*c.* 1375):

And that penance is wel hidous[a] and wel hard, for [b]al that the holy martires suffrede ever althermost ne womman that travaileth is no more to acounte ayens here peyne that to bathe a man in cold water to regard of thilke brennynge ovene, there that the soules brenneth al for to[c] they ben purged and clensed there; as a body that is fyned and tried[d] bi fier al for to it be fyn[e] and no more filthe is left, for that fier is of such kynde that al manere of filthe that it fyndeth in the soule of dede, of speche or of thought, that longeth[f] to synne, be it litle or mochel, al it brenneth and clenseth.[8]

The influence of French is immediately obvious in the vocabulary of the passage ('penance', hidous', 'martires' and so on), and in the awkward negatives ('ne ... no more ...'). But it is the conjunctions which best reveal the extent of the dependence: 'to regard of', 'there that' and 'al for to' are clumsy attempts to render French into English. Long 'trailing' sentences of this sort, in which the syntax is disjointed and each clause seems to generate the next without regard to the overall structure of the sentence, are the staple mode of many late Middle English prose writers, particularly those who had pretensions to 'courtly' sophistication.

By the end of the fifteenth century, however, another stylistic influence becomes apparent on Middle English prose: the self-conscious Latinity of the new humanists. Throughout the century various Englishmen – the most notable being Humphrey, Duke of Gloucester – had been acquiring humanistic books and seeking to persuade Italian humanists to come to England.[9] One such, Poggio Bracciolini (1380–1459), who had been briefly in England, in 1449 translated from Greek into Latin the first five books of Diodorus Siculus's *Bibliotheca Historica*, a history of the world from the origin of man to 59 B.C. Shortly before 1490 John Skelton translated Poggio's version into English and sought to imitate his Latin style as well. The following brief sentence is from the Prohemy:

We, therfore, advertysynge[g] in our remembraunce how famous reporte endureth with theym that be historyens,[h] of theyr exemplefyed demenour moeved which have put their dilygent endevoirment[i] in wrytynge, we have enforced[j] this historye to recounte.[10]

_____

a severe, b all that the holy martyrs ever suffered most of all or that a woman suffers who is in labour is as insignificant in comparison with their pain as is the giving of a cold bath to a man in comparison to that burning oven, c until, d refined and purified, e pure, f appertains, g taking heed, h influenced by their exemplary behaviour, i effort, j undertaken.

The 'aureate' vocabulary, the participial constructions, and the dislocation of the normal English word-order in imitation of the order of a Latin periodic sentence ('we have enforced this historye to recounte') are all marks of the effort to imitate humanistic style in English. Caxton admired the 'polysshed and ornate termes' of Skelton's translation;[11] but this style was not very widely written until it was adopted by the Tudor humanists of the sixteenth century.

Historical considerations, therefore, have some bearing on the nature of Middle English prose; but generally speaking it is a particular choice of style (whether more or less deliberate, or more or less involuntary) which is the decisive factor in what sort of prose is produced.

The simplest types of Middle English prose are those which apparently come closest to speech. Of course, authentic speech is nowhere exactly recorded, but because a great many English men and especially English women were virtually illiterate,[12] there do survive a number of documents which were taken down from the speech of those who could not themselves write. The following, the opening of a letter from Margaret Paston to her son John, dated 14 September 1469, refers to the siege of Caister Castle (a Paston holding) by John Mowbray, fourth Duke of Norfolk. Though it is formally from Margaret, it is written (presumably from dictation) in the hand of James Gloys, family chaplain to the Pastons, who acted frequently as secretary to the almost illiterate Margaret:

I grete you wele, letyng you wete*a* that your brothere and his felesshep*b* stond in grete joparte*c* at Cayster and *d*lakke vetayll, and Dawbeney and Berney be dedde and diverse othere gretly hurt, and thei fayll*e* gonnepowder and arrowes, and the place sore brokyn*f* wyth gonnes of the *g*toder parte, so that, but thei have hasty help, thei be like to lese*h* bothe there lyfes and the place, to the grettest rebuke to you that ever came to any jentilman, for every man in this countre marvaylleth gretly that ye suffre them to be so longe in so gret joparte wythought help or othere remedy.[13]

There survives the merest gesture towards epistolary formality[14] in the opening of the letter – 'I grete you wele' – but this is replaced at once by the querulous, almost hysterically insistent rhythms of Margaret's voice. These manifest themselves in the breathless piling up of one disastrous detail after another (sometimes, indeed, she gets things

*a* know, *b* company, *c* danger, *d* are short of food, *e* lack, *f* badly destroyed, *g* other side, *h* lose.

wrong, for Osbern Berney was not killed at the siege), in the almost unstoppable sequence of clauses which by turns convey information and berate her son, and in the occasional infinite clauses – 'and the place sore brokyn wyth gonnes of the toder parte'. The most notable feature of the passage though is the presumably unconscious stylistic gestures of emphasis: co-ordination is the rule rather than the exception – 'your brothere and his felesshep', 'stond in grete joparte . . . and lakke vetayll', 'Dawbeney and Berney', 'gonnepowder and arrowes', 'bothe there lyfes and the place'; key words are repeated – 'joparte . . . joparte', 'help . . . help'; and the modifiers insist on the seriousness of the situation – 'grete joparte', 'gretly hurt', 'grettest rebuke', 'marveylleth gretly', 'gret joparte', 'sore brokyn', 'hasty help'. One is left, as John must have been, with an almost audible sense of Margaret's voice.

Somewhat more ambitious and a little more formal than these letters is *The Book of Margery Kempe*, the autobiography of a Norfolk bourgeoise, who in 1413 persuaded her husband to live in mutual chastity with her and devoted herself thenceforth to a quest for self-knowledge and spiritual health. The selective record of her life, travels and experiences which makes up her 'book' may have been modified by at least three intermediaries (and the reference to Margery in the third person singular may be a facet of this), yet something of the flavour of her original account seems to survive in a passage such as that describing the summoning before Thomas Peverel, Bishop of Worcester, from 1407 to 1419, in the summer of 1417:

And anon aftyr sche was putt up befor the Bischop of Worcetyr that lay[a] iij myle beyondyn Bristowe & [b]moneschid to aper befor hym ther he lay. Sche ros up erly on the next day & went to the place wher he lay hymselfe, yet beyng in bedde, & happyd[c] to metyn on of hys worschepfulest men in the town, & so thei dalyid[d] of God. &, whan he had herd hir dalyin a good while, he [e]preyd hir to mete, & sithyn[f] he browt hir into the Bischopys halle. &, whan sche cam into the halle, sche saw many of the Biscophys men [g]al to-raggyd & al to-daggyd in her clothys. Sche, lyftyng up hir hande, [h]blissed her. & than thei seyd to hir, 'What devyl eyleth the'? Sche seyd ayen[i] 'Whos men be ye?' Thei answered ayen[j], 'The Bischopys men.' And than sche seyd, 'Nay, forsothe[k], ye arn lykar[l] the Develys men'. Than thei weryn wroth[m] and chedyn[n] hir & spokyn angrily unto hir, and sche suffryd hem well and

---

[a] was staying, [b] charged to appear, [c] chanced, [d] spoke, [e] invited her to a meal, [f] afterwards, [g] with their garments fashionably slashed and with the edges cut into points, [h] crossed herself, [i] is annoying, [j] replied, [k] truly, [l] more like, [m] angry, [n] reproved.

mekely. & sithyn sche spak so sadly[a] ageyn syn & her mysgovernawns that thei wer in sylens & held hem wel plesyd wyth her dalyawns[b], thankyd be God, er than sche left.[15]

Almost everything about the passage is simple. The sentences are con-joined by plain parataxis ('And anon . . .', '& than . . .', 'And than . . .', '& sithyn . . .'). Otherwise they depend on simple correlatives ('&, whan . . .', '&, whan . . .'). And within the sentences subordinate clau-ses are rare. The vocabulary, too, is simple, though traces of Mar-gery's distinctive idiolect appear – like the use of 'dalyid' for her conversation about God. In short, for the most part, the characteristics of this passage seem very like those of speech. There are sentences in which the subject alters quickly (like the second); the choice of vocab-ulary is sometimes inelegantly repetitive ('lay', for example, appears three times in the opening three lines); and sometimes the second of two clauses adds little to the first (as in, 'and chedyn hir & spokyn angrily unto hir'). Sometimes a fairly colloquial phrase appears, like 'putt up befor' or 'a good while'. The whole gives the impression of a rather self-righteous woman striving, discursively and not very precisely, to give a coherent account of her not very tidy life.

Only slightly more formal than these examples of essentially speech-based prose are those types of writing usually to be associated with the preserving and communicating of information. Narrative history, for example the following extract from *The Peterborough Chronicle* for 1137, provides the most obvious examples of this sort of prose:

I ne can ne I ne mai tellen alle the wunder ne alle the pines that hi diden wrecce men on this land, & that lastede tha xix wintre wile Stephne was king, & æure it was werse & werse. Hi læden gældes on the tunes æure um wile, & clepeden it 'tenserie'. Tha the wrecce men ne hadden nammore to gyven, tha ræveden hi & brendon alle the tunes, that wel thu myhtes faren al a dæies fare, sculdest thu nevre finden man in tune sittende ne land tiled. Tha was corn dære, & flesc & cæse & butere, for nan ne was o the land. Wrecce men sturven of hungær. Sume ieden on ælmes the waren sum wile rice men. Sume flugen ut of Iande. Wes nævre gæt mare wreccehed on land ne nævre hethen men werse ne diden than hi diden.[16]

I do not know how to, nor am I able to tell all the atrocities nor all the torments that they inflicted on the miserable people of this land; and that lasted the nineteen years while Stephen was king, and all the time it got worse

[a] seriously, [b] speaking.

and worse. They imposed taxes on the towns at regular intervals, and called it 'tenserie' [protection money]. When the wretched people had no more to give they robbed them and set fire to the villages, so that you could travel for a whole day and never find anyone inhabiting a village nor land cultivated. Then was corn dear, as well as meat cheese and butter, for there was none in the country. Wretched people died of starvation. Some who had at one time been rich men took to begging for alms. Others fled the country. Never before had there been greater misery in the country, nor had the heathens ever done worse than they did . . .

But much the same manner of writing appears in that which purports to be fact, even when it is not. 'Sir John Mandeville' tells the reader that he was born in St Albans, that on 29 September 1322 he left England to travel widely over almost all the known world and that he returned in 1356. There he wrote up his *Travels*, originally in Latin, and then he translated his account into English and French. But all this is fiction: there does not seem to have been a 'Sir John Mandeville' and the 'travels' are derivative. Nevertheless, the author records events and describes places as if he, or his informants, were there. The following passage describes Paradise, which even 'Mandeville' does not claim to have seen:

Of Paradys ne can I not speken propurly[a], for I was not there. It is fer beyonde, and that forthinketh[b] me, and also I was not worthi. But as I have herd seye of wyse men beyonde, I schalle telle you with gode wille. Paradys Terrestre[c], as wise men seyn, is the highest place of erthe that is in alle the world, and it is so high that it toucheth nygh to the cercle[d] of the mone, there as the mone maketh hire torn[e]. For sche is so high that the Flode of Noe[f] ne myght not come to hire, that wolde have covered alle the erthe of the world alle abowte and aboven and benethen, saf[g] Paradys only allone.[17]

Yet he still claims to be giving a true account.

Though the passage from *The Peterborough Chronicle* is based on true events (or at any rate events the author thought were true) and the whole of the 'Mandeville' passage is fictitious, both authors use roughly the same sort of prose. Both use the first and second person

*a* fittingly, *b* grieves, *c* Earthly Paradise, *d* orbit, *e* turn, *f* Noah's flood, *g* except.

pronouns and imply an intimate affinity with their respective audiences. Both use a fairly simple vocabulary: the only hard word *tenserie* is explained in the text itself. Both also use a limited range of conjunctions which force the readers to make up their own minds about the relative significance of the various facts and events recorded. The extract from *The Peterborough Chronicle* begins with some variation in syntax, but in the main keeps to the basic signposts of speech ('&', 'Tha'). The quotation from *Mandeville's Travels* is similar in its limited range of clausal types, but there are some differences, the main one being that the syntax of 'Mandeville' reflects the style of the French source where one clause 'trails' on from another ('and', 'for', 'as', 'so that'). Even so the *Travels* reads as idiomatic English, with no sense of strain.

Both pieces look unselfconscious but are not. The chronicler is concerned to stress the terror of the reign of Stephen and he does this by means of a few tactfully used stylistic devices: the modesty formula 'I ne can ne I ne mai tellen alle ...' suggests unspoken and unspeakable horrors, as does the repeated use of 'werse'; the direct address gives the piece immediacy ('tha ... tha ...'); and emphasis is given by the repetition of words and roots ('wrecce', 'wrecched') and the parallelism of sentences ('Sume ...', 'Sume ...'). In 'Mandeville' the modesty formulae ('I was not ther ...', 'I was not worthi ...') serve to disarm the reader because they contrastively persuade him to believe the 'wise men' on whom the account is based. But the author also emphasizes the preeminence and uniqueness of paradise – the first by means of a superlative ('highest') and a whole series of phrases connoting extent ('fer beyonde', 'in all the world', 'so high', 'all aboute and aboven and benethen'), the second by means of the emphatic phrase implying singleness ('only allone'). These two passages, separated in time by more than two centuries, exhibit the capacity of vernacular prose of this level of style for handling quite sophisticated narration and description.

Somewhat more elevated in style are those late fourteenth- and early fifteenth-century treatises written by contemplatives to record their mystical visions and to instruct other contemplatives. Here, for example, is Dame Julian of Norwich on the subject of a vision she received in May 1373:

Botte I sawe noght synne, fore[a] I lefe it has na manere of substaunce, na partye[b] of beynge, na it mygth nought be knawen bot be the paynes that it is cause of. And this payne, it is sumthynge, as to my syght, for a tyme[c]: for it purges us and makes us to knawe oureselfe and aske mercye. For the passionn of oure lorde is comfort to us agaynes alle this, and so is his blyssyd wille. To alle that schalle be saffe[d], he comfortes redely and swetlye be his wordes, and says: 'Botte alle schalle be wele, and alle maner of thynge schalle be wele.' Thyes wordes ware[e] schewed wele tenderlye, schewande na manere of blame to me, na to nane that schalle be safe. Than were it a grete unkyndenesse[f] of me to blame or wondyr of God for my synnes, syn[g] he blames not me for synne. Thus I sawe howe Cryste has compassyon of us for the cause of synne, and ryght as I was before with the passyon of Cryste fulfilled with payne and compassion, lyke in this I was in party[h] fyllyd with compassion of alle myn evencristene[i]; and than sawe I that[j] ylke kynde compassyone that man hase of his evencristene with charyte, that it is Criste in hym.[18]

The doctrinal content of this passage is relatively simple and orthodox. Earlier in the vision Christ has explained to her that sin is necessary ('Synne is behouelye'), and here she extrapolates from this, reasoning that a consciousness of sin makes one appreciate more fully the significance of Christ's redemption of mankind through the crucifixion, and that a contemplation of that causes one to seek to imitate Christ in his lovingkindness.

Julian describes herself in one place as a 'symple creature unlettryd' and in another as 'leued', which may be characteristic gestures of modesty and unworthiness, but alternatively may mean that she either did not know Latin or that she could not read or write. If she were illiterate it must be the case that her experiences were taken down from dictation, in much the same way as Margery Kempe's. Once or twice the syntax hesitates within the sentence, as in speech ('And this payne, it is sumthynge . . .', '. . . that it is Criste in hym'); but, for the most part, this is assured and sophisticated prose. The passage is, in its own way, argumentative and coercive, as is plain from the conjunctions: 'For . . .', 'Than . . .', 'synn . . .', 'Thus . . .', 'And than . . .'. But the persuasiveness also depends on a skilful verbal art, a wordplay which is at once witty and moving. The way in which a sense of one's own sinfulness is a prior necessity to apprehending the love of Christ is conveyed by the contrast between 'purges' and 'ful-filled', 'in party fyllyd'. The sense that Christ's suffering may produce

a believe, b part, c temporary, d saved, e revealed very tenderly, f act lacking in natural gratitude, g since, h partly, i fellow Christians, j same natural.

a reciprocal gesture in mankind is emphasized by the play on 'passyon' and 'compassyon' which runs through the second half of the passage. Most of all, perhaps, the passage suggests how spiritual revelation can be transmuted into an intellectual conviction: at the beginning of the passage 'sawe' means the sort of witnessing 'as to my syght', but in its occurrences towards the end it means rather 'realised intellectually'.

Something of the same conscious resourcefulness in choice of language is apparent in *The Cloud of Unknowing*. The author, who was from the North-east Midlands, possibly a priest and almost certainly a trained theologian, seeks to instruct a young disciple in the difficult exercise of contemplation, as in the following fairly representative passage:

Do on than fast; lat se how thou berest*a* thee. Seest thou not how he stondeth & abideth*b* thee? For schame! *c*travaile fast bot awhile, & thou schalt sone be esid*d* of the gretnes & of the hardnes of this travayle. For thof*e* al it be hard & streyte*j* in the byginnyng, when thou hast no devocion, nevertheles yit after when thou haste devocion, it schal be maad ful restful & ful light*g* unto thee, that bifore was ful harde; & thou schalt have outher litil travaile or none. For than wil God worche som-tyme al by him-self; bot not ever, ne yit no longe tyme togeders, bot *h*when him lyst, & as hym list, & *i*than wil thee thenk it mery to late hym alone. Than wil he sumtyme paraventure*j* seend oute a beme of goostly*k* light, peersyng*l* this cloude of unknowing that is bitwix thee & hym, & schewe thee sum of his privete*m*, the whiche man may not, ne kan not, speke. Than schalt thou fele *n*thine affeccion enflaumid with the fiire of his love, fer more than I kan telle thee, or may, or wile, at this tyme.[19]

What is being said is not particularly difficult or arcane: the union of the contemplative with God depends partly on the rigour and enthusiasm of the contemplative and partly on the will of God. But the style is elegant and lucid to a quite exceptional degree.

The most striking aspects of this passage are the two extended images (both of which appear elsewhere in the treatise): the 'beme of goostly liyt' that pierces the dark 'cloude of unknowing' and causes the contemplative's affection to be 'enflaumid'; and the idea of the fellow-workers at the 'travayle' of contemplation, the disciple who

*a* behave, conduct, *b* waits for, *c* work hard for a short time, *d* eased, *e* although, *f* rigorous, *g* easy, *h* when it pleases him and as it pleases him, *i* then it will appear pleasant to you to leave him alone, *j* perhaps, *k* spiritual, *l* piercing, *m* mystery, *n* your disposition fired with the burning of his love.

has to work 'fast' initially so that he will 'sone be esid', and God who will 'worche some-tyme al by him-self'. The author's real triumph, though, is in his tone: he manages to suggest to the disciple that his own efforts are valuable and will produce results – this initially by way of colloquial imperatives ('Do on than fast . . .', 'lat se how thou berest the'), then by the parallelisms between the work which will be 'harde and streyte' when he has no devotion, and 'ful restful and ful liyt' when he has acquired it. But the author, at the same time, shows the disciple his dependence, both on the grace of God (who will certainly work 'but not ever, ne yit no longe tyme to-geders, bot when him lyst, & as hym lyst . . .) and on the capacity and good-will of the author (who stresses that he is dealing with subjects which involve 'fer more than I can telle thee, or may, or wile, at this tyme'). The instructions to the disciple – that he must work hard at acquiring the right attitudes and then wait with humility for the light of revela-tion – are expressed with a graceful clarity and a persuasive subtlety.

If an author wished to elevate his prose further he could embellish and adorn it by means of a particular choice of vocabulary, by allitera-tion and rhythm. An example of this sort of prose is John Gaytryge's *Sermon* (1357), written at York, a free translation of the Latin catechism made by Archbishop Thoresby. Gaytryge's piece deals with the basic tenets of the Church (the Ten Commandments, the Seven Deadly Sins, and so on). In this passage he is talking about Pride and Envy:

The secunde dedely synn es hatten[a] envy, that es a sorowe and a syte[b] of the welefare[c] and a joy of the evyllfare[d] of our even-cristen[e]. [f]Of whilke synn many spyces [g]sprenges and spredes: ane es hateredyn[h] to speke or here oghte be spoken that may [i]sown unto gude to thaym that they hate; ane other [j]false juggynge or dome of thair dedis, and ay[k] turne unto evyll that es done to gude; the thirde es bakbyttynge, to saye behynde tham that we will noghte avowe ne saye before tham – whare noghte anely he that spekes the evyll bot he that heres it be spoken es for to blame, [l]for ware thare na herere thare ware na bakbyttere.[20]

The most notable feature of this passage is the alliteration, which is unsystematic but deliberate. But there is much else that marks the

*a* called, *b* distress, *c* success, *d* misfortune, *e* fellow Christian, *f* from which sin, *g* arise and spread, *h* hatred, *i* contribute to the good, *j* false judgement or censure, *k* always, *l* for were there no listener there would be no backbiter.

style. The sentences tend to fall naturally into short units of roughly the same number of syllables, and this imparts a strong rhythmical beat 'ane es hateredyn to speke / or here oghte be spoken / that may sown unto gude / to tham that thay hate;/ ane other false juggynge / or dome of thair dedis'. In the clause 'to saye behynde tham that we will noghte avowe ne saye before tham', Gaytryge is obviously aiming at balance, as in 'for ware thare na herere thare ware na bakbyttere', where the rhythm is strengthened by the rhyming ending –*ere*. Another embellishment is the antithesis 'welefare' and 'evyllfare'. The vocabulary is, for the most part, simple and plain, but in the sentence 'Of whilke synn many spyces sprenges and spredes' there appears to be a play on words: 'spyces' means primarily 'species'; but Gaytryge, in using the horticultural verbs 'sprenges' and 'spredes', evidently wishes to suggest the meaning 'spices' as well.[21]

An even more heightened example of this sort of prose can be found in the anonymous *Life of St Margaret* (*c.* 1225), a text from the 'Katherine Group', written in the West Midlands, presumably by a cleric. In the following passage the author describes the visit by a devil to the heroine, who has been imprisoned in a cell for rejecting a powerful man's advances:

Hire vostermoder wes an thet frourede hire, & com to the cwalmhus & brohte hire to fode bred & burnes drunch, thet ha bi livede. Heo, tha, & monie ma, biholden thurh an eilthurl as ha bed hire beoden. & com ut of an hurne hihendliche towart hire an unwiht of helle on ane drakes liche, se grislich thet ham gras with, thet sehen: thet unselhthe glistinde as thah he al overguld were. His lockes & his longe berd blikeden al of golde, & his grisliche teth semden of swart irn. His twa ehnen steareden steappre then the steoren & ten yimstanes, brade ase bascins, in his ihurnde heaved on either half on his heh hokede nease. Of his speatewile muth, sperclede fur ut, & of his neasethurles threste smorthrinde smoke, smecche forcuthest; & lahte ut his tunge, se long thet he swong hire abuten his swire; & semde as thah a scharp sweord of his muth scheate, the glistnede ase gleam deth & leitede al o leie.[22]

Her foster-mother was one who comforted her, and [she] came to the torture-chamber and brought her, for food, bread and a drink of spring water, by which she sustained life. Then she [i.e. the foster-mother] and many more, looked through an eye-hole as she [i.e. Margaret] said her prayers. And there came out from a corner quickly towards her a fiend of hell in the form of a dragon, so horrible that they were terrified of it – those who saw that evil creature glistening as if he were completely covered with gold. His hair and his long beard glittered entirely of gold and his horrible teeth seemed [to be made] of black iron. His two eyes shone more brightly than the stars and the precious stones, as wide as basins, in his horned head on either side of his high hooked nose. From his dribbling mouth fire sparkled forth, and from his nostrils issued stifling smoke, which left a foul taste in the mouth [*lit.* 'foulest of tastes']. And he darted out his tongue, which was so long that he swung it around his neck, and [it] seemed as if a sharp sword darted out of his mouth, which glistened as a flame does and blazed all along its length.

The comparisons used in this passage are fairly conventional ones, but they are chosen skilfully so as to emphasize the shiny and metallic appearance of the visitor from hell ('... al of golde', '... of swart irn', '... steappre then the steoren ant ten yimstanes', 'brade as bascins', '... as thah a scharp sweord'). The alliteration which is the most obvious feature of the passage, starts in a relatively sporadic way but becomes more insistently repetitive and emphatic ('brohte ... bred ... burnes', 'monie ma', 'bed ... beoden', 'hurne hihendliche ... hire ... helle', 'grislich ... gras' and so on). The alliteration is powerfully reinforced by the rhythm, an effect the author achieves by chopping up the material into short units containing approximately the same number of syllables (for example, 'Of his speatewile muth / sperclede fur ut, / & of his naesethurles / threste smorthrinde smoke, / smecche forcuthest.'). Both this piece and the extract from Gaytryge show the aptitude of the medium of prose for expressing didactic matter in a striking way. The stylistic embellishments observable here are found more often in verse, and, indeed, there was controversy among earlier editors of Gaytryge's sermon as to whether it was prose or poetry.[23]

Middle English prose, therefore, varies in style from that which is close to speech to the more highly figured sort which is closer to poetry. A descriptive analysis such as that above, however, misrepresents the situation a little to the extent that in some works, especially long works, more than one sort of prose is in evidence.

Perhaps the best example of this sort of work is *Ancrene Wisse* (Guide for Anchoresses), written in the West Midlands in about 1225. The author was almost certainly an Augustinian canon, perhaps, as has recently been suggested, Brian de Lingen.[24] The work was immensely popular: Latin and French versions were made; it was expanded, abridged and reused for a variety of purposes. But in its original form it was written at the request of three anchoresses, sisters not just in religion but in family, who had left the world to take up the life of recluses. The author divides his work into eight parts: Parts I and VIII, which he calls the 'outer rule', concern the non-spiritual side of the recluses' lives (what prayers to say in Part I, and what their general behaviour should be in Part VIII). The middle Parts, II to VII, he calls the 'inner rule': here he provides copious advice on such matters as temptations and how to overcome them, the sacrament of penance and how to prepare for it, the nature of human and divine love, and so on. The author is theologically learned but unfailingly humane; he is also an articulate, self-confident writer with a command of a variety of styles.

Something of this author's range may be deduced from the following extracts:

(a) The Neddre of attri Onde haveth seove hwelpes: *Ingratitudo*, this cundel bret hwa se nis icnawen goddede, ah teleth lutel throf, other forget mid alle ——'goddede' ich segge, nawt ane thet mon deth him, ah thet Godd deth him, other haueth idon him, other him other hire . . .
The Beore of heui Slawthe haveth theose hwelpes. Torpor is the forme, thet is, wlech heorte, unlust to eni thing, the schulde leitin al o lei i luve of Ure Lauerd.

(*a*) The Serpent of poisonous envy has seven young: Ingratitude – this is produced by anyone who is not mindful of good deeds, but thinks little of them or forgets them completely. 'Good deeds', I say, not only those that are done to him, but those that God does or has done to him, or her . . . The Bear of heavy Sloth has these offspring: the first is Torpor, that is a lukewarm heart (unwillingness to do anything) that should blaze all over with love for Our Lord.

(b) A leafdi wes mid hire fan biset al abuten, hire lond al destruet, & heo al poure inwith an eorthene castel. A mihti kinges luve wes thah biturnd up on hire, swa unimete swithe thet he for wohlech sende hire his sonden, an efter other, ofte somet monie, sende hire beawbeles bathe feole & feire, sucurs of liveneth, help of his hehe hird to halden hire castel . . . 'Thi luve', he seith 'other hit is forte yeoven allunge, other hit is to sullen, other hit is to reavin & to neomen with strengthe. Yef hit is forte yeoven, hwer maht tu biteon hit betere then up o me? Nam ich thinge feherest? Nam ich kinge richest? . . . Nam ich thinge freoest?'

(b) A Lady was completely surrounded by her enemies, her land totally destroyed, and she herself quite hapless in an earthen castle. However, the love of a powerful king was set on her, so extravagantly that in order to woo her he sent her his messengers, one after another, often many together. He sent her many jewels, a supply of food, the help of his noble army to hold her castle ... 'Your love', he says, 'either it is to be given completely, or it is to be sold, or ravished and taken by force. If it is to be given, where can it be better bestowed than on me? Am I not the fairest of men? Am I not the richest of kings? ... Am I not the most generous of men?'

(c) Ye schulen in an hetter ant igurd liggen, swa leotheliche thah thet ye mahen honden putten ther under. Nest lich nan ne gurde hire with na cunne gurdles, bute thurh schriftes leave, ne beore nan irn, ne here, ne ilespiles felles, ne ne beate hire ther with ne, with scurge ileadet, with holin, ne with breres, ne biblodgi hire seolf, withute schriftes leave.[25]

(c) You must sleep in a robe belted so loosely that you can get your hand between [it and the gown]. Let no one wear any kind of belt next to the body, except with her confessor's permission, nor let her wear any iron nor hair nor hedge-hog skins, not strike herself with them, nor with a leaded scourge, with holly, nor with thorns, nor make herself bloody, without her confessor's permission.

The first extract comes from the section in Part IV where he is dealing with the Seven Deadly Sins. It is explanatory prose but by no means dull. In places it possesses a distinctively conversational energy; for example, in the phrase 'goddede ich segge' the author doubles back on himself in the manner of speech and then supplies four neatly turned explanations of what he means by 'goddede'. In other places the author quickens the reader's attention by alliteration ('leitin al o lei i luve of Ure Lauerd'). The third extract comes from Part VIII which concludes what the author has to say about the 'outer rule'. It is instructional prose of great explicitness and clarity, but also of some subtlety: not only does the author specify what should be done ('ye schulen ... liggen') but he indicates the extent ('swa leotheliche thet ...'); not only does he say what should not be done ('nan ... ne ... na ... ne ...') but he also suggests what exceptional conditions might allow the injunctions to be disregarded ('bute thurh ... withute ...").

The second extract comes from one of the narrative *exempla* which the author uses from time to time – the famous allegorical piece in Part VII in which he compares the love of Christ for the soul to the love of a great king for a poor lady. Usually in this *exemplum* the author keeps the literal and allegorical levels separate, but there is a punning reference here in the adjective 'eorthene' to the allegorical level. Literally the word means 'composed or made of earth' and refers here to the earth walls or ramparts of castles; figuratively, however, the word carries with it the Biblical sense 'made from dust' and refers to the body.[26] Wordplay of this sort, however, is not frequent. More striking is the alliteration and other stylistic embellishments. The alliteration is sporadic ('sende ... sonden', 'feole & feire', 'help ... hehe hird ... halden ...') but it enlivens the surface of the discourse. A more elaborate sort of prose, more appropriately perhaps, appears in the next five sentences (taken from the lover's wooing speech) which are highly artificial. There are rhetorical questions ('hwer ...', 'Nam ich ...'), balanced clauses ('other hit is ... other hit is ... other hit is'), rhyme ('thinge ... kinge ... thinge'), like endings ('feherest ... richest ... freoest'). The whole speech, of which these sentences are merely the opening, abounds in figures of this sort.

The major imaginative effort of English writers in the Middle Ages did not go into prose but into poetry. Until the vogue for prose romances in the latter part of the fifteenth century, prose was essentially a utilitarian medium: it was used to record information, to inform, to instruct, and to exhort. Nevertheless, it was a medium in which a wide variety of styles was available (some of them deriving from pre-Conquest models) and in which there was some development between the eleventh and the fifteenth centuries. Throughout the Middle Ages prose was a mature and flexible medium in which a good many people wrote competently and in which a few wrote very well.

## NOTES

1. For a discussion of the distinction between poetry and prose see Christopher Ricks's review of John Sparrow's *Visible Words* (1969) in *Essays in Criticism*, XX (1970), 259–64.

2. See, for example, the frontispieces to the two volumes of Layamon's *Brut*, ed. G. L. Brook and R. F. Leslie (EETS, 250, 277, 1963, 1978).

3. See, for example, N. F. Blake '*The Form of Living* in Prose and Poetry', *Archiv*, CCXI (1974), 300–308.

4. *The Works of Sir Thomas Malory*, ed. Eugene Vinaver (2nd edn, 1967), I, 202.

5. For a survey of the varieties of Old English prose see Ian A. Gordon, *The Movement of English Prose* (1966), 35–44.

6. See R. W. Chambers, *On the Continuity of English Prose from Alfred to More and his School* (EETS 191A, 1932).

7. On this subject see J. Orr, *The Impact of French upon English* (1948); and A. A. Prins, *French Influence in English Phrasing* (1952).

8. Quoted from the extract given by N. F. Blake, *Middle English Religious Prose* (1972), 136.

9. See Roberto Weiss, *Humanism in England during the Fifteenth Century* (2nd edn, 1957), especially III and IV.

10. *The Bibliotheca Historica of Diodorus Siculus*, ed. F. M. Salter and H. L. R. Edwards (EETS, 233, 239, 1956, 1957), 9.

11. From Caxton's Prologue to *Eneydos* (*c.* 1490) in *Caxton's Own Prose*, ed. N. F. Blake (1973), 80.

12. Nicholas Orme, *English Schools in the Middle Ages* (1973), 52–55; and M. T. Clanchy, *From Memory to Written Record: England 1066–1307* (1979), 175–201.

13. *Paston Letters and Papers of the Fifteenth Century*, ed. Norman Davis (1971), I, 344 (No. 204).

14. For a good brief account of epistolary practice see Norman Davis, 'The *Litera Troili* and English Letters', in *Review of English Studies*, XVI (1965), 233–44.

15. *The Book of Margery Kempe*, ed. S. B. Meech and H. E. Allen (EETS, 212, 1940), 109.

16. *The Peterborough Chronicle 1070–1154*, ed. Cecily Clark (2nd edn, 1970), 56–7.

17. *Mandeville's Travels*, ed. M. C. Seymour (1967), 220.

18. *Julian of Norwich's Revelations of Divine Love: The Shorter Version*, ed. Frances Beer (MET 8, Heidelberg 1978), 60–61.

19. *The Cloud of Unknowing and The Book of Privy Counselling*, ed. Phyllis Hodgson (EETS, 218, 1944), 62.

20. *Middle English Religious Prose*, ed. N. F. Blake (1972), 84–5.

21. The words both derive ultimately from Latin *species* and in Middle English were often spelt in the same way: see OED *spice* sb. 1, 3; and the obsolete *spece* sb. 2, 3.

22. *Seinte Marherete the Meiden ant Martyr*, ed. Frances M. Mack, (EETS 193, 1934), 20.

23. See David A. Lawton, 'Gaytryge's Sermon, *Dictamen*, and Middle English Alliterative Verse', in *Modern Philology*, LXXVI (1979), 329–43; and for an interesting more general view Elizabeth Salter, 'Alliterative Modes and Affiliations in the Fourteenth Century', in *Neuphilologische Mitteilungen*, LXXIX (1978), 25–35.

24. E. J. Dobson, *The Origins of Ancrene Wisse* (1976).

25. *Ancrene Wisse*, ed. from MS. Corpus Christi College, Cambridge, 402 by J. R. R. Tolkien (EETS, 249, 1962), f.53b 10–15; f.54a 28–f.54b 2; f.105a 18–24; f.107b 4–10; f.113a 28–f.113b 6 (our punctuation).

26. See MED *erthen* adj. (a) and *erthe n* (1) 9. This play on words is the basis for the widely known *Erthe upon Erthe* text (see the edition by Hilda Murray, EETS, 141, 1911).

# PART III

# THE LANGUAGE OF
# ENGLISH MEDIEVAL LITERATURE

DEREK BREWER

In the early twelfth century one Brother William, a friend of the Somersetshire Saint Wulfric, performed a linguistic miracle. By the laying on of hands he made a dumb man speak not only English but French. Another friend, the local parish priest, called Brihtric, complained to Wulfric of the unfairness of this, having served Brother William faithfully for a long time; for he had not been given any French, and had to remain dumb even in the presence of his bishop.

This little story illustrates the linguistic dilemma brought about by the Conquest, and the nature of the English language itself cannot be understood without understanding the problems caused by the presence of French and Latin. English could not but continue as the main speech of the English people, but after the Conquest French became the language of the controlling classes. There are a number of references from the twelfth to the fourteenth centuries which reveal a strong resentment against French. The author of Robert of Gloucester's *Chronicle*, writing at the end of the thirteenth century, with a strong pro-English bias itself of some significance, points out that the Normans spoke French, and he maintains that this tradition continued. He says that nowadays 'unless a man knows French he is little thought of', but all the same, 'low men' still stick to English. There is a vein of slightly paranoid class-consciousness in this and some similar references which other evidence suggests should not be taken too seriously, but even if it almost certainly misrepresents the complex facts, it illustrates a widespread feeling. The heart of the matter is that while all classes before the Conquest had used their mother tongue for political, administrative and personal communication, after the Conquest for a long while the principal language of the higher classes was French, to which the lower classes had less access. This was a deprivation to the bulk of the population. It was a division far more rankling than that of class, which all societies must for practical purposes accept, but it deepened and embittered class-division and affected the further history of the English language, of education, and of attitudes to education. Up to the middle of the fourteenth century French was the language of social and political power and prestige. Such a situation was not the result of policy (William the Conqueror even tried to learn English). There was no prejudice against English. There was plenty of intermixture of marriages and eventually of languages. Many Englishmen learnt French, if less easily than Brother William's dumb friend: but the point was that they had to learn it. Paradoxically, in families French by origin, even if now English by nationality, they spoke French so naturally that French in England became a dialect of its own, called Anglo-Norman or Anglo-French, with an impressive literature from the late twelfth to the fourteenth centuries. The literature of medieval England rightly includes this French writing. But looked at in terms of the national culture French was a burden to the majority and the story of the English language in the medieval centuries is of how English first lost its prime position as the leading language of the English people and then regained it.

Although French had taken such a dominant social position in England its actual position was weaker than it seemed. Even the upper classes spoke English. One of the chronicles about St Thomas à Beckett tells how a noble lady, wife of a Norman knight, Hugh de Morevile, tried to seduce a young friend, whose name, Lithulf, reveals English ancestry. The virtuous young man resisted, so the lady tried to pay him out by getting him first to draw his sword in play, then calling out to her husband that Lithulf was about to attack him from the rear. The chronicler, writing in Latin, gives her words in *English*: 'Hugh de Morevile, ware! ware! ware! Lithulf heth his swerde adrege (*drawn*)!' English was the language of emergency and feeling, even for high-born Normans. Meanwhile, Anglo-Norman became a provincial dialect of French, losing prestige to continental French, so that by the end of the fourteenth century Chaucer has his joke at the expense of the would-be courtly Prioress that she spoke the French of 'Stratford-atte-Bow', a suburb of London, for the French of Paris was unknown to her. Once Anglo-Norman had lost its snob-value it was doomed as the dialect of a small class all of whom, for various practical reasons (including shouting to their husbands and, no doubt, talking the language of love to attractive young Englishmen), were continually also speaking English. Froissart tells us that the Black Prince in Aquitaine in the 1370s spoke French to his French barons and English to his English barons. He was bilingual, perhaps even in continental French, but they were not. French lost its hold in schools after the Black Death of 1348–9 and thus faded out naturally as a national language. In 1362 the Chancellor opened Parliament for the first time with a speech in English, and a statute was passed that certain law-court proceedings were to be held in English. French was not immediately discarded. It long retained its hold on law, where such technical words as *tort* reveal its influence, but in general it did not last long into the fifteenth century.

The presence of Latin made a further complication. Latin was at first more of a benefit and less of an irritation, but eventually it turned into a deadly enemy. It is a strange story. Christianity had brought to the English in the seventh century a superior and powerful religion based on a truly remarkable book, the Bible, supported by other books, liturgies, histories, etc., and with some hint of the implicit powers of the secular culture of Classical Rome. But all was in Latin. It was a severe disadvantage to the English to have so important a part of their higher culture in a foreign language, but the disadvantages were offset in the earlier centuries by the real benefits of entering so much greater an imaginative, religious and intellectual world than was otherwise available to them. There was much translation, and no specially privileged foreign class of Latin speakers. Ignorance of Latin may have been a spiritual disadvantage but it carried no social or political stigma. You could be both rich and noble and yet ignorant of Latin but not, until the fifteenth century, of French. But Latin proved to be a time-bomb. The Church itself had a mission to spread the good news and that meant education, and thus the use of English, especially after the resolutions of the Fourth Lateran Council at Rome of 1215. Educational and religious tracts were produced in English. Sermons translated passages from the Bible. Education is an appetite which grows by what it feeds on. It grew slowly in the small population and primitive physical conditions of medieval England, but by the end of the fourteenth century the effect of the Church's own admirably educative policies was a widespread passion felt by laymen to have the sacred text itself in English. This natural but unplanned consequence of an educational programme which had always envisaged *Latin* as the inevitable language of learning and liturgy was passionately resented by the educators themselves. Schoolteachers and parents are often upset by the unforeseen results of their own instructions. Educated churchmen could not easily relinquish the superior position which possession of the sacred mystery of Latin conferred. Only the Oxford philosopher Wycliffe, with a handful of associates, some of whom later recanted, argued for the Bible in English. In the late fourteenth century followers of Wycliffe produced first a literal translation and then a more idiomatic revision of the Latin Bible. The laymen, and the few priests who sympathized, who led the movement for the English Bible, for reforms and a new spirituality were called Lollards, and they were soon cruelly repressed. Although an underground Lollard movement persisted throughout the fifteenth century, most of the nation in the fifteenth century accepted for English the intellectual stagnation and comfortable sentimentality of extravagantly devout saints' lives and emotionally pious religious lyrics, untouched by the harder edges of the New Testament. Meanwhile, in the fifteenth century complex religious movements developed on the Continent, where an increasing number of people also wanted the Bible in their mother tongue, together with other profound changes in religious feelings and practices. The Czech reformer and martyr John Huss (1373–1415) had been influenced by Wycliffe. Huss's influence spread on the Continent and the movement of reform eventually culminated in the potent personality of Luther, who produced a great translation of the Bible in his own German vernacular. In the sixteenth century Continental influences (reinforced by Englishmen like Tyndale – persecuted for their desire to have the Scriptures in English – who took refuge on the Continent) affected the situation in England. Latin, too long defended, shrivelled away, and the mother tongue was at last established at the outset of the Reformation as the main language of English religious culture in the sixteenth century, at the cost of many religious martyrs burnt at the stake, and of estrangement with many European fellow-Christians who did not, at least directly, accept the Reformation. Latin remained the international language of science but even there its days were numbered.

The nature of the English language, and its availability for litera-

ture can only be understood as part of these large historical movements, and also as stemming from its Old English origins. Old English
(sometimes called Anglo-Saxon), the language of the English before
the Conquest, was a Germanic language with some resemblance to
modern German. It had already absorbed some Latin words, mainly
religious (like *church*) and some Norse words and forms. Some of these
latter only emerge in the Middle English period. Old English was an
inflected language; that is, the endings of words changed according to
whether they were verbs or nouns, and according to the part they
played within the group of words amongst which they operated.
Furthermore, Old English had developed a standard spelling based on
the form of the language used in Wessex. Although all languages
develop and change, the existence of a written standard stabilizes the
language and improves communication, while concealing sound
changes and often many other variations in common speech – in
vocabulary, word-order, loss of endings, etc.

After the Conquest English-trained scribes were gradually super-
seded by French-trained scribes, and standard written English as it had
been known was lost. This took some time. A useful index is the
*Anglo-Saxon Chronicle*, which had been maintained in various
monastic centres which copied and modified the text from each other.
The *Chronicle* is the major index of Old English general culture, the
steady witness of national identity and self-consciousness. William did
not suppress it. It slowly faded out, the copy at Peterborough lasting
longest. It records William's own death in 1087, with a vivid
character-sketch of him. The last entry is for 1154, nearly 100 years
after the Conquest. The language changes before our eyes. The entries
usually begin, for example, in good Old English, 'Her on thisum
ʒeare' (Here, in this year), until in 1106 we have 'Her on thyson
ʒeare', an easily recognizable variant; then in 1120, 'On this ʒeare',
where an inflection has gone (though the next entry begins 'On
thyssum ʒeare'); and then the phrase beginning the year 1125 'On
this ʒear' has lost further inflection. From 1131 we begin to get the
modern phrase 'This ʒear' (This year), and from now on the language
may be called Middle English, not Old English. There are many
other changes in the text, and the entries from 1122 to 1155 give us
an authentic record of Early Middle English in the Peterborough area.
Sounds, word-endings, word-order and vocabulary are all different

from, but except for some items of new vocabulary are clearly related to, Old English.

Very little survives in Middle English from before the end of the twelfth century. A few Old English sermons continued to be copied, but little new material was composed. But around 1200 in England there is a general increase of all kinds of documentation, and though most is non-literary, and in Latin or French, English texts begin to appear. We can piece together what *had* happened, and from that date onwards can fairly closely follow what *was* happening, to the English language. It is a fascinating but technical story of which only a few simplified details can be given here.

The loss of a standard, the consequent tendency of scribes to try to write what the words sounded like, and the use of different spelling conventions (e.g. either *k* or *ch* for the two sounds formerly represented only by *c*), reveal a great variety of regional dialects in Middle English, most of which can be faintly recognized even today, and which had their origin in Old English. Dialects varied in vocabulary and pronunciation to a very considerable extent and were distinctive to their areas, though they merged into each other at the edges of regions. They seem to have had no particular social status. We can easily distinguish the Derbyshire dialect of *Sir Gawain and the Green Knight* from the South-east Midland London of Chaucer. He himself gets comic effects from imitating the Northern dialect of the clerks in the *Reeve's Tale*. The centre of influence in the national language came to be London, and Modern English sounds essentially descend from London's South-east Midland dialect, with a casual admixture of a few Kentish, Western and Northern forms.

It is often wondered how scholars can recreate the sounds of a long silent language. In fact the language is not silent, for the English now spoken in Britain is derived from it, and the variants in modern pronunciation of British and indeed American English, are in part a clue to earlier pronunciations. Our pronunciations of *breath* and *death* compared with *heath* and *sheaf*, for example, tell us something about the earlier differing vowel sounds represented now by the same letters, *ea*. The varying spellings of the same word from Old to Modern English, as *ham* and *home*, *hal* and *whole*; comparisons to be made through rhyme; datings and placings in legal documents; in a word, the collection and comparison of millions of small facts by many hundreds of scholars, all add up to an almost complete account of the language as it looked and sounded in almost any period. The interested reader can begin this process himself by vigilant attention to the texts he reads and by comparing different spellings and forms. He will soon recognize the characteristic open *a*s and the present participle ending in -*ande*, not -*inge*, of Northern and Scottish texts, and the softer burr of the South-western. The language was changing in sounds all the time, but the diphthong-vowels so characteristic of modern English were not used in a big way till the late fifteenth century, so that a rough approximation of Middle English vowel sounds is achieved by pronouncing them single or 'pure', as in Modern European languages. Most consonants were pronounced, so that a very tolerable mock-up of the pronunciation of Middle English can be easily acquired. It is important to practise this, even when reading to oneself, for Middle English has a clear, bell-like beauty (like modern Italian) which modern English has lost. It is also important to pronounce words correctly for the sake of the metre, paying particular attention to the presence of inflections, which by the time of Chaucer had in many places decayed to no more than the so-called 'obscure' vowel, represented by final -*e*, which is still vital to the metre. To pronounce Chaucer even to oneself in only modern speech, paying no attention to the preservation of the metre, is frankly barbarous. Thus one must read such a line as

> O yongė fresshė folkės, he or she
> (*Troilus*, V, 1835)

sounding the inflected endings both of the adjectives and of the noun *folkės*, all in the plural form. The loss of a standard allowed many spelling variants until the practice of the fifteenth-century Chancery clerks in London, and finally the regularity of printing, more or less fixed our spelling in the first half of the sixteenth century. But in the earlier period spelling gives a fair guide to pronunciation for an experienced reader.

While the vocabulary of English remained basically English it underwent the most radical and important changes in its history within England during the medieval period, and the nature of these changes was also important for their effects on the remarkable development of English as a universal language with many dialects in the nineteenth and twentieth centuries. The root stock of English speech, the words with which we live and love and die, eat and breed, hope and fear, is still as English as all these words. Those stark four-letter words which are central to the language, words like *from* and *with* (not to say *like*), the even starker three- and two-letter words *and*, *but*, *by*, *to* – that is, the structural, most *linguistic* words, with least out-side reference but crucial to the internal structures of the language – all remained English. But the vocabulary, which more directly reflects changing social circumstance, intellectual culture, and to some extent feelings, changed very considerably. In particular many French words came into use, with the result that of all the Northern European Germanic languages English has the highest proportion of French and thus, more generally, of 'Romance' words, i.e. words which origi-nated in Latin, the language of Rome. This had the effect of building an educational barrier into the very structure of the language, since a native speaker could not easily discover the meaning of a word new to him by analysing its simpler components, as to some extent a German speaker still can. So the modern English speaker needs to be more specifically educated to achieve the same equivalent vocabulary, and hence knowledge, as a German speaker. On the other hand, the already mixed English vocabulary made it easier in later centuries to adopt new words from any language. The new words also probably helped break down the inflection of old words and thus made the syntax depend more on word-order. English is perhaps in con-sequence easier to speak badly and harder to speak well, than other European languages.

The new French words were taken in for a variety of social and practical reasons, and often displaced a perfectly good English word that was already in use, as *pais* (*peace*) replaced Old English *grith*. Other borrowings reflect Norman dominance, as *curt* (*court*), *castel*, *prisun*, and amount to about two hundred up to 1200. The celebrated example noted by Scott in *Ivanhoe* comes in here; the English *cow*, *ox*, *calf*, turn up cooked on the Norman table as *beef* and *veal*.

In the thirteenth and fourteenth centuries the major influence became Central French, partly as a wave of French-speaking French-men came into the English court and upper reaches of government, but partly as evidence of borrowing from the now intellectually and culturally more advanced French. By Chaucer's time the French

element was considerable, and in the first eighteen lines of the general
Prologue to the *Canterbury Tales* there are eighteen French words.
Chaucer is the first recorded user of many French words which
illustrate new concepts or new things from France, such as *scissors*.
One line of his illustrates in small measure the development of the
English vocabulary up to his time:

> Welcome, my knyght, my pees, my suffisance.
> (*Troilus*, III, 1309)

*Welcome my knyght* are all original English words, plain and warm,
though *knight* has undergone a great change of meaning from Old
English *cniht* (boy) to one who is a member of the upper social class
and exemplar of the elaborate ethos of chivalry. *Peace*, already noted,
was one of the first French words recorded in medieval English in
the middle of the twelfth century. *Suffisance* is a fourteenth-century
borrowing, rather a favourite with Chaucer, and a grand, abstract,
general word for 'satisfaction' (which has a similar meaning, is first
recorded in about 1300 in a religious sense, and has ousted *suffisance*.
Chaucer uses *satisfaction* nine times but only in the technical religious
sense.) The vocabulary of the *Gawain*-poet, however, is remarkably
different, drawing both on many Northern forms, influenced by
Norse, and on a large but somewhat different selection of French
courtly language.

It is significant that the more English came to be used, the more
French words were borrowed. Each process was part of the same
general development of domination and unification. A somewhat
similar situation arises in Latin. A small number of Latin words were
borrowed in the medieval period, though it is often difficult to tell
whether they came direct or through French, but the great period
of absorption of Latin into English was in the sixteenth century, when
intellectual functions formerly restricted to Latin began to be more
and more active in English. The fullness and unification of the
language which is almost complete in the great writers of the fourteenth century were at last achieved in the sixteenth.

Though vocabulary is the most easily demonstrable and socially
most directly affected of linguistic elements, syntax also developed.
The loss of inflections promoted regular word-order. (It is interesting
to see how often, for all his mastery of a colloquial style, Chaucer has

to change normal word-order in order to fit his metrical pattern, and gets little help from inflections.) Grammatical gender was early lost in the medieval period for the same reason, and to our great benefit. Verb forms developed a very flexible and rich system through the use of many auxiliaries.

Middle English had become a more flexible, varied, loose language than Old English. At first it was deprived of social status but in the end though scars, such as a somewhat irregular spelling system, remained it had become an instrument of immense potentiality. The use that Chaucer, the *Gawain*-poet and Langland, to mention only the three great fourteenth-century poets, could make of it, varying from plain, even coarse colloquialism to the richest descriptions and the heights of exalted feeling, show how that potentiality could be realized.

## NOTE

The story of William and Brihtric may be found in *Wulfric of Haselbury by John, Abbot of Ford*, ed. Dom Maurice Bell, Somerset Record Society XLVII (1933), privately printed. The story of Hugh de Moreville's wife is referred to by G. E. Woodbine, 'The language of English Law', *Speculum* XVIII (1943), 395–436, and is to be found in *Materials for the History of Thomas Beckett*, Rolls Series, I, 128. *The Peterborough Chronicle 1070–1154* is edited by Cecily Clark (Oxford, 1970, 2nd edn). Amongst several valuable histories of English may be noted A. C. Baugh, *A History of the English Language* (2nd edn, London, 1959), and Barbara Strang, *A History of English* (London, 1970).

# CHAUCERIAN THEMES AND STYLE IN THE *FRANKLIN'S TALE*

JILL MANN

The *Franklin's Tale* is not only one of the most popular of Chaucer's tales, it is also one whose emotional and moral concerns lie at the centre of Chaucer's thinking and imaginative activity. It is usually thought of as a tale about 'trouthe' – or perhaps about 'gentillesse' – but it is equally concerned with the ideal of patience and the problems of time and change, which are subjects of fundamental importance not in this tale alone but in the *Canterbury Tales* as a whole. What follows is intended to be not only a close discussion of the *Franklin's Tale*, but also an attempt to indicate how a proper reading of it can help with a proper reading of the rest of the *Tales* – and indeed, of Chaucer's work in general.

The *Franklin's Tale* begins by introducing a knight who has, in best storybook fashion, proved his excellence through 'many a labour, many a greet emprise*ᵃ*' and thus finally won his lady who, likewise in best storybook fashion, is 'oon the faireste under sonne'. 'And they lived happily ever after' is what we might expect to follow. And so far from trying to dispel the reader's sense of the familiar in this situation, Chaucer takes pains to increase it. He refers to the actors only in general terms ('a knyght', 'a lady'), and attributes to them the qualities and experiences normally associated with tales of romantic courtship (beauty, noble family, 'worthynesse', 'his wo, his peyne and his distresse'). Only after eighty lines are the knight and the lady given the names of Arveragus and Dorigen. This generality cannot be accidental, for Chaucer's apparently casual comments are designed precisely to emphasize that this individual situation takes its place in a plural context:

> But atte laste she, for his worthynesse,
> And namely for his meke obeisaunce,

*a* exploit.

Hath such a pitee caught of his penaunce<sup>a</sup>
That prively<sup>b</sup> she fil of his acord
To take him for hir husband and hir lorde,
Of swich lordshipe *as men han over hir wives.*

(738–43; my italics)

What is more, they stress this plural context even in describing the feature of the situation which seems to make it an unusual one: the knight's promise to his lady that he

Ne sholde upon him take no maistrye<sup>c</sup>
Again hir wil, ne kithe<sup>d</sup> hire jalousye,
But hire obeye, and folwe hir wil in al,
*As any lovere to his lady shal.*

(747–50; my italics)

And after the lady's delighted promise of her own faithfulness and humility, we have a warm outburst of praise which again consistently sets this mutual understanding in the context of a whole multiplicity of such relationships.

For o thing, sires, saufly<sup>e</sup> dar I seye,
That freendes everich oother moot<sup>f</sup> obeye,
If they wol longe holden compaignye.
Love wol nat been constreined by maistrye<sup>g</sup>.
Whan maistrye comth, the God of Love anon
Beteth his winges, and farewel, he is gon!
Love is a thing as any spirit free.
Wommen, of kinde<sup>h</sup>, desiren libertee,
And nat to been constreined as a thral;
And so doon men, if I sooth seyen shal.

(761–70)

'Love . . . maistrye . . . freendes . . . wommen . . . men' – the terms are abstract, plural, general. They relate general human experience to this situation, and this situation to general human experience, with no sense of conflict or discontinuity between the two.

I stress the importance of the general here for two reasons. The first is that this interest in the *common* features of human experience is characteristic of Chaucer. The parenthetical comments which transform the singular of the story into the plural of everyday experience

*a* suffering, *b* inwardly, *c* dominance, *d* show, *e* confidently, *f* must, *g* power, *h* by nature.

134

are not confined to this passage or this tale alone; on the contrary, they are so ubiquitous in Chaucer that we may take them for granted and fail to question their significance. The second reason is that the unusualness of the relationship between Arveragus and Dorigen has often been taken as a sign that it is aberrant – that it represents an attempt to break away from the normal pattern of marital relationships which inevitably invites problems to follow.[1] Against this view we should note that however unusual the *degree* of generosity and humility in this relationship, Chaucer very firmly roots it in the normal desires and instincts of men and women.

Nor is there any reason given for supposing that these desires and instincts are merely human weaknesses. Chaucer's own comments, some of which have been quoted, constitute an unhesitating endorsement of the wisdom of this situation and of the participants in it. The relationship between the knight and his lady is called 'an humble wys accord', and the knight himself 'this wise, worthy knight'. It would not affect this point were anyone to argue that the comments are the Franklin's, not Chaucer's. For in either case any reader who wishes to dissociate him- or herself from the warm approval in these lines will face the same difficulty – and that is the difficulty of finding a location in the tale for true wisdom and worthiness, if both characters and narrator offer only false images of these qualities. The only way out of this difficulty would be to claim that the reader already knows what true wisdom and worthiness are, and brings this knowledge to bear on the tale, in criticism of its values. But this idea assumes that it is possible for his or her knowledge to remain detached from the tale in a way that the passage we are considering simply refuses to allow. For if the reader is a woman, to refuse to acknowledge the truth of what is said about her sex is, *ipso facto*, to accept the legitimacy of her own 'thraldom':

> Wommen, of kinde, desiren libertee,
> And nat to been constreined as a thral.

If, on the other hand, the reader is a man, and feels inclined to respond to these lines with a knowing smile at the ungovernable nature of women, then the following line –

> And so doon men, if I sooth seyen shal

– immediately challenges him in turn to measure the reasonableness of the female desire for liberty by matching it against his own. The result is that both men and women readers are made aware of the need for the liberty of the opposite sex through the recognition that it is a need of their own. The use of the plural, the appeal to the general, is indeed an invitation to readers to bring their own experience and feelings to bear, but it invites them to an identification with the narrative, not to a critical dissociation from it.

Chaucer's use of the plural is thus intimately connected with his use of the second person, an equally pervasive and significant feature of his style. His appeals to the reader as judge have often been discussed – 'Who hath the worse, Arcite or Palamon?' (*Knight's Tale*); 'Which was the moost fre, as thinketh yow?' (*Franklin's Tale*). But to emphasize these formal appeals alone is to imply, again, that the reader, in the role of judge, remains detached from and superior to the narrative. If, on the other hand, we look at the whole series of addresses to the audience in Chaucer, we shall see that the situation is more complicated. Certainly it is true that the narrative is subordinate to the reader, in the sense that it acknowledges that it relies on a particular experience of the reader for its life and depth; the appeal for judgement on the situations of Arcite and Palamon, for example, is specifically addressed to 'Yow loveres'. The opening of *Troilus and Criseyde* similarly invites 'ye loveres' to read the narrative in the light of their own experience. This call for 'supplementation' of the narrative from one's own experience is often implicitly, as well as explicitly, made. Such an appeal can, for example, be felt in the rhetorical question that concludes the praise of the marriage in the *Franklin's Tale*:

> Who koude telle, but*a* he had wedded be,
> The joye, the ese, and the prosperitee
> That is betwixe an housbonde and his wif?
>
> (803–5)

The rhetorical question here makes a space for the reader's own experience to give full meaning to the description, just as it makes space for a very different kind of experience to give a very different kind of meaning to the apparently similar question in the *Merchant's*

*a* unless.

*Tale* (1337–41). But if the story needs the reader, it can also make claims on the reader. Precisely because the narrative is based on 'common knowledge', on experiences and feelings shared by the narrator, the readers, and the characters in the story, it is possible for its third-person generalizations to issue into second-person imperatives. Thus, when Troilus falls in love, the generalizations about Love's all-conquering power ('This was, and is, and yet men shal it see') issue naturally into a command:

> Refuseth nat to Love for to ben bonde,
> *ª*Syn, as himselven list, he may yow binde.
> (I, 255–6)

We can thus see that in the narrator's comments on the marriage of Arveragus and Dorigen, the apparently casual insertion of 'sires' in the first line is a deliberate preparation for the intensification of the narrative's claims on the reader – claims which make themselves known not only as commands but also as threats.

> Looke who that is moost pacient in love,
> He is at his avantage al above.
> Pacience is an heigh vertu, certeyn,
> For it venquisseth, as thise clerkes seyn,
> Thinges that rigour sholde never atteyne.
> For every word men may nat chide or pleyne.
> Lerneth to suffre, or elles, *ᵇ*so moot I goon,
> Ye shul it lerne, wherso*ᶜ* ye wole or noon;
> For in this world, certein, ther no wight is
> That he ne dooth or seith somtime amis.
> (771–80)

The command 'Lerneth to suffre' does not stand alone; if we disobey it, we face a threat, an 'or elles'. If we search for the authority on which we can be thus threatened, we find it, I think, in the appeal to *common* human experience that I have been describing, in the generalizations from which the imperative issues and into which it returns. And because the experience is common, the speaker himself is not exempt from it; it is perhaps possible to detect in the parenthetical 'so moot I goon' a rueful admission that he has learned the truth of his statement the hard way. At any rate, the phrase stands

*a* since, as he pleases, *b* as I live, *c* whether.

as an indication that the speaker offers his own individual experience as a guarantee of the truth of the generalizations.

It is because Chaucer wishes to appeal to the general that he so often uses proverbs as the crystallizations of episodes or whole narratives. The proverb which underlies the description of the marriage in the *Franklin's Tale* is perhaps the most important one of all to him; the attempt to understand the paradoxical truth 'Patience conquers' is at the heart of the *Canterbury Tales* and much of Chaucer's other work besides. It animates the stories of Constance and Griselda; it is celebrated in Chaucer's own tale of Melibee. It undergoes, as we shall see, a comic–realistic metamorphosis in the *Wife of Bath's Prologue*, and it also stimulates Chaucer's exploration of the qualities that represent a rejection of patience – 'ire', 'grucching', 'wilfulnesse'. It is tinged with a melancholy irony in *Troilus and Criseyde*, where Criseyde quotes another version of the proverb – 'the suffrant overcomith' – in the course of persuading Troilus of the wisdom of letting her go to the Greeks. This latter instance shows us that an understanding of the truth to be found in such proverbs does not give us clues to the instrumental manipulation of life – quite the reverse, in fact. The parallel truism that Criseyde also quotes – '*a*Whoso wol han lief, he lief moot lete' – does not become the less true because in this case Troilus fails to keep possession of his happiness even though he follows her advice. It is precisely the knowledge that proverbs carry with them the memory of human miseries as well as human triumphs and joys that gives depth and emotional power to the apparently worn phrases.

But of course it is also the story, the new setting which will give fresh meaning, that gives new depth and emotional power to the old words, and we should therefore look to the rest of the *Franklin's Tale* to see how much it can help us to understand the nature of patience and 'suffrance'. The first thing that the story shows us is the link between patience and change. In the first place, it is because human beings are inevitably and constantly subject to change, not just from day to day but from moment to moment, that the quality of patience is needed. In his list of the influences that disturb human stability, Chaucer makes clear that they come both from within and from without the person.

*a* whoever is willing to possess, must be willing to give up.

> Ire, siknesse, or constellacioun[a],
> Win, wo, or chaunginge of complexioun[b]
> Causeth ful oft to doon amis or speken.
> On every wrong a man may nat be wreken[c].
> After[d] the time moste be temperaunce[e]
> To every wight that [f]kan on governaunce.
>
> (781–6)

All these things disturb the stability of a relationship by altering the mood or feelings or behaviour of an individual. Thus, the only way that the stability and harmony of a relationship can be preserved is through constant adaptation, a responsiveness by one partner to changes in the other. The natural consequence of this is that patience is not merely a response to change; it *embodies* change in itself. And this is at first rather surprising to us, since we tend to think of patience as an essentially static quality, a matter of gritting one's teeth and holding on, a matter of eliminating responses rather than cultivating them. But it is the responsive changeability of patience which is emphasized in Chaucer's final lines of praise for the marriage of Arveragus and Dorigen.

> Heere may men seen a humble, wys accord:
> Thus hath she take hire servant and hir lord –
> Servant in love, and lord in mariage.
> Thanne was he bothe in lordshipe and servage.
> Servage? nay, but in lordshipe above,
> Sith he hath bothe his lady and his love;
> His lady, certes, and his wif also,
> The which that lawe of love acordeth to.
>
> (791–8)

It is often said that this passage illustrates Chaucer's belief in an ideal of equality in marriage. But the patterning of the language does not give us a picture of equality; it gives us a picture of alternation. The constant shifts in the vocabulary suggest constant shifts in the role played by each partner: 'servant ... lord ... servant ... lord ... lordshipe ... servage ... servage ... lordshipe ... lady ... love ... lady ... wif'. The marriage is not founded on equality, but on alternation in the exercise of power and the surrender of power. The image it suggests is not that of a couple standing immutably on the same level

---

*a* planetary influence, *b* the physiological balance of the body, *c* revenged, *d* according to, *e* adjustment, *f* is skilled in.

and side-by-side, or marching in step, but rather of something like the man and woman in a weather-house, one going in as the other comes out. Except of course that this image gives a falsely mechanical idea of what is, as Chaucer describes it, a matter of a living organic responsiveness, and that it is also incapable of expressing an important aspect of the relationship – that the ceaseless workings of change lead to an unchanging harmony, and to the creation of a larger situation in which each partner simultaneously enjoys 'lordshipe' and 'servage', as the passage itself stresses. The result of these constant shifts could be called equality (though I should prefer to call it harmony), but the term equality is too suggestive of stasis to be an accurate description of the workings of the ideal involved here. The ideal of patience better befits the way human beings are, because the simplest and most fundamental truth about people, for Chaucer, is that they change. 'Newefangelnesse', the love of novelty, is part of their very nature ('propre kinde'; *Squire's Tale*).

Human being are not only subject to change in themselves; they also live in a changing world. The opening of the *Franklin's Tale* might seem at first to belie this, since it reads more like an ending than a beginning, so that the story seems, with the long pause for the eulogy of the marriage, to have reached a full stop before it has begun. What prevents a sense of total stagnation is that the unusualness of the situation – of Arveragus' surrender of absolute control – creates a powerful expectation that something is going to happen. This is not just a stratagem for holding our interest; on the contrary, Chaucer uses narrative expectation as a way of indicating the persistence of change even when events have apparently reached a standstill, of making us feel the potentiality for change within the most apparently calm and closed of situations. Thus, as Chaucer allows himself his leisured commentary on the 'humble, wys accord', we find ourselves asking not 'Is this a good thing?', but 'How will this turn out?' We await the completion which the development of events will bring to our understanding and evaluation, and we are thus taught to expect development, the breaking of stasis, as natural.

The stasis is first broken in a very simple way: Arveragus departs for England, and Dorigen's contentment changes into a passionate grief. This grief is described in a long passage (815–46) which takes us from her first agonies, through her friends' attempts at comfort, to her final subsidence into a kind of resignation which creates a new, if provisional, stasis. Two features of this passage are important: the first is that Dorigen's experience is, once again, placed in a general context.

> For his absence wepeth she and siketh[a],
> *As doon thise noble wives whan hem liketh[b]*.
> (817–18; my italics)

Secondly, her experience is not only generalized, it is also abbreviated:

> She moorneth, waketh, waileth, fasteth, pleyneth[c].
> (819)

Dorigen experiences her grief intensely and at length, but it is described summarily and – *ipso facto* – with a sort of detachment. This does not mean, however, that we need to qualify what was said earlier about the identification established between character, writer and reader; the detachment here is not due to lack of sympathy or to criticism, but to a difference of position in time. Dorigen moves slowly through a 'process' which is for her personally felt and unique; the image of the slow process of engraving on a stone emphasizes its gradualness, its almost imperceptible development. The teller of the story (and the reader of it), on the other hand, can from the outset see Dorigen's experience in a general context of human suffering, and from a knowledge of the general human experience which is embodied in the formulae of traditional wisdom – 'Time heals', 'It will pass' – can appreciate not only what is pitiable about Dorigen's misery but also the inevitability of its alleviation, and thus, what is slightly comic about it. The amusement denotes no lack of sympathy, no sense that Dorigen's grief is melodramatic or insincere; it is the kind of amusement which might well be felt by Dorigen herself, looking back on her former agonies six months after her husband's safe return. As time goes on, and Dorigen succumbs to the natural 'proces' of adjustment, she herself comes nearer to this view, so that the passage ends with a rapprochement between her position and that of the storyteller and the reader, and the calmer wisdom of 'wel she saugh that it was for the beste' is shared by all three.

---

*a* sighs, *b* it pleases them, *c* laments.

The celebrated Chaucerian 'ambiguity of tone', of which this passage might well be taken as an example, is often regarded as an equivocation between praise and blame, a confusion in our impulse to approve or disapprove. Complex the tone may be, but it does not lead to confusion if we read it aright. The complexity is often due, as it is in this case, to Chaucer's habit of fusing with the narrative account of an event or situation the differing emotional responses it would provoke – and with complete propriety – at different points in time. Different contexts of place and time allow and even demand quite different emotional and intellectual responses. In common experience we take this for granted; we find it entirely proper and natural that a widow should be consumed with grief at her husband's death and equally proper and natural that several years later she should have found equanimity. Time thus affects not only decorum, but also morality; were the widow to show at the time of her husband's death the reactions of a widow several years later, we should find her behaviour unfeeling and wrong. Chaucer's complexity arises from the fact that he encourages us to bring to bear our knowledge of both points in the process at the same time. He is helped in this by the fact that a story always abbreviates experience; the protracted time-scale of experience is condensed in the time-scale of the narrative, so that we can more easily and more swiftly achieve those shifts of perspective which are in life so laboriously accomplished. This is, of course, even more true in short narrative, because in such a narrative the disparity between the time-span of the occurrences and the time-span of the relation of them is most striking. Chaucer's interest in short narrative, the beginnings of which can be seen in the *Legend of Good Women*, and which finally achieved success in the *Canterbury Tales*, seems to me, therefore, to be a natural consequence of what he sees as interesting in human experience. The short narrative is a powerful way of provoking reflection on the process of change and of vitalizing our sense of the moral and emotional complications created by change, by our existence in the 'proces' of time. And a multiplicity of short narratives can suggest the multiple individual forms in which a common experience manifests itself, and the constitution of common experience out of a multiplicity of variant instances.

The processes of time and change are not all, however, a matter of the development of inner feeling; change, as we have already observed, can equally originate in the outer world – in its most dramatic form, in the kind of sudden chance or accident for which Chaucer uses the Middle English word 'aventure'. This is a word that can be used with deceptive casualness to refer to the most mundane and minimal sort of occurrence, but also, more emphatically, to refer to the strange and marvellous. The other words which Chaucer uses to mark the operations of chance are 'hap', 'cas' and 'grace', the last of these being usually reserved for *good* luck unless accompanied by an adjective like 'evil' or 'sory'. Chaucer's concern with the problems of chance, with human helplessness before it, and with the difficulties it opposes to any belief in the workings of a co-ordinating providence, is something that can be observed throughout his literary work. The operations of 'aventure' are often examined, (as they are in the *Franklin's Tale*) in the sphere of love, and for good reason. The disruptive, involuntary, unforeseeable and unavoidable force of love is perhaps the most powerful reminder of the power of chance over human lives. What is more, it increases human vulnerability to other chances, as Dorigen, in her persistent fears for her husband's possible shipwreck on the 'grisly rokkes blakke', is only too well aware. What she at first fails to perceive is her possible vulnerability to an 'aventure' which is closer at hand: the 'aventure' of Aurelius' love for her.

> This lusty*a* squier, servant to Venus,
> Which that ycleped*b* was Aurelius,
> Hadde loved hire best of any creature
> Two yeer and moore, as was his aventure.
>
> (937–40)

Chaucer's description of the wearing away of Dorigen's grief means that we can dimly see several possible patterns into which the coalescence of inner 'proces' and outer 'aventure' might fall. Were Arveragus' ship in fact, to be wrecked, we could visualize not only Dorigen's passionate grief but also its susceptibility to slow assuagement, so that when healing processes of time have done their work, Aurelius *might* hope at last to win his lady (as Palamon does). Or Arveragus might

---

*a* gallant, *b* called.

simply be forced to stay away so long that by the same process of imperceptible adaptation, Dorigen finds Aurelius a more vivid and powerful presence to her thoughts and feelings than her husband, and changes her initial rejection into acceptance – in which case the story would come closer to the pattern of *Troilus and Criseyde*. The openness of Chaucer's stories to other possible developments makes us aware that they are not fixed into inevitable patterns; like life itself, they are full of unrealized possibilities. In this case, the menace symbolized in the black rocks is not realized, and the other possibilities thus evaporate. 'Aventure' does not take the form of shipwreck and Arveragus returns. But that there is no other kind of disaster is due also to the power of patience, of the ability to 'suffer' the shocks of 'aventure'.

In order to understand this conception of 'suffering' more fully, I should like to make some comparisons with another example of the genre to which the *Franklin's Tale* belongs, the Breton lay, a comparison which will have the incidental advantage of suggesting why Chaucer assigns the tale to this genre, even though his source was probably a tale of Boccaccio.[2] The *Franklin's Prologue* suggests that the Breton lays are centrally concerned with 'aventures':

> Thise olde gentil Britouns in hir dayes
> Of diverse aventures maden layes...
> (709–10)

The notion that this is the proper subject of the lays can be traced back to one of their earliest composers, the late twelfth-century writer Marie de France, who says that each lay was written to commemorate some 'aventure'.[3] There is no direct evidence that Chaucer knew Marie's work,[4] but a brief comparison with some aspects of the lay of *Guigemar* will help to illustrate the literary tradition which lies behind Chaucer's thinking on 'aventure', and also to understand the imaginative core of the *Franklin's Tale*, the underlying pattern of experience which it shares with a lay like *Guigemar*. Like the *Franklin's Tale*, *Guigemar* deals with 'aventure' in relation to love; it is interested both in the way that love is challenged by 'aventure', by the shocks of chance, and equally in the way that love itself *is* an 'aventure', a force which is sudden and overwhelming in its demands, and to which the only fitting response is surrender or commitment of the self. What we also find in Marie's lays is the idea that such a surrender acts as a release of power. It is this pattern – surrender to 'aventure' followed by release of power – which can be linked with the 'Patience conquers' of the *Franklin's Tale*.

The hero of the lay, Guigemar, is a young man endowed with every good quality, but strangely resistant to love. One day while out hunting he shoots a white deer; the arrow rebounds and wounds him in the thigh, and the dying deer speaks to him, telling him that he will only be cured of this wound by a woman who will suffer for love of him greater pain and grief than any woman ever suffered, and that he will suffer equally for love of her. Guigemar's actions indicate an immediate and unquestioning acceptance of the doom laid on him by the deer. He invents an excuse for dismissing his squire, and rides off alone through the wood, not following any predetermined direction, but led by the path. That is, he follows not the dictates of his own wishes, but the dictates of chance. Eventually he comes to the sea, and finds a very rich and beautiful ship, entirely empty of people. Having boarded the ship, Guigemar finds in the middle of it a bed, sumptuously and luxuriously arrayed. The bed is an emblem of an invitation to rest, to relax, to surrender control – or rather to surrender it still further, since he in fact lost control at the moment when he shot the white deer. He climbs into the bed and falls asleep; the boat moves off of its own accord, taking him to the lady who is to be his love, and who is kept imprisoned by her jealous husband in a castle surrounded by a high walled garden, open only to the sea. The castle and the sea, and their relation to each other, are images that the tale endows with symbolic meaning. The sea (as often in medieval literature) is an image of flux or chance, of something vast and unpredictable which can carry one with the force of a tide or a current to strange harbours. The image of the imprisoning castle which is nonetheless open to the sea suggests the openness of even the most restrictive marriage relationship to the threat of 'aventure'. The jealous husband cannot shut out the power of chance; his marriage – and equally the generous marriage of the *Franklin's Tale* – must remain vulnerable to the assaults of chance.

Guigemar, in contrast, surrenders to the dictates of chance. When he wakes from his sleep on the boat, he finds himself in mid-ocean. Marie's comment on this situation brings a new extension to our notion of 'suffering'; she says

> Suffrir li estut l'aventure.

Both the infinitive 'suffrir' and the noun 'aventure' seem to call for a double translation here. 'Aventure' simply means, in the first place, 'What was happening'; but the word also emphasizes the strangeness and arbitrariness of the event, its lack of background in a chain of causes. 'Suffrir' seems to ask to be translated not only as 'suffer, endure', but also as 'allow', a usage now familiar to us only in archaic biblical quotations such as 'Suffer the little children to come unto me'. So that the line cannot be confined to a single interpretation: 'He had to endure / allow / what was happening / chance'. Guigemar prays to God for protection, and goes back to sleep, another acknowledgement that control is not in his hands. So it is in the surrender or abandon of sleep that he arrives at the lady's castle, is found by her, and becomes the object of her love.

Guigemar's 'suffering' can help with the understanding of the 'suffering' urged in the *Franklin's Tale*:

> Lerneth to suffre, or elles, so moot I goon,
> Ye shul it lerne, wherso ye wole or noon.

This sort of 'suffering' is not simply a matter of enduring pain or vexation; it is a matter of 'allowing', of standing back to make room for, the operations of 'aventure', and thus of contributing to the creation of something new by allowing the natural process of change to work. It is the generous in spirit who do this, in both Marie's work and Chaucer's, and it is the mean-spirited, such as the lady's jealous husband, who vainly try to close off possibilities for change, to wall up what they have and to preserve it in a state of fixity.

It is a later moment in the lay, however, that provides the most powerful image of a surrender of the self which miraculously releases power. After Guigemar and the lady have enjoyed each other's love for some time, his presence is discovered by the lady's husband, and he is put back on to the magic ship (which has miraculously reappeared) and sent back to his own country. After his departure, the lady suffers intensely, and finally she cries out with passion that if only she can get out of the tower in which she is imprisoned, she will drown herself at the spot where Guigemar was put out to sea. As if in a trance, she rises, and goes to the door, where, amazingly, she finds neither key nor bolt, so that she can exit freely. The phrase that Marie uses is another that seems to call for a double translation:

Fors s'en eissi par aventure.

'Par aventure' is a casual, everyday phrase, meaning simply 'by chance, as it happened'; thus on one level, all this line means is 'By chance she got out'. But the miraculous nature of the event, and the way that the phrase recalls the other miraculous 'aventure' of the ship, suggest something like 'By the power of "aventure", she got out'. The intensity of the lady's surrender to her grief, which is imaged in her wish to drown herself, to 'immerse' herself in her love and sorrow, magically transforms external reality. 'Aventure', which had earlier been a force that impinged on people and acted on them, here becomes something which is itself acted on by emotion, which miraculously responds to its pressure. When the lady goes down to the harbour she finds that the magic ship is once again there, so that instead of drowning herself, she boards it, and is carried away to an eventual reunion with Guigemar. Her readiness to 'suffer', the depth of her surrender, magically transforms her external situation and releases the power for a new departure. A surrender paradoxically creates power.

The surrender that leads to the release of power is also at the heart of the narrative in the *Franklin's Tale*. It can be seen, first of all, in Arveragus' surrender of 'maistrye', which wins in return Dorigen's promise of truth and humility. Neither of them knows what their promises are committing them to, and it is precisely such ignorance that makes the commitments generous ones. But the underlying principle can operate in far less noble and generous situations, as Chaucer shows us by repeating such a pattern of reciprocal surrender in varying forms, through the rest of the *Canterbury Tales*. The most comic and 'realistic' version is to be found at the end of the *Wife of Bath's Prologue*, in the quarrel provoked by the Wife's fifth husband, who insists on reading to her his 'book of wikked wives'. The Wife, in fury, tears three leaves from his book, and he knocks her down. With instinctive shrewdness, the Wife exploits the moral advantage that this gives her, and adopts a tone of suffering meekness.

> 'O! hastow slain me, false theef?' I seyde,
> 'And for my land thus hastow mordred me?
> Er[a] I be deed, yet wol I kisse thee'.
>
> (800–802)

Such a display of submissiveness elicits a matching submissiveness from the aghast Jankin, and he asks for forgiveness. The quarrel ends with the establishment of a relationship that follows, in its own more robust way, the pattern of that between Arveragus and Dorigen: the husband's surrender of 'governance' is met by unfailing truth and kindness on the part of his wife. The description of this reconciliation stays within the sphere of comic realism, however, not least because every gesture of surrender carries with it an accompanying gesture – albeit softened and muted – of self-assertiveness: the 'false theef' of the Wife's first speech; Jankin's excusing of himself for striking the blow by insisting that she provoked him; the Wife's final tap on his cheek to settle the score and make their kind of equality. The generosity here is a matter of letting these last little pieces of self-assertiveness pass, of 'allowing' them to be submerged in the larger movements of self-abasement which are being enacted. Such a comic-realistic version of the notion that surrendering power gives one back power enables us to see that although its operations may be 'magical' in the sense that they are not easy to rationalize, the roots of this principle lie in the everyday world of instinctive interaction between human beings. The fairyland world where wishes come true is not an alternative to this everyday experience, but a powerful image of its more mysterious aspects.

Such an image is offered us, of course, by the end of the Wife's tale, in the account of the working out of the relationship between the knight and the ugly old lady he has been forced to marry. After lecturing the knight on the value of age, ugliness and poverty, the old lady offers him a surprising choice: whether he will have her 'foul and old', but a 'trewe, humble wif', or whether he will have her 'yong and fair', and take the chance ('take the aventure') that others will compete to win her favours away from him. The knight's response is to make the choice over to her, to put himself in her 'wise govern-aunce', and the miraculous result of this is that the ugly old lady is transformed into a beautiful young one, who promises to be faithful in addition. As in the lay of *Guigemar*, a mental surrender has magical effects on physical reality. But the magical transformation in physical reality is the manifestation of an equally magical inward transfor-mation which accompanies and causes it: the knight who began the tale with a particularly brutal assertion of masculine 'maistrye', the rape of a young girl, is transformed into a husband who humbly relinquishes control to his wife. What is more, he must accept that possession can never be complete in the sphere of human relations; to accept happiness is to accept the possibility of its loss, and to take a beautiful wife is to incur the risk of unhappiness at losing her ('Whoso wol han lief, he lief moot lete', as Criseyde puts it).

In the *Franklin's Tale*, the magic has rather a different role to play. The magic does not bring about the dénouement of the tale: on the contrary, it creates the problem. The clerk from Orléans uses it to remove all the rocks from the coast of Brittany so that Aurelius may fulfil the apparently impossible condition for winning Dorigen's love. As Dorigen herself says of their removal: 'It is agains the proces of nature'. The magic is used to create an 'aventure' – a sudden, disruptive happening that interrupts the gradual rhythms of natural change. It is as an 'aventure' that the situation created by the removal of the rocks presents itself to Arveragus; he says to Dorigen, 'To no wight telle thou of this aventure.' But he has also told her, 'It may be wel, paraventure, yet today.' There is the same kind of 'hidden pun' in the qualifying 'paraventure' here as there is in Marie de France's use of the phrase. On the face of it, it simply means 'perhaps'. But it also suggests a deeper appeal to the power of chance – the power of 'aventure' which has created the problem and which has, therefore, also the power to resolve it *if* it is allowed to operate. Arveragus allows it; he stands back, as it were, to make room for it, subduing his own claims and wishes. The test of his relinquishment of 'maistrye' is that he must submit himself to his wife's independently-made promise so far that he is forced to order her to keep it; the test of Dorigen's promise to be a 'humble trewe wyf' is that she must obey her husband's command that she fulfil her independent promise to be unfaithful. The structure of their relationship at this point, therefore, is a poignant illustration of the simultaneity of 'lordshipe' and 'servage' which had earlier been described; each of the marriage-partners is following the will of the other and yet also acting out an assertion of self. And just as this moment in the tale provides an illustration of the fusion of 'lordshipe' and 'servage', so it provides an illustration of what is meant by the command 'Lerneth to suffre'. Arveragus 'suffers' in the double sense of enduring pain and 'allowing'; in bidding his wife to keep her promise, he provides a compelling example of patience in Chaucer's sense of the word, of adaptation to 'aventure', of allowing events to take their course. And he shows us very clearly that such an adaptation is not, as we might idly suppose, a matter of lethargy or inertia, of simply letting things drift. The easy course here would be to forbid Dorigen to go; Chaucer makes clear the agonizing effort that is required to achieve this adaptation.

> 'Trouthe is the hyeste thing that man may kepe.'
> But with that word he brast*ª* anon to wepe.
> (1479–80)

In this tale, as in *Guigemar*, a surrender to 'aventure' is met by a response of 'aventure'. In this case, it takes the form of the meeting between Dorigen and Aurelius, as she sets out to keep her promise. Chaucer emphasizes the chance nature of this meeting: Aurelius 'Of aventure happed hire to meete', he says, and a few lines later, 'thus they mette, of aventure or grace'. Yet nothing is more natural, since we are told that Aurelius was watching and waiting for Dorigen's departure. These comments point, therefore, not so much to the fact that this meeting is an amazing coincidence, as to the operation of 'aventure' within it. The intensity of Dorigen's surrender to the situation in which she has been trapped, perceptible in her anguished cry 'half as she were mad',

> 'Unto the gardin, as min housbonde bad,
> My trouthe for to holde, allas! allas!'
> (1512–13)

has a dramatic effect on Aurelius; it mediates to him Arveragus's surrender to 'aventure' and stimulates him to match that surrender with his own. He releases Dorigen from her promise and sends her back to her husband. He accepts the chance by which he has come

*a* burst (into).

too late, by which his love for Dorigen post-dates her marriage – one of the arbitrary cruelties of time – and having perceived the inner reality of the marriage, the firmness with which each is linked in obedience to the other in the very act of consenting to Dorigen's 'infidelity', Aurelius 'allows' that relationship its own being, undisturbed; he too exercises patience and 'suffers' it.

But what if he had not? What if he had insisted on the fulfilment of the promise? For if Chaucer is pointing to the power of chance in human lives, he is bound to acknowledge that chance might well have had it so. One critic who correctly observes the perilous ease with which either development could realize itself at this point has written a conclusion to the episode in which Aurelius does just that.[5] The freedom and openness of events in the Chaucerian world means that romance is always open to turn into fabliau – or into tragedy. But I think that in this tale the nature of such a tragedy would be qualified by our sense that Aurelius would have 'enjoyed' Dorigen in only a very limited sense; his possession of her would have been as much a matter of 'illusion' and 'apparence' as the removal of the rocks that made it possible. The magic, in this tale, suggests the illusory, forced quality of Aurelius's power over Dorigen (in contrast to the natural power won by Arveragus, spontaneously springing into life at the end of the long process of his courtship). That is why the magic removal of the rocks is presented as a laborious, technologically complex operation, rather than the wave of a sorcerer's wand.[6] The real magic in this tale is Aurelius's change of heart, which is as miraculous as that of the knight in the *Wife of Bath's Tale*. The magic removal of the rocks is merely a means by which we can measure the immensity of this 'human magic'; we can gauge as it were, the size of the problem it is able to solve. And this 'human magic' is nothing other than the human power to change. What the development of the tale brings to our notion of the human tendency to change is that it is not just an everyday, humdrum matter of our moods fluctuating with the passage of time, but that it is a source of power; its role can be creative.

As I have already suggested, Chaucer is well aware of the tragic aspects of the human propensity to change, as his constant preoccupation with the theme of betrayal shows. He is also aware of the saving power of human resilience, a sort of comic version of patience, which can nullify the tragic aspects of 'aventure'; thus beside the serious transformation of the rapist knight in the *Wife of Bath's Tale* we can set the figure of Pluto in the *Merchant's Tale*, the ravisher who has clearly been worn down by feminine rhetoric so that he presents the ludicrous picture of a henpecked rapist. Romances such as the tales of the Knight and Franklin, however, offer us a serious celebration of patience, of the creative power of change. 'Pitee' may be the quality that leads Criseyde's emotions away from Troilus to Diomede, or it may be ironically appealed to as the cause of May's amazing readiness to respond to Damian's advances (*Merchant's Tale*), but it is also the quality that enables Theseus to adapt himself to each new claim that chance events impose on him (*Knight's Tale*), or that leads Dorigen to accept Arveragus' suit, and it is 'routhe' (another word for pity) that leads Aurelius to release Dorigen. Moreover, as the passage on patience makes clear, the responsiveness implied in the ideals of patience and 'pitee' must be exercised continually; the balance and poise achieved at the end of the *Franklin's Tale* is reached by a 'proces', a chain of ceaseless adjustment in which the magician-clerk, as well as the other three figures, must play his part.[7] Ceaseless adjustment is, as we saw, something that characterizes the marriage, with its endless alternation of 'lordshipe' and 'servage', and it is for that reason that it can survive 'aventure'; it is founded on it. Only through cease-less change can there be stability. Only through a perpetual readiness to adapt, to change, in each of the actors in the tale, can the status quo be preserved. Or, in Chaucerian language, 'trouthe' is the product of patience.

Chaucer's strength is that he gives us a creative sense of order; he makes us aware that static formulae, of whatever nature – the husband's sovereignty, equality in marriage – are inappropriate to human beings, since they are subject to change from within and chance from without. What is needed instead is an ideal such as the ideal of patience, which is founded on change, on the perpetual readi-ness to meet, to accept and to transform the endless and fluctuating succession of 'aventures' that life offers.

## NOTES

1. See, for example, D. W. Robertson, *A Preface to Chaucer* (Princeton, New Jersey, 1962) 470–72.

2. Boccaccio tells the story in the *Filocolo* (IV, 4) and the *Decameron* (X, 5). See the section on the *Franklin's Tale* in W. F. Bryan and G. Dempster, *Sources and Analogues of Chaucer's Canterbury Tales*, (New York, 1941).

3. Marie's *Lais* are edited by A. Ewert (Oxford, 1944). There is an English translation by Eugene Mason, *Lays of Marie de France and Others* (London, 1911). For Marie's statement about the *lais* and *aventures*, see her Prologue, 35–36.

4. Although her *lais* achieved a high degree of popularity; see Ewert's Introduction, xviii. For a full discussion of the fortunes of the lay in England, see John B. Beeston, 'How Much was Known of the Breton Lai in Fourteenth-Century England?', *The Learned and the Lewed: Studies in Chaucer and Medieval Literature*, ed. L. D. Benson (Cambridge, Mass., 1974), 319–36.

5. Ian Robinson, *Chaucer and the English Tradition* (Cambridge, 1972), 195–6.

6. The magic in the *Filocolo* story is of a much more traditional kind, involving the concoction of a magic potion from exotic herbs, roots, stones, etc.

7. Even this has its comic version, in the *Shipman's Tale*, where a chain of unshaken selfishness creates the same sort of final balance and poise.

# THE *PARDONER'S PROLOGUE* AND *TALE*

JOHN SPEIRS

The *Physician's Tale* and the *Pardoner's Prologue* and *Tale*, wherever they would finally have stood in relation to the other tales, are expressly intended to stand together. The *Pardoner's Prologue* and *Tale* are organically one, a dramatization of the Pardoner, and unmistakably one of Chaucer's maturest achievements.

The Chaucerian dramatic interest is less in the *Physician's Tale* itself than in the Host's reaction to it. The good-natured fellow is powerfully affected, his Englishman's sense of justice outraged:

> 'Harrow!' quod he, 'by nayles and by blood!
> This was a fals cherl and a fals justyse! . . .'

He declares he is in need of a drink to restore his spirits, or else of a merry tale; so he calls upon the Pardoner. At that the 'gentils' are fearful of hearing some 'ribaudye' and insist 'Tel us som moral thing'. The Pardoner has, as he says, to 'thinke up-on som honest thing' while he drinks. The irony is that he does indeed tell a moral tale with a vengeance.

But first, after this interlude, comes the *Pardoner's Prologue* to his *Tale*. This consists, as he drinks, of his 'confession' – a 'confession' of the same order as that of the Wife of Bath. The 'confession' should simply be accepted as a convention like those soliloquies in Elizabethan plays in which the villain comes to the front of the stage and, taking the audience entirely into his confidence, unmasks himself ('I am determined to prove a villain'). The consideration that the rogue is here apparently giving away to his fellow-pilgrims the secrets he lives by will intervene only when we refuse (incapacitated, perhaps, by modern 'naturalistic' conventions) to accept the convention – and that would be just as unreasonable as if we were to refuse to accept the other convention by which he speaks in verse. Even by 'naturalistic' expectations the phenomenon is not outrageously improbable.

In an excess of exhibitionism, glorying and confident in his invincible roguery, his tongue loosened by drink, the Pardoner is conceivable as sufficiently carried away to boast incautiously as well as impudently. But such considerations are hardly the relevant ones here. A conventionalized dramatic figure – such as could not be met with off a stage – is not necessarily less living or less of a reality than one that has not been treated conventionally. It partly depends on the vitality of the convention itself, which may concentrate instead of dissipate, eliminate all but essentials, sharply define, focus, and intensify. Within the frame of the present convention – the 'confession' – a dramatization of spectacular boldness, remarkable intensity and even subtlety is presented. By its means the Pardoner exhibits himself (like the Wife of Bath) without reserve.

The themes of the Pardoner's initial characterization in the great *Prologue* are developed and illustrated dramatically in both the *Pardoner's Prologue* and his *Tale*, which together may be regarded as all the Pardoner's monologue. He combines several rôles. His chief rôle, in which he most prides himself, is that of the fraudulent preacher who preaches against the sin which he himself typifies – Avarice. The object of his emotional and vivid sermons against Avarice is to loosen his hearers' heart-strings and purse-strings for his own profit. To this immoral end he is consciously the declamatory preacher, the spellbinder, in the guise of holiness. He presents, for admiration, the image of himself in the pulpit, incidentally revealing his contempt for the 'lewed peple' whom he deceives:

> I stonde lyk a clerk in my pulpet,
> And whan the lewed peple is doun y-set,
> I preche, so as ye han herd bifore,
> And telle an hundred false japes more.
> Than peyne I me to strecche forth the nekke,
> And est and west up-on the peple I bekke,
> As doth a dowve sitting on a berne.
> Myn hondes and my tonge goon so yerne,*a*
> That it is joye to see my bisinesse.
> Of avaryce and of swich cursednesse
> Is al my preching, for to make hem free
> To yeve her pens*b*, and namely un-to me.
>
> (63–74)

*a* briskly, *b* money.

He will do no honest work (such as weave baskets). His other profitable rôles are those of a pedlar of pardons and sham relics, and a
medicine-man selling false remedies and formulas to induce people to
feel and believe what they would like to – against the evidence of
their own senses – and to multiply the crops and cure sick animals:

> For, though a man be falle in jalous rage,
> Let maken with this water his potage,
> And never shal he more his wyf mistriste,
> Though he the sooth of hir defaute wiste;
> Al had she taken preestes two or three.
> Heer is a miteyn eek, that ye may see,
> He that his hond wol putte in this miteyn,
> He shal have multiplying of his greyn . . .
>
> (39–46)

Part of the power he exerts is unmistakably as a survival of the traditional medicine-man. As the eternal charlatan, showman, or quack,
his rôles are still being played not only in market-places and at street
corners.

The *Pardoner's Tale* has the dual character of a popular sermon and
a moral tale. The tale itself is such as might have been grafted on to
a popular sermon on Gluttony and Avarice as an *exemplum*, to show
Death as the wages of sin. It belongs (though in its origins clearly an
old traditional tale) with the Pardoner's own preaching as he has been
describing and enacting it in his *Prologue*. But the order by which the
tale is subsidiary to the sermon is in this case reversed. Instead of the
tale growing out of the sermon, the sermon here grows out of the tale;
instead of incorporating the tale, the sermon is here incorporated in
the tale; and the tale concludes, not only with a final condemnation of
the sins of Gluttony and Avarice, but a confident attempt by the
Pardoner to make the most of its terrifying effect by yet another production of the scandalous bulls and relics. The Pardoner's preaching
and entertaining are entangled, perhaps confused in his own mind,
share an identical lurid life, and are calculated by him to promote his
private business ends.

The lurid opening of the tale startles us sensationally into attention
with its images of ferocious riot, and with the tone of moral indignation which accompanies these images, a moral indignation that on examination turns out (as frequently with moral indignation) not to be

so moral after all, but to be itself an accompanying emotional orgy
on the part of the Pardoner:

> ... yonge folk, that haunteden folye,
> As ryot, hasard, stewes, and tavernes,
> Wher-as, with harpes, lutes, and giternes,
> They daunce and pleye at dees[a] both day and night,
> And ete also and drinken over hir might,
> Thurgh which they doon the devel sacrifyse
> With-in that develes temple, in cursed wyse,
> By superfluitee abhominable;
> Hir othes been so grete and so dampnable,
> That it is grisly for to here hem swere;
> Our blissed lordes body they to-tere;
> Hem thoughte Jewes rente him noght y-nough;
> And ech of hem at otheres sinne lough,
> And right anon than comen tombesteres[b]
> Fetys[c] and smale, and yonge fruytesteres[d],
> Singers with harpes, baudes, wafereres,
> Whiche been the verray develes officeres
> To kindle and blowe the fyr of lecherye,
> That is annexed un-to glotonye;
> The holy writ take I to my witnesse,
> That luxurie is in wyn and dronkenesse.
>
> (136–156)

The images are presented along with a thunderous overcharge of
shocked and outraged half-superstitious, half-religious feeling:

> ... they doon the devel sacrifyse
> With-in that develes temple, in cursed wyse.

Blasphemy is visualized as an act monstrously unnatural and ghastly,
the mutilation of the body of Christ.

Our imagination having been seized by these sensational means, we
find ourselves launched first not into a tale but into a sermon. This
'digression' – a sermon on gluttony and drunkenness, gambling and
swearing – again serves an integrating and dramatic purpose. Not
only are the themes of the sermon themes which the suspended tale
will illustrate, but the sermon is a further exhibition by the Pardoner
of his powers, and also a further exhibition of himself. He consciously
dramatizes certain aspects of himself – he is a play-actor by nature and

*a* dice, *b* female tumblers, dancing girls, *c* neat, *d* fruit-sellers.

profitable practice – but equally is unconscious of other aspects. He is half-horrified and half-fascinated by the subject-matter of his sermons. He unconsciously gloats over the sins he zestfully condemns. There is in his sermon (as, according to T. S. Eliot, may lurk even in some of Donne's sermons on corruption) a sly yielding to what for him is the grotesque fascination of the flesh. The dramatization here is more inclusive than the Pardoner's own conscious self-dramatization as a popular preacher, and it completely detaches and objectifies even the sermon as comic dramatic art.

After a succession of popular *ensamples* from the Bible, the Pardoner in his sermon dwells on the original instance of 'glotonye' – the eating of the forbidden fruit by Adam and his wife – and this produces a succession of indignant (or mock-indignant) apostrophes and exclamations – 'O glotonye . . . O glotonye . . .':

> Allas! the shorte throte, the tendre mouth,
> Maketh that, Est and West, and North and South,
> In erthe, in eir, in water men to-swinke
> To gete a glotoun deyntee mete and drinke!
>
> (189–192)

The idea corresponds to the Jacobean feeling that the fine clothes on a courtier's or lady's back may have cost an estate – evidence again that the Jacobean social conscience was inherited from the medieval religious attitude. The poetry here depends particularly on the contrasts arising from the conjunction of vigorous popular speech with scholastic phraseology:

> O wombe! O bely! O stinking cod,
> Fulfild of donge and of corrupcioun!
> At either ende of thee foul is the soun.
> How greet labour and cost is thee to finde!
> Thise cokes*a*, how they stampe, and streyne, and grinde,
> And turnen substaunce in-to accident,
> To fulfille al thy likerous talent!
> Out of the harde bones knokke they
> The mary*b*, for they caste noght a-wey,
> That may go thurgh the golet softe and swote*c*.
>
> (206–215)

A fantastic-comic effect is produced by the virtual dissociation of the belly and gullet – as, just before, of the throat and mouth – from the

*a* cooks, *b* marrow, *c* sweet.

rest of the body, their virtual personification and consequent magnification; and by the impression of the wasted labour and sweat of the cooks in the contrasting metaphysical phrase – 'turnen substaunce in-to accident'. The vigorous coarseness and the metaphysics come together, momentarily, in the term 'corrupcioun'. How close Chaucer can sometimes come, in some of the elements of his art, to the vernacular sermons and *Piers Plowman*, is once again shown in the Pardoner's farcical impression of Drunkenness:

> O dronke man, disfigured is thy face,
> Sour is thy breeth, foul artow to embrace,
> And thurgh thy dronke nose semeth the soun
> As though thou seydest ay 'Sampsoun, Sampsoun';
> And yet, god wot, Sampsoun drank never no wyn.
> Thou fallest, as it were a stiked swyn ...
>
> (233–8)

Gluttony has been visualized in the sermon as parts of the body that have taken on a kind of independent life of their own as in the fable of the rebellious members; drunkenness is impersonated realistically as a drunk man.

The tavern scene is before us again – on the resumption of the suspended tale – and has as its sombre and sinister background one of those periodic visitations of the pestilence (the Death) which made such a profound impact on medieval religious feeling as retribution for sin. The 'ryotoures' seated in the tavern are suddenly confronted in the midst of their ferocious lusts by an image of death:

> And as they satte, they herde a belle clinke
> Biforn a cors, was caried to his grave.
>
> (336–7)

Death was a person to the medieval mind, with its deep-rooted personifying impulse, and Death's victim is correspondingly seen as a sharp visual image:

> He was, pardee, an old felawe of youres;
> And sodeynly he was y-slayn to-night,
> For-dronke, as he sat on his bench up-right;
> Ther cam a privee theef, men clepeth Deeth,
> That in this contree al the people sleeth.
>
> (344–8)

In their drunken rage the rioters therefore rush forth to seek and to slay Death:

And we wol sleen this false traytour Deeth;
He shal be slayn, which that so many sleeth.

(371–2)

As they are about to cross a stile they do, indeed, meet someone who is equally anxious for death, an old man:

Right as they wolde han troden over a style,
An old man and a povre with hem mette.
This olde man ful mekely hem grette,
And seyde thus, 'now, lordes, god yow see!'
The proudest of thise ryotoures three
Anserde agayn, 'what? carl, with sory grace,
Why artow al forwrapped save thy face?
Why livestow so longe in so greet age?'
This olde man gan loke in his visage,
And seyde thus, 'for I ne can nat finde
A man, though that I walked in-to Inde,
Neither in citee nor in no village,
That wolde chaunge his youthe for myn age;
And therefore moot I han myn age stille,
As longe time as it is goddes wille.
Ne deeth, allas! ne wol nat han my lyf;
Thus walke I lyk a resteless caityf,
And on the ground, which is my modres gate,
I knokke with my staf, bothe erly and late,
And seyes, 'leve moder, leet me in!
Lo, how I vanish, flesh, and blood, and skin!
Allas! whan shul my bones been at reste? . . .'

(384–405)

The huge power of the impression of that old man seems to proceed from the sense that he is more – or at least other – than a personal old man; that he possesses a non-human as well as a human force; that he seems, in Yeats' phrase, 'to recede from us into some more powerful life'. Though it is not said who he is, he has the original force of the allegorical Age (Elde). As Age he is connected with Death, comes as a warning of Death, knows about Death, and where he is to be found:

To finde Deeth, turne up this croked wey,
For in that grove I lafte him . . .

(433–4)

('Croked wey' belongs to the traditional religious allegorical land-scape.) The old man therefore knows more, is more powerful, for all his apparent meekness and frailty, than the proudest of the rioters who foolishly addresses him as an inferior and who may be supposed to shrink from the suggested exchange of his youth for the old man's age. The bare fact that we are impelled to wonder who or what the old man is – he is 'al forwrapped' – produces the sense that he may be more than what he seems. He has been guessed (too easily) to be Death himself in disguise. Since that idea evidently occurs, it may be accepted as an element of the meaning; but there is no confirmation, though he says that he wants to but cannot die and has business to go about. He has the terrible primitive simplicity – and therefore force – of an old peasant man whose conception of death is elementary and elemental.

> And on the ground, which is my modres gate,
> I knokke with my staf, bothe erly and late,
> And seye, 'leve moder, leet me in! . . .'
>
> (401–3)

When the rioters come to the tree to which the old man directs them, they find not Death, a person, but a heap of bright new florins. We are thus brought round again to the theme of Avarice. The florins are the cause of their discord and several mutually inflicted deaths. The heap of florins turns out to have been indeed Death in one of his diverse shapes. The recognition that Death is not after all a person, as we have been led to expect, and as the rioters as medieval folk had imagined, but that Death is more subtle, elusive, and insidious – in this instance, the deadly consequences of Avarice – comes as the last shock in the tale's succession of disturbing surprises.

Presuming his tale to have awakened in the company the full terrors of death and damnation, the Pardoner loses no time in producing his bulls and relics and offering them as a kind of insurance policy against accidents on the journey:

> Peraventure ther may falle oon or two
> Doun of his hors, and breke his nekke atwo.
>
> (607–8)

He has the effrontery to call first upon the Host – 'for he is most envoluped in sinne' – to kiss, for a small fee, his assoiling relics; but he quite loses his good humour when at last he gets the answer from the Host he has richly deserved:

Thou woldest make me kisse thyn old breech,
And swere it were a relic of a seint.

(620–21)

Yet even the Pardoner had deepened to a momentary sincerity (we cannot mistake it) when he said:

And Jesu Crist, that is our soules leche,
So graunte yow his pardon to receyve;
For that is best; I wol yow nat deceyve.

(588–590)

Thus the conclusion provides a final view of the queer teller of the tale and by so doing sets the tale in a completed frame. With much the same skill, the opening description of the peasant widow's poverty frames the tale of the brilliant Chauntecleer and provides a contrast between the widow's life of sensible sobriety and the pretensions that so nearly cause Chauntecleer's downfall.

# NOTE

This essay is taken from *Chaucer the Maker*, by John Speirs (London, 1951), and is reproduced, slightly revised, by kind permission of the publishers.

# THE NUN'S PRIEST'S TALE

### DAVID HOLBROOK

The *Nun's Priest's Tale* can be read, with very little explanation of words and phrases, to an audience of people who have never come across Chaucer before, and they will enjoy it immensely. The witty and vivid story of the cock and the fox, and the other subsidiary stories in it of medieval life, make an immediate impact. What need is there, then, to say any more about it? Can the *Tale* not stand for itself? In theory it can: but at a time when one feels that Chaucer's poetry can give us an understanding of civilization so different from our own, many things said about Chaucer today tend to have a limiting effect, getting between us and the full life of the poetry.

The kinds of limiting attitudes to Chaucer I mean are perhaps fairly summarized by saying that he is held either to be 'having his little joke' or, if he is allowed to be serious, to be offering a slight improving moral, after the fashion of an Aesop's *Fable*. So even when we are told that the *Nun's Priest's Tale* is concerned with 'central truths about human nature' and about 'moral disorder'[1], we remain unconvinced, asking. What central truths? What moral disorder? The answer – and this is a significant point – is there in the poetry: the moral concern of the *Tale* cannot be simply summarized. The life of the *Tale* is there in the living language, and it comes to our senses and mind, our feeling and thought, through the poetry: in reading it, we experience the medieval community, its values, and something of the way human life was carried on in it.

The judgements which most limit Chaucer, and which prevent his achievement from being seen as standing behind Shakespeare, spring from a failure to treat his poetry as poetry. There is evidence enough of this in the amount of translation and modernization of Chaucer which appears without any apparent recognition of what is lost in the process. Compare, for instance, the first lines of the *Prologue* of the *Canterbury Tales* with two 'translated' versions[2]:

Whan that Aprille with his shoures sote
The droghte of Marche hath perced to the rote ...

When the sweet showers of April fall and shoot
Down through the drought of March to pierce the root ...

When April with sweet showers has ended the drought of March ...

Look at the soft fall of Chaucer's first line – the voice falls assuredly on 'shoures sote' after the light stresses of 'with his', but is softened by the consonance of the long vowels and by the gliding transition from 'sh' to 's'. And then note how this liquidness of sound ('Aprille ... shoures sote') is followed by the arid contrast of 'droghte ... Marche' and by the strong movement and feel of 'perced' – for it is the 'shoures sote', the light fall of rain, that is piercing to the root with such force. What is lost by the 'translations' isn't simply 'rhythm' as part of the 'style', but a rhythm and movement which are an integral part of the very meaning of the poetry itself. The reader feels the spring coming, feels the light fall of water stirring the parched ground: and the better he feels it, the more he is aware of the sense of harmony between man and Nature as the medieval poet experienced it. If one pays the same attention to the first translation, one can only be disturbed by that 'shoot down' – 'shoot', coming on the line-break with such emphasis, brings with it a degree of *activity* that quite inappropriately suggest storm and pandemonium. In the Chaucer it is the drought which is pierced, not the root, so that all this activity of 'fall', 'shoot', and 'pierced' destroys the image completely, and with it the poetry by which we can respond to the experience offered.

The *Nun's Priest's Tale*, then, needs to be read with a higher degree of seriousness and with greater expectations than the general account of Chaucer would suggest. In fact, the *Tale* could only have been written for a medieval audience which looked at life seriously, and which had a sensitive popular tradition of its own; and written by a mind which could add to that tradition complexities of its own. If we turn to the poetry, we can see that it is of a kind which could only proceed from a fine moral concern. Take, for instance, the masterly opening. On the one hand there is the old widow:

Thre large sowes hadde she, and namo,
Thre kyn<sup>a</sup>, and eek a sheep that highte<sup>b</sup> Malle.

(10–11)

On the other hand there is the cock:

This gentil cok hadde in his governaunce
Sevene hennes, for to doon al his plesaunce,
Whiche were his sustres and his paramours,
And wonder lyk to him, as of colours.
Of whiche the fairest hewed on hir throte
Was cleped faire damoysele Pertelote.

(45–50)

The difference in rhythm, imagery, and words chosen does not simply show an ability to use English to its full range in order to establish a comic, mock-heroic prince-of-a-cock in a dirty farmyard. The Cock is, of course, inflated as a character in the same way as Dryden's characters in his satire are inflated, and the French words, the long words, and the glorious trappings of Chauntecleer contribute to this effect. But to call it mere 'comic effect' is to limit the poetry, and to miss the way it brings to life for us different ways of living, different attitudes to life, so that we can judge what we see and feel 'in the round', alongside the considerations of good and evil which are raised.

The widow represents, as do the parson and the plowman in the *Canterbury Tales*, a simplicity and a goodness which were a standard in the medieval community:

Hir bord was served most with whyt and blak,
Milk and broun breed, in which she fond no lak.

(23–4)

She represents also the plain human life which exists underneath the graces and trappings of cultivated life, and beside which man's theories of life must be set. The physical simplicity of her life is realized in poetry in which the plain rural idiom predominates: the sound and movement here are not elegant:

*a* cows, *b* was called.

A povre widwe, <sup>a</sup>somdel stape in age,
Was whylom<sup>b</sup> dwelling in a narwe cotage...
(1–2)

Notice the words that Chaucer associates with the widow – 'Stape',
'hogges', 'kyn', 'sowes', 'narwe cotage', 'full sooty', 'sklendre' – those
harsh consonants reproduce audibly the rough simplicity of her life,
and 'stape' (lit.: 'stepped') and 'narwe' give a sense of movement as
of years of tramping in and out of a cramped hovel. She is not free of
drudgery or weariness of the flesh: indeed, the contrary is suggested
by 'narwe', 'stape', 'by housbondrye, of such as God hir sente, She
fond', 'sooty'. The repetition of 'fond' and the negative phrase
'fond no lak' imply a livelihood *won* from life. She is a member of
the medieval community, whom the community could recognize as
good and who has 'hertes suffisaunce' in the very arduousness of her
husbandry.

Chauntecleer and his wives are set in the midst of this, not only by
way of visual and comic constrast, but morally, and in such a way as
to give the poem more depth than is allowed by saying it has 'a
moral'. For all the wit and comedy, the interest in Chauntecleer is
serious, and it is of the same kind which later was to produce Shakespeare's consideration of 'man, proud man ... most ignorant of what
he's most assured: his glassy image...' In the lines quoted above,
'gouvernaunce', 'pleasaunce', 'paramours', 'damoysele' bring forward for examination, against the recognizably real background of
the yard, the graces and trimmings of the cultivated life. The 'glassy
image' of Pertelote is this:

Curteys she was, discreet, and debonaire,
And compaignable<sup>c</sup>, and bar hir self so faire ...
(51–2)

Yet the plain facts are that she is a hen in a hen-run, a wife ('fy on
yow, hertelees!'), and her gracious social life, when we see it for what
it is, amounts to this: 'He feathered Pertelote twenty tyme, And trad
her eke as ofte, er it was pryme'. The 'glassy image' of Chauntecleer
is portrayed, against the widow's 'white and black', in heraldic words
and phrases, he is a painted image: 'jet', 'azure', 'lyle flour', 'burned

a somewhat advanced, b once, c companionable.

gold'. Against the widow's 'narwe cotage', his comb is 'batailled as it were a castel wal'. Contrasted with her 'hertes suffisaunce', his achievements are of voice, appearance, 'knowledge', and social grace. And just as, in the first page or so, the 'courtesy' of the yard is revealed as a surface deception, so the rest of the story concerns the consequences of Chauntecleer's self-deception, in being 'ravished' with these, his own achievements. In those opening lines Chauntecleer is established as being compounded of 'the lust of the eyes, the lust of the flesh, the pride of life' – and later we find that it is by a tabulated appeal to these that the fox has him 'hente by the gargat'[a].

The *Nun's Priest's Tale* is, in effect, an expansion of an *exemplum* common in the popular medieval sermon: there were thousands of such homiletic stories taken from the Classics, the Bible, from local history and folk-lore, and used by popular preachers to illustrate religious precepts.[3] These stories presented the abstract moral consideration in terms of everyday life: the figure of a broken mirror would serve to explain the doctrine of Transubstantiation, and the story would be offered as Chaucer offers his *Tale*:

> But ye that holden this tale a folye,
> As of a fox, or of a cok and hen,
> Taketh the moralitee, goode men.
> (617–19)

Yet the strength of this *Tale* lies in Chaucer's individual development from the tradition: the *exemplum* here takes on a life of its own, and enacts in complex living terms something far more subtle than the plain moral. As Chaucer remarks elsewhere in the *Tale*, he is not dealing with the abstract but with a piece of life felt and seen; referring to a scholastic argument, he says:

> I wol nat han to do of swich mateere;
> My tale is of a cok, as ye may heere.
> (430–31)

This sermon-tradition explains how the comic *Tale* can have, at so many points, most serious religious references. Chauntecleer is Adam:

> Wommanes conseil broghte us first to wo,
> And made Adam fro paradys to go,
> Ther as he was ful mury, and wel at ese.
> (437–9)

[a] seized by the throat.

> When that the month in which the world began,
> That highte March, whan god first maked man ...
> Bifel that Chauntecleer, in al his pryde ...
>
> (367–71)

and the col-fox, black-tipped, is the Devil – Pertelote speaks of 'black devels', referring to Chauntecleer's dream, and the fox, ironically enough, says he 'were worse than a feend' if he should harm Chauntecleer. The farmyard chase at the end is, in its own way, the moral confusion following the Fall of Man:

> They yelleden as feendes doon in helle ...
> It seemed as that hevene sholde falle.
>
> (568–80)

As L. A. Cormican has written, in an article on *The Medieval Idiom in Shakespeare*[4]:

The medieval ethic saw all human actions as replicas either of Adam sinning or of Christ redeeming ... the principle that 'no man liveth to himself or dieth to himself' meant not only the practice of brotherly love towards neighbours; it implied the vast reverberations of actions, both good and evil ... the medieval doctrine of the power of concupiscence over man (the lust of the eyes, the lust of the flesh, the pride of life) comes from Adam's rejection of the objective divine law ... Lechery was the perverted, frustrated abuse of the body (or rather the abuse of the free control of the body by the will); pride was the abuse of the highest power, the intellect.

In a world pervaded by such a religious reality it would be apparent that Chauntecleer's dream did mean there was something wrong with him, something which was not simply the 'superfluytee' of his 'rede colera': it was a supernatural warning of his evil state of soul. Neither the dream, nor his seeing the fox by daylight, brings him to that conclusion, and much of the poem deals with recognizably human ways of failing to see what is wrong, with self-deception. When troubled by the dream, Chauntecleer turns in the end to the lust of the eyes, the lust of the flesh:

> For when I see the beautee of your face,
> Ye ben so scarlet-reed about your yen,
> It maketh al my drede for to dyen; ...
> For whan I fele a-night your softe syde,
> Al-be-it that I may nat on you ryde,
> For that our perche is maad so narwe, alas!

> I am so ful of joye and of solas,
> That I defye bothe sweven and dreem!
>
> (340–51)

But he also turns in his pride to 'abuse of the intellect', sheltering behind theories, odd scraps of knowledge, old examples. In the lines missed out above, for instance:

> For also siker as *In principio*,
> <sup>a</sup>*Mulier est hominis confusio*;
> Madame, the sentence of this Latin is –
> Womman is mannes joye and al his blis.
>
> (342–5)

The irony of Chauntecleer's 'recchlessnesse' is pointed to: his self-deceit shelters behind mistranslation, misuse of his knowledge.

Indeed, much of the force of the *Tale* derives from the intention summed up by the two lines at the end of this passage:

> But what that god forwoot mot nedes he,
> After the opinioun of certeyn clerkis.
> Witnesse on him, that any perfit clerk is,
> That in scole is gret altercacioun
> In this matere, and greet disputisoun,
> And hath ben of an hundred thousand men.
> But I ne can not <sup>b</sup>bulte it to the bren,
> As can the holy doctour Augustyn,
> Or Boece, or the Bishop Bradwardyn,
> Whether that goddes worthy forwiting<sup>c</sup>
> Streyneth<sup>d</sup> me nedely for to doon a thing,
> (Nedely clepe I simple necessitee);
> Or elles, if free choys be graunted me
> To do that same thing, or do it noght,
> Though God forwoot it en that it was wroght;
> Or if his witing streyneth nevere a del
> But by necessitee condicionel.
> I wol not han to do of swich matere;
> My tale is of a cok, as ye may here …
>
> (414–32)

Presenting a piece of life, Chaucer seems to say, produces a more useful consideration of the philosophical problem than could be dealt with in such terms as these. Chaucer does not treat lightly of scholastic debates, for instance, simply because he was so well grounded in

---

*a* Woman is man's downfall, *b* sift it down to the bran, *c* foreknowledge, *d* constrains.

them. It is rather part of his whole intention to set theories, attitudes, and assumptions against experience. The self-assured intellect (ours or Chauntecleer's) can be blind to something which happens in front of it:

> O destinee, that mayst nat be eschewed!
> Allas, that Chauntecleer fleigh fro the bemes!
> Allas, his wyf ne roghte *a* nat of dremes!
>
> (518–20)

– we know that whether Chauntecleer stayed on the beams or not has very little to do with his characteristic vulnerability to temptation: destiny is not something which can excuse his free choice. Again, in the debate between cock and hen on the significance of dreams, both fail, in their retreat into bogus knowledge, to recognize the evidence before them. Pertelote, in recommending laxatives, errs on the side of common sense and gives the practical answer to fear of temptation. But her 'lauriol, centaure and fumetere' seem less alien than Chauntecleer's retreat into 'old ensamples' (while in the end refusing the laxatives because he doesn't like them).

That this criticism of misused intellect, allied with pride, is part of the underlying intention of the *Tale* is indicated by the following passage:

> And on a Friday fil al this meschaunce.
> O Venus, that art goddesse of plesaunce,
> Sin that thy servant was this Chauntecleer,
> And in thy service dide al his poweer,
> More for delyt, than world to multiplye,
> Why woldestow suffre him on thy day to dye?
> O Gaufred, dere mayster soverayn,
> That, whan thy worthy king Richard was slayn
> With shot, compleynedest his deth so sore,
> Why ne hadde I now thy sentence and thy lore,
> The Friday for to chyde, as diden ye?
>
> (521–31)

There are references elsewhere in the *Tale* to significant dates ('the month in which the world bigan') and the medieval mind would associate Friday with the death of Christ. It is appropriate that the poem should draw no parallel between Chauntecleer and Christ

---

*a* took account.

(though the fox is the 'newe Scariot'), and appropriate too that Chauntecleer should *not* die on a Friday. But the reference amounts to a damning comment on the invocation to Venus, Chauntecleer's goddess because of his sensuality, and to Gaufred, the author of *Nova Poetria*, whose kind of rhetoric Chaucer parodies in those passages when the world of the hen-run is taken at its face-value: ('O destinee . . .' etc.) Venus and Gaufred are invoked because of Chauntecleer's associated 'abuse of body and mind'.

Such references do not come to our minds at first reading as they would have done to the medieval audience. But when explored they reveal the strength of the moral interest that Chaucer could draw on, and they show how, in turning to examine life as it is lived, he could achieve such range in his poetry, a range which gives the *Tale* its satisfying structure. The flexibility of the poetry, its varying notes from satirical inflation to lively dialogue (as in the debate between cock and hen), from 'rhetoric' to speeches 'in character' (often like the speeches of Polonius):

> Macrobeus, that writ th'avisioun
> In Affrike of the worthy Cipioun,
> Affermath dremes and seith that they been
> Warning of thinges that men after seen . . .
> Read eek of Joseph, and there shul ye see
> Wher dremes ben somtyme (I sey nat alle)
> Warning of thinges that shul after falle.
>
> (301-7)

– this flexibility is controlled by the poetry in which Chaucer establishes his main reference: the medieval community on the ground. The description of the widow, for instance, seems to have a symbolic weight, and in the way it makes use of popular idiom for such a purpose, is in a tradition on which Shakespeare was to draw to explore profounder complexities in his later plays. This symbolic use of language, as in the Liturgy, is there too, in Chaucer's reference to Saint Paul: 'Taketh the fruyt and let the chaf be stille'.

It is in this kind of poetry that the medieval community itself is brought to us in the *Tale*. It is the poetry of the two vivid stories Chauntecleer tells about murder and shipwreck. These are too good to be 'in character' – they are part of the total effect of the dramatic poem: they take us out into the streets and harbours, to the daily life where the moral considerations dealt with in the tale of cock and hen will count. They bring into the *Tale* its only murder, robbery, and sudden death, without making it anything other than a comedy, though adding to the serious bearing of it.

The kind of poetry I mean is represented at its best by this:

> 'Ha! Ha! the fox!' and after him they ran,
> And eek with staves many another man;
> Ran Colle our dogge, and Talbot, and Gerland,
> And Malkyn, with a distaf in hir hand;
> Ran cow and calf, and eek the verray hogges
> So were they fered for berking of the dogges
> And shouting of the men and wimmen eke,
> They ronne so, hem thoughte hir herte breke,
> They yelleden as feendes doon in helle;
> The dokes cryden as men wolde hem quelle;
> The gees for fere flowen over the trees;
> Out of the hyve cam the swarm of bees . . .
>
> (561–72)

Some of the most important characteristics of medieval civilization are evident in this poetry:

> In medieval England social organization was marked by three general characteristics; the close connexion of the whole population with the soil; the large corporate or co-operative element in the life of the people; and the extent to which the whole structure rested upon custom, and not upon either established law or written contract. (E. P. Cheyney, *Social Changes in England in the Sixteenth Century*.)[5]

> The first fundamental assumption which is taken over by the sixteenth century from the Middle Ages is that the ultimate standard of human institutions and activities is religion. (R. H. Tawney, *Religion and the Rise of Capitalism*.)[6]

Through the excitement of the rhythm, that community reaction ('many another man', 'they ronne so, hem thoughte hir herte breke'), and those 'hogges', 'bees', 'Malkyn with a distaf in hir hande' give solidity to the traditions of husbandry and 'God's plenty.' And the religious reality, as we have seen, is there too.

The range and flexibility of this poetry, and the dramatic qualities of the *Tale* derive from a moral concern which grew out of the religious and traditional community, and they represent a great individual achievement at the same time. Both the community and the

achievement are behind Shakespeare and much else in English literature: Chauntecleer is conceived out of the same kind of moral purpose, and performs in some ways a similar function in the poem, as
Shakespeare's Falstaff in the chronicle plays. Which is only to say that
Chaucer's great art, even in the lighter comedy, springs from a profound concern with man's being and the ultimate ends of his
existence.

## NOTES

1. By John Speirs, in his essay on this *Tale* in his book *Chaucer, the Maker*, to
which I am indebted both for its positive suggestions and as providing a point
of departure.
2. By Nevill Coghill and by Eleanor Farjeon.
3. See G. R. Owst, *Literature and Pulpit in Medieval England.*
4. In *Scrutiny*, vol. XVII, iv (1951).
5. Quoted by L. C. Knights, in *Drama and Society in the Age of Jonson.*
6. As note 5.

# TROILUS AND CRISEYDE AND THE KNIGHT'S TALE

IAN BISHOP

Chaucer is popularly and justly celebrated as one of the supreme masters of comedy in the English language. But we should not let this view of him as comic genius lead us to overlook his great achievements in tragedy. It is, therefore, salutary to recall that his earliest important poem, the *Book of the Duchess*, is about the attempt to console a bereaved husband, isolated in his grief, and that the most powerful of the Canterbury Tales, the *Pardoner's Tale*, is haunted by the spectre of Death. Another 'tale', the *Monk's Tale*, consists of a series of 'tragedyes' – a gloomy sequence of anecdotes that illustrate how men, when at the height of prosperity, have fallen into misery as the result of an unexpected stroke of Fortune. The image of Fortune and her wheel (symbol of the mutability of earthly affairs) is a medieval commonplace that derives principally from *The Consolation of Philosophy* by the late Roman philosopher, Boethius (d. 524). Chaucer's *Boece* is a prose translation of this work. At the point where this treatise associates Fortune with 'tragedies' Chaucer's translation supplies the following gloss: 'Tragedye is to seyne a dite*a* of a prosperite for a tyme, that endeth in wrecchednesse'.[1]

'Tragedye' is the designation that Chaucer applies to one of the two major poems that are the subject of this chapter: *Troilus and Criseyde* (written *c.* 1385). Although the *Knight's Tale* ends with the wedding of Palamon and Emelye, the shadow cast by the death of Arcite – killed accidentally in his hour of triumph – extends almost to the poem's last line. Both works have, as their principal source, an Italian poem by Boccaccio: whereas *Troilus* expands and adapts the 'novella', *Il Filostrato* (*c.* 1335), the *Tale* reduces and transforms the romantic epic, *Il Teseida* (*c.* 1340).[2] Both works also incorporate

*a* poem, discourse.

passages from *The Consolation of Philosophy*; but Chaucer's use of Boethius is somewhat oblique. It is not my intention to use these two poems in order to argue that there is a peculiarly Chaucerian tragic mode. Any attempt to do so would necessarily involve a gross over-simplification of these subtle and complex works. So I shall consider each poem separately in its own right.

Most of us first encounter the story of Troilus and Cressida in the theatre, as we watch Shakespeare's disillusioned and somewhat embittered contribution to the epic and romance traditions concerning the siege of Troy. Those of us whose opportunities for theatre-going include the opera house may also have witnessed a modern version of the story: William Walton's setting of the libretto by Christopher Hassall, which claims to be based not on Shakespeare but Chaucer. In fact Hassall sees Chaucer's poem through the spectacles of a particular twentieth-century critic, C. S. Lewis, who had diagnosed 'fear' as Criseyde's 'ruling passion'.[3] Accordingly, one of the more thrilling features of Walton's score is a *leitmotiv* that represents her fear. Although the opera (like Lewis's oddly seventeenth-century psychological nomenclature) oversimplifies Chaucer's subtle, complex and ambivalent presentation of his heroine, we are already far from the girl who provokes Shakespeare's Ulysses into exclaiming: 'her wanton spirits look out / At every joint and motive of her body' (*Troilus and Cressida*).

The operatic possibilities of Chaucer's poem are worth bearing in mind for another reason: they may act as a partial corrective to G. L. Kittredge's celebrated, though no less anachronistic, eulogy of it as 'the first novel, in the modern sense, that ever was written in the world'.[4] Although there is indeed, as in a psychological novel, much vividly naturalistic dialogue (especially in scenes involving Pandarus), there are also long speeches and soliloquies, epistles, invocations, 'complaints', hymns and songs, culminating in the sustained 'love-duet' in Book III. There is also much formal patterning in the poem's structure. The story of 'the double sorwe of Troilus' falls into two contrasted sections. Books I–III tell of the ascent of his fortunes in love *[a]*'Fro wo to wele' corresponding to the medieval

*[a]* from misery to happiness.

notion of a 'comedye'; Books IV and V record his descent 'out of joie', the medieval definition of a 'tragedye' – the generic term which Chaucer applies to the whole narrative.

There are several carefully contrived correspondences between the 'ascending' and 'descending' action; some of these extend to whole episodes, others consist of significant details or verbal echoes. The 'love-duet' in Book III, for example, is contrasted pointedly (cf. IV, 1247–51) with another dialogue between the lovers in bed, after the Trojan 'parlement' has decreed that Criseyde shall be exchanged for Antenor and re-united with her treacherous father, Calchas, in the Grecian camp. Moreover, the whole narrative is poised between a prelude (I, 1–56) that declares allegiance to the cult over which Venus and her son preside, and an epilogue (V, 1835–end) that affirms the only true source of love to be the religion of Christ and his mother. These contrasts are one manifestation of a dialectical spirit that informs the whole poem.[5]

Criseyde is no further from Shakespeare's Cressida than she is from her counterpart in *Il Filostrato*. Whereas the behaviour of Boccaccio's heroine causes him to conclude his narrative with a cynical moral about women's fickleness, Chaucer, addressing 'yonge, fresshe folkes, *he or she*' (my italics), urges them to seek the love of Christ instead of (unspecified) 'feynede[a] loves'. The account of her betrayal of Troilus with Diomede (the very raison d'être of the original story) occupies comparatively few stanzas in Book V, which is mostly concerned with Troilus's anxieties and grief. The lovers are shown together in only three long scenes: those of the declaration and consummation of love in Book III and the sharply contrasted scene that closes Book IV. The first two Books present them separately, for the most part alone or in conference with their confidant, Pandarus. The central interest of the poem thus lies in the attempt by two souls of diverse origins and dissimilar destinies – and endowed with contrasted modes of consciousness – to establish the deepest of human relationships. The representation of this relationship involves something more than a dialogue: the demands of love impose a rigorous dialectic that worries out the true nature of their personalities, and the process involves a searching anatomy of love itself.

Troilus is introduced as a young military hero, who scorns the

[a] false.

god of love as 'Seynt Idyot, lord of thise foles alle'. His conversion, as the result of an unwitting glance from Criseyde, is as sudden and total as that which transformed Saul into Paul. Although he receives practical help from the untiring Pandarus (himself a stricken lover), he sees the 'proces' of his life as shaped by what he conceives of as numinous powers, Fortune and Cupid himself. It is characteristic of him that, when he at last has his lady naked in his arms, his first impulse is to sing a hymn of thanksgiving to Cupid, Venus and Hymen. When the exchange of Criseyde for Antenor is decreed by the Trojan 'parlement', he is prepared to sacrifice everything for the sake of an elopement that will ensure his remaining with her. When death releases this tried and faithful lover from the vicissitudes of this world, his disembodied soul catches a glimpse of eternal truth, the power

<sup>a</sup>uncircumscript, and al maist circumscrive.

On the other hand, the widowed Criseyde, the sceptical daughter of a treacherous priest, is more apt to see the 'proces' of her life as manoeuvred by merely human manipulators – and with good cause. No sooner has she re-established her 'name'<sup>b</sup> after her father's desertion, and secured the protection of Hector, than her uncle, Pandarus, tries to inveigle her into a secret affair with the King's youngest son. When even Hector is unable to prevent her being traded by the politicians, she resolves upon suicide, but, in a revealing soliloquy, gradually recognizes that she has not the constitution of a tragic heroine. She rejects Troilus's defiant plan for elopement in favour of one of her own devising which will ensure the preservation of her 'name'. Ironically, it merely leads her into the society of Diomede, a less subtle but no less effective manipulator than her uncle, who causes her to lose her 'name of trouthe in love, for evermo'. It is characteristic of her that, when she yields to Troilus, she allows no gods to come between them, but declares: 'Welcome, my knyght, my pees, my suffisaunce!' Chaucer eventually leaves her, still circumscribed by secular life, as she makes her pathetic resolution of eternal stability: 'To Diomede algate<sup>c</sup> I wol be trewe'.

Chaucer's poetic language is able to present Criseyde dramatically from without and sensitively from within. When Pandarus even-

<sub>a</sub> uncircumscribed and can encompass all, <sub>b</sub> reputation, <sub>c</sub> at any rate.

tually discloses that he has come to urge Troilus's suit, she exclaims bitterly and resentfully:

> 'What! is this al the joye and al the feste$^a$?
> Is this youre need$^b$? Is this my blisful cas$^c$?
> Is this the verray mede of youre byheeste?
> Is al this peynted proces seyd, allas!
> Ryght for this fyn$^d$?'
>
> (II, 421–5)

William Empson has commented upon the Shakespearean complexity of these lines.[6] But the dramatic quality of this outburst can be fully appreciated only when we recognize that it consists of a tart anthology of the choicest phrases from Pandarus's devious prolegomena to his announcement. She continues to fence with her uncle in a dialectical process that is both witty and a little sinister. One of his schemes is to arrange that Troilus shall pass by her window when he is at her elbow so that he may commend the prince's parts to her; but his plan is anticipated by the genuine accident of Troilus's triumphal progress past her house while she is alone. From this moment the poet explores the inward effects of love upon her, beginning with her interior 'debate', in which she contemplates the attractions of love, until 'A cloudy thought gan thorugh hire soule pace' and she herself considers the 'stormy lyf' of love: 'For evere som mystrust or $^e$nice strif / Ther is in love, som cloude is over that sonne'. A series of images ('synken'; 'myne') describes how love penetrates her subconscious mind and finally her 'unconscious' – in the account of her dream about the white eagle that exchanges its heart for hers without causing her any fear or pain.

After much more 'business' by Pandarus (who behaves like the ennobled descendant of a *fabliau* intriguer), the moment arrives when the lover holds his lady in his arms:

> Hire armes smale$^f$, hire streghte bak and softe,
> Hire sydes longe, flesshly, smothe and white
> He gan to stroke, and good thrift bad$^g$ ful ofte
> Hire snowisshe throte, hire brestes rounde and lite$^h$:
> Thus in this hevene he gan hym to delite,
> And therwithal a thousand tyme hire kiste,
> That$^i$ what to don$^j$, for joie $^k$unnethe he wiste.
>
> (III, 1247–53)

*a* rejoicing, *b* advice, *c* occurrence, *d* end, *e* foolish contention, *f* slender, *g* wished good fortune to, *h* little, *i* so that, *j* do, *k* scarcely knew.

The ante-penultimate line of this frankly sensuous stanza is more than a piece of conventional amatory hyperbole. Criseyde was introduced as 'an hevenyssh perfit*ᵃ* creature, / That down were sent in scornynge of nature'; and she is first manifested to Troilus remotely in a temple so that he wonders whether she is a woman or a goddess. Now the goddess has become incarnate so that she may raise him to the quakes like an aspen leaf when he embraces her, and his 'steere'*ᵇ*, ordained by God to guide him, and who causes him to experience in his life 'a newe qualitee' – as if she had inaugurated for him (as Beatrice did for Dante) a veritable *Vita Nuova*. In a hymn he expresses his belief that he is joined to her by the love that binds together in harmony the whole of creation.

In such language the poet evokes the sense of the 'eternal moment' of love; but the poetry also conveys sharply an impression of its transient and fleeting character:

> That nyght, *bitwixen drede and sikernesse*ᶜ,
> [They] Felten in love the grete worthynesse.
> (III, 1315–16 – my italics)

The moment of consummation is approached through a beautifully varied series of comparisons which reiterate the theme that the lovers' joy was all the greater on account of sorrows previously endured. There is a Mozartian blend of smiles and tears as the equipoise is achieved and they 'passed wo with joie contrepeise'*ᵈ*. But hardly has equilibrium been achieved than the scales are tipped the other way. With the necessity of parting at dawn, Troilus feels

> The bloody teris from his herte melte,
> As he that nevere yet swich hevynesse
> Assayed hadde, out of so gret gladnesse.
> (III, 1445–7)

They join in their antiphonal *aubade*: Criseyde rebukes the night for going 'off duty' so hastily, and Troilus chides the sun as a pestilential salesman of light. He urges him to sell his commodity to those whose business it is to engrave small seals and calls him 'Fool' for leaving the bed of Aurora who lay beside him all night. The playful language will remind the reader of Donne's variation on the same basic *topos*.[7]

---

*a* perfect, *b* helmsman, *c* security, *d* counterbalance.

But this is mere bravado in the face of inexorable necessity; and these dawn partings foreshadow the permanent separation that will follow in the 'tragedye'.

When, at the beginning of Book IV, the action turns from 'comedye' to 'tragedye', its revolution is attributed by the narrator to a personified Fortune. Moreover, Troilus himself, in the course of a labyrinthine meditation, based obliquely on Boethius, finds that philosophical speculation cannot help him to escape from his gloomy premonition that

> '...al that comth, comth by necessitee:
> Thus to ben lorn, it is my destinee.'
> (IV, 958–9)

Certainly the way in which public events interfere with the lovers' private relationship is the cruellest of misfortunes. Nevertheless, the tale shows that there is rather more scope for voluntary human action than the teller is prepared to admit. This becomes particularly evident in the crucial debate in which Criseyde rejects the only plan that Troilus believes will save their love. So alarmed is he by the ill-considered (and ultimately ill-fated) stratagem that she substitutes for his own that this devout lover becomes almost sarcastic in his destructive criticism. Symptomatic of the change is the way his language falls into a vigorous, proverbial idiom of the kind we have come to associate with Pandarus. But the more he criticizes her scheme, the more she becomes wedded to it. Her motives are left ambiguous: are her arguments genuinely altruistic or merely specious? But the apportioning of blame is not the point of the scene: what is so distressing is to hear the couple whose voices blended in the 'love-duet' now involved in acrimonious altercation, seizing upon salient words and ideas in their respective arguments and turning them against each other. When Troilus capitulates, agreeing to let her go temporarily to Calchas – 'Which that his soule out of his herte rente' – we realize, as he leaves her chamber, that their relationship is doomed, even before Diomede has been mentioned.

This, however, by no means renders Book V superfluous. The debate has diagnosed a cancer in the relationship whose lingering death we watch helplessly throughout the final book. We see Criseyde, having failed to persuade Calchas to allow her to return secretly to Troy (to fetch out his treasure), realize too late that she had placed herself in a 'snare' when she rejected Troilus's plan for elopement. It is only after this that she begins to pay serious attention to 'this sodeyn*a* Diomede', who has been making advances from the moment when he escorted her to her father, while 'Troilus to Troie homward he wente'. Diomede has been described as a 'degraded replica' of the courtly hero;[8] and the comparison with Troilus affords a certain grim humour (cf., for example, III, 92–100 and V, 925–30). Moreover, Criseyde recognizes the superiority of her discarded lover, even in the very act of 'falsyng' him. Her yielding to the predatory Greek reads almost like an act of self-immolation in order to compromise herself so that she may acquire a guiltily adequate reason for her merely unheroic failure to return to Troilus, as promised, after ten days. She desecrates her former relationship by giving Diomede the bay horse Troilus had given her and even the brooch – 'and that was litel nede' – she had received from him at parting. It is when Diomede is wounded *by Troilus* that the narrator surmises: 'Men seyn – I not*b* – that she yaf*c* hym hire herte.'

Diomede had urged Criseyde not to 'spille a quarter of a tere' on any lover she may have in the 'prisoun' of Troy. But Chaucer spends most of the final book inside that prison as he describes – in some of the most anguished and slow-moving stanzas he ever wrote – the diminution, day by day, of Troilus's hopes for Criseyde's return. Even after he realizes 'That al is lost that he hath been aboute' and the faithful Pandarus declares that he hates his niece, Troilus, apostrophizing his faithless lady, declares that he cannot find it within his heart 'To unloven yow a quarter of a day'. The only hope for one who is thus 'despeired out of Loves grace' is that he may be granted 'soone owt of this world to pace'. This he accomplishes, not (as he had hoped) in internecine combat with Diomede, but at the hands of Achilles, his country's most formidable enemy. The hero's soul ascends to the Ogdoad, whence, having acknowledged the 'vanite'*d* of all worldly aspirations compared to the 'pleyn*e* felicite' of heaven, he is conducted by Mercury to an undisclosed abode.

The poem's narrator is both engaged with, and detached from, its action. He is characterized, on the one hand, as a devotee of Cupid's religion, though disabled from active 'service' of the god 'for myn unliklynesse'*f*; on the other hand, he is the student of antiquity who

*a* sudden, *b* I do not know, *c* gave, *d* emptiness, *e* full, *f* unattractiveness.

does not write out of 'sentement', but claims to follow a Latin 'auctour', 'Lollius', a supposed authority on the Trojan war. As the love relationship prospers, the enthusiastic devotee is continually at our elbow; but when it comes to the narration of Criseyde's infidelity he shrinks from his task in embarrassment and pity, tending to place responsibility upon the authority of his archive: 'Men seyn – I not – that she yaf hym hire herte'. Eventually, when defeated by the 'tragedye', he distances himself completely from his pagan narrative and addresses his young contemporaries, 'In which that love up groweth with youre age', urging them to repair home from 'worldly vanyte' and to love Christ, who alone, on account of His supreme sacrifice, is worthy of the wholehearted devotion exercised by the romantic lover or practitioner of *fine amour*:

> For *He* nyl*ª* falsen no wight*ᵇ*, dar I seye,
> That wol his herte al holly*ᶜ* on *Hym* leye.
> And syn*ᵈ* He best to love is, and most meke,
> *ᵉ*What nedeth feynede loves for to seke?
> (V, 1845–8 – my italics and capitals)

Whereas the significant part of the action in *Troilus* takes place in secret (even in such public scenes as I, 155–322; II, 610–58, 1555–end; IV, 141–219, 680–730), that of the *Knight's Tale* is set in the public eye. Except in the prison scene in Part I, we are continually aware of the presence of a 'chorus', applauding or weeping at the 'gentil'*ᶠ* behaviour exhibited before it. When he eventually urges the marriage of Emelye and Palamon, Duke Theseus, instead of taking the young couple aside, makes the proposal in a public assembly, calculating like an actor how to produce the maximum effect upon his audience (*Canterbury Tales*, I, 2981–6). Palamon and Arcite – the 'sworn brothers' turned into mortal foes through rivalry in love – cannot even fight their secret duel in the grove without being interrupted by Theseus, the ladies and his hunting party to produce a moving ensemble to conclude the Second Part. I almost wrote 'the Second Act', because Chaucer has transformed *Il Teseida* into a more dramatic poem than Boccaccio's epic, though it is far from being a true drama like *The Two Noble Kinsmen*, the version of the tale made by Shakespeare and Fletcher.

*a* will not, *b* anybody, *c* wholly, *d* since, *e* what need is there to seek false loves?, *f* noble.

My anachronistic analogy from opera may again be helpful. Indeed, the *Knight's Tale* – with its solemn processions, spectacular pageantry, grand tournament, ritual and ensemble scenes – would seem to have a more obvious appeal for a librettist than *Troilus* does. Its plot tolerates disguise and coincidence, and its actors are hardly individualized. Emelye is represented as the object of desire: unlike Criseyde, she never develops beyond the lyrical, initial description of her when she enters a-Maying into the garden beneath the tower where Theseus has imprisoned the youths, 'And as an aungel hevenysshly she soong'. It is impossible to prefer one of the Theban knights to the other on moral or psychological grounds. Because Chaucer wishes to show that neither 'deserves' his particular fate, they are presented as an equal pair whose sentiments are expressed antiphonally, not only while they are imprisoned together, but even when in separate countries. These 'compleyntes' (based partly on passages from Boethius's *Consolation of Philosophy*) are no more intended to be 'naturalistic' than is an operatic duet. Each youth in turn advances from bewailing his personal plight to a lament for the cruelties and ironies of man's universal predicament. In a moving poetic *rallentando*, the dying Arcite utters a similarly universalized sentiment:

> 'What is this world? What asketh men to have?
> Now with his love, now in his colde grave
> Allone, withouten any compaignye!'
>
> (2777–9)

before he concludes his long solo by generously commending his old rival to Emelye. It is characteristic of Chaucer that this lyrical utterance is accompanied by an objectively clinical commentary on the physiological process of dying.

The poetic strength of the tale is most evident in Part III, in which the 'gods' (conceived of both anthropomorphically and astrologically) decide their clients' fate. Since Jupiter is unable to resolve the quarrel between Venus (the patroness of Palamon) and Mars (the sponsor of Arcite), it falls to his father, Saturn, the most ancient of gods and most wide-ranging of planets, to resolve it by means of one of his malicious accidents, which causes Arcite's death after his victory in the tournament. Saturn declares his nature in the chilling couplets:

Myn is the drenchyng[a] in the see so wan;
Myn is the prison in the derke cote[b];
Myn is the stranglyng and hangyng by the throte,
The murmure and the cherles rebellyng,
The groynynge, and the pryvee empoysonyng...

                                        (2456–60)

This is matched in horror by the famous series of portraits in the Temple of Mars ('The smylere with the knyf under the cloke...'), which expose the stark realities of violence and martial combat that are invested elsewhere in the tale with the trappings of chivalric pageantry. Even Venus is depicted as essentially a troublemaker.

Just as the suggestion that the world is controlled by such forces is frightening, so the feeling that men's fortunes are determined by the family squabbles of such deities is insulting. The human actors acquire, by contrast with such a pantheon, a certain tragic dignity. Most striking is the contrast with Theseus. This humane ruler is both less and more than a god. The gods are omnipotent within their limited planetary spheres of influence; but their adamantine power is inflexible and their functions determined. Theseus is vulnerable, not only to irrational chance (Arcite's death), but also to the pleas of alien suppliants; and this allows him the freedom to develop. The supplications of the Theban widows cause him (quite literally) to change direction; and in the great scene that concludes Part II he modulates, through a whole spectrum of moods (and linguistic registers), from his stern condemnation of the duelling Theban knights to the setting up of the tournament, subsequently modified to a kind of animated game of chess to ensure that no combatant is killed. It is at this point, when Theseus has imposed his reasonable solution upon events, that Chaucer turns his attention (for virtually the whole of Part III) to the gods. At the beginning of Part IV Theseus is allowed a little more glory: the account of the preparations for the tournament culminates in his appearance at a window 'Arrayed right as he were a god in trone'. But this act of hubris calls forth its nemesis when Saturn contrives the accident that results in the death of the victorious Arcite.

Theseus's humane and even-tempered scale of cosmic harmony is untuned by this seemingly senseless accident: his philosophy is no

*a* drowning, *b* cottage.

longer able to 'save appearances', to borrow a phrase from Milton.[9]
He can be comforted only by 'his olde fader Egeus' who knew 'this
worldes transmutacioun ... Joye after wo, and wo after gladnesse'.
In other words, the aged man's bleak philosophy of contempt for
the world –

> 'This world nys but a thurghfare ful of wo,
> And we been pilgrymes, passynge to and fro'
> (2847–8)

– is the only one that will allow for the activities of the most ancient
of the 'gods'. Theseus, as an active ruler of men, cannot yet afford
to clothe himself in his shroud and turn his back upon life. Nevertheless, the influence of his father's counselling is evident in the great
speech that prepares the way for his eventual urging of the marriage
of Emelye to Palamon.

Starting from 'The Firste Moevere' (the Aristotelian definition
of God), the duke's gaze slowly descends 'the cheyne of love', that
binds the whole of Creation, until he arrives at the immediate,
practical issue. He recognizes that stability exists only in the realm
of Eternity. In the contingent world everything goes by 'pro-
gressiouns' and 'successiouns': the cycle of birth, life and death
inevitably revolves. Because of prolonged mourning for Arcite, the
cycle has been arrested for long enough at the moment of death.
So he deploys a battery of the traditional 'topics' of consolation and
employs all his eloquence to urge a renewal of life.[10] In this context
the wedding of Palamon and Emelye becomes something more than
the customary device for providing the happy ending of a romance;
marriage is seen as no less solemn than death.

There is an inconsistency in the poem's cosmology that becomes
evident in Theseus's speech. We have noted how, in Part III, Jupiter
appears as one of the seven planetary 'gods', and is unable to resolve
the contention between Venus and Mars. But Theseus lifts him out
of the system of the planets, raises him above the *Primum Mobile*
(the outermost sphere of Creation) and identifies him with 'The
Firste Moevere' Himself. It seems to me that the inconsistency is
deliberate: the 'world picture' presented in this speech is an alternative
to, rather than a refutation of, the cosmologies of the earlier episodes.
It no more 'explains away' the tragedy of Arcite's death than the

mythological machinery of Part III provides an adequate teleological explanation of it. In any case, the poetry of Part III burns too intensively to be extinguished by any system of metaphysics. The speech stands in relation to the *Knight's Tale* much as Ulysses's speech on 'degree' does to Shakespeare's *Troilus and Cressida*. We should hesitate before regarding either as a statement of the poet's own philosophy of cosmic order; for each is spoken by a skilful politician to meet the exigencies of a particular situation. An effective monarch must act as if he believes the world to be governed by 'Juppiter, the kyng', the symbol of Justice and Order.

On the other hand, we must beware of taking a cynical view of this oration. We may feel particularly encouraged to do so when we observe that, before Theseus addresses the assembly, the narrator mentions his political motives for marrying Emelye to the surviving Theban knight. But, for any hereditary monarch, the dynastic implications of marriage must be paramount. At the end of this tale there is, in fact, a felicitous confluence of dynastic considerations, of the expected 'romantic' ending, and of the fulfilment of Arcite's dying wish – so providing a kind of resolution of the conflict between love and friendship. Nevertheless, it is a resolution rather than a solution: the final chord of a work that has looked tragedy in the face rather than the triumphant conclusion of a theorem that claims to have 'saved the appearances'.

## NOTES

1. F. N. Robinson, ed., *The Complete Works of Geoffrey Chaucer* (London, 1957), 331. All my references to Chaucer's works are to this edition. On the medieval notion of tragedy, see further W. Farnham, *The Medieval Heritage of Elizabethan Tragedy* (Berkeley, 1936).

2. For modern translations, see N. R. Havely, ed., *Chaucer's Boccaccio* (Woodbridge and Totowa, N.J., 1980).

3. *The Allegory of Love* (London, 1936), 185.

4. *Chaucer and his Poetry* (Cambridge, Mass., 1915, 1946), 109.

5. I discuss this, and other aspects of the poem, in greater detail in my book, *Chaucer's 'Troilus and Criseyde': A Critical Study* (Bristol, 1981).

6. *Seven Types of Ambiguity* (2nd edn, London, 1947), 58ff.

7. cf. 'The Sun Rising', and compare Criseyde's response with 'Break of Day'.

8. J. Speirs, *Chaucer the Maker* (London, 1951), 79.

9. *Paradise Lost*, viii, 82; and cf. C. S. Lewis, *The Discarded Image* (Cambridge, 1964), 14.

10. On consolatory 'topics' in the *Knight's Tale*, see I. Bishop, *'Pearl' in its Setting* (Oxford, 1968), 21–2; also 'Chaucer and the Rhetoric of Consolation' (*Medium Aevum*, forthcoming), from which I have reproduced a few sentences here.

# LANGLAND'S *PIERS PLOWMAN*

## DEREK TRAVERSI

Of the author of *Piers Plowman* almost nothing is known except what the poem has to tell us. He seems to have been born, perhaps in 1331, in the region of the Malvern Hills.[1] He was educated, according to his own account, at the Benedictine school at Malvern, probably took minor orders and devoted most of the rest of his life to the writing and expansion of his poem. Evidently a poor man, he seems to have lived largely by offering prayers for the dead in the course of a wandering lifetime. We may assume that he died somewhere near the turn of the century. Perhaps the lack of significant biographical information is not altogether a misfortune. *Piers Plowman*, although it bears the mark of an unmistakable and powerful personality, is not, in the same sense as the *Canterbury Tales*, a purely personal creation. The language of the poem is the product of a long and mainly anonymous process, associated with developments particularly evident in medieval sermons and in the great dramatic cycles which were their natural extension in making the teachings of the Church available to a largely unlettered public. In these eminently popular forms of expression, the need to deal with abstract qualities, virtues and vices carefully differentiated by the processes of orthodox theology, was wedded to the popular instinct for realistic description to produce a remarkable development of the possibilities of common speech. The preacher came to the pulpit armed with an abstract survey of human failings, accurately analysed in the shape of the Seven Deadly Sins, but he had still to put them vividly before an audience who were accustomed to translate everything into terms of their own experience. The sermons thus conceived made extensive use of a technique which we might call proverbial; for the proverb is nothing more than the translation of general law into terms of particular knowledge.[2] They abound in such expressions as 'Pore be hanged bi the necke; a rich man bi the purs' or 'Trendle the appel so far, he conyes[a] from what tree he cam'. From these it was only a natural step to bring the well-worn virtues and vices to life, giving each of them an easily recognizable and vivid embodiment. As time passed these personifications assumed conventional shapes and were handed from preacher to preacher, or from play to play, until they became part of the common stock from which a writer like Langland could readily draw.

The poetic qualities which this tradition made available to Langland are present everywhere in his poem. His picture of Covetousness may be taken as typical:

> Thenne cam Covetyse · ich can nat hym discryve,
> So hongerliche and so holwe · Hervy[b] hym-self lokede.
> He was bytelbrowed and baberlupped · with two blery eyen,
> And as a letherene pors · lollid hus chekus,
> 'Wel sydder than hys chyn · ychiveled for elde:
> As bondemenne bacon · hus berd was yshave,
> [d]With hus hod on his heved · and hus hatte bothe;
> In a toren tabarde · of twelve wynter age.

>                                   (C Text, VII, 196–203)

The qualities of this passage are clearly visual qualities, and their ancestry will by now be obvious. They derive from centuries of effort on the part of preachers to bring home to their audience the true nature of the common vices of their time. Even the alliteration, with its long literary ancestry, is as much a device of the speaker as an accepted poetic technique; note how it falls again and again upon the descriptive epithets which are the key to the whole effect. The words chosen, moreover, are those which a preacher could be certain of sharing with his audience, intense, but in no way 'poetic', if by this we mean mere elaborations of feeling or a refined decoration of not too pressing emotions. These merits, once we admit them, are seen to be more than personal, more even than the qualities of Langland's own tradition; they are a general characteristic of much of the best English poetry. They are the product of an extraordinary ability to describe personal experience in terms of a common idiom, founded upon the simple but fundamental activities of a society closely connected with the land. Langland's close contact with rural

---

*a* knows, *b* Harvey. Skelton also gives this name to a covetous man., *c* much lower, *d* with his hood on his head.

life is apparent on every page of his poem. It opens with the wanderings of a shepherd on the Malvern hills, and never moves far away from them in spirit. Piers Plowman, its hero, is a universal-izing of the English rural way of living, a life which readers of the poem would understand and in terms of which they could establish a common idiom with its author.

A reading of the opening lines of *Piers Plowman* will illustrate the linguistic foundation on which the process of transformation rests:

> In a somere seyson · whan softe was the sonne,
> Y shop me in-to shrobbis*a* · as y a shepherde were,
> In abit as an ermite · unholy of werkes,
> Ich wente forth in the worlde · wonders to hure,
> And sawe meny*b* cellis · and selcouthe thynges.
> Ac on a May morwenyng · on Malverne hulles
> Me byfel for to slepe · for weyrenesse of wandrynge
> And in a launde as ich lay · lenede ich and slepte,
> And merveylously me mette*c* · as ich may yow telle;
> Al the welthe of this worlde · and the woo bothe,
> Wynkyng as it were · wyterly*d* ich saw hyt,
> Of tryuthe and of tricherye · of tresoun and of gyle,
> Al ich saw slepynge · as ich shal yow telle.

> (C Text, I, 1–13)

The advantages of scansion by stress rather than by mechanical counting of syllables are obvious here. Langland may not have been aware of the metrical subtleties of Anglo-Saxon verse, but he realized that the break at the centre of each alliterative line was the key to the whole effect; his lines rise up to the pause, and fall as definitely away from it, and are so preserved from the dangers of a mere invertebrate flow. The exigencies of the language, in turn, dictate the position of the stresses within the individual line, and these are determined by 'the ebbing and lifting emotion'.[3] The break in the middle of the line may serve to give point to a balanced contrast, or to emphasize a significant parenthesis in the flow of the narrative. Langland's metre, in fact, was the natural setting of a living language. One very important indication of this was the fact that he showed, in the passage just quoted, that he could do what very few modern poets have been able to accomplish – that is, handle a plain, unadorned narrative in verse, bringing out its full implications without interrupt-

*a* shrubs, but the A Text has 'schroud' and B 'schroudes' (garments), *b* cells and strange things, *c* dreamed, *d* truly.

ing its natural flow. He has succeeded in telling us that his poem is to be a complete survey of human life under the aspect of good and evil (for he saw 'Al the welthe of this worlde · and the woo bothe') without distracting in any way from the preliminary statement of the circumstances of his dream. In its way, this is an achievement not less remarkable than that which enabled Chaucer to turn the highly organized stanza of *Troilus and Criseyde* to the ends of conveying the flow of natural dialogue and a keen presentation of character.

If *Piers Plowman* draws part of its individuality from contact with a still living tradition of writing in verse, it also owes much to its foundations in medieval allegory. The allegorical habit of mind (for it was this as much as any consciously formulated philosophy that influenced Langland) is so remote from modern ways of thinking that it is hard for us to imagine that it could once have served as the basis for a satisfying and inclusive view of life. Allegory means for us the projection of abstract qualities – virtues, vices, spiritual states – into a tangible representation. This, however, is barely the husk of the complete thing. The allegorical outlook, in its full medieval form, implied the capacity to see a situation simultaneously under different aspects, each existing, on its own level, in its own right, but at the same time forming part of a greater order in relation to which its complete meaning is to be ascertained.

The figure of Piers Plowman himself is a perfect example of the way in which this convergence of attributes upon a single point enriches our understanding by conferring upon it moral significance without detracting from the concreteness of the original conception. Piers is in the first place the English countryman of his own time and place, and none of his subsequent transformations will make this primary aspect of his nature irrelevant: rather they will complete it, by setting it in what the poet believes to be its natural spiritual context. This context, in turn, is indicated through the gradual transformation of Piers, which springs so naturally from his normal being that we are hardly aware of it; for Piers, simply by living in accordance with the values he has inherited in his calling, is able to pass judgement upon the world around him, to denounce its failings and to indicate the way which leads to spiritual health. So far, factually and morally, the figure is still a projection of contemporary realities. It is only in the later and more daring stages of his allegorical

transformation that Piers becomes something more than a fourteenth-
century farmer concerned with the evils of contemporary society
and with the simple, severe code by which these evils can be
mastered. First as the Good Samaritan, the bodily representation of
the supreme Christian virtue of Charity, and then – by the most
far-reaching and inclusive transformation of all – as symbol of the
humanity assumed by Christ in his Incarnation, dying on the Cross,
harrowing Hell, and rising again in triumph from the dead, he
becomes the key, not merely to the time and place in which he
originally appeared, but to the destiny of the whole human race.
The successive phases of his transformation have by the end of the
poem been gathered together, assumed into the unity of the complete
conception.

This allegorical structure may even throw some light upon the
long process of growth by which the poem appears to have assumed
its final and complete form. The facts continue to be under dispute,
and there has even been some question as to whether the poem, in
its longer versions, is the work of a single hand.[4] A reading of the
successive forms taken by the poem indicates, in any case, the
existence of a single continuous development, in the course of which
the complete conception came into being. The first editors of the
poem distinguished three texts – A, B and C – which appear to grow
from one another, a process by which social realities are related to
developing moral judgements, and both in turn to a universal
spiritual interpretation. The so-called A Text, which may have been
written around 1370, consists of a Prologue and twelve sections or
Passus; it contains some 2,400 lines of verse. The B Text, which on
internal evidence can be plausibly dated between 1377 and 1379 (the
first years of the reign of Richard II) expands to twenty Passus,
extends the matter of the A version to 3,200 lines, and adds about
4,000 lines of completely new matter. This is the version of the poem
which contains the greatest number of strikingly 'poetical' passages
and which gives the strongest impression of the author's 'personality';
it is the text upon which most critics have chosen to base their interpretation of the work. The C Text, which has been variously dated
from as early as 1380 to as late as 1399, expands the twenty Passus
of B to twenty-three, modifies a considerable number of passages,
and adds in all about 100 lines to the B version. The C Text is the

most controverted of the three, and some scholars continue to express reservations concerning Langland's authorship of it.[5] Generally speaking, it seems to aim at further clarifying or developing points already made in B, at somewhat reducing the dramatic or 'poetic' effect of certain passages in the interests of doctrinal consistency, and at giving rather less prominence to descriptions of the social scene. It has to be added, however, that there are notable exceptions to these general tendencies; at least one passage (C Text, x, 71ff.) commenting powerfully on the condition of the poor is a new addition in C, and the opening of C Text, vi takes the form of a long autobiographical statement (C Text, vi, 1–106) which gives us most of the information we possess concerning the poet. In general, it seems impossible to deny that the C version is a natural develop-ment from B, written by someone who at least had an intimate under-standing of the nature of the poem, and whose modifications of the text stand in close connection to the original sources of inspiration.

Essential to an understanding of the work is a grasp of the *organic* nature of Langland's allegorical proceedings. Attempts have been made to interpret his allegory rigidly in the light of the methods developed by medieval theologians for the interpretation of scriptural texts. Scholars who favour this approach rely on the famous fourfold levels of exegesis – literal, allegorical, moral, and anagogical – familiar in such writers as Aquinas and summarized by Dante in his late letter to Can Grande commenting on his own *Paradiso*.[6] The comparison can be of value inasmuch as it illustrates the tendency of medieval thought to see the facts of human experience as significant on different levels, each simultaneously valid in its own right and incomplete, pointing to a higher order of reality beyond itself. This way of looking at things can be fruitful for poetry, as both Dante and Langland show in their work; but, in order to find it so, the reader of either poet is required to bear in mind the essential differences that separate scriptural commentary from poetic creation. To attempt to force the developing argument of Langland's poem into this or any other abstract framework is finally to do violence to the nature of the work, which is essentially more free, less constrained, than this kind of approach would indicate: not only because Langland's proceedings are sometimes less logically defined, even more confused, than such an interpretation might suggest, but because it is in the nature of his poem to move with relative freedom between different levels which tend to exist simultaneously beneath the successive transformations which the poetic experience dictates. Piers the Plowman's growth into a figure for the humanity of Christ does not obscure, or annul, his original nature. At the close the poem, and Piers with it, returns to where it began, to the human life in the world which has been throughout its undeviating concern.[7]

A summary consideration of the general plan will make this clear. The early manuscripts divide the poem into two parts, distinguished by rubrics which describe them respectively as the *Visio* of Piers Plowman and as the *Vita* of Do-Wel, Do-Bet, and Do-Best. The first part, the *Visio*, consists of the Prologue and – in the C Text – of Passus I to X; the material contained in it is essentially that of the A version of the poem. It opens with the poet's opening dream of 'a fair feld, ful of folke', combining universality of reference with a limited, even familiar environment. The field itself might easily be a part of the poet's local experience, expressly related to Malvern and its surroundings, but in it he finds

> Alle manere of men · the mene and the ryche,
> Worchynge and wandrynge · as the world asketh,
> (C Text, I, 19–20)

and it is bounded, on the east, by the Tower of Truth and, on the west, by the Dale of Death. From the first, therefore, the setting of the poem is at once local and universal, descriptive and allegorical. Its allegorical content, however, though present from the first, deals at this stage with relatively simple ideas, themselves pictorially expressed. As we pass from the Prologue to the main body of the poem, the awakened dreamer is concerned to show us the 'meaning' of his dream. To this end 'a loveliche lady ... in lynnen y-clothid' comes down from the Tower. She is 'Holy Church' and she tells him that salvation is to be obtained by living in accordance with the Truth which is the object of man's search during his earthly life:

> 'Whanne alle tresours ben tried,' quath hue · 'treuthe is the beste;
> Ich do hit on *Deus caritas* · to deme the sothe.
> Hit is *as derworthe a druwery · as dere god him-selve.
> (C Text, II, 81–3)

*a* as dear a dowry.

To arrive at truth, in turn, it is necessary to live by the law which the teachings of Holy Church enjoin and which is written in the hearts of men as a manifestation of creative love:

> Hit is a kynde*ᵃ* knowyng · that kenneth in thyn herte
> For to louve thy lord · levest of alle,
> And deye rathere than to do · eny dedlich synne,
> And this ich trowe be treuthe.
>
> (C Text, II, 142–5)

The state of affairs revealed to the poet in his dream, however, indicates that the teachings of 'Truth' have been neglected in the world of men, and so the next stage of the 'vision' is concerned with the contrasted appearance of Lady Meed, representing the desire for reward, material advancement, which is the occasion of all social disorder. She makes her appearance as a woman 'wonderliche riche clothed', clad in the luxury which was, for Langland, an infallible sign of degeneration:

> *ᵇ*Hue was purfild with peloure · non purere in erthe,
> And coroned with a corone · the kynge hath no betere;
> On alle hure fyve fyngres · rycheliche yrynged,
> And ther-on rede rubies · and other riche stones.
>
> (C Text, III, 10–13)

The contemplation of this figure provokes in the poet a conflict between fascination and moral condemnation which he expresses with direct simplicity when he says 'Hure a-raye with hure rychesse · ravesshede myn herte' (16).

The temptation, however, does not prevail. In Passus III and IV Lady Meed is brought to trial at the king's court, and accused by Conscience and Reason, who in this are shown as united with the king. Yet the condemnation does not in itself change the way of the world. From the superficial splendour of Lady Meed we pass to a picture of the clerical and courtly corruption which she spreads in a world where rank and responsibility are divorced from one another. This prompts the poet to resume the search for truth, which is found at last accompanying, in the contrasted figure of Piers, simple dedication to honest toil. 'Ich knowe hym as kyndeliche · as clerkus don huew bokes':

*a* natural, *b* She (her robe) was edged with fur.

Ich have yben his folwer · al thes fourty wynter,
And served Treuthe sothlyche · somdel<sup>a</sup> to paye;
In alle kynne craftes · that he couthe devyse
Profitable to the plouh · he putte me to lerne.
(C Text, VIII, 188–91)

This contrast between Lady Meed and Piers is the point of departure
for the allegorical development that follows. The later, and fuller,
versions expand this first direct enunciation of the main theme of
the poem in the light of a more ample vision of the universal spiritual
context of the immediate problems; but their foundation, as laid
down in these early Passus, is the poet's concern with the gap that
separated society, as he saw it, from true simplicity of life.

The transition from the early to the later versions of the poem
is marked by a passage which has inspired a variety of interpretations
but which is evidently intended to prepare for the transformed
character of Piers in the *Vita*. At the beginning of Passus X in the
C Text Truth offers Piers a 'pardon' which seems to be a confirmation
of his function as we have already described it:

Treuthe herde telle here-of · and to Peers sente
To take hus teeme · and tulye<sup>b</sup> the erthe;
And purchased hym a pardon · *a pena et a culpa*,
For hym and for hus heyres · for evere to be asoiled<sup>c</sup>;
And bad hym halde hym at home · and <sup>d</sup>erye hus leyes,
And alle that hulpe hym to erye · to setten other to sawe,
Other eny maner myster · that myght Peers a-vayle,
Pardon with Peers plouhman · perpetuel he graunteth.
(C Text, X, 1–8)

The 'pardon' is mediated to him, in the dream, by a priest, who
evidently assumes that Piers is unable to read or write and who offers
to 'translate' the Latin words into English for his understanding.
Opened by Piers, the 'pardon' is seen to consist of two lines which
are in effect a confirmation of the absolute nature of the law and
of its inescapable implications for the conduct of human life on earth:

In two lynes hit lay · and no lettere more,
And was ywryte ryght thus · in witnesse of treuthe.
*Qui bona egerunt ibunt in vitam eternam;*
*Qui vero mala, in ignem eternum.*

*a* somewhat, *b* till, *c* absolved, *d* plough his fallow lands.

'Peter!' quath the prest tho · 'ich can no pardon fynde.
Bote "do wel and have wel · and god shal have thy saule,
Do evel and have euel · and hope thow non other
Bote he that evel lyueth · evel shal ende!"'

(C Text, X, 286–91)

The teaching contained in these words is orthodox, and other passages make it clear that Langland has no intention of rejecting the Church's doctrine on 'pardons', but only of attacking the well-known abuses to which it gave rise. Piers, however, in a passage which is confined to the B text, reacts violently. He tears up the pardon 'in pure tene', quotes the words of Psalm XXII: – *si ambulavero in medio umbrae mortis, non timebo mala, quoniam tu mecum es* – and announces his intention to cease in his labour and to devote himself more directly to prayer and penance:

'I shal cessen of my sowyng', quod Pieres · 'and swynk nought so harde
Ne about my bely-ioye · so bisy be namore!
Of preyers and of penaunce · my plow shal ben herafter,
And wepen whan I shulde slepe · though whete-bred me faille'.

(B Text, VIII, 117–20)

In justification for this changed attitude he points to the Gospel words which speak of the birds who are careless about the future and which urge men to be less anxious about their material prospects and to live by faith in the care of Providence.

The episode is indeed puzzling, and it may be significant that the C writer, perhaps aware both of its illogicality – for the 'pardon' was after all offered to Piers by 'Truth' and does no more than stress the main theme of the preceding episodes – and of the possibility of heretical interpretations, chose to leave it out. It does, however, clearly mark an essential point in the transition from the *Visio* to the *Vita*. Piers, faced by a world which seems little inclined to accept the absolute injunction to live according to the law, and which in consequence will continue to be unredeemed by 'honest labour' and to suffer the consequences – plague, famine and social strife – which will inevitably result, rejects what he now sees as short cuts to salvation. Recognizing that the redemption of society depends finally on the divine will, Piers resolves to be less anxious about his daily sustenance and to devote himself to the search for that *personal* fulfilment which does lie in his power. Having taken this decision he will for a time disappear from the poem, only to re-enter it in due course in a transformed guise.

The transition from the *Visio* to the *Vita*, therefore, follows a logic of its own in moving from the particular to the universal, from a statement of facts to a consideration of their spiritual meaning. The pattern of the *Vita* is built up, primarily if at times loosely, on a triple conception of Christian obligation, summed up in the three successive stages Do-Well, Do-Bet, and Do-Best. These states have received a variety of allegorical interpretations, according to the preferences of different scholars. For one, they correspond respectively to the active, contemplative, and 'mixed' lives. For another, the emphasis is more directly vocational: the life of Do-Well is that appropriate to the laity, that of Do-Bet to the clergy, and that of Do-Best to the episcopal office. A third theory would find in the three states a parallel with the successive stages of the contemplative life – purgative, illuminative, and unitive – as described by St Bernard and other writers of the life of the spirit.[8] It needs to be stressed, perhaps, that there is no need to believe that the poet was exclusively concerned with any one of these triads, or with any others that might be proposed. As we have already argued it is of the essence of his plan to move freely on different levels of interpretation, passing from one to another as his imaginative purpose requires. To seek to confine the poem to a single level of interpretation is to be untrue to the heart of its conception and to subject to undue intellectual constriction what was freely and imaginatively conceived.

Each state is successively related to the facts of human behaviour as observed by the poet in the society which surrounds him; and the fact that the contrast assumes, as the allegorical progression advances, an air of increasing darkness prepares the way finally for the direct introduction of the central Christian symbols. When Piers tore up the offered 'pardon' and declared his determination to be *less* anxious about his material activities he was in fact accepting the need for faith, for belief in a providential ordering which the sorry state of the world might *seem* to contradict but which would finally, in its own good time, redeem or justify – make just – the process of human life in time. What is implied finally is a shift of emphasis from a temporal to an eternal, from a human to a divine perspective.

The first stage in this construction turns on the life of Do-Well (Passus XI to XVII in the C Text). Do-Well represents the acceptance of the conditions of daily life, lived truly in the sight of God and in accordance with the precepts of the Church. The philosophy of

> Who-so is trewe of hys tonge · and of hus two handes,
> And thorw leel[a] labour lyveth · and loveth his emcristine[b],
> (C Text, XI, 78–9)

is sufficient, when truly followed, for salvation. By contrast with this, the lowest form of the Christian ideal, Langland continues to set his sombre picture of the state of the world, and more especially his denunciation of the incapacity of the privileged and those to whom spiritual authority has been entrusted to follow even the elementary precepts of their own moral code:

> Clerkus and knyghtes · carpen[c] of god ofte,
> And haveth hym muche in hure mouthe · ac mene men in herte . . .
> so is pruyde en-hansed
> In religion and al the reame · among ryche and poure,
> That preyeres han no power · these pestilences to lette.
> For god is def now a dayes · and deyneth nouht ous to huyre,
> And good men for oure gultes · he al to-grynt to dethe.
> (C Text, XII, 52–3; 58–62)

It is this contrast between precept and reality, presented with a wealth of observed detail, that gives life at this stage to the abstract structure of the poem.

The main body of the life of Do-Well is devoted to a series of encounters with allegorical figures personifying the various human faculties: Wit, Study, 'Clergy' (Learning) and his wife Scripture, 'Imagynatyf'. In the course of these the dreamer is made to understand that the authority of the Law is absolute and that, in its almost universal neglect by men, the only hope of avoiding the retribution it promises lies in faith in the divine *mercy* which both includes and fulfils it. This section of the poem is brought to a close (Passus XIII and XIV in the B version) with the figure of Haukyn, in whom we are to see the ordinary sensual man involved in the life of the world. Haukyn wears a tattered coat ('the flesh') which he obstinately and unendingly fails to 'wash'. The failure gives tangible form to

*a* loyal, *b* fellow-Christian, *c* talk.

what has by now become the principal issue of the poem: the inveterate failure of human societies and of the individuals who compose them to live in accordance with the Law and to engage by so doing the only path which can lead to their temporal and eternal redemption. The way to that goal lies, as the dreamer now understands, through *faith*, in acceptance of the necessary incompleteness of *all* purely human perspectives: and so Haukyn is instructed by Patience to be less 'busy', less concerned about his worldly circumstance, to make confession of his sins, and to offer restitution for them as the Law enjoins; and – for the rest – to live by that faith of which good works are the natural and indispensable expression. The search finally is for 'Charity', the love which is the fulfilment of the Law; and when Haukyn, at the end of Do-Well, asks where it is to be found – 'Where woneth Charite?' – he is told to seek her in the 'parfit treuthe and pouere herte' which is required of all men in their necessarily incomplete and imperfect understanding.

Do-Well is, in any case, no more than a first step on the road to perfection. Beyond it, including and transcending its qualities, is the life of positive dedication to spiritual realities and to the practice of Charity. This, the state of Do-Bet, normally though not necessarily should find its consummation in the religious life. Do-Bet retains all the qualities of Do-Well, but – as the poet puts it – 'he doth more'. As we have already been told:

> He is lowe as a lombe · and loveliche of speche,
> And helpeth herteliche alle men · of that he may aspare.
> The bagges and the by-gurdeles*a* · he hath to-broke hem alle . . .
> And is ronnen in-to religiun · and rendreth hus the bible,
> And precheth to the peple · seint Poules wordes.
>
> (C Text, XI, 83–5; 88–9)

On this new level, the contrast between precept and behaviour looms larger than ever. Langland does not hesitate to underline it, more especially in the B version, with all the peculiar pungency of phrase at his command:

> He is worse than Judas · that giveth a Japer siluer,
> And biddeth the begger go · for his broke*b* clothes.
>
> (B Text, IX, 90–91)

*a* containers, *b* broken, torn.

Only now, more clearly than before, man's lack of Charity stands out against the direct evocation of God's providence:

> For owre ioye and owre hele · Jesu Cryst of hevene,
> In a pore mannes apparaille · pursueth us euere.
>
> (B Text, XI, 179–80)

With God thus incarnate in the garb of the poor, the identification of Christ, in his human nature, with Piers is clearly foreshadowed.

The allegorical pattern, however, has still to be completed. In spite of the greater moral discernment which it implies, Do-Bet is not the last step in the ladder of perfection. Beyond it and Do-Well, combining both in a higher perfection, is the state of *active* spiritual dedication in which a human being, having grasped true spiritual values and responded to them with a total offering of the self in poverty, is entrusted with the unending task of remoulding the world to their pattern: the state, in other words, of Do-Best. This is, in its most complete form, the life of spiritual authority entrusted to the rulers of the Church by Jesus Christ himself after the victory gained by him in favour of mankind. It implies the obligations described in the poet's own words:

> Dobest bere sholde · the bisshopes croce,
> And halye*a* with the hoked ende · ille men to goode,
> And with the pyk putte adoune · *prevaricatores legis*,
> Lordes that lyven as hem lust · and no lawe a-counten;
> For *b*here mok and here meeble · such men thynken
> That no bisshop sholde · here byddinge with-sitte.
> Ac Dobest sholde nat dreden hem · bote do as god hihte.
>
> (C Text, XI, 92–8)

As a combination of the active and contemplative virtues, the life of Do-Best is the highest destiny open to man on earth; but precisely because this is so, it bears the greatest responsibilities and is the most open to corruption. In his statement of its privileges, therefore, and in the accompanying denunciations of failure and neglect, spiritual ideal and social reality finally come together in the most universal contrast of the whole poem.

The conflict between good and evil, indeed, far from being settled in accordance with the dictates of reason, needs to be resolved by

---

*a* haul back, *b* their muck (trashy wealth) and their movable property.

other means. The solution cannot come from man alone; it requires an intervention of the divine which lies at the heart of Langland's Christian affirmation. At the end of the life of Do-Bet we are brought to the last vision of all, that which transforms Piers into the human semblance of God incarnate and crucified. Free will, we are told,

> for love hath undertake
> That this Jesus of hus gentrise · shal jouste in Peers armes,
> In hus helme and in hus haberion · *humana natura*;
> That Crist be nat knowe · for *consummatus deus*,
> In Piers plates the Plowman · this prikiere*<sup></sup>* shal ryde.
> (C Text, XXI, 20–24)

By this supreme transformation the scope of the whole vision is transformed. The decisive duel between good and evil is described in terms of a 'joust', a courtly tournament. Jesus has become a knight riding out to meet his challenger, and his armour, the humanity he has assumed for the purpose of battle, is that of Piers, who has borne his active representation of the Christian virtues through the successive stages of his pilgrimage and is now ready to play his part in the final encounter. The conflict between light and darkness, good and evil, Christ and Satan is given in a form that evidently derives much of its power from the example of the familiar 'miracle' plays in which it was dramatically presented.[9] Christ approaches the gates of Hell and is challenged by Lucifer:

> For eft that light bad unlouke · and Lucifer answerede,
> 'What lord art thou?' quath Lucifer; · a voys a-loude seyde,
> 'The lord of myght and of mayn · that made alle thynges.
> Duke of this dymme place · a-non undo the gates,
> That Crist mowe comen in · the kynges sone of heuene'.
> (C Text, XXI, 362–6)

In response to this command the gates of darkness are opened – 'with that breth helle brake' – and the Victor, addressing himself to Satan with superb power, announces his triumph in the name of the humanity which his action has redeemed:

> 'The biternesse that thow hast browe · now brouk hit thyself;
> That art doctour of deth · drynk that thow madest!
> For ich that am lord of lyf · love is my drynke,

*a* champion.

And for that drynke to-daye · deyede, as hit semede.
Ac ich wol drynke of no dich · ne of no deop cleregie,
Bote of comune coppes · alle Cristene soules;
Ac thi drynke worth deth · and deep helle thy bolle[a]
Ich fauht so, me fursteth[b] yut · for mannes soule sake;

      *Sicio.*

May no pymente ne pomade · ne presiouse drynkes
Moyste me to the fulle · ne my thurst slake,
Til the vendage falle · in the vale of Iosaphat,
And drynke ryght rype most · *resurreccio mortuorum.*
Then shal ich come as a kyng · with coroune and with angeles,
And have out of helle · alle mennes soules.

                    (C Text, XXI, 404–17)

As *humana natura*, the human element in the Word made flesh, Piers is united to the divinity of Christ and so participates in the great Christian victory over the enemies of God and mankind.

From beginning to end, indeed, the manifold richness and continuity of Langland's allegorical pattern is balanced by a deeply tragic view of the realities of the world. The life of Do-Best gives us no easy, or simply redemptive solution to the problems which the poem has so insistently posed. Like all human states it is subject to failure and required to face an unending process of degeneration. Once the victory over death, sin, and time has been affirmed, Piers is enjoined by Grace to make preparation for the gathering of its fruits:

'Ageynst that thi greynes', quath Grace · 'bygynneth to growe,
Ordeyne the an hous, Peers · to herberghen in thi cornes'.
'By god, Grace,' quath Peers · 'ye mote gyve me tymber,
And ordeyne that hous · er ye hennes wende'.
And Grace gaf hym the croys · with the corone of thornes,
That Crist up-on Calvarie · for mankynde on peynede;
And of hus baptisme and blod · that he bledde on rode
He made [c]a maner morter · and Mercy hit hihte.
And ther-with Grace by-gan · to make à good foundement,
And watelide[d] hit and wallyde hit · with hus peynes and hus passion,
And of alle holy writt · he made a roof after,
And cald that hous Unite · holychurche in English.

                    (C Text, XXII, 319–30)

This 'harvest' is to be the consummation of Piers' efforts throughout the poem, the fulfilment to which his successive transformations have

---

*a* bowl, *b* I thirst, *c* a kind of mortar, *d* wattled.

tended. The 'victory' has to be consolidated in terms of the battle of daily living in the temporal order; and, until the final confirmation which lies inscrutably hidden in the purposes of a divinity which is, necessarily and logically, 'in infinite excess'[10] of all created understanding, the battle will be an endless compound of temporary successes shadowed by unending failure. The final vision of the poem is that of Conscience, assaulted by Sloth and Pride, calling in vain on Clergy (Study) to help him and Contrition to 'keep the portal'. Faced by this discouraging prospect Conscience announces his determination to resume his apparently endless journey in search of justice:

'By Crist', quath Conscience tho · 'ich wole by-come a pilgryme,
And wenden as wide · as the worlde regneth,
To seke Peers the Plouhman · that Pruyde myghte destruye,
And that freres haden a fyndynge · that for neode[a] flateren,
And counterpleideth me, Conscience; · nowe Kynde me a-venge,
And sende me hap and hele · til ich have Peers Plouhman!'
And suthe[b] he gradde after grace · til ich gan a-wake.
(C Text, XXIII, 380–86)

By a last superb and characteristic touch the poet, having witnessed the consummation of his dream, wakes to the world to realize that the endless struggle must continue until the temporal process is wound up and the divine purpose finally fulfilled. Here, too, *Piers Plowman* is faithful to the Saxon origins of its inspiration. Like the pagan Beowulf many centuries earlier, the Christian hero, if not defeated, is given no rest in this life from the conflict with evil.

The allegorical conception thus sketched, however, is not to be appreciated except in the light of the literary virtues that went with it. The foundation of these is a capacity to see the highest spiritual conceptions in terms of a rooted concreteness, a firm grasp of the particular. When Langland desires to express his deepest feelings, and when these break through the sometimes cumbrous garb of his allegorical inventions, he finds it natural to rely on the simplest imagery. He writes of the Incarnation in terms of the most universal physical processes:

Love is the[c] plonte of pees · and most preciouse of vertues;
For hevene holde hit ne myghte · so hevy hit semede,
Til hit hadde on erthe · goten hym-selve.

*a* gain, *b* then, *c* plant of peace.

Was nevere lef up-on lynde · lyghter ther-after,
As whanne hit hadde of the folde · flesch and blod ytake;
Tho was it portatyf[a] and pershaunt[b] · as the poynt of a nedle,
May non armure hit lette · nother hye walles;
For-thy is love leder · of oure lordes folke of hevene.

(C Text, II, 149-56)

Langland's language here is the vehicle of a finely integrated experience, alive and sensitive to every point of contact and crystallizing suavely into poetry. The effect of 'pershaunt', preceded by 'portatyf' and followed by 'as the poynt of a nedle', is not so inferior to Hamlet's 'bare bodkin'; it is certainly of the same kind and depends upon a similar keen intensity of perception. The simple alliteration of the second and third lines, charged with the sense of ripeness, reflects the 'heaviness' of the spiritual burden which leads finally, after the process of begetting which follows so naturally from it, to the sense of joyous relief beautifully conveyed in the evocation of the leaf fluttering in the breeze. In writing of this kind, words become transparent vehicles for the emotion that underlies them and demands the simplest, most vital expression. Their value is, so to speak, sacramental (the word has a special relevance in view of the nature of Langland's allegory) and the presence of universal physical experiences illuminates even the most spiritual reality.

What is true of the language is equally true of the symbolic figures of the poem. Langland's allegory, like his language, grew out of his experience in the process of sublimating it. The symbol of Piers has a content that most later allegorical creations, whatever their other merits, lack; he is fully natural before and after he touches the supernatural. In this respect Langland's attitude reflects his 'philosophy' and the attitude to temporal experience which his tradition afforded him. He did not share the metaphysical preoccupation of the Renaissance with the idea of impersonal Time, as expressed in Shakespeare's line –

Devouring Time, blunt thou the lion's paws.
(Sonnet XIX)

The feeling of the sonnets is something new and complex. It is obtained here by transferring the epithet 'devouring', which belongs naturally to the lion, to Time, subjecting the classical commonplace

*a* easily carried, *b* piercing.

*tempus edax rerum*[11] to a new and complex emotional situation. The lion naturally raises associations of splendid life and boundless energy; but the transfer of 'devouring' suggests that all this energy is self-consuming, that it involves the ultimate wearing-down of life into pure annihilation. Shakespeare's tendency, in fact, as far as this sonnet is concerned (for it is only one of his many tendencies) is to subdue the nervous apprehension of life to the idea of Time, 'metaphysically' apprehended. In Langland, similar poetic resources are used to a different end. Time is regarded as the condition under which living moral action takes place. Full value is given to the human and spiritual tragedy represented by his personifications of sin. The tragedy is – to quote Shakespeare again – that of 'the expense of spirit in a waste of shame', and Langland's moral judgement recognizes not only the 'waste' and the 'expense' but the fact that it is 'of spirit' and therefore redeemable. As always, the allegory of *Piers Plowman* follows the principle of its author's central conviction – the Christian Incarnation. Far from imposing itself upon reality as an abstraction, it works from the body to the soul, from natural life to the consummation of grace in which its author believed. And, in so doing, it bears witness to a main source of strength in English literature.

## NOTES

All quotations from Langland's poem are taken from W. W. Skeat's edition of the three texts (Oxford, 1886, reprinted in 1954). I have chosen to quote from the C Text, as representing what is presumably the final version of the poem, drawing from B only for passages relevant to the argument but omitted in C.

1. A note in the Dublin MS states that Langland was the illegitimate son of Stacy de Rokayle, who held land in Shipton-under-Wychwood, Oxford.

2. On this subject, G. R. Owst's *Literature and Pulpit in Medieval England* (2nd edn, New York, 1961) is still the outstanding authority.

3. D. H. Lawrence, letter to Edward Marsh, 19 November 1913.

4. The theory of divided authorship was first authoritatively stated by J. M. Manly in *The Authorship of Piers Plowman* (Early English Text Society, 1910). The balance of later scholarship tends, with whatever reservations, to incline towards a recognition of single authorship. A review of the present state of the controversy is given in G. Kane, *Piers Plowman: The Evidence for Authorship* (London, 1965).

5. E. T. Donaldson, in his study *Piers Plowman: The C Text and its Poet* (New Haven, Conn., 1949), argued strongly in support of Langland's author-

ship of the C Text, and in favour of the philosophical and doctrinal validity of the changes introduced by it into B. His conclusions have been received favourably by many scholars.

6. Dante, *Letter to Can Grande*, paras. 7, 8. Some scholars have questioned the attribution of this Latin letter to the poet, against what still seems to be the consensus of opinion on this point. In any case, whatever uncertainty may exist does not affect the point here in question.

7. On the question of the 'figural' nature of medieval allegory, and on its implications for literature, reference should be made to Erich Auerbach's essay on *Figura*, published in translation in *Scenes from the Drama of European Literature* (New York, 1959).

8. The first of these interpretations was proposed by H. W. Wells in two articles published in *Proceedings of the Modern Languages Association*, XLIV, 123–40, and LIII, 339–49. The second was advanced by Nevill Coghill in *Medium Aevum*, II, 108–35. The third view is referred by E. T. Donaldson, in his book already cited, to a paper delivered by Howard Meroney to the Modern Language Association of America in 1946.

9. The Harrowing of Hell is represented in both the York and Chester cycles of plays.

10. The phrase is Dante's. See *Paradiso*, XIX, 45.

11. The phrase is from Ovid.

# SIR GAWAIN AND THE GREEN KNIGHT

### J.A. BURROW

The characteristic subject of medieval romance is adventure. By performing feats of arms and encountering marvels, the knightly hero shows his courage and prowess. Indeed, as Erich Auerbach says in his classic essay, the world of romance 'is a world specifically created and designed to give the knight opportunity to prove himself'.[1] In simple and popular romances a knight can prove himself by overcoming numerous adversaries in jousts and battles; but more sophisticated writers, such as the great twelfth-century French poet Chrétien de Troyes,[2] put their heroes to more subtle kinds of proof. Adventure, in a romance such as Chrétien's *Yvain*, exposes to test and scrutiny not only the prowess and courage of the hero, but also other ethical qualities specially valued in the polite society of the Middle Ages – fidelity to the pledged word, loyalty to women, courtesy, and the rest.

The finest of medieval English romances, *Sir Gawain and the Green Knight*, was composed by an unknown contemporary of Chaucer, some time in the latter part of the fourteenth century, somewhere in the counties of Staffordshire, Cheshire or Lancashire.[3] Scholars have attempted without success to track the author down; but it is at least clear that he must have written his poem for some sophisticated audience capable of appreciating an adventure as subtle as any of Chrétien's. The adventure, as it unfolds, reveals at every stage new subtleties. The reader learns to understand the story only by degrees; and his understanding is hardly allowed to settle into finality even at the very end, where the hero's moral secrets are exposed to a searching but far from simplifying scrutiny. Like the original circle of listeners, we are kept in suspense, not only about the outcome of Sir Gawain's adventure, but also about its true nature and significance. In the present essay, I shall attempt to retrace this process of discovery, so skilfully paced and controlled by the poet, through which the reader is led towards an understanding of what, in this poem, adventure really means.

The poem opens with a promise of wonders. No country, says the poet, has more marvels (ferlyes) in its history than Britain; and no British king was nobler than Arthur. Therefore:

> <sup>a</sup>Forthi an aunter in erde I attle to schawe,
> That a selly<sup>b</sup> in sight summe men hit holden,
> And an outtrage<sup>c</sup> awenture of Arthurez wondrez.
>
> (27–9)

The poet defines his subject precisely. This is not to be one of those Arthurian romances which follows the life of a hero through a whole series of adventures (the *Perceval* of Chrétien, for instance); nor does it claim (as Malory does) to treat the whole matter of Arthur and his knights. The biography of Sir Gawain and the history of the Round Table are both, we will find, irrelevances in a poem which maintains strict standards of relevance. The poet's subject is, as he declares, a single adventure: the Adventure of the Green Chapel ('the chaunce of the grene chapel', 2399).

The action begins briskly, with a description of a great feast on New Year's Day at Camelot. The poet, rather surprisingly, goes out of his way to explain at length why King Arthur had not taken his seat at the festive table; but, like this thrifty writer's later explanation of the pentangle on Gawain's shield, the passage serves more than its ostensible purpose. It establishes, in fact, the poem's first idea of adventure. Arthur, the poet tells us in his firm, clear way, had two reasons for not taking his seat: he was so young and sprightly that he could not bear to be still for any longer than he had to – 'So bisied him his yonge blod and his brayn wylde' – and also he had taken a vow not to eat on great feast days until he had either heard or seen some marvellous adventure. The effect of this double explanation is complex. It is a sign of Arthur's nobility that his adventurousness of spirit can overcome his appetite for roast swan; yet his idea of adventure also owes something to his 'young blood'. He makes no distinction between a tale of adventure and adventure itself – either will do – and his conception of the latter, while recognizing that lives will be in jeopardy, lays emphasis on

---

<sup>a</sup> Therefore I intend to declare an adventure in the land, <sup>b</sup> marvel, <sup>c</sup> extravagant.

good fortune and good sportsmanship, as if a joust were little more than a game to be played between gentlemen.

Yet the *Gawain*-poet's Arthur is not an absurd figure like Don Quixote, out of touch with the realities of the world in which he lives. In this land of marvels, Arthur's extravagant vow meets with an almost instantaneous response. Indeed, the remarkable episode which follows might be taken as the beginning of a quite conventional 'adventure from among the wonders of Arthur'. A knight rides into the hall, as hostile challengers were accustomed to do, and proposes to test the reputation of the Round Table in a contest with one of its knights. But this Knight of the Green Chapel (as he calls himself) is gigantic and green all over; and the contest which he proposes has a bizarre character. The Beheading Game seems both more and less threatening than an ordinary adventure – an ambiguity portrayed emblematically in the figure of the Green Knight himself, carrying in one hand a fearsome axe and in the other a bough of festive holly. The challenger has left his armour at home, he says, for he proposes nothing more than a 'Christmas game'; and the rules of that game would seem to require nothing of his adversary but one good blow of the axe. Yet the very generosity of the rules is unnerving; and the appearance of the knight confirms suspicions that ordinary canons of probability may not apply in this case. From the start, in fact, the Adventure of the Green Chapel presents a challenge to interpretation, for participants and readers alike.

In his account of the court's response to this unsettling visitation, the poet displays his characteristic realism – a realism which, unlike most of its modern counterparts, does not exclude the reality of courage. Although many of the diners are frankly afraid, Arthur chooses to treat the Green Knight's proposal as simply foolish; and Gawain, when he undertakes the adventure, calls it a silly business. The poet later admits that strong drink may have played a part in this grand behaviour; but Gawain is sober enough to restate with precision the terms of the proposed game and to pledge his knightly troth with due solemnity. Yet neither he nor we are prepared for the bizarre events which the poet goes on to describe in his vigorously realistic alliterative verse: Gawain's axe-blade 'shindering' the bone and slicing through the white flesh of the Green Knight's neck, ending up stuck in the floor ('the bit of the broun stel bot on the grounde'); the decapitated challenger picking up his head, remounting his horse, and turning his body in the saddle to speak his parting words:

> *He brayde his bulk aboute,
> That ugli body that bledde.
>
> (440–41)

The stark and hideous plainness of these lines marks the beginning of a new phase in the adventure, which is now unambiguously a serious affair ('sturne werk'). Gawain faces a difficult journey at the worst time of the year to find the mysterious Green Chapel; and at the end of that journey, on the next New Year's Day, he seems to face certain death at the hands of the Green Knight. After the challenger has left the hall, Arthur attempts to restore the festive mood with some tough jokes; but the opening of the Second Fit makes it clear that the affair is now no laughing matter:

> This hanselle*b* hatz Arthur of aventurus on fyrst
> In yonge yer, for he yerned yelpyng*c* to here.
> Thagh hym wordex were wane*d* when thay to sete wenten,
> Now ar thay stoken of*e* sturne werk, stafful*f* her hond.
> Gawan watz glad to begynne those gomnes*g* in halle,
> Bot thagh the ende be hevy haf ye no wonder.
>
> (491–6)

From the moment when Gawain sets off on his arduous journey, ten months later, until his arrival at the Green Chapel in the fourth and final fit, the poet keeps the hard realities of his adventure steadily in view. The noble knight never wavers in his resolution to vindicate the honour of himself and the Round Table by keeping his solemn promise to the Green Knight; but this is not the easy, weightless heroism of many romances. The end in prospect really is 'hevy', and it weighs on hero and reader alike. At the moment of Gawain's departure from Camelot, his likely fate is expressed in a single piercing phrase: he is to be 'hadet wyth an alvisch mon' – 'beheaded by an elvish man'.

Gawain's journey in search of his elvish man differs from the timeless and untraceable travels of many romance heroes. A masterly

---

*a* He twisted his body round, *b* New Year's gift, *c* challenge, *d* lacking, *e* stuck full of, fully provided with, *f* cram-full, *g* games.

description of the passing of the seasons establishes once and for all the reality of time in this poem. When Gawain sets out on 2 November (All Souls' Day, ominously) he has left himself almost two calendar months in which to find the Green Chapel; and those months are needed for a journey which takes him, not only through Logres and later through 'contrayes straunge', but also through real territory, no doubt familiar to the original audience of northwesterners – along the coast road in North Wales, across the River Dee and into the Wirral. He encounters monsters and marvels on the way; but the poet lays more stress on the troubles anyone would encounter, travelling in North Wales and Northern England during the months of November and December:

> [a]For werre wrathed hym not so much that wynter nas wors,
> When the colde cler water fro the cloudez schadde[b],
> And fres er hit falle myght to the fale[c] erthe;
> Ner slayn wyth the slete he sleped in his yrnes
> Mo nyghtez then innoghe in naked rokkez,
> Ther as claterande fro the crest the colde borne[d] rennez.
>
> (726–31)

This passage, like the description of the beheading of the Green Knight, shows the full power of alliterative verse, in the poet's hands, to communicate physical reality with heightened intensity – '*naked* rocks', '*clattering*'. The journey is indeed 'no gomen'.[e]

The next stage of the adventure manifests itself, like the first, in mysterious response to human needs and wishes. Gawain, deep in a tangled wood on Christmas Eve, prays for some place to hear Mass at Christmas; and no sooner has he crossed himself three times than he sees a castle in a clearing. He even hits 'ful chauncely' on the main road leading to the drawbridge. The world of the poem, for all its palpable solidity, is still a world 'specifically created and designed' for adventure, where statistical probability is suspended and apparent chances are saturated with significance. The significance of Gawain's stay at the castle, however, appears only when it is over. The reader – the ideal first-time reader – must suspect that there is more to the episode than meets the eye, if only because the author devotes more than half his poem to it. But Gawain is not reading the poem, and his suspicions are never aroused – not even

*a* For combat did not trouble him as much as the winter did, *b* fell, *c* pallid, *d* burn, stream, *e* no joke.

when his host's wife proves to be wearing a belt of green and gold, the challenger's colours. The poet does not confine the narrative to what Gawain himself sees, as strict point-of-view practice would require; but the scenes where the host goes hunting while the hero lies in bed contain nothing which would have caused Gawain surprise if he had been present. The reader is therefore allowed only a marginal advantage over the hero in his interpretation of events. Like Gawain, he has to wait until the last fit for full understanding – a retrospective understanding which, as we shall see, entirely justifies the poet in his elaborate and leisurely treatment of what might have seemed a mere interlude.

Gawain arrives at the castle on Christmas Eve and leaves on New Year's Day, having spent seven full days as a guest. Suppressing 28 December (unless a line is missing after 1022, as some editors think), the poet divides this period into two three-day sequences. In the three days of full Christmas festivity, Gawain finds himself in a household matching Camelot in luxury, civility and piety. As at Camelot, feasts are served, party games played, Masses heard. When the party breaks up after three days, however, Gawain prepares to leave with the rest. It is at this point that he tells his host for the first time of his 'high errand' and expresses his determination to keep his appointment at the Green Chapel:

> ᵃNaf I now to busy bot bare thre dayez,
> And me als fayn to falle feye as fayly of myn ernde.
>
> (1066–7)

The idiomatic 'bare', pointed by alliteration, is richly expressive. Time is running out, for Gawain as well as for his adventure; and the heroic declaration of the next line is shadowed by the realization that success in the mission will itself mean death. Gawain, to all appearances, *is* 'feye', doomed. Yet the host responds with laughter: Gawain does not need to 'busy' himself to find the Green Chapel:

> Mon schal yow sette in waye,
> Hit is not two myle henne.
>
> (1077–8)

The effect of this last short line is troubling, for the flat revelation

---

ᵃ Now I have only barely three days to work in, and I would rather die than fail in my mission.

carries a teasing note of humorous bathos. Gawain, however, responds with thanks and a promise to stay:

> Now acheved is my chaunce[a], I schal at your wylle
> Dowelle, [b]and ellez do quat ye demen.
>
> (1081–2)

'Now acheved is my chaunce . . .' Gawain's courageous determination to find the Green Chapel has never been in question; but the reader does not share his confident conviction that, now he is sure of finding it, the adventure is as good as 'achieved'. The very proximity of the Green Chapel confirms suspicions that all is not as it seems at the castle.

The poet's command over his powerful plot nowhere shows better than here, where Gawain's polite promise to stay and do his host's bidding provides the impulse for the next phase of the story – which starts, as it were, in an off-beat moment immediately following an apparent climax ('Now acheved is my chaunce'). The host, eagerly taking up Gawain's polite promise, proposes at once a kind of party game – what scholars call the Exchange of Winnings. This game occupies the greater part of the Third Fit, which follows; yet it bears no evident relation to the course of the adventure. The host seems simply to have hit upon a hospitable device for avoiding the flatness which always threatens a single guest when the rest of the party has broken up; and the poet likewise may seem to be using a bit of irrelevant business to fill up those 'bare three days' in which his hero has now nothing to do. Christmas game and knightly adventure, confused together in the First Fit, here seem to be absolutely distinct.

Throughout most of the Third Fit this distinction is maintained. On the one hand, there are festivities, field sports and party games; on the other, the ominous approach, as the Old Year dies, of the return match with the Green Knight. On each of the three days the narrative follows the same pattern: descriptions of the host out hunting alternated with descriptions of his wife's visits to Gawain's chamber, and at the end of each day an evening of merry-making at which the two men exchange their winnings. The rich and varied detail of life in the castle and on the hunting field, contained within this strictly recurring pattern, creates an effect of good cheer and ordered security; but this is broken into at irregular intervals by

a mission, b and do whatever else you require.

chilling reminders that the hero is shortly to be 'hadet wyth an alvisch mon'. The beheading of the deer carcase on the first day may pass unnoticed, but not the moment when, on the second day, the host marches back to his home with a huge boar's head carried before him in triumph. Gawain takes this in his stride – he even *pretends* to be afraid of the head, to flatter his host – but when the lady visits his room next morning, on the last day of the old year, he is in the grip of nightmare:

> <sup>a</sup>In dregh droupyng of dreme draveled that noble,
> As mon that watz in mornyng<sup>b</sup> mony thro<sup>c</sup> thoghtes,
> How that destiné schulde that day dele hym his wyrde<sup>d</sup>
> At the grene chapel, when he the gome<sup>e</sup> metes.
>
> (1750–53)

In the last scene with the lady, which immediately follows, a direct connection is established for the first time between Gawain's agreeable life as a guest and his increasingly nightmarish private experience as a knight errant. By this time the reader will already have drawn his own conclusions about the lady's stealthy visits to Gawain's bedside. On the previous day, the lady had frankly suggested love-making. A knight, she declared, should always have a mistress, for whom he can risk his life in combat. But that view of knightly adventure should appear, at best, charmingly irrelevant – the lady has been reading too many romances, perhaps. Gawain clearly ought to resist her advances. Ordinary moral rules require this, particularly where the wife of one's host is concerned; and there are also special rules for a knight 'on errand', requiring him to avoid diverting amorous entanglements. Understanding the matter in some such way, a reader will be duly relieved when Gawain, on New Year's Eve, resists the lady's last assaults, and the lady prepares, with pathetic protestations, to say good-bye. Another phase of the adventure – if that is what it was – has been successfully achieved. But here, as at the end of the Second Fit, the moment of achievement is immediately followed, in its slack and unguarded aftermath, by further developments. After Gawain has politely declined to give or receive a parting gift – in both cases, because he is 'on errand' – the lady makes what appears to be her last and weakest bid for a

*a* In his heavy and troubled sleep the knight was dreaming and muttering, *b* troubled by, *c* dire, *d* doom, *e* man.

concession. He has refused her ring; but will he not at least accept her belt? Gawain again declines, until the lady reveals that the belt has a magical property. It saves its wearer from violent death:

> Then kest[a] the knyght, and hit come to his hert
> [b]Hit were a juel for the jopardé that hym jugged were:
> When he acheved to the chapel [c]his chek for to fech,
> [d]Myght he haf slypped to be unslayn, the sleght were noble.
>
> (1855–8)

Such an offer, on such a day, could not fail to go straight to Gawain's heart. Nor does there seem any reason why he should not enlist magic against an adversary who himself proved capable of surviving decapitation. But there is more to the 'sleght' than that. He must agree – and he does agree – to conceal the belt from his host that evening at the exchange of winnings.

The adventure enters, at this moment, its darkest phase. The hero's conduct can no longer be taken as exemplary; and a number of episodes in what remains of the Third Fit arouse unsettling reflections. After Gawain has accepted the belt, the lady kisses him, as she has done before – once on the first day, twice on the second, and now three times on the third. The action is almost routine; but here it has an air of ominous finality, coming in the sensitive last short lines of the stanza:

> Bi that on thrynne sythe[e]
> Ho hatz kyst the knyght so toght[f].
>
> (1868–9)

Then Gawain, after hiding the belt 'holdely' (faithfully – a dubious epithet here) where he can find it later, goes off to confession and spends the rest of the day in revelry. That first action, confirming his fixed resolution to deceive the host, casts a shadow over the priest's absolution, as does the poet's reference – on the face of it merely hypothetical – to doomsday 'on the morn':

> He asoyled[g] hym surely and sette hym so clene
> As domezday schulde haf ben dight[h] on the morn.
>
> (1883–4)

---

a considered, b That it would be a precious thing in the dangerous affair that faced him, c to suffer his fate, d It would be a noble trick if he could escape with his life, e three times, f doughty, g absolved, h appointed.

The poem then returns, as it has on the two previous occasions, to the hunting field; but here the effect is again uneasy. The quarry, previously deer and boar, is on this occasion a fox; and the description of the wily beast failing, despite all its tricks, to escape from its adversary calls to mind Gawain's recent 'sleight' in the face of death and predicts for it, symbolically, an unhappy outcome. There follows a last exchange of winnings, repeating a pattern set up on previous days, but with disturbing variations. Gawain appears in a mantle of blue, the colour of fidelity ('true blue'); but his eagerness to get his side of the exchange over with (previously it was the host who paid his winnings first) betrays some uneasiness about the act of infidelity which he is on the point of committing. And when, in response to that act, the host apologizes for his own meagre winnings and presents Gawain with a 'foul fox fell', the moment is fraught with ironies. If Gawain handed over the belt, the fox skin would indeed have been a very inadequate return; but, as things are, it seems entirely appropriate.

Gawain has now secured possession, at a price, of his talisman; and when he sets out for the Green Chapel next morning, he wraps the belt firmly round his waist – '*That* forgat not Gawayn for gode of hymselven'. In the ambiguous world of this romance, magic, though always possible, is never entirely free from the suspicion of trickery, as when the courtiers at Camelot referred to the Green Knight as an illusion ('fantoum') and Arthur dismissed his head-trick as a Christmas show ('enterlude'). Hence, although Gawain's belief in the magic power of the belt must not appear ridiculous, the poet is free to make flesh creep as the crisis approaches. The Fourth Fit opens before dawn on New Year's Day, Gawain lying in bed, eyes shut but unable to sleep, listening to the snow-storm outside and the ominous periodic crowing of the cock. The effect of this chilling opening is to bring home the reality of the case, a reality which is intensified when Gawain leaves the castle and rides out into the bleak northern moorland. A damp morning mist covers the hills with grotesque hats and sinister cloaks of vapour:

> *a*The heven watz uphalt, bot ugly thereunder;
> Mist muged*b* on the mor, malt*c* on the mountez,
> Uch hille hade a hatte, a myst-hakel*d* huge.
>
> (2079–81)

*a* The clouds were high, *b* lay damp, *c* condensed, *d* cloak of mist.

Such piercing evocations of 'morning-care' and 'winter-care' (expressions used by Anglo-Saxon alliterative poets) set the Adventure of the Green Chapel apart from more routine wonders of Arthur, with their easy heroisms and unresisting landscapes.

Gawain's determination to keep his appointment undergoes one last trial when his guide, stopping him after sunrise on a high hill, warns him of the perils of the place and offers to keep his mouth shut if Gawain chooses to avoid the encounter. The Green Knight acquires, in the guide's account, something of the indiscriminate destructiveness of Death itself – he kills everyone who rides past his Chapel – but Gawain is determined not to be found a 'knyght kowarde', and he rides alone down into the valley of death. The scene *is* a heroic one; yet the valley proves a place of surprises and anti-climaxes, from the moment when Gawain finds, instead of a Green Chapel, only a queer hollow mound by a stream:

> nobot an olde cave,
> Or a crevisse of an olde cragge, [a]he couthe hit noght deme
> with spelle
>
> (2182–4)

There follows, in this desolate and uncanny setting, the return match between Gawain and his adversary, the moment when the hero finally will 'achieve his chance'. The finality is later to prove deceptive; but the poet in the meantime does full justice to the beheading scene, as he did to the corresponding episode in the First Fit. Gawain first hears the sound of the Green Knight sharpening his axe somewhere up in the crags, and then sees him whirling out of a fissure, vaulting the stream on the long handle of his weapon, and striding towards him over the snow. The art lies not only in the unexpected physical details, such as the axe-borne vault, but also in the imaginative adoption of Gawain's point of view, especially when the hero comes at last to the moment when, against all knightly impulse and training, he has to stand still and bow his bared neck for the return blow. He is afraid, though he has behaved as if he is not; and when the Green Knight heaves the axe up, he glances round at it and 'shrinks a little with his shoulders'. The same tension is felt as the Green Knight prepares for a second time to strike, with Gawain

[a] he could not say what it was.

standing rigidly still as if rooted to the spot. And when, at the third stroke, he finally sees the blood from his cut neck gleam on the snow, Gawain's great leap, more than a spear's length, gives expression to his sense of relief. He has survived, and the honour of the Round Table has been vindicated. His adventure is 'achieved'.

In this adventure, however, moments of achievement have a way of being overtaken at once by new developments, as we saw during Gawain's stay at the castle; and here this deep rhythm asserts itself again, and decisively, at a moment when the adventure may appear to be truly over. The immediate aftermath of the return blow is a moment of humorous anti-climax. Finally released from the constraints of the Beheading Game, Gawain springs into a posture of defence; but the Green Knight responds by leaning on his axe and gazing at the hero with a look in which admiration is mixed with a certain affectionate paternal humour. He has an advantage over Gawain which the reader may suspect, but the hero does not; and in the crucial speech which follows (2338–68) he reveals that advantage in his own teasing, casual way. This speech, in fact, places the whole adventure in a quite new light. Obligations and rights under the Beheading Game agreement no longer seem to matter very much. The fact that Gawain has fulfilled those obligations, by turning up on time and submitting to the return blow, is mentioned only casually, earlier; and the Green Knight refers to his own corresponding rights only to dismiss them. He could, he implies, easily have decapitated Gawain, as he was entitled to do under the 'covenant'; but he refrained, for reasons which have nothing to do with the Beheading Game.

The revelation that Gawain's fate depended upon his conduct in the Exchange of Winnings profoundly alters both his and our understanding of the adventure which has just ended. It adds greatly to the moral and human significance of the affair. The Beheading Game, once the Green Knight had survived decapitation, presented a challenge to Gawain's courage and good faith which was only too grimly obvious; and the poet, as we have seen, did full justice to that challenge. He now reveals, however, that the critical challenge to Gawain's 'trawthe' or integrity lay elsewhere, in an episode which was to all appearances no more than an interlude or diversion in the Adventure of the Green Chapel. The Exchange of Winnings, after all, really *was* a Christmas game; and Gawain might well be excused here, as he could not be in the case of the Beheading Game, for failing to realize that his pledge of troth would have to mean what it said. Yet the poem insists that his 'trawthe' is even here – indeed, here above all – at stake.

There is something in this, certainly, of the extravagance and artificiality of chivalric romance. Yet the *Gawain*-poet is no mere casuist of courtly manners. Like his French predecessor, Chrétien de Troyes, he sees in the magic world of romance an image of life itself. The word 'adventure' itself originally means 'that which happens without design', and in the world of adventure apparently accidental events will turn out to be important. Just so, in life, unforeseen consequences can often flow from trifling and unregarded actions – for moral issues do not always present themselves as such. Social life, as the *Gawain*-poet sees it, is itself a kind of adventure, in which the greatest moral challenge can take the most unexpected form. In his account of the pentangle on Gawain's shield, the poet laid particular emphasis upon the fact that, just as each of the five lines in the pentangle touches every other, so the corresponding virtues which make up Gawain's 'trawthe' are all connected one with another: *a* 'uchone halched in other, that non ende hade'. The conclusion of the poem justifies this emphasis, for the Green Knight's revelations display, not only the unity of the poem's plot, but also the unity of the hero's moral experience. His conduct at the castle over Christmas proves to have had an unforeseen bearing upon the outcome of his adventure. Beheading Game and Exchange of Winnings are 'uchone halched in other'; and the very same moral quality, 'trawthe', which the hero displays when he arrives at the Green Chapel on New Year's Day has already been tested in the chambers and halls of the castle during the last three days of the Old Year. 'Trawthe', as the poet expounds it at the beginning of the Second Fit, is a complex thing; but it is not more complex than life itself, as the rest of the poem portrays it.

The events in the last part of the poem follow a conventional course: the Green Knight reveals his true name and explains why Morgan le Fay contrived the adventure, and Gawain rides back to Camelot. Yet the poem ends strangely, too, for it arrives at no

*a* each one joined in to the others, so that none had any end.

settled conclusion about the outcome of the Adventure of the Green Chapel. Bertilak praises Gawain as a pearl among knights and [a]'on the fautlest freke that ever on fote yede'. Yet the epithet 'faultless' loses, in the superlative, its absolute force; and Bertilak concludes his first speech of explanation with the observation that Gawain did, after all, withhold the magic girdle, contrary to his pledged word:

> here yow lakked a lyttel, sir, and [b]lewté yow wonted;
> Bot that watz for no [c]wylyde werke, [d]ne wowyng nauther,
> Bot for ye lufed your lyf; the lasse I yow blame.
>
> (2366–8)

The assessment is eminently fair, even comradely, with its emphasis on the alleviating circumstance; yet we may reflect that to fail, even 'a lyttel', in *lewte* or fidelity can hardly be a trivial matter for the knight of the pentangle.

It is not. Gawain responds to Bertilak's revelations with violent self-reproaches. The fact that he has upheld the collective honour of the Round Table at the Green Chapel is quite lost, for him, in the personal shame of his act of 'trecherye and untrawthe' (his own words) at the castle of Hautdesert. What Bertilak calls 'love of life', he calls 'cowardice'; and he even accuses himself of covetousness, so referring in unsparing terms to the fact that he withheld something which was due to another (an act classified by the manuals of penance under Covetousness). Many modern readers are inclined to take all this, more or less sympathetically, as a first, emotional overreaction on Gawain's part; but the poem hardly justifies a liberal view of his case. His words are less wild than they may appear. The hero gives, in fact, a precise account of what he has done, according to the manner of moral self-analysis then cultivated in the confessional. He employs exactly the same three terms – cowardice, covetousness and untruth – again much later when, after returning to Camelot, he displays the green belt to his companions:

> This is the lathe[e] and the losse that I laght[f] have
> Of couardise and covetyse that I haf caght thare;
> This is the token of untrawthe that I am tan[g] inne.
>
> (2507–9)

---

*a* quite the most faultless man that ever trod ground, *b* your fidelity failed you, *c* fine workmanship, *d* nor wooing either, *e* injury *f* incurred, *g* taken, detected.

'The token of untrawthe' – that phrase is enough in itself to explain and justify Gawain's shame and his remorse; for he had set out from Camelot bearing on his shield the pentangle, described as 'a syngne that Salamon set sumquyle / In bytoknyng of trawthe': 'a sign that Solomon established in days gone by as an *emblem of fidelity*'.

But this poet is fond of unexpected twists. Just as Bertilak stood back and leaned on his axe when Gawain sprang to arms at the Green Chapel, so at Camelot the hero's mortification is met with an unexpectedly friendly response. Arthur 'comforts' Gawain, the whole court laughs, and the Round Table adopts the green belt as a new badge of honour. A reader who has felt the full force of Gawain's self-reproaches may be tempted to discount the court's reaction as immature or frivolous; but that interpretation impoverishes the rich and complex ending. Camelot had not expected to see Gawain again after he set out on his perilous adventure. Now he has returned, having fulfilled the arduous conditions of the Beheading Game and so maintained the 'renoun of the Rounde Table'. Gawain has told them what happened at the castle; but as far as they are concerned, his adventure was the 'chance of the Chapel'. It is right that they should celebrate his success there and the collective glory which he has won. His partial failure in the Exchange of Winnings remains, as it were, a private and uncovenanted matter, arising from developments in the adventure which are no concern of theirs; and it would not be fitting for public pride to yield to private shame.

The reader, however, cannot split things up in this way. The final impression of the adventure is rather one of complex unity. Although the grand orchestral effects of the Green Chapel contrast sharply with the chamber music of the castle, the moral themes are the same in both. Gawain's encounter with the lady, of course, raises issues which play no part in his dealings with her husband; but it is not the subtle chamber conflict between courtesy and 'cleanness' which causes him to slip with her, but that very same fear of death which has haunted him since the Green Knight picked up his head; and the fault itself, 'untrawthe', lies at the heart of those values which Gawain seeks to uphold in his dealings with his adversary. The poet's emblem for those values, the pentangle, asserts that they form an indivisible whole; and the action of the poem itself demonstrates the truth of this. The unforeseeable complexities of life, imaged here in the mysterious world of romance where accidents form themselves into a hidden pattern of adventure, can only be met and mastered by a perfect and uncompromising integrity – something which even Gawain, for all his 'grete trawthe', cannot quite achieve.

## NOTES

1. Erich Auerbach, *Mimesis: The Representation of Reality in Western Literature*, trans. Willard Trask (New York, 1957), 119. This chapter ('The Knight Sets Forth') provides one of the most penetrating discussions of medieval romance. See also Eugène Vinaver, *The Rise of Romance* (Oxford, 1971) and John Stevens, *Medieval Romance: Themes and Approaches* (London, 1973).

2. See the essay on Chrétien de Troyes' *Yvain* by Tony Hunt in the companion volume, *Medieval Literature: The European Inheritance*, gen. ed. Boris Ford (Penguin, 1982).

3. The standard edition is that of J. R. R. Tolkien and E. V. Gordon, very thoroughly revised by Norman Davis (2nd edn, Oxford, 1967). Quotations in this essay are taken from that edition.

# *PEARL*: POETRY AND SUFFERING

IAN ROBINSON

*Pearl* is the least approachable of the fine English poems of the four-teenth century, but well worth the effort.[1] The first obvious difficulty is the language: the same dialect as that of *Sir Gawain and the Green Knight* is used for a far more laborious style of verse.[2] The modern reader has no alternative (the available 'translations' are of use but not an alternative) to a good deal of work with notes and glossary. As to style: the first trap is that the four-beat lines look as if they must be read quickly. By modern standards they have numbers of hypermetrical syllables, and the temptation is to take the verse as a time-metre in which all the unstressed syllables are compressed into similar times. This temptation, I am sure, should be resisted: the verse moves much better if the rhythmic phrasing more than hinted at by the very frequent alliteration is given at least as much say as the four-beat metre. Syllable-count does not come in at all, I think. My advice is to take these lines quite slowly and let the phrases and attendant tones form from the stress-patterns as they would in modern English.[3] This will allow some of the poem's expressive powers to emerge; till when we cannot read or form a judgement.

The second and main difficulty is inherent to the poetry which is, necessarily as I shall argue, rather teasing. But here at least we may hope: with any subtle or teasing poem there is nothing to be done but stay with it and follow it until it gives itself. I think this is not impossible with *Pearl*.

The indirectness appears as soon as we try to state the subject. It is a little untrue to the poem's spirit to say simply that it is an elegiac poem in which a father is reconciled to the death of his young daughter by a vision of her in heaven, for the poem itself refrains from any such simple disclosure of theme. It has in fact been seriously denied that this is the story. One scholar, for instance, could not believe that such fuss could be made over a 'dead baby' and interpreted *Pearl* as about the poet's relations with his own soul.[4] It seems to me that the fuss can be made, if the poet is grasping some sense from his feelings of loss; but, especially for the happy few who read *Pearl* before its Introductions and critics, the sense has to be grasped from a teasingly oblique presentment.

It begins with a use of the curious central image of jewellers and pearls, together with a forceful but still puzzling evocation of the jeweller's grief at the loss of his pearl:

> Perle plesaunte to prynces paye
> To clanly clos in golde so clere
> Oute of oryent I hardyly saye
> Ne proved I never her precios pere
> So rounde so reken in uche araye
> So smal so smothe her sydez were
> Quere so ever I jugged gemmez gaye
> I sette hyr sengeley in synglere
> Allas I leste hyr in on erbere
> Thurgh gresse to grounde hit fro me yot
> I dewyne fordolked of luf daungere
> Of that pryvy perle wythouten spot

> Sythen in that spote hit fro me sprange
> Ofte haf I wayted wyschande that wele
> That wont watz whyle devoyde my wrange
> And heven my happe and al my hele
> That dotz bot thrych my hert thrange
> My breste in bale bot bolne and bele
> Yet thoght me never so swete a sange
> As stylle stounde let to me stele
> For sothe ther fleten to me fele
> To thenke hir color so clad in clot
> O moul thou marrez a myry juele
> My privy perle wythouten spotte

Pearl, delightful for princes' pleasure, chastely set in gold so pure – from the Orient, I boldly say, I never assayed her precious equal. So round, so fresh in every setting, so slender, so smooth her curves were, that wherever I judged gay gems I put her uniquely alone. But oh! I lost her in a grassy plot: through the grass to the ground it fell away from me. I am pining, terribly wounded by the refusal of that special pearl without a spot.

Afterwards, at the spot it sprang from me I have often watched, longing for that wealth which used formerly to purge my evil and lift up my good fortune and make me whole – but which now only pierces my heart, terribly, only makes my breast in torment swell and burn. Yet there seemed to me

never so sweet a song as that still time let steal to me. Truly there floated
to me many, musing on her colour so clothed in clay. O mould, you're
marring a vivid jewel, my special pearl without a spot!

I think any doubts one has about the reality of a loss expressible
in so elaborate a conceit are the same as wondering what exactly
it can mean. To the extent that there is anything here beyond a
jeweller lamenting the loss of a pearl of great price, the hinted human
loss seems to be that of a lover, and to have about it the desperation
of Donne's 'Twickenham Garden'. The 'small, smooth sides' are of
course those of a girl, of the approved courtly style of beauty, as well
as of a pearl, and the poet makes good use of the absence from Middle
English of a neuter possessive pronoun. Although the pearl can be 'it'
the 'sides' have to be 'her' sides. The last lines of the first stanza are
a much plainer evocation of the love of man for woman, though
misinterpreted by E. V. Gordon.[5] The 'luf daungere' can only be
the refusal personified in the *Romaunt of the Rose* as the fierce ruffian
who at a hopeful moment sends the lover about his business. The
Pearl has refused her jeweller's love in the most final way, and he
seems to be pining away because like Arcite in the *Knight's Tale*
he is suffering from the medically recognized malady of Eros. Still
in the second stanza his longing seems to be that of the 'starved lover
... best quitted with disdain'. The loss is expressed in symptoms
straightforwardly physical, very like those of Troilus writhing in
agony as he so often does. The Jeweller's heart just ('but') swells
with trouble.

The violence of feeling turns out to be characteristic of him,
and goes with the poem's intensity of sense-impression – its oddly
sensuous response for instance to the shiningness of heaven. At the
end of this first section the dreamer doesn't just go to sleep, he is
felled by sleep: at line 80 the leaves of the paradisal trees shine *shrilly*
– a word industriously flattened by editors and the NED but which
means what it says.[6] I feel a certain reality in the trouble at the
beginning, and a certain questioning about whether he has hit on
the right image for expressing it. But both in the love-language and
the violent suffering of stanza two all I am sure of is intensity of
feeling. What it means remains to be seen. He seems to have had the
experience but missed the meaning. The physical reality that she
is in the earth is plainly, wryly faced (something of Anglo-Saxon

lyric feeling in 'O moul thou marrez a myry juele') but how can that let a sweet song steal to him? The question must be answered by what is irreplaceably poetry in the poem.

We have as always to distinguish what the poet does from what, perhaps, he only would do if he could. Of course we (I am certainly not excluding myself) feel at a disadvantage because the poem's language is far from ours and its style tricky. Moreover, it is impossible to solve all the problems: there is such scarcity of the dialect that even a lifelong quest for the exact nuances of the words would often fail. There will always be a number of quite unknown words in *Pearl*. I must repeat that I don't think the verse-form improves matters: it tends to increase the obscurity. Defences have been offered of its complication: perhaps it is in itself the discipline of the violence of feeling and perception, the necessary mode of control. I am just not sure. I do suspect that the rhyme-sounds repeated in one case four and in another six times within the twelve-short-line stanza, and the semi-refrain line repeated or varied at the end of each stanza of a section and then as the opening line of the next, together force the poet to push words arbitrarily far. Can *mote* or *date* really be pushed so many ways as the poet must for the sake of his rhyme? I suspect old-fashioned poetic licence: but the dialect is too far off for me to be sure. I am sure that the rhymes on 'segh hit / justyfyet' (698, 700) are too Samuel Butler-like for the context and that the rhymes on 'flot / knot / clot' (786ff.) are too earthy for the Pearl's evocation of heaven.

This however is a hopeful comment: we can sometimes judge. The poem is not so obscure as to prevent us from distinguishing what is alive in it from what is not. Where else can criticism begin?

At first readings there are several moments in *Pearl* when one's ears prick up. The second group of stanzas, with its vision of crystal cliffs – of heaven or earthly paradise – in such contrast with the very-much-this-earth mound of the end of the first section, is startling and compelling. The vision leads with a convincing touch to the gradually dawning recognition of the Pearl girl at the end of Section III. The dream here is more than convention. Already so early in the poem the dreamer is yearning to cross the stream to 'the fyrre londe' (the farther land – haunting phrase!) and it is then that he begins to see her, not leaving behind a certain wryness in his gradual recognition

('I knew hyr wel, I had sen hyr ere'), but with it, with knowing her more and more, expressing something of wonder. But the recognition of wonder makes us, as well as the poet, ask what the vision means, which is as yet not sure.

The dreamer has still not understood what it means that he sees her in the shining land, nor why he cannot come to her (she has to explain that as if *he* were a child of two); and she uses to him a perfectly courtly image of love, a reversal of 'Oh my love's like a red red rose' which limits his love, still, to the order of nature:

> For that thou leste watz bot a rose
> That flowred and fayled as kynde hyt gef.
> (269)

For what you lost was only a rose that bloomed and failed as nature made it.

The second reappearance of the Pearl at the end of the poem is even more compelling, I think, and the dreamer's mad (as he says) effort to get across the stream to her immediately strikes the reader. I will come back to this passage.

On the other hand at least one longish passage is unmistakably uninspired. The vision of the New Jerusalem comes to the dreamer as a sort of uncovenanted reward for good reception of the Pearl's lessons, but the poet fails to make Heaven anything like as visionary as his glimpses of the Pearl. It may be thought that a poet who attempts to depict Heaven is attempting the impossible (and if our poet is indeed indebted to Dante perhaps he is only repeating the failure of the *Paradiso*) but not perhaps by anyone who has recently been inside Suger's Abbey of St Denis, or the Chapter House at Salisbury. Our poet is reduced to a rather relentless list of the precious stones of each successive 'tablement' of the walls; the jewellery imagery becomes a misfortune and we have indeed, as D. H. Lawrence said of the Apocalypse, a 'jeweller's paradise of a new Jerusalem'. The sign of our poet's failure of nerve is his anxiety to rest all the time on the authority of 'the apostle John'. He can't really see Heaven for himself.

We could continue the list of elementary discriminations: but the further we go with them the more insistently they will raise the question what the good things mean, what whole the poet is trying to make.

In one way this is not in doubt.

> Deme Dryghtyn, ever him adyte,
> Of the way a fote ne wyl he wrythe
>
> (349–50)

says the Pearl rather snappishly: Judge the Lord, make all kinds of accusations against him, he still won't turn a foot out of the way. Instead the narrator must [a]'seche hys blythe ful swefte and swythe'. He has to take his great loss as the will of God. But to find mercy, the poet also has to be granted the right ways. He needs also the grace of creation.

What the Jeweller must do for the redemption of his grief is clearly stated in the first section:

> Thagh kynde of Kryst me comfort kenned
> My wreched wylle in wo ay wraghte.
>
> (55–6)

– though the nature of Christ taught him strength, his vile will all the time thrashed about in grief. But to accept the offered strength he has to achieve faith in the love of God even for himself and his beloved child dead before her second birthday: to do that he has to be able to find the right words.

I think it is clear from the beginning that the poet is expressing the pain of a great loss: what is at first unclear is that there is anything beyond quasi-physical pain: without the meaning the experience is not quite complete. The recognition that she is in the earth, for all the artifice of the imagery of jewels and the language of courtly love, is very very plain: the first section is largely devoted to this establishing of the plain physicality of her death. The flowers and spices that grow out of her in the third stanza are very much of this world of nature – later in the poem her beauty is *not* from nature – and

> Ther wonys that worthyly I wot and wene
> My precious perle wythouten spot.
>
> (47–8)

---

*a* look for his mercy as quickly and eagerly as possible.

The mound is where she dwells now, buried in that piece of the external world, almost, like Lucy,

> Roll'd round in earth's diurnal course
> With rocks, and stones, and trees,

so that in the last line of the section the dreamer actually lies 'on' her. The rest of the poem is the effort to see the matter otherwise; so he next has to 'spring from the spot' and leave time and space.

I think the long middle section, in which the Pearl preaches to the poet, is a successful finding of a necessary mode of expression. After his longing and his first glimpse the whole part may seem anticlimatic, and she is certainly without the otherworldly glow the poet manages to give her before and after. The comic intention of her lecturing her old father in a rather schoolmarmish way is surely apparent. He makes three mistakes in the first three things he says, and is duly ticked off; he muddles makelez[a] with maskelez[b] and so on. The tone of what is happening here follows naturally enough from the Anglo-Saxonate wryness of some of the earlier evocations of her (he recognizes her easily, he has seen her before; they meet so seldom now).

I think the point of the rather comic didacticism is to show the dreamer's doubts and pains rising in another form, as doubts and pains do. He has seen her: but then how can what he has seen fit with his common-sense notions of fair play? He turns into a rather pettifogging theologian and asks some silly questions. If she lived less than two years on our earth (483) he is aggrieved she should be made queen the first day in Heaven. The comedy of her answers, using and imitating that of the Gospel parables, shows the simplicity of the truth she offers. Nowadays the Jeweller would have been a negotiator for his union. The parable of the labourers in the vineyard isn't meant to demonstrate that the arrangements in Heaven are fair in trades union terms, but to reject his niggling frame of reference. Beside his rather small questionings she places the overwhelming Christian troth, so commonplace as hardly to be theology at all, that the noble Chief is no niggard because the grace of God is sufficient. (That is one chorus line, 612 etc., admirably placed.) Questions of

---

*a* matchless, *b* spotless.

greater and less are not pursued in His kingdom. In her comic way she is giving the Jeweller an authentic song of innocence; peculiarly appropriate.

'How his audit stands, who knows save heaven?' even Hamlet says about even his father. St Peter's power of binding and loosing, of remitting or retaining sins, did not give the medieval Christian any certainty that his departed loved ones were safe in heaven. There is always the alarming possibility of the other place, or the more hopeful but still alarming prospect of purgatory. Pearl, though, is absolutely secure of salvation, for she is innocent: that is to say, her original sin has been washed away in baptism and her new birth there has not been sullied by post-baptismal sin for she has not attained the age of responsibility for sin. *If* he can believe, he can be certain! She has grown when he sees her – that is right too. The 'dead baby', had she lived, would have grown into a woman and been loved in the terms the dreamer does use: his vision is that she does live, in the love of God.

It remains true that the central section depends for its force on the higher moments that precede and succeed it.

What the dreamer glimpses at first is just the well-known beloved child; moreover, it is she who rescues the poem's Heaven from dullness, not vice versa. The poetry comes back to life quite suddenly when he sees *his* little queen there. At line 1111 we are still in the midst of the unassimilated Apocalyptic imagery. If 'the Lamb' is sanctioned by other tradition, it is still hard to know what to do with the information that he has seven horns of red gold. But the attendant virgins are 'mylde as maydenez seme at mas' and with the return to comparisons with this world, life and sense re-enter the poem. But this must mean the abandonment of any effort at transcendence if that is understood as having no point of contact with this world. The dreamer can only see Heaven as the recognition of his beloved; moreover, he has to bring the meaning of the vision back to the grave-mound, as the sweet song that the still hour lets steal to him.

Yet there is transcendence and the Heaven is truly, poetically Heaven. 'Then saw I there my little queen' (1,147) inevitably stresses *then*, *there* and *my*: but these bits of the personal and the 'this worldly' apply to him as he sees, not to what he sees, beyond space, time and, momentarily, beyond personal craving. Here the teasingness of the jewellery image hints its point: it comes to mean an indirect or flawed expression of love compared with this true sight. The jeweller has lost an uninsured pearl. The love of fathers for daughters can have an element of possessiveness (Lear's first state) but not as necessarily as the love of jewellers for their stock, though that possessiveness may include appreciation and may be thought of as a form of love. Now, when he sees his little queen there, there is momentarily nothing of self in his love. The experience becomes one of Eliot's (Kierkegaardian) moments, an intersection of the timeless with time. The vision is our jeweller's redemption and makes a new man of him. But he is still a man in this world and only human. The consequence of seeing his little queen is humanly inevitable. How can he not long to join her, even though the vision is of her irretrievable removal from him? The immediate humanizing of the tone, after New Jerusalem, is right:

> [a]'Lorde much of mirthe watz that ho made
> Among her ferez that watz so quyt.
>
> (1149)

This is the alienation of the parent who with a pang in his delight sees his child wholly absorbed in play with others; the 'luf-longyng' is still that of man for woman, both feelings of this world, of the human self.

The longing and the thoughts of heaven go together for this poet. Inevitably the love-longing brings him hard up against the will of God. [b]'Hit watz not at my Prynces paye' that he should rejoin his pearl: she is in Heaven and he in earth. But how can he not long to be with her to the extent that he is a man and his love human? What is the point of saying 'Thy will be done' unless our will is in conflict?

The narrator himself calls this longing to join the Pearl madness and he is rebuked for it by several commentators as well as by the Pearl herself earlier in the poem. He is punished by being suddenly awoken from his vision and finding himself back once more on the

---

*a* Lord! how merry she made, so white among her companions, *b* it was not to my prince's pleasure.

Pearl's grave-mound – after the high requiem once more, so to speak, on the sod.

I do not wish to rebuke him, though it is right that he should rebuke himself. But that rebuke is no more the whole story than the moral Wordsworth extracts at the end is the whole story of 'Resolution and Independence'.

What *Pearl* really creates, the true poetry, is a repetition of an experience the dreamer cannot pass beyond: two climaxes which illustrate not development but the fixity of necessary conditions. In his grief he is granted a vision of the beloved in Heaven; he recognizes the well-known face in that new setting. For all the effort of instruction and description the second climax only repeats the first, more strongly: he again sees his little girl in Heaven, again longs to reach her and is again refused by what Carlyle would have called 'eternal Fact'.

The dreamer must want the perfect, angelic conformity to the divine will as peace (as at line 1190): he is twice granted by grace momentarily to attain this state of the pure vision of the beloved free from desire. But only as the attainment is momentary, as he is still a man, subject to human desire.

*Patience*, the 'voluntary acceptance of inevitable evil', as Peter Winch calls it, is the great theme of the poetry of the age of Chaucer, in *Sir Gawain and the Green Knight*, time and again in *Piers Plowman*, in the *Knight's Tale* and the *Clerk's Tale*. In this last Chaucer too shows, very poignantly, the impossibility in human terms of the demand made upon Griselda.[8] The loss of beloved children is not to grieve us at all if it be the will of God. But Griselda's patience can only be good, only a true submission, if her 'not grieveth me at all' is extracted from deep grief.

More is necessary to the success of *Pearl* than the girl's teaching. That is necessary, but without the suffering the question of patience would not arise: if the suffering were surmounted to the point of not being suffering, if the poet had rested happily in his glimpse of the New Jerusalem and lost sight of his little queen, he would not have seen his love transmuted by grace, he would have killed it. His reward for offering his Pearl and his grief up to God is at last the cure of suffering, not just by going past it as we do in life, but in being able to report that God is a 'frende ful fyin'. This is unecstatic but faithful, which I think is right. He cannot escape from this world into his visions, and if he could have done he would not have been better.

These elements, then, contribute to the chancy but genuine success of *Pearl*: the irreplaceable experience of loss, the Christian ideas, and the poetic power to bring them truly together. Without all, none. I think the real explanation for the difficulty of this poem is that it is necessary. Without it we miss something of what Lawrence called our 'fulfilment in the past'. In all its trickiness *Pearl* says something we do not hear with quite the same purity elsewhere in English.

## NOTES

I quote the text of *Pearl* as printed in the anthology accompanying this volume, but without modern editorial punctuation. A prose paraphrase of the whole poem which sometimes differs from my glosses can also be found in the anthology.

1. I am grateful, as with all my work on Chaucer and his contemporaries, for substantial help from Mr David Sims, who differs, however, from my adverse criticisms of the *Pearl*'s versification.

2. The consensus that all four poems of MS. Cotton Nero A.x. are by the same author – a view that originated in a cataloguing error in the British Museum – has been definitively criticized in a dissertation by Mrs Anne Samson (University of Wales, 1970).

3. On the rhythmic habits of Middle English cf. my *Chaucer's Prosody* (London, 1971).

4. Sr Mary Madeleva, *Pearl, A Study in Spiritual Dryness* (New York, 1925).

5. *Pearl*, ed. E. V. Gordon (Oxford, 1953). 'I am pining away, grievously wounded, through the power of my love for my own pearl,' Gordon translates. The *daungere* can only be hers to him. *Daungere* can mean 'power' but here certainly has its ordinary courtly-love sense.

6. 'Clearly, brightly', says *NED*, but cites no other instance!

7. I am much indebted to Robert Marchant's *Principles of Wordsworth's Poetry* (Swansea, 1975) and its demonstration that the attitude of the whole poem to the Leech Gatherer differs from that of the poet.

8. I discuss this in my *Chaucer and the English Tradition* (London, 1971).

# DREAM-POEMS

A. C. SPEARING

The dream-poem was one of the most popular and long-lasting of medieval literary forms. It was attempted by virtually every major English and Scottish poet from Chaucer to Gavin Douglas, and there are also many anonymous examples. We might feel tempted to attribute its popularity to that deep orientation towards the ideal that characterizes medieval culture, or to a natural wish to escape momentarily from a world of pain, labour, plague and famine to a pleasanter realm of imagination. There would be some truth in those explanations, but the whole truth is more complicated. The origins of medieval dream-poetry lie in the remote past when, as in 'primitive' cultures today, poets were seers who in prophetic ecstasy saw and told of the other world. In classical times prophetic visions were recounted by Plato, Cicero, and others. In the Old Testament God speaks to his prophets in dreams and visions; in the New Testament St Paul is 'caught up into paradise', and the Bible ends with St John the Divine's vision of the other world and the end of this. Otherworld visions recur in the succeeding centuries; one common type is a vision of Heaven and hell from which the visionary brings back doctrines taught by 'a parent, or a pious or revered man, or a priest, or even a god' (as Macrobius wrote in his influential fifth-century commentary on Cicero's *Dream of Scipio*). Doubtless some writers really had dreams of this type, *oracula* in which they were taught by a father- or mother-figure; but soon the *oraculum* became an established literary form, in which instruction was cloaked in the authority of vision. A further development occurred with the rise of courtly literature from the twelfth century onwards: the courtly cult of secular love produced fictional visions where the place visited was a secular pseudo-paradise, a walled garden of Cupid inhabited by mythological and personified figures, and the doctrine was an erotic pseudo-theology. The key example is the thirteenth-century *Roman de la Rose* of Guillaume de Lorris and Jean de Meung. This most widely influential of all dream-poems was translated by Chaucer, and a part of his version survives.

In the light of this history, it might be supposed that the purpose of a dream-framework would always be to confer supernatural or quasi-supernatural authority on its contents. Sometimes this is so, but we must also take account of the fact that the Middle Ages had a keen interest in dreams of all kinds, and that theorists divided dreams into various categories, not all of which were of supernatural origin. Besides the *oraculum* and other types of inspired dream, Macrobius mentions the *insomnium*, or anxiety-dream, and the *visum*, or hallucination seen in drowsiness. By Chaucer's time there was widespread agreement on a rough division of dreams into *somnia naturalia*, with physical causes such as indigestion or a disturbance of the humours; *somnia animalia*, caused by the preoccupations of the waking mind; and *somnia coelestia*, with supernatural causes.[1] It was hard to tell to which category any particular dream belonged, and this uncertainty was of value to the creators of literary dreams. From the fourteenth century onwards, poets began to ponder the uncertain nature of their own work as producers of imaginative fictions; and fictions could be seen as sharing the dubious status of dreams. Like a dream, a fiction is not literally true, yet neither is it simply a lie; and poems and dreams were both products of *vis imaginativa*, the image-making faculty of the mind.

The earliest English dream-poems of any substance date from the 1350s or 1360s, and by this time the dream-framework is a well-established literary convention in French. It has many uses, but it is always a first-person narrative, and it tends to frame experiences that could not occur in normal waking life – visions of the world beyond death, encounters with the dead, or meetings with personified, allegorical, mythological, or symbolic beings. Even if contents of these kinds were thought to possess a higher degree of reality than men's everyday lives, still they existed for the mind only, detached from the waking world men shared with their neighbours. Much medieval literature contains such material, but not all such literature is framed in dreams. Thus in *Summer Sunday*[2] the narrator goes hunting, then wanders off alone and has a vision of Fortune and her wheel. This would be appropriate material for a dream, but we are not told that he is dreaming. The dream-framework is only an option, and its effect when used is not to establish a separate genre, but to make possible a sharper consciousness of the fictionality of a certain type of literary fiction – its existence as something made, not a part of the natural world.

In this brief survey I can give only a sample of some different types of Middle English dream-poem. I begin with one that, for all its sophistication of technique, remains close to the authoritative vision of earlier times. This is *Pearl*, a poem found in the same manuscript as *Gawain and the Green Knight* and generally attributed to the same poet writing in the latter half of the fourteenth century. It is discussed more fully elsewhere in this volume; I consider it here only as a literary vision. Its narrator, a jeweller lamenting the loss of a precious pearl, falls asleep and is carried in spirit to the other world. There, in a brilliantly glittering landscape, he sees, beyond a river, a maiden dressed in pearls, who is the pearl he has lost. As the poem's complex symbolism unfolds itself, it emerges that the narrator is a father mourning the death of his infant daughter, and that the pearl-maiden is that daughter, now one of the Brides of the Lamb seen by St John in Revelation 14. There is no question as to the dream's status: it is a 'veray avysyoun', and the dreamer sees the heavenly city across the river just 'As devysez[a] hit the apostel John'. Like John in Revelation, but unlike Paul in Corinthians, he knows that while 'dreaming' he was out of the body, for

> Hade bodyly burne[b] abiden that bone[c],
> Thagh alle clerkes hym hade in cure[d],
> His lyf were loste anunder mone[e].
>
> (1090–92)

His experience is in fact a mystical vision, only metaphorically a dream: 'he sleeps and sees a dream who, through ecstasy of the mind, rises into the contemplation of divine things' (Richard of Saint-Victor, *De Eruditione Hominis Interioris*). The heavenly Jerusalem of his vision is no literal city but is the mystic's goal, for, as the poet's contemporary Walter Hilton explains, 'Jerusalem ... betokeneth contemplation in perfect love of God'. Though the poem is a fiction, within it no question arises as to the truth of its content.

*a* describes, *b* man, *c* favour, *d* under their care, *e* beneath the moon (i.e. on earth).

*Pearl*, however, does not merely invite us to escape into a world of happiness beyond death; rather it conveys a strenuous tension between the earthly and the heavenly. In one sense the dream is an *oraculum*, intended to teach that a child dying in infancy can justly receive the fulness of heavenly reward. Yet it is an inverted *oraculum*, for the child is instructor, and her father her pupil. The father feels the unnaturalness of this, and takes into the heavenly world an earthly jeweller's scepticism and materialism. Repeatedly he fails to understand or believe what his daughter tells him, and he ends by attempting to swim across the river-barrier to join her in the heavenly Jerusalem, thereby bringing his vision to an untimely halt. In the closing stanzas he regrets his folly, and commits his pearl, now lost for a second time, to Christ. The poem, concluding not with joy but with sad acquiescence in human limitation, leaves us with a renewed sense of the gap between earthly and heavenly values.

*Pearl* is unique in the wholeheartedness with which it defines dream as 'veray avysyoun', but there are many dream-poems that glance obliquely at their visionary origins. In the *House of Fame* Chaucer's dreamer is a burlesque St Paul, saying, as he is carried precariously through the heavens by an eagle,

> Y wot wel y am here;
> But wher*a* in body or in gost
> I not*b*, ywys; but God, thou wost!
> (980–82)

Dunbar (*c.* 1460–*c.* 1520) has a dream-poem in which St Francis urges him to become a friar; but when Dunbar refuses, on the grounds that friars are flatterers rather than saints, the alleged saint 'vaneist away with stynk and fyrie smowk' and the supposed *oraculum* reveals itself as a diabolic illusion.

Another poem of Dunbar's, *The Thrissill and the Rois*, offers a secular parallel to *Pearl*, evoking an ideal vision but also acknowledging the gap between the ideal and the everyday. It celebrates the wedding in 1503 of James IV of Scotland to the English princess, Margaret Tudor, and the world it discloses is one of harmonious order and beauty. In a paradisal garden, Dame Nature summons a gathering of the birds, beasts, and plants. She crowns the lion king

*a* whether, *b* do not know.

of beasts, raising him into the rampant posture of the lion in the Scottish royal arms. Then she crowns the eagle king of birds, and the thistle king of plants. All three kings symbolize James, and each is to sustain the hierarchy of species within its kingdom. Nature also crowns 'the fresche Ros of cullour reid and quhyt[a]' – the Tudor rose, symbolizing the English princess – and unites her with the thistle, while all the birds sing in her praise. In this dream-world of heraldry and neo-Platonic allegory, personal union and political concord are seen as aspects of a natural order which finds its fullest expression in music.

A parallel might be drawn with the wedding masque *Hymenaei* created by Jonson for another Stuart court a century later, or with the betrothal masque in Shakespeare's *Tempest*. By framing his vision in a dream, Dunbar gains an effect equivalent to Prospero's dismissal of the *Tempest* masque as an 'insubstantial pageant'. From the very beginning Dunbar admits that his dream-world is a fictional artifice. As he lies sleeping, May comes to urge him to write something in her honour; his immediate reaction is to refuse, because the real Scottish May is quite unlike the May of literary convention:

> 'Quhairto[b],' quod I, 'sall I uprys at morrow,
> For in this May few birdis herd I sing?
> Thai haif moir caus to wepe and plane[c] thair sorrow!
> Thy air it is nocht holsum nor benyng;
> Lord Eolus dois in thy sesson[d] ring[e] ...'

> (29–33)

Having vigorously protested, he nevertheless proceeds with the visionary celebration; yet even there we are kept aware of the precarious foundations of the harmony celebrated. Nature has to command Neptune and Aeolus 'Nocht to perturb the wattir nor the air', and she warns the thistle not to let any 'nettil vyle and full of vyce' or 'wyld weid' rise above its proper place. James IV was a notorious philanderer, and the nettles and weeds must symbolize his mistresses. Even the song of the birds is not only music but noise, a 'schout' that breaks the dream. The dream offers a glimpse of the ideal, but the poem wryly admits the distance between that ideal and our daily waking world.

*a* white, *b* what purpose, *c* lament, *d* season, *e* reign.

I now turn to a different type of dream-poem, in which the dream-world is no paradise, but this world seen with deeper insight. An early example is *Winner and Waster*, an alliterative poem of about 1350–70,[3] whose narrator has a dream in which 'Me thoghte I was in the werlde, I ne wiste[a] in whate ende'. He sees two armies drawn up to fight; but the king sends a knight to summon their leaders before him. They are Winner and Waster, personifications of the two great forces seen by the poet as underlying the economic activity of his time – gathering possessions and spending them. In place of the threatened battle, these two engage in a disputation – a matter not of graphs and statistics, as in a modern economic analysis, but of graphically descriptive satire, in which the concreteness and muscularity of the alliterative style are used to their fullest extent. Winner sees Waster's life as a matter of lands uncultivated, tools sold, fallen dovehouses, dried-up pools; while Waster sees Winner's as accumulation for its own sake, benefiting neither the possessor nor the poor –

> . . . wyde howses full of wolle-sakkes, –
> The bemes benden at the rofe, siche bakone there hynges[b],
> 'Stuffed are sterlynges undere stelen bowndes.
>
> (250–52)

Economic issues are considered not with 'scientific' objectivity, but in relation to moral and religious values. Waster assures Winner that, since his expenditure feeds the poor, 'It es plesynge to the Prynce that paradyse wroghte', while Winner expresses his horror at the extravagance of Waster's table by the brilliant incongruity of comparing it with a jewelled cross:

> To see the borde overbrade[d] with blasande dishes,
> [e]Als it were a rayled rode with rynges and stones!
>
> (342–3)

The poem's conclusion is missing, though probably little has been lost. There can be no victory for either of the two complementary tendencies; instead the king sends each to its appropriate place. Winner is to lie in silk sheets among the avaricious cardinals at Rome, while Waster is to encourage the extravagance of London's shopping

---

*a* knew, *b* hangs, *c* silver coins are crammed into a steel-bound chest, *d* overspread, *e* as if it were a cross bejewelled.

streets. In a sense, the two abstractions have changed places, for instead of being examples of two ways of life, they become patrons of those who follow such ways; but this change only serves to emphasize their mutual dependence, for 'Whoso wele*a* schal wyn, a wastour moste he fynde'. The dream offers no solution, only an acute analysis of the way things are.

There are several other alliterative dream-poems belonging to the same tradition as *Winner and Waster*, among them *The Parliament of the Three Ages*, *Mum and the Sothsegger*, *Death and Life*, and *Piers Plowman*. The last is justly the most famous; here I consider it only briefly as a dream-poem. It seems likely that when Langland (b. *c.* 1330) began writing the A Text of *Piers Plowman*, he intended a work similar in kind to *Winner and Waster*: a vision of England, in which problems of economic morality would be enacted by personified abstractions beneath the unchallenged authority of a king. From the beginning, however, Langland's work has a larger scope: his dreamer has Lady Holychurch as guide, and he wishes to know 'How I may saven my soule'.[4] This very largeness of scope leads to fragmentation; alone among dream-poems, *Piers Plowman* consists of a series of dreams, separated by intervals in which we glimpse the dreamer's waking life. It is not an autobiography, but it is a poem made out of the poet's life, rewritten in successive versions as new inner experience challenges what seemed fixed, until eventually it has the intriguing density of a palimpsest. The dreams have a genuinely dreamlike fluidity and fragmentariness, and the poem's turning-points – scenes such as Piers's tearing of the pardon, and the vision in which he knocks down the fruit from the Tree of Charity and thereby sets off the Annunciation – have an authentically visionary effect. It is easy to believe that, rather than constructing allegories to express preconceived ideas, Langland really had visions which were not fully susceptible of rational analysis. The deepest mystery is the figure of Piers himself, the symbol of the means by which man can achieve divine grace. Taking on a variety of forms (ploughman, overseer, Humanity of Christ, ideal Pope), ever more urgently desired as the poem proceeds, enigmatically appearing and disappearing, Piers is concrete yet elusive in a way that reminds us

*a* wealth.

why medieval mystics wrote of contemplation as dreaming.

In *Winner and Waster* the dreamer was no more than an observer. In *Piers Plowman* he is from the first a questioner and a seeker. Like the author, he is called Will, and even in the A Text he is as deeply implicated in the subject-matter of his visions as a real dreamer in his own dreams. Repentance, urging the Sins to confess, 'made Wil to wepe watir with his eiyen'. The dreamer-poet knows that he too is a sinner, and this knowledge means that the poem cannot remain, like *Winner and Waster*, a satire. At first Langland seems to have been unprepared to pursue the consequences of his own insight, and the A Text ends untidily, brought to a halt by the poet's doubts. A vision aiming at intellectual clarity has disintegrated into nightmarish confusion.

When he revised his work, some dozen years later, Langland seems to have recognized that he could proceed only by incorporating his own life more directly into the poem. It must be not an objective but a reflexive vision, explicitly calling in question the position of the poet and focusing on his own doubts and difficulties in continuing his work. After revising A, Langland added two passus (B Text, XI–XII) which look back over his own life. After Scripture has reminded him of the need for self-knowledge, he falls into an inner vision in which he is assured that he is justified in satirizing known abuses, but is so shamed by a reminder from Reason of his impatience and imperfection that he wakes, wishing that he had slept longer. Next Ymagynatyf (*vis imaginativa*, the faculty responsible for memory as well as for dreams and poems) questions him sharply for writing poetry when he might pray:

> ... thow medlest thee with makynges[a] – and myghtest go seye thi Sauter[b],
> And bidde[c] for hem that yyveth[d] thee breed ...
>
> (B Text, XII, 16–17)

He has no satisfactory answer, but only by exposing such self-doubt can he proceed beyond the impasse of A. By looking back over his past with Ymagynatyf's aid, Will is able to acquire the self-knowledge which is the condition of his moving forward. The climax of the B Text comes with his vision of the Crucifixion and Harrow-

---

*a* poetic compositions, *b* Psalter, *c* pray, *d* give.

ing of Hell, a true *somnium coeleste* at the end of which he wakes to the ringing of Easter bells: dream and reality are one. But Langland's tough honesty does not permit the poem to end here; it plunges deeper into nightmare, with a vision of the corruption of the Church, the ageing of Will, and the imminent triumph of Antichrist. The B and C Texts both end with a new beginning: a final quest for Piers and divine grace by the individual Conscience, unaided by the institutional Church.

Langland was driven to innovation by powerful inner forces; Chaucer, always an experimentalist, was fascinated by the dream-form itself and used it differently in each of his four dream-poems. Passages throughout his work indicate his interest in medieval dream-psychology: even the cock and hen of the *Nun's Priest's Tale* quarrel about whether dreams are prophetic or merely symptoms of an imbalance of the humours. His first experiment is the *Book of the Duchess*, a poem commemorating the death of John of Gaunt's first wife, Blanche, in 1368. He begins by presenting himself in the traditional courtly role of unhappy lover. Sick with melancholy, he cannot sleep, and passes the night by reading a tale from Ovid. In it, after Ceyx is drowned, his wife Alcyone prays to the gods to send her a dream to disclose his fate. They do so, Ceyx himself appears to tell of his death, and she dies of grief. The narrator is moved by this tale, and excited by the thought that he too could gain sleep by praying to the gods. Vowing a feather-bed to Juno and Morpheus, he at once falls asleep. He dreams that on a May morning he hears the noise of a hunt. He goes out to join it, learns that a hart is being hunted, follows a puppy into the forest, and there finds a knight in black lamenting the loss of his lady. The main part of the dream consists of a dialogue between the dreamer and the mourning knight, in which the latter tells of his love for his lady, 'goode faire White'. The dreamer persistently misunderstands the nature of his loss, until eventually he says plainly, 'She ys ded'. At this we are told that the hart-hunt is over, the knight rides back to his castle, and the narrator wakes with his book in his hand.

The lengthy prologue to the dream serves to attach it to waking life by an intricate variety of threads. The narrator is suffering from melancholy, the black humour which causes 'sorwful ymagynacioun' and 'fantasies'; it is therefore natural that he should dream of a black knight. The dream may thus be seen as a *somnium naturale*. However, it also functions as a *somnium animale*, which reflects the dreamer's waking preoccupations. His melancholy is provoked by unrequited love; he therefore dreams of an unhappy lover, a grander version of himself; and his stubborn inability to grasp that the knight's loss is caused by death surely derives from his obsession with his own cause of grief, rejection by his lady. Moreover, his last waking thoughts were of the Ovidian story, and this reappears in his dream in an inverted form, with the wife mourning her husband transformed into the knight mourning his lady. However, this connection of the dream with the story also suggests that the dream may be a *somnium coeleste*. Alcyone's dream had a divine origin; the Chaucerian narrator imitates her prayer, and his dream immediately follows. We are not meant to take seriously the Christian narrator's prayer to pagan gods, but it does work; moreover, like Alcyone's, the dream reveals a truth. As dreams do, it requires interpretation: it is an allegory, in which the black knight represents John of Gaunt and 'good faire White' is Blanche, the duchess who was really dead.

In the *Book of the Duchess*, then, the connection between waking life and dream can be explained in three different ways. The explanations merge at times, clash at others: the black knight, for example, illustrates what Freud would call 'condensation', symbolizing both John of Gaunt and the melancholy dreamer. What does Chaucer gain by this multiplication of possibilities? One gain is the pleasure of structural intricacy. From a study of the subtle cohesiveness that underlies the superficial incoherence of real dreams, Chaucer learned a new way of making poems. Thus the apparently divergent motif of the hunt becomes a metaphor of the dreamer's quest for the cause of the knight's grief; and once 'She ys ded' has been spoken, the hunt is over. Even small details are used to connect different parts of the poem: the horn blown by Juno's messenger to wake the sleepy Morpheus reappears in the dream to mark the different stages of the hunt.

A second gain from the multiple interpretation of the dream is one of tact. John of Gaunt doubtless did mourn Blanche, yet for a man so important marriage could not be only a matter of personal feeling, and negotiations for his second marriage began almost immediately. Who was the young Chaucer either to offer him sympathy

or to suggest that he could escape from melancholy only by acknowledging the fact of death? A dream provided neutral territory
for an encounter between two men separated by social rank, and
it could avoid giving offence because it could always be repudiated
as mere fantasy. For a medieval poem about death, the *Book* is
strikingly secular: the consolation offered is not the promise of
heavenly reunion, but only the recollection of past happiness; and
this too was tactful if a second marriage was imminent.

A last gain lay in the equation 'dream equals poem' implied by
the *Book*'s closing line: 'This was my sweven; now hit ys doon'. Like
dreams, poems have their origins somewhere outside the rational
mind: we would say, in the unconscious mind, that 'derke valeye'
from which Juno's messenger summons up the dream-image of the
dead Ceyx. In a period that valued rationality highly, fictions of
such dubious origin could best be admitted if identified with dreams,
strangely charged with meaning and yet of uncertain status, precariously balanced between prophetic vision and personal fantasy.

Two of Chaucer's later dream-poems are more directly concerned
with poetry itself. The *House of Fame*, a hair-raisingly centrifugal
work, not surprisingly left unfinished, is concerned on one level with
the dependence of the 'tidynges' that form the subject-matter of
literature on the arbitrariness of fame and rumour. On another level,
it can be read as Chaucer's meditation on his own work as a poet
who had become dissatisfied with merely derivative writing about
love, and was excited by, yet unable to take quite seriously, a new
and higher conception of the poet as inspired prophet, gained from
reading Dante. Many late-medieval dream-poems are written under
Chaucerian influence, and among those that recognizably derive
from the *House of Fame* and its concern with the poetic vocation
Skelton's *Garland of Laurel* deserves special mention. This strange late
Gothic or early Renaissance masterpiece articulates Skelton's sense
of his relation to an English poetic tradition springing from Chaucer
and to a larger classical and European tradition to which Chaucer
first dared to attach writing in English. The dream leads up to the
crowning of Skelton with a laurel garland made by his patroness,
the Countess of Surrey, and her ladies; but the 'laurel' which is then
praised by Chaucer, Gower and Lydgate as 'the goodlyest / That
ever they saw, and wrought it was the best' is also the poem recounting

the dream, which itself constitutes Skelton's final claim to laureate fame.

Chaucer's next dream-poem, the *Parliament of Fowls*, will not be discussed here. It is a meditation on the varieties of love, in which philosophical concepts are translated into the concrete imagery of dreams, and it has a structural intricacy comparable to that of the *Book of the Duchess*. It too had many late-medieval offspring, Dunbar's *The Thrissill and the Rois* among them. Chaucer's final dream-poem, the *Prologue* to the *Legend of Good Women*, on which he was still working in his last decade, once more focuses on the poetic vocation, with a beguiling mixture of comedy and seriousness. The dreamer who, while performing Maytime devotions to the daisy, is carried in sleep to a courtly paradise where he meets the God of Love and a lady who is a transfigured daisy, is the author of Chaucer's poems. Indeed, Cupid scolds him for having written against the religion of love by impugning the fidelity of women. The lady, Alcestis, defends him by saying that his works were only translations, which he wrote 'Of innocence, and *a*nyste what he seyde'; but his penance is to write the collection of legends of Cupid's saints which the dream prefaces. A eulogy of the daisy before the dream begins has an unusual fervour: it is the only light of the poet's world, 'The maistresse of my wit', to whom his voice is as obedient as a harp to the harpist. In all Chaucer's work, this is the passage which speaks most openly of his inspiration or muse, the force outside himself that makes him a poet, and that is personified in his dream as Alcestis. She, by dying, rescued her husband from death's power. Poetry has the same ability to recall the dead, as the actual legends testify; but it can do so only in the insubstantial form of words, dream-images such as that of Ceyx in the *Book of the Duchess*.

Chaucer's use of the dream-prologue also proved influential on later poets, especially in Scotland. Its obvious function is to account for the existence of a literary work by introducing the inspiration or authority that caused it to be written. Henryson's (*c.* 1425–*c.* 1500?) *Moral Fables* purport to be translated from Aesop; the central fable is framed in an *oraculum* in which Aesop himself appears to the narrator. He is an impressive figure, this 'pious or revered man'

*a* did not know.

dressed as an antique poet, and the effect of the dream is not only to give the *Fables* authority but to express doubts that Henryson may really have felt about the moral justification of his work. Aesop is reluctant to agree to the narrator's request to tell a story, for in these godless days

> ... quhat is it worth to tell ane fenyeit*a* taill,
> Quhen haly preiching may nathing availl?
> (1389–90)

He nevertheless tells the fable of the Lion and the Mouse, followed by its *moralitas*; then, with a prayer that 'king and lord' may take in its implications and put them into effect, he vanishes and the dreamer wakes. As we have come to expect, the dream-framework is used to discuss the poetic fiction itself, and in doing so to convey its essential ambiguity: authoritative yet fragile, true yet impossible, fantasy yet vision.

## NOTES

1. See W. C. Curry, *Chaucer and the Mediaeval Sciences* (London, 1960), 2nd edn ch. 8. For a classification of this type known to Chaucer, see Robert A. Pratt, 'Some Latin Sources of the Nonnes Preest on Dreams', *Speculum*, 52 (1977), 538–70.

2. Ed. R. H. Robbins, *Historical Poems of the XIVth and XVth Centuries* (New York, 1959), 98–102.

3. *Winner and Waster* has traditionally been dated 1352–3. Elizabeth Salter, 'The Timeliness of *Winner and Waster*', *Medium Aevum*, 47 (1978), argues convincingly for being less specific, but an early date remains probable.

4. I quote the A Text from the edition of George Kane (London, 1960), and the B Text from that of A. V. C. Schmidt (London, 1978).

*a* fictional.

# MEDIEVAL LYRICS AND MUSIC

## JOHN STEVENS

Some fifty years ago a historian at King's College, Cambridge, was preparing some medieval charters for inspection. The charters related to the privileges of a small cell of Cluniac monks, the Priory of St James by Exeter. One of them contained a finely written contemporary copy of a Papal bull dated 1199. Turning the parchment roll over, the searcher, John Saltmarsh, noticed on its back some words in the vernacular and scribbled musical notes.[1] The words turned out to be an English love-poem of the thirteenth century:

> Bryd one brere, brid, brid one brere!
>   <sup>a</sup>kynd is come of love, love to crave.
> blithful biryd on me thu rewe,
>     or <sup>b</sup>greyth, lef, greith thu me my grave.

> 2. <sup>c</sup>Hic am so blithe so bryhit brid on brere
>     quan I se that hende in halle.
> yhe is quit of lime, loveli, trewe,
>     yhe is fayr, and flur of alle.

> 3. <sup>d</sup>Mikte hic hire at wille haven,
>     stedfast of love, loveli, trewe,
>   of mi sorwe yhe may me saven;
>     <sup>e</sup>joye and blisse were eere me newe.

The melody is written out once – for the words of the first verse. The words of verses 2 and 3 follow on, written (as is quite normal) as prose.

This little song raises a number of problems and it is as well to be aware of them before attempting to comment on the poem. First of all, what is the song? Can we rely on the text before us? To judge from the published versions of it, the answer is no. The scribe who

---

*a* nature has come of (God's creative) love and demands love in return, *b* prepare, my love, prepare my grave for me, *c* I am as happy as a beautiful bird on a briar / when I see that gracious (lady) .../ she is white of limb ..., *d* if I might have her, ..., *e* joy and bliss would ever be renewed in me.

Bryd o-nē bre-rē, brid, brid onē bre-rē

2 Kynd is co-me of love, love to cra-vē

3 Blith-ful biryd, on me thu re-wē

4 Or greyth, lef, greyth thu me—my gra-vē

jotted it down so casually does not seem to have distinguished
properly between *d* and þ (= th) in *greith*, for example. And he did
not bother to rule his stave-lines; he drew them by eye. According
to some editors, he did not understand the metre he was writing
in, nor did he notice that he had made an error of clef in the second
line of the melody. Another problem arises from our modern system
of punctuation. We cannot remind ourselves too often that almost
all the medieval texts we have, have been punctuated for us by their
editors. So, in the first line of the second verse we have to choose
between 'Hic am so blithe, so bryhit, brid on brere', 'I am so happy,
so resplendently happy (?), o bird on the briar', and the line without
commas, which means 'I am as happy as a beautiful bird ...' (the
preferred reading in my view). The difference is a rhythmical one,
as well as one of plain sense. In brief, medieval lyrics do not grow
in neatly printed books arranged in lines and stanzas with full-stops,
commas and the rest. They have to be edited. And every edition
is an interpretation.

Another problem which 'Bryd one brere' presents to us is its lack
of context. It must presumably have been written down (from
memory? from a copy? in the act of composition itself?) whilst the
charter was in the keeping of the Priory of St James. But why? The
back of a finely written official document hardly seems the natural
place to copy out a song which you expected to sing or encourage
someone else to. And again, if the author or copyist was a member
of this small community of monks, on what sort of occasion did
he expect to make use of it? (This question is not otiose; most
medieval lyrics, and longer poems too, served a social purpose.)

To these questions we have no answers. In the end we are left face to face with the text – words and, in this rare case, music. The first impression the poem makes is one of freshness and spontaneity. There is an emotional force in the repetition of the key-phrase 'bryd one brere', of 'love, love', of 'greyth, lef, gryith' – an effect lightly echoed by other alliterative phrases 'hende in halle', 'lime, loveli', 'love, loveli'. The freshness is real; but at the same time there is a sophistication in the poem, a selfconscious awareness of other ways of saying things. The association of the 'bird' with love is of course an age-old one; 'notes swete of nyhtegales' all too often accompany the happy loves of spring and the 'lenten' (lengthening of days) that comes 'with love to toune'. In the English of the thirteenth century this association is all the more natural because the word for bird (bryd, brid) is virtually a homonym (that is, makes the same sound) with the word for maiden (burde). To what extent the writer of this song regarded himself as playing on two different words, and to what extent he was just using similar sound and associated meaning in an unselfconscious way, it is not easy to say.

The line that follows is also elusive in meaning but tends to support the idea that the poet was no naïve versifier. 'Kynd' (the creative force that runs through the universe) has come from 'love' (? love, God's love for his creation) 'love to crave' (to ask for, demand, love, i.e. from the lover and his lady, whose duty it is to obey the dictates of nature). These are common medieval concepts, much used by Chaucer, for instance (see his *Parliament of Fowls* and *Troilus*); but perhaps they are rather too lofty for this song? The line will certainly bear a simpler interpretation. If we punctuate it with a single comma after 'come', it then means 'Nature (the creative force) has come (? with the spring) to ask for love of Love (the goddess of love, or simply his lady-love?)'. But this reading, too, involves a certain pretentiousness – it is not quite natural to refer to the lady baldly as 'love' – and is less interesting. After this the meanings and verbal associations become clearer. The physicality of the 'grave' is reminiscent of folk-song; courtly lovers tend to talk more abstractly of their inevitable death. Other phrases seem to come out of the vocabulary of popular lyric and romance – the alliterative tag 'hende in halle', the description 'quit of lime'. ('Popular' art may be distinguished from 'folk' art as having qualities which unmistakeably connect it to a particular time and place.) The last two lines of the poem are the purest cliché from popular or courtly-popular lyric, and if the rest of it were on this level of conventionality, it would scarcely merit our attention. Why it does so is not easy to analyse but seems to rest on a particularly subtle combination of rhythms. Some editors have tried to turn the poem into a regular balanced alliterative lyric by repeating certain words and phrases – e.g. 'yhe is fayr, and flur · and flur of alle'. But to my ear the charm of the rhythm – 'charm' with some of its root sense of incantatory power – is precisely derived from its shifting and mixed mode: the stanza form is a favourite one of popular poetry, rhyming *a b c* (or *a*) *b*, with four main stresses to a line; and with this are combined suggestions, through alliteration and repetition, of other traditions of versifying. It is a moving little piece, and one that in my judgement is as elusively fresh in its movement as in its choice of word and phrase. The judgement is subjective, someone might say. To which the proper answer is that in the study of medieval literature as of all other there comes a moment at which neither philology, nor metrics, nor any other 'science' can take the place of a considered personal response.

I have said so far nothing about the music. It is time to ask what it is, how it fits the poem and whether as literary readers we can learn anything from it. It looks from its spacing out on the page as if a two-part song was intended; one stave is left blank and there is room for another. Simple two-part songs are represented in the English repertory by 'Foweles in the frith', one mutilated version of 'Angelus ad virginem' and, from *c.* 1400, by numerous carols and a few other songs. But in the twelfth and thirteenth centuries most of the songs in English manuscripts, whether their words are in English, French (i.e. Anglo-Norman) or Latin, are monophonic – that is, they are, as most oriental music still is, conceived for a single voice, a single line of melody. However, the possible absence of a second part does not in medieval song greatly matter, since the construction of even polyphonic music was essentially *linear* well into the fifteenth century. To compose part-music you wrote a complete melody, then added another, and perhaps others. 'Bryd one brere' is, then, a melody complete in itself. It differs from most other early songs in one important respect: it makes use of the mensural (i.e. proportionately measured) notation which was developed from around 1250 onwards for the presentation of polyphonic music. Neither in this song nor in any others are there any directions as to performance; indications of speed, dynamics, style and accompanying instruments (if any), are completely absent.

The melody of 'Bryd one brere' seems at first sight as artless as the poem also seemed. But closer analysis shows that consciously or unconsciously it is a well-wrought and tautly constructed piece. Like all medieval song it follows the form of the poem precisely, line by line. Typically, again, the setting is syllabic; only occasionally is there any ambiguity as to the way the words fit the notes. The movement of the melody is smooth. What more can be said about the words and music of this song? Very little I believe. There is no sign, to my mind, of any direct intellectual or emotional response on the composer's part to the words of the poem. He does not point up words rhetorically nor does he respond rhythmically to their syntax or meaning. Moreover, there is only the faintest suggestion in the melodic contours that the musician 'felt' the sounds of individual words or phrases. These negatives, as we shall see further, are of the first importance for our understanding of medieval songs. Until we have rid ourselves of the wrong expectations (expectations, primarily, that music as a 'language' must provide in song a further 'linguistic' dimension, of emotional commentary and so forth) we cannot properly respond to what medieval song does richly offer – the perfect paralleling of one sound-structure with another. This 'parallelism' is the very life even of a miniature like 'Bryd one brere'.

This discussion of 'Bryd one brere' has been lengthy, but with reason, because it has introduced a number of general issues. With these in mind we may now consider the three main traditions of the lyric in medieval England – the popular, the clerical, the courtly. To name them separately is a convenience of discussion; it will soon be evident that the three traditions are no more separate, no more individually isolated, than the streams of traffic on a three-lane highway. We may begin with the 'popular'.

*The Popular Tradition*

Our knowledge of popular lyric is bafflingly fragmentary. Popular song is indeed the lost art of medieval England. The sort of problem encountered may be summed up by this poem, written as prose on a single discoloured strip of parchment[2]:

> Maiden in the mor lay
> in the mor lay
> sevenyst[a] fulle
> sevenyst fulle.
> Maiden in the mor lay
> in the mor lay
> sevenistes fulle ant a day.
>
> 2. [b]Welle was hir mete.
> wat was hire mete?
> the primerole ant the –
> the primerole ant the –
> Welle was hire mete.
> wat was hire mete?
> the primerole ant the violet.
>
> 3. Welle was hire dryng.
> wat was hire dryng?
> the chelde[c] water of the –
> the chelde water of the –
> Welle was hire dryng.
> wat was hire dryng?
> the chelde water of the welle-spring.
>
> 4. Welle was hire bour.
> wat was hire bour?
> the red rose an te –
> the red rose an te –
> Welle was hire bour.
> wat was hire bour?
> the rede rose an te lilie flour.

This haunting little piece has been subjected to a great burden of commentary. Some scholars see it as a religious allegory which it takes some learning to unravel: the 'maiden' is Mary, or the penitent Magdalene, suffering in the wilderness of this world. The fact that such a poem could have been allegorized in the Middle Ages is not in dispute. Medieval thinkers, even quite modestly endowed ones, were capable of 'reading sermons' in every work of creation from the 'cart of the fayth' to a minstrel's coat, from a man eating an apple to one playing a trumpet. Typology was very much their business. But

_a_ seven nights, _b_ her food was good, _c_ cold.

we need to get behind this activity to the elusive thing-in-itself. Fortunately there are at least two contemporary references to 'Maiden in the mor'. One is in the margin of a book of Latin songs compiled by an Irish bishop in the fourteenth century for his clergy. What he wanted to do was to replace 'dirty' (*turpis*) songs in the vernacular with pious and uplifting texts in Latin, but keeping the original tunes. The Latin text, 'Peperit virgo', celebrating the birth of Christmas, matches the metrical structure of 'Maiden in the mor lay' quite well and could obviously have been sung to the same tune. Equally obviously, Bishop Richard de Ledrede saw nothing particularly edifying in the English song. This is helpful. As a basis of interpretation it has been strikingly confirmed by another recent find: the preacher of a sermon against Wycliffe refers to 'a certain song, viz. a *karole* that is called "The mayde be wode lay" ... [they drank] "the colde water of the welle-spryng"'.[3]

'Maiden in the mor lay' seems, then, to have been not only a popular song but a popular *dance*-song. As such it may have dramatized a game, as such songs often did, but what the game was about can now only be conjectured. Most dance-songs have a refrain – a line or two for the chorus repeated from verse to verse. This song strictly has none; but its highly patterned repetitive structure may have achieved the same effect. And in each verse, except the first, question and answer again suggest some sort of action. The mystery remains, but we can savour it in the curious broken lines (a rather unusual feature), the short repeated rhythms, and most of all in the succession of concretely presented, but never elucidated, images. Such use of images, lucid *foci* of attention, occurs in some other poems – the famous *Corpus Christi* carol, for example. But they are a small group. The great majority of medieval lyrics are all too explicit. One could wish for more imaginative riddles like 'Maiden in the mor', or its companion-piece on the leaf:[4]

> Al nist by the rose, rose,
>   al nist bi the rose I lay.
> darf[a] ich noust the rose stele
>   and yet ich bar the flour away.

There must have been many dance-songs in the lost repertory of English songs. Not all of them were 'popular'. (I use this ill-defined

*a* dared.

term reluctantly to cover a large variety of lyrics which were, at least in their original associations, *non*-courtly, *non*-clerical.) The *carole* of the thirteenth and fourteenth centuries was as much a courtly recreation as it was a popular one; but what complicates the whole question is the existence of many in French and some in English, which are neither the one nor the other. Such a courtly-popular *carole* is 'Now sprinkes the sprai' of *c.* 1300[5]:

> Now sprinkes the sprai;
> Al for love icche am so seek
> That slepen I ne mai.

1. Als I me rode this endre[a] dai
   O mi pleyinge,
   [b]Seih I hwar a litel mai
   Bigan to singge:
   [c]"The clot him clingge!
   [d]Wai es him i louve-longinge
   Sal libben ai.'

2. [e]Son icche herd that mirie note,
   Thider I drogh;
   I fonde hire in an herber swot[f]
   Under a bogh
   With joie inogh.
   Son[g] I asked, 'Thou mirie mai,
   [h]Hwi sinkes tou ai?'

3. Than answerde that maiden swote
   Midde wordes fewe:
   'Mi lemman[i] me haves bihot[j]
   Of louve trewe.
   He chaunges anewe;
   [k]Yiif I mai, it shal him rewe
   Bi this dai!'

The song is in carol form, one of the earliest of the type in English. This means that the first three lines, which form a separate self-contained unit, the 'burden', are repeated after each verse. If performed as a dance-song (*carole*), the leader would have sung the verses, and the group the burden.

---

*a* other, *b* I saw where a little maiden, *c* may the earth shrivel him up *or* may his corpse wither away, *d* wretched is he who must live in a continual state of desire, *e* as soon as I heard … I drew near, *f* sweet, *g* straightway, *h* why do you sing? *i* sweetheart, *j* promised, *k* if I may (bring it about), he shall regret, i.e. and no mistake.

Once again one is struck by the freshness of the language, and fresh it is – perhaps because learned poets had not been doing this kind of thing for long *in English*, though they had *in England*, in the other and more favoured languages of courtly-clerical entertainment, French and Latin. This poet probably knew, perhaps wrote in, French, since for all its freshness this is not a naïve poem; it has a context. It belongs to the genre of the *chanson d'aventure* – that is, a song about a happening. To ask, about a medieval poem, 'Of what *kind* is it?' can never be a stupid question. The art of a medieval lyric is far more likely to consist of delicate variation on a known theme, within a known genre, than of creation *de novo*, original invention. A *chanson d'aventure*, of which there are scores in French and in English, invariably begins with 'Lautre jor me chivachai' or 'Als I me rode this endre dai' or something like it; and it usually continues with the poet meeting a 'may', or dreaming about one.

'Now sprinkes the sprai' may well be modelled on a French song. In fact, a fairly close analogy has been spotted between it and a French *pastourelle*. (A *pastourelle* is a special kind of *chanson d'aventure* in which a knight meets a country maiden and makes advances to her which may or may not be repulsed. We learn our first *pastourelle* in the nursery: 'Where are you going to, my pretty maid?') The French poem has no 'burden', but it has a refrain (that is, an internal repeat within the verse structure). 'Jamais n'amerai / nullui de cuer gai' (Never shall I love anyone with a happy heart). This refrain probably had a separate existence as an amorous tag and also a tune which went with it. The parallel gives us a hint as to what sort of a melody 'Now sprinkes the sprai' may have had – something tuneful and measured (dance must be metrical) and regularly associated with the words of the 'burden', which has a detachable quality and may have existed as a popular song-fragment before the carol / *carole* was written. The 'burdens' of carols often raise this possibility.

The principal type of popular song in medieval England was the carol; it flourished from the fourteenth century up to the Reformation. One should, if awkwardly, refer to it as *mainly* popular, since its transformations and uses were manifold. The carol has, in this period, to be seen as a fixed form of the kind already described; its scheme is Burden Verse1 B V2 B V3 ... B. This means that one or two modern favourites such as 'Adam lay ibounden' and

'I sing of a maiden' are not carols in the clearly accepted medieval definition because they have no burden. The chief use to which this form was put was religious; the central tradition of the carol as it survives (and Richard Greene has collected some 470 texts) is of a popular religious song.[6]

It cannot be doubted that the earliest carols were true songs. Unfortunately almost all their melodies have been lost, perhaps quite all. The snatches that survive are all in later manuscripts. This lullaby-carol from the Winchester area is so simple, so easy to memorize, that one wonders why it ever found its way on to the written page[7]:

This is one of a number of carols in which the baby Jesus is not only articulate about his present sufferings ('Slepe I wolde / I may not for colde / And clothys hav I non') but also about his Passion to come. This totally unhistorical attitude to the Christian story pervades the popular religious carol as it does the medieval drama of the mystery cycles; the two belong to the same imaginative world, prosaic, literal, everyday, and yet magnificent in its assured truth.

A carol which vividly and colourfully captures the everyday is this one of the apostles and saints at Mass[8]:

> 2. Sente Thomas the bellys gane ryng
> And Sent Collas[a] the Mas gane syng;
> Sente Jhon toke that swete offeryng
> And by a chapell as I came.

More characteristic than this somewhat 'folky' carol with its 'ryche rede gollde' and fine disregard for liturgical anachronism, to say no more, is this semi-learned carol about St Stephen[9]:

a ? Nicholas.

2. Stonyd he was wyth stonys grete
   [a]Fervore gentis impie;
   Than he say Cryst sitte in sete
   [b]Innixum Patris dextere.

3. Thou preydyst Cryst for thin enmyse
   [c]O martir invictissime;
   Thou prey for us that hye Justyse
   [d]Ut nos purget a crimine.

This carol, one of five in honour of St Stephen which survive, is found on a parchment roll in Trinity College, Cambridge. The roll is in three sections sewn together and seems to have had a practical purpose. The carol is not the most colourful of the St Stephen carols – one refers to the 'gret yell' of the Jews when 'gret stones and bones at hym they caste' – but it is typical of the genre in several respects. Like so many other carols, it belongs to the Christmas season; the feast of St Stephen the first martyr is celebrated on 26 December. The linguistic style is simple and direct, without syntactic or metrical sophistication – except, paradoxically, that the Latin lines are perfectly fitted into the argument; the verses were written by someone, presumably a cleric, who understood Latin. These lines do not seem to come directly from the liturgy of the day, nor from any well known hymns or antiphons – though these were common sources for borrowing. But they have a well-worn stamp upon them: phrases like 'Qui triumphavit hodie' hardly had to be minted afresh. The carols are a tissue of commonplaces. Formally, the four-line verse is standard, though it more often rhymes *a a a b* and frequently the *b*-rhyme links the verse with the burden.

Musically this early fifteenth-century carol represents the simplest polyphony that could be devised: it is copied out *in score* in the Trinity Roll, a procedure which was beginning to be old fashioned. This means that the two voices are presented one above the other, just as in a modern edition. The tenor, the lower voice, is structurally the more important and was written first; this does not necessarily mean that it has the better 'tune'. Practically all carols are in the same musical metre (modern $\frac{3}{8}$ or $\frac{3}{4}$) in which ♪♪ alternates freely with ♪♩ . In the more elaborate later carols there are many rhythmic complica-

*a* through the rage of an ungodly people (the Jews), *b* leaning on the right hand of the Father, *c* O most invincible martyr, *d* that he may cleanse us from sin.

tions of the kind foreshadowed in mm. 14–15 (voice ii) and m. 26 (voice i) of our example. The words are written in only to the tenor part but both parts were sung, the burden by a chorus and the verse by solo voices. There is no evidence that instruments ever accompanied polyphonic carols.

Does the music in fact 'do' anything for the words? The relationship between the words and the music is largely a formal one. Their structures are closely parallel: each line of the verse is fitted to, or with, a phrase of the music; and the music is rounded off at the end (mm. 26–8) by a cadence which 'rhymes' briefly with the cadence of the burden (mm. 6–8). Tonally the piece is clear and stable (in a transposed D-mode). In effect, then, the impression of verbal directness, the almost prosaic communication of the awesome mystery of Stephen's painful martyrdom, is not one whit altered by the musical setting. The strong, impersonal melody leaves no opening for emotionalizing or dramatization of any sort.

Such a carol as 'Eya, martir Stephane' stands in the middle of the carol tradition – in the middle not only chronologically (it dates from the first part of the fifteenth century) but in other ways as well. It seems to mark a point of departure: this is where the polyphonic carol begins to branch off from the presumed main tradition of the carol as a popular religious song and to take on a life of its own as a musical ornament to not the liturgy itself but some ritual associated with it, such as processions at Christmastide to the altars of the saints.

During the course of the fifteenth century the carol developed in various ways. It did not cease to be a popular song, and especially a popular religious song, as numerous texts and a few fragments of music attest. But at the same time it produced the important ecclesiastical and musical phenomenon just mentioned – the first substantial corpus of English vernacular songs, over one hundred of them in a homogeneous style. The verbal texts remain in character unchanged; but the music becomes gradually more complex in its polyphony. These were songs for professional men's choirs with skilled soloists. The carol also developed as a literary form, and one of the interesting features of the last decades of the fifteenth century is a repertory of songs and carols from the court of Henry VII which have quite a new look[10].

Jhesu, mercy, how may this be,
That God hymselfe for sole mankynd
Wolde take on Hym humanite?
My witt nor reson may hit well fynd:
   Jhesu, mercy, how may this be?

1.  Crist, that was of infynyt myght,
    Egall to the Fathir in deite,
    Inmortal, inpassible*a*, the wordlis lyght,
    And wolde so take mortalite.
      Jhesu, mercy, how may this be?

3.  A Jhesu, whi suffyrd thou such entretyng*b*,
    As betyng, bobbyng*c*, ye spettyng on thi face?
    Drawne like a theffe, and for payne swetyng
    Both water and blode, ye, crucified *d*an hevy case!
      Jhesu, mercy, how may this be?

The conscious art and affective piety of this Passion poem are far removed from the naïve craft and prosaic directness of the popular carol. The vocabulary is deliberately elevated, Latinate ('humanity', 'immortal', 'impassible', 'mortality' are late medieval words, and their novel strangeness may still have been felt). The rhythms, too, however we account for them, are not the strong-stress metres of, for instance, 'O sisters too / How may we do / For to preserve this day ... ?'; they are nearer to the 'balanced' line of alliterative verse ('Dráwne like a théffe and for páyne swétyng'). The emphasis on the physical details of the Passion is absolutely in keeping with the general tradition of late medieval devotions; and with dozens of poems written within it. Their motto might well be (in the words of another Passion carol) 'Wofully araid / My blode, man, / for thee ran: / ... Wofully araid'.

## The Clerical Tradition

It is no easier to define a clerical tradition of verse than it was a popular one. Perhaps a way out of some difficulties is to think of the intended *audience* as the principal defining factor? *Authorship* clearly will not do, since, as we have seen, a great deal of popular verse, like the popular religious drama, was written by clerics for the benefit of layfolk. But the concept of a specific audience is also

*a* incapable of suffering, *b* treatment, *c* buffeting, *d* in grievous condition.

hard to apply. A festive carol such as the following would presumably have been sung in 'the Hall' at a celebration attended by the various estates[11]:

> Lett no man cum into this hall,
> Grome, page, nor yet marshall,
> But that sum sport he bryng withall,
>> For now ys the tyme of Crystmas.

As the burden says 'Make we mery, *bothe more and lasse* ...' We can be sure that good pieces, whether pious, amorous, moral or convivial, would have found an appreciative audience wherever they were performed – at court, in monastery refectory, in the town square.

There are, however, some kinds of lyric for which the term clerical seems, if not fully apt, at least more apt than any other. One of these is the lyric based on a liturgical model. 'Liturgical' lyrics range from simple hymn translations ('Wikked Herode, thou mortall foo' translating 'Hostis Herodes impie') to more elaborate paraphrases ('What is he, thys lordling that cometh from the fyht', based on a Holy Week reading from Isaiah, ch. 63, 1–7). The latter is extraordinarily impressive in the way it (unconsciously?) transforms a passage of Old Testament prophecy into a triumphant presentation of Christ the epic warrior[12]:

> So fayre ycontised[a], so semlich in syht
> [b]So styflyche yongeth, so douhti a knyht.
> 'Ich hyt am, Ich hyt am, that[c] ne speke bote ryht,
> Chaunpyon to helen monkunde in fyht.'

No part of the liturgy was richer in imaginative symbol, action, gesture and word than Holy Week, the week before Easter. William Herebert's poem 'My volk, what habbe I' is based on a passage from the liturgy of Good Friday, the *Improperia* or 'Reproaches'. In them Christ speaks to the Jewish people and contrasts his goodness (as God) to them with their cruelty to him (as Jesus)[13]:

> My volk, what habbe I do the
> Other[d] in what thyng toened[e] the?
> Gyn nouthe[f] and onswere thou me:

*a* apparelled, *b* advances so valiantly, *c* speak only what is righteous, *d* or, *e* grieved, *f* now.

Vor vrom Egypte Ich ladde the,
Thou me ledest to rode troe[a]
  My volk, what habbe I do the? &c.

Ich delede[b] the see for the,
 And Pharaon dreynte[c] for the;
 And thou to princes sullest[d] me. My volk, &c.

In bem[e] of cloude Ich ladde the;
 And to Pylate thou ledest me. My volk, &c.

Wyth aungeles mete Ich vedde the;
 And thou bufetest and scourgest me. My volk, &c.

Of the ston Ich dronk[f] to the;
 And thou wyth galle drincst to me. My volk, &c.

Kynges of Chanaan Ich for the boet;
 And thou betest myn heved[g] wyth roed. My volk, &c.

Ich gaf the croune of kynedom;
 And thou me gyfst a croune of thorn. My volk, &c.

Ich muchel worshype doede to the;
 And thou me hongest on rode troe. My volk, &c.

What are the characteristics of the Latin liturgical 'Reproaches'? Despite the personal nature of Christ's 'reproach', the presentation is austerely stylized. Christ is not depicted as a dramatic character – his words are sung by two priests whose actions and garments are symbolic; the people's response, *our* response, comes not in the form of a congregational prayer for pardon but is divided between two deacons, singing the praises of God in Greek, and the choir, repeating them in Latin. The whole exchange is sung, but not to music of an overtly emotional or dramatic character; to music, rather, that impersonalizes and distances the suffering implied in the utterances of Christ.

What does Herebert do with this liturgical ceremony? In a phrase, he brings it down to earth. The resounding Latin words are replaced by homely 'Anglo-Saxon' ones: *contristavi* becomes 'toened'; *columna nubis* becomes 'bem of cloude'; *aqua salutis de petra*, 'Of the ston ich dronk to the'. He seems to deliberately avoid 'up-to-date' English words of romance origin. Herebert is not able to match the compactness possible in an inflected language (*Ego propter te flagellavi* . . . ;

*a* the tree of the cross, *b* divided, *c* drowned, *d* sellest, *e* pillar, *f* gave drink, *g* head with reed.

*et tu me flagellatum tradidisti*) but through the directness of his syntax and the roughness of his rhythm he gives Christ an ordinary speaking voice, the voice of a man addressing men. And this is, I suppose, why we bother with him. Herebert is not a great poet but his poems convey to us through words the power and immediacy of a lost world. This lost world of the medieval religious imagination was one in which the most sublime mysteries could be grasped and handled in a preposterously familiar manner. The medieval poet sometimes seems rather like Cain who blasphemes in the mystery play, shouting rudely at God, 'Who is that hob-over-the wall?' The familiarity is quite unlike the deeply cultivated, self-conscious, humbling and personal, friendship which a later religious poet, George Herbert, aspires to ('How sweetly doth "My Master" sound, "My Master" ') though it can sometimes catch a note of warmth and sweetness of its own ('Suete Jhesu, King of blysse / myn huerte love, min huerte lisse'). The familiarity is unaware, unquestioning, natural, and in the last resort curiously impersonal, or at least unindividual. If we are to understand the medieval Herebert's poem aright, we have to grasp the fact that the poet is not, *in his poem*, an individual with a unique utterance; he is a voice. But the voice is worth hearing for two reasons: first, because it has behind it the authority of a great liturgical tradition; and, secondly, because it makes the tradition alive here-and-now with all the vividness of contemporary life and experience.

The liturgy was an ever fecund source of ideas, images and texts. One text which achieved wide popularity all over Europe was the *Letabundus* sequence; a sequence is, at its simplest, a sacred piece which changes its melody, and usually its metrical form, every second verse (A'A BB CC DD . . .).

> 1a Letabundus exultet fidelis chorus,
>      Alleluia.
> 1b Regem regum intacte profundit torus,
>      Res miranda.
> 2a Angelus consilii natus est de virgine,
>      Sol de stella.
> 2b Sol occasum nesciens, stella semper rutilans
>      Semper clara . . .

(Let the choir of the faithful resound joyfully, Alleluia.
The touch of a virgin brings forth the King of Kings, a
  marvellous thing.
The Angel of Counsel is born of a virgin, the sun
  from a star.
The sun that knows no setting, the star that ever
  glows, ever bright . . .)

This sequence[14], attributed to St Bernard of Clairvaux, survives in over 200 manuscripts in various shapes and forms. In addition it was imitated and parodied and pillaged. In fifteenth-century England it was still popular; witness, one of the best-loved of medieval carols – 'Ther is no rose of swych vertu / As is the rose that bare Jhesu / Alleluia'[15]. Each verse ends with a short line from the sequence: *Alleluia . . . Res miranda . . . Sol de stella* etc. The carol has its own music; but many imitators of the sequence used its melody as well. This was the case of the French Christmas song 'Hui enfantez fu li fiz dieu; chantez chantez *Alleluia*' and of the drinking-song 'Or hi parra! La cerveyse nos chauntera *Alleluia*' – the beer will sing Alleluia to us.

The practice of writing new words to pre-existent tunes (for which the technical term is *contrafactum*) was very prevalent in the Middle Ages. For us it is important in two ways. First, if one finds a translation or paraphrase which is in the same metre as the original, one can be almost sure it was sung to the same tune. John Awdelay, for example, the blind carol-poet of the early fifteenth century, imitated closely the metre of *Angelus ad virginem* in his translation, 'The angel to the vergyn said'; it must have been sung to the well-known tune. Secondly, this widespread practice of writing not just popular songs but sometimes art-songs to melodies that had previously been used for other words tells us something essential about the attitude of medieval poets to the relationship of music and poetry. In brief, it was a matter of pattern; this was the first criterion of appropriateness and in most cases the only criterion. It was essential that the new text should have the same syllabic count and line structure as the old; in some melodic styles coincidence of stress, even, was irrelevant. It is virtually meaningless to say such things as 'In this and the four following poems the singing quality is evident . . .'; there is no verbal 'quality' as such which will tell us whether a poem was sung or not.

It is tempting to call more lyrics 'clerical' than perhaps one should. One reason for this is the overwhelming preponderance of surviving manuscripts of which the ownership can be traced to monasteries or houses of friars. This should not mislead us; such ownership was the condition of their survival, not evidence of any monopoly. There is, of course, another and more significant reason for the preponderance: clerics, if by this we mean all men in some kind of ecclesiastical orders (not necessarily ordained priests), were the most numerous class of writers, in both senses of the word. As authors they produced, as we have seen, a great bulk of 'literature' for popular consumption and edification; they wrote also for court audiences; and they wrote for themselves. Many moralistic poems cannot with any surety be assigned to any single milieu. *De contemptu mundi* was a favourite theme throughout the centuries: *Memento, homo, quod cinis es* ... 'Dust thou art, and unto dust shalt thou return.' No poem on dusty death was more popular than this one with its grim wordplay. I give it here in its simplest and earliest version from *The Harley Lyrics* (early fourteenth century)[16]:

> Erthe toc*a* of erthe erthe wyth woh;
> Erthe other erthe to the erthe droh*b*;
> erthe leyde erthe in erthene throh*c*.
> *d*Tho hevede erthe of erthe erthe ynoh.

('Erthe' may mean the stuff of man's flesh, or the earth he is buried in; in longer versions of the poem it refers also to the earth as the place we live on and to the muck which is the 'earth' of our possessions.)

Sombre moralizing poems are just as frequently found with music as any other kind of poem: 'Worldes blis ne last no throwe', 'Mirie it is while sumer ilast', 'Man mei longe him lives wene', all have messages of gloom and all have melodies. The third of these was scrappily written in the midst of miscellaneous material in Latin and French sometime in the middle of the thirteenth century when the manuscript belonged to a Cistercian abbey in Lincolnshire. There are no stave lines and the notation is unmeasured[17] (see opposite page).

The song, despite the casual way it has been notated, is quite a complex melody: it follows the standard form of the courtly *chanson* of the troubadours and trouvères (A A B, where B, the *cauda*, consists of

---

*a* took, *b* drew down, *c* grave, *d* then had 'earth' enough 'earth' from 'earth'.

Man mei longe him lives wene
2. ac of -te him li -yet the wreinch.
3. Fair weder ofte him went to re - ne
4. an fer -li - che ma -ket is blench.
5. Thar - fo -re, man, thu thee bi - thench,
6. al sel va -lu - i the gre - ne,
7. Wel - a - wey! nis king nor que - ne
8. that ne sel drinke of dethis drench.
9. Man, er thu fal -le of thi bench,
10. thu sinne a - quench

( ♪ indicates a lighter note)

Man may expect a long life,
but he is often deceived.
Fair weather often turns to rain and suddenly plays a trick.
Therefore man, bethink you, everything that is green must fade.
Wel-a-wey! There is neither king nor queen that will not have to drink the
drink of death.
Man, before you fall at your (tavern) bench, put an end to your sin.

lines 5–10); the word-setting is syllabic, with slight notational adjustments for diphthongs and sounded consonants ('Man' has two notes; 'mei' the same); the opening with its rising major triad, *c–e–g*, is not characteristic, but the general structure of the melody, its mostly stepwise movement, and its tendency to repeat melodic motifs (line 11 'rhymes' with 2 and 4) is quite in keeping with *chanson* style – variety within unity. There is no evident emotional connection between the words and the music, unless perhaps the single word 'Welawey' catches the intonation of speech. If it does, and it certainly seems to, this is a rare instance indeed of the sound of an individual word being represented in melody. The 'just note and accent' approach to a text is more or less an invention of the sixteenth century, in England; its absence is a thing we have to come to terms with in medieval song.

## The Courtly Tradition

The apparent total disappearance of evidence for English courtly lyric will seem very curious until we reflect on it and recall that the language of the English court and of courtly activity from the twelfth to the fourteenth century was not English but French. The manuscript which contains the celebrated canon 'Sumer is icumen in' has no other English songs in it at all; but it does give us the *lais* in French of the Anglo-Norman poetess, Marie de France (a *lai* is a short romance story in verse). What is in fact more curious is the absence of any surviving Anglo-Norman song-book as such – though there are a good number of separate songs and lyrics.

The reasons are mostly literary for envisaging some of the lyrics in the Harley collection as courtly[18]:

> Bytuene Mersh ant Averil
>   when spray biginneth to springe,
> the lutel foul hath hire wyl
>   on hyre lud*a* to synge
>   Ich libbe*b* in lovelonginge
>   for semlokest*c* of alle thynge;
>   he may*d* me blisse bring;
>     *e*icham in hire baundoun.
>       An *f*hendy hap ichabbe yhent,
>       ichot*g* from heuene it is me sent;
>       from alle wymmen mi love is lent*h*
>         ant lyht on Alysoun.

*a* their language, *b* live, *c* loveliest, *d* she can, *e* I am in her power, *f* I have had fine fortune, *g* I know, *h* gone away, departed.

The thoughts and images of this poem, of which I have given only verse I with its refrain, are almost wholly 'conventional' – and none the worse for that (a convention is simply what people have agreed to do or say in a given situation; all medieval and Renaissance poetry, good and bad, is reliant upon convention). The season is early spring (as usual), the birds are singing (as usual). The poet-lover's thoughts are all on the loveliest creature there ever was; he is totally enthralled. The fact that she is called 'Alysoun' scarcely signifies, since she is like all courtly ladies a fiction of the idealizing imagination. There are no warts on her; the catalogue of her charms includes a neck whiter than the swan, fair hair, black eyes, a slim waist. The lover is equally unindividualized: he knows his good fortune is sent him from heaven, and he will die if he can't have her; he lies awake and is weary with his suffering; he begs her to have pity on him. These are the topics of a thousand lyrics in Provençal, French and Italian.

There is another respect in which this poem may be thought of as belonging to a courtly tradition, its form. The attempt at a fairly elaborate stanza with an unusual rhyme-scheme is in keeping with *trouvère* (N. French) style; so is the tendency not to use too many rhymes. On the other hand the continental style is based on an absolute and precise syllabic count. This the Harley poet fails to achieve; the second and fourth lines of the stanza seem to be especially unstable – sometimes there are six or seven syllables with three stresses ('When spráy bigínneth to springe') sometimes eight with four ('forthí myn wónges wáxen wón'). However, this sort of irregularity in a stress-language like English, or German, which obeys different phonological rules, is not so pronounced that it countermands one's general impression that the Harley poet is trying to do the kind of thing that elegant poets were doing in French *and in Latin* – that is, construct an interesting artefact in sound and pattern. The question of the poem's 'aesthetic', if that is not too grand a term, is relevant when we come to ask whether it was sung or not. There is no music in the Harley MS. and only one poem, translated from a Latin sequence, is found with music elsewhere. The answer can only be guessed at, but I believe there is a good case for thinking that any poem which approximates to the model of *la grande chanson courtoise* was regarded as having an inherent *musica*, that is to say, a pattern, a deducible structure, to which a melody could be fitted.

However, before jumping to this tentative conclusion, one must ask whether 'courtly' *is* the right description even for such a lyric as *Alysoun*. There is, I suggest, for better or worse, something incorrigibly insular, not to say provincial, about the Harley lyrics compared with their continental equivalents, and the reason for this lies in the English language – or in that version of the language which was current in Herefordshire in the early fourteenth century. A phrase like 'ant feye fallen adoun' is reminiscent of the fallen heroes of epic who are 'doomed' (*feye*) rather than of a sick lover; and the easy alliteration of 'geynest under gore' recalls the popular alliterations of English narrative. (Some of the Harley lyrics, incidentally, are totally within the alliterative tradition as used for serious narrative verse.) So far as we can tell, the very English vocabulary of *Alysoun* is almost entirely wanting in 'romance' resonances: 'baundoun' (1.8) and 'bounte' (3.6) are the only words that spring redolent from the page; in 'lossum chere' (*lovesome face*) the adjective overweighs the pale French substantive. These are delicate matters for us to judge, at this distance of time. But perhaps the main point can be made with another example which I believe catches the spirit of courtliness in a way that the poet of *Alysoun*, imprisoned in a 'Saxon' vocabulary, could not do:

> Madame, ye ben of al beaute shryne
> As far as cercled is the mapemounde *a*,
> For as the cristal glorious ye shyne,
> And lyke ruby ben your chekes rounde.
> Therwith ye ben so mery and so jocounde
> That at a revel whan that I see you daunce,
> It is an oynement unto my wounde,
> Thogh ye to me ne do no daliaunce.

This *balade* by Chaucer[19] has three verses, each with the refrain-line 'Thogh ye to me ne do no daliaunce'. The third raises interesting problems of tone and intention:

> Nas never pyke *b*walwed in galauntyne
> As I in love am walwed and ywounde,
> For which ful ofte I *c*of myself devyne

*a* map of the world, *b* steeped in bread sauce, *c* conjecture of myself that.

That I am trewe Tristam the secounde.
My love may not *refreyde nor affounde;
I brenne ay in an amorous plesaunce.
Do what you lyst, I wyl your thral be founde,
Thogh ye to me ne do no daliaunce.

The literary allegiances of this poem are in no doubt. Chaucer has chosen a French form, the *balade*, and treated it in the strict French manner; the use of the same rhyme-sounds throughout the poem is typical. Most striking of all is a new register of words and images. Rosemounde is the 'shrine' of all beauty; the lover burns in 'amorous plesaunce' (a Frenchified expression, surely); and 'daliaunce', suggesting the delights of social intercourse, the refined gambits of love, is the desired end – or means to an end. Words like 'refreyde' and 'affounde' add to our sense of rarefied emotion. Chaucer has not only understood 'the courtly experience' as transmitted and *formed* by literature written in French, but has succeeded in making it at home in English. It is tempting at this point to say that Chaucer has also kept his 'English commonsense' in stanza 3 with the image of the 'pyke'. Certainly the Anglo-Saxon 'walwed' comes in pat; but the delightful self-mockery whereby the poet admits the ridiculous side of his situation ('falling in love' *is* rather comic – in someone else) is a dimension of sophisticated romance from earliest years. Chrétien de Troyes, in the latter half of the twelfth century, is fully capable of ironic hyperboles like Chaucer's reference to 'trewe Tristam'.

Was *Rosemounde* a song? No music survives for it. On the other hand, the general style and form of the piece closely corresponds, as I have suggested, to what Guillaume de Machaut (d. 1377) and his younger contemporaries were doing. Although there are very few surviving English songs from this period, there is a large repertory in French, to which Machaut himself, reputed the greatest composer of his generation, contributed. The lyric poems are in three main 'fixed forms', *rondeau, virelai* and *balade*, and these were now usually set polyphonically i.e. for more than one voice (three was the norm). Of these intricately patterned and rhythmically elaborated part-songs there are no examples with English texts; but it is evident from the continental examples that any words could be set to music. In keeping with the centuries-old tradition of the courtly chanson, from the

*a* grow cold or become chilled.

troubadours onward, the metrical structure of the verse was reproduced, reflected in the music; but the closeness of the two 'movements', musical and verbal, which led Dante to use images of the
hand and the glove, a man and his shadow, to describe it, is now a
thing of the past. It was never the case at any time in the Middle
Ages that poems had to be written in a special way in order to be 'set
to music'. But in the earlier centuries stricter conventions and more
limited resources brought about a closer association of the two arts,
based though it was almost entirely on concepts of number, proportion and pattern and not on those things which later ages have seen as
'marrying' them together – careful declamation, sensitivity to mood,
witty pictorialism. Deschamps' distinction between *musique artificiele*
(music proper) and *musique naturele* (the 'music' of poetry) was no new
conception; but by Chaucer's time the great increase in musical
virtuosity must have led to an increased feeling of independence,
perhaps generally of indifference on both sides. *Rosemounde* is, first
and foremost, a poem to be read.

   Courtly lyric continued to be written in the expected and familiar
forms, whether by courtiers themselves or by court 'servants' such as
Chaucer and the Benedictine monk, John Lydgate. This suited
composers well; they needed set forms, having as yet no 'pure'
musical forms (e.g. sonata-form) to work with. So when a composer
of the late fifteenth or early sixteenth century had to write a song he
could choose a text in the 'rhyme-royal' stanza (closely akin to
*balade*), or a carol, and he would automatically know the conventions
which applied to it. An example from an early Tudor songbook
(*temp.* Henry VII) will show how interestingly a court-poet and composer could work together (or, at least, alongside each other) with a
rich weave of conventional forms and images.[20]

(The vocalized passage at the end of the burden to which no words are set is typical of the composer's still largely abstract approach to song.)

This day day dawes,
This gentill day day dawes,
This gentill day dawes,
And I must home gone.

1. In a glorius garden grene
   Sawe I syttyng a comly quene
   Among the flouris that fressh byn.
   She gaderd a flowr and set betwene [a],
       The lyly-whighte rose methoughte I sawe,
       The lyly-whighte rose methoughte I sawe,
           And ever she sang:
           [This day day dawes . . .]

In the second verse the lady asserts 'The white rose is most trewe / This garden to rule by ryghtwis lawe'. The song was perhaps written in honour of the white rose, Queen Elizabeth of York, the wife of Henry VII. 'On the literary side, it inherits the favourite form of the fifteenth century, the carol, it interweaves the central symbols of courtly love (lovely lady sits in rose-garden) with a popular *aubade* [the traditional song of lovers at dawn] "This day day dawes" . . . and makes the whole serve a political purpose.'[21] There are many earlier and contemporary examples of ceremonial carols; celebration of one kind or another is an intrinsic part of the carol phenomenon. Musically this court song interweaves what may have been the tune of the popular *aubade* into an attractive contrapuntal setting in contemporary style. There could perhaps be some intention on the composer's part to suggest joyfulness through the use of triple dance-like rhythms; but it is hard to be sure since these are the rhythmic idioms of many songs in this book.

'This day day dawes' is a song with a context, a song which plays with several traditions and conventions. Many medieval lyrics, as we have seen, are without contexts; and this is what makes their study at the same time fascinating and baffling. The masterpieces of English literature – and this includes the great poems of Chaucer and his contemporaries – do not need contexts; they create the conditions on which they may be read and understood. You do not have to make a study of 'courtly love' to enter into *Troilus*. Medieval lyrics are for the most part in a different category; they are parasitic upon the imaginative traditions of church and court as well as on popular

a sat amongst [the flowers].

custom and festivity. The traditions of the church we can easily recover – the liturgy survives, and there is no reason why we should fail to comprehend a poem like 'My volk, what habbe I do the?' The traditions of court and aristocratic life are a sort of lost liturgy, but one of which parts can be pieced together out of fragments. Whether, finally, we shall ever know anything securely helpful about the imaginative life of the common folk of these islands is extremely doubtful. Poems (songs? dances?) like 'Maiden in the mor lay' and this *Corpus Christi* carol are liable to go on teasing us for ever with their enigmatic power[22]:

> Lully lulley lully lulley
> The fawcon hath born my mak away.

1. He bare hym up, he bare hym down,
   He bare hym into an orchard brown.

2. In that orchard ther was an hall,
   That was hangid with purpill and pall.

3. And in that hall ther was a bede;
   Hit was hanged with gold so rede.

4. And yn that bed ther lythe a knyght,
   His wowndes bledyng day and nyght.

5. By that bedes side ther kneleth a may
   And she wepeth both nyght and day.

6. And by that beddes side ther stondith a ston,
   'Corpus Christi' wretyn theron.

# NOTES

Throughout this chapter quotations have been modernized in their spelling; I have occasionally also emended the punctuation. When editions are cited, therefore, the quotations should be regarded as 'based on' the edited texts. Works referred to by short title here are listed with full details in the Bibliography (p. 609).

1. John Saltmarsh, 'Two Medieval Love-songs set to Music', *The Antiquaries Journal*, XV (1935), with facsimile. Transcription in text by John Stevens.

2. R. H. Robbins, *Secular Lyrics*, no. 18.

3. E. J. Dobson and F. Ll. Harrison, *Medieval English Songs*, no. 16b, 188–9, 269–70, 306, texts and discussion. The recent find is reported by S. Wenzel in *Speculum*, XLIX (1974). See also P. Dronke, *Medieval Lyric*, 195–6, for another interpretation.

4. R. H. Robbins, *Secular Lyrics*, no. 17. One meaning of the riddle is, of course, obvious.

5. R. L. Greene, *Early English Carols*, no. 450.

6. R. L. Greene, *Early English Carols*, prints all the texts; J. Stevens, *Medieval Carols, Music at the Court of Henry VIII, Early Tudor Songs & Carols*, prints the music.

7. J. Stevens, *Medieval Carols*, appendix no. 1A.

8. R. L. Greene, no. 323.

9. R. L. Greene, no. 98; J. Stevens, *Medieval Carols*, no. 12.

10. J. Stevens, *Music & Poetry*, 367 (original text); *Early Tudor Songs and Carols*, no. 51 (music).

11. R. L. Greene, no. 11, st. 1.

12. Carleton Brown, *XIV Century*, no. 25.

13. *ibid.*, no. 15.

14. Full text in R. L. Greene, introd., p. xcviii.

15. R. L. Greene, no. 173; J. Stevens, *Medieval Carols*, no. 14.

16. G. L. Brook, *Harley Lyrics*, no. 1.

17. New transcription by John Stevens. A different transcription of the melody with an edited text is in E. J. Dobson and F. Ll. Harrison, *Medieval English Songs*, no. 6a.

18. G. L. Brook, *Harley Lyrics*, no. 4.

19. F. N. Robinson, *The Works of Geoffrey Chaucer* (2nd edn, London 1957), 533.

20. J. Stevens, *Music & Poetry*, p. 381 (text); *Early Tudor Songs & Carols*, no. 55 (music).

21. As note 20.

22. R. L. Greene, no. 322A; no medieval setting survives.

# THE MIRACLE PLAYS OF NOAH

## RICHARD AXTON

For Chaucer's Wife of Bath 'pleyes of miracles' were a sociable summer pastime, where preaching and church processions were mingled with popular festivities, with drinking, dancing and display. To the followers of John Wycliffe, neo-puritan opponents of the drama, miracles were 'sights of sin' which turned holy scripture into a blasphemous 'game'. The surviving religious plays, though mostly a century later than Chaucer, show this same double aspect, a happy blend of sacred and profane, their theological and moral 'text' conveyed in a holiday spirit of 'playing'.

Chaucer, as Clerk of the King's Works, with responsibility for erecting lists and scaffolds for spectacular tournaments at Smithfield, must have seen the open-air plays of biblical history performed by London clerks in the presence of Richard II and lasting three – or sometimes five – days. But these cycles plays, running from Adam's fall to doomsday and lingering in graphic detail on the sufferings of Christ's Passion, do not seem to stirred his poetic imagination. Chaucer would not have thought of drama as a high poetic art – his contemporary English playwrights remain anonymous – and he does not mention any ancient dramatists in his gallery of authors in the *House of Fame*. The name of Euripides disappears in Chaucer's translation of Boethius and Chaucer's definitions of tragedy say nothing about live performance. The splendid classical 'theatre' of Athens, described in the *Knight's Tale* with wonder and pseudo-scientific care, is a forum for heroic spectacle rather than a scripted play. A passage in the *Franklin's Tale* describes the shows conjured up by 'tregetoures': 'water and a barge' suddenly appear in a banquet hall, together with 'a grym leoun', flowers 'as in a mede' and 'a castel al of lym and stoon'. This *trompe l'oeil* pageantry or 'science of apparence' probably recalls elaborate historical plays Chaucer had seen at the royal palaces in Paris.[1] Similarly, it is the notion of drama as illusion that delights Chaucer in the *Miller's Tale*, where the parish clerk Absolon vainly tries to catch Alison's attention by his acting:

> Somtyme, to shewe his lightnesse and maistrye,
> He pleyeth Herodes upon a scaffold hye.

As the plot of the *Miller's Tale* unfolds, a playful parody of the miracle plays of Noah's flood is revealed like a sort of puppet drama. The Oxford astrologer-student Nicholas predicts a flood and sets his carpenter landlord to work adapting wooden food troughs as miniature arks. While Nicholas enjoys Alison, her cuckold husband 'floats', suspended from his own rafters, experiencing the terrors of 'Nowelis flood' as if his imagination had been deranged by the contemporary stage. Alone among Chaucer's tales, the Miller's requires a special 'set', constructed by a 'wright', and a scenario that is carefully rehearsed.

Plays of Noah were popular and widespread in medieval England. As six survive in Middle English (two from the York cycle, one from Chester, Wakefield, Newcastle, 'N-town') and one in Cornish, I have decided that it would be more valuable to concentrate on these than to try to deal with the Miracle plays as a whole. With the possible exception of the creation of the world, there could not be a more unlikely subject for dramatic representation. Yet in all the plays but one the audience sees the ark built before its eyes, and Noah's ordeal enacted. There is no question of a photographic illusion though; this is a delightful 'game', as Chester stage directions make clear:[2]

Then Noe with all his familye shall make a signe as though they wrought upon the shippe with divers instruments.

Members of Noah's family identify their different tasks: 'I have a hatchett wonder keene', 'And I can well make a pynne / And with this hammer knocke yt in', 'And I will goe gather slytche', and Japhet's wife sweeps up wood chips to light the fire for dinner. The problem of the animals is solved by a boldly transparent device:

Then Noe shall goe into the arke with all his familye, his wyffe excepte, and the arke muste bee borded rownde aboute. And on the bordes all the beastes and fowles hereafter rehearsed muste bee paynted, that ther wordes may agree with the pictures.

The words are no mere list of exotic species: there is room here for cats, rats, mice – and for cabbage to feed 'hares hoppinge gayle'. The verse delights in the energy of creation ('And here are doves, digges, drakes, / redshanks ronninge through lakes'). This ark is no mausoleum. When this miniature play-world has been assembled, the chosen cast disappear from our sight:

Then shall Noe shutt the windowe of the arke, and for a little space within the bordes hee shal be scylent.

All attention is focused, waiting for the window to open. In the 'little space' of silence the imagination is made to work. The opening and closing of the window find their parodic echo (scatological rather than escatological) in the *Miller's Tale* too.

Chaucer's single reference to dramatic *speech* is disparaging: the drunken Miller pushes himself forward as story-teller and begins to rant and swear 'in Pilates voys'. Here is the voice of Pilate from the opening of the thirtieth play in the York cycle, commanding silence in his judgement hall (he is later shown to be a great drunkard).[3]

> Yhe cursed creatures that cruelly are cryand
> Restreyne you for stryvyng for strength of my strakis.
> *a*Youre pleyntes in my presence use plately applyand,
> Or ellis this brande*b* in youre braynes schall brestis and brekis.

The alliterative lines are over-full of slack syllables, creating a sense of spluttering affectation and comic violence. Chaucer imitates this in the Miller's oath 'By armes and by blood and bones', proving, in passing, how free his own poetry normally is from the pounding stress of alliterative cliché. Chaucer attuned his own verse to the gentler rhythms of indoor speech and has taught us to expect the same. Pilate's speech, in contrast, is outdoor speech, strongly accented, propelled by alliterating consonants, meant to carry in the open air. This is an important consideration, for no known Middle English plays use prose: prose does not project as well as verse (even in the interludes intended for more intimate playing in Tudor halls prose is only used for special effects), and is harder than verse to memorise. The strong rhythms and well-trussed, rhyming stanzas of the Middle English plays are primarily functional, helping the actor remember his lines and his cues, and to project his voice.[4]

In an age when vernacular translation of the Latin bible was considered 'heretical', the nearest most people came to the word of God

*a* Make your complaints perfectly, *b* sword.

was in *listening* to a paraphrase in a sermon or a play. Listen, then, to two verses from the first Wycliffite translation of Genesis (VI, 7–8), in which God voices his resolve to drown creation:

'I schall do awey', he seith, 'man whome I made of nought from the face of the erth, fro man unto thingez having soul, fro creping beeste unto the foulez of heven, forsoth it athinkith me to han made hem.' Noe forsoth fond grace byfor the lord.[5]

By following the word order of the Vulgate, the inhibited translator produces a syntax foreign to English speech, hobbled by prepositions, lacking shape and rhythm, weak in sense. In the corresponding lines of the York Shipwrights' play the obscurity vanishes, God's speech is rhythmic, free and clear:

> DEUS.
>> Al newe I will this worlde be wrought,
>> And waste away that wonnys[a] ther-in,
>> A flowyd above thame shall be broght,
>> To stroye medilerthe, both more and myn[b].
>> 'Bot Noe alon lefe shal it noght,
>> To[d] all be sownkyn for ther synne,
>> He and his sones, thus is my thoght,
>> And with there wyffes away sall wynne[e].
>>> (Y, VIII, 25–32)

The lines are balanced and sonorous, two stresses to each half, the halves linked by alliteration. Emphasis falls naturally on the words which carry meaning. God's creative purpose comes first ('Al newe ...'); the moral meaning of the flood is rendered concretely in the coupling of 'sownkyn' and 'synne' and in the balance of 'Noah alon' contrasted with 'noght'; deliverance is fittingly foretold in the last word of the stanza, 'wynne'. Even the phrase 'thus is my thoght' which seems to mark time, makes a bridge between male and female, so that God's speech seems to enact his developing thought that wives will be necessary if the new world is to breed.

Noah's trouble in getting his wife aboard was legendary, according to Chaucer:

---

*a* live, *b* great and small, *c* nothing shall be left except Noah, *d* until, *e* escape.

'Hastou nat herd,' quod Nicholas, 'also
The sorwe of Noe with his felaweshipe,
Er that he myghte get his wyf to shipe?
Hym hadde be levere, I dar wel undertake,
At thilke tyme, than alle his wetheres blake
That she hadde had a ship hirself allone.'

The tradition is as English as it is unbiblical and it goes back before the Conquest. Explanation of how an archetypal stage shrew came to dominate the biblical drama of Noah's flood must be postponed for a moment, for it begs more fundamental questions: Why were there plays of Noah's flood at all? How did it come about that the dominant form of drama in England from the time of Chaucer to the birth of Shakespeare consisted of short plays on biblical subjects, many of them from the Old Testament?

It would be wrong to imply that medieval playwrights chose their stories freely from the Bible. This choice of significant events had already been made for them by the Church, in the centuries of selection and interpretation which patterned the liturgical services, providing the key figures of church painting, sculpture and stained glass. The story of Christ's birth, ministry, passion, and resurrection was read in its narrative detail, but the Jewish Old Testament history could only be of interest to the Christian Church when considered as prophecy or prefiguration. According to the Church fathers, Noah's tribulations and deliverance prefigured Christ's sufferings and resurrection; this is why the ark of Genesis, with its puzzlingly precise specifications, is shown in early Christian art as a sort of sepulchre. In the fifteenth-century Cornish play *Origo Mundi*, the ark is 'our grave' and when the flood subsides it comes pointedly to rest on 'the fairest of hills', Mount Calvary.[6] In the later Middle Ages, as naturalism smothered symbolism, the ark became a masted sailing vessel. When the subjects of sacred history were parcelled out to guilds ('mysteries') of English craftsmen to stage as pageant-plays ('mystery plays') in summer processions, Noah fell naturally to shipwrights or mariners, who could display professional skills. God must instruct the York Noah in the correct technique of clinkering, ('of burds and wands betwen ... not over-thin'), while at Newcastle Noah knows the difference between 'spyer, sprund, sprout, nor sprot' (all apparently kinds of spar). Yet even in this world of tar and tackle there is vestigial symbolism, as when the labouring Wakefield Noah rests against the mast and bends his bones to 'this tree' in the name of the Trinity.

One drama contains neither a ship building nor an obstreperous Mrs Noah and concentrates purely on exposition of moral and theological sense. This is the so-called N-town play, from East Anglia, which may have been performed in church.[7] Here Noah goes 'off' to fetch his vessel, which presumably ran on a wheeled carriage (like the one used annually by the Mariners Guild of the Trinity at Hull and over-wintered in church). The N-town Noah is an ancient didact, explaining to the congregation that he is father of the 'second age' after Adam; his wife then warns them of the penalty of sin at 'dredfull domys day', a theme echoed by her three sons and three daughters-in-law. The poet of this insipid pageant has no way of indicating that the Noah family represents the fellowship of the righteous, saved at judgement by the ark of the church, than by filling his museum ship with trinities of prayerful little moralists preaching and singing anthems. The human experience remains unexplored, and there is little dramatic interest in the show-and-tell pageant because there is no conflict.

To provide the conflict necessary to good drama is the purpose of Noah's wife. Her crabbedness can be traced from the English plays back into the folk tales of Eastern Europe. In some of these she is in league with the devil and acts as man's traditional enemy to frustrate God's purpose. But she also voices the apocryphal – and perfectly rational – view that Noah's scheme was absurd: either his preparations are delusion or, if he is right about the flood, then why should not the rest of the world be warned? The popular tales of her resentment thus focus on Noah's secrecy. In the Newcastle play, after the sleeping Noah has received his instructions from an angel, a devil with a 'long snout' goes to his wife and offers her a potion which will make her husband reveal the secret. The shadows of Adam and Eve thus fall across the action; Noah succumbs and tells all, at which she scolds him for his presumptuous workmanship, 'Who devil made thee a wright?', implying that the matter concerns the whole guild:[8]

> When thou began to smite
> Men should have heard wide-where.
>
> (N, 172–3)

According to the folk-tale followed here, Noah's axe was silent while he kept secret, but afterwards rang throughout the world. So the Newcastle angel rebukes him:

> Thy strokes shall fair be kend[a]
> For thou thy wife has told.
> (N, 194–5)

and the play ends with the devil gloating over a temporary victory.

Noah's wife is most energetically developed in the Wakefield play, the most ambitious Middle English treatment (558 lines – about forty-five minutes playing). Matrimonial scolding and three distinct 'rounds' of Punch-and-Judy style combat occupy the centre. The delight in physical violence, the explosive colloquial exchanges and salty proverbial wit link the play to others composed or remodelled in distinctive nine-line stanzas by the so-called Wakefield Master (killing of Abel, the two Shepherds plays, Herod the Great, the Buffeting, and parts of other plays).[9] Yet the moral and theological themes are also developed more fully than in other Noah plays and are woven into the fabric of domestic speech. The flood is framed between visions of creation and judgement, so that the play presents in miniature the shape of the whole cycle of thirty-two plays.

Wakefield begins with seven stanzas in which Noah recalls God's creation, the fall of Lucifer, the fall of Adam and Eve from paradise, and man's life on earth, encumbered by the seven sins. His own great age and impotence are those of earth itself, crying for renewal:

> O therfor I drede lest God · on us will take veniance
> For syn is now alod[b], · witout any repentance.
> Sex hundreth yeris and od · have I, without distance[c]
> In erth, as any sod, · liffyd with grete grevance
> Allway;
> And now I wax old,
> Seke, sory, and cold:
> As muk upon mold[d]
> I widder away;
>
> But yit will I cry · for mercy and call:
> No[e], this servant, am I, · Lord over all!

*a* known afar, *b* widespread, *c* dispute, *d* earth, *e* Noah.

Therfor me, and my fry · shal with me fall,
Save from velany, · and bryng to thi hall
In heven;

The ordeal in the ark lasts almost exactly a year and its happy outcome is foreseen in cosmic tokens ('the son shynes in the eest' ... 'We shuld have a good feest'). When the family emerges joyfully ('with gle and with gam') and united ('all sam') the world is green and untilled. But Noah's sober astonishment hints rather that this is an image of doomsday:

NOE.

Behald on this greyn! · Nowder cart ne plogh
Is left, as I weyn[a], · nowder tre then bogh,
Ne other thyng,
Bot all is away;
Many castels, I say,
Grete townes of aray,
Flitt has this flowyng.

and the torment of all sinners:

To dede ar thai dyght, · prowdist of pryde
Everich a wyght · that ever was spyde
With syn:
All ar thai slayn,
And put unto payn.

UXOR.

From thens agayn
May thai never wyn?[b]

NOE.

Wyn? No, iwis, [c]bot he that myght hase
Wold [d]myn of thare mys, and admytte thaym to grace.

Her question is simple and natural, almost concealing its theological purpose; but Noe repeats the cue-word *wyn* so as to deepen its sense: the way to escape from death is through God's grace.

Within this cosmic frame is developed a boisterous domestic comedy. From the first rhyming of 'wife' and 'strife', and from Noah's apprehensive confidings as he goes home –

And I am agast · that we get som fray
Betwixt us both,

*a* believe, *b* escape, *c* unless the mighty one, *d* remember their tribulation.

> For she is full tethee*a*,
> For litill oft angre;
> If any thyng wrang be,
> Soyne is she wroth –

the audience is primed to expect trouble. This proverbial hostility of man and wife is provoked through scolding and verbal taunts until physical violence is inevitable. In turn the partners appeal to the audience to support and sustain the antagonism of the sexes. This Mrs Noah is no mere shrew but a cunning actress, relishing the role of persecuted martyr as much as the prospect of fisticuffs with an abusive husband:

> We women may wary*b* · all ill husbandys;
> I have oone, bi Mary · that *c*lowsyd me of my bandys!
> If he teyn*d*, I must tary, · howsoever it standys,
> With seymland*e* full sory, wryngand both my handys
> For drede;
> Bot yit otherwhile,
> What with gam and with gyle,
> I shall smyte and smyle,
> And *f*qwite hym his mede.

NOE.
> We! hold thi tong, ram-skyt*g*, or I shall the still!*h*

Her woman's weapon is her distaff and she enthrones herself on a little hill, where she spins, issuing a clear challenge to the men, both in the family and in the audience:

> Sir, for Jak nor for Gill · will I turne my face,
> Till I have on this hill · spon a space
> On my rok*i*
> Well were he myght get me!
> Now will I downe set me;
> Yit reede*j* I no man let*k* me,
> For drede of a knok.

It seems that the act of spinning, which is associated with fate and the ancient domain of women, enshrined in such folk festivals as St Distaff's Day (the day after Plough Monday) epitomizes her defiance of male authority.[10]

---

*a* peevish, *b* curse, *c* delivered me, *d* is angry, *e* countenance, *f* pay him back, *g* ramshit, *h* quieten, *i* distaff, *j* warm, *k* prevent.

Medieval preachers explained that Noah's wife signifies the rebellious flesh, chastised before it can be accepted into the Ark of the Church. Yet such a *post facto* interpretation of the drama hardly regulates the gusto of these domestic combats. The third and fiercest bout takes place after she has rushed into the ark ('Yei, water nyghys so nere · that I sit not dry') refusing to move a step further. Up there, in plain view of the audience, Noah prepares an exemplary thrashing ('Cry me mercy, I say!'), but she returns as good as she gets, until they are both finally exhausted.

NOE.

> Yee men that has wifis, · whyls they ar yong,
> If ye luf youre lifis, · chastice thare tong:
> Me thynk my hert ryfis, · both *a*levyr and long,
> To se sich stryfis · wedmen emong;
> Bot I,
> As have I blys,
> Shall chastyse this.

UXOR.

> Yit may ye mys,
> Nicholl Nedy!

NOE.

> I shall make the still as stone, · begynnar of blunder!
> I shall bete the bak and bone, · and breke all in sonder.
>
> [*They fight*]

UXOR.

> Out, alas, I am gone! · Oute apon the, mans wonder!

NOE.

> Se how she can grone, · and I lig under*b*,
> Bot, wife,
> In this hast let us ho,
> For my bak is nere in two.

UXOR.

> And I am bet so blo
> That I may not thryfe.

I FILIUS.

> A, whi fare ye thus, · fader and moder both?

II FILIUS.

> Ye shuld not be so spitus, · standyng in sich a woth*c*.

III FILIUS.

> Thise [weders] ar so hidus, · with many a cold coth*d*.

---

*a* liver and lung, *b* lie underneath, *c* danger, *d* illness.

NOE.

    We will do as ye bids us; · we will no more be wroth,
    Dere barnes!
    Now to the helme will I hent,
    And to my ship tent.

UXOR.

    I se on the firmament,
    Me thynk, the seven starnes.

In this final exchange the sexual taunting and grotesque battle end with the sexual roles turned topsy-turvy. Noah lying on his back belaboured with a distaff is a poor figure of God's authority. Admonished by their children for behaviour as *spitus* as the weather, the Noahs come to their senses, the sky begins to clear, and Noah prays for God's help ('As thou art stere-man good'). A catharsis of comic violence is skilfully used here – as in the two Wakefield Shepherds Plays – to prepare the audience to contemplate the more sober but wonderful reality of 'God's high miracle'.

    The behaviour of the Wakefield Noahs prompts the thought that God was mistaken in His judgement of them. Are they worthy to be saved? What has happened to Noah as a 'figure' of God? One problem is that Mrs Noah's carnival crabbedness is not focused on the business at hand. This aspect is better handled in the delightful and less ambitious Chester play, where Noah ruefully admits to the audience that his wife has the mastery by festival custom:

    Lord, that weomen bine crabbed aye,
    And non are meeke, I dare well saye
    That is well seene by mee todaye
    in witnesse of you echone.
    Good wiffe, lett be all this beare[a]
    that thou makest in this place here,
    for all they weene that thou arte mastere –
    and soe thou arte by sayncte John.

                (C, 105–12)

At Chester plays were performed at the feasts of Corpus Christi, Whitsun, and Midsummer or St John's Day, which was founded on that pagan feast and immemorially associated with women's midsummer practices. The Chester Wife's crabbedness is expressed by defiant drinking with her cronies. This refusal to enter the ark without 'my gosseppes all' is thus both amusing and sympathetically moral,

*a* noise.

for in expressing concern for those who will be lost, she shows herself worth saving. The family's singing celebrates the joy of salvation and the drama leaves aside the terror of those who are drowned. A humanist reading (like Turner's apocalyptic painting of The Deluge) must stress the agony of those who missed the boat, and cannot help but ask: was not Noah's acceptance of God's plan partly a betrayal of mankind? (Such a notion is implicit in the Newcastle use of folk-tale motifs.) The problem cannot be solved by merely insisting on Noah's piety, because a Noah family convinced of its own righteousness (like those of N-town) can hardly kindle our emulation.

In the end it is the humanity of man and wife that matters most. The second York play is most successful in this respect, for God does not appear and it is Noah who controls the action, thoughtfully keeping the reasons for their adventure to himself until they are safely dry. His wife's objections are thus thoroughly natural:

> Trowes thou that I wol leve the harde lande
> And tourne up here on toure deraye?[a]
> Nay, Noye, I am nought[b] bowne
>     To fonde nowe over there ffellis,
> Doo barnes, go we and trusse[c] to towne.
>
> (Y, IX, 77–81)

With an almost visible gesture she dismisses the absurdity of sailing upon the Yorkshire fells and summons her children to go shopping. Blamed for her delay in packing her kitchen gear, she reproaches Noah for not giving her more notice, finally striking him, exasperated at secrecy a hundred-winters-long. Once in the ark, she points out in the distance the 'commodyrs' and 'cosynes' for whom she interceded, all 'overe flowen with floode'. Through all this Noah displays exemplary patience and practicality, leading family prayers, ordering his sons to give hay to the cattle and his daughters-in-law to feed the chickens. Disappointed to find fifteen cubits of water still beneath his plumb line, he interrupts his casting to reassure the family. Here is a father to be trusted and loved, one worthy of God's secret counsel, capable of pioneering the new world. It is Noah rather than God who blesses the seed of his children, urges their cattle to breed, and consecrates anew the everyday work of medieval life:

a utter confusion, b ready to go exploring the hills, c make ready.

Beastes and foules sall forth be bredde,
And so a worlde be-gynne to bee,
Now travaylle sall ye taste
    To wynne you brede & wyne,
For all this worlde is waste;
They beestes muste be unbraste,
And wende we hense in haste,
    In goddis blissyng & myne.
                (Y, IX, 322–33)

The concern is homely and practical, but the simple words carry also a spiritual judgement of 'this worlde' which is not separate from the action but embodied in it, as is the case in all good drama.

## NOTES

1. L. H. Loomis, 'Secular dramatics in the Royal Palace, Paris, 1378, 1389 and Chaucer's *tregetoures*', in *Medieval English Drama*, ed. J. Taylor and A. H. Nelson (Chicago, 1972).

2. *The Chester Mystery Cycle*, ed. R. M. Lumiansky and David Mills (EETS) (Oxford, 1974). Another text of the Chester Noah with Latin stage directions is printed by P. Happé, *English Mystery Plays* (Penguin, 1975).

3. Happé, 485.

4. The experience of directors confirms this priority. However ignorant of the precise sense of the Middle English, modern amateurs, given the option, will usually prefer to learn to speak the original text 'because it sounds better'.

5. Genesis VI, 7–8 in MS. Bodley 959. *Genesis and Exodus*, ed. Conrad Lindberg (Stockholm Studies in English VI, 1959).

6. *The Ancient Cornish Drama*, ed. E. Norris, 2 vols (Oxford, 1859): *Origo Mundi*, line 1180.

7. 'N-town' because of the reference in the prologue, 'We gynne oure play / In N.town', indicating a touring play cycle. Text: *Ludus Coventriae or The Plaie Called Corpus Christi*, ed. K. S. Block (EETS) (Oxford, 1922).

8. Newcastle play: *Non-Cycle Plays and Fragments*, ed. N. Davis (EETS) (Oxford, 1970).

9. *The Wakefield Pageants in the Towneley Cycle*, ed. A. C. Cawley (Manchester, 1958). *Noah* and all except the *Herod* are printed in Happé, *English Mystery Plays*.

10. cf. The Wife of Bath:

    For al swich wit is yeven us in oure byrthe:
    Deceit, wepyng, spynnyng God hath yeve
    To wommen . . .

# THE VISUAL WORLD OF THE MIDDLE AGES

DEREK PEARSALL

To attempt to recover 'the visual world' of our medieval English poets is both a necessary and a hopeless task: necessary, because their visual experience is an immediate part of the imaginative experience that is communicated in their poetry, and the whole purpose of our reading is to absorb this experience into our own; hopeless, because, though we may momentarily inhabit their visual world through their communication of its presence, we can never truly annex it to ourselves. The world has changed, and the way of seeing it has changed. The domestic and urban and rural environment, the tools, clothes, furniture, the very landscape, which were so intimate a part of the experience of the past that they needed no special remark, are different from what we are familiar with. Our own modes of cognition condition us to select and emphasize different elements even from what we may conceive of as common reality, such as natural forms. We may think we have glimpses of the world they inhabited – of the noisome alleys and squalid hovels of medieval London, for instance, when we hear of Langland's Lyare 'lorkyng thorw lanes' and of 'the wo of this wommen that wonyeth in cotes' or of the secluded refinements of a large town house when we find Criseyde and her maidens reading from a romance in 'a paved parlour' with steps leading down to the garden – but they are no more than glimpses.

Nevertheless, the task of recovery is one that must constantly be taken up, and there is perhaps one area of the medieval poet's visual experience to which we may reasonably claim a more direct access. The visual world of the poet is in one sense the world that the poet conceives of as being uniquely visual; that is, the world of the visual arts, and here, in the paintings, illustrated books, fine buildings, sculpted figures and ornaments, tiles and textiles of the age, in so far as they survive, we have common ground, and we can share more

fully their experience, particularly their experience of what was inno-
vative and exciting. There are still barriers, of course: the types of
spiritual understanding which informed appreciation of religious art
and architecture, the devout frame of mind in which a beautifully
decorated book of hours may (or may not) have been used and
inspected by its owner, are not readily recovered. Furthermore, much
of what survives has changed in many respects from what once
existed. Cathedrals and churches have not only undergone constant
reshaping – as they were being reshaped in the fourteenth century
itself – but they have also largely lost the brightness and richness of
colour, the profusion of ornament, which once made them visual
experiences of a very different order. The stained glass, the decorative
programmes of wall-painting, the colouring and gilding applied to
sculpted figure and ornament and canopied niche, have been largely
swept away by revolutions of taste, and what remains is of an un-
medieval austerity. Ornaments, objets d'art, alabaster figurines and
ivory panels, which once had a living context in everyday visual
experience, are now unnaturally sealed in the antiseptic hush of
museums and galleries. Only illustrated manuscripts remain exactly
as they were.

Yet much survives to stimulate our imaginations, to inspire by its
beauty or to astonish by its extraordinariness as well as to take us into
the visual world of the medieval poets. In what follows, the hints
provided by Chaucer and his contemporaries to what they found
notable in the art and architecture of their day will be used as the
starting points for a brief survey of the development of the arts in
fourteenth-century England, with some particular emphasis on the
last quarter of the century. What will not be attempted is any
drawing of analogies between developments in the arts and developments in literature. Such analogies, where they have no foundation
in common iconographic content or other subject-matter, where,
that is, they are drawn from a perception of 'stylistic' similarities, tend
to be based on large and dubious assumptions about cultural change,
and to betray an ignorance of professional and technical practice.
They involve a high degree of abstraction, whereby stylistic features
said to be discerned in the visual arts are clothed in abstract language
(realism, structural coherence, stylization, organic form, etc.)
matched with features of literary works similarly described, and a

wonderful similarity perceived. It is not a difficult game to play, and intelligent readers of medieval literature can be left to play it among themselves.

★　　★　　★

> But many subtil compassinges,
> Babewynnes and pynacles,
> Ymageries and tabernacles,
> I say; and ful eke of wyndowes,
> As flakes falle in grete snowes.
> And eke in ech of the pynacles
> Weren sondry habitacles,
> In which stoden, al withoute –
> Ful the castel, al aboute –
> Of alle maner of mynstralles,
> And gestiours, that tellen tales . . .
> (Chaucer, *House of Fame*, 1188–98)

The rebuilding of Westminster Abbey under the direct royal patronage of Henry III in the years after 1245 introduced an emphasis on decorative refinement which was to have a profound influence on the development of English Gothic architecture. In the Abbey, this new taste is best evidenced in the decorative treatment of the interior, with elaborate traceries for the interior arches, and diaper patterning and foliage sculpture, even figure sculpture, wherever a featureless blank space threatens. This emphasis on functionless decoration may be seen as significantly related to the motives of the secular patron, where love of display and ostentation (and, in Henry's case, the desire to compete with France) may be expected to figure large. Nevertheless, the new influences are soon at work in the remodelling of the choirs of Lincoln in the 1260s and Exeter in the 1280s. But it was Edward I's decision to build a series of twelve crosses to mark the stages of his dead queen's journey from Hardby, in Lincolnshire, to Westminster in 1290 that gives us the most striking evidence of the new style. These tall, delicate, ornamented monuments, pure in the ostentation of grief, are ideal vehicles for decoration, and one of the surviving examples of the 'Eleanor Cross', the one at Hardingstone (Northants.), has not only crocketed gables with foliate finials and naturalistic foliage but also, apparently for the first time in England, the ogee arches which are the most defiantly functionless of all major features of the style. A tomb was built for Eleanor in Westminster

*Tomb of Edward II, Gloucester Cathedral*

Abbey, but it was surpassed by that of Edmund Crouchback (d. 1296), the king's brother, which must have looked extremely rich when all its crestings and pinnacles were gilt, as they were meant to be, its sculpted figures of 'weepers' painted, and its canopy inlaid here and there with stained glass set on tinfoil. Tombs, indeed, provide some of the best surviving examples of the decorative style in all its essential features, and that of Edward II (d. 1327) in Gloucester Cathedral, with its bewildering tintinnabulation of ogival canopies and slender pinnacles, its 'malediction of little tabernacles', might have provided the very spur of outrage for Vasari. Even that, though, can barely match the dizzy splendours of the Percy tomb (c. 1342–5) in Beverley Minster, which represents perhaps the efflorescence of the style, insofar as encrustation with sculptured ornament is concerned.

Throughout the church-building of the period, the emphasis is on decorative rather than structural innovation: multiplication and exaggeration of ribs in vaulting, flowing window tracery (as in the west window at York), hectic and sinuous line in figure sculpture, ballflower ornament and foliage sculpture everywhere. The canopied niche (or 'tabernacle', in Chaucer's term), rhythmically repeated, becomes a decorative feature in its own right in the York chapter house, while in the Lady Chapel at Ely the protruding ogival arch, or 'nodding arch', proclaims itself ostentatiously useless. There is a proliferation, too, of slender, crocketed pinnacles, and the heads of the flying buttresses, themselves made necessary by the increasing size of the windows, provide a perch for yet more pinnacles, and, with them, more arcades, niches, tracery and sculpture.

Foliage-carving is a favourite opportunity for the decorative artist to display his skill, and there is a phase in the late thirteenth and early fourteenth century, at Lincoln (in the Angel Choir), Exeter (in the presbytery) and above all at Southwell (in the Chapter House and its vestibule), when foliage-sculpture achieves a high degree of naturalistic accuracy. The ease with which leaves of oak, maple, vine, may, rose, hop and fig may be identified at Southwell has led some enthusiasts to proclaim here a revolution in perception. But it hardly seems to be so. The fashion soon dies out, very abruptly at Exeter with the arrival of a new carver in 1308, and may be due to no more than the mislaying of a pattern book and the catching-on of a new fashion. More purely ornamental and conventionally decorative leaf-carving soon takes over, and those elements in foliage are emphasized which contribute to a generally rhythmical patterning. How deep the dedication to 'realism' goes is indicated at Lincoln, where we find naturalistic primrose or periwinkle flowers growing among microscopically perfect oak-leaves. In truth, it needs more

*Stone capital, Passage, Southwell Minster, Nottinghamshire*

than a localized imitation of nature, however exact, to make it possible to talk about a revolution in perception, and this fragmentary 'realism' is to coexist for a long time with generally decorative or symbolic aesthetic programmes without affecting their essential nature. The beautifully observed flora and fauna in the margins of English illuminated manuscripts are a case in point. The excellent herring gull on the *bas de page* boss in the late thirteenth-century Tenison Psalter,[1] the superb array of birds gathering at the angel's call in an early fourteenth-century Apocalypse[2] – where hoopoe, magpie, kingfisher, wren, green woodpecker, goldfinch, bullfinch, woodcock, stork, crane and parrot are readily identifiable – or swarming around God's head in the creation scenes of the Holkham Bible Picture Book or Queen Mary's Psalter,[3] are points of rapport for the modern observer, but they are not part of a new composition of the world of experience, such as we find in Giotto.

It is to the margins of the illustrated manuscripts that we should also turn to find the most elaborate examples of another favourite decorative feature of the period – the grotesques or *babewynnes*. In association with genre-scenes of domestic life and images drawn from the bestiaries, as well as more traditional iconographic motifs, these misshapen and aborted beast-and-human figures appear here and there in hidden or distant corners of churches, on roof-bosses or misericords, occasionally in stained glass, as in the scenes of the monkey's funeral and the monkey-physician in the glass of the north aisle of the nave at York. But it is in the margins of the East Anglian psalters of the first half of the fourteenth century that we find the most riotous assemblies of such grotesques. The beginnings can be traced in manuscripts of the late thirteenth century, such as the Tenison Psalter, made for the marriage of Alfonso, son of Edward I, but left unfinished, presumably because of his death in 1284. The marginal decoration and illustration here is of a marked freedom, with finely drawn grotesques, birds, beasts and plants, but it does not threaten the overall decorative plan of the page. The Peterborough Psalter[4] was done about 1300 by a travelling group of secular artists for a monastic patron, and was given by the abbot of Croyland to a French nephew of Pope John XXII, which is what brought it eventually to Brussels. The *Beatus* page (the illustrative page accompanying Psalm 1, 'Blessed is the man') is enormously elaborate, and the borders are packed with detail, including a scene of a fox making off with a cock over his shoulder, as in Chaucer's *Nun's Priest's Tale*. The Queen Mary Psalter, done about twenty years later, is one of the finest and most fully achieved of these manuscripts, and it is, for its period, remarkably restrained. The illustration additional to the main miniatures is confined to the *bas de page*, and consists of a series of quite carefully composed pen-and-ink scenes of courtly, domestic and rural life. The manuscript is a prime example of the emphasis on fine draughtsmanship and linearity which remains such a permanently distinctive feature of medieval English manuscript illumination.

It is, however, to another group of manuscripts, notably the Ormesby, Gorleston and St Omer Psalters[5] that one turns for the most lavish border decoration. Here the margins rampage with ingeniously misconceived grotesques, as well as menageries of exquisitely drawn animals, genre-scenes and bestiary motifs, all in, on and around formal border ornament of overpowering lushness. Certain pages, especially the *Beatus* pages, are clearly regarded as opportunities for virtuoso displays of decorative ingenuity. The *Beatus* page of the St Omer Psalter, for instance, is almost incredibly elaborate: on a stippled gold ground, there is a panelled border with medallions (containing Old Testament scenes) enfolded and linked by a complex network of interlaced cords; from every part of the border grow curling tendrils and delicate sprays of foliage of oak, holly, ivy, daisy and maidenhair fern. Then, in every crevice of the page, a bewildering variety of animal and human activity – a peacock, a man drinking from a wide-lipped goblet, a boy leaping over and spearing a unicorn, a raven picking at a dead horse, two men straining at a rope attached to the Ark (being built in one of the roundels), other men working with axe and auger, mounting a ladder and felling an oak, a wild man of the woods, a porcupine, a stag and a bear, two men mounted pick-a-back wrestling, a female dancer, rams butting, swine, a horse grazing, birds, rabbits and squirrels, a swan, a heron, a hawk striking a duck, a caterpillar, a fly and a butterfly. The *Dixit dominus* page of the Ormesby Psalter is still more bizarre. At the top, an owl seated backwards on a rabbit is pursued by a monkey wearing falconer's gloves and seated on a greyhound, while at the bottom, two naked men seated on a lion and a bear fight fisticuffs. On the left, a half-naked man, with upper and lower halves of his body facing in opposite directions, blows a trumpet from which a pennant flaps.

What such images signify, if they signify anything at all, it is hard to say. It would need the exercise of an almost perverse ingenuity to argue that they are all part of an ordered and coherent iconographic programme, with every scene and image reinforcing a point of doctrine derived from the text or the main miniature. The fact that this is sometimes so does not mean that it is always so. We should allow something for the imaginative ingenuity and comparative freedom from clerical constraint of the secular artists who by now were almost entirely responsible for the decoration of such manuscripts. In other words, they did it because they enjoyed doing it. Emile Male comments similarly on the carvings on the porch at Rouen, where quatrefoils swarm with ingeniously carved grotesques: a rearing centaur wearing a cowl and bearded like a prophet shows two horse's hooves as forelegs, two human feet in boots behind; a doctor inspecting a test-tube is a man to the waist and then becomes a goose; a philosopher with a pig's head meditates as he holds his snout. 'If ever works of art were innocent of ulterior meaning,' says Male, 'surely these are.'

We should allow something, too, in the magnificently exuberant Psalter pages, for the interests of the growing class of secular patrons, and indeed for the interests of rich clerics who may have welcomed the absorbing distractions of these complicated pages, and enjoyed the diversion they provided by their wit and ingenuity. Certainly, this seems very clearly to be the function of the Books of Hours made by Jean Pucelle in Paris during roughly this same period of the early to mid fourteenth century. They are fashionable accessories for wealthy ladies, for whom the marginal digressions provided a source of amusement. The Belleville Breviary, for instance, was done for Jeanne de Belleville when as a young widow she was contemplating entering a convent. She did not do so, but married again, and the book passed into the hands of the crown when her husband was later executed. (It was later given by Charles VI to Richard II when the English king married the French king's daughter; Henry IV returned it to France.) The margins are full of brilliant naturalistic drawing, contrasting markedly with the ostentatious Italianate foreshortening and over-ambitious architecture of the main pictures. The Hours of Jeanne d'Evreux, done for the queen of Charles le Bel, and painted in grisaille throughout, contain a riotous abundance of *drôleries*, in the borders, in and around the initials, at line-endings, and as caryatids to support the main miniature. They exhibit an inexhaustible interest in natural appearances, combined with a lively sense of the ridiculous.

The life of this particular fashion, at least in its most vigorous and fully achieved form, is comparatively brief, and by the time

*East Anglian: Marginal Scene and Grotesque, from Luttrell Psalter*

the Luttrell Psalter[6] was executed, about 1340, for the family of that name, genre scenes of domestic and rural life and coarsely drawn grotesque monsters have broken free of the decorative composition. Manuscripts like this, and like the Taymouth Hours and the Smithfield Decretals,[7] have acquired a special fame for their realistic depiction of contemporary life, of games and sports and daily work, and in this respect they are extremely valuable, but they hold little for the lover of decorative art.

★ ★ ★

> The burne bode on bonk, that on blonk hoved,
> Of the depe double dich that drof to the place.
> The walle wod in the water wonderly depe
> Ande eft a ful huge heght hit haled upon lofte,
> Of harde hewen ston up to the tables,
> Enbaned under the abataylment, in the best lawe;
> And sythen garytes[a] ful gaye gered bitwene,
> Wyth mony luflych loupe that louked ful clene;
> A better barbican that burne blusched upon never.
> And innermore he behelde that halle ful hyghe,
> Towres telded bytwene, trochet ful thik,
> Fayre fylyoles that fyed, and ferlyly long,
> With corvon coprounes, craftyly sleye.
> Chalk-whyt chymnees ther ches he innoghe,
> Upon bastel roves that blenked ful whyte.
> So mony pynakle payntet was poudred aywhere
> Among the castel carneles[b], clambred so thik,
> That pared out of papure purely hit semed.
>
> (*Sir Gawain and the Green Knight*, 785–802)

The magnificence of English secular architecture in the fourteenth century has to be largely reconstructed from the eroded remains, but there is enough to suggest that the poet's description of Bercilak's castle is not pure fantasy. Splendour, opulence and comfort are what the last two Plantagenet kings looked for in their new building, and where his grandfather had pressed all the kingdom's masons into service on his great Welsh castles, Edward III brought them south to turn castles into palaces. The great work was at Windsor, where the royal lodgings were refurbished (1357–65) on a most sumptuous scale. The king had a first, second, third and fourth chamber, a

---

*a* look-out turrets, *b* embrasures.

chamber called 'La Rose', a painted chamber and a great chamber and closet as well as a chapel and hall. The queen had a first chamber, a second with a chapel, a chamber with mirrors, and 'la daunsyng chambre'. Leeds, in Kent, was another royal castle that had its residential quarters upgraded, while the new royal castle at Queenborough, on the Isle of Sheppey, completed in 1371, with its beautifully symmetrical concentric fortifications, combined military strength with domestic splendour. Queenborough has disappeared,

*Bodiam Castle, Sussex*

but a spectacular example of the new style of castle architecture survives at Bodiam, in Sussex, completed by Sir Edward Dalyngrigge in 1386 from the proceeds of the French wars, where the lord's apartments are completely secluded from those of his retainers. The great residential castles of the fifteenth century, such as Caister (1432), Tattershall (1434) and Hurstmonceux (1440), continue this tradition.

Edward III was also enlarging and improving the royal houses around London, where he preferred to spend most of his later years. The improvements at King's Langley (1359–77) included a large and elaborate bath-house with hot running water, while a new suite of royal lodgings of considerable opulence was built at Eltham.

Richard II also favoured Eltham, where he had a new bath-house and 'dancing chamber' installed (1384–8), an oriel chamber for Queen Anne, apartments for the court, an almonry, a spicery, and a saucery. His favourite, though, was Sheen, where his grandfather had built a whole set of new apartments, expensively decorated and glazed. Richard added a new bath-house, tiled with 2,000 painted tiles, as well as a separate 'summer-house' on an island in the nearby river. He had the whole palace of Sheen demolished as a mark of his grief when Anne died in 1394.

*John of Gaunt's Hall, Kenilworth Castle, Warwickshire*

Richard was, for the most part, adding to and improving the work of his grandfather, who was indeed 'besy and corious in bildyng'. His own great achievement was the commissioning of the rebuilding of the great hall at Westminster Palace, where the king's mason, Henry Yevele (who had recently been at work on the nave at Winchester, and possibly at Canterbury too), and the king's carpenter, Hugh Herland, combined to reshape the largest royal hall in Europe. With its magnificent hammerbeam roof, it survives as the masterpiece of medieval English secular architecture. Begun in 1393, it was almost complete for the King's deposition in 1399.

Others were not idle. Kenilworth was transformed by John of Gaunt (1390–93) from a feudal stronghold into a palace, with a bay-windowed great hall roofed in a single span, splendid apartments, and much elaborate interior and exterior decoration. New College, built by William of Wykeham at Oxford (1386), set the model for the monumental collegiate building of the future. Some of the new abbey gatehouses, such as that at Thornton Abbey in Lincolnshire (*c.* 1385), built to provide fitting accommodation for important guests, are like miniature palaces in themselves. Castles like Bodiam, or Wardour Castle in Wiltshire, residences with a military air rather than castles with accommodation, might have given a hint of *Gawain*-like richness when they had their full complement of towers and turrets. But it is probably to France that one has to go to find Bercilak's Castle, if it, or its like, is to be found anywhere outside the fantasy of a cake-decorator. Jean, duc de Berry, the greatest artistic patron of late medieval Europe north of the Alps, had a series of castles built which yield nothing to fiction. The castle at Mehun-sur-Yèvre, where the great sculptor and artist André Beauneveu was established as artistic director, was famous enough by 1393 for Froissart to rhapsodize over it, and for Philip of Burgundy to send his own painter and sculptor to study it. The Duke, with a nice sense of irony, had it painted by the Limbourgs as the foreground to *The Temptation of Christ* in the *Très Riches Heures*, and there, with its pinnacles and gables, pinnacles upon turrets upon towers, its elaborate statuary, all gilded and coloured, it is as it was. The first visual evidences of this taste in England are in the vertiginous architecture behind the figure of Chaucer in the famous frontispiece to *Troilus and Criseyde*.[8]

★   ★   ★

> Thanne y [a]munte me forth, the mynstre to knowen,
> And [b]awaytede a woon wonderlie well ybeld[c],
> With arches on everiche half and [d]belliche ycorven,
> With crochetes on corners with knottes of golde,
> Wyde wyndowes ywrought, ywritten ful thikke,
> Schynen with schapen scheldes to schewen aboute . . .
> Tombes opon tabernacles tyld[e] opon lofte,
> Housed in hirnes[f], harde set abouten
> Of armede alabaustre clad for the nones,
> Made upon marbel in many maner wyse,
> Knyghtes in her conisantes[g] clad for the nones,
> All it semed seyntes ysacred opon erthe;
> And lovely ladies ywrought leyen by her sydes
> In many gay garmentes that weren gold-beten.
>
> (*Piers the Ploughman's Creed*, 171–88)

*a* went, *b* saw a building, *c* built, *d* beautifully, *e* built, *f* niches, *g* coats of arms.

The anonymous early fifteenth-century poet records here his vision of a great Dominican church, crowded with tombs in their canopied niches. Churches had become the mausoleums of the great, and the church generally, and the friars particularly, welcomed the endowments of those who desired and could pay for a pompous incarceration. Heraldic shields appear everywhere, as the mark of this secular patronage. Marble gives way to more easily carved stone, such as alabaster, for the tomb-effigy, and alabaster relief sculpture and statuettes fill every niche or tabernacle of the shrine. Alabaster-carving becomes, in fact, something of an industry in England, and figurines and carved retables are exported in quantities to the Continent. The funerary industry in its turn imports incised brass slabs from Flanders, which enable every knight and his lady to be commemorated in church, without taking up too much valuable space. Styles grow simpler, less inventively decorative, in this kind of funerary ornament, though the change may have as much to do with methods of production as with revolutions of taste. At the same time, some measure of deliberate restraint characterizes the monumental gilded bronze effigies of the Black Prince at Canterbury and of Richard II and his queen in Westminster Abbey. The latter was tremendously expensive, further evidence of the conscious ostentation of Richard's artistic patronage.

The friars may also have had something to do with another important fourteenth-century development. The origins of English Perpendicular have traditionally been traced to the transepts and choir at Gloucester (*c.* 1331–6 and *c.* 1337–60 respectively), and certainly there is here the classic surviving statement of the characteristic features of the style: strong vertical emphasis, geometrical uniformity rather than decorative variety, vast window area, and the carrying of the repetitive panel structure of the window from the floor below the window to the very top of the flattened arch. But it was the influence of the masons attached to the Royal Works that made itself felt at Gloucester, through Edward III's interest in providing a fitting expression of his pious memory of his father, and that style was foreshadowed in St Stephen's chapel (part of Westminster Palace), now destroyed, and possibly in other building in London. The origins of 'Perpendicular' are thus meshed with the origins of 'Decorated', which is a warning against simple chronological division

*Gloucester Cathedral, Interior*

of styles. In London, too, was begun in 1306 the vast church of the Franciscans in Newgate Street (which, unlike other mendicant churches, survived the Reformation, only to be destroyed in the Great Fire of 1666), where the emphasis on light and air and unity of space, which were to characterize the new Perpendicular style, would have matched well the ambitions of the friars, who wanted nothing so much as a large, well-lit hall where they could win folk over by their preaching.

Whatever its origins, rebuilding in the dignified new style proceeded apace, reaching its climax in the remodelling of the nave at Winchester, the complete rebuilding of the nave at Canterbury, begun in 1379, and the transformation of the east end of York minster into a dignified and harmonious late Gothic composition. 'Babewynnerie' is out, and the move from the flowing traceries of the west window at York, and the rich diversity of the nave glass, to the monumental east window (1405-8) is the history of a transformation in style. The chapel of New College, Oxford, built by William of Wykeham (1383), has the same unity of design, as do many new or rebuilt parish churches in thriving towns or ports, such as Newark, Hull (Holy Trinity) and Lynn (St Nicholas). With their high vaults, slender columns and great windows, and with their magnificent hammerbeam timbering and carved rood-screens, they are the epitome of the medieval parish church. Even a piece of church-furniture as exquisitely elaborate as the Neville screen in Durham Cathedral (1372-80), from one point of view a manifestation of the purely decorative, can be seen from another point of view, and in comparison with the tomb of Edward II, as the product of an almost mathematical purity of design.

★　★.　★

> The firste was a ferse freke*a*, fayrere than thies othire ...
> A hathelle*b* on ane heghe horse with hauke appon hande ...
> A chaplet one his chefe-lere*c*, chosen for the nones,
> Raylede alle with rede rose, richeste of floures,
> With trayfoyles and trewloves of full triede perles,
> With a chefe charebocle*d* chosen in the myddes.
> He was gerede alle in grene, alle with golde byweuede,
> Embroddirde alle with besanttes*e* and beralles full riche;

*a* fierce fellow, *b* man, *c* hair, *d* carbuncle, *e* small gold ornaments, coins.

*East front, York Minster*

His colere with calsydoynnes clustrede full thikke,
With many dyamandes full dere dighte one his sleves.
The semys with saphirs sett were full many
With emeraudes and amatistes appon iche syde,
With full riche rubyes raylede by the hemmes;
The price of that perry*a* were worthe powndes full many.

(*Parliament of the Three Ages*, 109–29)

Richard II cared much for the things he was surrounded by, and the latter part of his reign is one of unparalleled luxury in the minor decorative arts as applied to costume, ornament and personal objets de luxe – the new insignia of rank and taste. The fashion had been begun by Edward III, who had his clothes, plate, horse-harness, beds and hangings liberally sprinkled with coats of arms, badges and other decorative devices; but it is after Richard's marriage to Anne of Bohemia in 1382 that the English court begins to rival those of the Continent in the richness, intricacy and expensiveness of its appurtenances. We read of a white satin doublet that Richard had, embroidered with golden orange-trees bearing a hundred silver-gilt oranges, the white satin sleeves hung with fifteen silver cockles and thirty mussels and whelks in silver gilt. It was imported luxury for the most part, the English art of embroidery, *opus anglicanum*, having gone into a decline in the face of the fashion for imported fabrics. When Richard had some books rebound in 1386, it is the same taste that finds expression: they are to be covered, as the account books put it, 'de satyn pale blu et albo, liniatorum cum satyn rube, garnitato cum serico blu et botanatorum de auro de cipre et tassellis de serico'. Robert de Vere, earl of Oxford, Richard's favourite, had a bed of blue camoca, embroidered in gold with owls and fleur-de-lis, and valued at £68 13s. 4d. Clearly, the bed that Chaucer promised Morpheus, in the *Book of the Duchess*, 'ryght wel cled in fyn blak satyn doutremer', is not the meretricious finery of mere imagination. Costliness may seem to be the essence of the matter, and it is all we are likely to hear about in what survives, that is, the account books; but taste and discrimination and the appreciation for fine workmanship should be allowed their part too. The poet of *The Parliament of the Three Ages* perhaps looks at things with a jaundiced eye in stressing how many pounds' worth of *perry* are lavished on

---

*a* outfit of precious stones.

the costume of Youth, but the *Gawain*-poet shows a more refined taste in describing the hero's *urysoun*,

> Enbrawden and bounden wyth the best gemmes
> On brode sylkyn borde, and bryddes on semes,
> [a]As papjayes paynted perving bitwene,
> Tortors and trulofes entayled so thyk
> [b]As many burde theraboute had ben seven wynter / In toune
>> (*Gawain*, 609–14)

For him, clearly, it is the quality of the workmanship, and the infinite care of the seamstresses, that is to be admired.

Domestic objects of all kinds are similarly enriched with ornament – an ivory looking-glass in a gold frame with enamelled and jewelled roses, a silver ewer enamelled with birds, caskets with ivory lids of imported workmanship done with elegant scenes of courtly dalliance. The taste and style is French, and the models for such artifice may be found in the inventory of the duke of Anjou (d. 1385), Berry's elder brother. Here, amongst other things, there is described a golden salt-cellar which took the form of a tree, with a brook running around its base; in the tree, in allusion to the story of Tristram and Yseult, King Mark spies on the lovers, his face reflected in the enamelled brook below. Everywhere, function is swallowed in ornament, nature conjured into exquisite and costly artifice.

It is possible to see the same 'international style' at work in the English painting of the period. There is a marked decline in the quality of English illustrated manuscripts after about 1350, which may be in part due to the Black Death, in part to the availability of imported French work. Among the few signs of vigour are the group of psalters and books of hours done for Humphrey de Bohun, seventh earl of Hereford (d. 1373), and his daughter Mary (d. 1394). The smaller initials, as well as the borders of the full-page illustrations, are done with a good deal of inventiveness, and the occasional grotesques are lively, but the drawing of the main pictures is usually undistinguished. Perhaps the most striking feature of the group is the extensive use of architectural allusion: slender crocketed pinnacles spring in profusion, like inverted icicles, out of the top border of

---

*a* Such as parrots painted between periwinkles, turtledoves and true-love flowers . . . ,
*b* The suggestion is that many maidens must have been engaged for seven winters on this elaborate embroidery.

the Beatus page in the Exeter psalter,[9] in a manner reminiscent of the Neville screen, whilst many main and border scenes are framed in quite elaborate architectural canopies. This love of intricate architectural decoration remains a feature of English illustrated manuscripts in the international style, and reaches its most perfect expression in the Annunciation which is now to be found bound up with the 'Beaufort' Hours,[10] itself of somewhat later date (after 1430). The scene is set in a beautiful architectural shrine, and the colouring, with ultramarine and soft pink against a green and gold backdrop, is most delicate.

There are other examples of this bejewelled style of illumination in the late fourteenth century, amongst which may be mentioned the *Liber Regalis* (1382). But the triumph of the international style in England is of course the Wilton Diptych, in which the young Richard, backed by John the Baptist, King Edmund the Martyr, and Edward the Confessor, kneels in homage to the infant Jesus, whose mother and accompanying angels bear Richard's badge of the white hart. The draughtsmanship is of the utmost delicacy and precision, the figures of the Baptist and his companions achieve a stateliness far beyond mere elegance, and the exquisite monotony of blue in the angels' costumes is highly sophisticated. With all this, it is difficult to be more than charmed by the painting, and possible to be less than charmed by the atmosphere of privileged affectation or by the spoilt adolescent who takes Richard's part. There is nothing here to move the observer: it is high-class ornament, no more, and it is doubtful whether a more certain knowledge of the occasion for which the work was produced would make much difference to this view of it.

\* \* \*

A womman travaillynge was hire biforn;
But for hire child so longe was unborn,
Ful pitously Lucyna gan she calle,
And seyde, 'Help, for thou mayst best of alle!'
Wel koude he peynten lifly that it wroughte;
With many a floryn he the hewes boghte.

(Chaucer, *Knight's Tale*, 2083–8)

Praise of realism is a familiar theme in classical writing on the appreciation of art, as in Pliny, and remains throughout the Middle

*Sherborne Missal*

Ages as a *topos*, even though art itself has no dedication to realism but is rather, as Emile Male put it, 'at once a script, a calculus and a symbolic code'. But there are signs in the late fourteenth century, as earlier in Italy in Boccaccio's praise of Giotto, that verisimilitude is becoming more than a *topos* of praise. Chaucer's comment on the picture in the temple of Diana is derived from a similar comment in the *Roman de la Rose*, but where Guillaume de Lorris was describing an iconographic image of Vilanye, Chaucer is referring to a whole scene expressive of drama and emotion. This is an important change, for, as we have seen, a 'fragmentary realism' had long been a feature of medieval art, and had been brought to a high degree of naturalistic accuracy in English manuscripts of the early fourteenth century. This surface verisimilitude, which is interested in line rather than volume, is epitomized in the exquisite bird-painting of English artists, a tradition which can be seen continued in the Pepysian Sketch Book[11] begun in the 1380s, and still later in the painting of John Siferwas in the Sherborne Missal. But the dedication of a whole composition to the representation of observed reality, with human figures realized as solid forms in their relation to each other and to their spatial environment, and with the commitment to human experience, human drama and emotion that is necessarily involved thereby, is a different matter.

Such observed reality is rare in England in this period, it must be admitted. The manuscripts of the period have been scoured for signs of Giottesque influence, and a few experimental figures have been thrown up, often in margins, which were generally more receptive to innovation. The figure with the trumpet in the *Dixit dominus* of the Ormesby Psalter has, for instance, been cited as an example of an Italianate interest in the modelling of unusual figure poses. The superb *Beatus* page of the St Omer Psalter has an interesting male figure in the border, straining to take the weight of the border decoration above him with head bent towards the observer and skilfully foreshortened. We can see a similar figure, with his back to the viewer, promoted to the main picture later on, in the Crucifixion scene in the Lytlington Missal (1383–4). This picture also has some rather self-conscious attempts at face and figure modelling, and some notion of the realization of the scene in depth (which actually results only in overcrowding). Some of the Bohun manuscripts go after similar effects, suggesting dramatic interconnections between figures where earlier painters would have isolated them in set poses. Again, it is interaction within the compositions that is important, with its suggestion of a reality that has an existence beyond the artist's statement, for the 'humanization' of individual figures had been a feature of representation for a long time: an early example is the warmly affectionate Virgin and Child in the Chichester roundel of about 1250 (a wall-painting in the chapel of the bishop's palace), which is not so very different in spirit from the more delicate representation of the same scene in the De Lisle Psalter[12] (c. 1325) or in the Jesse Window of Winchester College Chapel (1392–4).

At the very end of the century, these fragmentary indications of a shift in the preoccupation of English artists with primarily decorative compositions come together in the work of two foreign artists working in England. One is the master of the great Carmelite Missal (1393–8), which now survives only in part. Here there is a new mastery of face and figure modelling, a sense of depth in the buildings which accommodate such scenes as the Birth of the Virgin or the Presentation in the Temple, and a new coherence of spatial realization. The other is Herman Scheere (c. 1400–15), whose work, though it lacks the monumentality of composition of the Carmelite master, combines sensitivity in the rendering of human feeling with considerable technical control of the elements of modelling and of spatial composition. His masterpiece is the Bedford Psalter and Hours.[13] The contrast with native-born artists is still striking, as with John Siferwas, whose Crucifixion in the Sherborne Missal (c. 1396), though crowded and dramatic, with lively figures in rich costumes, lacks the conviction of a fully harmonized composition. The illustrator of the *Livres du Graunt Caam*,[14] about 1400, has a similar taste for strong colour, crowded detail, and drama, but his work is still closer to the fastidiously decorative preoccupations of the international style.

Even the most advanced painters in England, however, can hardly bear comparison with contemporary artists in France such as the Boucicaut Master and the Limbourgs. Their realization of scenes, their mastery of figure and space, their inexhaustible inventiveness in meeting the challenge of new subjects, exhibit a technical control of representational realism so complete that we must believe that the occasional restraints placed by them upon the exploration of that realism are deliberate. The careful 'framing' of the pictures of the Visitation or of the Flight into Egypt by the Master of the Boucicaut Hours, for instance, are reminders to the observer of the limitations of pictorial realism, and of the necessity of meditation as well as aesthetic enjoyment. The superbly atmospheric rendering of the distant landscape, with its precocious suggestions of aerial perspective, is likewise counterpointed against the wholly formal representation of the sun, the rays of which dart down as independently drawn golden beams so as to irradiate the scene with a super-real presence. The work of the Limbourg brothers is still more technically advanced, and the different preoccupations of the three brothers, Paul (or Pol), Jean and Herman, can be seen in fascinating juxtaposition in a manuscript like the *Belles Heures* of Jean, duc de Berry, in the Cloisters Museum in New York. Paul's mastery of Tuscan painting is complete, of its solid forms, its colours, its sense of space, and he matches this technical mastery with a powerful sense of drama, of the significance in human terms of the events that he paints, which leads him into a multitude of naturalistic innovations. The faces and postures of the participants in the Lamentation are expressive, in a fully controlled way, of the intensely felt human drama of the occasion; the drama of figure-relationship in the Flight into Egypt does not exclude the more intimate view of the world shown in the representation of the very prints of hoofs and feet in the dust of the road; in the scene of the beheading of St Catherine, the saint's hair falls in natural disarray over her breast and between her praying hands. Jean's copy of this scene, in his beheading of St Lucy, shows an altogether different view of the event. He has made it more elegant, less dramatic, more fragile and pathetic: the praying hands droop, the stray lock over the breast is gone, the fold of the cloak is elegantly draped over the left arm instead of accidentally caught. This is the true international style, which we may see too in the elegant scene of Eustace's loss of his sons, also by Jean, where Eustace, watching his sons being carried off by wild animals on either side of the river he is wading through, is not so disturbed as to allow his expression or his costume to be much disarrayed.

★　　★　　★

And so shaltow come to a court as cleer as the sonne.
The mote is of Mercy, the manere[a] in the myddes,
And al the wallyng is of Wyt, for Wil ne sholde it wynne.
The carneles[b] ben of Cristendom, that kynde to save,
Ybotresed with Bileve-so-or-thow-best-not-ysaved;
And alle the hous been yheled[c], halles and chaumbres,
With no leed but with love, and with lele[d]-speche.
(Langland, *Piers Plowman*, C Text, VII, 232–8)

It is worth remembering, finally, that there were many humbler forms of expression in the visual arts which would have had an altogether more permanent presence in the medieval mind. The wall-paintings in churches would have made everyone familiar with the iconography of the Last Judgement, and with biblical scenes and their typological significance. Some churches, such as that at Hoxne, in Suffolk, include more systematic programmes of doctrinal instruction in their wall-paintings, with representations of the seven deadly sins, the Seven Works of Mercy and the Seven Ages of Man. Others have more schematized allegorical representations of the trees of the Vices, or the ladder of Virtue. Such schemes are not confined to churches: at Longthorpe Tower, near Peterborough, there is a room that contains some of the best surviving wall-painting of the period, with a diagrammatic Wheel of the Senses and a representation of that favourite *memento mori*, the meeting of the Three Living and Three Dead. Similarly schematized didactic drawings are found in manuscripts of the period: sometimes they are there to illustrate allegorical and other works of instruction, such as the *Hortus Deliciarum* or the *Somme le Roi*, with its labelled diagrammatic trees, but there are also manuscripts which themselves constitute a kind of 'spiritual encyclopaedia' and which contain a carefully contrived text-and-picture programme of didactic instruction. Manuscripts like B.L. MS. Add. 37049, a Carthusian compilation, or B.L. MS. Arundel 507, a fourteenth-century collection of texts and drawings owned by a monk of Durham, use pictures rather as 'figures' would be used now in a technical or scientific treatise. They are there to inform, to provide an aid to understanding and an aid to memory. The allegorical building called *turris sapientiae*, 'tower of wisdom', portrayed in Arundel 507 (f. 20v), is an example of the kind of thing that must have been familiar to a man like Langland. Like the

*a* manor, *b* battlements, *c* roofed, *d* true.

schematized illustrations of MS. Add. 37049, it is a pragmatic and unlovely art, but a useful reminder of an aspect of the medieval visual world that we are likely to pass over completely.

## NOTES

1. B. L. MS. Add. 24686, f.11.
2. B.L. MS. Royal 19.B. xv, f.37v.
3. B.L. MS. Add. 47682, f. 2v; B.L. MS. Royal 2.B. vii, f.2.
4. Bibl. Royale, Brussels, MSS 9961.2.
5. Bodl. MS. Douce 366; B.L. MS. Add. 49622; B.L. MS. Yates Thompson 14.
6. B.L. MS. Add. 42130.
7. B.L. MS. Yates Thompson 13; B.L. MS. Royal 10.E. iv.
8. Corpus Christi College, Cambridge, MS. 61.
9. Exeter College, Oxford, MS. 47, f.33v.
10. B.L. MS. Royal 2.A. xviii.
11. Magdalene College, Cambridge, Pepysian MS. 1916.
12. B.L. MS. Arundel 83.
13. B.L. MS. Add. 42131.
14. Bodl. MS. 264.

## BIBLIOGRAPHY

Derek Brewer, *Chaucer and his World* (London, 1978).

C. J. P. Cave, *Roof Bosses in Medieval Churches* (Cambridge, 1948).

C. J. P. Cave, *Medieval Carvings in Exeter Cathedral* (Penguin, 1953).

M. V. Clarke, *Fourteenth-Century Studies* (Oxford, 1937).

H. M. Colvin, *The History of the King's Works*, Vol. I, *The Middle Ages*, by R. Allen Brown, H. M. Colvin and A. J. Taylor (London, 1963).

Joan Evans, *English Art 1307–1461* (Oxford, 1949).

Samuel Gardner, *English Gothic Foliage Sculpture* (Cambridge, 1927).

F. E. Halliday, *Chaucer and his World* (London, 1968).

George Henderson, *Gothic* (Penguin, 1967).

Maurice Hussey, *Chaucer's World: A Pictorial Companion* (Cambridge, 1967).

M. R. James, *The Bohun Manuscripts* (Roxburghe Club, Oxford, 1936).

A. Katzenellenbogen, *Allegories of the Vices and Virtues in Medieval Art* (London, 1939).

R. S. Loomis, *A Mirror of Chaucer's World* (Princeton, 1965).

Emile Male, *The Gothic Image: Religious Art in France of the Thirteenth Century* (original French edition, 1910; translated by Dora Nussey, London, 1913).

Gervase Mathew, *The Court of Richard II* (London, 1968).

Millard Meiss, *French Painting in the time of Jean de Berry: the Boucicaut Master* (London, 1968).

Millard Meiss and Elizabeth H. Beatson, *Les Belles Heures de Jean Duc de Berry* (London, 1974).

Kathleen Morand, *Jean Pucelle* (Oxford, 1962).

Walter Oakeshott, *The Sequence of English Medieval Art* (London, 1950).

E. R. Panofsky, *Early Netherlandish Painting* (Cambridge, Mass., 1953).

Derek Pearsall and Elizabeth Salter, *Landscapes and Seasons of the Medieval World* (London, 1973).

Nikolaus Pevsner, 'English Architecture in the Late Middle Ages', in the Pelican *Age of Chaucer*, ed. Boris Ford (Penguin, 1954), 229–51.

Margaret Rickert, *Painting in Britain: The Middle Ages* (Penguin, 1954; 2nd edn, revised, 1965).

Elizabeth Salter, 'Medieval Poetry and the Visual Arts', *Essays and Studies*, 22 (1969), 16–32.

Elizabeth Salter, '*Piers Plowman* and the Visual Arts', in *Encounters: Essays on Literature and the Visual Arts*, ed. John Dixon Hunt (London, 1971), 11–27.

Lucy Freeman Sandler, *The Peterborough Psalter in Brussels and other Fenland Manuscripts* (London, 1974).

O. Elfrida Saunders, *A History of English Art in the Middle Ages* (Oxford, 1932).

Lawrence Stone, *Sculpture in Britain: The Middle Ages* (Penguin, 1955).

Geoffrey Webb, *Architecture in Britain: The Middle Ages* (Penguin, 1956).

# TWO SCOTS POETS:
# DUNBAR AND HENRYSON

PATRICK CRUTTWELL

Of Dunbar's life we know almost nothing. He was born about 1460 and had died by 1513. He lived in and wrote for the court of James IV; his life was that of a court-poet at a court, which, it would seem, had little use for poetry. His verse shows all the uneasiness, the spiritual discomfort and self-disgust, the financial anxieties, the bitter brew of envy and contempt for those more favoured, which seem the inevitable lot of the artist who must be also a courtier. Sometimes he is familiar and jaunty; sometimes envious, disgruntled, and melancholy; sometimes obsequious and mendicant; sometimes 'polished' and artificial. His work, though its compass is comparatively small, is as varied as his personality.

Within it, there are immediately apparent two styles, two dictions; one could almost say, so great is the difference, two poets. The one is ornate, artificial, and English; the other colloquial, natural, and Scottish. Of the former, the two allegorical poems, *The Goldyn Targe* and *The Thrissill and the Rois*, are the most complete examples. In one thing, at least, these poems are remarkable: they succeed in enclosing, in small compass, virtually every commonplace of their age and *genre*, the allegorical poem of the Middle Ages. They are both dreams, both dreamed on a May morning. Both use a quasi-religious language; both assemble companies of mythological personalities; both draw up lists of allegorical abstractions. Both, above all other resemblances, are written in that medieval 'poetic diction' which is just as lifeless and conventional as the worst that the eighteenth century can show and which, indeed, in many ways resembles it. 'Fresh anamalit termes celicall' is Dunbar's own phrase for it (praising Chaucer in *The Goldyn Targe*) – 'anamalit' (*enamelled*) is one of his favourite epithets when he writes in this style. 'Naturis nobil fresh anamalyng'; 'anamalit was the felde wyth all colouris'; 'annamyllit richely with new asur lycht' – these are all from these two poems. And the word is unintentionally appropriate: this diction *is* like enamel, applied from above, rootless, indiscriminate. It abounds in repetitive clichés. 'Quhois[a] armony to heir it wes delyt' says *The Thrissill and the Rois* of the birds singing, and 'quhat throu the mery foulys armony' answers *The Goldyn Targe*. In the latter also, when 'Omer' and 'Tullius' are praised, it is for their 'lippis suete' and their 'aureate tongis'; Lydgate and Gower, a somewhat dissimilar pair, have 'sugurit lippis and tongis aureate'. In such a diction, fixed and prefabricated, living poetry can hardly be made. Its essential method and fatal effect is to reduce the natural to the artificial, as do these lines of *The Goldyn Targe*, which imprison the living world in the compass of a jeweller's shop:

> The cristall air, the sapher firmament,
> The ruby skyes of the orient,
>    Kest berriall[b] bemes on emerant bewis[c] grene;
> The rosy garth depaynt and redolent
> With purpur, azure, gold, and [d]goulis gent....

The modern reader may be reminded of Yeats's cock in *Sailing to Byzantium*, made 'of hammered gold or gold enamelling' – symbol of the dead life of 'artifice', set against the true life of the 'salmon-falls, the mackerel-crowded seas'. Such lines remind one of the 'quaint enamelled eyes' of Milton's flowers in *Lycidas*, and then of Gray's 'Idalia's velvet-green'; and the latter recalls the comment it evoked from Dr Johnson, which will stand as the final judgement on all such writing, be it Augustan or medieval: 'An epithet or metaphor drawn from nature ennobles art; an epithet or metaphor drawn from art degrades nature'.

It is not in such writing that the greatness of Dunbar makes its true contribution, but in his other style, in the 'colloquial, natural, and Scottish'. An analysis of one poem in this style will have to stand for all; I have chosen the *Tretis of the Tua Mariit Wemen and the Wedo* because it is perhaps the finest of all his poems, and it is certainly the most remarkable. There is nothing like it in the language. It cannot be denied, though, that the general reader of the twentieth century may not, at first sight, find it attractive. For this, three reasons may be suggested. The language is, or seems to be, somewhat more

*a* whose: qu = w, *b* beryl, *c* boughs, *d* beautiful gules.

'crabbed' and obscure than that of the average of Dunbar's writings; the alliterative unrhymed metre is strange to modern ears; above all, the tone and intention are apt to be wrongly taken. For the language it need only be said that in this poem Dunbar is not using the cosmopolitan poetic diction I have glanced at above, but the full colloquial resources of his native Scots. The metre is that alliterative line most familiar to us through *Piers Plowman* and *Sir Gawain and the Green Knight*. This poem is one of the latest known examples of the metre; but it is clear that the line survived, as a lively form and not a selfconscious archaism, much later in the North than it did in the South.

The *Tretis* describes a conversation between two married women and a widow; all three, thoroughly tipsy, and increasingly so as the poem proceeds, relate with alcoholic frankness their matrimonial experiences. Marriage, for them, is nothing but a means of securing sexual satisfaction; and all of them are, or have been, bitterly disappointed by their husbands' sexual capacities. The first is married to an old man, the second to a worn-out lecher, and the third, the widow, has had, first, a dotard and, second, a merchant, her inferior in all things but money. The theme of the poem was possibly suggested by the *Wife of Bath's Prologue*; but the difference between them is radical: the poems differ as their personae differ. Dunbar's women have none of the Wife of Bath's genial tolerance; they are creatures savage in their frustration and primitive in their lust. The whole poem, indeed, under its comic surface, is a terrible creation.

It is also a satirical creation. It cannot be understood unless it is seen to contain a great deal of *parody*; to be, indeed, in a certain sense, a parody as a whole. Two things are parodied: the literary pastoral idealism, so dear to part of the medieval mind and exploited so mechanically (in the allegorical poems) by Dunbar himself, and the great medieval convention of courtliness and courtly love.

The parody of the former is rendered by the poem's setting. It begins and ends with passages, beautiful and lyrical in themselves, evoking the ideal beauty of nature and the 'literary' mood that traditionally accompanied it:

> Appon the Midsummer evin, · mirriest of nichtis,
> I muvit furth allane, · neir as midnicht wes past,
> Besyd ane gudlie grein garth, · full of gay flouris,

Hegeit[a], of ane huge hicht, · with hawthorne treis:
Quhairon ane bird, on ane branshe, · so burst out hir notis,
That never ane blythfullar bird · was on the beuche[b] harde:
Quhat throw the sugarat sound · of hir sang glaid,
And throw the savour sanative · of the suet flouris,
I drew me in derne[c] to the sky · to dirkin[d] efter mirthis;
The dew donkit[e] the daill, · and dynnit[f] the feulis.

(1–10)

So it opens; and it ends in the same 'aureate' style:

The morow myld wes meik, · the mavis did sing,
And all remuffit[g] the myst, · and the meid smellit;
Silver shouris doune shuke · as the shene cristall,
And berdis shoutit in shaw · with their shill notis.

(513–16)

The language of these passages, with their 'sugarat sound' and 'silver
shouris', is clearly akin to the 'anamalit termes' of the two allegorical
poems; the word itself appears in the introductory passage: 'nature
full nobillie annamalit with flouris'. But the language and the content
that come between these framing passages are very different. This
is the first wife describing her husband:

I have ane wallifrag[h], ane worme, · ane auld wobat[i] carle,
A waistit wolroun[j], na worth · but wourdes to clatter;
Ane bumbart, ane dron bee, · ane bag full of flewme,
Ane skabbit skarth[k], ane scorpioun, · ane scutarde behind;
To see him scart[l] his awin skyn · grit scunner[m] I think.

(89–93)

So, too, with the looks of the ladies themselves. They, like the landscape, are rendered with stylized idealism, in ironic contrast with
the stories they tell:

I saw thre gay ladeis · sit in ane grene arbeir,
All grathit[n] into garlandis · of freshe gudlie flouris;
So glitterit as the gold · wer thair glorius gilt tressis,
Quhill all the gressis did gleme · of the glaid bewis;
Kemmit[o] was thair cleir hair, · and curiouslie shed
Attour thair shulderis doun shyre[p], · scyhning full bricht ...

a hedged, b branch, c secret, d listen, e moistened, f made noise, g removed, h sloven,
i caterpillar, j boar, k cormorant, l scratch, m disgust, n decked, o combed, p clear.

> Of ferliful<sup>a</sup> fyne favour · war thair faceis meik,
> All full of <sup>b</sup>flurist fairheid · as flou is in June;
> Quhyt, seimlie, and soft, · as the sweit lillies
> New upspred upon spray, · as new spynist<sup>c</sup> rose.
> (17–29)

Parody, again, is the opening of the widow's speech, the most out-
rageous and immoral of the three; she begins with the pious unction
of a sermon's exordium:

> Now tydis me for to talk; · my taill it is nixt;
> God my spreit now inspir · and my speche quykkin,
> And send me sentence to say, · substantious and noble;
> So that my preching may pers · your perverst hertis,
> And mak yow mekar to men · in maneris and conditiouns.
> (246–50)

With all these parodies, the stage is set for the mockery of courtliness and courtly love. Here the third speaker, the widow, is the main
means of making the satirical effect. She claims for herself the qualities
and virtues of courtliness (her claims, of course, are totally negatived
by her actual behaviour). She despises her second husband not only
for his amorous feebleness, but also because he is a mere merchant,
below her in birth:

> The severance wes meikle<sup>d</sup>
> Betwix his bastard blude · and my birth noble.
> (311–12)

And she claims also the virtue of pity, the proper virtue of the conventional Lady adored by conventional Lover:

> Bot mercy in to womanheid · is a mekle vertu,
> For never bot in a gentil hert · is generit ony ruth.
> (315–16)

The irony of that is given force by the fact that the last line goes
straight to the centre of its target, echoes, and in its context ridicules,
one of the central sayings of courtly love. It derives from Chaucer's
'pity renneth soon in gentil hert'; that comes from Dante's 'amor,
che in cor gentil ratto s'apprende'; both go back to Provence and
the deepest roots of the whole tradition. The satire is both moral and
social, for the meaning of 'gentil' hovered between gentle and genteel.

---

*a* wonderful, *b* blooming beauty, *c* blown, *d* much.

It is not only the hypocrisy of one woman that Dunbar is here satirizing; he is commenting also on the gulf between the courtly idealism and the reality of flesh-and-blood women. (The reality itself is caricatured, to match what it exposes; the women are turned into creatures not much more than animals.) It is satire in exactly the spirit of Donne's:

> Love's not as pure, and abstract, as they use
> To say, who have no Mistresse but their Muse

– a collocation which may serve to remind us both that Donne is largely medieval and that the Middle Ages carried within themselves the criticisms of their own extravagances.

What the women represent, positively, is the life of the natural body, rebellious against any restraint, whether of Church or of society. On this the first speaker is the most explicit:

> It is agane the law of lufe, · of kynd, and of nature,
> Togiddir hairtis to strene · that stryveis with uther;
> Birdis hes ane better law · <sup>a</sup>na bernis be meikill,
> That ilk yeir with new joy, · joyis ane maik,
> And fangis<sup>b</sup> thame ane freshe feyr<sup>c</sup>, · unfulyeit<sup>d</sup>, and constant,
> And lattis thair fulyeit feiris · flie quhair thei pleis.
> <sup>e</sup>Crist gif sic ane consuetude · war in this kith haldin!
>
> (58–64)

Again one is reminded of Donne, of the remarkably close parallel in *Confined Love*:

> Are birds divorced, or are they chidden,
> If they leave their mate, or lie abroad a night?
> Beasts doe no joyntures lose,
> Though they new lovers choose,
> But we are made worse then those.

But, whatever Donne may have felt about it, Dunbar shows no sympathy for the attitude he is dramatically rendering: much less than Chaucer shows for *his* young girl who is married to a dotard, in the *Merchant's Tale*. Chaucer is Shakespearean in his balancing of irony and sympathy; Dunbar, who is a real Scot, fiercer, narrower, more doctrinaire, degrades his women's 'naturalness' to utter animal-

---

*a* 'than men, by much', *b* gets, *c* lover, *d* untired, *e* 'If only human beings had a custom like that!'

ism. Animal comparisons abound: worm, caterpillar, boar, drone-bee, cormorant, scorpion are in the five lines (cited above) with which the first woman begins her description of her husband; and when he makes love, she tells us, he fidgets like a sick cart-horse lusting for a mare ('he fepillis like a farcy · aver that flyrit one a gillot'). The husband of the other wife

> dois as dotit[a] dog · that damys[b] on all bussis[c],
> And liftis his leg apone loft, · thoght he nought list pishe.
>
> (186–7)

And the widow, having established her sovereignty over her second man, compares herself with a cock crowing in triumph:

> I crew abone that craudone[d], · as cock that wer victour.
>
> (326)

The women are dominant throughout; the reversal of sex in that line (woman likened to cock) is surely intentional. The men are nothing but the humble (and inadequate) servitors of their lusts: a point that is rammed home by the consistent use of the word 'courage' (what should be the male prerogative) with the meaning of virility – and its equally consistent degradation:

> He has a luke without lust, · and lif without curage.
>
> (188)

> Wariand[e] oft my wekit kyn · that me away cast
> To sic a[f] craudoune but curage, · that kynt my cler bewte.
>
> (214–15)

This meaning gives to the ending a particular irony:

> The sweit savour of the sward · and singing of foulis,
> Myght confort ony creatur · of the kyn of Adam,
> And kindill again his curage, · thocht it were [g]cald sloknyt.
>
> (520–2)

It is a dubious renewal for the 'kin of Adam', whose inadequate 'courage' the whole poem has been exposing. The poetic convention, a bodiless worshipping of all-pure Lady by adoring Lover, is thus reversed and animalized; the result is not far from the spirit of Swift

---

*a* foolish, *b* makes water, *c* bushes, *d* craven, *e* cursing, *f* craven without, *g* extinguished cold.

(the last book of *Gulliver*), but preserved from the anarchy of Swift's negation. The parallel is closer with those passages of *King Lear* which strip mankind down to the 'poor, bare, forked animal' – with lines like these:

> Behold yond simpering dame,
> Whose face between her forks presages snow,
> That minces virtue, and does shake the head
> To hear of pleasure's name –
> The fitchew nor the soiled horse goes to 't,
> With a more riotous appetite . . .

Dunbar, like Shakespeare, has his positives; implied in this poem, they are explicit in others. In these lines, for instance (they come from the ode *Of the Nativitie of Christ*):

> Now spring up flouris fra the rute,
> Revert yow upwart naturaly,
> In honour of the blissit frute
> That rais up fro the rose Mary.

By the 'naturaly' of those lines, by their unforced, unselfconscious assimilating of the religious and miraculous Nativity to its natural and seasonal equivalent, the degraded 'law of nature' as preached and practised by the 'tua mariit wemen and the wedo' is judged and condemned. The life of the fields and the life of devotion, in the time of Dunbar, were not yet hostile to each other, for all the strivings of ascetics to make them enemies; but for Burns, some two hundred and fifty years later, the Kirk stood as *opponent* of Nature, a negative and bodiless force in face of which the life of the body was furtive and guilty – or else (the obverse of the same medal) uneasily defiant. Hence, when Dunbar is bawdy, his bawdiness is never distorted by self-consciousness or poisoned by self-justifying, as it is sometimes with Burns. Though Dunbar himself, it would seem, was a dissatisfied, melancholy, restless individual, yet the age he lived in, though standing on the edge of chaos, still held together and held him with it.

Henryson, the man, is known even less than Dunbar. He lived in the second half of the fifteenth century, was 'chief schoolmaster in Dunfermline', and was dead by 1508. His work comprises a number of short poems, mostly devotional, of no great merit; one pastoral (*Robene and Makyne*) of real charm; and two major works, the *Morall Fabillis* and the *Testament of Cresseid*. To these two this study will be confined.

The *Morall Fabillis* consist of thirteen animal-fables. Most, though not all, are taken from Aesop; with the modesty incumbent upon a medieval author, Henryson represents his work as a mere translation, but he is, in fact, as original as Shakespeare: like him, he takes the bare bones and nothing else. The Fables are completely recreated; they emerge as a product conceivable only in the time and place that produced them, in medieval Scotland; and in them, better than in any other work of art, its life is preserved. A first reading will probably pick out the obvious qualities: the life and quickness of narrative, the charm of personal details, and the wealth of discursive comment. But of Henryson as of Chaucer it can be said that the picturesque detail owes its effectiveness to the solidity and seriousness of what it grows from. Henryson's Fables (like La Fontaine's – they deserve the comparison) do more than present types of human beings in animal guises and animals comically behaving like human beings; they build up a total and consistent *society*, both rendered and criticized. The types of humanity are shown in their relationships as well as their individualities; they form the particular pattern of the society that Henryson lived in.

At the basis of this society stands the peasant. Him the Fables observe with detail and accuracy, and with sympathy and anger for the hardness of his lot. Henryson's comment is often political, often stinging in its denunciations of the peasant's oppressors; but it springs from a feeling more primitive than politics. Throughout the Fables the sense of the rural life, the agricultural process, is deeply felt, far more deeply than it is by Dunbar, who has by comparison an urban mind. No one could call Henryson – as one might call, for instance, the author of *Piers Plowman* – a revolutionary mind. His conclusions are thoroughly orthodox: prayer, resignation, and hopes of a better world. He accepts the hierarchical structure of society, and has nothing but contempt for those who would climb above their stations – La Fontaine, once more, comes to mind, for that conclusion is also his:

> Le monde est plein de gens qui ne sont pas plus sages;
> Tout bourgeois veut bâtir comme les grands seigneurs;

> Tout petit prince a des ambassadeurs;
> Tout marquis veut avoir des pages.

Kindness and common sense, conformity in fundamentals and outspoken criticism of details, acceptance of authority and sympathy with the victims of its abuse: these are Henryson's qualities as a social commentator, and all shot through with a deep, unobtrusive Christianity. The words of the mouse, pleading with the lion –

> Quhen Rigour sittis in the Tribunall,
> The equitie of Law quha may sustene?
> Richt few or nane, but[a] mercie gang betwene,

give the essence of Christian doctrine, that God's mercy outweighs strict justice and is greater than man deserves: the essence which Renaissance and Reformation alike left untouched, to appear in Hamlet's 'use every man after his desert, and who should scape whipping?' and in Isabella's words in *Measure for Measure*:

> Why, all the souls that were were forfeit once,
> And he that might the vantage best have took,
> Found out the remedy.

Here, as elsewhere, there is a real kinship with Chaucer. Henryson leaves an impression somewhat similar to Chaucer's, of a man who has no deep quarrel with his world and no real difference with the ideas of his age, and who did not find it too difficult to love his fellow-creatures, but who was not made complacent, unobservant, or uncritical by his conformity and his tolerance. He is, in fact, the only 'Scottish Chaucerian' who is at all like Chaucer, and he is so by a genuine temperamental affinity much more than by literary discipleship.

The affinity is no less clear, but the discipleship is clearer, when we turn from the Fables to the *Testament of Cresseid*. It is, of course, a platitude of literary criticism that there is no plainer proof of true originality than the ability to borrow and learn from another writer, especially a greater one, without becoming lost in his shadow. As Mr Speirs has observed in his Literary Survey in this volume, Chaucer's great poem is the springboard for Henryson's; the emotional power which Chaucer has given to his heroine and her

*a* unless.

story is there for Henryson to exploit and develop. This he does,
in his own way. He begins with an introduction which is no formal
and separate Prologue in the usual medieval mode, but merges with
the story in a miracle of artistic skill, and prepares for it with a
subtle interplay of resemblances and contrasts and hinted forebodings.
The first lines warn us, with the bitter weather foreshadowing the
tragic tale:

> Ane doolie*a* sessoun *b*till ane cairfull dyte
> Suld correspond, and be equivalent.
> Richt sa it was quhen I began to wryte
> This tragedie . . .

The stars also forbode it; for Venus, whom Cresseid has displeased
and by whom she is punished, is dominant in the sky; she rises 'in
opposition' to Phoebus, god of tenderness and comfort, as she is to
rise against Cresseid. The author would pay his tribute of prayer
to her in the fields; but the cold drives him in and his own age restrains
him, setting him free from the passions of the young, 'of quhome
the blude is flowing in ane rage' (as it flowed in Cresseid and Troilus).
So much for the correspondences: then comes the contrast – a picture,
delightful in its domestic snugness, of the middle-aged bachelor (so
he would seem, for he 'does' for himself), saved, as he hopes, like
Horace, from Venus's attentions, making himself comfortable with a
fire, a drink, and a book. And the book is Chaucer's poem:

> Writtin by worthie Chaucer glorious
> Of fair Cresseid, and worthie Troilus.

*Suave mari magno* – it is the Lucretian explanation of why tragedy
appeals to us: but Henryson has no Epicurean indifference to the
sufferings of others. He is a thoroughly Christian writer, and the
*Testament* is one of the most Christian of poems, although (or because)
it is quite devoid of preaching. Its keynote is set at once, in the first
of the few comments that the author allows himself:

> I have pietie thou suld fall sic mischance.

'Pity' and 'piety' have the same root: in Henryson's language, as
in his mind, they are virtually the same. The *Testament* is an exercise

*a* dismal, *b* 'to a tragic tale'.

328

in Christian pity for sinners and unfortunates. It has its 'moral', if such is desired: Cresseid, before her punishment, blames the gods:

> O fals Cupide, is nane to wyte*a* bot thow

but after it, she recognizes her own responsibility:

> Nane but myself as now I will accuse.

The mood is one of pity and resignation; the language and mode of narrative are appropriately restrained. The poem is a masterpiece in the art of leaving unsaid; its greatest moments are lines or phrases of almost Dantesque bareness and brevity:

> Quhen Diomeid had all his appetyte,
> And mair, fulfillit of this fair ladie . . .

The two words 'and mair' suggest a terrible weight of satiety and humiliation. So, in the passage describing the grief of Cresseid and her father, when she has been smitten with leprosy:

> Thus was thair cair aneuch betwix thame twane

the love between the two is very quietly, very movingly realized; her overwhelming shame ('Father, I wald not be kent') and his complete lack of reproachfulness when she comes back to him disgraced:

> 'Welcum to me, thou art full deir ane gest'

are certainly reminiscent – it may be deliberately – of the father's welcome to the prodigal son: but the parallel is not enforced. In all the dramatic moments of the story, the effect is clinched by such restraint and brevity; in the climax of the whole, when Troilus in full knightly splendour ('with greit tryumphe and laude victorious') meets but does not know Cresseid the begging leper, the essence of the episode is given in the plain concluding statement:

> And nevertheless not ane ane uther knew.

This sober tension is now and then relieved: by the vivid and some-times humorous pageant of the seven planets; by an occasional strik-ing detail, such as this line, brilliant in aural and visual beauty:

> Cupide the King ringand ane silver bell

*a* blame.

and by one passage, perhaps the only one, in which full eloquence rises from the prevailing control:

> Nocht is your fairnes bot ane faiding flour,
> Nocht is your famous laud and hie honour
> But wind inflat in uther mennis eiris.
> Your roising reid to rotting sall retour . . .

In subtlety of characterization, Henryson does not try, or need, to rival Chaucer; his heroine is 'given' him by his forerunner, and he does not try to change her. But his grasp of the original has the flexible sureness of life; he can modify his Cresseid to fit the situation of his own poem, more utterly tragic than any in Chaucer's, and this he can do with no awkwardness and no incongruity. Neither dramatic irony nor psychological insight are beyond his powers when he needs them. There is irony when the 'chyld' reports to Cresseid that her father wonders why she is praying so long – 'the goddis wait (*know*)', says he, 'all your intent full weill' – for the gods have already decided her fate and awarded her her punishment: she knows it, though her father does not, yet. And for insight, one may cite the sudden cry with which she breaks off the making of her 'testament':

> O Diomeid, thou hes baithe Broche and Belt,
> Quhilk Troylus gave me in takning[a]
> Of his trew lufe . . .

Such things are enough to avoid the monotony that unrelieved soberness might bring with it; the poem stands as one of the most moving, and most completely accomplished, in the canon of medieval English.

[a] token.

# MALORY: KNIGHTLY COMBAT IN
## *LE MORTE D'ARTHUR*

JILL MANN

Malory's popularity is undoubted, but in some ways surprising, for the simple reading of his work presents considerable difficulties. The events of the narrative are repetitive and hard to connect with each other; since it is difficult to see them as a meaningful sequence, it is difficult to remember them, even over the span of a few pages. The vast numbers of people to whom we are introduced are barely differentiated from each other in terms of individual personality, and what distinguishing traits they have are liable to shift in a disconcerting fashion. Gawain is now a traitor and murderer, now a noble knight, and we cannot see what governs the change from one role to the other. Although Malory is a master in conveying human emotion, and at catching the rhythms of human speech, terse or plangent, dignified or touching, he seems to have little interest in 'character', in the web of emotions and motives that lie behind human speech and action. Furthermore, this means that it is difficult for us to assess these actions in moral terms – and yet moral terms are by no means banished from the narrative. The knightly world is a world dedicated to abstract moral values – to 'worthynes', 'jantylnes' and 'trouthe' – and yet the knight's most characteristic activity is within the physical sphere, in physical combat, often undertaken for its own sake, or as the result of a randomly-imposed 'custome'. At the end of the work, the relation between the physical and the moral becomes an acute problem when Lancelot offers to prove Guinevere's 'truth' to Arthur by means of bodily combat.

Clearly we cannot read Malory with the equipment of expectations and responses we bring to other kinds of narrative. What modern Malory criticism needs to do – and has to some extent begun to do[1] – is to work out a critical vocabulary and a way of reading that is appropriate for the structure and nature of his particular kind of narrative. We could begin, in my view, by banishing from this

331

critical vocabulary the word 'character' as inappropriate to his representation of human figures, and also by ceasing to impose on his work the opposition between feudal loyalty and romantic love which critics have for so long tried to read into it, but for which the text itself provides little or no evidence. Instead, the terms on which we should build our reading of Malory are those suggested by the work itself; the (deliberate, as I believe) narrowness and simplicity of his vocabulary directs our attention, by insistent repetition, to the key words and concepts of his narrative. I cannot discuss or even list them all here, but some of the most important are: *aventure*, *worship*, *body*, *departe*, *hole*, *togidir*, *felyship*. These words are not, for Malory, a decorative clothing for his subject; they form the skeletal structure of his work. For example, Malory invests with import the double significance of the word 'departe' in Middle English; it means both 'to leave' and 'to separate'.[2] The reiteration of this word (and its variants) lays cumulative stress on this double significance, and this means that we feel the poignancy of separation as an emotional pressure behind even the most routine of knightly departures. It also creates in us a corresponding yearning for that which negates separation, for 'wholeness' – both the wholeness of the individual person, and the wholeness of the Round Table fellowship.[3] Each individual departure adumbrates that final division of fellowship, and departure from life itself, which is realized at the end of the work. Correspondingly, at the end we are also reminded of the wholeness once achieved, and now passed away, in the solemn recording of the number of the Round Table knights 'whan they were holé togidirs'. The deepest division at this point, however, is not that which separates them from each other, but that which separates us from them, locked in the past. Yet even as we register this, we are made conscious that only by means of this intervening distance can a different kind of wholeness be achieved – that of the 'hoole book', which is only now made complete.

Study of the use of 'departe' leads logically, if to us somewhat surprisingly, to a realization of the importance of what might be called the 'choreography' of Malory's narrative. What I mean is that in this work, emotional and moral aspirations, frustrations and satisfactions are expressed simply by movement, by motion away and toward, by departure and return. The Grail Quest, for example, is initiated because of Gawain's desire for greater closeness to the Grail, the sight of it without the distancing veil; it is a 'movement towards'. Yet Galahad, the knight who does achieve full contact with the presence of the Grail, is separated from his fellows not only geographically, by the sea-journey to the city of Sarras, but also by the 'departure' of his soul 'to Jesu Cryste', and his integration into the new 'fellowship' of the son of Joseph of Arimathaea. Our longing for wholeness must instead be satisfied by the return of Bors to the Round Table fellowship, and by Lancelot's assurance to him: 'ye and I shall never departe in sundir whilis our livis may laste'.

A discussion of these key words and concepts in Malory which was in any way adequate to the richness and subtlety of his use of them would, however, be a full-length study, and it would have to go far beyond vocabulary alone. As a preliminary to such a full-scale study, what I should like to sketch here is the role of the knightly combat in Malory, to show how it acts as a focus for two of his key concepts: 'aventure' and the body.

Knights are, of course, dedicated to adventures. But it is important in Malory, as in Chaucer, to remind ourselves that the primary meaning of the Middle English word 'aventure' is 'chance'. The knight's dedication is therefore a dedicated submission to chance. The knight puts himself at the disposal of chance; he does not decide his exploits in advance, but rides out so as to expose himself to the claims that chance may lay on him in his travels – or, alternatively, he responds to chance intrusions into the sphere of the court. The adventure is beyond the knight's control; it is something that comes to him. The knights who are least successful in the Grail Quest are not those who fail in adventures, they are those who simply do not have any. Nor can the knight ensure his success by effort; it is determined by 'aventure'. The most concisely-formulated example with which this aspect of Malory's work can be illustrated is to be found in one of his French sources; King Pellinore explains to Arthur that he hunts the Questing Beast because it is destined to be killed by the best knight of his lineage,

and because I wanted to know for a truth whether I was the best of our lineage, I have pursued it for so long. And I haven't said this to exalt myself, but to know the truth about myself.[4]

Normally, we assume that titles follow on actions, and are merely their consequence, that it would be the action of killing the Questing Beast that gave rise to and justified the title of 'best knight'. But here the situation is reversed; the action is reduced to a mere sign that the title is to be claimed, and any knight to whom it is not destined to be awarded will not be able to kill the Beast. The title and the ability to perform the action are granted simultaneously by some third, mysterious agency. It is the discovery of self, not the creation of self, that is the function of knightly 'aventure'.

The importance of knightly combat is that it offers a structure within which 'aventure' can operate, within which the revelatory movements of chance can realize themselves. With this notion of combat we can compare the ideas underlying the historical tradition of the judicial combat – that is, the use of battle in deciding cases of law. The judicial combat was introduced to England by the Normans, and it was never a major element of English law; in Malory's time, it had long fallen into disuse. But the ideas on which it was founded seem to have had a more vigorous life in imaginative literature than in historical actuality. To us, the recourse to a judicial combat might look like a cynical decision to let physical force settle a quarrel, but this was far from being the governing principle. As the authors of the standard history of early English law put it, 'the judicial combat is an ordeal, a bilateral ordeal', and like the ordeal, it constitutes an 'appeal to the supernatural'. 'It was a sacral process. What triumphed was not brute force but truth.'[5] As in the ordeal, the exposure of the body to hazard is the medium through which non-physical realities are revealed.

So it is with the knightly combat in Malory; the knight realizes himself and his destiny, the nature and the events that chance has willed to him, in the long succession of physical engagements with his fellows. But to see the relation of Malory's combats to the judicial combat of history is also to see the need to distinguish between them. The ideas that lie behind the judicial combat remain within the realm of historical interest. The notions behind the knightly combat in Malory, by contrast, take on a serious and perennially relevant significance. The significance of the battle in Malory is metaphysical; it becomes a means of asking 'why?'. If we regard the question 'why did that knight win that battle?' as answered when we say 'because he was the stronger', or 'because he was the better fighter', we are obscuring the fact that the 'why' is only put back a stage; if we pursue it and ask '*why* was he the stronger?', we shall see that ultimately there is no possibility of answering except that so it is, for reasons we do not understand. The world that Malory constructs is a world that manages to perform the nigh-impossible task of bringing us face to face with the unanswerable nature of these questions, of making us feel and accept the arbitrariness that lies at the very roots of experience and existence. Because the physical is made the medium for the revelation of the non-physical, the very absoluteness of the gulf between them teaches us to recognize how mysterious are the sources of the immaterial qualities which reside in the bodily person or the material world, and how unidentifiable are the agencies that assign them to one resting-place or another.

It is not only in combat, of course, that the bringing together of the physical and the non-physical is used to make us conscious of this mysterious arbitrariness; it is also in the multifarious tests and ordeals which likewise rank as 'aventures'. The physical act of pulling a sword from a sheath, for example, mysteriously signals that Balin is the knight 'moste of worship withoute treson, trechory, or felony'. His possession of these qualities cannot be explained, nor can the statement that he possesses them be seen as a derivative of his actions, since his success in the test of the sword is its only basis. The sword-test makes clear that it is as a result of the uncomprehended mechanisms of existence that these qualities reside in him.

The combat, then, is a way of engaging with 'aventure', and this engagement is accomplished through the body. The knight 'puts his body in aventure', or he 'jeopardies' it, or he offers to prove his truth against an accuser 'my body to his body'. Over and over again Malory introduces the word, in phrases like these, in his alterations of his French sources. When Tristram takes his leave of the Irish court, for example, he challenges any knight who has a grievance to declare it 'now or ellis never, and here is my body to make it good, body ayenste body!'. It is true that the Middle English word 'body' has a wider meaning than its modern English counterpart; it can refer to the person as a whole, rather than his or her physical aspect alone. But Malory's insistent use of the word in physical contexts places an emphasis on the corporeal as that within which the non-corporeal person mysteriously resides. The connections between the two are not fully explicable, but (as in the ordeal) they are strong; the condition of the body signals the condition of the person.

It is not only the knight's own body that is important in this process, it is also the body of his opponent. Tristram declares to Sir Marhalt that he proposes 'to be worshipfully proved uppon thy body'. Through engagement with the body of his opponent the knight 'proves' or 'assays' his own quality; but equally he 'proves' that of his fellow. It is this, and not a sort of military *Blutbruderschaft*, that leads to the paradoxical situation in which conflict becomes the means to achieve fellowship. We naturally think of combat either as strategic (designed to fend off aggression or oppression), or as expressive (venting anger or malice). In Malory, the role of knightly combat is often purely neutral; it is unrelated to the affective state of its participants. On occasion, in the *Book of Tristram*, a knight about to engage in combat is asked whether he requests it 'of love othir [or] of hate'. In both cases, the answer is 'for loove'. Understandably puzzled by this response, critics have sought to explain it as a sign of decadence infecting the chivalric world. But this explanation fails to understand the nature of combat in Malory – the way in which acceptance of battle, just as much as renunciation of it, demonstrates an acceptance of the arbitrary in the qualities and destiny assigned to one.

There is a particularly good illustration of this in the account of the opposition between Tristram and Lamorak and its reconciliation. The form taken by the arbitrary here is the creation of Lamorak's ill-will towards Tristram; it is formed not by any voluntary action of Tristram's, but by Mark's command that he belatedly enter a tournament to engage with Lamorak, who has had the upper hand in it all day. Tristram's protests that this is 'ayenste knighthode' are overruled, but having technically complied with Mark's order by jousting with Lamorak and unhorsing him, he refuses to fight further. Lamorak, who is eager to win back the honour he has lost, is enraged by this refusal (and rightly, since from his point of view it looks like an unknightly refusal to follow through 'aventure' to the end, an attempt to use it opportunistically by shaping it to the pattern of one's own advantage). Later, therefore, he takes his revenge on

Tristram by sending to Mark's court a magic horn, drinking from which will reveal adulterers. (We may note in passing that this is another example of the revelation of spiritual states by physical means.) When Tristram and Lamorak next meet, in the 'Ile of Servage', however, Tristram refuses to protract this hostile relationship; he accepts, as it were, the arbitrary in Lamorak's enmity; or we could say that he accepts it as the 'aventure' that comes with his own obedience to Mark's commands. Tristram's renunciation of hostility wins from Lamorak an instant admiration for his 'knighthode': 'Hit may nat be false that all men sey, for of youre bounté, nobles, and worship of all knightes ye are pereles.'

Renunciation of battle here leads to reconciliation, and this we find unsurprising (though we might ponder on the paradox that renunciation of battle had of course created the hostility in the first place). What is surprising is that later in the narrative we find that the reconciliation is to be achieved all over again, and this time not through renunciation of battle, but through insistence on it. This time, on meeting, instead of expressing a spirit of mild forgiveness, Tristram in fury admonishes Lamorak 'bethinke the now of the despite thou dedist me of the sendinge of the horne unto kinge Markis courte', and asserts 'the tone [*one*] of us two shall dy or [*before*] we departe'. It is not that Malory has simply forgotten the earlier episode, because Lamorak's response is the mild reminder: 'that time we were togidirs in the Ile of Servage ye promisid me bettir frendeship'. (Tristram's refusal to allow separation without battle to the death is a grim travesty of the 'togetherness' achieved earlier, signalled by the recurrence of two key terms, 'departe' and 'togidirs'.) Lamorak's reminder is perhaps designed to point to the fact that this time it is he who accepts the arbitrary – which is the belated expression of Tristram's violent fury. And he demonstrates this acceptance by entering the proffered battle. This time it is Tristram who comes to feel Lamorak's knighthood, through his bodily qualities.

So sir Tristramis wolde make no lenger delayes, but lajsshed at sir Lamerok, and thus they faught till aithir[a] were wery of other. Than sir Tristrams seide unto sir Lamorak, 'In all my liff mette I never with such a knight that was so bigge[b] and so well-brethed. Therefore', saide sir Tristramis, 'hit were pité that ony of us bothe sholde here be mischeved[c]'.

(295–6)[6]

*a* each, *b* strong, *c* hurt.

Lamorak's response is to offer his sword in surrender, but Tristram insists that the surrender is to be his. The image of fighting men on their knees offering their swords to each other is, when we think about it, an odd one, but it is a frequent one in romance, and expresses the spirit of the romance world. It does not imply a rejection of battle; on the contrary, it symbolizes the acceptance of engagement with the unknown that is at the heart of battle. Thus opposition becomes a means of achieving union. It is fitting, then, that the climax of the relationship between Tristram and Lancelot should be their (unwitting) battle against each other; it is likewise fitting that at the end of the Tristram book it should be battle that brings about Palomides' final reconciliation with Tristram, his acceptance of the arbitrariness that makes Tristram his superior and the beloved of Isolde, and leads to his final integration into Christian fellowship.

From this vantage-point, we can see that it is significant that the phrases used of combat are phrases implying union. Often, as in the passage just quoted, the knight talks of 'meeting' his opponent; in another favourite phrase, they 'come together' like thunder; battle is 'joined'. The destruction of their bodily wholeness paradoxically reveals – and in that sense brings into being – the wholeness of their selves (their 'integrity', to use the etymologically appropriate word), the wholeness of fellowship between them, and the integration with the external world that comes from acceptance of the independence and inexplicability of its operations. Malory's image of the body has its roots in romance, but his development of it, and the uses to which he puts it, are, I think, unique. In Malory, the body is not a clumsy encumbrance to the spirit, nor even its humble tool. It is the medium through which a knight's worship is revealed, and the testing-ground of its validity; it is what the knight opposes to his fellows and yet what unites him with them. It is a field of action, and a repository of truths.

Malory's image of the body is a deliberately stylized one; there is none of the Rabelaisian sense of the body's functions, of eating, excreting, giving birth, of bodily fecundity or decay. Its most important element in Malory is blood, which is the creator of wholeness in two ways: firstly, as the creator of kinship, the fellowship between those of the same blood, and secondly, as the creator of personal wholeness through its powers of healing. The images of the body and of blood find their apotheosis in the Grail book, which gives a central position to the mystery of the Eucharist, the re-creation of the Body and Blood of Christ, and the commemoration of His suffering. If, then, we are tempted to think of the body as a crude irrelevance to the spiritual, we are powerfully reminded in this book that it is through *bodily* suffering that human kind is redeemed. Through the shedding of God's blood men are healed, made whole in their own nature and united with the divine.

The Grail book, then, does not represent an indictment or even a qualification of the values of chivalry; on the contrary, it is their sublimation. It is the profoundest example of the mysteries accomplished in the body. Like a true knight, God (in Langland's phrase) 'auntred himself', and by exposing His body to suffering, by 'accepting' human sin, miraculously re-constituted the wholeness between Himself and His creation.

## NOTES

1. I have in mind in particular Mark Lambert's *Style and Vision in Le Morte Darthur* (New Haven and London, 1975).

2. Malory's use of the word in both senses is noted by P. J. C. Field, *Romance and Chronicle* (London, 1971), 82.

3. Mark Lambert has sensitively analysed the way that the two kinds of 'wholeness' are brought into relation in 'The Healing of Sir Urr', which is based on a 'kind of pun' on the word 'whole' (*op cit.*, 63–5).

4. This is my translation of the French *Suite du Merlin*, edited by Gaston Paris and Jacob Ulrich as *Merlin: Roman en Prose du XIII$^e$ Siècle* (Société des Anciens Textes Français, 2 vols, Paris, 1886), I, 151.

5. Sir Frederick Pollock and Frederic William Maitland, *The History of English Law Before the Time of Edward I* (2nd edn, 2 vols, Cambridge, 1968), 598–600. For a full account, see George Neilson, *Trial by Combat* (Glasgow, 1890).

6. Page references are to Vinaver's one-volume edition of Malory, in its revised form (1971).

# THE MORALITY TRADITION

RICHARD AXTON

According to Aristotle, the action of drama is primary; speech and ideas which explain the action are of secondary importance. Certainly the primacy of action is the only guide in making sense of the most primitive form of English drama – the folk plays orally preserved in the mummers' tradition described by Thomas Hardy in Book Two of *The Return of the Native*. The surviving texts are so garbled by transmission by word of mouth that they seem nonsensical, mixing St George (or King George) with the Turkish Knight, Beelzebub, the Fool, the 'Lady', Pickle Herring, Big-Head, and Father Christmas – to mention just a few. Any coherence or meaning must be sought in the action of the plays; and this emerges, in spite of scores of local variants, as a pattern known to folklorists as 'combat-and-cure'. A champion boasts of his invincible power and issues a challenge. His 'evil' opponent replies. They fight and one of them falls. Someone (mother, father or wife) laments the hero and calls for a doctor. He comes, boasting of his miraculous power and works a cure. The champion rises to fight again. The performance ends with the mummers begging money (the *quête*) and a fresh stock of bizarre characters is often 'brought in' with collecting pans. Performance of these folk plays begins with sweeping or clearing the acting place with cries of 'Room, room' and each new character steps into the magic circle with the formula 'In steps I, Saint George' etc. It ends, after the collection, with song, dance, and blessings on the audience of the house.

Folklorists have seen in these ancient relics the survival of a pagan ritual drama of man's life cycle. But while it is true that birth, copulation and death can be found (usually obscured and grotesquely distorted) in many of the plays, these themes hardly control the action, and much recourse to *The Golden Bough* has been needed to produce a paradigm of this 'life cycle drama'.[1] On the other hand, the common core of action in the combat plays is clear and simple: the champion boasts his invincibility; this is both denied, in that he is slain, and affirmed, when he is revived to fight again. The action moves through death in a comic manner, making an affirmation of life as part of a seasonal rejoicing. It might be thought of as a pagan underplot of a Christian story pattern.

With these observations in mind it is interesting to consider the earliest morality play in English, *Pride of Life* or, more properly, *King of Life*.[2] Its date, *c.* 1350, makes it earlier by a century than any of the extant biblical plays in Middle English (a fact that has been obscured in traditional accounts of medieval drama), and this earliness suggests the closeness of this moral play to the popular play pastimes of the common people.

Only 502 lines of *King of Life* have been preserved, but the lengthy prologue outlines the plot and moral theme of 'oure gam', which is performed outdoors with the principal characters housed in tents, tournament-fashion. The protagonists are the Kings of Life and Death. Life's Queen warns him to beware his end, for 'Deth over-comith al thinge / How-so-ever we wende'. When he scorns her advice she sends for the Bishop who preaches the same theme until the King sends him packing. A messenger then comes from Death to the King, telling him that his master 'wold com into his ouin lond / On him to *kyt his mit'. Death comes as the King dreams a dreadful dream. Death and Life fight and Life is killed. But the conflict does not end here, because Life's soul is now liberated and must struggle with his body for its own salvation. Devils take the soul, but the Virgin Mary intercedes for it and, says the prologue, you will see how it ends.

Life establishes his power over the place and audience in the manner of the folk-play; threatening to 'ding down' any man who says him nay, for no man of woman born may stand against his strokes. He is supported in the delusion 'I shal lyve evermo' by two champion knights named Strength and Health, who promise in folk-play manner to fight against Death and 'make his sides bleed'. The King's messenger Solas runs among the audience, challenging any man so bold to fight his master; here the fragment ends.

*a* show his might.

In this tournament it is impossible for Life to defeat Death, and though the audience must associate themselves with Life's worldly presumption, they must wish to see him defeated by the mysterious stranger champion for flouting the rules of life and drama. However, the moral point is not quite so simple, because of the reversal which will take place after death: the final triumph of the soul is not assured in the drama, because it must depend on an act of will to be made by every individual in the audience:

> Thinke, thou haddist beginninge
> Qwhen thou were ibore[a];
> And bot[b] thou mak god endinge,
> Thy sowle is forlore[c].

The audience is simultaneously at the centre of the drama, represented by Life, and at the periphery, able to see and condemn his – and its own – folly.

There is a clear line of development running from *King of Life* to the best known of all allegorical plays, *Everyman*, even though the latter is immediately based on a Dutch play. Where the dominant motif of action in *King of Life* is combat, *Everyman* uses the journey towards death. Both plays gain by contracting man's life-time so as to focus on the clarification of self-awareness that comes with the prospect of death.

*Everyman* was printed (the first English morality to be so) for private reading four times between 1510 and 1525. It is quite short (921 lines) and has seventeen parts, playable by ten actors doubling. Described by the printer as 'a treatyse . . . in maner of a morall playe', it sets out as an allegory the medieval Christian doctrine concerning Holy Dying. The dramatic interest comes from development of Everyman's first moment of recognition, 'O Deth, thou comest whan I had thee leest in mynde!' as a series of encounters in which he discovers which parts of his nature are friends unto death. The allegory of death as a pilgrimage gives the mind an image of action in a play that would otherwise be very static. It also puts a veil between Everyman and the prospect of death, a veil such as we normally hold there, in order to keep removing it. Recognition is made more sobering by the dramatization of man's evasions, which first take the form of proverbial self-comfort (Everyman pitifully hopes that

*a* born, *b* unless, *c* lost.

Good will help him make his 'reckoning', 'For it is sayd ever among / That money maketh all ryght that is wronge'). In the climactic moment Everyman reaches his destination accompanied by Strength (shown here as one of the champions of Christendom) and Beauty. The chilling force of his discovery is the greater because the spare, unemotional quality of his language contrasts so well with Strength's ironic boasts and Beauty's proverbial bustle. The language insists on both the physicality of experience and the negativeness of death;

STRENGTH.
> Everyman, I wyll be as sure by thee
> As ever I dyde*a* by Iudas Machabee.

EVERYMAN.
> Alas, I am so faynt I may not stande;
> My lymmes under me do folde.
> Frendes, let us not tourne agayne to this lande,
> Not for all the worldes golde;
> For in to this cave must I crepe
> And tourne to erth, and there to slepe.

BEAUTE.
> What, in to this grave? Alas!

EVERYMAN.
> Ye, there shall ye consume, more and lesse.

BEAUTE.
> And what, sholde I smoder*b* here?

EVERYMAN.
> Ye, by my fayth, and never more appere.
> In this worlde lyve no more we shall,
> But in heven before the hyest Lorde of all.

BEAUTE.
> I *c*crosse out all this. / Adewe, by Saynt Iohan!
> I take my tappe*d* in my lappe*e* and am gone.

(E, 786–801)

The spareness of the language is notable. A. C. Cawley comments,[3] quoting T. S. Eliot on poetry and drama: '. . . the freely rhythmical verses of *Everyman* harmonize inconspicuously with its neutral style, so that we find ourselves "consciously attending, not to the poetry, but to the meaning of the poetry".'

*a* did, *b* smother, *c* cancel my promise, *d* distaff, *e* fold of a garment, pocket.

In the final sequence Everyman commends his spirit into God's hands and Knowledge describes his passing. The soul is carried to the upper storey of the House of Salvation, where it is welcomed in marriage as God's 'electe spouse', having now become female. This sequence forms the only real spectacle in *Everyman*, which in some ways resembles the oldest Christian ritual drama: a procession to a sacred place to witness a miracle. In the *Visitatio Sepulchri* man witnessed the miracle of Christ's resurrection. In *Everyman* man himself is transformed at the House of Salvation. This property marks the goal of Everyman's journey and occupies the centre of the acting place.

In *The Castle of Perseverance*, a colossal East Anglian morality dated *c.* 1425, the image of the house of the soul is elaborated to explore psychological allegory and develop dramatic action. Mankind's whole life is shown as a kind of journey, but the central action of the play is a siege of the castle itself; this provides many opportunities for vivid conflict between the virtuous occupants of the castle and their besiegers. Allegorical castles are sometimes described in medieval homiletic writing as an aid to memorizing moral truths; what distinguishes the dramatic use of the castle is, of course, the occupation of an actual play castle by live actors. The form of the play's action, reduced to its simplest dimension, is that of many children's games.[4] Mankind must journey to his goal without being captured; he has a home-base where he is safe and has a team to protect him; outside this base he is hunted by the enemy. In the courts of medieval Europe elaborate siege games were known, mostly, it seems of an erotic kind: a lady or ladies were besieged in a model castle, known in England as the 'maydens castle', and might protect themselves from capture by amorous knights by showering the besiegers with flowers and sweets.

According to the staging plan in the Macro manuscript, the *Castle* was played, like several other East Anglian plays, 'in the round'.[5] The acting circle has scaffolds at its perimeter to raise the chief characters to the audience's view: God, the Devil, Flesh, World, and Covetousness. At the centre is the castle itself, a two-storey building, open at ground-level to show the bed where Mankind will die, and with an upper gallery for the embattled Virtues. The castle is surrounded by a ditch with 'water abowte the place'; alternatively it is to be 'strongly barred al a-bowt' against the enemy – and inquisitive audiences. This splendid arena accommodates thirty-six actors and embodies the whole world of man, both macrocosm and microcosm. The audience can see invisible moral and spiritual processes happen before their eyes: vices and virtues strive for man's company and for his body; at the body's death the soul is 'born', emerging as a child actor from under Mankind's bed, to be carried physically by the Bad Angel to Hell and finally snatched back for God by the troupe of motherly Daughters of God. The castle, then, directly represents the psychological and metaphysical space that man inhabits; it is not an image of something physical (as might be the case in a play about the Siege of Jerusalem); rather, it projects into three-dimensional space and time those elements in man which we could not otherwise see.

An audience's need for spectacle and for conflict is well catered for. In the siege, which occupies a third of the playing time, each of the three captains of vice leads his troops and war machines against the castle and is repelled; there are also individual combats across the moat between the female Virtues protecting Mankind and their opposite Vices outside. Analysis of the cast list reveals matched 'teams' of good and evil figures who struggle sixteen-a-side for possession first of Mankind's body, then his soul. (This principle of matching 'friend' and 'foe' is even extended to Heaven, where the 'older' two of God's daughters want to damn Mankind and two 'younger' to save him.) The siting of 'camps' by points of the compass makes visible many elemental conflicts: God (East) is confronted by both the Devil (in the 'nip of the North' as was traditional) and by World (West), so that the contrasts of salvation / damnation and immortality / mortality are ever present. Flesh rules over his trio of Gluttony, Lechery, and Sloth in the warm South. In the frosty North-East there is a scaffold specially for Covetousness, who has particular power over Mankind in old age. There is also an opposition of male vices (all but Lechery) and female saving virtues.

The play's meaning is conveyed mainly by spectacle and movement. Consequently, speech is of secondary importance, though the verse is lively and well crafted. The speeches enliven the action and interpret the moral and theological point of the visual images. Thus Sloth uses a spade to dig through the bank of the castle moat to let out the water of Grace, and he hyperbolically urges 30,000 of the audience to join in the assault. But he is soundly beaten by his busy female opponent and finds himself appropriately suffering from the symptoms of Sloth and burning from his association with Lechery, so that he must call for water:

ACCIDIA.

> Out, I deye! Ley on watyr!
> I swone, I swete, I feynt, I drulle![a]
> Yene qwene[b], with hir pityr-patyr,
> Hath al to-days,chyd[c] my skallyd[d] skulle!
>
> It is as softe ass wulle.
> [e]Or I have here more skathe,
> I schal lepe awey, [f]by lurkinge lathe;
> There I may my ballokys bathe,
> And leykyn[g] at the fulle.

The Vices are defeated when the Virtues in the tower drop roses on them, emblems of Christ's Passion. This emblematic action is doubly allegorical, showing the triumph of Christian virtues over vice and also the historical battle of the Passion, which is related. Patience responds to Wrath's abusive speech with an account of Christ's own patience:

PATIENTA.

> [h]Fro thy dowte, Crist me schelde
> This iche day, and al mankinde!
> Thou wrecchyd Wrethe, wood[i] and wilde,
> Paciens schal thee schende!
> [j](Quia ira viri justitiam Dei non operatur.)
> For Marys sone, meke and milde,
> Rend[k] thee up, rote and rinde[l],
> Whanne he stod meker thanne a childe
> And lete boyes[m] him betyn and binde.
> Therfor, wrecche, be stille!
> For tho pelourys[n] that gan him pose[o],
> He myth a[p] drevyn hem to dros;
> And yit, to casten him on the cros
> He sufferyd al here[q] wille.

*a* stagger, *b* you wench, *c* broken, *d* scabby, *e* before I take more harm, *f* through some dark lane, *g* refresh myself, *h* from fear of you, *i* mad, *j* For the wrath of man does not produce the justice of God, *k* tore/root and, *l* skin, *m* fellows, *n* despoilers, *o* push, *p* might have, *q* their.

The pattern of man's individual life coincides with that of Christian history in the conclusion, when God the Father 'sitting in judgement' speaks of doomsday 'whanne Mihel his horn blowith at my dred dom' and delivers the same warning to the audience as concludes *King of Life* and *Everyman*:

> Thus endith our gamys.
> To save you fro sinninge,
> Evyr at the beginninge
> Thinke on your last endinge.

Whereas the *Castle of Perseverance* has 3,648 lines and is constructed on an epic scale, demanding four or five hours playing time and relying on spacious explanation of allegorical action, *Mankind*, in the same Macro manuscript but dating from about 1465, is altogether different: it offers slick theatrical entertainment and brilliant verbal comedy in 914 lines (about seventy minutes playing). It seems to have been designed for touring by a company of six in East Anglia between Cambridge and King's Lynn, playing in manorial halls (some local gentry are named in the dialogue) as well as at inn yards and in the canvas-covered 'game-places' found in fifteenth-century East Anglia.[6]

In *Mankind* there is no symbolic structure to house the protagonist; nowhere he is safe from his worldly enemies, who come at him from the audience with boasts of thievery and violence. In this portable drama Mankind has only a spade with which to demonstrate man's lot since the Fall of Adam and to use eventually as a sword; the vices have a mere rope halter with which to urge him to suicide. Life and death are thus economically suggested in this contest. The teams in this Shrovetide 'game' are unevenly matched: on one side Mankind and his father confessor Mercy; on the other Mischief, foreman of a foul-mouthed, rough-and-tumbling trio, Nought, Nowadays and Newguise, and their diabolic master Titývillus 'that goth invisibele'. The Lenten virtues of prayer, abstinence, and hard work are set against the grosser attractions of carnival riot and licentious speech.

The image of Mankind digging the earth and planting his corn connects a complex of themes ingeniously developed through dialogue in the lively manner of a popular sermon. Mankind's spiritual adviser Mercy preaches on the Last Judgement, when 'The corn shall be savyde, the chaffe shall be brente', warning the vices that 'such as they have sowyn, such shall they repe', and these texts are imprinted in the audience's minds even as they are mocked by Mischief ('Misse-masche, driff-draff, / Summe was corn and sume was chaffe', 'Corn servit bredibus, chaffe horsibus, straw firybusque') who cheekily offers himself as a 'winter corn-thresher'. Mankind's strenuous labouring at his 'earth' contrasts with the mockery of idlers who make fun out of the conventions of the play, drawing attention to the size and unpromising nature of the hall floor as a corn field.

A second Shrovetide theme is the conflict in man between soul and body ('my soull, so sotyll in thy substance', 'my flesch, that stinking dunghill'). Mankind's predicament is graphically suggested in the excremental language and threats of the vices. (Nought suggests that if Mankind wants a good crop: 'If he will have reyn, he may over-pisse it; / Ande if he will have compasste, he may over-blisse it / a lityll with his ars'.) Mercy warns,

> Ther is ever a batell betwix the soull and the body:
> *Vita hominis est militia super terram.*

The Old Testament text (*The life of man on earth is a battle*) connects Mankind himself with Job, sitting (as the Vulgate Bible has it) on a dung heap, patiently refusing to speak evil of God.[7] Mankind must imitate 'the grett pacience of Job in tribulacion'; he sits upon the earth, having hung about his own neck a motto from *Job*:

> *Memento homo, quod cinis es, et in cenerem reverteris.*
> (*Remember, O man, that you are dust and to dust you will return.*)

This penitential text belongs to Ash Wednesday, the beginning of Lent and end of the carnival season which lasted from Christmas to Shrove Tuesday. (There is some evidence from the later Middle Ages that plays were prohibited during Lent.) While Mankind digs earnestly, the vices create a carnival atmosphere and teach the audience a 'Cristemas songe', taking delight in excremental parody of the *Sanctus* of the Mass. With the obscene gusto of Swift's Yahoos they discover the bodily meaning lurking within the word 'holy':

> *Cantant Omnes:* Hoylyke, holyke, holyke! Holyke, holyke, holyke!

By such 'idle language' and 'delight in derision' the three N's show themselves 'wers then bestys'. Indeed, at their first entrance Nought is made to dance to music by being beaten by the other two as if he was a performing bear, and the suggestion of a recent editor that the actor should inhabit a bear-skin makes good sense of the comic lines in which the bear-head is removed to address the audience.[8] The temptations of his enemies finally turn Mankind himself into a beast; leaving aside his spade and prayers, despairing of Mercy, he is sworn into the fraternity of rioters; his jacket is removed and cut so short that it no longer covers his body and, when Mercy approaches to reclaim him, Mankind is driven like an animal to the tavern to cries of 'Hay, doog! hay, whoppe! whoo! Go yowr wey lightly', and 'lende us a football'. When Mischief threatens to defile the audience, their disenchantment with vice should be complete. Mercy is left to mourn for Mankind's unnaturalness ('Man on-kinde') and to think of death as a comfort.

The apprehension of death which is central to many plays in the morality tradition is not of final importance in *Mankind*. This may be because the playwright concentrates on life itself as a battle in which the inevitable descent into sin should lead to contrition (Mankind is ashamed to be 'so bestially disposyde'), confession, and mercy in the course of everyday living. Another reason is that the play's comic action is developed along lines from the old folk drama. In the following sequence Mankind's spade is used in a mock-beheading / castration (Newguise sits on Nowadays' shoulders). The vices then prime the audience for the appearance of Tityvillus. They will only show him if the audience will pay:

NEWGUISE.
> Alasse, master, alasse, my privite!*a*

MISCHIEF.
> A, wher? Alake, fayer babe, ba me!*b*
> Abide! Too sone I shall it se.

NOWADAYS.
> Here, here, se my hede, goode master!

MISCHIEF.
> Lady, helpe! Sely darlinge, *vene, vene!*c*
> I shall helpe thee of thy peyn:
> I shall smyte off thy hede and sett it on again.

> *a* privy parts, *b* kiss me, *c* come.

NOUGHT.

> By Owr Lady, ser, a fayer playster!
> Will ye off with his hede? It is a schrewde charme!
> As for me, I have none harme –
> I were loth to forbere mine arme.
> Ye pley: *In nomine patris*, choppe!

NEWGUISE.

> Ye shall not choppe my jewellys, and[a] I may.

NOWADAYS.

> Ye, Cristys crose! Will ye smight my hede awey?
> Ther, wher, on and on? Oute! Ye shall not assay –
> I might well be callyde a foppe.

MISCHIEF.

> I kan choppe it off and make it again.

NEWGUISE.

> I had a schrewde *recumbentibus*[b], but I fele no peyn.

NOWADAYS.

> Ande my hede is all save and holl again.
> Now, towchinge the mater of Mankinde,
> Lett us have an interleccion[c], sithen ye be cum hethere.
> It were goode to have an ende.

MISCHIEF.

> How, how? A minstrell! Know ye ony ought?

NOUGHT.

> I kan pipe in a Walsingham whistill, I, Nought, Nought.

MISCHIEF.

> Blow apase, and thou shall bring him in with a flowte[d].

TITYVILLUS.

> I com, with my leggys under me!     [*off stage*]

MISCHIEF.

> How, Newguise, Nowadays, herke or[e] I goo:
> When owr hedys wer together, I spake of *si dedero*[f].

NEWGUISE.

> Ye, go thy wey, we shall gather mony onto[g] –
> Ellys ther shall no man him se.

[*To the audience*]

> Now gostly[h] to owr purpos, worschipfull soverence.
> We intende to gather mony, if it plesse yowr necligence,
> For a man with a hede that is of grett omnipotens –

(M, 429–61)

*a* if, *b* knockdown blow, *c* consultation, *d* flute, *e* before, *f* if I give, *g* for the purpose, *h* devoutly.

As happens in the mummers' plays, the collection develops a life of its own, with the actors commenting on their takings. In return for gold and silver (Tityvillus 'Lovith no groats') they will 'bring in' the devil-with-the-great-head. The collection gives the actor who plays Mercy time to change into this 'abhominabull presens'. The players make sure they are paid and take the opportunity to chastise stinginess.

The theatrical sophistication of *Mankind* depends on skilful professionals harnessing the energies of popular carnival plays within a framework of moral homily: a joining of 'sermon' and 'game' which is first seen in *King of Life*. This was an effective pattern interlude which would be acceptable to all kinds of audience, and playable by small travelling troupes during the later fifteenth century. These companies, often the liveried servants of nobles, thrived by offering a different sort of theatre from the large-scale spectacular outdoor miracle-play cycles produced by amateur communities. Increasing private patronage and professional rivalry stimulated dramatic experiment; the possibility of printing play texts gave playwrights new scope and prestige. From the turn of the fifteenth century playwrights are no longer anonymous: we know of Henry Medwall, who wrote interludes for performance in Cardinal Morton's household, where Thomas More grew up, and of John Skelton, John Rastell and John Heywood. The early Tudor playwrights found fresh inspiration for their interludes in humanist debate, French farce, and Spanish novel,[9] but the morality tradition remained strong.[10] Dramatists were still little interested in 'story', preferring to conceive plays as conflicts between vice and virtue. Man is at the centre, he chooses his company, is tempted, resists, falls, repents, and starts anew. The same pattern of action that conveyed sacramental and penitential wisdom was adapted for political analysis (Skelton's *Magnificence*, *c.* 1520, Lyndsay's *Satire of Three Estates*, *c.* 1540), for educational allegory (Redford's *Wit and Science*, *c.* 1535), and for popular scientific instruction (Rastell's *Four Elements*, *c.* 1518). Some of the interludes were acted for élite audiences at court, in schools and colleges, and at the private houses of humanist scholars; but they did not lose touch with the popular theatrical tradition. They were didactic but they were 'merry'. The dramatic models based on the popular games of the Middle Ages remained potent into the age of Marlowe and Shakespeare.

# NOTES

1. See Alan Brody, *The English Mummers and Their Plays* (Stony Brook and London, 1971).

2. *Pride of Life* is printed by N. Davis, ed. *Non-Cycle Plays and Fragments*, EETS (Oxford, 1970), and by Peter Happé, ed. *Tudor Interludes* (Penguin, 1972). I have partly modernized the spelling.

3. *Everyman*, ed. A. C. Cawley (Manchester, 1961), Introduction, xxviii.

4. cf. Iona and Peter Opie, *Children's Games in Street and Playground* (Oxford, 1969), 172–3, 223–4.

5. Richard Southern, *Medieval Theatre in the Round* (London, 1957), discusses the staging of *The Castle of Perseverance* in detail but comes, I think, to the wrong conclusion in arguing that the ditch surrounds the audience too, rather than dividing them from the castle. The plan is reproduced by David Bevington, ed. *Medieval Drama* (Boston, 1975), 79.

6. *Mankind*'s professional qualities are discussed by Bevington in *From Mankind to Marlowe* (Cambridge, Mass., 1962).

7. See the excellent discussion by Paula Neuss, 'Active and Idle Language: Dramatic Images in *Mankind*' in *Medieval Drama*, ed. N. Denny, Stratford-upon-Avon Studies, 16 (London, 1973). 41–67.

8. Ed. Glynne Wickham, *English Moral Interludes* (London, 1976), 5.

9. e.g. Medwall's *Fulgens and Lucres*, *c*. 1495; Heywood's *Johan Johan*, 1533; anon. *Calisto and Melebea*, *c*. 1525. On the repertory see T. W. Craik, *The Tudor Interlude* (Leicester, 1958).

10. See Robert Potter, *The English Morality Play* (London, 1975).

# THE POETRY OF WYATT

D. W. HARDING

After lively appreciation and serious respect in his own time, Wyatt as a poet was embalmed for several hundred years in a few paragraphs of the literary histories and two or three anthology poems. In the twentieth century the worth of his poetry began to be more widely appreciated; and this had the effect of attracting so much academic attention that he is once again in danger of being lost to living enjoyment, this time in a mausoleum of scholarship. The originals, Latin, French, Italian, of his translations and adaptations, the conventional fictions of chivalry and the court of love that survived vestigially in the Tudor court, and the literary forms that expressed them, the theology behind his translations of the penitential Psalms, the sources of his metres and stanzas, all these (amply expounded by Patricia Thomson, H. A. Mason and John Stevens – see Appendix: Authors and Works) are of great interest but much less important than the fact that he wrote English poems dealing sensitively and vividly with lasting human concerns.

Only two difficulties may hinder our immediate enjoyment. In some of the poetry the rhythm creates a barrier, one that was heightened in the past by misunderstanding but now seems troublesome at fewer points and in fewer poems. The second difficulty, more serious, is that the tradition of courtly love and its stereotyped expression which he was at times content to follow made some of his short poems conventional exercises, serving a social purpose for his own time but having too little pressure of personal intent to be humanly important 400 years later. For a few critics, especially Mason and Stevens, this has been a major obstacle to enjoyment. Mason showed that many of the lover's complaints and supplications, and the imagery and rime used by Wyatt and the other young men of Henry VIII's court, were stock materials going back to Chaucer and largely borrowed by him from French writers. Stevens suggests that the 'game of love', deriving from medieval fictions of the Court of Love, was a framework within which the ladies of the court could be flattered with conventionalized love-pleas (at times also a cover for serious wooing), the verses being mainly a skilled performance contributed to courtly entertainment.

Wyatt of course took part in the game, sometimes with verse as trifling and stereotyped as the common run. If this were all he could be put aside. Stevens in fact believes that Wyatt's lyrics 'are on the whole dull', and 'except for one or two' he does not find in them 'any serious attempt to come to terms with life'. Mason becomes even more sweeping. After quoting conventional ideas, cliché phrases and standard rimes persisting from Chaucer's short poems through the scantly surviving lyrics of later writers down to Wyatt himself, he exclaims: 'Can we doubt that if we had *all* the songs sung at court between Chaucer and Wyatt we should be able to show that every word and phrase used by Wyatt was a commonplace and had been used by many of his predecessors?' What is meant as a rhetorical question has to be answered seriously: Yes, we can well doubt it, except in the sense that every writer uses the words and phrases of a common language. The Mason–Stevens view that the short poems merely manipulate clichés and make no 'serious attempt to come to terms with life' strangely overlooks the substance of a large proportion of the poetry and its direct relevance to Wyatt's serious experience.

Whether in original writings or in what he chose to translate, Wyatt's verse was fused with his active life and its vicissitudes. The dangers of Henry VIII's court were those that are always met with in the inner circle of a totalitarian state: hostile intrigues, sudden disgrace and overthrow, imprisonment, banishment to remote estates, rigged trials, and death. Wyatt pursued a difficult diplomatic career, he had the usual experiences of fairweather friends and malicious enemies, he was involved in the sexual liaisons of the court, he was plunged into disillusionment and sobered penitence during periods of political disgrace. He was twice imprisoned in the Tower, under threat of death, though each time released and eventually restored to royal favour. The second of these arrests resulted from a shift of power among the factions and the execution of his patron, Thomas Cromwell. The first illustrates another of the hazards of the court, for it came with the fall of Anne Boleyn. Before her marriage to the King she had had a love affair with Wyatt and may have been his mistress; he was arrested immediately after the men who were convicted of having been her paramours, but whether because he was suspect too or might have been a useful witness is unknown. As the French ambassador said on the occasion of Wyatt's second arrest, the true cause would be hard to learn, for the English 'condemn people without hearing them; and when a man is prisoner in the Tower none dare meddle with his affairs, unless to speak ill of him, for fear of being suspected of the same crime' (quoted by Thomson, p. 71). Anne's lovers were executed while he awaited his fate. Whether in the Tower or the Lubyanka these are experiences that leave a mark. Through the grating of his cell Wyatt is thought to have seen Anne's execution, and in poem CXLIII*, with its refrain, *circa Regna tonat*, he renounces the ambitions of court life:

> These bloody days have broken my heart:
> My lust, my youth did them depart,
> And blind desire of estate,
> Who hastes to climb seeks to revert:
>     Of truth, *circa Regna tonat*.
>
> The bell-tower showed me such sight
> That in my head sticks day and night:
> There did I learn out of a grate,
> For all favour, glory or might,
>     That yet *circa Regna tonat*.
>
> By proof, I say, there did I learn
> Wit helpeth not defence to earn,
> Of innocency to plead or prate:
> Bear low, therefore, give God the stern,
>     For sure, *circa Regna tonat*.

And CXLIX, addressing Anne's supposed lovers at the time of their execution –

> The axe is home, your heads be in the street –

states bleakly the reality of the danger he himself had faced.

In spite of the risks, people in these circumstances want to express their feelings. The lament in CXLIX for the victims of Henry VIII's axe prudently acknowledges in the second stanza that of course they

---

* References are to the numbers of poems in Daalder's edition.

deserved death, and by implication repeats the avowal as each man is named; for instance:

> Ah! Weston, Weston, that pleasant was and young,
> In active things who might with thee compare?
> ...
> But that thy faults we daily hear so rife,
> All we should weep that thou art dead and gone.

The acknowledgement of their guilt is perfunctory, the grief vivid. But besides poems like this with explicit reference to political events and the personal disasters they bring, the conventional love poem too can be pressed into service to voice a range of feelings – depression, protest at bad faith, weariness from unrewarded service – that could arise from quite other sources than love, such as the difficulties and disappointments of his diplomatic work, fluctuations in the King's favour, and the hazards of his position as a courtier among intriguing rivals. Poem XXXIX offers a simple demonstration.

> Patience: do what they will
> To work me woe or spite
> ...
> Patience, withouten blame,
> For I offended nought:
> I know they know the same,
> Though they have changed their thought.
> Was ever thought so moved
> To hate that it hath loved?
>
> Patience of all my harm,
> For fortune is my foe;
> Patience must be the charm
> To heal me of my woe.
> Patience without offence
> Is a painful patience.

But an earlier version of the same poem had been given disguised reference by different pronouns throughout, with 'she' for 'they' and 'her' for 'their' (see Daalder's note to XL), giving the superficial impression of a conventional love plaint, something far more prudent than a protest at being wronged politically. Tottel's editor helped to establish the idea that all Wyatt's short poems dealt with love, titling even CLXXVI, 'The lover suspected blameth ill tonges', a poem obviously referring to his political enemies, the angry exclamation of the last stanza echoing the mood of his hard-hitting attack against Bonner, Bishop of London, in the magnificent *Defence* he wrote from the Tower during his imprisonment of 1541:

> Mistrustful minds be moved
> To have me in suspect
> . . .
> Though falsehood go about
> Of crime me to accuse
> . . .
> Such sauce as they have served
> To me without desert,
> Even as they have deserved,
> Thereof God send them part!

And Tottel similarly gave the title 'The lover lamentes the death of his love' to CLX, 'The pillar perished is whereto I leant', now taken to convey Wyatt's bitter sadness at the execution of his patron, Thomas Cromwell. Some ambiguity or vagueness of reference was an ordinary prudence in lamenting the death of a 'traitor'. The ease with which feelings of melancholy and protest could be assimilated to the conventions of love poetry made that genre an inviting outlet, whatever the real source of the feelings may have been.

Yet there can be no doubt that there was a close connection between Wyatt's depression and his attitude to women. He was one of a circle of fashionable and promiscuous people; 'I grant I do not profess chastity', he admitted in the *Defence*, while rebutting Bonner's charge of the 'abomination' of having sexual relations with nuns in Spain. But he gives clear evidence in his poems of valuing more keenly than most the things that the court's easy promiscuity slighted, notably secure affection, mutual trust, kindness. In the third Satire (poem CVII) he expresses his attitude in one of the pieces of bitter advice he gives for worldly advancement:

> In this also see you be not idle:
> Thy niece, thy cousin, thy sister or thy daughter,
> If she be fair, if handsome by her middle[a],
> If thy better hath her love besought her,
> Advance his cause, and he shall help thy need:
> It is but love, turn it to a laughter.

> *a* in her waist.

Much of his most characteristic love poetry is a retort to the attitude 'It is but love'. Although the sexual liaisons at court were combined with the business of family advancement and factional intrigue they were also, we have to remember, the ordinary love affairs of young people. Wyatt was seventeen at the time of his marriage, and he left his wife, within six years or so, on account of her infidelity. Anne Boleyn seems (the date of her birth is uncertain) to have been about twenty when the King took her up and she had already been involved with Wyatt, then in his early twenties. Whatever the constraints of career and family ambition, and whatever the décor of the game of love – with 'disguises' (costume revels), songs, symbolic gifts, poems to be circulated and copied (thoroughly discussed by Stevens) – there were still the underlying inevitabilities of strong sexual attraction, transient infatuations, jealousy and hurt, and for some people (Wyatt among them) an insistent longing to share a relation in which sexual passion could be fused with affection and fidelity, a longing that turned to depression when it was baulked.

Denouncing fickleness and lamenting unrequited love were, it scarcely needs saying, commonplaces of the more trivial court verse (just as they continued to be in popular songs of, say, the 1920s and 1930s) and some of the verse Wyatt put together for superficial social purposes has no more significance than that; whether or not the emotion was genuine the verse is deadened with the convention and cliché that fill the foreground for a critic like Mason. But in other poems the words and the feeling react together to produce something that is much more a language creation than an expressive cry and much sharper emotionally than a language exercise. Even within the same poem it is sometimes possible to see the standard format of court verse suddenly transformed by fresh language conveying urgent emotion. In poem LXXXIV, for instance, 'All heavy minds', he begins conventionally, proposing to ease his depression by expressing it to his lute, since among women there is no one who will give him solace in his dejection:

> (1) All heavy minds
>     Do seek to ease their charge,
>     And that that most them binds
>     To let at large

(2) Then why should I
Hold pain within my heart,
And may my tune apply
To ease my smart?

(3) My faithful lute
Alone shall hear me plain,
For else all other suit
Is clean in vain.

(4) For where I sue
Redress of all my grief,
Lo, they do most eschew
My heart's relief.

So far, one could say it is an exercise along conventional lines, though highly polished and competent. The next two stanzas develop the familiar idea of the unkind mistress:

(5) Alas my dear,
Have I deserved so
That no help may appear
Of all my woe?

(6) Whom speak I to,
Unkind and deaf of ear?
Alas, lo, I go,
And wot not where.

But those last two lines introduce a note of bewildered loss of direction and uncertainty about his true need, a note that grows urgent and personal:

(7) Where is my thought?
Where wanders my desire?
Where may the thing be sought
That I require?

The exclamatory questions have an insistence, from their grammatical repetitiveness together with their rhythmical variety and crescendo (with 'where' successively stressed, unstressed, and stressed again), which gives an intensity totally different from the rhythmically staid question of stanza (2). Then comes the statement of his real need – the sincerity and faith that he knows to be lacking in the girl:

(8) Light in the wind
Doth flee all my delight
Where troth[1] and faithful mind
Are put to flight.

(9) Who shall me give
Feathered wings for to flee,
The thing that doth me grieve
That I may see?

The next three stanzas elaborate the idea of the unkind mistress, along the usual lines though with a recurrence of the special note of bewildered seeking:

(10) Who would go seek
The cause whereby to pain?
Who could his foe beseek
For ease of pain?

(11) My chance doth so
My woeful case procure
To offer to my foe
My heart to cure.

(12) What hope I then
To have any redress?
Of whom, or where, or when,
Who can express?

Finally Wyatt returns to the opening theme and completes the formal structure of his poem, with sighs and complaints to his lute offering little to distinguish the stanzas from other competent court verses:

(13) No, since despair
Hath set me in this case,
In vain oft in the air
To say alas,

(14) I seek nothing
But thus for to discharge
My heart of sore sighing,
To plain at large,

(15) And with my lute
Sometime to ease my pain,
For else all other suit
Is clean in vain.

If we left out stanzas (5) to (9) inclusive and ran straight on from 'My heart's relief' to 'Who would go seek' we should have a neat court poem of high craftsmanship. It is the middle stanzas, with the urgent and hopeless wish for a love that he could trust, which colour the whole poem and give it a lasting relevance to the relation between lovers.

Biographically we know that Wyatt did establish a steady relation in the latter part of his life with Elizabeth Darrell by whom he had a son and to whom he bequeathed lands. He seems to refer to that stability in poem CXXVI, although there the word 'love' allows him a deliberate ambiguity about the renunciation of his youthful mode of love in favour of his present steadfastness:

> Now such as have me seen or this,
> When youth in me set forth his kind
> And folly framed my thought amiss,
> The fault whereof now well I find,
> Lo since that so it is assigned
> That unto each a time there is,
> Then blame the lot that led my mind
> Sometime to live in love's bliss.
>
> But from henceforth I do protest
> By proof of that that I have passed
> Shall never cease within my breast
> The power of love so late outcast:
> The knot whereof is knit full fast,
> And I thereto so sure professed,
> For evermore with me to last
> The power wherein I am possessed.

(This is to assume that the poem is in fact Wyatt's; to authenticate some of the unascribed poems with any show of certitude would demand the aplomb of a Berenson. But Daalder's edition, which does include this, wisely withdraws the benefit of the doubt from many that earlier editors assembled.)

What can be pointed to with conviction is the strength of yearning in many of the poems for mutual trust in a love relation, and the painfulness of loss and betrayal. Poem XXXVII, 'They flee from me', may be remembered for its vivid record of the bedroom kiss but its theme is his desertion, and the implication that his own gentleness itself causes the casually promiscuous girl to turn away from him:

> It was no dream: I lay broad waking.
> But all is turned thorough my gentleness
> Into a strange fashion of forsaking,
> And I have leave to go of her goodness,
> And she also to use newfangleness.

The force of personal feeling in a poem like this makes a sharp contrast with the mere exercises in courtly verse, such as LXXII:

> Since ye delight to know
> That my torment and woe
> Should still increase
> Without release,
> I shall enforce me so
> That life and all shall go,
> For to content your cruelness.

But verse exercises form no large proportion of Wyatt's poetry (compared for instance with Thomas Hardy's); even a rather dilute poem like XXXVIII is given substance by personal emotion and the evocation of real incident:

> There was never nothing more me pained,
> Nor nothing more me moved,
> As when my sweetheart her complained
> That ever she me loved.
>  Alas the while!
> . . .
> She wept, and wrung her hands withal,
> The tears fell in my neck.  .
> She turned her face, and let it fall,
> Scarcely therewith could speak.
>  Alas the while!

Wyatt with the weeping girl in his arms, feeling her tears on his neck, is the same observer who could meet Henry VIII's requirement that his ambassadors should not just summarize an interview but give details of occasion, behaviour and manner. His despatches (in Muir, see Appendix: Authors and Works) contain the elements of much later novel-writing. The scenes are set with concrete detail, as when the French king takes Wyatt's letter of credence to a sideboard while the Cardinal holds a square candle for him to read by; active incidents are made as lively as they must actually have been, notably the cloak-and-dagger enterprise of capturing Brancetour; dialogue is given verbatim, for instance in the record of a tense and difficult interview between the increasingly angry emperor and Wyatt trying to hold his own with diplomatic tact and firmness. Not only are the observation and the recording vivid, but the English is sinewy and colloquial: 'This far had I written at Losches in evil favoured lodging and worse bedding . . .': or, complaining to Cromwell of the high costs in Flanders, 'the least fire I make to warm my shirt by stands me in a groat'.

It is the conversational manner and the colloquial, terse English that give life to much of the verse too. The satires, verse letters giving Wyatt's views of the courtier's life and contemporary moral standards, are of course explicitly conversational:

> By God, well said! But what and if thou wist
> How to bring in as fast as thou dost spend?
> 'That would I learn.' And it shall not be missed
> To tell thee how. Now hark what I intend.
>
> (CVII)

The same quality is a more notable achievement in the short poems, where the manner and usages of speech are fused remarkably with the 'musical' qualities. The refrains, for instance, often consist of those rhythmical short phrases that mark the more concentrated, exclamatory moments of everyday speech. He warns his friend against letting her eyes betray the fact that she is in love:

> For some there be of crafty kind;
> Though you show no part of your mind,
> Surely their eyes ye cannot blind.
>   Therefore take heed!
>
> For in like case theirselves hath been,
> And thought right sure none had them seen;
> But it was not as they did ween.
>   Therefore take heed!
>
> (CIX)

Or poem CXI:

> Is it possible
> That so high debate,
> So sharp, so sore, and of such rate,
> Should end so soon, and was begun so late?
> Is it possible?

Nor is the personal statement just a technical device; in many of the poems it seems beyond doubt that he intended a serious communication with his friends, using the poem as a means of putting his case or framing his advice in a form that gave it maximum force as effective statement. The puzzling and interesting poem CXXXVI, 'Greeting to you both in hearty wise', is an example. Another is CLXV, 'Sighs are my food', addressed from prison to his friend Sir Francis Brian whose political influence might help him, and proclaiming his ill-usage and his continued hope:

> Sure I am, Brian, this wound shall heal again,
> But yet alas the scar shall still remain.

And the intention of personal communication is unmistakable in XCIII, a reproach to his mistress who has been flirting by eye with someone else; he picks up a cliché of courtly love, the eye that can slay, to introduce a direct justification of himself after a quarrel with the girl:

> And if an eye may save or slay
> And strike more deep than weapon long,
> And if an eye by subtle play
> May move one more than any tongue,
> How can ye say that I do wrong
> Thus to suspect without desert?
> For the eye is traitor of the heart.
> . . .
> And my suspect is without blame,
> For as ye say, not only I
> But other mo have deemed the same.
> Then is it not of jealousy,
> But subtle look of reckless eye
> Did range too far, to make me smart,
> For the eye is traitor of the heart.

The poem clearly continues a broken-off argument in which Wyatt's reproaches had been met by the girl's counter-accusation of his unreasonable jealousy; in the poem he returns to the charge, restating his reproach in the most effective way he can and in the end rather hesitatingly accepting a reconciliation:

> But I your friend shall take it thus,
> Since you will so, as stroke of chance,
> And leave further for to discuss
> Whether the stroke did stick or glance.

The references back are to such specific points in the previous argument (including her incautious reproach that he was just like the others in suspecting her) that one cannot think of the poem as a mere exercise in dramatic form; its role as a contribution for a manuscript book and circulation among friends seems likely to have been secondary to its other purpose of personal communication.

Although the conversational aspect of the poetry is important, and appreciated particularly nowadays when the Miltonic convention of poetry has been placed in a longer perspective, it would be misleading to emphasize it to the extent of slighting Wyatt's obvious concern with the 'formal' features of his verse. His evident zest in developing a great range of skill in handling patterns of verbal sound points to what must have been one of the chief appeals of verse-writing to him.

The use he makes of refrains is highly characteristic and appears to have been a marked advance on what was usual in court songs of the time.[2] One of their purposes is to bring about a cumulative forcefulness in the main theme of the poem as the effect of successive stanzas increasingly explains and justifies the exclamatory refrain. This happens, for instance, in poem CXXIX:

> Forget not yet the tried intent
> Of such a truth as I have meant,
> My great travail so gladly spent
> Forget not yet.
> ...
> Forget not yet, forget not this,
> How long ago hath been and is
> The mind that never meant amiss,
>     Forget not yet.
>
> Forget not then thine own approved,
> The which so long hath thee so loved,
> Whose steadfast faith yet never moved,
>     Forget not this.

In several poems the refrain also provides an emphatic rhythmical anchorage to which the verse can return after wandering freely through more varied and expressive rhythms:

> Is it possible
> That any may find

> Within one heart so diverse mind
> To change or turn as weather and wind?
> Is it possible?
>
> (CXI)

Hallett Smith notes one effect of a repeated, contrasting rhythm at the end of each stanza in the example of poem LVIII:

> To wish and want and not obtain,
> To seek and sue ease of my pain,
> Since all that ever I do is vain,
>     What may it avail me?

He comments that 'this curious difference of effect between the monotonously rhyming first three lines, slow and heavy in their movement, and the rapid energy of the question is carried through to the end ...'

Enough has been said, though more examples can easily be found, to put it beyond doubt that Wyatt had an extremely sensitive ear for the effects of rhythm and high skill in managing his words rhythmically. He came at a point when rather simple regularity of metre was just beginning to dominate English verse. The tradition of ballads and carols and the neo-Latin poetry of the *vagantes* had maintained a flowing metrical form, though a very varied one, and this was the background of those of Wyatt's lyrics that run most smoothly to metre-habituated ears.[3] But side by side with this line of metrical form there existed the discursive poetry of the fifteenth century in which regular flowing rhythms played little or no part. The so-called broken-backed line that such verse tolerated may have been influenced by, though much less disciplined than, the older alliterative line with its well-marked pause separating two distinct rhythmical units; it is part of the rhythmical tradition that includes plainsong, where diverse units of rhythm are divided from one another by pauses and are not intended to flow together in the way that creates regular metre.

Wyatt drew both on the carol tradition and on that of pausing verse. Traces even of the alliterative line are fairly frequent:

> This maketh me at home to hunt and to hawk ...
> In lusty lease at liberty I walk.
>
> (CV)

More important than these vestiges of actual alliterative organization is Wyatt's readiness to combine in one line two differently patterned rhythmical units which have to be held apart by a slight pause in reading. He and his scribes no longer inserted the virgula at the pivotal point of the line, but some slight pause is still as necessary as it was in Langland's verse. Without it the effect is specially disturbing if, as often happens, pausing lines are interspersed among flowing lines:

> There was never file · half so well filed
> To file a file for every smith's intent,
> As I was made a filing instrument
> To frame other, · while I was beguiled.
>
> (XVI)

Again:

> Sighs are my food, drink are my tears,
> Clinking of fetters such music would crave;
> Stink and close air away my life wears,
> Innocency · is all the hope I have;
> Rain, wind, or weather · I judge by mine ears …
>
> (CLXV)

Where it is the last line of a stanza that has to be detached in this way from previous metrical lines the pausing rhythm can more readily be accepted; it is often vivid in its own right:

> So unwarely was never no man caught
> With steadfast look upon a goodly face
> As I of late: for suddenly me thought
> My heart was torn · out of his place.
>
> (CXIV)

and in XCI:

> The sun, the moon doth frown on thee,
> Thou hast darkness in daylight's stead,
> As good in grave as so to be:
> Most wretched heart, · why art thou not dead?

That Wyatt was fully aware of the ordinary demands of metrical writing is evident from the occasions on which he did commit himself to a regular scheme of metre and rime, as in the penitential psalms; there at times he lapses into mechanical regularity achieved through the w ak devices of unidiomatic inversions of word order, auxiliary verbs used as metrical fillers, redundant phrases inserted for the sake of rime. So the Prologue to Psalm 143 opens with

> This word redeem that in his mouth did sound
> Did put David, it seemeth unto me,

clumsy lines unworthy of the more impressive passage they introduce on David's foreknowledge of the Incarnation:

> As in a trance to stare upon the ground
> And with his thought the height of heaven to see,
> Where he beholds the Word that should confound
> The sword of death, by humble ear to be
> In mortal maid, in mortal habit made,
> Eternal life in mortal veil to shade.

> (CVIII)

Had Wyatt wanted to write in regular metre he would obviously have done so, and we must assume that in many other poems he wanted to do something else.

Indeed, no assumption is necessary; the fact happens to be demonstrated in Poem XLIV, 'Alas, madame! for stealing of a kiss', where we have both Wyatt's early version and his own revisions. The fifth and sixth lines run:

> Then revenge you, and the next way is this:
> Another kiss shall have my life ended.

*Tottel's Miscellany*, published in 1557 when simple metrical regularity had become standard, altered the fifth line to

> Revenge you then, the rediest way is this.

But in fact Wyatt's version is a revision of what he first wrote, and what he first wrote was as regular as Tottel:

> Revenge you then and sure ye shall not miss
> To have my life with another ended.

In this and many other poems Wyatt deliberately avoided the repetitive thump of regular metre.

The forcefulness of many of the irregular lines is beyond doubt. In other lines, especially in the sonnets, the rhythm is more defeating, and Wyatt's criterion for a satisfactory line is difficult to fathom. He was experimenting widely at a period when several forms of rhythmical organization were either current or only recently obsolete in English, and he was familiar with Latin, Italian, French and Spanish, with their different conventions of verse. In several of the rhythmically awkward poems he seems to have been using the merely intellectual criterion of counting a specified number of syllables to the line instead of creating a directly perceived pattern of stressed and unstressed syllables. In others the difficulty seems to lie in our expectation that all the lines will fall into roughly the same rhythmical mould and therefore flow easily into one another, while Wyatt was content to separate one line rhythmically from its neighbours and link them only by rime:

> Like to these unmeasurable mountains
> Is my painful life, the burden of ire,
> For of great height be they, and high is my desire,
> And I of tears, and they be full of fountains.
> Under craggy rocks they have full barren plains,
> Hard thoughts in me my woeful mind doth tire.
> Small fruit and many leaves their tops do attire,
> Small effects with great trust in me remains.
> The boistous winds oft their high boughs do blast,
> Hot sighs from me continually be shed.
> Cattle in them, and in me love is fed.
> Immovable am I, and they are full steadfast,
> Of that restless birds they have the tune and note,
> And I always plaints that pass thorough my throat.
>
> (XXXIII)

This is the sort of mechanical and uninspired translation in which one would expect strict adherence to whichever convention of verse was being followed – and yet no ordinary convention is recognizable. Whatever the solution of puzzles like this, we can at least put aside the older idea that Wyatt was groping and fumbling towards a regularity of metre from which he was debarred by lack of skill; when he wished to, he wrote metrically with dexterous variations on an underlying pattern. The irregular lines were the outcome of some other intention, however obscure it may now be.[4]

While he experimented alertly among the literary possibilities of his day and made graceful contributions of verse to the pastimes of the court, Wyatt's deeper concern as a writer was to shape and express an attitude to his own experience in a stimulating and dangerous social milieu. This by itself would have given his work mainly historical and psychological interest. That it has literary value springs from his having been a talented writer, rhythmically fertile, forceful in his command of idiomatic and often colloquial English, with a grasp of real incident and concrete fact to anchor intense feelings. His work continues to be rewarding because he used these resources to handle lasting human concerns as they presented themselves to a man of high intelligence and sophisticated civilization who was also sensitive and emotionally vulnerable.

## NOTES

1. *troth*. The MS. 'trouth' could also be modernized 'truth' as in Daalder's edition. But Dr Daalder now thinks 'troth' preferable in this context (personal communication).

2. See Hallett Smith, 'The Art of Sir Thomas Wyatt', *The Huntingdon Library Quarterly*, vol. IX, 323–55 (August, 1946).

3. See E. K. Chambers, *Sir Thomas Wyatt and Some Collected Studies*, and E. M. W. Tillyard, *The Poetry of Sir Thomas Wyatt*, who have pointed this out.

4. For a further discussion of his rhythm, see Hallett Smith (above), D. W. Harding, 'The Rhythmical Intention in Wyatt's Poetry', *Scrutiny*, vol. XIV, 90–102 (December, 1946); and Alan Swallow, 'The Pentameter Lines in Skelton and Wyatt', *Modern Philology*, vol. XLVIII, 1–11 (August, 1950).

# THOMAS MORE AND THE
# COURT OF HENRY VIII

DOMINIC BAKER-SMITH

One of the most notable signs of cultural change in sixteenth-century Europe is the advent of the courtier. Courts, needless to say, were nothing new but the novelty lay in the elaboration of a philosophy for those who inhabited them. The key text in this philosophy was Castiglione's *The Book of the Courtier*, first printed in Italy in 1528 and translated into English in 1561. As early as 1530 Thomas Cromwell was acquainted with it and it is a basic source for Sir Thomas Elyot's *Book of the Governor* (1531). Castiglione replaces the knightly ideals of medieval chivalry (still vigorously stated by Caxton in his *Order of Chivalry* in 1484) with a new style of omnicompetent individual, based on Cicero's pattern of the perfect orator. Like the orator, the courtier is versed in eloquence and the arts of persuasion; to military competence he adds the duties of counsellor and diplomat. While this was the dominant ideal, in the courts north of the Alps tensions can be discerned between the assumptions of an established feudal class and the values of humanism derived from Italy. Elyot's *Governor* is a characteristic attempt to modify humanist education so as to fit the needs of a traditional knightly class. Its outcome is the magistrate, that backbone of Tudor administration.

This pattern of adjustment can be traced quite clearly in the court of Henry VIII. At his succession (1509), just twenty-five years after Caxton's plea for a chivalric revival, Henry inherited a style of courtliness directly based on the medieval grandeurs of the Burgundian court. Within a decade the modes had changed to the Renaissance style of the French court under Francis I. By the Eltham ordinance in 1526 the new style is confirmed and a new kind of courtier is established. Men like Sir Thomas Wyatt and Sir Francis Bryan, who can joust with the king and yet take an interest in poetry and classical literature, mark this transition.

Not all those attracted by the humanist revival were so conciliatory. John Colet, Thomas More (1478–1535) and Erasmus (1466/7–1536), all born outside the knightly class, show only contempt for those literary myths which served to disguise the horrors of war. Colet, who deeply influenced More and Erasmus in their early years, even preached an anti-war sermon before the king in Holy Week, 1513, as Henry was preparing an expedition against the French. The sermon had only a local impact but the same note can be heard in Erasmus's bitter satires against war and in the ruthless warfare of the Utopians. Thomas More, like his friends, had little sympathy with the ethos of courtly life, but throughout life his assessment of the Court was ambivalent. On one hand it is less a place than a moral option, an artificial world of display and deceit, full of snares for the unwary. On the other, it is the centre of power, the only means to social and political reform. The moralist is repelled and the practical realist drawn. This double attitude is evident in aristocratic courtiers as well: Wyatt's third Satire, addressed to Sir Francis Bryan, is an extreme indictment of the Court, and Bryan himself translated de Guevara's *Dispraise of the life of a Courtier* with its succinct advice,

> If a man know himself to be ambicious, impacient, and covetous, let him go hardely to the court: And contrary, if the courtier feel his nature content, peacable, and desiryng rest and quietnes, let him be dwellyng in the village.

Yet Wyatt remained a diplomat, 'runnyng day and nyght / From Reaulme to Reaulme …'; Bryan maintained his position as court favourite; and More spent fifteen years as Henry's trusted servant. Only Erasmus kept clear of princes.

Perhaps that fact can guide us to the reason. Erasmus was a man of letters, and it is clear that we are dealing here with conventions, literary attitudes. The sharp contrast of court and village in Bryan's book is a variation on the classical contrast between town and country, *urbs* and *rus*, corrupt sophistication and natural simplicity. It is the contrast which underlies the satires of Horace and Juvenal when they place Rome against the purity of rural life. In the early years of the sixteenth century, when the friendship of More and Erasmus led to literary collaboration, they practised their Greek by Latin translations from the Greek Anthology and from the dialogues of Lucian. The dominant tone of these works is ironical, and in Lucian they encountered one of the most effective satirists of antiquity. The result was a recognition of the power of irony as a means of social influence. More's first performance as a humanist, the publication of his translations from Lucian in 1505, is justified in its dedicatory letter as an exposure of superstition and the fantasies of hagiographers. Lucian, More asserts, 'everywhere remarks and censures with very honest and at the same time very amusing wit, the shortcomings of mortals'. This adoption of a notorious atheist as an ally in the campaign against social and religious decadence is a daring step. The literary basis of this campaign is satire; irony is used to reveal the gap between ideals and sordid reality.

The satiric output of Erasmus is a brilliant performance, although it should be stressed that it is only one part of his achievement. Over a period of thirty years, in his *Adages*, the *Colloquys* and *The Praise of Folly*, he castigated the dead forms of medieval life; whether in courts, universities, or the Church. But his satire is not the same as More's complex irony; and this is surely the point. Erasmus stood outside the court and exposed its evil; he could only see one aspect, the moral option. More, however, could see both sides; he was in the court but not of it. This double-faced apprehension is characteristic of More. It explains the force of his irony and the deeply serious foundation of his popular reputation for wit. That familiar epithet, 'a man for all seasons', slides too easily over the complexity of the man.

This must explain why dialogue is such a basic feature of More's literary style. This is the case not only in those works which adopt dialogue form but also in those univocal ones which reveal a plurality of voices. The sense of speech is constant, and this is clearly linked to More's habit, as a lawyer, of 'putting cases', of exploring dispassionately the arguments that can be summoned for a particular course of action. Legal training links up here with the rhetorical habit of role-playing, of appropriating fictional *personae*. A valuable comparison would be the poetry of John Donne. More's instinct for dramatic elaboration is reported by his son-in-law, William Roper, who describes how the young More would 'at Christmas tyde sodeynly steppe in among the players, and never studying for the matter, make a part of his own there presently among them, which made the lookers on more sporte then all the plaiers beside'. One of his most persistent habits, it seems, was this dramatic exploration of his inner concerns in dialogue form. It also explains the virtuosity by which More is able to engage on several levels at once, as in his letters to his family from the Tower. The paradox is that, in a writer so chary of the first person, the sense of self-revelation is so strong.

More's first wholly original work, *The History of Richard III*, written around 1513, is no exception to these tendencies. Like Erasmus, he instinctively saw history in dramatic terms as a repertory of moral *exempla* which could demonstrate the limits of human possibility in the face of man's deceptive passions. In this respect his influence on Shakespeare's history plays is more than a mere source. While this work is closely modelled on classical historians – More had absorbed Thucydides, Livy, Sallust and Tacitus in particular – it is dominated by a Christian perspective which is strongly ironical. Events are disposed outside man's control. The figure of Richard is no biographical portrait but rather the type of the tyrant, a powerful image of political manipulation. More's concern with this theme is clear, too, in his Latin epigrams where he deals not only with the vulnerability of the ruler but also with the dangers of uncontrolled power. Thus a courtier is warned of the danger of intimacy with a king,

> This is like playing with tamed lions – often it is harmless, but every time there is the danger of harm. Often in anger he roars for no known reason, and suddenly what was just now a game brings death.

This is the irony of court life: no one knows what others truly intend. There is often a startling continuity between More's literary works and his recorded words; his *exempla* were given practical application: at Chelsea he offered Cromwell practical advice:

> in your councell gevinge unto his grace, ever tell him what he ought to doe, but never what he is able to doe ... For if [a] Lion knew his owne strengthe, harde were it for any man to rule him.

This moral vantage point suggests the advisability of withdrawal from court. *Richard III* is an exercise in the 'rustic' mode of Bryan's *Dispraise*, and this is nowhere more clearly shown than in the vivid comparison of court life to a play when Richard is persuaded, with apparent reluctance, to take the crown. More at once moves on to a more conventional example, the enthronement of a bishop after his formal refusal. There is a world of public role-playing, and a world of private affairs, and the two must be kept separate; call an actor by his own name and you wreck the play:

And so they said that these matters bee Kynges games, as it were stage playes, and for the more part plaied upon scafoldes. In which pore men be but the lokers on. And thei that wise be, wil medle no farther. For they that sometyme step up and playe with them, when they cannot play their partes, they disorder the play and do themself no good.

Within a short while of writing these words More was offered a part.

At this point it will be useful to cast a quick glance over More's public career. It has already been suggested that More's life and his writings have a curious relation; this gives us some understanding of the way in which a Renaissance author might use the conventional roles and situations of his rhetorical models to explore and define his understanding of life and of self. In May 1515 More took part in a diplomatic mission to the Low Countries where, in Antwerp, he wrote the introductory pages and the greater part of the second book of *Utopia*. That is to say, he devised the actual fiction of Utopia, an ideal commonwealth. On his return More seems to have been offered a place on the King's Council and he had accepted it by mid 1517. But before September 1516 he had completed Book One of *Utopia*, which contains the so-called Dialogue of Counsel, and thus set the polity of Utopia within a complex fictional frame. As John Guy has shown, More had been working steadily towards service of the Crown; yet the fact that he did not tell Erasmus for the best part of a year suggests some tension. Erasmus would not, in any case, have understood. By accepting a place on the Council More discarded the 'rustic' viewpoint of the satirist and became involved in the dangerous world of the Court.

It is important to recognize the dilemma which faced men of More's reforming disposition. Given that dark view of institutional life revealed in *The Praise of Folly* (1511) one could either stand apart or risk soiling one's hands. The reforming movement stimulated by humanism, seeking to replace present decadence with purer models from the past, was powerless without institutional support. But such support required compromise. Erasmus's refusal to compromise meant that, in spite of his enormous influence, his ideals had little practical impact. The key to success lay in capturing the ear of the king. The whole endeavour of Castiglione's courtier 'is to purchase him the good will and favour of the prince he is in service withall'. Only by these means can ideals be given practical expression. This problem is fundamental to humanism in the early decades of the century, and it is fundamental to *Utopia* as well.

There is a lot to be said for approaching *Utopia* in the order in which More wrote it. It was composed in Latin, the international language, because it arose from some intellectual game in Peter Giles' house in Antwerp. More called it *The best state of a commonwealth* because the island of Utopia is only part of its theme. The work draws heavily on Plato, in particular on *The Republic*, and on the *Seventh Epistle* in which Plato reflects on his effort to introduce philosophy into practical politics. Plato's problem is that of the humanists: how to mediate ideals into active life.

Firstly, there are the ideals which are manifest in the account of the island of Utopia. These can be summarized under the label of community. While this is a significant factor in Plato, to More it is undoubtedly based on his youthful experience of the Carthusian life. Certain features such as the regular exchange of houses, the material uniformity of life, the communal meals, the public reading and moral conversation reflect a monastic ethos. All are designed to wither egotism. Since there is no privacy there is no property, all goods are held in common. As a result goods are those things which are socially beneficial; gold, as an artificial symbol of status, has no value. The Utopians have a clear scheme of natural values which support their idea of man as a social and reasonable being.

The most original element in this fictional society is its attitude to pleasure. According to the Utopians nature prescribes pleasure as the end of all human operations. Since they also define virtue as living in accord with nature it seems that pleasure and virtue are inseparable. This hardly fits with the view that virtue must be solemn or gloomy. Yet it soon becomes evident that true pleasure is far from vicious; no true pleasure can be at another's expense, nor can it violate man's true nature. Since man has a soul as well as a body, spiritual pleasures outweigh the merely physical. In the end Utopian pleasure amounts to an extremely elevated concept of human potential. Through the fictional Utopians More here presents a view of pleasure, of the fulfilment of our natural desires, which is remarkably similar to that of Marsilio Ficino (1433–99), the most influential Platonist of the Renaissance who had corresponded with Colet.

Ficino's ideas seem to be echoed, too, in the account of Utopian religion. More's imaginative account of a purely natural religion does emphasize those articles of faith which are fundamental to human dignity: that man has an immortal soul, that providence guides events, that all will be punished or rewarded after death. These are those under-props of Christian faith which Ficino declared to be available to natural reason. That, indeed, is the point: the Utopians are pegs on which More can hang satirical points or witty schemes, but they are above all the ideal natural men of the pagan moralists. They realize the virtues praised by Plato, by Epictetus and by Seneca, those authors who led men like Erasmus and Wyatt to a gnawing dissatisfaction with their own society.

This implied contrast between Utopia and the state of Europe is the most obvious thrust of the satire. Europe, with its sterile education, its warring monarchs and its legalistic priests, when placed beside Utopia, seems to be a conspiracy of the rich. But there are deeper contrasts than this. The Utopians adopt any good innovation they encounter, while in Europe vested interests block progress. At the end of Book II, when the traveller Raphael completes his account of the island, he castigates Europe for its pride:

This serpent from hell entwines itself around the hearts of men and acts like the suckfish in preventing and hindering them from entering on a better way of life.

The condition of Europe is, in other words, the consequence of original sin. When we look again at the Utopians we notice that with them ideas lead directly to action, they are *simply* rational and do not even need to will the good, it happens as a reflex. This explains why there is little evidence of love in Utopia. The Utopian scheme, like pagan wisdom, may serve as a spur but it fails to allow for the harsh reality of pride, of self-interest. As More's fictional self observes, 'it is impossible that all should be well unless all men were good, a situation which I do not expect for a great many years to come'.

So far we have considered that part of *Utopia* written in Antwerp in 1515. To understand the full force of the work we must look now at the fictional frame which More devised on his return, that is Book I and the final paragraph of Book II. More creates for himself a rather slow-witted *persona* (a trick he may have learnt from Chaucer) who is the perfect foil for the fiery idealism of the Portuguese sailor Raphael Hythlodaeus. They meet in Antwerp, in conditions reminiscent of the opening of Plato's *Republic*, and they repair to a garden where the rest of the dialogue is set. More starts off the discussion by his suggestion that Raphael, given his experience, should enter the service of a king. Raphael reacts strongly: there can be no freedom in courts. More tries to be idealistic; whatever the personal loss royal service can be a benefit to the nation. By way of reply Raphael gives two examples of European decadence: the debate at Cardinal Morton's household and an imaginary session of the French council. In the former Raphael describes his dispute with a lawyer and friar, representative of a stagnant society, about the irresponsible use of wealth and its social consequences. In the council session we encounter all those abuses of power and position which Erasmus held up to ridicule. As Book I draws to a close the two speeches offer two different responses to these parables. Raphael sees any participation in public affairs as participation in lunacy; he intends to preserve the integrity of his ideals at all costs. More, on the other hand, tries to suggest a compromise.

The dilemma at the heart of the 'dialogue of counsel' is that which faced More in the form of a royal invitation to join the Council. The full force of Raphael's case for non-participation can be sensed if we glance back at an earlier point of More's life. When, as a young man, he decided against a monastic vocation someone – probably Colet – suggested the precocious Italian scholar, Giovanni Pico della Mirandola, as a model for the layman. More translated Pico's biography as *The Life of John Picus Erle of Myrandula* which was first printed in about 1510. In that book we learn that Pico, like Raphael, sold off his property and estates to relatives for a nominal price and that he refused to marry or enter public life so that he could give himself wholly to philosophical contemplation. When one Andrew Corneus urged him to leave his studies and enter the service of some prince, expressing at the same time dismay at the divorce between philosophers and courts, Pico indignantly rejected the idea as a betrayal of his liberty. It seems reasonable to suppose that when More created the figure of Raphael he based him on this *alter ego* of his early life. This, then, is More 'putting cases', exploring a range of options by means of an imaginary dialogue.

Confronted by Raphael's withering exposure of court life the fictional More tries to define a moderate course, achieved by 'the indirect approach'. Raphael's academic purism is all very well in conversation but what is needed, says More, is a philosophy responsive to the realities of life (*philosophia civilior*).

> You must not force upon people new and strange ideas which you realise will carry no weight with persons of opposite conviction. On the contrary, by the indirect approach you must seek and strive to the best of your power to handle matters tactfully. What you cannot turn to good you must at least make as little bad as you can.

In terms of the imaginary debate More gives no final resolution; at the close of Book II Raphael is adamant and the fictional More discreetly unconvinced. The options of retirement or involvement remain open. Some twenty years later one of the most gifted of the younger generation of humanists, Thomas Starkey (*c.* 1499–1538), provided an interesting gloss on the issue in his *Dialogue between Reginald Pole and Thomas Lupset*. Pole plays something like the role of Raphael and shies away from practical politics, for which he is roundly blamed by Lupset. It is an error to wait for an apt time before entering public life, as some do.

> They loke, I trow, for Plato's commyn wele, in such expectatyon they spend theyr lyfe, as they thynke wyth grete polityke wysdome, but in dede wythe grete frantyke foly. For of thys I am sure, that such exacte consyderyng of tyme hath causyd in many placys much tyranny, wych myght have byn amendyd, yf wys men, in tyme and in place, wold have bent themselfe to that purpos, levyng such fon*a* respect of tyme and of place.

As it turned out, the historical More followed the advice of his fictional self and entered the Council. It was a move that baffled Erasmus, but obviously More recognized in a way that escaped his brilliant friend the real problem of humanist reform and intended to find some manner of solving it. To 'make as little bad as you can' might seem a reasonable course, mediating between the opposed conventions of court and 'village'. By 1518 More was serving as secretary to the king, which suggests that Raphael, like Swift's Gulliver, must be seen as a disowned narrator.

*a* affected.

More remained close to the king throughout the 1520s, largely because Wolsey could rely on his integrity. While it would overstate the case to call him Henry's tame intellectual, it is true that he had little influence on affairs until 1529, perhaps because Wolsey could not fathom him. His acceptance of the Chancellorship in 1529 in Wolsey's place was a different matter since it opened the way to much-needed legal reform. It also committed More by oath to assist the suppression of heresy, a duty that he took seriously and supported by his polemical writings. It is at this point that he appears as virtual leader of the 'Aragonese' party, opposed to the king's divorce and determined to spin out matters until the king wearied of Anne Boleyn. But the Submission of the Clergy in the spring of 1532, which overthrew the safeguards against state control of the Church, made his position untenable; he resigned and returned to the private independence of Pico and Raphael, leaving behind a significant legacy of legal reform. However, privacy was no longer a real option for him; he had lost that by the decision of 1517.

During the months of imprisonment from April 1534 until his execution on 6 July 1535 More was engaged on his 'Tower works', a varied body of writing which includes the final letters to his family and a number of devotional works. The letters are complex, aiming at several levels of readership: his own family, the officials who would read them first, and posterity. Others, like the *Treatise on the Passion*, are the basis for a deeply personal identification with Christ. The work that is the greatest achievement of this period, and More's best vernacular writing, is *A Dialogue of Comfort against Tribulation*. Apart from its use of a common mode, *A Dialogue* invites comparison with the 'Dialogue of Counsel' in *Utopia* by the way in which it uses dramatized discussion to resolve a personal problem.

More's choice of a vehicle for his heavily charged theme is brilliantly apt. Anthony, an aged Hungarian, and his nephew, Vincent, are faced by the near certainty of Turkish invasion and ponder on the alarming implications. The issue is nothing less than martyrdom. Vincent is the voice of realism, even of fear, while Anthony, at the end of a long life, provides the Christian perspective. Both viewpoints have their validity and the resolution must take account of this. By the adoption of this fictional but historically plausible scenario the dialogue is able to touch on matters nearer home under a figurative disguise. As in the prefatory letters to *Utopia* there is a deliberate blurring of the boundary between fiction and reality: the titlepage informs us that *A Dialogue* has been 'made by an Hungaryen in Laten, and translatyd out of Laten into French, and out of French into Englysh'. But the technique has its resemblance to that of *Richard III* where Tacitus provided a model for the recent history of England, and Richard's tyranny was a warning to the young Henry VIII. In *A Dialogue*, however, More is less concerned with Henry than with himself. The king is, by implication, Suleiman the Magnificent, poised to invade Hungary while the Christians quarrel and intrigue among themselves, and the time is the tense lull before the Turkish invasion of 1529. By adopting such a recent event as his fictional vehicle More ensured that no one could miss this point. Henry's tyranny is designed, no less than Suleiman's, to destroy Christendom. The divisive intrigues of Suleiman's enemies figure the lack of sustained opposition to Henry's attack on the Church. Above all, the threat of persecution and martyrdom which faces the Hungarians is already More's situation.

A parallel that must have occurred to More is that of Boethius, composing the *Consolation of Philosophy* just a thousand years earlier while awaiting death at the hands of Theodoric. Both men faced the harshest consequence of court life and both braced themselves with something more positive than the rhetoric of rustic solitude. More, however, kept clear of the dream allegory and relied on the impact of his historical metaphor. It was a bold and effective choice. As a result the book does not offer an impersonal and abstract solution but the process of reasoning is completed through personal identification with Christ's sufferings by means of meditation. The method is not allegorical so much as typological.

Book I of *A Dialogue* opens with the recognition that pagan wisdom can provide some comfort but it is inadequate. For the medicine against tribulation we must turn to Christ, not only in the sense that his sufferings are the ground for Christian hope but also in the sense that his sufferings absorb and transform all human pain, making it a means of identification with him. In a sense the remainder of *A Dialogue* builds up this process of identification; seeking to give the abstract argument subjective force by a complex rhetorical development. The comparison with a preacher which opens Book II clarifies this function of rhetoric, of 'a mery tale', in relating the objects of belief to the actual world, thus making them emotionally compelling. As a result the movement is from fear to love, from the present plight of Hungary to an apocalyptic vision of the Trinity.

The complex working of the dialogue can best be grasped if we allow that More envisaged three classes of reader: the ordinary reader who would relate the book to the general theme of consolation, More's intimate circle who could recognize the personal allusions and ironies inserted in it, and More himself, attempting to objectify his situation. Thus the literal surface may be directed at the general reader, but an episode like Mother Mawd's Tale (II, XIV), a beast fable on scrupulosity, would be heavily ironical to those who recognized it as the fable told by Sir Thomas Audley, More's successor as Chancellor, to More's stepdaughter Alice Alington. Audley intended by the tale to imply that More was excessively scrupulous in his stand, but More shoots back the fable with interest, with the new application that scrupulosity, however painful to the individual, is less harmful to the world than 'a conscience over large'.

For those who could penetrate beyond the surface, *A Dialogue* spoke very directly of the contemporary scene. Reference to the Lutheran threat is open and even muted. But the sharp attack on those who practise external conformity while holding to an inner faith – when translated from Hungary to England – forcefully conveys More's impatience with those who shared his beliefs but ducked the consequences. This is an important element in the book since it reveals More's apparent obduracy as a public declaration of the threat to Christendom, not from the Turks but from Henry. Henry in his infatuation with Anne is thinly disguised as Herod with Herodias. The role held out to the reader is that of John the Baptist.

In order to speak to More himself the text had to embody the real tensions of his isolated stand. Thus Anthony, the older man, urges heroic fidelity while Vincent firmly insists on the reality of pain:

> But surely good uncle, whan I bethynke me ferther on the greefe and the payne that may tourne unto my flesh: here fynd I the feare that forceth myne hart to tremble

(III, 17).

This insistence on an objective apprehension of the difficulties ahead is what gives *A Dialogue* its extraordinary power and conviction. Quite methodically each stage of suffering is imaginatively antici- pated so that it can be recognized and borne. Grace may be the chief support, but psychology is given its place, 'the affections of mens myndes toward the increase or decrease of dreade maketh much of the matter' (III, 21). The affections are the proper target for rhetorical persuasion, and More's dialogue engages the imagination in order to draw them towards his intended goal. Classical rhetoric is linked to the discipline of meditation. The final chapter takes the form of a vivid meditation on Christ's death which completes the transition from the abstract argument of Book I to a deeply felt personal response, and translates death into an act of love.

It is often said that the More of 1535 is not the More of 1515; certainly few intelligent men remain the same for twenty years. But there is a certain formal continuity. When More was in the Tower Lady More was allowed to visit him and William Roper recalls that she expressed amazement that 'you, that have bine alwaies hitherto taken for so wise a man, will nowe so play the foole to lye heare in this close, filthy prison'. To which, we learn, More replied, 'Is not this house ... as nighe heaven as my owne.' One of Raphael's constant sayings, it is reported in *Utopia*, was, 'From all places it is the same distance to heaven.' More offers a particularly instructive example of the way in which a writer trained in the art of rhetoric could adopt familiar conventions in an uncompromisingly personal way. It is clear that rhetorical themes or models provided valuable instruments for the analysis of a situation or the definition of a role, and to More this sort of exercise was a life-long habit. Just as his court career can be read as a realization of the analysis offered in the 'Dialogue of Counsel', so his death manifests the argument of *A Dialogue of Comfort*.

# PART IV

# AN ANTHOLOGY OF MEDIEVAL POEMS AND DRAMA

### EDITED BY THORLAC TURVILLE-PETRE

# INTRODUCTION

The purpose of this selection of medieval verse is to give the reader who has been interested by the essays in the first part of this volume the opportunity to enjoy some of the literature itself. The selection does not include such works as *Sir Gawain and the Green Knight*, *Sir Orfeo*, or any poems by Chaucer, since all of these are widely available in excellent editions for the non-specialist. By excluding some of the more readily obtainable works, I have been able to find room for interesting but less well-known pieces, such as *Winner and Waster*, *Sir Launfal*, and tales from Gower and Henryson. I have included nothing from before the fourteenth century, because from the earlier period there is less that is interesting, and what is interesting is so difficult that it can only properly be presented with a full commentary and glossary. The latest piece here is one of Robert Henryson's *Fables*, written at the end of the fifteenth century.

I have tried to give the reader some idea of the variety of the literature of these two centuries. Here will be found examples of the three main genres of medieval verse: narrative, drama and lyric. Both alliterative and rhymed verse are represented. In subject-matter there is the secular and the religious, the comic and the serious; there are examples of the dream-vision, the debate and the *exemplum*; satire of contemporary conditions finds its place together with Arthurian romance and works of doctrine and ethics. The poems range from the easy to the very difficult; the inexperienced reader would be well advised to begin with *Sir Launfal*, John Gower and the Sloane Lyrics, and to leave some of the more difficult pieces, such as *Winner and Waster*, *Pearl* and the York *Crucifixion*, until later.

Snippets from longer poems are generally neither interesting nor fair to the works from which they are taken. The texts here are either complete, or are self-contained sections of long poems: a *passus* (chapter) from near the end of *Piers Plowman* (to which is appended an earlier passage that introduces the narrator of the poem), a tale from Gower's *Confessio Amantis*, a play from each of the Towneley and York cycles, and one of Henryson's thirteen *Fables*. The whole of *Pearl* is included, despite its length, because the poem consists of a developing argument which cannot properly be represented by a selected passage. Though the poem is one of the gems of medieval literature, the non-specialist has been hindered from appreciating its power by its lexical and syntactic difficulties, and has previously been offered either a text with a mass of glosses, or a verse- translation which conveys neither the beauty nor the exact sense of the original. Here I have presented a prose-translation to accompany the text. This is not meant as a substitute for the poem, but as a 'crib', an aid to grappling with the text itself. I have therefore not hesitated to sacrifice felicity in an attempt to convey as precisely as possible the meaning of the text, a text whose interpretation is still doubtful in many places.

All other texts apart from *Pearl* are provided with glosses at the foot of the page. These are numbered,★ and consist of a translation either of the complete line or of a word or phrase.

In editing the poems, I have in each case taken one manuscript from which to reproduce the text, though, as it happens, most of the pieces chosen are recorded only in one manuscript. Any print of a manuscript-text misrepresents the original to some extent; I have tried to keep this misrepresentation down to a minimum, though I have at the same time borne in mind the convenience of the reader, to whom the individual habits of a medieval scribe are unlikely to be of any interest. Abbreviations have been expanded; the obsolete letters þ and ȝ have been replaced by appropriate modern equivalents; *u/v* and *i/j* have been distinguished as vowel and consonant; *y* has been printed as *I* when it represents the personal pronoun. Punctuation, capitalization and word-division follow modern practice. All other substantial variations from the manuscripts are recorded in the textual notes that follow the selection.

Each of these texts has been newly edited from the manuscript specified in the introductory note, though I have, of course, profited from the work of earlier editors, and I acknowledge my indebtedness by referring the reader to what I consider to be the best modern

---

★ In the rest of the volume glosses are lettered. In this anthology they often run to more than twenty-six per page and so are numbered.

edition of the text concerned. I am grateful to the Trustees of the Huntington Library of San Marino, California, for permission to print the selections from *Piers Plowman* and Hoccleve's poems from their manuscripts, and to many other libraries for supplying me with photographs of their manuscripts.

## Notes on Pronunciation

1. All consonants are pronounced, including the *k* in *know* etc. In words such as *knight*, *gh* is pronounced like *h* in modern *huge*.

2. Short vowels have approximately the same values as in modern English.

3. Long vowels are as follows (with approximate modern equivalents and medieval examples): *a* as in modern *spa* (e.g. *game*, *make*, *table*); *e* may be either close, to rhyme with modern *say*, or more exactly German *See* (e.g. *be*, *se* 'see', *ded* 'deed', and other words spelt *-ee-* in modern English), or open, to rhyme with modern *there* (e.g. *gret* 'great', *se* 'sea', *ded* 'dead', and other words spelt *-ea-* in modern English); *i* and *y* as *i* in modern *routine* (e.g. *lyf*, *ryde*, *wis*); *o* may be either close, rather as in modern *go*, or more accurately as in German *Sohn* (e.g. *gode* 'good', *sone* 'soon', and other words spelt *-oo-* in modern English), or open, to rhyme with modern *saw* (e.g. *go*, *ston*, *bote* 'boat'); *u* and *ou* as *oo* in modern *moon* (e.g. *hous*, *cuth*, *out*).

4. Final *-e* may be sounded or dropped to suit the metre. In short words the plural ending is generally sounded as a syllable (e.g. *stones*).

## Notes on Metre

There are many metrical forms represented here. At one end of the spectrum are the regular octosyllabic rhyming couplets of Gower's *Confessio Amantis*. At the other end are the unrhymed alliterative lines of *Winner and Waster* and *Piers Plowman*. In between is a range of metrical forms, some with rhyme, some with alliteration, some with both.

The basic features of the unrhymed alliterative line deserve some attention. Each line is of four stresses. Structurally it consists of two halves, with two stresses in each half-line. The stresses are not regularly placed, though there are a number of stress–patterns which are particularly common. The alliterative patterns also vary to some extent, though in the predominant pattern the first three stresses of the line alliterate together, while the last does not alliterate. An example is the first line of *Winner and Waster*:

> Sythen that *B*rétayn was *b*íggede, and *B*rúyttus it áughte.

In *Pearl*, the four stresses are placed more regularly in the line, but the alliteration upon them is less regular. The poem is in twelve-line rhyming stanzas, which fall into twenty groups of five stanzas (except group XV, which has six). A common refrain runs through the stanzas of each group, and each stanza is linked to the next by repetition of word or phrase.

The *Second Shepherds' Play* is in stanzas of nine lines, the first four lines of four stresses, the fifth of one stress, and the last four lines of two stresses. The rhythm of the line is very like that of the alliterative line, although there is in fact not much alliteration. Instead there is end-rhyme, as well as internal rhyme in the opening quatrain of each stanza.

The *Crucifixion Play* is in twelve-line stanzas which are heavily but irregularly alliterative. The rhythm of the line is predominantly iambic.

These lyrics are preserved in B.L. MS. Harley 2253 which was copied in Herefordshire in about 1340. The manuscript contains texts in English, French and Latin, and includes a large and important collection of secular lyrics, three of which are printed here. The standard edition is G. L. Brook, *The Harley Lyrics* (4th edn, Manchester, 1968).

## I. ALISON

Bytuene Mersh and Averil[1]
When spray[2] biginneth to springe,
The lutel foul hath hire wyl[3]
On hyre lud[4] to synge.
Ich libbe[5] in love-longinge      5
For semlokest[6] of alle thynge;
He[7] may me blisse bringe –
Ich am in hire baundoun[8].

    An hendy hap ich'abbe yhent![9]
    Ich'ot[10] from hevene it is me sent.      10
    From alle wymmen mi love is lent[11],
    And lyht[12] on Alysoun.

On heu hire her is fayr ynoh[13],
Hire browe[14] broune, hire eye blake;
With lossum chere he on me loh[15],      15
With middel smal and wel ymake[16].
Bote he[17] me wolle to hire take
For te buen hire owen make[18],
Longe to lyven ich'ulle forsake[19],
And feye[20] fallen adoun.      20

    An hendy hap, etc.

1. Between March and April, 2. branch, 3. The little bird wishes, 4. language, 5. I live, 6. fairest, 7. She, 8. power, 9. I have had good fortune, 10. I know, 11. gone, 12. has fallen, 13. Her hair is very beautiful in colour, 14. eyebrow, 15. She smiled on me with a lovely expression, 16. made, 17. Unless she, 18. To be her own partner, 19. I shall refuse to live long, 20. dead.

Nihtes when I wende[1] and wake[2] –
Forthi myn wonges waxeth won[3] –
Levedi[4], al for thine sake
Longinge is ylent[5] me on.                                      25
In world nis non so wyter mon[6]
That al hire bounté[7] telle con;
Hire swyre[8] is whittore then the swon,
And feyrest may[9] in toune.


    An hendy, etc.                                              30


Ich am for wowyng al forwake[10],
Wery so[11] water in wore[12],
Lest eny reve[13] me my make[14]
Ych'abbe y-yirned yore[15].
Betere is tholien whyle sore[16]                                 35
Then mournen evermore.
Geynest under gore[17],
Herkne to my roun[18].


    An hendy, etc.


## II. LENTEN IS COME

Lenten[19] ys come with love to toune[20],
With blosmen and with briddes roune[21],
That al this blisse bryngeth.
Dayeseyes in this dales,
Notes suete of nyhtegales,                                        5
Uch[22] foul song singeth.
The threstelcoc him threteth oo[23],

---

1. turn, 2. remain sleepless, 3. For which reason my cheeks grow pale, 4. Lady, 5. come, 6. there is no man so wise, 7. excellence, 8. neck, 9. maiden, 10. deprived of sleep, 11. as, 12. motion (?), 13. take away from, 14. partner, 15. Whom I have long yearned for, 16. It is better to suffer bitterly for a time, 17. Loveliest of women (lit. under gown), 18. song. 19. Spring, 20. the world, 21. With blossoms and bird-song, 22. Each, 23. The thrush chides all the time.

Away is huere[1] wynter wo,
When woderove[2] springeth.
This foules singeth ferly fele[3],                    10
Ant wlyteth on huere wynne wele[4],
That al the wode ryngeth.

The rose rayleth hire rode[5],
The leves on the lyhte wode
Waxen[6] al with wille.                                15
The mone mandeth[7] hire bleo[8],
The lilie is lossom[9] to seo[10],
The fenyl and the fille[11].
Wowes this wilde drakes[12],
Miles murgeth huere makes[13],                        20
Ase strem that striketh stille[14].
Mody meneth, so doth mo[15];
Ich'ot ych am on of tho
For love that likes ille[16].

The mone mandeth hire lyht,                           25
So doth the semly sonne bryht,
When briddes singeth breme[17].
Deawes donketh the dounes[18],
Deores with huere derne rounes
Domes for te deme[19].                                30
Wormes woweth[20] under cloude[21],
Wymmen waxeth wounder[22] proude,
So wel hit wol hem seme[23].
Yef me shal wonte wille of on
This wunne weole I wole forgon                        35
Ant wyht in wode be fleme[24].

1. their, 2. woodruff, 3. in amazing numbers, 4. And warble in their great joy, 5. The rose displays its colour, 6. Grow, 7. sends forth, 8. light, 9. lovely, 10. see, 11. thyme, 12. These wild drakes court, 13. Animals gladden their mates, 14. Like a stream that flows quietly, 15. The man fired with love (*mody*) complains, as do others, 16. I know I am one of those who is unhappy for love, 17. loudly, 18. Dews moisten the hills, 19. Animals with their secret sounds to speak their minds, 20. woo, 21. the earth, 22. become extremely, 23. So well it (love) will suit them, 24. If I am to be deprived of the joy of one of them, I shall abandon all happiness and at once become a fugitive in the woods.

### III. WHEN THE NIGHTINGALE SINGS

When the nyhtegale singes
The wodes waxen grene;
Lef and gras and blosme springes
In Averyl, I wene[1];
Ant love is to myn herte gon                          5
With one[2] spere so kene;
Nyht and day my blod hit drynkes –
Myn herte deth me tene[3].


Ich have loved al this yer
That I may love na more,                               10
Ich have siked moni syk,
Lemmon, for thin ore[4];
Me nis love never the ner[5],
And that me reweth[6] sore.
Suete lemmon, thench[7] on me –                        15
Ich have loved the yore[8].


Suete lemmon, I preye the
Of love one speche[9];
Whil I lyve in world so wyde
Other nulle I seche[10];                               20
With thy love, my suete leof[11],
Mi blis thou mihtes eche[12];
A suete cos[13] of thy mouth
Mihte be my leche[14].


Suete lemmon, I preye the                              25
Of a love-bene[15];
Yef[16] thou me lovest ase men says,
Lemmon, as I wene,
Ant yef hit thi wille be,


1. believe, 2. a, 3. pains me, 4. I've sighed many a sigh, dear one, for your mercy, 5. nearer, 6. grieves, 7. think, 8. a long time, 9. word, 10. I will not look for another, 11. darling, 12. You could increase my joy, 13. kiss, 14. doctor, 15. For a love-favour, 16. If.

Thou loke[1] that hit be sene[2].                          30
So muchel I thenke upon the
That al I waxe grene[3].

Bituene Lyncolne and Lyndeseye[4],
Norhamptoun ant Lounde[5],
Ne wot I non so fayre a may                               35
As I go fore ybounde[6].
Suete lemmon, I preye the
Thou lovie me a stounde[7].
I wole mone my song
On wham that hit ys on ylong[8].                          40

1. see to it, 2. evident, 3. fall ill, 4,5. Lindsey and Lound in Lincs., 6. As she for whom I go in chains, 7. while, 8. About the one who has caused it (i.e. my sorrow).

*Winner and Waster* deals with a perennial theme, the virtues of saving money as against those of using it. The arguments are set in the economic and social context of the mid fourteenth century. The poem survives in only one manuscript, B.L. Additional MS. 31042, where the ending is lacking. It was edited by Sir I. Gollancz (London, 1920, 1931).

### PROLOGUE

Sythen that Bretayne was biggede, and Bruyttus it aughte[1]
Thurgh the takynge of Troye with tresone withinn,
There hathe selcouthes[2] bene sene in seere[3] kynges tymes,
Bot never so many as nowe by the nyne-dele[4].
For nowe alle es witt and wyles that we with delyn,     5
Wyse wordes and slee, and icheon wryeth othere[5];
Dare never no westren wy[6], while this werlde lasteth,
Send his sone southewarde to see ne to here,
That he ne schall holden byhynde when he hore eldes[7].
Forthi[8] sayde was a sawe of Salomon the wyse –     10
It hyeghte harde appone honde, hope I no nother[9] –
When wawes waxen schall[10] wilde, and walles bene doun,
And hares appon herthe-stones schall hurcle in hire fourme[11],
And eke[12] boyes[13] of no blode, with boste and with pryde
Schall wedde ladyes in londe, and lede[14] tham at will,     15
Thene dredfull domesdaye it draweth neghe aftir.
Bot who-so sadly[15] will see and the sothe telle,
Say it newely will neghe, or es neghe here[16].
Whylome[17] were lordes in londe that loved in thaire hertis
To here makers of myrthes that matirs couthe fynde[18],     20

---

1. Since Britain was founded and Brutus possessed it (alluding to the belief that Brutus, descendant of Aeneas of Troy, founded Britain), 2. strange things, 3. several, 4. ninth part, 5. For now all is cunning and trickery that we have to deal with, wise and clever words, and yet each word conceals another intention, 6. man of the west, 7. Lest he should be badly off (without his son) when he grows old and grey, 8. Therefore, 9. It will rapidly come to pass, I believe, 10. waves shall grow, 11. And hares shall crouch on hearth-stones as if in their lair (an established item in medieval prophecies), 12. also, 13. rascals, 14. control, 15. seriously, 16. Say it is about to come or is nearly here, 17. Once, 18. To hear writers of delightful poems who could find suitable subjects.

And now es no frenchipe in fere[1] bot fayntnesse of hert,
Wyse wordes withinn that wroghte were never[2],
Ne redde in no romance that ever renke[3] herde.
Bot now a childe appon chere[4], withowtten chyn-wedys[5],
That never wroghte thurgh witt three wordes togedire[6],    25
Fro[7] he can jangle als[8] a jaye and japes telle,
He schall be levede[9] and lovede and lett of[10] a while
Wele[11] more than the man that made it[12] hymselven.
Bot never the lattere[13] at the laste, when ledys bene knawen[14],
Werke wittnesse will bere who wirche kane beste[15].    30

### FIT I

Bot I schall tell yow a tale that me bytyde ones,
Als I went in the weste wandrynge myn one[16]
Bi a bonke of a bourne[17], bryghte was the sone,
Undir a worthiliche[18] wodde by a wale[19] medewe;
Fele floures gan folde[20] ther my fote steppede.    35
I layde myn hede one ane hill, ane hawthorne besyde,
The throstills full throly[21] they threpen[22] togedire,
Hipped up heghwalles fro heselis tyll othire[23],
Bernacles with thayre billes one barkes thay roungen,
The jay janglede one heghe, jarmede[24] the foles[25],    40
The bourne full bremly rane the bankes bytwene.
So ruyde were the roughe stremys, and raughten[26] so heghe,
That it was neghande[27] nyghte or I nappe[28] myghte,
For dyn of the depe watir, and dadillyng of fewllys[29].
Bot as I laye at the laste, than lowked myn eghne[30],    45
And I was swythe in a sweven sweped belyue[31].
Me thoghte I was in the werlde, I ne wiste in whate ende[32],
One a loveliche lande that was ylike[33] grene,

---

1. among people, 2. With wise words that were never put into action, 3. man, 4. in appearance, 5. a beard, 6. Who never composed with skill three words together, 7. When, 8. chatter like, 9. believed, 10. appreciated, 11. Much, 12. wrote the poem (that the child is reciting), 13. less, 14. men are known in their true colours, 15. Deeds will demonstrate who can do best, 16. alone, 17. stream, 18. fine, 19. lovely, 20. Many flowers bent down, 21. vigorously, 22. contend in song, 23. Woodpeckers hopped up from hazels to other trees, 24. Barnacle geese (thought to grow on trees), 25. the birds sang, 26. reached, 27. approaching, 28. sleep, 29. chattering of birds, 30. my eyes closed, 31. And I was very quickly swept up in a dream, 32. did not know in what part, 33. all over.

That laye loken[1] by a lawe[2] the lengthe of a myle.
In aythere holte was ane here in hawberkes full brighte[3],⠀⠀⠀⠀50
Harde hattes appon hedes and helmys with crestys,
Brayden owte thaire baners, bown for to mete[4],
Schowen[5] owte of the schawes[6], in schiltrons[7] thay felle,
And bot the lengthe of a launde[8] thies lordes bytwene.
And alle prayed for the pese till the prynce come,⠀⠀⠀⠀55
For he was worthiere in witt than any wy ells,
For to ridde and to rede and to rewlyn the wrothe
That aythere here appon holte had untill othere[9].
At the creste of a clyffe a caban[10] was rerede[11],
Alle raylede[12] with rede the rofe and the sydes,⠀⠀⠀⠀60
With Ynglysse besantes[13] full brighte, betyn of golde,
And ich one gayly umby-gone[14] with garters of inde[15],
And iche a gartare of golde gerede[16] full riche.
Then were ther wordes in the webbe werped of he[17],
Payntted of plunket[18], and poyntes[19] bytwene,⠀⠀⠀⠀65
That were fourmed full fayre appon fresche lettres,
And alle was it one sawe[20], appon Ynglysse tonge,
'Hethyng have the hathell that any harme thynkes[21].'

'Now the kyng of this kythe[22], kepe hym oure Lorde[23]!'
Upon heghe one the holt ane hathell[24] up stondes,⠀⠀⠀⠀70
Wroghte als a wodwyse, alle in wrethyn lokkes[25],
With ane helme one his hede, ane hatte appon lofte[26],
And one heghe one the hatte ane hattfull[27] beste,
A lighte lebarde and a longe, lokande full kene[28],
Yarked[29] alle of yalowe golde in full yape wyse[30].⠀⠀⠀⠀75

1. enclosed, 2. hill, 3. In each wood was an army in bright coats of mail, 4. Unfurled their banners ready to engage battle, 5. Rushed, 6. woods, 7. troops, 8. field, 9. For he had more ability than any other man to settle a quarrel and to advise, and to control the anger that each army on wooded hill had towards the other, 10. pavilion, 11. set up, 12. adorned, 13. English gold coins, 14. surrounded, 15. blue (alluding to the Order of the Garter), 16. embellished, 17. woven in the cloth up high, 18. light blue, 19. dots, 20. motto, 21. 'May the man who thinks any evil be dishonoured' (i.e. 'Honi soit qui mal y pense'), 22. country, 23. May our Lord preserve him, 24. man, 25. Dressed as a wild man with twisted locks of hair. (The *wodwose* was a heraldic figure associated with Edward III and the Garter), 26. a 'cap of maintenance' above it (as on the helmet of the Black Prince at Canterbury Cathedral), 27. savage (with pun?), 28. staring fiercely (i.e. 'guardant'), 29. Made, 30. very skilful way.

Bot that that hillede¹ the helme byhynde in the nekke  
Was casten² full clenly in quarters foure  
Two with flowres of Fraunce, before and behynde³,  
And two out of Ynglonde with sex grym bestes,  
Thre leberdes one lofte⁴, and thre on lowe undir⁵;        80  
At iche a cornere a knoppe⁶ of full clene perle,  
Tasselde of tuly⁷ silke, tuttynge⁸ out fayre.

And by the cabane I knewe the kynge that I see,  
And thoghte to wiete, or I went, wondres ynewe⁹.  
And, als I waytted, withinn I was warre sone¹⁰        85  
Of a comliche kynge crowned with golde,  
Sett one a silken bynche¹¹, with septure in honde,  
One of the lovelyeste ledis¹², who-so loveth hym in hert,  
That ever segge under sonn¹³ sawe with his eghne.

This kynge was comliche clade in kirtill and mantill,        90  
Bery-brown was his berde, brouderde with fewlys¹⁴,  
Fawkons of fyne golde, flakerande¹⁵ with wynges,  
And ich one bare in ble blewe¹⁶ als me thoghte,  
A grete gartare of ynde¹⁷ girde in the myddes¹⁸.

Full gayly was that grete lorde girde in the myddis,        95  
A brighte belte of ble¹⁹, broudirde with fewles,  
With drakes and with dukkes, daderande tham semede²⁰  
For ferdnes²¹ of fawkons fete, lesse²² fawked²³ thay were.  
And ever I sayd to myselfe, 'full selly me thynke²⁴  
Bot if this renke to the revere ryde umbestounde'²⁵.        100  
The kyng biddith a beryn²⁶ by hym that stondeth,  
One of the ferlyeste frekes²⁷, that faylede hym never:  
'Thynke I dubbede the knyghte with dynttis²⁸ to dele!  
Wende wightly thy waye my willes to kythe²⁹.  
Go bidd thou yondere bolde batell that one the bent hoves³⁰,    105

---

1. which covered (referring to the 'mantling'), 2. divided, 3. Two – the first and last – with the flowers (i.e. lilies) of France, 4. above, 5. below. (In 1340 Edward III adopted the arms of France quartered with those of England), 6. stud, 7. red, 8. projecting, 9. And I determined to discover, before I went, many marvels, 10. I quickly noticed within (the pavilion), 11. seat, 12. men, 13. a man anywhere, 14. (his clothes) embroidered with birds, 15. flapping, 16. bore in a blue colour, 17. blue, 18. wrapped around the middle, 19. A belt of bright colour, 20. they appeared to be trembling, 21. fear, 22. lest, 23. caught, 24. it would be very strange, 25. If this man were not sometimes to ride out hawking, 26. man, 27. most wonderful men, 28. blows, 29. Go quickly to make known my commands, 30. army waiting on the field.

That they never neghe nerre[1] togedirs;
For if thay strike one stroke, stynte thay ne thynken[2].'
'Yis, lorde', said the lede, 'while my life dures[3].'
He dothe hym[4] doun one the bonke, and dwellys a while,
Whils he busked and bown[5] was one his beste wyse[6].                     110
He laped[7] his legges in yren to the lawe[8] bones,
With pysayne and with pawnce[9] polischede full clene,
With brases[10] of broun[11] stele brauden[12] full thikke,
With plates buklede at the bakke the body to yeme[13],
With a jupown full juste[14], joynede by the sydes                         115
A brod chechun[15] at the bakke, the breste had another,
Thre wynges inwith, wroghte in the kynde[16],
Umbygon[17] with a gold wyre. When I that gome[18] knewe,
What[19], he was yongeste of yeris, and yapeste[20] of witt,
That any wy[21] in this werlde wiste of his age.                           120
He brake a braunche in his hande, and caughten it swythe[22],
Trynes[23] one a grete trotte, and takes his waye
There bothe thies ferdes[24] folke in the felde hoves[25].


Sayd, 'loo, the kyng of this kyth, ther kepe hym oure Lorde!
Send his erande[26] by me, als hym beste lyketh,                           125
That no beryn be so bolde, one bothe his two eghne[27],
Ones[28] to strike one stroke, no stirre none nerre[29],
To lede rowte[30] in his rewme[31], so ryall[32] to thynke
Pertly[33] with youre powers his pese to disturbe.
For this es the usage here and ever schall worthe[34],                     130
If any beryn be so bolde with banere for to ryde
Withinn the kyngdome riche bot the kynge one[35],
That he schall losse the londe and his lyfe aftir.
Bot sen ye knowe noghte this kythe ne the kyngeryche[36],
He will forgiffe yow this gilt of his grace one[37].                       135

1. get closer, 2. they don't intend to stop, 3. as long as I live (I shall obey you), 4. goes, 5. dressed and equipped, 6. manner, 7. covered, 8. lower, 9. With neck- and body-armour, 10. protection for the arms, 11. bright, 12. wrought, 13. protect, 14. a well-fitting tunic, 15. escutcheon, 16. depicted in natural colours, 17. Enclosed, 18. man, 19. Indeed, 20. liveliest, 21. man, 22. quickly, 23. Hurries, 24. armies', 25. wait, 26. Has sent his message, 27. i.e. on pain of severe punishment, 28. Once, 29. nor move any nearer, 30. an army, 31. realm, 32. arrogant, 33. Openly, 34. be, 35. alone, 36. kingdom, 37. through his mercy only.

Full wyde hafe I walked amonges thies wyes one[1],
Bot sawe I never siche a syghte, segge, with myn eghne;
For here es alle the folke of Fraunce ferdede[2] besyde,
Of Lorreyne, of Lumbardye, and of Lawe Spayne;
Wyes of Westwale[3], that in were duellen[4];                140
Of Ynglonde, of Yrlonde, Estirlynges[5] full many,
That are stuffede[6] in stele, strokes to dele.
And yondere a banere of blake that one the bent hoves,
With thre bulles of ble white brouden withinn[7],
And iche one hase of henppe hynged a corde[8],              145
Seled with a sade lede[9]; I say als me thynkes,
That[10] hede es of Holy Kirke, I hope[11] he be there,
Alle ferse to the fighte with the folke that he ledis.
Another banere es upbrayde with a bende of grene,
With thre hedis white-herede with howes one lofte[12],      150
Croked full craftyly, and kembid[13] in the nekke:
Thies are ledis of this londe that schold oure lawes yeme[14],
That thynken to dele this daye with dynttis full many.
I holde hym bot a fole that fightis whils flyttynge[15] may helpe,
When he hase founden his frende that fayled hym never.      155

The thirde banere one bent es of blee whitte,
With sexe galegs[16], I see, of sable withinn,
And iche one has a brown brase[17] with bokels twayne.
Thies are Sayn Franceys folke, that sayen alle schall fey worthe[18];
They aren so ferse and so fresche thay feghtyn bot seldom.  160
I wote wele for wynnynge[19] thay wentten fro home;
His purse weghethe full wele that wanne thaym all hedire[20].

The fourte banere one the bent was brayde appon lofte[21],
With bothe the brerdes[22] of blake, a balle in the myddes,

---

1. on my own, 2. assembled, 3. Westphalia, 4. live, 5. Hanseatic merchants, 6. fitted out, 7. With three white papal bulls embroidered in it, 8. a hempen cord hanging down, 9. heavy lead, 10. He who, 11. think, 12. lawyers' caps above them, 13. Curled very skilfully and combed, 14. guard (referring to lawyers), 15. debate, 16. sandals (worn by Franciscan friars), 17. strap, 18. die (alluding to the Franciscans' hell-fire sermons), 19. to make money, 20. He who persuaded them to come here had a heavy purse, 21. unfurled aloft, 22. borders.

Reghte siche as the sone es in the someris tyde,　　　　165
When it hase moste of the mayne one Missomer Even[1].
That was Domynyke this daye, with dynttis to dele,
With many a blesenande beryn his banere es stuffede[2].
And sythen the pope es so priste[3] thies prechours to helpe,
And Fraunceys with his folke es forced besyde[4],　　　　170
And alle the ledis of the lande ledith thurgh witt[5],
There es no man appon molde[6] to machen thaym agayne[7],
Ne gete no grace appon grounde[8], undir God hymselven.

And yitt es the fyfte appon the folde[9] the faireste of tham alle,
A brighte banere of blee whitte with three bore-hedis[10];　　175
Be any crafte that I kan[11] Carmes[12] thaym semyde,
For thay are the ordire that loven oure Lady to serve.
If I scholde say the sothe, it semys no nothire
Bot that the freris with othere folke schall the felde wynn.

The sexte es of sendell[13], and so are thay alle,　　　　180
Whitte als the whalles bone, who-so the sothe tellys,
With beltys of blake, bocled togedir,
The poyntes pared off rownde, the pendant awaye,
And alle the lethire appon lofte that one lowe hengeth[14]
Schynethe alle for scharpynynge of the schavynge iren[15].　　185
The ordire of the Austyns, for oughte that I wene[16],
For by the blussche[17] of the belte the banere I knewe.

And othere synes I seghe sett appon lofte,
Some wittnesse of wolle, and some of wyne tounnes[18],
Some of merchandes merke[19], so many and so thikke　　　190
That I ne wote in my witt, for alle this werlde riche,
Whatt segge under the sonne can the sowme[20] rekken.

---

1. When it is strongest on Midsummer's Eve (the sun symbol signifies the Dominicans' pride), 2. His banner is supported by many a magnificent man, 3. eager, 4. also reinforced, 5. And he (i.e. Francis, the Franciscan) craftily controls all the people of the country, 6. earth, 7. match up to them, 8. favour anywhere, 9. battlefield, 10. boars' heads (signifying gluttony), 11. If I have any judgement, 12. Carmelites, 13. silk, 14. hangs down, 15. Shines because the razor has been sharpened on it. (The Austin friars, who wore black belts, were clean-shaven), 16. for anything I know (i.e. I am certain), 17. shining, 18. Some depict wool, some wine casks, 19. signify, 20. total.

And sekere[1] one that other syde are sadde[2] men of armes,
Bolde sqwyeres of blode, bowmen many,
That, if thay strike one stroke, stynt thay ne thynken[3]          195
Till owthir here appon hethe be hewen to dethe[4].

Forthi[5] I bid yow bothe that thaym hedir broghte
That ye wend with me, are any wrake falle[6],
To oure comely kyng that this kythe owethe[7],
And fro he wiete wittirly where the wronge ristyth,          200
Thare nowthir wy be wrothe to wirche als he demeth[8]'.
Off[9] ayther rowte[10] ther rode owte a renke[11], als me thoghte,
Knyghtis full comly one coursers attyred,
And sayden, 'Sir sandisman, sele the betyde[12]!
Wele knowe we the kyng; he clothes us bothe,          205
And hase us fosterde[13] and fedde this fyve and twenty wyntere.
Now fare thou byfore, and we schall folowe aftire.'
And now are thaire brydells upbrayde[14], and bown[15] one thaire
     wayes.
Thay lighten doun at the launde, and leved thaire stedis,
Kayren[16] up at the clyffe, and one knees fallyn.          210
The kynge henttis[17] by the handes, and hetys[18] tham to ryse,
And sayde, 'welcomes, heres[19], as hyne[20] of oure house bothen.'
The kynge waytted one wyde[21], and the wyne askes;
Beryns broghte it anone in bolles[22] of silvere.
Me thoghte I sowpped so sadly it sowede bothe myn eghne[23].          215
And he that wilnes[24] of this werke to wete[25] any forthire,
Full[26] freschely and faste, for here a fitt endes.

---

1. certainly, 2. determined, 3. they don't intend to stop, 4. Until one of the armies in the field is cut to death, 5. Therefore, 6. before any harm occurs, 7. owns, 8. And when he knows for certain where the wrong lies, let neither man be angry at acting according to his judgement, 9. From, 10. army, 11. man, 12. envoy, may happiness befall you, 13. provided for, 14. taken up, 15. (they have) set out, 16. Go, 17. seizes (them), 18. commands, 19. lords, 20. retainers, 21. looked about, 22. cups, 23. It seemed as if I drank so deep it pained both my eyes, 24. wishes, 25. know, 26. Fill up.

### FIT II

Bot than kerpede[1] the kynge, sayd, 'kythe[2] what ye hatten[3],
And whi the hates aren so hote youre hertis bytwene.
If I schall deme yow this day, dothe[4] me to here.'                    220
'Now certys, lorde', sayde that one, 'the sothe for to telle,
I hatt Wynnere, a wy that alle this werlde helpis[5],
For I lordes cane lere, thurgh ledyng of Witt[6].
Thoo that spedfully will spare[7], and spende not to grete,
Lyve appon littill-whattes[8], I lufe hym the bettir;                   225
Witt wendes me with, and wysses[9] me faire;
Aye when gadir my gudes[10], than glades myn hert.
Bot this felle[11] false thefe that byfore yowe standes
Thynkes to strike or he styntt[12], and stroye[13] me forever.
Alle that I wynn thurgh witt he wastes thurgh pryde;                    230
I gedir, I glene, and he lattys goo sone[14];
I pryke and I pryne[15], and he the purse opynes.
Why hase this cayteffe[16] no care how men corne sellen?
His londes liggen alle ley[17], his lomes[18] aren solde,
Downn bene his dowfehowses, drye bene his poles[19];                    235
The devyll wounder one the wele he weldys at home[20],
Bot[21] hungere and heghe howses and howndes full kene!
Safe a sparthe and a spere sparrede in ane hyrne[22],
A bronde[23] at his bede-hede, biddes[24] he no nother
Bot a cuttede capill to cayre[25] with to his frendes.                  240
Then will he boste[26] with his brande, and braundesche hym[27] ofte,
This wikkede weryed[28] thefe, that Wastoure men calles,
That if he life may longe, this lande will he stroye.
Forthi deme us this daye, for Drightyns[29] love in heven,
To fighte furthe with oure folke to owthire fey worthe[30].'           245

1. spoke, 2. make known, 3. are called, 4. allow, 5. who helps the whole world, 6. instruct by the guidance of Good Sense, 7. Those who profitably will save, 8. a small amount, 9. guides, 10. Always when my goods mount up, 11. cruel, 12. before he desists, 13. destroy, 14. dissipates it at once, 15. I assemble it neatly, 16. villain, 17. lie quite untilled, 18. tools, 19. fish-ponds, 20. The Devil may marvel at the wealth he has at home (i.e. there isn't any left), 21. Apart from, 22. Except for a battle-axe and a spear shut in a corner, 23. sword, 24. asks for, 25. gelding to ride, 26. threaten, 27. swagger, 28. accursed, 29. God's, 30. until either of us is killed.

'Yee, Wynnere,' quod Wastoure, 'thi wordes are hye;
Bot I schall tell the a tale that tene[1] schall the better.
When thou haste waltered and went and wakede[2] alle the nyghte,
And iche a wy in this werlde that wonnes the abowte[3],
And hase werpede[4] thy wyde howses full of wolle sakkes –          250
The bemys benden at the rofe, siche bakone there hynges[5],
Stuffed are sterlynges[6] undere stelen bowndes[7] –
What scholde worthe[8] of that wele[9], if no waste come?
Some rote, some ruste, some ratons[10] fede.
Let be thy cramynge of thi kystes[11], for Cristis lufe of heven!          255
Late[12] the peple and the pore hafe parte of thi silvere;
For if thou wydwhare[13] scholde walke, and waytten[14] the sothe,
Thou scholdeste reme[15] for rewthe[16], in siche ryfe[17] bene the pore.
For and[18] thou lengare thus lyfe, leve[19] thou no nother,
Thou schall be hanged in helle for that thou here spareste;          260
For siche a synn haste thou solde thi soule into helle,
And there es ever wellande[20] woo, worlde withowtten ende.'


'Late be[21] thi worde, Wastoure,' quod Wynnere the riche.
'Thou melleste of a mater, thou madiste it thiselven[22],
With thi sturte[23] and thi stryffe thou stroyeste up my gudes;          265
In playinge and in wakynge in wynttres nyghttis,
In owttrage, in unthrifte, in angarte pryde[24].
There es no wele[25] in this werlde to wasschen thyn handes
That ne es gyffen and grounden are thou it getyn have[26].
Thou ledis renkes in thy rowte wele rychely attyrede,          270
Some hafe girdills of golde, that more gude coste
Than alle the faire fre londe that ye before haden.
Ye folowe noghte youre fadirs that fosterde yow alle,
A kynde[27] herveste to cache, and cornes to wynn[28],
For[29] the colde wynttter and the kene with gleterand frostes,          275
Sythen dropeles drye in the dede monethe[30].


1. annoy, 2. tossed and turned and lain awake, 3. associates with you, 4. filled, 5. hangs, 6. coins, 7. bands of steel, 8. become, 9. wealth, 10. rats, 11. chests, 12. Let, 13. round about, 14. search out, 15. weep, 16. sorrow, 17. multitudes, 18. if, 19. believe, 20. surging, 21. Leave off, 22. You speak of a problem you created yourself, 23. violence, 24. In excess, extravagance and boasting, 25. wealth (with pun on 'well'), 26. That isn't given away and used up before you've got it, 27. good, 28. obtain, 29. Before, 30. And afterwards the rainless drought in the dead month (of March).

And thou wolle[1] to the taverne, byfore the toune-hede[2],
Iche beryne redy with a bolle to blerren[3] thyn eghne,
Hete[4] the whatte thou have schalte, and whatt thyn hert lykes,
Wyfe, wedowe, or wenche, that wonnes[5] there aboute.                    280
Then es there bott "fille in" and "feche forthe", "florence to
    schewe[6]",
"Wee-hee", and "worthe[7] up", wordes ynewe[8].
Bot when this wele es awaye, the wyne moste be payede fore.
Than lympis yowe weddis to laye[9], or your londe selle.
For siche wikked werkes, wery[10] the oure Lorde!                        285
And forthi[11] God laughte that[12] he lovede, and levede that other,
Iche freke one felde ogh[13] the ferdere[14] be to wirche.
Teche thy men for to tille and tynen[15] thyn feldes,
Rayse up thi rent howses, ryme up thi yerdes[16],
Owthere hafe as thou haste done, and hope aftir[17] werse –      290
That es firste the faylynge of fode, and than the fire aftir,
To brene the alle at a birre, for thi bale dedis[18]:
The more colde es to come, als me a clerke[19] tolde.'


'Yee, Wynnere,' quod Wastoure, 'thi wordes are vayne.
With oure festes and oure fare we feden the pore;               295
It es plesynge to the Prynce that paradyse wroghte.
When Cristes peple hath parte hym payes[20] alle the better,
Then here ben hodirde and hidde and happede in cofers[21],
That it no sonn may see thurgh seven wyntter ones;
Owthir freres it feche, when thou fey worthes[22],              300
To payntten with thaire pelers[23], or pergett[24] with thaire walles.
Thi sone and thi sektours[25], ich one slees[26] othere;
Maken dale[27] aftir thi daye, for thou durste never
Mawngery ne myndale[28], ne never myrthe lovediste.
A dale aftir thi daye dose[29] the no mare                      305

---

1. would rather go, 2. in the disreputable area of the town, 3. blear, 4. Offer, 5. lives,
6. show your money, 7. climb, 8. enough, 9. you are obliged to pawn valuables, 10.
curse, 11. because, 12. took the one (reference to Matthew 24, 40), 13. ought, 14.
keener, 15. harrow, 16. clear your enclosed land, 17. expect, 18. To burn you all in an
instant for your wicked deeds, 19. wise man, 20. it pleases Him, 21. Rather than that (the
money) should be covered up and hidden and shut in coffers, 22. die, 23. pillars (of their
rich churches), 24. plaster, 25. executors, 26. slays, 27. a share-out, 28. (Have a) feast or
memorial drink, 29. profits.

Than a lighte lanterne late appone nyghte,
When it es borne at thi bakke, beryn, be my trouthe.
Now wolde God that it were als I wisse couthe[1]
That thou, Wynnere, thou wriche[2], and Wanhope[3], thi brothir,
And eke ymbryne dayes[4], and evenes of sayntes,                    310
The Frydaye and his fere one the ferrere syde[5],
Were drownede in the depe see there never droghte come,
And dedly synn for thayre dede[6] were endityde with twelve[7];
And thies beryns one the bynches, with howes[8] one lofte
That bene knowen and kydde[9] for clerkes of the beste,            315
Als gude als Arestotle, or Austyn the wyse,
That alle schent[10] were those schalkes[11], and Scharshull[12] itwiste[13]
That saide I prikkede with powere his pese to distourbe!
Forthi, comely kynge, that oure case heris,
Late us swythe[14] with oure swerdes swyngen togedirs;            320
For nowe I se it es full sothe that sayde es full yore –
The richere of ranke wele[15], the rathere[16] will drede:
The more havande[17] that he hathe, the more of hert feble.'

Bot than this wrechede Wynnere full wrothely he lukes,
Sayse, 'This es spedles[18] speche to speken thies wordes.         325
Loo, this wrechide Wastoure, that wydewhare[19] es knawenn!
Ne es nothir kaysser[20], ne kynge, ne knyghte that the folowes,
Barone, ne bachelere[21], ne beryn that thou loveste,
Bot foure felawes or fyve, that the fayth owthe[22];
And he schall dighte[23] thaym to dyne with dayntethes so
     many                                                          330
That iche a wy in this werlde may wepyn for sorowe!
The bores hede schall be broghte with plontes appon lofte[24],
Buk-tayles full brode in brothes there besyde,
Venyson with the frumentee[25], and fesanttes full riche,
Baken mete[26] therby one the burde[27] sett,                     335

1. that I could arrange, 2. wretch, 3. Despair, 4. ember days (periods of fasting, as were eves of saints' days and Fridays), 5. companion on the further side (i.e. Saturday, the mass-day of the Virgin), 6. death (of Winner etc.), 7. i.e. by a jury, 8. judges' caps, 9. recognized, 10. destroyed, 11. men, 12. Chief Justice Sir William Shareshull, 13. together with them, 14. quickly, 15. excessive wealth, 16. sooner, 17. possessions, 18. pointless, 19. universally, 20. emperor, 21. young knight, 22. owe you allegiance, 23. set, 24. herbs on it, 25. wheat boiled in milk, 26. pies, 27. table.

Chewettes[1] of choppede flesche, charbiande fewlis[2],
And iche a segge that I see has sexe mens doke[3].
If this were nedles note[4], anothir comes aftir –
Roste with the riche sewes[5], and the ryalle[6] spyces,
Kiddes cloven by the rigge[7], quarterd swannes,     340
Tartes of ten ynche, that tenys[8] myn hert
To see the borde overbrade[9] with blasande[10] disches,
Als it were a rayled rode[11] with rynges and stones.
The thirde mese[12] to me were mervelle to rekken[13],
For alle es Martynmesse mete that I with moste dele[14],     345
Noghte bot worttes[15] with the flesche, withowt wilde fowle,
Save ane hene to hym that the howse owethe[16].
And he[17] will hafe birdes bownn[18] one a broche[19] riche,
Barnakes and buturs and many billed snyppes[20],
Larkes and lyngwhittes[21], lapped[22] in sogoure,     350
Wodcokkes and wodwales[23], full wellande[24] hote,
Teeles and titmoyses, to take what hym lykes;
Caudels of conynges[25], and custadis swete,
Dariels[26] and dische-metis, that ful dere coste,
Mawmene that men clepen[27], your mawes[28] to fill,     355
Aye a mese at a merke[29] bytwen twa men,
Thoghe bot brynneth for bale your bowells within[30].
Me tenyth[31] at your trompers, thay tounen[32] so heghe
That iche a gome[33] in the gate[34] goullyng[35] may here:
Than wil thay say to thamselfe, as thay samen[36] ryden,     360
Ye hafe no myster[37] of the helpe of the heven kyng.
Thus are ye scorned by skyll[38], and schathed[39] theraftir,
That rechen[40] for a repaste a rawnsom of silver.
Bot ones I herd in a haule of a herdmans[41] tong:
"Better were meles many than a mery nyghte." '     365

1. Meat dishes, 2. roast fowl, 3. duck, 4. expense, 5. sauces, 6. delicate, 7. split along the back, 8. it grieves, 9. covered, 10. shining, 11. As if it were a bejewelled cross, 12. course, 13. relate, 14. For it is all salted meat (eaten during winter) that I have to do with, 15. vegetables, 16. is master of, 17. i.e. Waster, 18. prepared, 19. spit, 20. Geese and bitterns and many long-billed snipes, 21. linnets, 22. covered, 23. woodpeckers, 24. boiling, 25. Rabbit stews, 26. Pastries, 27. What men call 'mawmene' (a wine sauce), 28. stomachs, 29. Every time a course costing a mark, 30. Though your bowels within just burn with discomfort, 31. I am angry, 32. sound, 33. man, 34. street, 35. howling, 36. together, 37. need, 38. with good reason, 39. insulted, 40. You who hand over, 41. servant's.

And he that wilnes of this werke for to wete forther,
Full freschely and faste, for here a fit endes.


### FIT III

'Yee, Wynnere!' quod Wastour, 'I wote[1] wele myselven
What sall lympe of the[2], lede, within fewe yeris,
Thurgh the pure plente of corne that the peple sowes.                370
That[3] God will graunte of his grace to growe on the erthe,
Ay to appaire[4] the pris, that it passe nott to hye,
Schal make the to waxe wod[5] for wanhope[6] in erthe,
To hope aftir an harde yere, to honge thiselven.
Woldeste thou hafe lordis to lyfe as laddes on fote?          375
Prelates als prestes that the parischen yemes?[7]
Prowde marchandes of pris[8] as pedders[9] in towne?
Late lordes lyfe als tham liste[10], laddes as tham falles[11];
Thay the bacon and beefe, thay botours and swannes,
Thay the roughe of the rye, thay the rede whete,          380
Thay the grewell gray, and thay the gude sewes;
And then may the peple hafe parte in povert that standes,
Sum gud morsell of mete to mend with thair chere[12].
If fewlis flye schold forthe, and fongen[13] be never,
And wild bestis in the wodde wone[14] al thaire lyve,          385
And fisches flete[15] in the flode, and ichone ete other,
Ane henne at ane halpeny by halfe yeris ende,
Schold not a ladde be in londe a lorde for to serve[16].
This wate[17] thou full wele witterly[18] thiselven.
Who so wele schal wyn, a wastour moste he fynde,          390
For if it greves one gome, it gladdes another.'


'Now', quod Wynner to Wastour, 'me wondirs in hert
Of thies poure penyles men that peloure[19] will by,
Sadills of sendale, with sercles[20] full riche.
Lesse and ye wrethe[21] your wifes, thaire willes to folowe,          395

---

1. know, 2. happen to you, 3. That which, 4. reduce, 5. go mad, 6. despair, 7. look after the parishioners, 8. importance, 9. pedlars, 10. they please, 11. they have to, 12. improve their conditions, 13. caught, 14. live, 15. swim, 16. i.e. if the rich did not consume the natural resources, they would become so cheap that the poor would have no incentive to work, 17. know, 18. certainly, 19. fur, 20. rings, 21. In order not to anger.

Ye sellyn wodd aftir wodde in a wale tyme[1],
Bothe the oke and the assche and all that ther growes;
The spyres[2] and the yonge sprynge[3] ye spare to your children,
And sayne God wil graunt it his grace to grow at the last
For to save to your sones; bot the schame es your ownn.          400
Nedeles save ye the soyle, for sell it ye thynken.
Your forfadirs were fayne[4], when any frende come,
For to schake to the schawe[5], and schewe hym the estres[6],
In iche holt that thay had ane hare for to fynde,
Bryng to the brod launde[7] bukkes ynewe[8],          405
To lache[9] and to late goo, to lightten thaire hertis.
Now es it sett[10] and solde, my sorowe es the more,
Wastes alle wilfully, your wyfes to paye[11].
That are[12] had lordes in londe and ladyes riche,
Now are thay nysottes[13] of the new gett[14], so nysely[15]
    attyred,          410
With sleghe[16] slabbande[17] sleves, sleght[18] to the grounde,
Ourlede all umbtourne[19] with ermyn aboute,
That es as harde, as I hope[20], to handil in the derne[21],
Als a cely symple[22] wenche that never silke wroghte.
Bot who-so lukes on hir lyre[23], oure lady of heven,          415
How scho fled for ferd[24] ferre out of hir kythe,
Appon ane amblande asse, withowtten more pride,
Safe a barne in hir barme[25], and a broken heltre[26]
That Joseph held in hys hande, that hend for to yeme[27],
Allthofe scho walt[28] al this werlde, hir wedes wer pore;          420
For to gyf ensample of siche, for to schewe other
For to leve pompe and pride – that poverte ofte schewes[29].'

Than the Wastour wrothly castis up his eghne,
And said, 'Thou Wynnere, thou wriche, me woundirs in hert,

---

1. in rapid succession, 2. shoots, 3. sapling, 4. glad, 5. To go to the wood, 6. coverts, 7. wide pasture, 8. many, 9. catch, 10. leased, 11. please, 12. Those (i.e. servant girls) who previously, 13. frivolous girls, 14. fashion, 15. foolishly, 16. skilfully made, 17. trailing in mud, 18. falling, 19. Trimmed all around, 20. believe, 21. dark, 22. innocent and decent. (Obscure; perhaps 'A night-time fumble with one of the new sophisticates encumbered with clothes is as difficult as with a decent, homely girl who never made a silk dress'), 23. appearance (in, e.g., a picture), 24. fear, 25. lap, 26. halter, 27. to guide that gentle lady, 28. Although she ruled, 29. poverty often demonstrates that.

What hafe oure clothes coste the, caytef, to by,   425
That thou schal birdes[1] upbrayd of thaire bright wedis,
Sythen that we vouchesafe that the silver payen.
It lyes wele for a lede his lemman to fynde,
Aftir hir faire chere to forthir hir herte[2].
Then will scho love hym lelely[3] as hir lyfe one,   430
Make hym bolde and bown[4] with brandes to smytte,
To schonn schenchipe[5] and schame ther schalkes[6] ere gadird;
And if my peple ben prode[7], me payes[8] alle the better
To fee[9] tham faire and free[10] tofore with myn eghne[11];
And ye negardes appon nyghte ye nappen so harde,   435
Routten at your raxillyng, raysen your hurdes;
Ye beden wayte one the wedir, then wery ye the while
That ye nade hightilde up your houses, and your hyne raysed[12].
Forthi, Wynnere, with wronge thou wastes thi tyme;
For gode day ne glade getys thou never.   440
The devyll at thi dede-day schal delyn thi gudis,
Tho thou woldest that it were, wyn thay it never;
Thi skathill sectours schal sever tham aboute[13],
And thou hafe helle full hotte for that thou here saved.
Thou tast tent one[14] a tale that tolde was full yore:   445
I hold hym madde that mournes[15] his make[16] for to wyn,
Hent hir that hir haf schal[17], and hold hir his while,
Take the coppe as it comes, the case as it falles,
For who-so lyfe may lengeste lympes[18] to feche
Woodd that he waste schall, to warmen his helys,   450
Ferrere[19] than his fadir dide by fyvetene myle.
Now kan I carpe[20] no more, bot, Sir Kyng, by thi trouthe,
Deme us where we duell schall: me thynke the day hyes[21].

---

1. ladies, 2. Since we agree to pay for it. It is proper for a man to provide for his lady, to gladden her heart in response to her pleasant behaviour, 3. faithfully, 4. ready, 5. dishonour, 6. warriors, 7. proudly arrayed, 8. it pleases me, 9. reward, 10. nobly, 11. in my presence, 12. You snore and yawn, lift up your buttocks; you order (your men) to await the weather, then you curse the day that you didn't repair your storehouses and procure servants. (i.e. Winner saves money by postponing action until it is too late.), 13. Those you would like to have it will never get it; your evil executors will divide it up, 14. Have heed to, 15. worries, 16. lady, 17. Whoever shall have her shall take her, 18. is obliged, 19. Further, 20. speak, 21. fast approaches.

Yit harde sore es myn hert and harmes me more
Ever to see in my syghte that I in soule hate.'                                      455

The kynge lovely[1] lokes on the ledis twayne,
Says, 'blynnes, beryns, of youre brethe and of youre brode worde[2],
And I schal deme yow this day where ye duelle schall,
Aythere lede in a lond ther he es loved moste.
Wende, Wynnere, thi waye over the wale stremys[3],                                   460
Passe forthe by Paris to the Pope of Rome;
The cardynalls ken the wele, will kepe the ful faire,
And make thi sydes in silken schetys to lygge,
And fede the and foster the and forthir thyn hert,
As leefe to worthen wode as the to wrethe ones[4].                                   465
Bot loke, lede, be thi lyfe, when I lettres sende,
That thou hy the to me home on horse or one fote;
And when I knowe thou will come he schall cayre uttire[5],
And lenge[6] with another lede, til thou thi lefe take;
For thofe thou bide in this burgh to thi berying-day                                 470
With hym happyns the never a fote for to passe[7].
And thou, Wastoure, I will that thou wonne[8] ther ever
Ther moste waste es of wele, and wynge theruntill[9].
Chese the forthe into the Chepe, a chambre thou rere[10],
Loke thi wyndowe be wyde[11], and wayte the[12] aboute,                              475
Where any potet beryn[13] thurgh the burgh passe;
Teche[14] hym to the taverne till he tayte worthe[15];
Doo[16] hym drynk al nyghte that he dry be at morow,
Sythen ken hym to the crete[17] to comforth his vaynes,
Brynge hym to Bred Strete, bikken[18] thi fynger,                                    480
Schew hym of fatt chepe[19] scholdirs ynewe,
Hotte for the hungry, a hen other[20] twayne,
Sett hym softe one a sege[21], and sythen send after[22],
Bryng out of the burgh the best thou may fynde,
And luke thi knave hafe a knoke[23] bot he the clothe spred;                         485

1. lovingly, 2. He says, 'cease, men, from your anger and your outspokenness', 3. swift
currents, 4. (They would be) as ready to go mad as ever to anger you, 5. he (Winner)
shall move further away, 6. stay, 7. You will never run across him, 8. stay, 9. hurry thither,
10. Go into Cheapside and equip yourself with a room, 11. wide open, 12. look, 13.
tippler (?), 14. Show, 15. gets drunk, 16. Make, 17. Then introduce him to the Cretan
wine, 18. beckon, 19. sheep, 20. or, 21. seat, 22. i.e. for supplies, 23. blow.

Bot late hym paye or he passe[1], and pik hym so clene
That fynd a peny in his purse and put owte his eghe!
When that es dronken and don, duell ther no lenger,
Bot teche hym owt of the townn, to trotte aftir more.
Then passe to the Pultrie, the peple the knowes,                    490
And ken[2] wele thi katour[3] to knawen thi fode,
The herouns, the hasteletez[4], the henne wele serve;
The partrikes[5], the plovers, the other pulled[6] byrddes,
The albus[7], this other foules, the egretes[8] dere;
The more thou wastis thi wele, the better the Wynner lykes.   495
And wayte[9] to me, thou Wynnere, if thou wilt wele chefe[10],
When I wende appon werre my wyes to lede;
For at the proude pales[11] of Parys the riche
I thynk to do it inded, and dub the to knyghte,
And giff giftes full grete of golde and of silver                    500
To ledis of my legyance[12] that lufen me in hert;
And sythen kayren[13] as I come, with knyghtis that me foloen[14],
To the kirke of Colayne ther the kynges ligges[15] . . .

*(Here the text breaks off.)*

1. before he leaves, 2. instruct, 3. buyer, 4. roast meats, 5. partridges, 6. plucked, 7. bullfinches, 8. herons, 9. attend, 10. prosper, 11. palace, 12. allegiance, 13. travel, 14. follow, 15. are buried (the shrine of the Three Magi in Cologne Cathedral).

# THE LORD OF LOVE

This poem examining the paradoxical power of divine love is taken from a late fourteenth-century manuscript in Glasgow University Library, MS. Hunter 512.

Crist makith to man a fair present,
His blody body with love brent[1];
That blisful body his lyf hath lent[2]
For love of man, that synne hath blent[3].
O love, love, what hast thou ment?               5
Me thinketh that love to wraththe is went[4].
Thi loveliche hondis love hath to-rent[5],
And thi lithe arme wel streit itent[6];
Thi brest is baar[7], thi bodi is bent,
For wrong hath wonne, and right is schent[8].     10

Thi mylde boones love hath to-drawe[9],
The naylis thi feet han[10] al to-gnawe[11];
The Lord of Love love hath now slawe[12];
Whanne love is strong it hath no lawe.

His herte is rent,                                15
His body is bent
Upon the roode tre;
Wrong is went[13],
The devel is schent,
Crist, thurgh the myght of thee.                  20

For thee that herte is leyd to wedde[14],
Swych was the love that herte us kedde[15],
That herte barst[16], that herte bledde,
That herte blood oure soulis fedde.

---

1. fired, 2. given, 3. blinded, 4. turned, 5. torn apart, 6. And stretched your gentle arms very tightly, 7. bare, 8. destroyed, 9. pulled apart, 10. have, 11. gnawed away, 12. Love has now slain the Lord of Love, 13. gone, 14. as a pledge, 15. showed, 16. burst.

That herte clefte for treuthe of love,                     25
Therfore in him oon[1] is trewe love;
For love of thee that herte is yove[2];
Kepe thou that herte and thou art above.

Love, love, where schalt thou wone[3]?
Thi wonyng-stede is thee binome[4],                        30
For Cristis herte that was thin hoome,
He is deed – now hast thou noone.
Love, love, whi doist thou so?
Love, thou brekist myn herte a-two.

Love hath schewid his greet myght,                         35
For love hath maad of day the nyght[5];
Love hath slawe[6] the Kyng of Right,
And love hath endid the strong fight.

So inliche[7] love was nevere noon;
That witith[8] wel Marie and Joon[9],                      40
And also witen thei everychon[10]
That love with hym is maad at oon[11].

Love makith, Crist, thin herte myn,
So makith love myn herte thin;
Thanne schulde myn be trewe al tym,                        45
And love in love schal make it fyn[12].

1. alone, 2. given, 3. live, 4. Your home is taken from you, 5. turned day into night (at Christ's death), 6. slain, 7. deep, 8. know, 9. St John the Evangelist, 10. everyone, 11. That love is one with Him, 12. bring a reconciliation.

# WILLIAM LANGLAND: *PIERS PLOWMAN*

The selections presented here are from the C Text, Langland's final revision of his poem, in MS. HM 143 in the Huntington Library, which has been edited by D. Pearsall, York Medieval Texts (London, 1978).

## APOLOGIA

This *apologia*, only in the C Text (V, 1–104), is preceded by an account of how the King asked Conscience and Reason (cf. l.6) to be his guides, and is followed by another confession, that of the Seven Deadly Sins.

Thus I awakede, wot God, whan I wonede[1] in Cornehull[2],
Kytte[3] and I in a cote[4], yclothed as a lollare[5],
And lytel ylet by[6], leveth[7] me for sothe,
Amonges lollares of Londone and lewede ermytes[8],
For I made of tho[9] men as resoun me taughte.                5
For as I cam by[10] Consience with Resoun I mette
In an hot hervest[11] whenne I hadde myn hele[12],
And lymes to labory with and lovede wel fare[13],
And no dede to do but to drynke and to slepe.
In hele and in inwitt[14] one me apposede[15];               10
Romynge in remembraunce, thus Resoun me aratede[16].
'Can thow serven,' he sayde, 'or syngen in a churche,
Or koke[17] for my cokeres[18] or to the cart piche[19],
Mowen or mywen[20] or make bond to[21] sheves,
Repe or been a rypereve[22] and aryse erly,                  15
Or have an horn and be hayward and lygge[23] theroute nyhtes
And kepe my corn in my croft fro pykares[24] and theves?
Or shap shon[25] or cloth, or shep and kyne kepe[26],

---

1. lived, 2. Cornhill in London, 3. his wife, 4. cottage, 5. idler, 6. esteemed, 7. believe, 8. ignorant hermits, 9. wrote about those, 10. passed, 11. autumn, 12. good health, 13. And limbs to work with, and I loved to enjoy myself, 14. good understanding, 15. questioned, 16. While I was thinking of the past, Reason thus rebuked me, 17. put hay into haycocks, 18. haymakers, 19. load (hay), 20. stack (hay), 21. bind, 22. head-reaper, 23. lie, 24. robbers, 25. fashion shoes, 26. guard.

Heggen[1] or harwen[2], or swyn or gees dryve,

Or eny other kynes[3] craft that to the comune nedeth[4],    20

That thou betere therby that byleve the fynden[5]?'

'Sertes[6],' I sayde, 'and so me God helpe,

I am to wayke to worche with sykel or with sythe,

And to long[7], lef[8] me, lowe to stoupe,

To wurche as a werkeman eny while to duyren[9].'    25

'Thenne hastow[10] londes to lyve by,' quod Resoun, 'or
    lynage ryche

That fynde the thy fode? For an ydel man thow semest,

A spendour that spene mot[11] or a spille-tyme[12],

Or beggest thy bylyve[13] aboute at men hacches[14],

Or faytest[15] uppon Frydayes or feste-day in churches,    30

The whiche is lollarne[16] lyf, that lytel is preysed

Ther[17] ryhtfulnesse rewardeth ryht as men deserveth.

    *Reddet unicuique juxta opera sua*[18].

Or thow art broke, so may be, in body or in membre

Or ymaymed thorw som myshap, whereby thow myhte be
    excused?'

'When I yong was, many yer hennes[19],    35

My fader and my frendes[20] fonde[21] me to scole,

Tyl I wyste witterly[22] what holy writ menede

And what is best for the body, as the bok telleth,

And sykerost[23] for the soule, by so I wol contenue[24].

And fond I nere[25], in fayth, seth[26] my frendes deyede,    40

Lyf that me lykede but in this longe clothes.

And yf I be[27] labour sholde lyven and lyflode deserven[28],

That laboure that I lerned beste, therwith lyven I sholde.

    *In eadem vocacione in qua vocati estis*[29].

And so I leve[30] in London and opelond bothe[31];

The lomes[32] that I labore with and lyflode deserve    45

1. Make hedges, 2. harrow, 3. kind of, 4. necessary to the community, 5. So that you thereby improve things for those that provide you with food, 6. Indeed, 7. tall (cf. B.XV.152 'My name is Long Wille'), 8. believe, 9. last out, 10. have you, 11. must waste money, 12. time-waster, 13. food, 14. folk's kitchen-doors, 15. beggest, 16. idler's, 17. Where, 18. He rewards each man according to his works, 19. ago, 20. relations, 21. paid for, 22. clearly, 23. safest, 24. provided I continue (to do good), 25. never, 26. after, 27. by, 28. earn my living, 29. (Remain) in the same vocation to which you are called, 30. live, 31. in the country as well, 32. tools.

Is *pater-noster* and my prymer, *placebo* and *dirige*[1],
And my sauter[2] som tyme and my sevene psalmes.
This I segge[3] for here[4] soules of suche as me helpeth,
And tho[5] that fynden me my fode fouchen-saf[6], I trowe,
To be welcome when I come, other-while[7] in a monthe,                  50
Now with hym, now with here; on this wyse[8] I begge
Withoute bagge or botel but my wombe one[9].

   And also moreover me thynketh, syre Resoun,
Me sholde constrayne no clerc to no knaves werkes[10],
For by the lawe of Levyticy that oure lord ordeynede,                   55
Clerkes ycrouned, of kynde understondynge[11],
Sholde nother swynke[12] ne swete ne swerien at enquestes[13]
Ne fyhte in no fannewarde[14] ne his foe greve[15].
      *Non reddas malum pro malo*[16].
For hit ben eyres[17] of hevene, alle that ben ycrouned[18],
And in quoer[19] and in kyrkes[20] Cristes mynistres.                   60
      *Dominus pars hereditatis mee. Et alibi: Clemencia non
         constringit*[21].
Hit bycometh[22] for clerkes Crist for to serve
And knaves uncrounede to carte and to worche.
For sholde no clerke be crouned but yf he come were[23]
Of frankeleynes[24] and fre men and of folke ywedded.
Bondemen[25] and bastardus and beggares children,                      65
Thyse bylongeth to labory, and lordes kyn to serve[26]
God and good men, as here degre asketh[27],
Somme to synge masses or sitten and wryten,
Redon and resceyven that resoun ouhte to spene[28].
Ac sythe bondemen barnes han be mad bisshopes[29],                     70
And barnes bastardus han be[30] erchedekenes,

---

1. Are the Our Father and my book of devotions, and Vespers, and Matins of the Dead,
2. psalter, 3. say, 4. their, 5. those, 6. guarantee me, 7. now and then, 8. manner, 9. stomach
alone, 10. Clergy should not be forced to do labourers' jobs, 11. Tonsured clergy, by
natural reason, 12. toil, 13. give evidence in law courts (by 'benefit of clergy', they had
their own ecclesiastical courts), 14. front line, 15. injure, 16. Do not repay evil with evil,
17. they are heirs, 18. tonsured, 19. choir, 20. churches, 21. The Lord is the portion of
my inheritance. And elsewhere (it says): Mercy does not hold itself in check, 22. It is
suitable, 23. unless he is descended, 24. country-gentry, 25. Serfs, 26. (it is proper for)
the nobly born to serve, 27. as befits their rank, 28. Advise and collect (at Mass) what
it is reasonable to spend, 29. But since serfs' children have been made bishops, 30. have
become.

And soutares[1] and here sones for sulver han be knyhtes,
And lordes sones here[2] laboreres and leyde here rentes to
    wedde[3],
For the ryhte of this reume[4] ryden ayeyn[5] oure enemyes
In confort of the comune[6] and the kynges worschipe[7],     75
And monkes and moniales[8], that mendenants sholde fynde[9],
Imade here kyn knyhtes and knyhtes-fees[10] ypurchased,
Popes and patrones pore gentel[11] blood refused[12]
And taken Symondes sones seyntwarie to kepe[13],
Lyf-holynesse[14] and love hath be longe hennes[15],     80
And wol, til hit be wered out[16], or otherwyse ychaunged.
Forthy rebuke me ryhte nauhte, Resoun, I yow praye,
For in my consience I knowe what Crist wolde I wrouhte[17].
Preyeres of a parfit man and penaunce discret
Is the levest[18] labour that oure lord pleseth.     85
*Non de solo*,' I sayde, 'for sothe *vivit homo*,
*Nec in pane et in pabulo*[19], the *pater-noster* wittenesseth;
*Fiat voluntas dei*[20], that fynt[21] us alle thynges.'
Quod Consience, 'By Crist, I can nat se this lyeth[22];
Ac[23] it semeth no sad[24] parfitnesse in citees to begge,     90
But[25] he be obediencer[26] to prior or to mynistre.'
'That is soth,' I saide, 'and so I beknowe[27],
That I have ytynt[28] tyme and tyme myspened;
Ac yut, I hope, as he that ofte hath ychaffared[29]
And ay loste and loste, and at the laste hym happed[30]     95
He bouhte suche a bargayn he was the bet[31] evere,
And sette al his los at a leef at the laste ende[32],
Suche a wynnyng hym warth[33] thorw wyrdes[34] of grace.
    *Simile est regnum celorum thesauro abscondito in agro.*
    *Mulier que invenit dragmam, etc.*[35]

---

1. cobblers, 2. (have become) their, 3. mortgaged their lands, 4. realm, 5. against, 6. people, 7. honour, 8. nuns, 9. should provide for beggars, 10. estates, 11. noble, 12. have rejected, 13. And appointed simoniacs to look after the church, 14. (Since all this has happened) holiness of life, 15. hence, 16. until it (the present evil state) has passed away, 17. wants me to do, 18. most desirable, 19. (Latin) Not by bread and food alone does man live, 20. God's will be done, 21. provides for, 22. applies (to you), 23. But, 24. proper, 25. Unless, 26. monastic officer, 27. acknowledge, 28. wasted, 29. traded, 30. it befell, 31. better, 32. And in the end regarded his loss as negligible, 33. he gained, 34. the agency, 35. The kingdom of heaven is like a treasure hidden in a field. The woman who found a piece of silver, etc. (see Luke 15.10).

So hope I to have of hym that is almyghty
A gobet[1] of his grace, and bigynne a tyme                    100
That alle tymes of my tyme[2] to profit shal turne.'
'I rede the[3],' quod Resoun tho[4], 'rape[5] the to bigynne
The lyf that is louable[6] and leele[7] to thy soule' –
'Ye, and contynue,' quod Consience; and to the kyrke I wente.


## THE HARROWING OF HELL

In this passage (C Text, XX) the Dreamer sees Christ coming to rescue
from Hell the souls of the just who have died before the Incarnation.
In an earlier dream he had witnessed how the Devil had seized them
from the Tree of Charity (cf. l.18), after which the Dreamer had met
Faith and Hope on their way to Jerusalem. They were joined by the
Good Samaritan who represents Charity, and is here (l.8) identified
with Christ. The description of the Harrowing of Hell that follows
is derived from the apocryphal Gospel of Nicodemus.


Wolleward and watschod[8] wente I forth aftur
As a recheles renk that recheth nat of sorwe[9],
And yede[10] forth ylike a lorel[11] al my lyf-tyme,
Til I waxe[12] wery of the world and wilnede efte[13] to slepe
And lened me to lenten[14] and long tyme I slepte.                    5
Of gurles[15] and of *gloria laus*[16] greetliche[17] me dremede
And how *osanna* by orgene olde folke songe.
One semblable[18] to the Samaritan, and somdeel[19] to Pers the
    Plouhman,
Barfot on an asse bake botles[20] cam prikynge
Withouten spores[21] other[22] spere – sprakeliche[23] he lokede,          10
As is the kynde[24] of a knyhte that cometh to be dobbet[25],
To geten here[26] gult spores and galoches ycouped[27].

---

1. morsel, 2. moments of my life, 3. advise you, 4. then, 5. hurry, 6. praiseworthy,
7. lawful, 8. With wool next to the skin, (in penance) and shoes full of water, 9. Like
a heedless man who does not care about sorrow, 10. went, 11. layabout, 12. grew, 13.
wished again, 14. idled about until Lent, 15. children, 16. 'glory, praise', 17. very much,
18. One resembling, 19. somewhat, 20. without riding boots, 21. spurs, 22. or, 23. lively,
24. manner, 25. dubbed, 26. their, 27. fashionable shoes.

And thenne was Faith in a fenestre[1] and criede '*A, filii*[2]
    *David!*'

As doth an heraud of armes when auntres[3] cometh to joustes.

Olde Jewes of Jerusalem for joye they songen,         15

    '*Benedictus qui venit in nomine domini*[4].'

Thenne I afraynede at[5] Fayth what al that fare bymente[6],

And who sholde jouste in Jerusalem. 'Jesus', he saide,

'And feche that[7] the Fende[8] claymeth, Pers fruyt[9] the
    Plouhman'.

'Is Peres in this place?' quod I, and he prente[10] on me:

'*Liberum-dei-arbitrium*[11] for love hath undertake     20

That this Jesus of his gentrice[12] shal jouste in Pers armes,

In his helm and in his haberjon, *humana natura*[13],

That Crist be nat yknowe for *consummatus deus*[14];

In Pers plates[15] the Plouhman this prikiare[16] shal ryde,

For no dount shal hym dere as *in deitate patris*[17].'     25

'Who shal jouste with Jesus', quod I, 'Jewes, or scribes?'

'Nay', quod Faith, 'bote the Fende, and Fals-dom[18]-to-deye.

Deth saith a wol fordo[19] and adown brynge

Alle that lyveth or loketh, a[20] londe or a watre.

Lyf saith that a[21] lyeth and hath leide his lyf to wedde[22]     30

That for al that Deth can do, withynne thre dayes to walke

And feche fro the fende Peres fruyt the Plouhman,

And legge hit[23] there hym liketh and Lucifer bynde

And forbete adown and bringe bale Deth for evere[24].

    *O mors, mors tua ero, morsus*[25]!'

Thenne cam Pilatus with moche peple, *sedens pro tribunali*[26],     35

To se how douhtyliche Deth sholde do, and demen ther beyre
    rihte[27].

The Jewes and the justices ayeyns[28] Jesus they were,

---

1. window, 2. son of, 3. adventurous knights, 4. Blessed is he who comes in the name
of the Lord, 5. asked of, 6. business meant, 7. what, 8. Devil, 9. the fruit of Piers, 10.
looked warningly, 11. The free will of God, 12. nobility, 13. coat of mail, that is to say
human nature. (At this point Piers represents God incarnate), 14. So that Christ is not
recognized as supreme God, 15. the armour of Piers, 16. horseman, 17. For no blow shall
injure him in the divine nature of the Father, 18. judgement, 19. he will destroy, 20. in,
21. he, 22. pledged his life, 23. put it, 24. And thoroughly beat and bring down eternal
destruction on Death, 25. O death, I will be your death, your sting, 26. sitting in the place
of judgement, 27. judge between them, 28. opposed to.

And alle the court cryede '*Crucifige*!' loude.

Thenne potte hym forth a pelour[1] bifore Pilatus, and saide:

'This Jesu of oure Jewene temple japed[2] and despised,                40

To fordon[3] hit on a day, and in thre dayes aftur

Edefien[4] hit eft[5] newe – here he stant[6] that saide hit –

And yut maken hit as moche[7] in alle manere poyntes[8],

Bothe as longe and as large, aloofte and o grounde,

And as wyde as hit evere was; this we witnesseth alle'.        45

'*Crucifige*!' quod a cachepol[9], 'he can of[10] wycchecrafte'.

'*Tolle*[11], *tolle*!' quod another, and tok of kene thornes,

And bigan of grene thorn a garlond to make

And sette hit sore on his heved[12], and sethe[13] saide in envye,

'*Ave, rabbi*,' quod that ribaud, and redes shotte up to his yes[14];   50

And nayled hym with thre nayles, naked upon a rode

And, with a pole, poysen potten up to his lippes

And beden hym drynke, his deth to lette[15] and his dayes
    lenghe[16],

And saiden, 'Yf he sotil[17] be, hymsulve now he wol helpe,

And yf thow be Crist – and Crist, godes sone –                 55

Come adoun of this rode and thenne shal we leve[18]

That Lyf the loveth and wol nat late[19] the deye'.

'*Consummatum est*[20]', quod Crist, and comsed[21] for to swone,

Pitousliche and pale, as prisoun[22] that deyeth.

The lord of lyf and of liht tho[23] leyde his eyes togederes,       60

The daye for drede therof withdrouh, and derke bicam the
    sonne;

The wal of the temple to-cleyef[24] evene al to peces,

The hard roch al to-rof[25], and riht derk nyht hit semede;

The erthe to-quasche and quok as hit quyk were[26],

And dede men for that dene[27] cam oute of depe graves          65

And tolde why the tempest so longe tyme durede[28].

'For a bittur bataile', the ded bodye saide,

'Lyf and Deth in this derkenesse here one fordoth her other[29],

---

1. accuser, 2. mocked, 3. destroy, 4. Build, 5. again, 6. stands, 7. great, 8. kinds of details, 9. court-officer, 10. understands, 11. Away with him, 12. head, 13. then, 14. Hail, master, said that villain, and thrust reeds up to his eyes, 15. prevent, 16. prolong, 17. clever, 18. believe, 19. let, 20. It is finished, 21. began, 22. prisoner, 23. then, 24. split apart, 25. was torn apart, 26. The earth shook and quaked as if it were alive, 27. noise, 28. lasted, 29. one is destroying the other.

Ac shal no wyht wyte witterlich who shal have the maistry[1]
Ar[2] a Soneday, aboute the sonne-rysynge', and sank with that
   til erthe.           70
Somme saide he was Godes sone that so fayre deyede,
    *Vere filius dei erat iste*[3],
And somme saide, 'He can[4] of sorcerie; god is that we assaie
Wher[5] he be ded or nat ded, down or[6] he be taken'.
Two theves tho tholed[7] deth that tyme
Uppon cros bisyde Crist, so was the comune lawe.    75
A cachepol cam and craked a-to her[8] legges
And here arme after, of evereche[9] of tho[10] theves.
Ac was no boie[11] so bold Godes body to touche,
For he was knyht and kynges sone, Kynde foryaf[12] that tyme
That hadde no boie hardynesse hym to touche in deynge.    80
Ac ther cam forth a blynde knyhte with a kene spere
   ygrounde,
Hihte[13] Longies, as the lettre[14] telleth, and longe hadde lore[15]
   his sihte;
Bifore Pilatus and othere peple in the place he hoved[16].
Maugre his mony teth[17], he was mad that tyme
Jouste with Jesus, this blynde Jewe Longies;    85
For alle were they unhardy[18], that hoved ther or stode,
To touchen hym or to trinen[19] hym or to taken hym down
   and graven[20] hym,
Bote this blynde bacheler[21], that bar[22] hym thorw the herte.
The blod sprang down by the spere and unspered[23] the knyhte
   yes[24];
Tho ful[25] the knyhte uppon knees and criede Jesu mercy –    90
'Ay eyn my will hit was', quod he, 'that I yow wounde made!'
And syhed and saide, 'Sore hit me forthenketh[26]
Of the dede that I have do; I do me in youre grace.
Bothe my lond and my licame[27] at youre likynge taketh hit,

---

1. But no man shall know for certain who shall have the upper hand, 2. Before, 3. Truly
this was the Son of God, 4. knows, 5. Whether, 6. before, 7. suffered, 8. their, 9. each,
10. those, 11. ruffian, 12. Nature (i.e. God) granted, 13. Was called, 14. text (the
apocryphal Book of Nicodemus), 15. lost, 16. waited, 17. Despite his many protests, 18.
afraid, 19. handle, 20. bury, 21. knight, 22. pierced, 23. opened, 24. eyes, 25. Then fell,
26. grieves, 27. body.

And have mercy on me, rightfol Jesu!' and riht with that he
    wepte.      95
Thenne gan Faith fouely the false Jewes to dispice,
Calde hem[1] caytyves, acorsed for evere,
'For this was a vyl vilanye, vengeaunce yow bifall
That made the blynde bete the dede – this was a boyes[2] dede!
Corsede caytifves! knyhtheed was hit nevere      100
To bete a body ybounde, with eny briht wypene[3].
The gre[4] yut[5] hath he geten, for[6] al his grete woundes,
For youre chaumpioun chivaler, chief knyht of yow alle,
Yelde hym recreaunt remyng[7], riht at Jesu wille.
For be this derkenesse ydo, Deth worth yvenkused,      105
And ye, lordeyns[8], han[9] lost, for Lyf shal have maistrie,
And youre franchise[10] that fre was yfallen is into thraldom,
And alle youre childerne cherles, cheve[11] shall nevere,
Ne have lordschipe in londe[12], ne no londe tulye[13],
And as bareyne[14] be, and by usure libbe[15],      110
The which is lif that oure Lord in all lawes defendeth[16].
Now ben youre gode dayes ydon, as Daniel of yow telleth,
When Crist thorw croos overcam, youre kyndom sholde to-
    cleve[17].

    *Cum veniat sanctus sanctorum, cessat etc.*[18]'
What for fere of this ferly[19] and of the false Jewes
I withdrow in that derkenesse to *descendit ad inferna*[20],      115
And there I seyh sothly, *secundum scripturas*[21],
Out of the west, as it were, a wenche, as me thouhte,
Cam walkynge in the way, to hell-ward she lokede.
Mercy hihte that mayde, a mylde thynge withalle,
And a fol benyngne buyrde, and buxum of speche[22].      120
Here suster, as hit semede, cam softly walkynge
Evene oute of the eest, and westward she thouhte[23],
A comely creature and a clene, Treuthe she hihte;

1. them, 2. villain's, 3. weapon, 4. victory, 5. even so, 6. despite, 7. Submits himself weeping as the one vanquished, 8. villains, 9. have, 10. freedom, 11. prosper, 12. own land (which Jews were forbidden to do), 13. till, 14. unproductive, 15. live (only Jews could lend money), 16. prohibits, 17. fall apart, 18. When the Holy of Holies comes, then ceases (your anointing of kings), 19. wonder, 20. he descended into hell, 21. according to the scriptures, 22. And a very lovely lady, courteous of speech, 23. intended (to go).

For the vertue[1] that her folewede, afered was she nevere.
When this maydones metten, Mercy and Treuthe,                    125
Ayther asked other of this grete wonder,
Of the dene and the derkenesse and how the day roued[2],
And which[3] a lihte and a leem[4] lay bifore helle.
'I have ferly of this fare[5], in faith,' seide Treuthe,
'And am wendynge to wyte[6] what this wonder meneth'.          130
'Have no merveyle therof', quod Mercy, 'murthe hit
    bitokneth.
A mayde that hoteth[7] Marie, a moder withouten velynge[8]
Of eny kynde[9] creature, conceyved thorw speche
And grace of the Holy Gost, wax grete with childe,
Withouten wommane wem[10] into this world brouhte hym;        135
And that my tale is trewe, I take God to witnesse.
Sethe[11] this barn was ybore ben thritty wynter ypassed,
Deyede and deth tholede[12] this day aboute mydday;
And that is the cause of this clips[13] that overcloseth now the
    sonne,
In menynge[14] that man shal fro merkenesse[15] be ydrawe,    140
The while this lihte and this lowe[16] shal Lucifer ablende[17].
For patriarkes and prophetes han preched herof ofte,
That[18] was tynt[19] thorw tre, tre shal hit wynne,
And that deth down brouhte, deth shal releve[20]'.
'That thow tellest', quod Treuthe, 'is bote a tale of
    walterot[21]!                                              145
For Adam and Eve, and Abraham with othere
Patriarkes and prophetes that in peyne liggen[22],
Leve[23] hit nevere that yone liht hem alofte brynge
Ne have hem out of helle – holde thy tonge, Mercy,
Hit is bote truyfle[24] that thow tellest; I, Treuthe, wot the
    sothe,                                                    150
That thyng that ones is in helle out cometh hit nevere.
Job the parfit patriarke repreveth thy sawes[25]:

> *Quia in inferno nulla est redempcio[26]*'.

---

1. because of the power, 2. dawned, 3. what, 4. glow, 5. event, 6. learn, 7. is called,
8. contact, 9. natural, 10. impurity, 11. Since, 12. suffered, 13. eclipse, 14. Signifying, 15.
darkness, 16. flame, 17. blind, 18. What, 19. lost, 20. restore, 21. nonsense, 22. lie, 23.
Believe, 24. rubbish, 25. disproves your words, 26. For in hell there is no salvation.

Thenne Mercy fol[1] myldely mouthed[2] this wordes:
'Thorw experiense', quod she, 'I hope they shal ben saved;
For venym fordoth[3] venym, ther feche I evydence                    155
That Adam and Eve have shullen bote[4].

For of alle fretynge[5] venymes the vilest is the scorpioun;
May no medecyne amende the place there he styngeth,
Til he be ded ydo[6] thereto, and thenne he destruyeth
The verste venemousté[7] thorw vertu of hymsulve.                    160
And so shal this deth fordo, I dar my lyf legge[8],
All that Deth and the devel dede formost[9] to Eve.
And riht as the gylour[10] thorw gyle bigiled man formost,
So shal grace, that bigan al, maken a god ende
And bigile the gilour, and that is a god sleythe[11]:               165
   *Ars ut artem falleret[12]*'.

'Now soffre[13] we', saide Treuthe, 'I se, as me thynketh,
Out of the nype[14] of the north, nat ful fer hennes,
Rihtwisnesse[15] come rennynge. Reste we the while,
For she wot more then we – she was ar[16] we bothe'.

'That is soth', saide Mercy, 'and I se here bi southe                170
Where cometh Pees pleiynge[17], in pacience yclothed;
Love hath coveyted here longe – leve[18] I non othere
Bote Love have ysente her som lettre what this liht bymeneth
That overhoveth[19] helle thus; she us shal telle'.

Whenne Pees, in pacience yclothed, aproched her ayther
   other[20],                                                        175
Rihtwisnesse reverenced Pees in here rich clothyng
And preyede Pees to tellen to what place she sholde[21],
And here gay garnementes, wham she gladie thouhte[22]?
'My wil is to wende', quod Pees, 'and welcomen hem[23] alle
That many day myhte I nat se, for merkenesse of synne,              180
Adam and Eve and other mo[24] in helle.

Moises and many moo mercy shal synge,
And I shal daunce therto – do thow so, sustur!

---

1. very, 2. spoke, 3. destroys, 4. shall have atonement, 5. destructive, 6. applied dead, 7. first poison, 8. wager, 9. first, 10. deceiver, 11. trick, 12. Art to deceive art, 13. be patient, 14. cold region, 15. Justice, 16. (in existence) before, 17. moving swiftly, 18. believe, 19. hangs over, 20. each of the others, 21. was going, 22. intended to please, 23. them, 24. more.

For Jesus joustede wel, joy bigynneth dawe[1].
    *Ad vesperum demorabitur fletus, et ad matutinum leticia*[2].
Love, that is my lemman[3], such lettres he me sente      185
That Mercy, my sustur, and I mankynde shal save,
And that God hath forgyve[4] and graunted to alle mankynde
Mercy and me to maynprisen[5] hem alle;
And that Crist hath converted the kynde[6] of rihtwisnesse
Into pees and pyte, of his puyr grace.      190
Loo, here the patente!' quod Pees, '*in pace in idipsum* –
And that this dede shal duyre – *dormiam et requiescam*[7]'.
'Ravest thow?' quod Rihtwisnesse, 'or tho wart riht dronke!
Levest thow that yone lihte unlouke[8] myhte helle
And save mannes soule? suster, wene hit nevere!      195
At the bigynnynge of the world, God gaf the dom[9] hymsulve
That Adam and Eve and al his issue
Sholde deye downriht and dwellen in payne evere
Yf that thei touchen that tre and of the fruyt eten.
Adam afturward, ayenes[10] his defense[11],      200
Freet[12] of the fruyt and forsoke, as hit were,
The love of oure Lord and his lore bothe,
And folewede that the Fend tauhte and his flesch will[13],
Ayeynes resoun; I Rihtwisnesse recorde hit with treuthe
That her peyne is perpetuel – no preyer may hem helpe.      205
Forthy hem cheve[14] as they chose, and chyde we nat, sustres,
For hit is boteles bale[15], the bite that they eten'.
'And I shal preye', quod Pees, 'here payne mot[16] have ende,
And that her wo into wele[17] mot wende[18] at the laste.
For hadde they wist of no wo, wele hadde thay nat knowen;      210
For no wiht wot what wele is, that nevere wo soffrede,
Ne what is hot hunger, that hadde nevere defaute[19].
Who couthe kyndeliche[20] whit colour descreve[21],
Yf all the world were whit, or swan-whit all thynges?
Yf no nyhte ne were, no man, I leve,      215

---

1. to dawn. 2. In the evening weeping shall have place, and in the morning gladness,
3. beloved. 4. freely allowed. 5. go bail for. 6. nature. 7. Lo, here is the authorization,
'in peace and in the selfsame', and so that this document shall always be valid, 'I shall
sleep and rest' (Ps. 4.9). 8. unlock. 9. judgement. 10. despite. 11. prohibition. 12. Ate.
13. desire of the flesh. 14. it happened to them. 15. an incurable evil. 16. may. 17. joy.
18. turn. 19. lack. 20. intuitively. 21. describe.

Sholde ywyte witterly[1] what day is to mene;
Ne hadde God ysoffred[2] of som other then hymsulve,
He hadde nat wist witterly where[3] deth were sour or swete.
For sholde nevere right[4] riche man, that lyveth in rest and in hele[5],
Ywyte what wo is, ne were the deth of kynde[6].                    220
So God, that bigan al, of his gode wille
Bycam man of a mayde, mankynde to save,
And soffred to be sold to se the sorwe of deynge,
The which unknytteth alle care and comsyng[7] is of reste.
For til moreyne[8] mete with us, I may hit wel avowe,          225
Ne wot no wyht, as I wene, what is ynow to mene[9].
Forthy God of his godnesse the furste man Adam
Sette hym in solace furste and in sovereyne merthe;
And sethe[10] he soffrede[11] hym to synne, sorwe to fele,
To wyte what wele was ther-thorw, kyndeliche to knowe.    230
And aftur, God auntred[12] hymsulve and tok Adames kynde,
To wyte what he hath soffred in thre sundry places,
Bothe in hevene and in erthe – and now to helle he thenketh,
To wyte what al wo is, that wot of alle joye.
    *Omnia probate; quod bonum est tenete*[13].
So hit shal fare bi this folk, here folye and here synne    235
Shal lere[14] hem what love is, and lisse[15] withouten ende.
For wot no wiht what werre is, ther as pees regneth,
Ne what is witterliche wele, til welaway[16] hym teche'.
Thenne was ther a wihte[17] with two brode yes[18],
Bok[19] hihte that beau-pere[20], a bolde man of speche.    240
'By Godes body', quod this Bok, 'I wol bere witnesse,
Tho that[21] this barn was ybore, ther blased a sterre,
That alle the wyse of the world in o wit[22] acordede
That such a barn was ybore in Bethleem the citee
That mannes soule sholde save and synne distruye.    245
And all the elementis', quod the Bok, 'hereof bereth witnesse.

---

1. know for certain, 2. suffered at the hands of, 3. whether, 4. a very, 5. health, 6. were it not for natural death, 7. the beginning, 8. plague, 9. what 'enough' means, 10. afterwards, 11. allowed, 12. put at risk, 13. Test everything, hold fast what is good, 14. teach, 15. joy, 16. sorrow, 17. man, 18. wide eyes (i.e. the O.T. and N.T.), 19. i.e. the Bible, 20. father, 21. When, 22. one judgement.

That he was god that al wrouhte, the welkene[1] furste shewede:
Tho[2] that weren in hevene token *stella comata*[3]
And tenden hit[4] as a torche to reverensen his burthe;
The lihte folewede the lord into the lowe erthe.                    250
The water witnesseth that he was God, for a[5] wente on hym
    druye[6]:
Peter the apostel parceyved his gate[7],
And, as he wente on the watur, wel hym knewe, and saide,
    "*Domine, jube me venire ad te*[8]."
And lo, how the sonne gan louke[9] here lihte in heresulve
When she sye[10] hym soffre, that sonne and se made!               255
Lo, the erthe, for hevynesse that he wolde soffre,
Quakid as a quyk[11] thyng, and also to-quasch[12] the roches!
Loo, helle myhte nat holde, bote opened, tho[13] God tholede[14],
And lette out Symondes sones[15] to sen[16] hym honge on rode.
    *Non visurum se mortem*[17], etc.
And now shal Lucifer leve[18] it, thogh hym loth[19] thynk,         260
For Jesus as a geaunt[20] with a gyn[21] cometh yende[22]
To breke and to bete adoun all that ben agaynes hym
And to have out alle of hem that hym liketh.
And yut I, Bok, wol be brente[23], bote[24] he aryse to lyve
And comforte alle his kyn and out of care brynge,                  265
And alle the Jewene[25] joye unjoynen[26] and unlouken[27],
And bote they reverense this resurexioun and the rode honoure
And bileve on a newe lawe, be[28] ylost lyf and soule.'
'Soffre[29] we', sayde Treuthe, 'I here and se bothe
A spirit speketh to helle and bit to unspere the yates[30].        270
    *Attollite portas*[31], etc.'
A vois loude in that liht to Lucifer saide:
'*Princepes*[32] of this place, prest[33] undo this gates,
For here a cometh with croune, the kynge of all glorie!'

---

1. heavens, 2. Those, 3. a comet, 4. lit it, 5. he, 6. it dry, 7. walking, 8. Lord, bid me come to you, 9. lock up, 10. saw, 11. live, 12. shattered, 13. when, 14. suffered, 15. Simeon's sons (who, in the apocryphal Book of Nicodemus, are raised from the dead to witness Christ's descent into hell), 16. see, 17. He should not see death (as promised to Simeon, Luke 2.26), 18. believe, 19. unpleasant, 20. giant (traditional symbol of Christ), 21. siege-engine, 22. yonder, 23. burnt, 24. unless, 25. Jews', 26. destroy, 27. dissipate, 28. (the Jews will) be, 29. Wait, 30. bids unbolt the gates, 31. Open the gates, 32. Princes, 33. quickly.

Thenne syhed Satoun and saide to helle,

'Suche a lyht ayenes oure leve Lazar hit fette[1];       275

Care and combraunce[2] is come to us all.

Yf this kyng come in, mankynde wol he fecche

And lede hit ther[3] Lazar is, and lihtliche[4] me bynde.

Patriarkes and prophetes han parled[5] herof longe,

That such a lord and a lihte shal lede hem alle hennes[6].      280

Ac[7] arise up, Ragamoffyn, and areche[8] me alle the barres

That Belial thy beel-syre[9] beet with thy dame,

And I shal lette[10] this lord and his liht stoppe,

Ar[11] we thorw brihtnesse be blente[12], go barre we the yates[13].

Cheke[14] and cheyne we and uch a chine[15] stoppe,      285

That no liht lepe in at lover[16] ne at loupe[17].

Astarot, hot[18] out, and have[19] out oure knaves,

Coltyng and al his kyn, the catel[20] to save.

Brumston boylaunt brennyng out cast hit[21]

Al hot on here hedes that entrith ney[22] the walles.      290

Setteth bowes of brake[23] and brasene gonnes

And sheteth out shot ynow his sheltrom to blende[24].

Set Mahond at the mangrel[25] and mullestones throweth

And crokes and kalketrappes, and cloye we hem uchone[26]!'

'Lustneth', quod Lucifer, 'for I this lord knowe,      295

Bothe this lord and this lihte, ys longe ygo I knewe hym.

May no deth this lord dere[27], ne develes quentyse[28],

And where he wol is his way – ac war hym[29] of the perelles:

Yf he reve[30] me of my rihte, a[31] robbeth me by his maistrie[32].

For bi riht and by resoun, the renkes[33] that ben here      300

Body and soule beth myne, bothe gode and ille.

For hymsulve said hit, that sire is of hevene,

That Adam and Eve and all his issue

Sholde deye with dol[34] and here dwelle evere

Yf they touched a tre or tok therof an appul.      305

---

1. A similar light without our permission took away Lazarus, 2. trouble, 3. where, 4. easily, 5. spoken, 6. from here, 7. But, 8. pass, 9. grandfather, 10. obstruct, 11. before, 12. blinded, 13. gates, 14. Obstruct, 15. chink, 16. roof-opening, 17. wall-slit, 18. shout, 19. fetch, 20. goods, 21. Throw out brimstone boiling and burning, 22. near, 23. crossbows, 24. And shoot out enough shot to blind his troops, 25. catapult, 26. And hooks and spikes (to injure horses), and lame each one of them, 27. injure, 28. trickery, 29. but let him beware, 30. deprive, 31. he, 32. power, 33. people, 34. misery.

Thus this lord of liht such a lawe made,
And sethe[1] he is a lele[2] lord, I leve that he wol nat
Reven us of oure riht, sethe resoun hem dampnede.
And sethen we han ben sesed[3] sevene thousand wynter,
And nevere was ther-ayeyne, and now wolde bigynne[4],     310
Thenne were he unwrast[5] of his worde, that witnesse is of
   treuthe'.
'That is soth', saide Satoun, 'bote I me sore doute,
For thow gete hem[6] with gyle and his gardyn breke[7],
Ayeyne[8] his love and his leve on his londe yedest[9],
Not in fourme of a fende bote in fourme of an addre     315
And entisedest Eve to eten by here one[10] –
   *Ve soli*[11]! –
And byhihtest[12] here and hym aftur to knowe,
As two godes[13], with God, bothe god and ille.
Thus with treson and tricherie thow troyledest[14] hem bothe
And dust[15] hem breke here buxumnesse[16] thorw fals
   bihestes[17],     320
And so haddest hem out, and hiddere[18] at the laste.
Hit is nat graythly ygete[19], ther gyle is the rote.'
'And God wol nat be gyled[20]', quod Gobelyne, 'ne byjaped[21].
We han no trewe title[22] to hem, for thy tresoun hit maketh.
Forthy I drede me', quod the devel, 'laste[23] Treuthe[24] wol hem
   fecche.     325
And as thowe bigyledest Godes ymages[25] in goynge[26] of an
   addre,
So hath God bigiled us alle in goynge of a weye[27].
For God hath go', quod Gobelyn, 'in gome liknesse[28]
This thritty wynter, as I wene, and wente aboute and prechede.
I have assayled hym with synne, and som tyme ich[29] askede     330
Where[30] he were God or Godes sone. He gaf me short answere.
Thus hath he trolled[31] forth lyke a tydy[32] man this two and
   thritty wynter;

---

1. since, 2. honourable, 3. in possession, 4. Without any opposition, and it is now
beginning, 5. he would be deceitful, 6. won them, 7. broke into, 8. In defiance of, 9. went,
10. alone, 11. Woe to him who is alone, 12. promised, 13. Like two gods, 14. deceived,
15. made, 16. obedience, 17. promises, 18. (brought them) hither, 19. properly obtained,
20. tricked, 21. fooled, 22. claim, 23. lest, 24. i.e. Christ, 25. i.e. Adam and Eve, 26.
manner, 27. man, 28. man's form, 29. I, 30. Whether, 31. strolled, 32. worthy.

And when I seyh hit was so, I sotiled[1] how I myhte
Lette[2] hem that lovede hym nat, laste[3] they wolde hym
   martre.
I wolde have lenghed[4] his lyf, for I leved, yf he deyede,    335
That if his soule hider cam, hit sholde shende[5] us all.
For the body, whiles hit on bones yede[6], aboute[7] was hit
   evere
To lere[8] men to be lele[9], and uch man to lovye other;
The which lyf and lawe, be hit[10] longe y-used,
Hit shal undo us develes and down bryngen us all.    340
And now I se where his soule cometh sylinge hidward[11]
With glorie and with gret lihte – God hit is, ich wot wel.
I rede[12] we flee', quod the fende, 'faste all hennes;
For us were bettere nat to be, then abyde in his sihte.
For thy lesinges[13], Lucifer, we losten furst oure joye,    345
And out of hevene hidore[14] thy pryde made us falle;
For we leved on[15] thy lesynges, ther loste we oure blysse.
And now, for a later lesynge that thow lowe[16] til Eve,
We han ylost oure lordschipe a[17] londe and in helle.
    *Nunc princeps huius mundi*[18] *etc.*
(Sethe that Satan myssaide[19] thus foule    350
Lucifer for his lesynges, leve I non other
Bote[20] oure lord at the laste lyares here rebuke
And wyte hem[21] al the wrechednesse that wrouhte is her on
   erthe.
Beth ywar, ye wyse clerkes and ye witty[22] men of lawe,
That ye belyen[23] nat this lewed[24] men, for at the laste David    355
Witnesseth in his writynges what is lyares mede[25]:
    *Odisti omnes qui operantur iniquitatem.*
    *Perdes omnes qui loquntur mendacium*[26].
A litel I overleep for lesynges sake,
That I ne sygg nat as I syhe, suynde my teme[27]!)

---

1. contrived, 2. Stop, 3. lest (an allusion to the dream of Pilate's wife, warning her that Christ must not be condemned; see Matt. 27.19), 4. prolonged, 5. destroy, 6. walked in the flesh, 7. busy, 8. teach, 9. faithful, 10. if it is, 11. gliding hither, 12. suggest, 13. lies, 14. hither, 15. Because we believed, 16. lied, 17. in, 18. Now the ruler of this world (shall be cast out), 19. rebuked, 20. I fully believe That, 21. blames them for, 22. skilful, 23. deceive, 24. ignorant, 25. reward, 26. Thou hatest all evildoers. Thou destroyest all liars, 27. I digressed a bit about lying, and failed to say what I saw, pursuing my theme.

For efte[1] that lihte bade unlouke, and Lucifer answeride:

'What lord artow[2]?' quod Lucifer. A voys aloude saide:    360

'The lord of myhte and of mayne, that made alle thynges.

Dukes of this demme[3] place, anon undoth this yates,

That Crist may come in, the kynges sone of hevene'.

And with that breth[4], helle brak[5], with alle Belialles barres;

For eny wey or warde[6], wyde open the yates.    365

Patriarkes and profetes, *populus in tenebris*[7],

Songen with seynt John '*Ecce agnus dei*[8]!'

Lucifer loke ne myhte, so liht hym ablende[9];

And tho[10] that oure Lord lovede, forth with that liht flowen[11].

'Lo me here', quod oure Lord, 'lyf[12] and soule bothe,    370

For alle synfole soules to save oure bothe rihte[13].

Myne they were and of me, I may the bet hem clayme.

Althouh resoun recordede, and rihte[14] of mysulve,

That if they ete the appul, alle sholde deye,

I bihihte[15] hem nat here helle for evere.    375

For the dedly synne that they dede, thi deseite hit made[16];

With gyle thow hem gete, agaynes all resoun.

For in my palays, paradys, in persone of an addere,

Falsliche fettest there that me biful to loke[17],

Byglosedest[18] hem and bigiledest hem and my gardyne
    breke[19],    380

Ayeyne[20] my love and my leve. The olde lawe techeth

That gylours be bigiled and in here gyle falle,

And who-so hit out a mannes eye or elles his fore-teth,

Or eny manere membre maymeth other herteth[21],

The same sore shal he have that eny so smyteth.    385

    *Dentem pro dente, et oculum pro oculo*[22].

So lyf shal lyf lete, ther lyf hath lyf anyented[23],

So that lyf quyte[24] lyf, the olde lawe hit asketh.

---

1. again, 2. art thou, 3. dark, 4. word, 5. broke, 6. Notwithstanding any man or guard, 7. the people in darkness, 8. Behold the Lamb of God, 9. blinded, 10. those, 11. hurried, 12. body, 13. preserve the just claim of both of us (i.e. Christ and Satan also, whose claim on men has now been satisfied), 14. justice, 15. promised, 16. caused, 17. Deceitfully you there took away what was mine to protect, 18. Tricked, 19. broke into, 20. Contrary to, 21. Or maims or hurts a limb of any kind, 22. Tooth for tooth, and eye for eye, 23. So a man shall forgo his life where a man has destroyed a life, 24. pay for.

*Ergo*, soule shal soule quyte, and synne to synne wende[1],
And al that men mysdede, I, man, to amenden hit;
And that deth fordede[2], my deth to releve[3],                    390
And bothe quykie[4] and quyte that queynte[5] was thorw synne,
And gyle be bigyled, thorw grace, at the laste.

    *Ars ut artem falleret.*

So leve hit nat, Lucifer, ayeyne the lawe I feche
Here eny synfole soule sovereynliche[6] by maistrie,
Bote thorw riht and thorw resoun raunsome here my lege[7].     395

    *Non veni solvere legem, set adimplere*[8].

So that with gyle was gete, thorw grace is now ywonne.
And as Adam and alle thorwe a tre deyede,
Adam and alle thorw a tre shal turne to lyve.
And now bygynneth thy gyle agayne on the[9] to turne
And my grace to growe ay wyddore[10] and wyddore.            400
The bitternesse that thow hast browe[11], now brouk[12] hit
   thysulve
That[13] art doctour of deth, drynke that thow madest!
For I that am lord of lyf, love is my drynke,
And for that drynke today I deyede, as hit semede.
Ac I wol drynke of no dische, ne of deep clergyse[14],          405
Bote of comune coppes, alle Cristene soules;
Ac thy drynke worth[15] deth, and depe helle thy bolle[16].
I fauht so, me fursteth yut[17], for mannes soule sake.

    *Scicio*[18].

May no pyement[19] ne pomade[20] ne precious drynkes
Moiste me to the fulle ne my furste slokke[21]                    410
Til the ventage valle[22] in the vale of Josophat[23],
And drynke riht rype must, *resureccio mortuorum*[24].
And thenne shal I come as kyng, with croune and with angeles,
And have out of helle alle mennes soules.
Fendes and fendekynes[25] byfore me shal stande                  415

---

1. Therefore a soul shall pay for a soul, and a sin (the Fall) result in a sin (the Crucifixion), 2. destroyed, 3. restore, 4. revive, 5. extinguished, 6. as a conqueror, 7. subjects, 8. I have not come to destroy the Law but to fulfil it, 9. against you, 10. even wider, 11. brewed, 12. enjoy, 13. You who, 14. learning, 15. will be, 16. bowl, 17. I am still thirsty, 18. I thirst, 19. sweet wine, 20. cider, 21. slake my thirst, 22. grape-harvest takes place, 23. scene of the Last Judgement (Joel 3.2), 24. And I drink the ripe new wine (which is) the resurrection of the dead, 25. little devils.

And be at my biddynge, at blisse or at payne.
Ac to be merciable to man thenne, my kynde asketh[1],
For we beth brethrene of o blod, ac nat in baptisme alle[2].
Ac alle that beth myn hole bretherene[3], in blod and in baptisme,
Shal nevere in helle eft[4] come, be he ones oute.                    420

    *Tibi soli peccavi, et malum coram te feci*[5].

Hit is nat used[6] on erthe to hangen eny felones
Oftur then ones, thogh they were tretours.
And yf the kynge of the kyngdom come in the tyme
Ther a thief tholie[7] sholde deth other jewyse[8],
Lawe wolde he yeve hym lyf, and he loked on hym[9].        425
And I, that am kynge over kynges, shal come such a tyme
Ther that dom[10] to the deth dampneth alle wikkede;
And if lawe wol[11] I loke on hem, hit lith[12] in my grace
Where[13] they deye or dey nat, dede[14] they nevere so ille.
Be hit enythyng abouhte, the boldenesse of here synne[15],        430
I may do mercy of my rihtwysnesse[16] and alle myn wordes
   trewe.
For holy writ wol that I be wreke of[17] hem that wrouhte ille,
As *nullum malum impunitum, et nullum bonum irremuneratum*[18].
And so of alle wykkede I wol here take venjaunce.
And yut my kynde[19], in my kene ire, shal constrayne my will –
    *Domine, ne in furore tuo arguas me*[20] etc. –
To be merciable to monye of my halve-bretherne[21].        435
For blod[22] may se blod bothe afurst[23] and acale[24],
Ac blod may nat se blod blede, bote hym rewe[25].

    *Audivi arcana verba, que non licet homini loqui*[26].

'Ac my rihtwysnesse and rihte shal regnen in helle,
And mercy and mankynde bifore me in hevene.
For I were an unkynde[27] kyng, bote[28] I my kyn helpe,        440

---

1. nature demands, 2. i.e. all belong to the brotherhood of mankind, even the
unbaptised, 3. full brothers (referring to baptised Christians), 4. again, 5. Against you
alone (i.e. Christ, who can forgive) have I sinned, and done evil in your sight, 6. the
practice, 7. suffer, 8. or punishment, 9. The law requires that he grant him life, if he saw
him, 10. Last Judgement, 11. decrees that, 12. lies, 13. Whether, 14. did, 15. If the gravity
of their sin is in any way atoned for, 16. justice, 17. avenged upon, 18. No evil unpunished,
and no good unrewarded, 19. (merciful) nature, 20. Lord, rebuke me not in your anger,
21. i.e. non Christians, 22. kindred, 23. thirsty, 24. cold, 25. without feeling pity, 26. I
heard secret words which man may not utter, 27. unnatural, 28. unless.

And namliche[1] at such a nede, that nedes helpe asketh.
    *Non intres in judicium cum servo tuo*[2].
Thus by lawe', quod oure Lord, 'lede I wol fro hennes
Tho that I lovye and leved in my comynge.
Ac for the lesynge that thow low[3], Lucifer, til Eve,
Thow shalt abyye[4] bittere', quod God, and bonde hym with
    chaynes.        445
Astarot and alle othere hidden hem in hernes[5],
They dorste nat loke on oure Lord, the leste of hem alle,
Bote leten hym lede forth which hym luste[6] and leve which
    hym likede.
Many hundret of angels harpeden tho and songen,
    *Culpat caro, purgat caro, regnat deus dei caro*[7].
Thenne piped Pees of poetes a note:    450
    '*Clarior est solito post maxima nebula Phebus:*
    *Post inimicicias clarior est amor*[8].
Aftur sharpest shoures', quod Pees, 'most shene[9] is the sonne;
Is no wedore warmore then aftur watri cloudes,
Ne no love levore[10], ne no levore frendes,
Then aftur werre and wrake[11], when love and pees ben maistres.
Was nevere werre in this world, ne wikkedore envye,    455
That Love, and hym luste[12], to louhynge[13] ne brouhte,
And Pees thorw pacience alle perelles stopede'.
'Trewes[14]!' quod Treuthe, 'thow tellest us soth, by Jesus!
Cluppe we[15] in covenaunt and uch of us kusse othere!'
'And lat no peple', quod Pees, 'parseyve that we chydde,    460
For inposible is no thynge to hym that is almyhty'.
'Thowe saiste soth', saide Rihtwisnesse, and reverentlich here
    custe,
Pees, and Pees here *per secula seculorum*.
    *Misericordia et veritas obviaverunt sibi; justicia et pax osculate*
    *sunt*[16].

---

1. especially, 2. Enter not into judgement with your servant, 3. lied, 4. pay for it, 5. corners, 6. wanted, 7. The flesh sins, the flesh atones, the flesh of God reigns as God, 8. The sun is brighter after the darkest clouds, and love is brighter after strife, 9. bright, 10. dearer, 11. destruction, 12. if he chose, 13. laughter, 14. Truce, 15. Let us embrace, 16. 'You are right,' said Justice, and reverently kissed her, Peace, and Peace (kissed) her, for ever and ever. Mercy and Truth have met each other, Justice and Peace have kissed.

Treuthe trompede[1] tho, and song '*Te deum laudamus*[2]'.
And thenne lutede[3] Love in a loude note, 465
    '*Ecce quam bonum et quam jocundum*[4]' etc.
Til the day dawed[5] thes damoyseles caroled,
That men rang to the resureccioun[6], and riht with that I
    wakede,
And calde Kitte my wyf and Calote my douhter:
'Arise, and go reverense Godes resureccioun,
And crepe to the cros on knees and kusse hit for a jewel 470
And rihtfollokest[7] a relyk, noon richore on erthe.
For Godes blessed body hit bar[8] for oure bote[9],
And hit afereth[10] the Fende, for such is the myhte,
May no grisly gost glyde ther hit shaddeweth!'

1. trumpeted, 2. We praise you, God, 3. played on a lute, 4. See how good and how pleasant (it is for brethren to dwell together in unity), 5. dawned, 6. i.e. Easter bells, 7. a most fitting, 8. bore, 9. salvation, 10. frightens.

*Sir Launfal* is from the late fourteenth century. Ultimately the story is of Celtic origin, and was retold in French in the late twelfth century by Marie de France. *Sir Launfal*, preserved in B.L. MS. Cotton Caligula A II, has been edited by A. J. Bliss (London, 1960). Nothing is known for certain about the author, Thomas Chestre, though a man of this name was ransomed from a French prison in 1360 (see M. Crow and C.C. Olson, *Chaucer Life Records* (Oxford, 1966), 24).

Be doughty Artours dawes[1],
That held Engelond yn good lawes,
  Ther fell a wondyr cas[2]
Of a ley[3] that was ysette[4],
That hyght[5] 'Launval', and hatte yette[6]:      5
  Now herkeneth how hyt was.
Doughty Artour somwhyle
Sojournede yn Kardevyle[7],
  Wyth joye and greet solas,
And knyghtes that wer profitable[8]      10
Wyth Artour, of the Rounde Table –
  Never noon better ther nas[9].


Sere Persevall and Syr Gawayn,
Syr Gyheryes and Syr Agrafrayn,
  And Launcelet du Lake;      15
Syr Kay and Syr Ewayn,
That well couthe[10] fyghte yn playn,
  Bateles for to take[11];
Kyng Ban Booght and Kyng Bos,
Of ham[12] ther was a greet los[13],      20
  Men sawe tho nowher her make[14];
Syr Galafre and Syr Launfale,
Wherof a noble tale
  Among us schall awake.

1. In the days of brave Arthur, 2. wondrous deed, 3. poem, 4. composed, 5. was called, 6. is still called, 7. Carlisle, 8. excellent, 9. There were never better, 10. could, 11. undertake, 12. them, 13. praise, 14. their equal.

Wyth Artour ther was a bacheler[1],        25
And hadde ybe[2] well many a yer:
   Launfal, forsoth, he hyght.
He gaf gyftys largelyche[3],
Gold and sylver and clothes ryche,
   To squyer and to knyght.        30
For hys largesse[4] and hys bounté[5]
The kynges stuward made was he
   Ten yer, I you plyght[6].
Of alle the knyghtes of the Table Rounde
So large ther nas noon yfounde[7],        35
   Be[8] dayes ne be nyght.

So hyt befyll, yn the tenthe yer
Marlyn was Artours counsalere,
   He radde[9] hym for to wende
To Kyng Ryon of Irlond, ryght,        40
And fette[10] hym ther a lady bryght[11],
   Gwennere[12], hys doughtyr hende[13].
So he dede, and hom her brought;
But Syr Launfal lykede her noght,
   Ne other knyghtes that wer hende,        45
For the lady bar los of swych word
That sche hadde lemmannys under her lord[14],
   So fele[15] ther nas noon ende.

They wer ywedded, as I you say,
Upon a Wytsonday,        50
   Before princes of moch pryde[16];
No man ne may telle yn tale
What folk ther was at that bredale[17],
   Of countreys fer and wyde.
Non other man was yn halle ysette[18]        55

1. young knight, 2. been, 3. generously, 4. generosity, 5. goodness, 6. assure, 7. None was found so generous, 8. By, 9. advised, 10. fetch, 11. beautiful, 12. Guenevere, 13. gracious, 14. For the lady bore the reputation that she had lovers in addition to her lord, 15. many, 16. glory, 17. wedding-feast, 18. seated.

But[1] he wer prelat other baronette,
  In herte ys naght to hyde[2];
Yf they satte noght all ylyche[3],
Har servyse[4] was good and ryche,
  Certeyn, yn ech a syde.　　　　　　　　　　60

And whan the lordes hadde ete yn the halle,
And the clothes wer drawen[5] alle,
  As ye mowe[6] her and lythe[7],
The botelers sentyn wyn[8]
To alle the lordes that wer theryn,　　　　　　65
  Wyth chere[9] bothe glad and blythe.
The quene yaf yftes[10] for the nones[11],
Gold and selver and precyous stonys,
  Her curtasye to kythe[12];
Everych knyght sche yaf broche other[13] ryng,　70
But Syr Launfal sche yaf nothyng:
  That grevede hym many a sythe[14].

And whan the bredale was at ende,
Launfal tok hys leve to wende
  At[15] Artour the kyng,　　　　　　　　　　75
And seyde a lettere was to hym come
That deth hadde hys fadyr ynome[16];
  He most[17] to hys beryynge[18].
Tho[19] seyde Kyng Artour, that was hende,
'Launfal, yf thou wylt fro me wende,　　　　　80
  Tak wyth the greet spendyng[20]!
And my suster-sones two,
Bothe they schull wyth the go,
  At hom the for to bryng[21].'

Launfal tok leve, wythoute fable[22],　　　　　85
Wyth knyghtes of the Rounde Table,

---

1. Unless, 2. i.e. to tell the truth, 3. on equal rank, 4. Their fare, 5. removed, 6. may,
7. hear, 8. The butlers served wine, 9. behaviour, 10. gave gifts, 11. occasion, 12. show,
13. or, 14. time, 15. From, 16. taken, 17. must go, 18. funeral, 19. Then, 20. lots of money,
21. To take you home, 22. truly.

And wente forth yn hys journé
Tyl he com to Karlyoun[1],
To the meyrys[2] hous of the toune,
Hys servaunt that hadde ybe[3].                          90
The meyr stod, as ye may here,
And sawe hym come ryde, up anblere[4],
Wyth two knyghtes, and other mayné[5];
Agayns hym he hath wey ynome[6],
And seyde, 'Syr, thou art wellcome!'                     95
How faryth our kyng? – tel me!'


Launfal answerede and seyde than,
'He faryth as well as any man,
And elles greet ruthe hyt wore[7].
But, Syr Meyr, wythout lesyng[8],                        100
I am departyd[9] fram the kyng,
And that rewyth[10] me sore;
Nether thar no man, benethe ne above[11],
For the Kyng Artours love
Onowre me nevermore[12]; –                               105
But, Syr Meyr, I pray the, par amour[13],
May I take wyth the sojour[14]? –


Somtyme we knewe us[15], yore[16].'
The meyr stod and bethoghte hym[17] there
What myght be hys answere,                               110
And to hym than gan he sayn:
'Syr, seven knyghtes han her har in ynom[18]
And ever I wayte whan they wyl come,
That arn of Lytyll Bretayne[19].'
Launfal turnede hymself and lowgh[20],                   115
Therof he hadde scorn inowgh[21],
And seyde to hys knyghtes tweyne:
'Now may ye se, swych ys service

1. Caerleon-upon-Usk, 2. mayor's, 3. Who had been his servant, 4. on horseback, 5. retinue, 6. He walked towards him, 7. Otherwise it would be a great pity, 8. lie, 9. estranged, 10. troubles, 11. Nor need anyone, high or low, 12. Ever honour me again, 13. please, 14. lodging, 15. one another, 16. formerly, 17. considered, 18. have here taken their lodging, 19. Who are from Brittany, 20. laughed, 21. much.

Under a lord of lytyll pryse[1],
   How he may therof be fayn[2]!'        120


Launfal awayward gan to ryde;
The meyr bad he schuld abyde,
   And seyde yn thys manere:
'Syr, yn a chamber by my orchard-syd
Ther may ye dwelle wyth joye and pryde,      125
   Yyf hyt your wyll were[3].'
Launfal anoonryghtes[4],
He and hys two knytes
   Sojournede ther yn fere[5];
So savagelych hys good he besette[6]      130
That he ward[7] yn greet dette,
   Ryght yn the ferst yere.


So hyt befell at Pentecost
(Swych tyme as the Holy Gost
   Among mankend gan lyght[8])      135
That Syr Huwe and Syr Jon
Tok her leve for to gon
   At[9] Syr Launfal the knyght;
They seyd, 'Syr, our robes beth torent[10],
And your tresour ys all yspent,      140
   And we goth ewyll ydyght[11].'
Thanne seyde Syr Launfal to the knyghtes fre[12],
'Tellyth no man of my poverté
   For the love of God almyght!'


The knyghtes answerede and seyde tho      145
That they nolde hym wreye nevermo[13],
   All thys world to wynne.
Wyth that word they wente hym fro[14]

---

1. esteem, 2. pleased, (i.e. Launfal's knights will not benefit from serving a lord who is in disfavour.), 3. If you want to, 4. at once, 5. together, 6. So extravagantly he bestowed his possessions, 7. fell, 8. Descended among men, 9. From, 10. are all torn, 11. And we are poorly equipped, 12. noble, 13. That they would never reveal his secret, 14. away from.

To Glastyngbery[1], bothe two,
   Ther Kyng Artour was inne.          150
The kyng sawe the knyghtes hende[2],
And ayens ham he gan wende[3],
   For they wer of hys kenne[4];
Noon other robes they ne hadde
Than they owt wyth ham ladde[5],          155
   And tho[6] wer totore[7] and thynne.

Than seyde Quene Gwenore, that was fel[8],
'How faryth the prowde knyght, Launfal?
   May he hys armes welde[9]?'
'Ye, madame!' sayde the knytes than,          160
'He faryth as well as any man,
   And ellys God hyt schelde[10]!'
Moche worchyp and greet honour
To Gonnore[11] the quene and Kyng Artour
   Of Syr Launfal they telde,          165
And seyde, 'He lovede us so
That he wold us evermo
   At wyll have yhelde[12].

But upon a rayny day hyt befel
An huntynge went Syr Launfel          170
   To chasy yn holtes hore[13];
In our old robes we yede[14] that day,
And thus we beth ywent away,
   As we before hym wore[15].'
Glad was Artour the kyng          175
That Launfal was yn good lykyng[16];
   The quene hyt rew well sore,
For sche wold wyth all her myght
That he hadde be bothe day and nyght
   In paynys mor and more.         180

1. Glastonbury, 2. noble, 3. And he went up to them, 4. kin, 5. took away with them (from court), 6. those, 7. in rags, 8. cruel, 9. maintain, 10. God forbid it should be otherwise, 11. Guenevere, 12. Have retained us willingly, 13. ancient woods, 14. went, 15. And thus we left him (dressed) just as we were, 16. state.

Upon a day of the Trinité[1],
A feste of greet solempnité
   In Carlyoun was holde.
Erles and barones of that countré,
Ladyes and borjaes[2] of that cité,           185
   Thyder[3] come, bothe yongh and old.
But Launfal, for hys poverté,
Was not bede[4] to that semblé[5];
   Lyte[6] men of hym tolde[7].
The meyr to the feste was ofsent[8];       190
The meyrys doughter to Launfal went,
   And axede[9] yf he wolde

In halle dyne wyth her that day.
'Damesele,' he sayde, 'Nay!
   To dyne have I no herte;         195
Thre dayes ther ben agon[10]
Mete ne drynke eet[11] I noon,
   And all was for povert.
Today to cherche I wolde have gon,
But me fawtede hosyn and schon,      200
   Clenly brech and scherte[12];
And for defawte[13] of clothynge
Ne myghte I yn wyth the peple thrynge[14].
   No wonder though me smerte[15]!

But o[16] thyng, damesele, I pray the:    205
Sadel and brydel lene[17] thou me
   A whyle, for to ryde,
That I myghte confortede be
By a launde under[18] thys cyté,
   Al yn thys underntyde[19].'       210
Launfal dyghte[20] hys courser,
Wythoute knave other squyer;
   He rood wyth lytyll pryde.

---

1. On Trinity Sunday, 2. citizens, 3. Thither, 4. invited, 5. gathering, 6. Little, 7. esteemed, 8. gone, 9. asked, 10. For the past three days, 11. have eaten, 12. But I lacked hose and shoes, clean breeches and shirt, 13. lack, 14. throng, 15. No wonder I'm upset, 16. one, 17. lend, 18. glade near, 19. morning, 20. equipped.

Hys hors slod[1], and fel yn the fen[2],
Wherfore hym scornede many men                    215
   Abowte hym fer and wyde.

Poverly[3] the knyght to hors gan sprynge;
For to dryve away lokynge[4]
   He rood toward the west.
The weder was hot, the undertyde;                 220
He lyghte adoun, and gan abyde
   Under a fayr forest;
And, for hete of the wedere,
Hys mantell he feld[5] togydere,
   And sette hym doun to reste;                 225
Thus sat the knyght yn symplyté,
In the schadwe, under a tre,
   Ther that hym lykede best.

As he sat yn sorow and sore
He sawe come out of holtes hore                    230
   Gentyll maydenes two:
Har kerteles wer of Inde-sandel,
Ilased smalle, jolyf and well[6] –
   Ther myght noon gayer go;
Har[7] manteles wer of grene felwet[8],           235
Ybordured[9] wyth gold, ryght well ysette,
   Ipelured wyth grys and gro[10];
Har heddys wer dyght[11] well, wythalle –
Everych hadde oon a jolyf coronall[12],
   Wyth syxty gemmys and mo.                    240

Har faces wer whyt as snow on downe,
Har rode[13] was red, her eyn[14] wer browne:
   I sawe never non swyche!
That oon bar[15] of gold a basyn,

---

1. slipped, 2. mud, 3. Wretchedly, 4. To escape attention, 5. folded, 6. Their tunics were of blue silk, tightly laced, and very prettily, 7. Their, 8. velvet, 9. Edged, 10. Trimmed with grey fur, 11. ornamented, 12. Each wore a lovely crown, 13. complexion, 14. eyes, 15. One of them carried.

That other a towayle[1], whyt and fyn,    245
   Of selk that was good and ryche.
Har kercheves wer well schyre[2],
Arayde wyth ryche gold wyre[3].
   Launfal began to syche[4]!
They com to hym over the hoth[5];    250
He was curteys, and ayens[6] hem goth,
   And greette hem myldelyche.

'Damesels,' he seyde, 'God yow se[7]!'
'Syr knyght,' they seyde, 'well the be!
   Our lady, Dame Tryamour,    255
Bad thou schuldest com speke wyth here,
Yyf hyt wer thy wylle, sere[8],
   Wythoute more sojour[9].'
Launfal hem grauntede curteyslyche,
And wente wyth hem myldelyche,    260
   They wheryn[10] whyt as flour;
And when they come the forest an hygh[11]
A pavyloun yteld he sygh[12],
   Wyth merthe and mochell[13] honour.

The pavyloun was wrouth[14], forsothe, ywys,    265
All of werk of Sarsynys[15],
   The pomelles of crystall;
Upon the toppe an ern[16] ther stod,
Of bournede[17] gold, ryche and good,
   Iflorysched wyth ryche amall[18];    270
Hys eyn wer carbonkeles bryght –
As the mone they schon anyght,
   That spreteth[19] out ovyr all.
Alysaundre the conquerour,
Ne Kyng Artour yn hys most honour,    275
   Ne hadde noon scwych[20] juell.

---

1. towel, 2. Their head-dresses were beautifully white, 3. thread, 4. sigh (in admiration), 5. heath, 6. towards, 7. preserve, 8. If you, sir, agreed, 9. delay, 10. were, 11. above, 12. He saw a pavilion pitched, 13. great, 14. made, 15. Entirely of Saracen workmanship, 16. eagle, 17. burnished, 18. Decorated with fine enamel tracery, 19. (The moon) that spreads, 20. no such.

He fond yn the pavyloun
The kynges doughter of Olyroun[1],
   Dame Tryamour that hyghte[2];
Her fadyr was kyng of Fayrye,          280
Of occient[3], fer and nyghe,
   A man of mochell myghte.
In the pavyloun he fond a bed of prys[4]
Iheled wyth purpur bys,
   That semylé was of syghte[5]:       285
Therinne lay that lady gent[6]
That after Syr Launfal hedde[7] ysent;
   That lefsom lemede[8] bryght.

For hete her clothes down sche dede[9]
Almest to her gerdylstede[10];         290
   Than lay sche uncovert.
Sche was as whyt as lylye yn May,
Or snow that sneweth yn wynterys day –
   He seygh never non so pert[11].
The rede rose, whan sche ys newe,    295
Ayens her rode nes naught of hewe[12],
   I dar well say, yn sert[13].
Her here schon as gold wyre;
May no man rede[14] here atyre,
   Ne naught well thenke yn hert[15].    300

Sche seyde, 'Launfal, my lemman[16] swete,
Al my joye for the I lete[17],
   Swetyng paramour[18]!
Ther nys no man yn Cristenté[19]
That I love so moche as the,        305
   Kyng neyther emperour!'

---

1. The daughter of the King of Oléron, 2. who was called, 3. the west, 4. value, 5. Covered with purple linen, lovely to see, 6. gracious, 7. had, 8. lovely one glowed, 9. put, 10. Almost to her waist, 11. lovely, 12. Compared with her complexion has no colour, 13. certainly, 14. describe, 15. Nor well imagine it, 16. beloved, 17. give up, 18. Dear beloved, 19. Christendom.

Launfal beheld that swete wyghth[1],
All hys love yn her was lyghth[2],
   And keste[3] that swete flour,
And sat adoun her bysyde,           310
And seyde, 'Swetyng, what so betyde,
   I am to thyn honour[4]!'

She seyde, 'Syr knyght, gentyl and hende[5],
I wot thy stat, ord and ende[6]:
   Be naught aschamed of[7] me!     315
Yf thou wylt truly to me take,
And alle wemen for me forsake,
   Ryche I wyll make the.
I wyll the yeve[8] an alner[9]
Imad of sylk and of gold cler,     320
   Wyth fayre ymages[10] thre;
As oft thou puttest the hond therinne,
A mark of gold thou schalt wynne,
   In wat place that thou be.

'Also,' sche seyde, 'Syr Launfal,     325
I yeve the Blaunchard, my stede lel[11],
   And Gyfre, my owen knave;
And of my armes oo pensel[12]
Wyth thre ermyns, ypeynted well,
   Also thou schalt have.     330
In werre ne yn turnement
Ne schall the greve no knyghtes dent[13],
   So well I schall the save.'
Than answerede the gantyl[14] knyght
And seyde, 'Gramarcy[15], my swete wyght!     335
   No bettere kepte I have[16].'

1. person, 2. placed, 3. kissed, 4. I am at your service, 5. noble, 6. I know your position from start to finish, 7. abashed because of, 8. give, 9. purse, 10. pictures, 11. faithful horse, 12. a streamer (worn as a badge of loyalty), 13. No knight's blow shall hurt you, 14. noble, 15. Thank you, 16. I have never had a better (lady).

The damesele gan her up sette[1],
And bad her maydenes her fette[2]
   To hyr hondys watyr clere;
Hyt was ydo wythout lette[3],         340
The cloth was spred, the bord was sette,
   They wente to hare sopere.
Mete and drynk they hadde afyn[4],
Pyement, claré[5] and Reynysch[6] wyn,
   And elles greet wondyr hyt wer.        345
Whan they had sowped, and the day was gon,
They wente to bedde, and that anoon,
   Launfal and sche yn fere[7].

For play lytyll they sclepte that nyght,
Tyll on morn hyt was daylyght;        350
   Sche badd hym aryse anoon.
Hy[8] seyde to hym, 'Syr gantyl knyght,
And[9] thou wylt speke wyth me anywyght[10],
   To a derne stede thou gon[11].
Well privyly I woll come to the –        355
No man alyve ne schall me se –
   As stylle as any ston.'
Tho was Launfal glad and blythe;
He cowde no man hys joye kythe[12],
   And keste her well good won[13].       360

'But of o thyng, syr knyght, I warne the,
That thou make no bost of me
   For no kennes mede[14]!
And yf thou doost, I warny the before,
All my love thou hast forlore[15]!'       365
   And thus to hym sche seyde.
Launfal tok hys leve to wende,
Gyfre kedde[16] that he was hende,
   And brought Launfal hys stede.
Launfal lepte ynto the arsoun[17]       370

1. sat up, 2. fetch, 3. delay, 4. in full, 5. spiced wines, 6. Rhine, 7. together, 8. She, 9. If, 10. ever, 11. Go to a secret place, 12. tell, 13. And kissed her often, 14. For a reward of any sort, 15. lost, 16. showed, 17. saddle.

And rood hom to Karlyoun
   In hys pouer wede[1].


Tho was the knyght yn herte at wylle[2];
In hys chaunber he hyld hym[3] stylle
   All that underntyde[4].           375
Than come ther, thorwgh the cyté, ten
Well yharneysyd[5] men
   Upon ten somers ryde[6];
Some wyth sylver, some wyth gold,
All to Syr Launfal hyt schold[7],        380
   To presente hym, wyth pryde,
Wyth ryche clothes and armure bryght.
They axede[8] aftyr Launfal the knyght,
   Whar he gan abyde[9].


The yong men wer clothed yn ynde[10],     385
Gyfre, he rood all behynde
   Up[11] Blaunchard, whyt as flour.
Tho seyde a boy that yn the market stod,
'How fer schall all thys good?
   Tell us, par amour!'         390
Tho seyde Gyfre, 'Hyt ys ysent
To Syr Launfal, yn present,
   That hath leved yn greet dolour.'
Than seyde the boy, 'Nys he but[12] a wrecche!
What thar[13] any man of hym recche[14]?    395
   At the meyrys hous he taketh sojour.'


At the merys hous they gon alyghte[15],
And presented the noble knyghte
   Wyth swych good as hym was sent;
And whan the meyr seygh[16] that rychesse,   400
And Syr Launfales noblenesse,
   He held hymself foule yschent[17].

---

1. In his poor clothes, 2. pleased, 3. kept himself, 4. morning, 5. armed, 6. Riding on ten horses, 7. was meant (to go), 8. asked, 9. lived, 10. blue, 11. Upon, 12. He is only, 13. need, 14. take notice, 15. dismounted, 16. saw, 17. He thought himself foully disgraced.

Tho seyde the meyr, 'Syr, par charyté[1],
In halle today that thou wylt ete wyth me!
   Yesterday I hadde yment           405
At the feste we wold han be yn same[2],
And yhadde solas and game,
   And erst thou were ywent[3]!'

'Syr Meyr, God foryelde[4] the!
Whyles I was yn my poverté           410
   Thou bede[5] me never dyne.
Now I have more gold and fe[6],
That myne frends han sent me,
   Than thou and alle thyne.'
The meyr for schame away yede[7];      415
Launfal yn purpure[8] gan hym schrede[9],
   Ipelured[10] wyth whyt ermyne.
All that Launfal hadde borwyd before
Gyfre, be tayle and be score[11],
   Yald[12] hyt well and fyne.          420

Launfal helde ryche festes,
Fyfty fedde pouere gestes[13],
   That yn myschef[14] wer;
Fyfty boughte stronge stedes,
Fyfty yaf[15] ryche wedes[16]          425
   To knyghtes and squyere;
Fyfty rewardede relygyons[17],
Fyfty delyverede pouere prysouns,
   And made ham quyt and schere[18];
Fyfty clothede gestours[19],         430
To many men he dede honours
   In countreys fer and nere.

---

1. please, 2. together, 3. And you departed too soon, 4. repay, 5. invited, 6. riches, 7. went, 8. purple cloth, 9. dress, 10. Furred, 11. by exact reckoning, 12. Paid, 13. Fed fifty poor guests, 14. distress, 15. gave, 16. clothes, 17. clerics, 18. Set free fifty poor prisoners, and cleared them of debt, 19. Provided clothes for fifty minstrels.

Alle the lordes of Karlyoun
Lette crye¹ a turnement yn the toun,
　　For love of Syr Launfel,　　　　　　　　435
And for Blaunchard, hys good stede,
To wyte how hym wold spede²
　　That was ymade so well.
And whan the day was ycome
That the justes were yn ynome³　　　　　　440
　　They ryde out also snell⁴.
Trompours gon har bemes⁵ blowe,
The lordes ryden out arowe⁶
　　That were yn that castell.

Ther began the turnement,　　　　　　　　445
And ech knyght leyd on other good dent⁷,
　　Wyth mases and wyth swerdes bothe;
Me myghte yse some therfore
Stedes ywonne, and some ylore⁸,
　　And knyghtes wonder wroghth⁹.　　　　450
Syth the Rounde Table was,
A bettere turnement ther nas,
　　I dar well say, for sothe!
Many a lord of Karlyoun
That day were ybore¹⁰ adoun,　　　　　　455
　　Certayn, wythouten othe¹¹.

Of Karlyoun the ryche constable¹²
Rod to Launfal, wythout fable;
　　He nolde no lengere abyde¹³.
He smot to Launfal, and he to hym;　　　　460
Well sterne strokes, and well grym,
　　Ther wer yn eche a syde.
Launfal was of hym yware;
Out of hys sadell he hym bar¹⁴

---

1. Arranged to be proclaimed, 2. To find out how he (Launfal) would get on, 3. On which the jousts were appointed, 4. at once, 5. trumpets, 6. in succession, 7. blow, 8. One might see, in consequence, some horses won, and some lost, 9. very angry, 10. brought, 11. oath, i.e. dispute, 12. chief officer, 13. He would delay no longer, 14. threw.

To grounde that ylke tyde[1];  465
And whan the constable was bore adoun
Gyfre lepte ynto the arsoun[2],
   And awey he gan to ryde.

The Erl of Chestere therof segh[3];
For wreththe[4] yn herte he was wod negh[5],  470
   And rood to Syr Launfale,
And smot hym yn the helm on hegh
That the crest adoun flegh[6] –
   Thus seyd the Frenssch tale.
Launfal was mochel of myght[7];  475
Of hys stede he dede hym lyght,
   And bar hym doun yn the dale.
Than come ther Syr Launfal abowte
Of Walssche knyghtes a greet rowte[8],
   The numbre I not[9] how fale[10].  480

Than myghte me[11] se scheldes ryve[12],
Speres to-breste and to-dryve[13],
   Behynde and ek before;
Thorough Launfal and hys stedes dent[14]
Many a knyght, verement[15],  485
   To ground was ibore.
So the prys of that turnay
Was delyvered to Launfal, that day,
   Wythout oth yswore[16].
Launfal rod to Karlyoun,  490
To the meyrys hous of the toun,
   And many a lord hym before.

And than the noble knyght Launfal
Held a feste, ryche and ryall,
   That leste[17] fourtenyght.  495
Erles and barouns fale[18]

1. same time, 2. the (constable's) saddle, 3. saw, 4. anger, 5. nearly mad, 6. flew, 7. very powerful, 8. multitude, 9. do not know, 10. many, 11. one, 12. split, 13. Spears shattered and splintered, 14. charge, 15. indeed, 16. Without any dispute, 17. lasted, 18. many.

Semely wer sette yn sale[1]
　　And ryaly[2] wer adyght[3].
And every day, Dame Triamour,
Sche com to Syr Launfales bour[4]　　　　　　　　500
　　Aday[5] whan hyt was nyght.
Of all that ever wer ther tho[6]
Segh her non but they two[7],
　　Gyfre and Launfal the knyght.


A knyght ther was yn Lumbardye,　　　　　　　　505
To[8] Syr Launfal hadde he greet envye[9],
　　Syr Valentyne he hyghte[10].
He herde speke of Syr Launfal,
That he couth justy[11] well,
　　And was a man of mochel myghte.　　　　　　510
Syr Valentyne was wonder strong,
Fyftene feet he was longe,
　　Hym thoghte he brente[12] bryghte
But[13] he myghte wyth Launfal pleye
In the feld, betwene ham tweye[14]　　　　　　　515
　　To justy other to fyghte.


Syr Valentyne sat yn hys halle,
Hys massengere he let ycalle[15],
　　And seyde he moste wende
To Syr Launfal, the noble knyght,　　　　　　　520
That was yholde[16] so mychel of myght;
　　To Bretayne he wolde hym sende.
'And sey hym, for love of hys lemman[17],
Yf sche be any gantyle[18] woman,
　　Courteys, fre other hende[19],　　　　　　　525
That he come wyth me to juste,
To kepe hys harneys[20] from the ruste
　　And elles hys manhod schende[21].'

1. Were fittingly seated in the hall, 2. royally, 3. treated, 4. bedroom, 5. Always, 6. then, 7. None but those two saw her, 8. Of, 9. hatred, 10. was called, 11. could joust, 12. burned (with anger), 13. Unless, 14. the two of them, 15. summoned, 16. regarded, 17. lady, 18. well-bred, 19. noble or gracious, 20. armour, 21. And if not, he will disgrace his manhood.

The messengere ys forth ywent
To do hys lordys commaundement;                    530
   He hadde wynde at wylle[1].
Whan he was over the water ycome
The way to Syr Launfal he hath ynome[2],
   And grette hym wyth wordes stylle,
And seyd, 'Syr, my lord Syr Valentyne,             535
A noble werrour and queynte of gynne[3],
   Hath me sent the tylle[4],
And prayth the, for thy lemmanes sake,
Thou schuldest wyth hym justes[5] take[6].'
   Tho lough[7] Launfal full stylle;              540

And seyde, as he was gentyl knyght,
Thylke[8] day a fourtenyght
   He wold wyth hym play.
He yaf[9] the messenger, for that tydyng,
A noble courser, and a ryng,                       545
   And a robe of ray[10].
Launfal tok leve at Triamour,
That was the bryght berde[11] yn bour[12],
   And keste[13] that swete may[14].
Thanne seyde that swete wyght,                     550
'Dreed the nothyng, Syr gentyl knyght,
   Thou schalt hym sle[15] that day!'

Launfal nolde nothyng wyth hym have
But Blaunchard hys stede and Gyfre hys knave
   Of all hys fayr mayné[16].
He schypede[17], and hadde wynd well good,         555
And wente over the salte flod
   Into Lumbardye.
Whan he was over the water ycome

---

1. He had favourable wind, 2. taken, 3. resourceful, 4. to you, 5. jousts, 6. engage in, 7. laughed, 8. (On) the same, 9. gave, 10. striped cloth, 11. lady, 12. bedchamber, 13. kissed, 14. maiden, 15. slay, 16. retinue, 17. took ship.

Ther the justes schulde be nome[1],                    560
   In the cyté of Atalye,
Syr Valentyn hadde a greet ost[2],
And Syr Launfal abatede her bost[3]
   Wyth lytyll companye[4].


And whan Syr Launfal was ydyght                        565
Upon Blaunchard, hys stede lyght,
   Wyth helm and spere and schelde,
All that sawe hym yn armes bryght
Seyde they sawe never swych a knyght,
   That hym wyth eyen beheld.               570
Tho ryde togydere thes knyghtes two,
That har schaftes to-broste bo[5]
   And to-scyverede[6] yn the felde;
Another cours togedere they rod,
That Syr Launfales helm of glod[7],                    575
   In tale as hyt ys telde.


Syr Valentyn logh, and hadde good game;
Hadde Launfal never so moche schame
   Beforhond, yn no fyght.
Gyfre kedde[8] he was good at nede                     580
And lepte upon hys maystrys stede,
   No man ne segh wyth syght;
And er than[9] thay togedere mette
Hys lordes helm he on sette[10],
   Fayre and well adyght.                    585
Tho was Launfal glad and blythe,
And thonkede Gyfre many sythe[11]
   For hys dede so mochel of myght.


Syr Valentyne smot Launfal soo
That hys scheld fel hym fro,                            590
   Anoonryght[12] yn that stounde[13];

---

1. appointed, 2. army, 3. their arrogance, 4. With a small force, 5. both shattered, 6. splintered, 7. fell off, 8. showed, 9. before, 10. replaced, 11. times, 12. Then, 13. instant.

And Gyfre the scheld up hente[1]
And broghte hyt hys lord, to presente,
 Er hyt cam doune to grounde.
Tho was Launfal glad and blythe,     595
And rode ayen the thrydde sythe[2],
 As a knyght of mochell mounde[3]:
Syr Valentyne he smot so there
That hors and man bothe deed were,
 Gronyng wyth grysly wounde.     600

Alle the lordes of Atalye
To Syr Launfal hadde greet envye[4]
 That Valentyne was yslawe[5],
And swore that he schold dye
Er he wente out of Lumbardye,     605
 And be hongede and to-drawe[6].
Syr Launfal brayde[7] out hys fachon[8],
And as lyght as dew he leyde hem doune
 In a lytyll thrawe[9];
And whan he hadde the lordes sclayn     610
He wente ayen ynto Bretayn,
 Wyth solas and wyth plawe[10].

The tydyng com to Artour the kyng
Anoon, wythout lesyng[11],
 Of Syr Launfales noblesse[12];     615
Anoon a let to hym sende[13]
That Launfall schuld to hym wende
 At Seynt Jonnys Masse[14],
For Kyng Artour wold a feste holde
Of erles and of barouns bolde,     620
 Of lordynges more and lesse.
Syr Launfal schud be stward of halle
For to agye[15] hys gestes alle,
 For he cowthe of largesse[16].

---

1. picked, 2. third time, 3. valour, 4. hatred, 5. slain, 6. torn apart, 7. drew, 8. sword, 9. time, 10. rejoicing, 11. falsehood, 12. prowess, 13. Then he ordered (a message) to be sent to him, 14. i.e. at Midsummer, 15. organize, 16. For he knew about generosity.

Launfal toke leve at Triamour                          625
For to wende to Kyng Artour,
   Hys feste for to agye.
Ther he fond merthe and moch honour,
Ladyes that wer well bryght yn bour,
   Of knyghtes greet companye.             630
Fourty dayes leste[1] the feste,
Ryche, ryall and honeste[2];
   What help hyt for to lye?
And, at the fourty dayes ende,
The lordes toke har leve to wende,                      635
   Everych[3] yn hys partye[4].


And aftyr mete[5] Syr Gaweyn,
Syr Gyeryes and Agrafayn,
   And Syr Launfal also,
Wente to daunce upon the grene                          640
Under the tour ther[6] lay the quene
   Wyth syxty ladyes and mo.
To lede the daunce Launfal was set;
For hys largesse he was lovede the bet,
   Sertayn, of alle tho.                          645
The quene lay[7] out and beheld hem alle;
'I se,' sche seyde, 'daunce large[8] Launfalle;
   To hym than wyll I go.


'Of alle the knyghtes that I se there
He ys the fayreste bachelere;                            650
   He ne hadde never no wyf.
Tyde me good other ylle,
I wyll go and wyte[9] hys wylle;
   I love hym as my lyf.'
Sche tok wyth her a companye,                           655
The fayrest that sche myghte aspye,
   Syxty ladyes and fyf;
And wente hem doun anoonryghtes,

1. lasted, 2. excellent, 3. each, 4. direction, 5. the meal, 6. where, 7. leaned, 8. generous, 9. ascertain.

Ham to pley[1] among the knyghtes,
   Well stylle, wythouten stryf.          660

The quene yede[2] to the formeste[3] ende
Betwene Launfal and Gauweyn the hende,
   And after her ladyes bryght;
To daunce they wente, alle yn same[4],
To se hem play, hyt was fayr game,       665
   A lady and a knyght.
They hadde menstrales of moch honours,
Fydelers, sytolyrs[5] and trompours,
   And elles hyt were unryght[6].
Ther they playde, forsothe to say,     670
After mete, the somerys day,

   Allwhat[7] hyt was neygh nyght.
And whanne the daunce began to slake
The quene gan Launfal to counsell take,
   And seyde yn thys manere:        675
'Sertaynlyche, Syr knyght,
I have the lovyd wyth all my myght
   More than thys seven yere!
But that[8] thou lovye me,
Sertes[9], I dye for love of the,       680
   Launfal, my lemman dere!'
Thanne answerede the gentyll knyght,
'I nell[10] be traytour, day ne nyght,
   Be God that all may stere[11]!'

Sche seyde, 'Fy on the, thou coward!   685
Anhonged worth thou[12], hye and hard!
   That thou ever were ybore,
That thou lyvest, hyt ys pyté!
Thou lovyst no woman, ne no woman the.
   Thow wer worthy forlore[13]!'     690

1. To enjoy themselves, 2. went, 3. top, 4. together, 5. citole-players, 6. Otherwise it would not have been fitting, 7. Until, 8. Unless, 9. Indeed, 10. will not, 11. rule, 12. May you be hanged, 13. You should be destroyed.

The knyght was sore aschamed tho;
To speke ne myghte he forgo,
   And seyde, the quene before:
'I have loved a fayryr woman
Than thou ever leydest thyn ey upon,        695
   Thys seven yer and more!

'Hyr lothlokste[1] mayde, wythoute wene[2],
Myghte bet[3] be a quene
   Than thou, yn all thy lyve!'
Therfore the quene was swythe wrogth[4],     700
Sche taketh hyr maydenes and forth hy[5] goth
   Into her tour, also blyve[6].
And anon sche ley doun yn her bedde,
For wrethe, syk sche hyr bredde[7],
   And swore, so moste sche thryve[8],     705
Sche wold of Launfal be so awreke[9]
That all the lond schuld of hym speke,
   Wythinne the dayes fyfe.

Kyng Artour com fro huntynge,
Blythe and glad yn all thyng;     710
   To hys chamber than wente he.
Anoon the quene on hym gan crye,
'But I be awreke, I schall dye!
   Myn herte wyll breke athre[10]!
I spak to Launfal, yn my game[11],     715
And he besofte me of schame[12]
   My lemman for to be;
And of a lemman hys yelp[13] he made,
That the lodlokest[14] mayde that sche hadde
   Myght be a quene above me!'     720

Kyng Artour was well wroth,
And be God he swor hys oth

---

1. ugliest, 2. doubt, 3. rather, 4. angry, 5. she, 6. at once, 7. She became ill with anger, 8. as she hoped to prosper, 9. avenged, 10. into three pieces, 11. jokingly, 12. And he shamefully asked, 13. boast, 14. ugliest.

That Launfal schuld be sclawe[1].
He wente aftyr doghty knyghtes
To brynge Launfal anoonryghtes                    725
   To be honged and todrawe.
The knyghtes softe[2] hym anoon,
But Launfal was to hys chaumber gon
To han[3] hadde solas and plawe[4];
He softe hys leef[5], but sche was lore[6],         730
As sche hadde warnede hym before;
   Tho was Launfal unfawe[7]!

He lokede yn hys alner[8],
That fond hym spendyng, all plener[9],
   Whan that he hadde nede,                    735
And ther nas noon, forsoth to say,
And Gyfre was yryde[10] away
   Up Blaunchard hys stede.
All that he hadde before ywonne,
Hyt malt[11] as snow ayens the sunne,               740
   In romaunce as we rede;
Hys armur, that was whyt as flour,
Hyt becom of blak colour,
   And thus than Launfal seyde:

'Alas!' he seyde, 'My creature[12],                 745
How schall I from the endure,
   Swetyng Tryamour?
All my joye I have forlore[13],
And the – that me ys worst fore[14] –
   Thou blysfull berde[15] yn bour!'           750
He bet[16] hys body and hys hedde ek[17],
And cursede the mouth that he wyth spek[18],
   Wyth care and greet dolour.
And for sorow yn that stounde[19]

---

1. slain, 2. sought for, 3. have, 4. enjoyment, 5. beloved, 6. lost, 7. unhappy, 8. purse, 9. Which supplied him with money in full, 10. had ridden, 11. melted, 12. adored one, 13. lost, 14. for which I suffer most, 15. lady, 16. beat, 17. as well, 18. spoke, 19. moment.

Anoon he fell aswowe[1] to grounde;                      755
   Wyth that come knyghtes four,

And bond hym, and ladde hym tho –
Tho was the knyghte yn doble wo –
   Before Artour the kyng;
Than seyde Kyng Artour,                                   760
'Fyle ataynte traytour[2],
   Why madest thou swyche yelpyng[3]?
That thy lemmannes lodlokest mayde
Was fayrer than my wyf, thou seyde;
   That was a fowll lesynge[4]!                   765
And thou besoftest[5] her, befor than,
That sche schold be thy lemman:
   That was mysprowd lykynge[6]!'

The knyght answerede wyth egre mode[7],
Before the kyng ther he stode,                            770
   The quene on hym gan lye[8].
'Sethe[9] that I ever was yborn,
I besofte her herebeforn
   Never of no folye!
But sche seyde I nas no[10] man,                          775
Ne that me lovede no woman,
   Ne no womannes companye;
And I answerede her, and sayde
That my lemmannes lodlekest mayde
   To be a quene was better worthye.               780

'Sertes, lordynges, hyt ys so!
I am aredy for to do
   All that the court wyll loke[11].'
To say the soth, wythout les[12],
All togedere how hyt was,                                 785
   Twelve knyghtes wer dryve to boke[13].
All they seyde ham betwene[14]

---

1. swooning, 2. Vile and guilty traitor, 3. boast, 4. lie, 5. requested, 6. That was arrogant lust, 7. angrily, 8. That the queen was lying about him, 9. Since, 10. was not a, 11. decree, 12. lie, 13. Twelve knights were ordered to swear on the Bible, 14. together.

That knewe the maners of the quene
    And the queste toke[1],
The quene bar los of swych a word[2]      790
That sche lovede lemmannes wythout[3] her lord;
    Har never on hyt forsoke[4].

Therfor they seyden alle
Hyt was long on[5] the quene, and not on Launfal –
    Therof they gonne hym skere[6];      795
And yf he myghte hys lemman brynge
That he made of swych yelpynge[7],
    Other[8] the maydenes were
Bryghtere than the quene of hewe,
Launfal schuld be holde[9] trewe      800
    Of that, yn all manere[10];
And yf he myghte not brynge hys lef[11],
He schud be hongede as a thef;
    They seyden all yn fere[12].

Alle yn fere they made proferynge[13]      805
That Launfal schuld hys lemman brynge;
    Hys heed he gan to laye[14].
Than seyde the quene, wythout lesynge,
'Yyf he bryngeth a feyrer thynge[15],
    Put out my eeyn[16] gray!'      810
Whan that wajowr was take on honde[17]
Launfal therto two borwes[18] fonde,
    Noble knyghtes twayn;
Syr Percevall and Syr Gawayn,
They wer hys borwes, soth to sayn,      815
    Tyll a certayn day.

The certayn day, I yow plyght,
Was twelve moneth and fourtenyght

---

1. And undertook the enquiry, 2. had a reputation, 3. apart from, 4. No-one denied it, 5. (The guilt) was attributable to, 6. acquitted him, 7. such boast of, 8. Or, 9. regarded as, 10. respects, 11. beloved, 12. together, 13. proposal, 14. pledged, 15. person, 16. eyes, 17. When that agreement was made, 18. sureties.

That he schuld hys lemman brynge.
Syr Launfal, that noble knyght,    820
Greet sorow and care yn hym was lyght,
   Hys hondys he gan wrynge.
So greet sorowe hym was upon,
Gladlyche hys lyf he wold a[1] forgon
   In care and in marnynge,    825
Gladlyche he wold hys hed forgo;
Everych man therfore was wo
   That wyste of that tydynge.

The certayn day was nyghyng[2];
Hys borowes[3] hym broght befor the kyng;    830
   The kyng recordede[4] tho,
And bad hym bryng hys lef[5] yn syght;
Syr Launfal seyde that he ne myght,
   Therfore hym was well wo.
The kyng commaundede the barouns alle    835
To yeve[6] jugement on Launfal,
   And dampny hym to sclo[7].
Than sayde the Erl of Cornewayle
That was wyth ham at that counceyle:
   'We wyllyth naght do so.    840

'Greet schame hyt wer us alle upon
For to dampny that gantylman,
   That hath be hende and fre.
Therfor, lordynges, doth be[8] my reed[9]!
Our kyng we wyllyth another wey lede[10]:    845
   Out of lond Launfal schall fle.'
And as they stod thus spekynge,
The barouns sawe come rydynge
   Ten maydenes, bryght of ble[11].
Ham thoghte[12] they wer so bryght and schene[13]    850
That the lodlokest, wythout wene[14],
   Har quene than myghte be.

---

1. have, 2. approaching, 3. sureties, 4. gave evidence, 5. beloved, 6. give, 7. And condemn him to be slain, 8. by, 9. advice, 10. direct, 11. complexion, 12. It seemed to them, 13. lovely, 14. doubt.

Tho seyde Gawayn, that corteys knyght,
'Launfal, brodyr, drede the nowyght[1]!
   Her cometh thy lemman hende.'          855
Launfal answerede and seyde, 'Ywys,
Non of ham my lemman nys[2],
   Gawayn, my lefly[3] frende!'
To that castell they wente ryght,
At the gate they gonne alyght,          860
   Befor Kyng Artour gonne they wende,
And bede hym make aredy hastyly
A fayr chamber, for her[4] lady
   That was come of kynges kende[5].

'Ho[6] ys your lady?' Artour seyde;         865
'Ye schull ywyte[7],' seyde the mayde,
   'For sche cometh ryde[8].'
The kyng commaundede, for her sake,
The fayryst chaunber for to take
   In hys palys that tyde.         870
And anon to hys barouns he sente
For to yeve jugemente
   Upon that traytour full of pryde.
The barouns answerede anoonryght,
'Have we[9] seyn the madenes bryght,         875
   Whe schull not long abyde.'

A newe tale they gonne[10] tho,
Some of wele and some of wo,
   Har lord the kyng to queme[11].
Some dampnede Launfal there,         880
And some made hym quyt and skere;
   Har tales wer well breme[12].
Tho saw they other ten maydenes bryght,
Fayryr than the other ten of syght,
   As they gone hym deme[13].         885

---

1. not at all, 2. None of them is my beloved, 3. dear, 4. their, 5. lineage, 6. Who, 7. learn, 8. riding, 9. When we have, 10. began, 11. placate, 12. And some judged him blameless; their arguments were fierce, 13. As they passed judgement on him.

They ryd upon joly moyles[1] of Spayne,
Wyth sadell and brydell of Champayne;
 Har lorayns lyght gonne leme[2].


They wer yclothed yn samyt tyre[3];
Ech man hadde greet desyre       890
 To se har clothynge.
Tho seyde Gaweyn, that curtayse knyght,
'Launfal, her cometh thy swete wyght
 That may thy bote[4] brynge.'
Launfal answerede wyth drery thoght     895
And seyde, 'Alas! I knowe hem noght,
 Ne non of all the ofsprynge[5].'
Forth they wente to that palys
And lyghte at the hye deys[6]
 Before Artour the kynge,       900


And grette the kyng and quene ek,
And oo[7] mayde thys wordes spak
 To the Kyng Artour:
'Thyn halle agraythe[8], and hele[9] the walles
Wyth clothes and wyth ryche palles[10],    905
 Ayens[11] my lady Tryamour.'
The kyng answerede bedene[12],
'Wellcome, ye maydenes schene[13],
 Be[14] Our Lord the Savyour!'
He commaundede Launcelot du Lake to brynge
 hem yn fere[15]        910
In the chamber ther har felawes were,
 Wyth merthe and moche honour.


Anoon the quene supposed[16] gyle,
That Launfal schulld, yn a whyle,
 Be ymade quyt and skere      915
Thorugh hys lemman, that was commynge;

---

1. mules, 2. Their bridles shone brightly, 3. silk dresses, 4. remedy, 5. young people, 6. dais, 7. one, 8. get ready, 9. cover, 10. hangings, 11. In readiness for, 12. quickly, 13. lovely, 14. By, 15. together, 16. suspected.

Anon sche seyde to Artour the kyng:
  'Syre, curtays yf thou were,
Or yf thou lovedest thyn honour,
I schuld be awreke[1] of that traytour        920
  That doth me changy chere[2].
To Launfal thou schuldest not spare,
Thy barouns dryveth the to bysmare[3],
  He ys hem lef[4] and dere.'


And as the quene spak to the kyng,        925
The barouns seygh come rydynge
  A damesele alone,
Upoon a whyt comely palfrey;
They saw never non so gay,
  Upon the grounde gone[5];        930
Gentyll, jolyf as bryd[6] on bowe,
In all manere fayr inowe[7]
  To wonye yn wordly wone[8].
The lady was bryght as blosme on brere[9],
Wyth eyen gray, wyth lovelych chere[10];        935
  Her leyre lyght schoone[11].


As rose on rys[12] her rode[13] was red;
The her schon upon her hed
  As gold wyre[14] that schynyth bryght;
Sche hadde a crounne upon her molde[15]        940
Of ryche stones, and of golde,
  That lofsom lemede[16] lyght.
The lady was clad yn purpere palle[17],
Wyth gentyll body and myddyll small,
  That semely was of syght;        945
Her mantyll was furryd wyth whyt ermyn,
Ireversyd[18] jolyf and fyn;
  No rychere be ne myght[19].


1. avenged, 2. Who upsets me, 3. disgrace, 4. dear to them, 5. travel, 6. bird, 7. very beautiful, 8. To live in an earthly dwelling, 9. briar, 10. complexion, 11. Her face glowed brightly, 12. branch, 13. complexion, 14. thread, 15. head, 16. lovely one glowed, 17. cloth, 18. Lined, 19. There could not be a finer one.

Her sadell was semyly set,
The sambus[1] wer grene feluet[2]  950
   Ipaynted wyth ymagerye[3];
The bordure was of belles
Of ryche gold, and nothyng elles
   That any man myghte aspye.
In the arsouns[4], before and behynde,  955
Were twey[5] stones of Ynde,
   Gay for the maystrye[6];
The paytrelle[7] of her palfraye
Was worth an erldome, stoute[8] and gay,
   The best yn Lumbardye.  960

A gerfawcon sche bar on her hond;
A softe pas her palfray fond[9],
   That men her schuld beholde.
Thorough Karlyon rood that lady;
Twey whyte grehoundys ronne hyr by,  965
   Har colers were of golde;
And whan Launfal sawe that lady,
To alle the folk he gon crye an hy,
   Bothe to yonge and olde:
'Her,' he seyde, 'comyth my lemman swete!  970
Sche myghte me of my balys bete[10],
   Yef[11] that lady wolde.'

Forth sche wente ynto the halle
Ther was the quene and the ladyes alle,
   And also Kyng Artour.  975
Her maydenes come ayens[12] her, ryght,
To take her styrop whan sche lyght,
   Of the lady, Dame Tryamour.
Sche dede of her mantyll on the flet[13],
That men schuld her beholde the bet,  980

---

1. saddle cloths, 2. velvet, 3. pictures, 4. saddle-bows, 5. two, 6. Extremely pretty, 7. breast-trappings, 8. splendid, 9. At an easy pace her horse walked, 10. She could rescue me from my misfortunes, 11. If, 12. up to, 13. She took off her mantle in the hall.

Wythoute a more sojour[1].
Kyng Artour gan her fayre grete,
And sche hym agayn[2], wyth wordes swete
  That were of greet valour[3].

Up stod the quene and ladyes stoute[4],                     985
Her for to beholde all aboute,
  How evene[5] sche stod upryght.
Than wer they wyth her also donne[6]
As ys the mone ayen[7] the sonne,
  Aday whan hyt ys lyght.                                   990
Than seyde sche to Artour the kyng,
'Syr, hydyr I come for swych a thyng,
  To skere[8] Launfal the knyght;
That he never, yn no folye,
Besofte the quene of no drurye[9],                          995
  By dayes ne be nyght.

Therfor, Syr Kyng, good kepe thou nyme[10]!
He bad naght her, but sche bad[11] hym
  Here lemman for to be,
And he answerede her and seyde                             1000
That hys lemmannes lothlokest mayde
  Was fayryr than was sche.'
Kyng Artour seyde: 'wythouten othe[12],
Ech man may yse[13] that ys sothe
  Bryghtere that ye be[14].'                               1005
Wyth that, Dame Tryamour to the quene geth[15],
And blew on her swych a breth
  That never eft[16] myght sche se.

The lady lep an[17] hyr palfray
And bad hem alle have good day;                            1010
  Sche nolde[18] no lengere abyde.
Wyth that com Gyfre allso prest[19],

1. delay, 2. in return, 3. worth, 4. elegant, 5. straight, 6. Compared with her they were
as colourless, 7. compared with, 8. acquit, 9. Asked the queen for her love, 10. take good
heed, 11. asked, 12. dispute, 13. see, 14. That you are more lovely, 15. goes, 16. again,
(cf. line 810), 17. leaped on, 18. would not, 19. at once.

Wyth Launfalys stede, out of the forest,
  And stod Launfal besyde.
The knyght to horse began to sprynge                    1015
Anoon, wythout any lettynge[1],
  Wyth hys lemman away to ryde.
The lady tok her maydenys achon[2]
And wente the way that sche hadde er[3] gon,
  Wyth solas and wyth pryde.                            1020


The lady rod thorth[4] Cardevyle
Fer ynto a jolyf ile,
  Olyroun that hyghte[5].
Every er[6], upon a certayn day,
Me[7] may here Launfales stede nay,                     1025
  And hym se wyth syght.
Ho that wyll ther axsy justus[8],
To kepe hys armes fro the rustus,
  In turnement other fyght,
Thar[9] he never forther gon;                           1030
Ther he may fynde justes anoon
  Wyth Syr Launfal the knyght.


Thus Launfal, wythouten fable,
That noble knyght of the Rounde Table,
  Was take ynto Fayrye.                                 1035
Seththe[10] saw hym yn thys lond no man,
Ne no more of hym telle I ne can,
  Forsothe, wythoute lye.
Thomas Chestre made thys tale
Of the noble knyght Syr Launfale,                       1040
  Good of chyvalrye.
Jesus, that ys Hevene Kyng,
Yeve[11] us alle Hys blessyng,
  And Hys modyr Marye!


---

1. delay, 2. every one, 3. previously, 4. through, 5. Called Oléron, 6. year, 7. One,
8. Whoever wants to ask for a joust there, 9. Need, 10. Afterwards, 11. Give.

# PEARL

*Pearl* is preserved in B.L. MS. Cotton Nero A.x, which also contains *Cleanness*, *Patience* and *Sir Gawain and the Green Knight*. All four poems were composed in the North-West Midlands in the second half of the fourteenth century. The standard edition of *Pearl* is by E. V. Gordon (Oxford, 1953).

### I

Perle, plesaunte to prynces paye
To clanly clos in golde so clere,
Oute of oryent, I hardyly saye,
Ne proved I never her precios pere.
So rounde, so reken in uche araye,   5
So smal, so smothe her sydez were,
Quere-so-ever I jugged gemmez gaye,
I sette hyr sengeley in synglure.
Allas! I leste hyr in on erbere;
Thurgh gresse to grounde hit fro me yot.   10
I dewyne, fordolked of luf-daungere
Of that pryvy perle wythouten spot.

Sythen in that spote hit fro me sprange,
Ofte haf I wayted, wyschande that wele,
That wont watz whyle devoyde my wrange   15
And heven my happe and al my hele.

### I

Pearl, pleasing to a prince's pleasure to enclose beautifully in gold so bright; I say certainly that I never found her precious equal from the Orient. So round, so lovely in every setting, so slender, so smooth were her sides; wheresoever I examined fair jewels, I set her apart as unique. Alas, I lost her in a garden; it fell from me through the grass into the ground. I languish, terribly wounded by the power of my love for that pearl of mine without spot.

Since it slipped from me in that spot, I have often kept watch, longing for that precious one that once used to dispel my sorrow and increase my happiness and all my well-being.

That dotz bot thrych my hert thrange,
My breste in bale bot bolne and bele;
Yet thoght me never so swete a sange
As stylle stounde let to me stele.                    20
For sothe ther fleten to me fele.
To thenke hir color so clad in clot!
O moul, thou marrez a myry juele,
My privy perle wythouten spotte.

That spot of spysez mot nedez sprede,                 25
Ther such rychez to rot is runne;
Blomez blayke and blwe and rede
Ther schynez ful schyr agayn the sunne.
Flor and fryte may not be fede
Ther hit doun drof in moldez dunne;                   30
For uch gresse mot grow of graynez dede,
No whete were ellez to wonez wonne.
Of goud uche goude is ay bygonne;
So semly a sede moght fayly not
That spryngande spysez up ne sponne                   35
Of that precios perle wythouten spotte.

To that spot that I in speche expoun
I entred in that erber grene,
In Auguste in a hygh seysoun,
Quen corne is corven wyth crokez kene.                40

That merely afflicts my heart painfully, my breast swells and festers with sorrow. And yet I thought there was never a song so sweet as that which a quiet moment allowed to steal over me. Indeed, many such moments came to me. To think her colour so covered in mud! O earth, you are spoiling a lovely jewel, my own pearl without spot.

That spot must inevitably be covered with plants, where such riches have mouldered; white, blue and red blooms shine there brightly in the sun. Flower and fruit may not fade where the pearl sank down into the dark earth, for every blade of grass must grow from dead seed, otherwise no wheat would be brought home. Each good thing springs from that which is good; a seed so fine could not fail to produce flourishing spices from that precious pearl without spot.

To that spot that I describe in that green garden, I came on a solemn festival in August, when the corn is cut with sharp scythes.

On huyle ther perle hit trendeled doun
Schadowed this wortez ful schyre and schene,
Gilofre, gyngure and gromylyoun,
And pyonys powdered ay bytwene.
Yif hit watz semly on to sene,                         45
A fayr reflayr yet fro hit flot.
Ther wonys that worthyly, I wot and wene,
My precious perle wythouten spot.


Bifore that spot my honde I spennd
For care ful colde that to me caght;                   50
A devely dele in my hert denned,
Thagh resoun sette myselven saght.
I playned my perle that ther watz spenned
Wyth fyrce skyllez that faste faght;
Thagh kynde of Kryst me comfort kenned,                55
My wreched wylle in wo ay wraght.
I felle upon that floury flaght;
Suche odour to my hernez schot,
I slode upon a slepyng-slaghte
On that precios perle wythouten spot.                  60


On the mound where the pearl rolled down, these bright and lovely plants cast their
shadow; gilly flower, ginger and gromwell, and peonies scattered among them. If it was
lovely to look at, lovely also was the scent that wafted from it. There, I know and believe,
dwells that noble one, my precious pearl without spot.

By that spot I clenched my hands, because of the chill sorrow that seized me. A desolating
grief lay in my heart, though reason offered me composure. With fierce and bitterly
contending arguments, I mourned for my pearl imprisoned there. Though the example
of Christ taught me comfort, my wretched self-will was always afflicted with sorrow.
I fell upon the flowery turf, and such a scent rose to my brain that I dropped into a deep
sleep on that precious pearl without spot.

## II

Fro spot my spyryt ther sprang in space;
My body on balke ther bod in sweven.
My goste is gon in Godez grace
In aventure ther mervaylez meven.
I ne wyste in this worlde quere that hit wace,            65
Bot I knew me keste ther klyfez cleven;
Towarde a foreste I bere the face,
Where rych rokkez wer to dyscreven.
The lyght of hem myght no mon leven,
The glemande glory that of hem glent;                     70
For wern never webbez that wyghez weven
Of half so dere adubbemente.

Dubbed wern alle tho downez sydez
Wyth crystal klyffez so cler of kynde,
Holtewodez bryght aboute hem bydez                        75
Of bollez as blwe as ble of Ynde;
As bornyst sylver the lef on slydez,
That thike con trylle on uch a tynde.
Quen glem of glodez agaynz hem glydez,
Wyth schymeryng schene ful schrylle thay schynde.        80
The gravayl that on grounde con grynde
Wern precious perlez of oryente:
The sunnebemez bot blo and blynde
In respecte of that adubbement.

## II

My spirit left that spot after a time; my body remained there dreaming on the mound.
My spirit went by the grace of God on an adventure where marvels occur. I did not know
where in the world I was, but I knew I was conveyed to where cliffs rose up to the sky.
I turned my face towards a forest where splendid rocks were to be seen. No one could
believe their brightness and the gleaming radiance that shone from them, for men have
never woven fabrics that were of half such lovely splendour.

All the hillsides were resplendent with crystal cliffs of great beauty. Bright woods are
situated around them with tree-trunks as blue as indigo. The leaves that quiver abundantly
on every branch slide against one another like burnished silver. When the light from the
glades falls on them, they shine dazzlingly with shimmering brightness. The gravel that
crunched on the ground was precious oriental pearls; the sunbeams were merely dark
and dim in comparison with that splendour.

The adubbemente of tho downez dere                    85
Garten my goste al greffe foryete.
So frech flavorez of frytez were,
As fode hit con me fayre refete.
Fowlez ther flowen in fryth in fere,
Of flaumbande hwez bothe smale and grete;          90
Bot sytole-stryng and gyternere
Her reken myrthe moght not retrete;
For quen those bryddez her wyngez bete,
Thay songen wyth a swete asent.
So gracios gle couthe no mon gete                    95
As here and se her adubbement.


So al watz dubbet on dere asyse
That fryth ther fortwne forth me ferez,
The derthe therof for to devyse
Nis no wygh worthé pat tonge berez.                 100
I welke ay forth in wely wyse;
No bonk so byg that did me derez.
The fyrre in the fryth, the feier con ryse
The playn, the plonttez, the spyse, the perez,
And rawez and randez and rych reverez,             105
As fyldor fyn her bonkes brent.
I wan to a water by schore that scherez –
Lorde, dere watz hit adubbement!

The splendour of those lovely hillsides caused my spirit to forget all its grief. So refreshing were the scents from the fruits that like food they revived me delightfully. Birds of dazzling colours, both small and large, flew in the wood together; but no citole-string and gytern player could reproduce their delightful music, for when those birds beat their wings, they sang with a sweet harmony. No one could have pleasure so enchanting as to hear and see their splendour.

That wood where fortune leads me forth was so gloriously resplendent that no one capable of speech is worthy to describe the beauty of it. I walked on and on in a blissful state; there was no hill big enough to hinder me. The further I went in the wood, the fairer grew the meadow, the bushes, the spice-flowers and the pear trees, the hedgerows, the water-edges and lovely brooks, their steep banks bright as fine gold-thread. I reached a stream that cuts along its banks – Lord, how wonderful was its splendour!

The dubbemente of tho derworth depe
Wern bonkez bene of beryl bryght.                    110
Swangeande swete the water con swepe,
Wyth a rownande rourde raykande aryght.
In the founce ther stonden stonez stepe,
As glente thurgh glas that glowed and glyght,
As stremande sternez, quen strothe-men slepe,        115
Staren in welkyn in wynter nyght;
For uche a pobbel in pole ther pyght
Watz emerad, saffer, other gemme gente,
That alle the loghe lemed of lyght,
So dere watz hit adubbement.                         120


### III

The dubbement dere of doun and dalez,
Of wod and water and wlonk playnez,
Bylde in me blys, abated my balez,
Fordidden my stresse, dystryed my paynez.
Doun after a strem that dryghly halez               125
I bowed in blys, bredful my braynez;
The fyrre I folwed those floty valez,
The more strenghthe of joye myn herte straynez.
As fortune fares ther as ho fraynez,
Whether solace ho sende other ellez sore,           130
The wygh to wham her wylle ho waynez,
Hyttez to have ay more and more.

---

Those splendid deep waters were adorned with beautiful banks of bright beryl. The water rushed past swirling merrily, flowing along with a whispering sound. On the bottom were brilliant stones that shone and glinted like a beam of light through glass, or like gleaming stars that shine in the sky on a winter night while men on earth are asleep; for every pebble set there in the water was emerald, sapphire or some elegant gem, so that the whole stream shone with light, so wonderful was its splendour.

### III

The lovely splendour of hills and dales, of wood and water and noble meadows, kindled joy in me, relieved my sorrows, dispelled my distress, ended my griefs. Joyfully I went down along a stream that flows steadily, my head full of happy thoughts. The further I followed those watery vales, the more strongly joy stirred my heart. As is fortune's practice when she makes trial of someone, whether she sends solace or misery, the man to whom she allots whatever she will finds he has ever more and more of it.

More of wele watz in that wyse
Then I cowthe telle thagh I tom hade,
For urthely herte myght not suffyse     135
To the tenthe dole of tho gladnez glade;
Forthy I thoght that Paradyse
Watz ther over gayn tho bonkez brade.
I hoped the water were a devyse
Bytwene myrthez by merez made;     140
Byyonde the broke, by slente other slade,
I hoped that mote merked wore.
Bot the water watz depe, I dorst not wade,
And ever me longed ay more and more.

More and more, and yet wel mare,     145
Me lyste to se the broke byyonde;
For if hit watz fayr ther I con fare,
Wel loveloker watz the fyrre londe.
Abowte me con I stote and stare;
To fynde a forthe faste con I fonde,     150
Bot wothez mo iwysse ther ware
The fyrre I stalked by the stronde.
And ever me thoght I schulde not wonde
For wo ther welez so wynne wore.
Thenne nwe note me com on honde,     155
That meved my mynde ay more and more.

---

There was more delight in that situation than I could relate even if I had the chance, for an earthly heart could not contain a tenth part of those happy joys. Therefore I thought that Paradise was there beyond those broad banks. I guessed the water was a dividing-line between delightful places made by pools. I supposed the city was situated beyond the brook by hill or vale. But the water was deep, I did not dare wade, and I yearned ever more and more.

More and more, and still more, I wished to see beyond the brook, for if it was beautiful where I walked, lovelier still was the country further off. I stopped and stared about me; I tried hard to find a ford, but in fact there were more dangers the further I walked along the bank. Always I thought I should not turn back because of difficulty where the joys were so delightful. Then something new caught my attention, it stirred my mind more and more.

More mervayle con my dom adaunt:
I segh byyonde that myry mere
A crystal clyffe ful relusaunt;
Mony ryal ray con fro hit rere.                            160
At the fote therof ther sete a faunt,
A mayden of menske, ful debonere;
Blysnande whyt watz hyr bleaunt.
I knew hyr wel, I hade sen hyr ere.
As glysnande golde that man con schere,                    165
So schon that schene anunder shore.
On lenghe I loked to hyr there;
The lenger, I knew hyr more and more.


The more I frayste hyr fayre face,
Her fygure fyn quen I had fonte,                            170
Suche gladande glory con to me glace
As lyttel byfore therto watz wonte.
To calle hyr lyste con me enchace,
Bot baysment gef myn hert a brunt.
I segh hyr in so strange a place,                          175
Such a burre myght make myn herte blunt.
Thenne verez ho up her fayre frount,
Hyr vysayge whyt as playn yvore:
That stonge myn hert ful stray atount,
And ever the lenger, the more and more.                    180


A more marvellous sight disconcerted my judgement: I saw beyond that lovely river a dazzling cliff of crystal. Many wonderful rays of light were reflected from it. At its foot sat a child, a courteous and gracious maiden; her mantle was shining white. I knew her well, I had seen her before. The fair girl beneath the cliff shone like bright gold that has been cut into threads. I looked long on her there; I knew her more and more the longer I did so.

The more I examined her beautiful face, after I had noticed her delicate figure, joyful adoration swept over me as it had seldom done before. Longing urged me to call her, but confusion struck my heart. I saw her in so strange a place; such a shock might numb my heart. Then she raises her lovely forehead, her face as white as polished ivory; that threw my heart into bewildered astonishment which grew more and more the longer it continued.

IV

More then me lyste my drede aros.
I stod ful stylle and dorste not calle;
Wyth yghen open and mouth ful clos
I stod as hende as hawk in halle.
I hoped that gostly watz that porpose;                    185
I dred onende quat schulde byfalle,
Lest ho me eschaped that I ther chos,
Er I at steven hir moght stalle.
That gracios gay wythouten galle,
So smothe, so smal, so seme slyght,                       190
Rysez up in hir araye ryalle,
A precios pyece in perlez pyght.


Perlez pyghte of ryal prys
There moght mon by grace haf sene,
Quen that frech as flor-de-lys                            195
Doun the bonke con bowe bydene.
Al blysnande whyt watz hir beau bys,
Upon at sydez, and bounden bene
Wyth the myryeste margarys, at my devyse,
That ever I segh yet with myn ene;                        200
Wyth lappez large, I wot and I wene,
Dubbed with double perle and dyghte;
Her cortel of self sute schene,
Wyth precios perlez al umbethyghte.


IV

My fear increased more than I liked. I stood very still and did not dare call. As silent as a hawk in a hall I stood, with eyes open and mouth quite closed. I supposed that the meaning of the vision was spiritual; I was afraid about what would happen, in case she I saw there escaped me before I could detain her with words. That lovely beautiful girl without impurity, so smooth, so slender, so becomingly slight, rises up in her splendid attire, a precious lady adorned in pearls.

By God's grace one could have seen pearls of exquisite excellence set there when that girl bright as a lily came swiftly down the slope. Her fine linen was glowing white, open at the sides and delicately fastened with, in my estimation, the loveliest pearls that I have ever set eyes on; with hanging sleeves, I know and believe, decorated and set with double pearls; her kirtle of matching beauty, adorned all around with precious pearls.

A pyght coroune yet wer that gyrle                           205
Of marjorys and non other ston,
Highe pynakled of cler quyt perle,
Wyth flurted flowrez perfet upon.
To hed hade ho non other werle;
Her lere-leke al hyr umbegon,                                210
Her semblaunt sade for doc other erle,
Her ble more blaght then whallez bon.
As schorne golde schyr her fax thenne schon,
On schylderez that leghe unlapped lyghte.
Her depe colour yet wonted non                              215
Of precios perle in porfyl pyghte.

Pyght watz poyned and uche a hemme
At honde, at sydez, at overture,
Wyth whyte perle and non other gemme,
And bornyste quyte watz hyr vesture.                         220
Bot a wonder perle wythouten wemme
Inmyddez hyr breste watz sette so sure;
A mannez dom moght dryghly demme,
Er mynde moght malte in hit mesure.
I hope no tong moght endure                                  225
No saverly saghe say of that syght,
So watz hit clene and cler and pure,
That precios perle ther hit watz pyght.

Also that girl wore a crown adorned with pearls and no other stone, with high pinnacles of clear white pearl, and flowers figured perfectly upon it. She had no other circlet upon her head. Her wimple enclosed her all around, her demeanour grave enough for a duke or an earl, her complexion whiter than ivory. As bright cut gold shone her hair that lay unbound lightly on her shoulders. Her pure white colour was not inferior to the precious pearls adorning the embroidery.

The wrist-band and each hem at the hand, at the sides and at the neck, were adorned with white pearl and no other gem, and her dress was shining white. A wonderful pearl without a flaw was placed securely in the middle of her breast. Human judgement would be utterly confused before the mind could comprehend the size of it. I believe no tongue would be able to give a proper account of that sight, so clean and clear and pure, that precious pearl set where it was.

Pyght in perle, that precios pyse
On wyther half water com doun the schore.                    230
No gladder gome hethen into Grece
Then I, quen ho on brymme wore.
Ho watz me nerre then aunte or nece;
My joy forthy watz much the more.
Ho profered me speche, that special spyce,                   235
Enclynande lowe in wommon lore,
Caghte of her coroun of grete tresore
And haylsed me wyth a lote lyghte.
Wel watz me that ever I watz bore
To sware that swete in perlez pyghte!                        240

v

'O perle', quod I, 'in perlez pyght,
Art thou my perle that I haf playned,
Regretted by myn one on nyghte?
Much longeyng haf I for the layned,
Sythen into gresse thou me aglyghte.                         245
Pensyf, payred, I am forpayned,
And thou in a lyf of lykyng lyghte,
In Paradys erde, of stryf unstrayned.
What wyrde hatz hyder my juel wayned,
And don me in thys del and gret daunger?                     250
Fro we in twynne wern towen and twayned,
I haf ben a joylez juelere.'

Adorned in pearl, that precious girl came down the bank on the opposite side of the river. There was no gladder man between here and Greece than I, when she was at the water's edge. She was closer to me than an aunt or a niece, and therefore my joy was much the greater. That exquisite person addressed me, bowing low in a woman's fashion, took off her crown of great value, and greeted me with a glad cry. Happy was I to have been born to answer that dear one adorned in pearls!

v

'O pearl', said I, 'adorned in pearls, are you my pearl that I have wept and grieved for alone at night? I have hidden much sorrow for you since you slipped from me into the grass. Miserable and broken, I am tormented, and you are settled into a life of enjoyment, in the land of Paradise, untroubled by strife. What fate has carried off my jewel here, and put me in this sorrow and great distress? Since we were drawn apart and separated, I have been a joyless jeweller.'

That juel thenne in gemmez gente
Vered up her vyse wyth yghen graye,
Set on hyr coroun of perle orient,                    255
And soberly after thenne con ho say:
'Sir, ye haf your tale mysetente,
To say your perle is al awaye,
That is in cofer so comly clente
As in this gardyn gracios gaye,                       260
Hereinne to lenge for ever and play,
Ther mys nee mornyng com never here.
Her were a forser for the, in faye,
If thou were a gentyl jueler.

'Bot, jueler gente, if thou schal lose                265
Thy joy for a gemme that the watz lef,
Me thynk the put in a mad porpose,
And busyez the aboute a raysoun bref;
For that thou lestez watz bot a rose
That flowred and fayled as kynde hyt gef.             270
Now thurgh kynde of the kyste that hyt con close
To a perle of prys hit is put in pref.
And thou hatz called thy wyrde a thef,
That oght of noght hatz mad the cler.
Thou blamez the bote of thy meschef;                  275
Thou art no kynde jueler.'


That jewel in elegant gems then raised up her face with her grey eyes, put on her crown of orient pearl, and then said severely: 'Sir, you have spoken mistakenly to say your pearl is quite lost, that is so beautifully enclosed in a jewel-box such as this pleasant and lovely garden, to stay and play here forever, where sorrow and mourning never come. Here indeed would be a casket for you if you were a truly noble jeweller.

'But, noble jeweller, if you are to lose your joy for a gem that was dear to you, I think you are set on a mad course, and concern yourself with a short-lived matter; for what you lost was only a rose that flowered and faded as its nature dictated. Now through the nature of the chest that encloses it, it has proved to be a pearl of great price. Yet you have called your fate a thief, that has clearly made for you something from nothing. You are blaming what is the remedy of your misfortune; you are not a right-minded jeweller.'

A juel to me then watz thys geste,
And juelez wern hyr gentyl sawez.
'Iwyse', quod I, 'my blysfol beste,
My grete dystresse thou al to-drawez.          280
To be excused I make requeste;
I trawed my perle don out of dawez;
Now haf I fonde hyt, I schal ma feste,
And wony wyth hyt in schyr wod-schawez,
And love my Lorde and al his lawez          285
That hatz me broght thys blys ner.
Now were I at yow byyonde thise wawez,
I were a joyful jueler.'

'Jueler', sayde that gemme clene,
'Wy borde ye men? So madde ye be!          290
Thre wordez hatz thou spoken at ene:
Unavysed, for sothe, wern alle thre.
Thou ne woste in worlde quat on dotz mene;
Thy worde byfore thy wytte con fle.
Thou says thou trawez me in this dene,          295
Bycawse thou may wyth yghen me se;
Another thou says, in thys countré
Thyself schal won wyth me ryght here;
The thrydde, to passe thys water fre.
That may no joyfol jueler.          300

This visitor was a jewel to me, and her noble words were jewels. 'Indeed', I said, 'my dear and best one, you quite banish my great distress. I ask you to forgive me. I believed my pearl was deprived of life; now I have found it I shall rejoice, and dwell with it in the bright groves, and praise my Lord and all His decrees, who has brought me to this bliss. Now if I were with you beyond these waves, I should be a joyful jeweller.'

'Jeweller', said that pure gem, 'why do you men joke? You are foolish! You have made three statements together: all three of them, in fact, were ill-judged. You do not know what in the world even one of them means. Your words escaped before you understood them. You say you believe me to be in this valley because you can see me before your eyes; further, you say you will live with me right here in this country; thirdly that you will cross this noble river. No joyful jeweller may do that.

VI

'I halde that jueler lyttel to prayse
That levez wel that he segh wyth yghe,
And much to blame and uncortayse
That levez oure Lorde wolde make a lyghe,
That lelly hyghte your lyf to rayse,                    305
Thagh Fortune dyd your flesch to dyghe.
Ye setten hys wordez ful westernays
That levez nothynk bot ye hit syghe.
And that is a poynt o sorquydrye
That uche god mon may evel byseme,                    310
To leve no tale be true to trye
Bot that hys one skyl may dem.

'Deme now thyself if thou con dayly
As man to God wordez schulde heve.
Thou saytz thou schal won in this bayly;             315
Me thynk the burde fyrst aske leve,
And yet of graunt thou myghtez fayle.
Thou wylnez over thys water to weve;
Er moste thou cever to other counsayle:
Thy corse in clot mot calder keve.                   320
For hit watz forgarte at Paradys greve;
Oure yorefader hit con mysseyeme.
Thurgh drwry deth boz uch man dreve,
Er over thys dam hym Dryghtyn deme.'

VI

'I regard that jeweller who believes only what he sees with his own eyes as scarcely commendable, and much to be blamed and discourteous to believe that our Lord would deceive, who faithfully promised to raise you to life, though fortune caused your flesh to die. You who believe nothing unless you have seen it, completely disregard His words. It is an instance of pride that ill befits any good man, to believe no statement be proved unless his own judgement can confirm it.

'Consider now yourself if you have spoken courteously as one should address words to God. You say you will live in this realm; I think you should first ask leave, and even then you might fail to get permission. You want to go over this river; first you must follow a different course: your corpse must sink quite cold into the ground, because it was forfeited in the Garden of Eden; our ancestor Adam neglected it. Each man must pass through cruel death before God will permit him over this river.'

'Demez thou me', quod I, 'my swete,                    325
To dol agayn, thenne I dowyne.
Now haf I fonte that I forlete,
Schal I efte forgo hit er ever I fyne?
Why schal I hit bothe mysse and mete?
My precios perle dotz me gret pyne.                    330
What servez tresor, bot garez men grete
When he hit schal efte wyth tenez tyne?
Now rech I never for to declyne,
Ne how fer of folde that man me fleme.
When I am partlez of perle myne,                       335
Bot durande doel what may men deme?'


'Thow demez noght bot doel-dystresse',
Thenne sayde that wyght. 'Why dotz thou so?
For dyne of doel of lurez lesse
Ofte mony mon forgos the mo.                           340
The oghte better thyselven blesse,
And love ay God, in wele and wo,
For anger gaynez the not a cresse.
Who nedez schal thole, be not so thro.
For thogh thou daunce as any do,                       345
Braundysch and bray thy brathez breme,
When thou no fyrre may, to ne fro,
Thou moste abyde that he schal deme.


'If you, my sweet, condemn me to sorrow again', said I, 'then I shall pine away. Now I have found what I lost, shall I lose it again before I die? Why shall I both find it and lose it? My precious pearl causes me great grief. What is the good of treasure except to make a man weep when he has to lose it again sorrowfully. Now I do not care at all if I go downhill, nor how far I am driven into exile. When I am deprived of my pearl, what can that be termed but lasting sorrow?'

'You speak of nothing but sorrow and distress', that girl said then. 'Why do you do so? In loud lament over lesser evils, many a man often misses the greater prize. You ought rather to call yourself happy, and always praise God in both prosperity and sorrow, for anger will get you nowhere. Anyone who has to suffer must not be impatient, for though you may leap about like a doe, struggle and bray out your bitter anguish, when you can go no further forwards or backwards, you must endure what He ordains.

'Deme Dryghtyn, ever hym adyte,
Of the way a fote ne wyl he wrythe. 350
Thy mendez mountez not a myte,
Thagh thou for sorwe be never blythe.
Stynt of thy strot and fyne to flyte,
And sech hys blythe ful swefte and swythe.
Thy prayer may hys pyté byte, 355
That mercy schal hyr craftez kythe.
Hys comforte may thy langour lythe,
And thy lurez of lyghtly leme;
For, marre other madde, morne and mythe,
Al lys in hym to dyght and deme.' 360

### VII

Thenne demed I to that damyselle:
'Ne worthe no wraththe unto my Lorde,
If rapely I rave, spornande in spelle.
My herte watz al wyth mysse remorde,
As wallande water gotz out of welle. 365
I do me ay in hys myserecorde,
Rebuke me never wyth wordez felle,
Thagh I forloyne, my dere endorde,
Bot kythez me kyndely your coumforde,
Pytosly thenkande upon thysse: 370
Of care and me ye made acorde,
That er watz grounde of alle my blysse.

'Sit in judgement on God, accuse Him continually – He will not turn one foot from the path. Your relief will not increase a jot, even though you are never happy in your sorrow. Give up your wrangling and stop arguing, and seek His mercy swiftly and quickly. Your prayer may stir His compassion, so that mercy shows her powers. His encouragement can lessen your anguish, and easily drive off all your sorrows; for you may lament or rave, mourn and fret, but all lies in Him to ordain and judge.'

### VII

Then I said to that damsel: 'May my Lord not be angry if I prattle thoughtlessly, stumbling in my words. My heart was greatly afflicted by my loss, overflowing like water pouring from a spring. I submit myself to His mercy always. Do not rebuke me with harsh words, my golden darling, even though I go astray, but graciously grant me your comfort, thinking compassionately of this: that you, who had been the foundation of all my joy, brought me and sorrow together.

'My blysse, my bale, ye han ben bothe,
Bot much the bygger yet watz my mon;
Fro thou watz wroken fro uch a wothe,     375
I wyste never quere my perle watz gon.
Now I hit se, now lethez my lothe.
And, quen we departed, we wern at on;
God forbede we be now wrothe!
We meten so selden by stok other ston.     380
Thagh cortaysly ye carp con,
I am bot mol and manerez mysse.
Bot Crystes mersy and Mary and Jon,
Thise arn the grounde of alle my blisse.

'In blysse I se the blythely blent,     385
And I a man al mornyf mate;
Ye take theron ful lyttel tente,
Thagh I hente ofte harmez hate.
Bot now I am here in your presente,
I wolde bysech, wythouten debate,     390
Ye wolde me say in sobre asente
What lyf ye lede erly and late.
For I am ful fayn that your astate
Is worthen to worschyth and wele, iwysse;
Of alle my joy the hyghe gate,     395
Hit is, and grounde of alle my blysse.'

'You have been both my joy and my torment, but my grief was much the greater; from the time when you were set free from all vicissitudes, I did not know where my pearl had gone. Now I see it, my grief eases. When we parted we were at one – God forbid we should now be angry! We meet so seldom in any place. Though you have spoken courteously, I am just dirt and have no manners. Yet Christ's mercy, and Mary and John, these are the foundations of all my joy.

'I see you happily steeped in joy, and I am a man quite sunk in grief. You take very little notice of that, though I often suffer burning sorrows. But now I am here in your presence, putting argument aside I beg you to tell me in a spirit of true reconciliation what life you lead from morning to night, for I am very glad indeed that your state has become an honourable and prosperous one. It is the main avenue of all my happiness, and the foundation of all my joy.'

'Now blysse, burne, mot the bytyde',
Then sayde that lufsoum of lyth and lere,
'And welcum here to walk and byde,
For now thy speche is to me dere.          400
Maysterful mod and hyghe pryde,
I hete the, arn heterly hated here.
My Lorde ne lovez not for to chyde,
For meke arn alle that wonez hym nere;
And when in hys place thou schal apere,     405
Be deth devote in hol mekenesse.
My Lorde the Lamb lovez ay such chere,
That is the grounde of alle my blysse.

'A blysful lyf thou says I lede;
Thou woldez knaw therof the stage.          410
Thow wost wel when thy perle con schede
I watz ful yong and tender of age;
Bot my Lorde the Lombe thurgh hys godhede,
He toke myself to hys maryage,
Corounde me quene in blysse to brede        415
In lenghe of dayez that ever schal wage;
And sesed in alle hys herytage
Hys lef is; I am holy hysse.
Hys prese, hys prys, and hys parage
Is rote and grounde of alle my blysse.'     420

'Now may joy come to you, sir', then said that girl lovely of body and face, 'and you are welcome to walk and linger here, for now your words are pleasing to me. I assure you that an arrogant attitude and overbearing pride are bitterly hated here. My Lord does not like to rebuke, for all those near Him are meek, and when you appear in His presence, be deeply devout with absolute humility. My Lord the Lamb, who is the foundation of all my joy, always loves such behaviour.

'You say I lead a joyful life, and you want to know my position in it. You know well when your pearl was lost I was very young and of tender age. But my Lord the Lamb, through His divine nature, took me in marriage, crowned me queen to prosper in bliss, for a span of time that will last for ever. His beloved is endowed with all His inheritance; I am wholly His. His worth, His excellence and His nobility are the root and foundation of all my joy.'

## VIII

'Blysful', quod I, 'may thys be trwe?
Dysplesez not if I speke errour.
Art thou the quene of hevenez blwe,
That al thys worlde schal do honour?
We leven on Marye that grace of grewe,                    425
That ber a barne of vyrgyn flour;
The croune fro hyr quo moght remwe
Bot ho hir passed in sum favour?
Now, for synglerty o hyr dousour,
We calle hyr Fenyx of Arraby,                             430
That freles flewe of hyr fasor,
Lyk to the Quen of cortaysye.'

'Cortayse Quen', thenne sayde that gaye,
Knelande to grounde, folde up hyr face,
'Makelez Moder and myryest May,                           435
Blessed bygyner of uch a grace!'
Thenne ros ho up and con restay,
And speke me towarde in that space:
'Sir, fele here porchasez and fongez pray,
Bot supplantorez none wythinne thys place.               440
That Emperise al hevenz hatz,
And urthe and helle, in her bayly,
Of erytage yet non wyl ho chace,
For ho is Quen of cortaysye.

### VIII

'Joyful one', I said, 'can this be true? Do not be angry if I speak in error. Are you the queen of blue heaven, whom all this world must honour? We believe in Mary from whom grace sprang, who bore a child from the flower of virginity. Who, unless she surpassed her in some quality, could take the crown from her? Now, because of the uniqueness of her sweetness, we call her the Phoenix of Arabia, that flew immaculate from her Creator, like the Queen of grace.'

'Gracious Queen', that lovely one then said, kneeling on the ground, her face raised, 'Peerless Mother and most joyous Maiden, blessed fount of every grace!' Then she stood up and paused, and spoke to me in that moment: 'Sir, many here strive for the prize and receive it, but there are no usurpers in this place; that Empress has all heaven and earth and hell in her domain, yet she will drive no one from his inheritance, for she is Queen of grace and hell.

'The court of the kyndom of God alyve                                445
Hatz a property in hytself beyng:
Alle that may therinne aryve
Of alle the reme is quen other kyng,
And never other yet schal depryve,
Bot uchon fayn of otherez hafyng,                                   450
And wolde her corounez wern worthe tho fyve,
If possyble were her mendyng.
Bot my Lady of quom Jesu con spryng,
Ho haldez the empyre over uus ful hyghe;
And that dysplesez non of oure gyng,                                455
For ho is Quene of cortaysye.

'Of courtaysye, as saytz Saynt Poule,
Al arn we membrez of Jesu Kryst:
As heved and arme and legg and naule
Temen to hys body ful trwe and tryste,                              460
Ryght so is uch a Krysten sawle
A longande lym to the Mayster of myste.
Thenne loke what hate other any gawle
Is tached other tyghed thy lymmez bytwyste?
Thy heved hatz nauther greme ne gryste                              465
On arme other fynger thagh thou ber byghe.
So fare we alle wyth luf and lyste
To kyng and quene by cortaysye.'

'The court of the kingdom of the living God has a property in its own nature: everyone
who arrives there is queen or king of the whole realm, and yet he will never deprive
another, but each one will be glad at what the others have and wish their crowns were
five times as precious, if improvement were possible. But my Lady from whom Jesu
was born holds sway high over us, and that displeases none of our company, for she is
Queen of grace.

'Through grace, as St Paul says, we are all parts of the Body of Christ. Just as the head,
arm, leg and navel belong firmly and absolutely to the body, so each Christian soul is
a limb belonging to the Master of divine mysteries. Then look, what hatred or jealousy
is there attached or fastened between your limbs? Your head has neither resentment nor
anger against your arm or your finger if you wear a ring. This is the way we all act with
love and joy towards those who are king and queen by grace.'

'Cortaysé', quod I, 'I leve,
And charyté grete, be yow among,                    470
Bot, my speche that yow ne greve,

.      .      .      .      .

Thyself in heven over hygh thou heve,
To make the quen that watz so yonge.
What more honour moghte he acheve                    475
That hade endured in worlde stronge,
And lyved in penaunce hys lyvez longe
Wyth bodyly bale hym blysse to byye?
What more worschyp moght he fonge
Then corounde be kyng by cortaysé?                   480

### IX

'That cortaysé is to fre of dede,
Yyf hyt be soth that thou conez saye.
Thou lyfed not two yer in oure thede;
Thou cowthez never God nauther plese ne pray,
Ne never nawther Pater ne Crede –                    485
And quen mad on the fyrst day!
I may not traw, so God me spede,
That God wolde wrythe so wrange away.
Of countes, damysel, par ma fay,
Wer fayr in heven to halde asstate,                  490
Other ellez a lady of lasse aray –
Bot a quene! Hit is to dere a date.'

'I believe', said I, 'there is great grace and charity among you, but – I hope my words will not offend you – you exalt yourself too high in heaven, to make yourself a queen, you who were so young. What greater honour might he achieve who had suffered steadfastly in the world, and lived in penance all his life to buy himself heavenly joy with bodily pain? What greater dignity might he receive than to be crowned king by grace?

### IX

'That grace is too liberal in its action, if what you say is true. You lived less than two years with us; you did not know how to please God or to pray to Him, not your Lord's Prayer or your Creed – and made a queen on the first day! I can not believe, God help me, that God would go so badly astray. Truly, damsel, on my honour, it would be pleasing to hold the position of countess in heaven, or else a lady of lesser rank – but a queen! That is too noble a position.'

'Ther is no date of hys godnesse',
Then sayde to me that worthy wyghte,
'For al is trawthe that he con dresse,                          495
And he may do nothynk bot ryght.
As Mathew melez in your messe,
In sothfol gospel of God almyght,
In sample he can ful graythely gesse,
And lyknez hit to heven lyghte.                                500
"My regne", he saytz, "is lyk on hyght
To a lorde that hade a vyne, I wate.
Of tyme of yere the terme watz tyght,
To labor vyne watz dere the date.

' "That date of yere wel knawe thys hyne.                      505
The lorde ful erly up he ros
To hyre werkmen to hys vyne,
And fyndez ther summe to hys porpos.
Into acorde thay con declyne
For a pené on a day, and forth thay gotz,                      510
Wrythen and worchen and don gret pyne,
Kerven and caggen and man hit clos.
Aboute under the lorde to marked totz,
And ydel men stande he fyndez therate.
'Why stande ye ydel?' he sayde to thos.                        515
'Ne knawe ye of this day no date?'

'There is no limit to His goodness', that noble person then said to me, 'for all that He ordains is just, and He can only do right. As Matthew tells you in your Mass, in the true gospel of almighty God – he visualizes it very neatly in a parable representing bright heaven: "My kingdom on high", he says, "is, I believe, like a lord who had a vineyard. The due time of year had come, and the season was right to work in the vineyard.

' "The workers well knew what season of the year it was. The lord rose very early to hire workmen into his vineyard, and he finds there some to his purpose. They reach an agreement on a penny a day, and out they go, toil and labour and greatly exert themselves, cut and tie and make secure. During the morning the lord goes to market and finds there men standing idle. 'Why do you stand idle?' he says to them. 'Do you not know the time of day?'

' " 'Er date of daye hider arn we wonne',
So watz al samen her answar soght.
'We haf standen her syn ros the sunne,
And no mon byddez uus do ryght noght.'          520
'Gos into my vyne, dotz that ye conne',
So sayde the lorde, and made hit toght.
'What resonabele hyre be naght be runne
I yow pay in dede and thoghte.'
Thay wente into the vyne and wroghte,          525
And al day the lorde thus yede his gate
And nw men to hys vyne he broghte,
Welnegh wyl day watz passed date.


' "At the date of day of evensonge,
On oure byfore the sonne go doun,          530
He segh ther ydel men ful stronge
And sade to hem wyth sobre soun,
'Wy stonde ye ydel thise dayez longe?'
Thay sayden her hyre watz nawhere boun.
'Gotz to my vyne, yemen yonge,          535
And wyrkez and dotz that at ye moun.'
Sone the worlde bycom wel broun,
The sunne watz doun and hit wex late.
To take her hyre he mad sumoun;
The day watz al apassed date.          540

' " 'We came here before daybreak' was the answer all gave together. 'We have stood here since the sun rose, and no one asks us to do anything at all.' 'Go into my vineyard, do what you can', the lord said, and made a firm agreement. 'Whatever reasonable wages have accrued by nightfall I shall pay you on the nail.' They went into the vineyard and worked, and all day the lord went his rounds like this and brought new men into his vineyard, until the day had almost reached an end.

' "At the time of evensong, one hour before sunset, he saw strong men idle there, and said to them in a grave tone, 'Why do you stand idle all day long?' They said they had no work arranged for them. 'Go to my vineyard, young men, and work and do whatever you can.' Soon the world became quite dark, the sun was set and it grew late. He summoned them to take their wages; the day had reached its end.

X

' "The date of the daye the lorde con knaw,
Called to the reve: 'Lede, pay the meyny.
Gyf hem the hyre that I hem owe,
And fyrre, that non me may reprené,
Set hem alle upon a rawe                              545
And gyf uchon inlyche a peny.
Bygyn at the laste that standez lowe,
Tyl to the fyrste that thou atteny.'
And thenne the fyrst bygonne to pleny
And sayden that thay hade travayled sore:            550
'These bot on ourè hem con streny;
Uus thynk uus oghe to take more.

' " 'More haf we served, uus thynk so,
That suffred han the dayez hete,
Thenn thyse that wroght not hourez two,               555
And thou dotz hem uus to counterfete.'
Thenne sayde the lorde to on of tho:
'Frende, no waning I wyl the yete;
Take that is thyn owne, and go.
And I hyred the for a peny agrete,                   560
Quy bygynnez thou now to threte?
Watz not a pené thy covenaunt thore?
Fyrre then covenaunde is noght to plete.
Wy schalte thou thenne ask more?

x

' "The lord knew it was the end of the day; he called to the bailiff: 'Pay the workers, man. Give them the wages that I owe them, and furthermore, so that none can find fault with me, set them all in a line and give each one alike a penny. Begin with the last ones who stand at the bottom, until you reach the first.' And then the first began to complain, and said that they had worked hard: 'These only exerted themselves for one hour. We think we ought to take more.

' " 'We reckon we who have endured the heat of the day have deserved more than these who worked for less than two hours, and you equate them with us.' Then the lord said to one of them: 'Friend, I will not give you a reduced amount; take what is your own, and go. I hired you for a penny as we agreed; why do you now begin to argue? Was your compact not for a penny? You cannot claim more than your compact. Why should you then ask for more?

' " 'More, wether louyly is me my gyfte,                565
To do wyth myn quat-so me lykez?
Other ellez thyn yghe to lyther is lyfte
For I am goude and non byswykez?'
Thus schal I'', quod Kryste, "hit skyfte:
The laste schal be the fyrst that strykez,              570
And the fyrst the laste, be he never so swyft;
For mony ben called, thagh fewe be mykez."
Thus pore men her part ay pykez,
Thagh thay com late and lyttel wore;
And thagh her sweng wyth lyttel atslykez,               575
The merci of God is much the more.

'More haf I of joye and blysse hereinne,
Of ladyschyp gret and lyvez blom,
Then alle the wyghez in the worlde myght wynne
By the way of ryght to aske dome.                       580
Whether welnygh now I con bygynne –
In eventyde into the vyne I come –
Fyrst of my hyre my Lorde con mynne:
I watz payed anon of al and sum.
Yet other ther werne that toke more tom,                585
That swange and swat for long yore,
That yet of hyre nothynk thay nom,
Paraunter noght schal to-yere more.'

' " 'Furthermore, is my giving within my own jurisdiction, to do whatever I want with my own? Or is your eye turned to evil because I am good and deceive no one?' '' Christ said "Thus shall I arrange it. The last shall be the first to come, and the first the last however swift he is, for many are called though the chosen ones are few." Thus poor men always get their share, though they came late and were lowly; and though their labour is spent with little result, the mercy of God is much the greater.

'Here I have more joy and bliss, great queenly estate and perfection of life, than anyone in the world might gain by demanding reward in accordance with justice. Although I began only recently – I came into the vineyard in the evening – my Lord remembered my wages first; I was paid in full at once. Yet there were others who spent longer, who laboured and sweated a long time, who have still not received wages, and perhaps will not for years to come.'

Then more I meled and sayde apert:
'Me thynk thy tale unresounable.                    590
Goddez ryght is redy and evermore rert,
Other Holy Wryt is bot a fable.
In Sauter is sayd a verce overte
That spekez a poynt determynable:
"Thou quytez uchon as hys desserte,                 595
Thou hyghe kyng ay pretermynable."
Now he that stod the long day stable,
And thou to payment com hym byfore,
Thenne the lasse in werke to take more able,
And ever the lenger the lasse, the more.'           600

XI

'Of more and lasse in Godez ryche',
That gentyl sayde, 'lys no joparde,
For ther is uch mon payed inlyche,
Whether lyttel other much be hys rewarde;
For the gentyl Cheventayn is no chyche,             605
Quether-so-ever he dele nesch other harde:
He lavez hys gyftez as water of dyche,
Other gotez of golf that never charde.
Hys fraunchyse is large that ever dard
To hym that matz in synne rescoghe;                 610
No blysse betz fro hem reparde,
For the grace of God is gret inoghe.

Then I said more and spoke openly: 'Your account seems to me unreasonable. God's justice is ready to act and always supreme, or Holy Writ is just a fable. There is an explicit verse in the Psalter that makes a definite statement: "High King ever omnipotent, you reward each according to his desert." Now if you came to payment before the one who stood steadfast all day long, then whoever performed less work would be entitled to take more, and the less he did, the more he would get.'

XI

'There is no question', that courteous one said, 'of more and less in God's kingdom, for there each man is paid alike, whether his merit is great or small. For the noble Lord is no niggard, whether He allots a pleasant or a hard fortune. He pours out His gifts as water from a drain, or as streams from depths that have never stopped flowing. His generosity is great to those who always submitted to Him who rescues sinners. No joy will be withheld from them, for the grace of God is great enough.

'Bot now thou motez, me for to mate,
That I my peny haf wrang tan here;
Thou sayz that I that com to late         615
Am not worthy so gret fere.
Where wystez thou ever any bourne abate
Ever so holy in hys prayere,
That he ne forfeted by sumkyn gate
The mede sumtyme of hevenez clere?     620
And ay the ofter, the alder thay were,
Thay laften ryght and wroghten woghe.
Mercy and grace moste hem then stere,
For the grace of God is gret innoghe.

'Bot innoghe of grace hatz innocent.     625
As sone as thay arn borne, by lyne
In the water of babtem thay dyssente;
Then arne thay boroght into the vyne.
Anon the day, wyth derk endente,
The niyght of deth dotz to enclyne:    630
That wroght never wrang er thenne thay wente,
The gentyle Lorde thenne payez hys hyne.
Thay dyden hys heste, thay wern thereine;
Why schulde he not her labour alow,
Yys, and pay hym at the fyrst fyne?     635
For the grace of God is gret innoghe.

'But now you argue, in order to shame me, that I have come by my penny wrongly here. You say that I who came too late am not worthy of such distinguished company. Where do you know of anyone who continued entirely holy in prayer, who did not sometime in some way forfeit the reward of bright heaven? And the older they were, the more often they forsook right and did wrong. Then mercy and grace had to direct them, for the grace of God is great enough.

'But the innocent have enough grace. As soon as they are born, straightaway they descend into the water of baptism; then are they brought into the vineyard. Soon the day, flecked with darkness, is brought to an end by the night of death. The noble Lord then pays His servants who never did wrong before they departed. They kept His commandment, they were in the vineyard; why should He not recognize their labour, yes, and pay them at once in full? For the grace of God is great enough.

'Inoghe is knawen that mankyn grete
Fyrste watz wroght to blysse parfyt;
Oure forme fader hit con forfete
Thurgh an apple that he upon con byte.    640
Al wer we dampned for that mete
To dyghe in doel out of delyt,
And sythen wende to helle hete,
Therinne to won wythoute respyt.
Bot theron com a bote astyt.    645
Ryche blod ran on rode so roghe,
And wynne water; then at that plyt
The grace of God wex gret innoghe.

'Innoghe ther wax out of that welle,
Blod and water of brode wounde.    650
The blod uus boght fro bale of helle
And delyvered uus of the deth secounde;
The water is bathtem, the sothe to telle,
That folwed the glayve so grymly grounde,
That waschez away the gyltez felle    655
That Adam wyth inne deth uus drounde.
Now is ther noght in the worlde rounde
Bytwene uus and blysse bot that he wythdrogh,
And that is restored in sely stounde;
And the grace of God is gret innogh.    660

'It is well enough known that noble mankind was first created for perfect bliss. Our first father forfeited it through an apple which he tasted. On account of that food we were all damned to die in misery cut off from joy, and then to go to the heat of hell, to remain there without reprieve. But then there quickly came deliverance. On the cross so cruel ran precious blood and water; then at that evil time the grace of God became great enough.

'Enough issued from that source, blood and water from the wide wound. The blood bought us from the torment of hell and delivered us from the second death. Truly the water that ran from the spear sharpened so cruelly is baptism, that washes away the deadly sins by which Adam drowned us in death. So now there is nothing in the round world separating us from bliss except what Adam removed, and that is restored in a blessed hour; the grace of God is great enough.

## XII

'Grace innogh the mon may have
That synnez thenne new, yif hym repente,
Bot wyth sorw and syt he mot hit crave,
And byde the payne therto is bent.
Bot resoun of ryght that con not rave          665
Savez evermore the innossent;
Hit is a dom that never God gave,
That ever the gyltlez schulde be schente.
The gyltyf may contryssyoun hente
And be thurgh mercy to grace thryght;          670
Bot he to gyle that never glente
As inoscente is saf and ryghte.

'Ryght thus I knaw wel in this cas
Two men to save is God by skylle:
The ryghtwys man schal se hys face,           675
The harmlez hathel schal com hym tylle.
The Sauter hyt satz thus in a pace:
"Lorde, quo schal klymbe thy hygh hylle,
Other rest wythinne thy holy place?"
Hymself to onsware he is not dylle:           680
"Hondelyngez harme that dyt not ille,
That is of hert bothe clene and lyght,
Ther schal hys step stable stylle";
The innosent is ay saf by ryght.

### XII

'The man who sins again may have enough grace if he repents, but he must beg for it with contrition and grief, and accept the penalty that accompanies it. Yet reason that cannot stray from what is right will always save the innocent; God never decreed that the guiltless should be punished. The guilty may experience contrition, and through mercy be thrust to grace. But he who never strayed towards wickedness is saved and justified as an innocent person.

'Just so I know well in this matter that God is to save two kinds of men in all reason: the righteous man shall see His face, the sinless man shall approach Him. In one passage the Psalter says: "Lord, who shall climb Thy high hill or rest within Thy holy place?" He is not slow to answer himself: "He who did no evil with his hands, who is both clean and pure of heart, shall there place his foot at rest." The innocent one is always saved as of right.

'The ryghtwys man also sertayn                                    685
Aproche he schal that proper pyle,
That takez not her lyf in vayne,
Ne glaverez her nieghbor wyth no gyle.
Of thys ryghtwys saz Salamon playn
How Koyntise onoure con aquyle;                                   690
By wayez ful streght ho con hym strayn,
And scheued hym the rengne of God awhyle,
As quo says, "Lo, yon lovely yle!
Thou may hit wynne if thou be wyghte."
Bot, hardyly, wythoute peryle,                                    695
The innosent is ay save by ryghte.


'Anende ryghtwys men yet saytz a gome,
David in Sauter, if ever ye segh hit:
"Lorde, thy servaunt draw never to dome,
For non lyvyande to the is justyfyet."                            700
Forthy to corte quen thou schal com
Ther alle oure causez schal be tryed,
Alegge the ryght, thou may be innome,
By thys ilke spech I have asspyed;
Bot he on rode that blody dyed,                                   705
Delfully thurgh hondez thryght,
Gyve the to passe, when thou arte tryed,
By innocens and not by ryghte.


'Certainly the righteous man will also approach that glorious castle, those that do not
spend their life in folly, nor deceive their neighbour with guile. Of this righteous man
Solomon says plainly how Wisdom gave him honour. She directed him along narrow
paths, and showed him the kingdom of God for a while, like one who says, "Behold,
yonder lovely region! You may reach it if you are valiant." But assuredly, and without
question, the innocent one is always saved as of right.

'Concerning the righteous, a certain man, David, also says in the Psalter, if you ever saw
it: "Lord, never bring Your servant to judgement, for no living man is justified before
You." Therefore, when you come to the court where all our cases shall be tried, if you
plead justification you may be trapped by this very passage I have pointed out. But may
He who died bloodily on the cross, horribly nailed through the hands, grant you to go
free when you are tried, by your innocence, and not as your right.

'Ryghtwysly quo con rede,
He loke on bok and be awayed                      710
How Jesus hym welke in arethede,
And burnez her barnez unto hym brayde.
For happe and hele that fro hym yede
To touch her chylder thay fayr hym prayed.
His dessypelez wyth blame "let be!" hym bede      715
And wyth her resounez ful fele restayed.
Jesus thenne hem swetely sayde:
"Do way, let chylder unto me tyght.
To suche is hevenryche arayed":
The innocent is ay saf by ryght.                  720

XIII

'Jesus con calle to hym hys mylde,
And sayde hys ryche no wygh myght wynne
Bot he com thyder ryght as a chylde,
Other ellez nevermore com therinne.
Harmlez, trwe, and undefylde,                     725
Wythouten mote other mascle of sulpande synne,
Quen such ther cnoken on the bylde,
Tyt schal hem men the yate unpynne.
Ther is the blys that con not blynne
That the jueler soghte thurgh perré pres,         730
And solde alle hys goud, bothe wolen and lynne,
To bye hym a perle watz mascellez.

'Whoever can read rightly, let him look at the Bible and be instructed how Jesus walked among the people of old, and men brought their children to Him. Because of the joy and healing that flowed from Him, they begged Him earnestly to touch their children. His disciples reprovingly ordered them to stop, and deterred very many by their words. Jesus then said gently to them: "Leave them alone; let children come to me. For such is the kingdom of heaven prepared." The innocent one is always saved as of right.

XIII

'Jesus called to Him His gentle disciples and said no one might attain His kingdom unless he came there just as a child; he would never enter otherwise. The innocent, the faithful, the pure, without stain or spot of polluting sin, when such as these knock there on the dwelling, the gate shall immediately be unfastened to them. There is the joy that cannot end, that the jeweller sought with precious stones, and sold all his goods, both wool and linen, to buy himself a pearl that was spotless.

'This makellez perle, that boght is dere,
The joueler gef fore alle hys god,
Is lyke the reme of hevenesse clere:       735
So sayde the Fader of folde and flode;
For hit is wemlez, clene, and clere,
And endelez rounde, and blythe of mode,
And commune to alle that ryghtwys were.
Lo, even inmyddez my breste hit stode.     740
My Lorde the Lombe, that schede hys blode,
He pyght hit there in token of pes.
I rede the forsake the worlde wode
And porchase thy perle maskelles.'

'O maskelez perle in perlez pure,     745
That berez', quod I, 'the perle of prys,
Quo formed the thy fayre fygure?
That wroght thy wede, he watz ful wys.
Thy beauté com never of nature;
Pymalyon paynted never thy vys,     750
Ne Arystotel nawther by hys lettrure
Of carped the kynde these propertez.
Thy colour passez the flour-de-lys;
Thyn angel-havyng so clene cortez.
Breve me, bryght, quat kyn offys     755
Berez the perle so maskellez?'

'This matchless pearl that is dearly bought, for which the jeweller gave all his goods, is like the bright kingdom of heaven, so said the Father of land and sea; for it is flawless, pure and clear, and endlessly round and lovely in character, belonging equally to all who were righteous. Behold, just in the middle of my breast it stood; my Lord the Lamb, who shed his blood, set it there as a symbol of peace. I urge you to abandon the mad world, and buy your spotless pearl.'

'O spotless pearl dressed in pure pearls', I said, 'wearing the pearl beyond price, who shaped your lovely form? The one who made your dress was very clever. Your beauty did not come from nature; Pygmalion never depicted your face, nor did Aristotle in his writings discuss the nature of these qualities. Your colour surpasses the lily, so pure and lovely is your angelic form. Tell me, beautiful one, what sort of position does the spotless pearl hold?'

'My makelez Lambe that al may bete',
Quod scho, 'my dere destyné,
Me ches to hys make, althagh unmete
Sumtyme semed that assemblé.                    760
When I wente fro yor worlde wete,
He calde me to hys bonerté:
"Cum hyder to me, my lemman swete,
For mote ne spot is non in the."
He gef me myght and als bewté;                  765
In hys blod he wesch my wede on dese,
And coronde clene in vergynté,
And pyght me in perlez maskellez.'


'Why, maskellez bryd that bryght con flambe,
That reiatez hatz so ryche and ryf,            770
Quat kyn thyng may be that Lambe
That the wolde wedde unto hys wyf?
Over alle other so hygh thou clambe
To lede wyth hym so ladyly lyf.
So mony a comly onuunder cambe                  775
For Kryst han lyved in much stryf;
And thou con alle tho dere out dryf
And fro that maryag al other depres,
Al only thyself so stout and styf,
A makelez may and maskellez.'                   780


'My peerless Lamb who can amend all things', she said, 'my dear Destiny, chose me as His bride, although that union once seemed unsuitable. When I left your rainy world, He called me to His gracious presence. "Come hither to Me, My beloved, for there is not a stain or spot in thee." He gave me strength and also beauty; on the dais He washed my apparel in His blood, and crowned me pure in virginity, and set me in spotless pearls.'

'Tell me, spotless maiden, you who shine so bright and have royal honours so noble and abundant, what sort of thing may that Lamb be, that He would take you as His wife? You have risen so high above all others to lead such an exalted life with Him. So many beautiful ladies have lived in great hardship for Christ, yet you were able to eject all those lovely ones, and dislodge all others from that marriage, yourself alone so bold and strong, a peerless and spotless maiden.'

## XIV

'Maskelles', quod that myry quene,
'Unblemyst I am, wythouten blot,
And that may I wyth mensk menteene;
Bot "makelez quene" thenne sade I not.
The Lambez wyvez in blysse we bene,        785
A hondred and forty thowsande flot,
As in the Apocalyppez hit is sene;
Sant John hem sygh al in a knot
On the hyl of Syon, that semly clot;
The apostel hem segh in gostly drem        790
Arayed to the weddyng in that hyl-coppe,
The nwe cyté o Jerusalem.

'Of Jerusalem I in speche spelle.
If thou wyl knaw what kyn he be,
My Lombe, my Lorde, my dere juelle,        795
My joy, my blys, my lemman fre,
The profete Ysaye of hym con melle
Pitously of hys debonerté:
"That gloryous gyltlez that mon con quelle
Wythouten any sake of felonye,            800
As a schep to the slaght ther lad watz he;
And, as lombe that clypper in hande nem,
So closed he hys mouth fro uch query,
Quen Juez hym jugged in Jerusalem."

### XIV

'Spotless', said that lovely queen 'and unblemished I am, without stain, and I can honourably affirm that, but I did not say "peerless queen". We are the wives of the Lamb in bliss, a company of a hundred and forty thousand, as is seen in the Apocalypse. St John saw them all in a throng on the hill of Sion, that lovely mountain; the apostle saw them in a spiritual vision, assembled for the wedding on that hill-top, the new city of Jerusalem.

'I speak of Jerusalem. If you want to know of what nature He is, my Lamb, my Lord, my precious jewel, my joy, my bliss, my noble lover, then the prophet Isaiah spoke compassionately of His gentleness: "That glorious, sinless one, killed though He was not charged with any crime, was there led like a sheep to the slaughter; and like a lamb seized by the shearer, He kept his mouth closed to every question, when Jews put Him on trial in Jerusalem."

'In Jerusalem watz my lemman slayn                805
And rent on rode wyth boyez bolde.
Al oure balez to bere ful bayn,
He toke on hymself oure carez colde.
Wyth boffetez watz hys face flayn
That watz so fayr on to byholde.              810
For synne he set hymself in vayn,
That never hade non hymself to wolde.
For uus he lette hym flyghe and folde
And brede upon a bostwys bem;
As meke as lomp that no playnt tolde          815
For uus he swalt in Jerusalem.

'In Jerusalem, Jordan, and Galalye,
Ther as baptysed the goude Saynt Jon,
His wordez acorded to Ysaye.
When Jesus con to hym warde gon,              820
He sayde of hym thys professye:
"Lo, Godez Lombe as trwe as ston,
That dotz away the synnez dryghe
That alle thys worlde hatz wroght upon.
Hymself ne wroght never yet non;              825
Whether on hymself he con al clem.
Hys generacyoun quo recen con,
That dyghed for uus in Jerusalem?"

'My beloved was slain in Jerusalem and torn on the cross by wicked ruffians. Full willing to bear all our sorrows, He took upon Himself our bitter sufferings. His face so lovely to look on was scourged with buffets. He who Himself was never sinful, sacrificed Himself for our sin. For us He allowed Himself to be scourged and bowed and stretched on a heavy cross. As meek as an uncomplaining lamb, He died for us in Jerusalem.

'In Jerusalem, Jordan and Galilee, where the good St John baptized his words accorded to Isaiah. When Jesus went towards him, he made this prophecy about Him: "Behold the Lamb of God, firm as a rock, who redeems the heavy sins that all this world has committed. He Himself committed not one, yet He took them all upon Himself. Who shall declare His generation who died for us in Jerusalem?"

'In Jerusalem thus my lemman swete
Twyez for lombe watz taken thare,                    830
By trw recorde of ayther prophete,
For mode so meke and al hys fare.
The thryde tyme is therto ful mete,
In Apokalypez wryten ful yare;
Inmydez the trone, there sayntez sete,               835
The apostel John hym sagh as bare,
Lesande the boke with levez sware
There seven syngnettez wern sette in seme;
And at that syght uche douth con dare
In helle, in erthe, and Jerusalem.                   840

XV

'Thys Jerusalem Lombe hade never pechche
Of other huee bot quyt jolyf
That mot ne masklle moght on streche,
For wolle quyte so ronk and ryf.
Forthy uche saule that hade never teche              845
Is to that Lombe a worthyly wyf;
And thagh uch day a store he feche,
Among uus commez nouther strot ne stryf;
Bot uchon enlé we wolde were fyf –
The mo the myryer, so God me blesse.                 850
In compayny gret our luf con thryf
In honour more and never the lesse.

'Thus in Jerusalem my dear beloved was twice recognized as a Lamb, on the true report of both prophets, on account of His meek nature and His whole disposition. The third occasion, described very clearly in the Apocalypse, accords with these exactly; in the middle of the throne where the saints sat, the apostle John saw Him distinctly, reading the book with thick leaves, on the border of which seven seals were set. And at that sight all the multitudes bowed down, in hell, in earth and in Jerusalem.

XV

'This Lamb of Jerusalem had no mark of any other colour but lovely white on which no spot or stain could rest, because the white fleece was so thick and luxuriant. Therefore each soul that never had a blemish is an honoured wife of that Lamb. And though He brings in a multitude every day, there is neither quarrel nor dispute among us, but we wish each single one of them were five – the more the merrier, God bless me! In a large company our love thrives, greater rather than less in honour.

'Lasse of blysse may non uus bryng
That beren thys perle upon oure bereste,
For thay of mote couthe never mynge, 855
Of spotlez perlez that beren the creste.
Althagh oure corses in clottez clynge,
And ye remen for rauthe wythouten reste,
We thurghoutly haven cnawyng;
Of on dethe ful oure hope is drest. 860
The Lombe uus gladez, oure care is kest;
He myrthez uus alle at uch a mes.
Uchonez blysse is breme and beste,
And never onez honour yet never the les.

'Lest les thou leve my tale farande, 865
In Appocalyppece is wryten in wro:
"I seghe", says John, "the Loumbe hym stande
On the mount of Syon ful thryven and thro,
And wyth hym maydennez an hundrethe thowsande,
And fowre and forty thowsande mo. 870
On alle her forhedez wryten I fande
The Lombez nome, hys Faderez also.
A hue from heven I herde thoo,
Lyk flodez fele laden runnen on resse,
And as thunder throwez in torrez blo, 875
That lote, I leve, watz never the les.

'No one can bring a lessening of bliss to those of us who bear this pearl on our breast, for they that wear the crown of spotless pearls could never think of quarrelling. Although our corpses decay in the earth, and you ceaselessly weep for sorrow, we have transcendent knowledge; our hope is entirely derived from one death. The Lamb makes us happy, our sadness is dispelled, He delights us all at every Mass. Each person's joy is intense and supreme, and no one's honour is any the less.

'Lest you should have less belief in my wonderful story, it is written in a passage of the Apocalypse: "I saw", John says, "the Lamb standing beautiful and glorious on the mount of Sion, and with Him a hundred and forty four thousand maidens. I found written on all their foreheads the name of the Lamb and also of His Father. I heard a voice from heaven, like the noise of many waters rushing in a torrent, and like thunder rolling in the dark hills – no less, I believe, was that sound.

' "Nautheles, thagh hit schowted scharpe,
And ledden loude althagh hit were,
A note ful nwe I herde hem warpe,
To lysten that watz ful lufly dere.                    880
As harporez harpen in her harpe,
That nwe songe thay songen ful cler,
In sounande notez a gentyl carpe;
Ful fayre the modez thay fonge in fere.
Ryght byfore Godez chayere                             885
And the fowre bestez that hym obes
And the aldermen so sadde of chere,
Her songe thay songen never the les.

' "Nowthelese non watz never so quoynt,
For alle the craftez that ever thay knewe,              890
That of that songe myght synge a poynt,
Bot that meyny the Lombe that swe;
For thay arn boght fro the urthe aloynte
As newe fryt to God ful due,
And to the gentyl Lombe hit arn anjoynt,               895
As lyk to hymself of lote and hwe;
For never lesyng ne tale untrwe
Ne towched her tonge for no dysstresse.
That moteles meyny may never remwe
Fro that maskelez mayster, never the les." '           900

' "Nevertheless, though it rang out powerfully, and although it was a loud voice, I heard
them utter a new sound that was very lovely to listen to. Just as harpists play on their
harp, so they sang that new song very clearly, noble words to sonorous notes; they catch
the harmonies together very beautifully. Directly in front of God's throne and the four
creatures that do Him homage and the elders so grave of face, they none the less sang
their song.

' "Nevertheless none, despite all the arts that they ever knew, were ever so skilful that
they might have sung a note of that song, except for the company that follow the Lamb;
for far from the earth they are redeemed, as first fruits due to God, and they are united
to the noble Lamb, resembling Him in behaviour and form. For no lie or untrue word
ever touched their tongue, whatever the inducement. That sinless company may never
in any circumstances be parted from that spotless master." '

'Never the les let be my thonc',
Quod I, 'My perle, thagh I appose;
I schulde not tempte thy wyt so wlonc,
To Krystez chambre that art ichose.
I am bot mokke and mul among,                                905
And thou so ryche a reken rose,
And bydez here by thys blysful bonc
Ther lyvez lyste may never lose.
Now, hynde, that sympelnesse conez enclose,
I wolde the aske a thynge expresse,                          910
And thagh I be bustwys as a bose,
Let my bone vayl neverthelese.

### XVI

'Neverthelese cler I yow bycalle,
If ye con se hyt be to done,
As thou art gloryous wythouten galle,                        915
Wythnay thou never my ruful bone.
Haf ye no wonez in castel-walle,
Ne maner ther ye may mete and won?
Thou tellez me of Jerusalem the ryche ryalle,
Ther David dere watz dyght on trone,                         920
Bot by thyse holtez hit con not hone,
Bot in Judee hit is, that noble note.
As ye ar maskelez under mone,
Your wonez schulde be wythouten mote.

'May my gratitude not be counted less', said I, 'though I question my pearl; I should not test the wisdom of one so gracious as to have been chosen for Christ's bridal chamber. I am merely muck mixed with dust, and you are a rose so fresh and glorious, and you live here by this lovely river-bank where the joy of life can never fail. Now dear one, in whom meekness resides, I wish to ask you a direct question, and though I am loutishly clumsy, let my request nevertheless be granted.

### XVI

'Nevertheless, I ask you frankly, as you are gloriously pure, if you can find a way to grant it, do not deny my piteous request. Have you no dwellings within the castle wall, no mansion where you can meet and live? You speak of Jerusalem the royal kingdom, where noble David was seated on the throne, but it cannot exist by these woods, because that noble place is in Judaea. Since you are entirely spotless, the places you live in should be without a blemish.

'Thys motelez meyny thou conez of mele,                     925
Of thousandez thryght so gret a route;
A gret ceté, for ye arn fele,
Yow byhod have, wythouten doute.
So cumly a pakke of joly juele
Wer evel don schulde lygh theroute,                          930
And by thyse bonkez ther I con gele
I se no bygyng nawhere aboute.
I trowe alone ye lenge and loute
To loke on the glory of thys gracious gote.
If thou hatz other bygyngez stoute,                          935
Now tech me to that myry mote.'


'That mote thou menez in Judy londe',
That specyal spyce then to me spakk,
'That is the cyté that the Lombe con fonde
To soffer inne sor for manez sake,                           940
The olde Jerusalem to understonde;
For there the olde gulte watz don to slake.
Bot the nwe, that lyght of Godez sonde,
The apostel in Apocalyppce in theme con take.
The Lompe ther wythouten spottez blake                       945
Hatz feryed thyder hys fayre flote;
And as hys flok is wythouten flake,
So is hys mote wythouten moote.


'You speak of this unblemished company, such a huge crowd of thousands thronging together; because you are so many you need to have a great city, without a doubt. Such a fine set of lovely jewels would be poorly treated if they had to sleep in the open, and I see no building anywhere around these slopes where I have been. I suppose you linger and stroll alone in order to look at the splendour of this lovely stream. If you have other strong buildings, show me that beautiful city now.'

'The city you mention in the land of Judaea', that precious maiden said to me then, 'that is the city to which the Lamb came to suffer in terribly for mankind's sake, that is to say the old Jerusalem, for there original sin was expiated. But it was the new Jerusalem, which descended at God's ordinance, that the apostle took as his subject in the Apocalypse. The Lamb without a spot of black has taken His fair company there, and as His flock is without a fault, so is His city without blemish.

'Of motes two to carpe clene,
And Jerusalem hyght bothe nawtheles –          950
That nys to yow no more to mene
Bot "ceté of God", other "syght of pes" –
In that on oure pes watz mad at ene;
Wyth payne to suffer the Lombe hit chese.
In that other is noght bot pes to glene          955
That ay schal laste wythouten reles.
That is the borgh that we to pres
Fro that oure flesch be layd to rote,
Ther glory and blysse schal ever encres
To the meyny that is wythouten mote.'          960


'Motelez may so meke and mylde',
Then sayde I to that lufly flor,
'Bryng me to that bygly bylde
And let me se thy blysful bor.'
That schene sayde: 'that God wyl schylde;          965
Thou may not enter wythinne hys tor,
Bot of the Lombe I have the aquylde
For a syght therof thurgh gret favor.
Utwyth to se that clene cloystor
Thou may, bot inwyth not a fote;          970
To strech in the strete thou hatz no vygour,
Bot thou wer clene wythouten mote.

'To speak clearly of the two cities, both even so called Jerusalem – which means no more than "city of God" or "vision of peace" – in the one our peace was established; there the Lamb chose to suffer pain. In the other there is nothing but peace to be had, that will last for ever without end. That is the city we hasten to when our flesh is buried and decays. There glory and bliss will increase for ever for the company that is without blemish.'

'Unblemished maiden so meek and gentle', I said then to that lovely flower, 'take me to that comfortable building and let me see your delightful chamber.' That radiant girl said: 'God will prohibit that; you may not enter His stronghold, but I have had permission from the Lamb for you to have a sight of it through His great favour. You may see that pure enclosure from outside, but you may not step a foot within it. You are not able to stroll in the street unless you are pure and without blemish.

### XVII

'If I this mote the schal unhyde,
Bow up towarde thys bornez heved,
And I anendez the on this syde                                    975
Schal swe, tyl thou to a hil be weved.'
Then wolde I no lenger byde,
Bot lurked by launcez so lufly leved,
Tyl on a hyl that I asspyed
And blusched on the burghe, as I forth dreved,                   980
Byyonde the brok fro me warde keved,
That schyrrer then sunne wyth schaftez schon.
In the Apokalypce is the fasoun preved,
As devysez hit the apostel Jhon.

As John the apostel hit sygh wyth syght,                         985
I syghe that cyty of gret renoun,
Jerusalem so nwe and ryally dyght,
As hit was lyght fro the heven adoun.
The borgh watz al of brende golde bryght
As glemande glas burnist broun,                                  990
Wyth gentyl gemmez anunder pyght,
Wyth bantelez twelve on basyng boun,
The foundementez twelve of riche tenoun;
Uch tabelment watz a serlypez ston;
As derely devysez this ilk toun                                  995
In Apocalyppez the apostel John.

### XVII

'If I am to reveal this city to you, walk up towards the source of this river, and I shall follow opposite you on this side till you come to a hill.' Then I had no intention of delaying longer, but stooped under branches beautifully covered with leaves, until from a hill I saw the city, and studied it as I moved forward. It had come down from God across the brook from me, and shone with beams brighter than the sun. Its shape is given in the Apocalypse, as the apostle John describes it.

Just as the apostle John saw it with his own eyes, so I saw that city of great splendour, Jerusalem so new and gloriously adorned, exactly as it was set down from heaven. The city was all of pure bright gold, burnished brilliantly like shining glass, with noble gems set below, and with twelve tiers fixed at the base, these twelve foundations elaborately joined together. Each coursing consisted of a single stone; just so the apostle John splendidly describes this city in the Apocalypse.

As John thise stonez in writ con nemme,
I knew the name after his tale:
Jasper hyght the fyrst gemme
That I on the fyrst basse con wale:                    1000
He glente grene in the lowest hemme;
Saffer helde the secounde stale;
The calsydoyne thenne wythouten wemme
In the thryd table con purly pale;
The emerade the furthe so grene of scale;             1005
The sardonyse the fyfthe ston;
The sexte the rybé he con hit wale
In the Apocalyppce, the apostel John.

Yet joyned John the crysolyt
The seventhe gemme in fundament;                      1010
The aghthe the beryl cler and quyt;
The topasye twynne-hew the nente endent;
The crysopase the tenthe is tyght;
The jacynght the enleventhe gent;
The twelfthe, the gentyleste in uch a plyt,           1015
The amatyst purpre wyth ynde blente;
The wal abof the bantels bent
O jasporye, as glas that glysnande schon;
I knew hit by his devysement
In the Apocalyppez, the apostel John.                 1020

As John identified these stones in the Bible, I knew the name according to his account. The first gem that I picked out on the first foundation was called jasper, which shone green in the lowest tier. The sapphire occupied the second step; then the chalcedony without flaw glimmered clearly in the third level. The fourth was the emerald with a surface so green, the fifth stone was sardonyx, the sixth the ruby, as the apostle John pointed out in the Apocalypse.

In addition John listed the chrysolite, the seventh stone in the foundation; the eighth is the clear white beryl; the ninth set in is the two-coloured topaz, the tenth fixed there is the chrysoprase, the eleventh fine stone is the jacinth; the twelfth, the finest against every evil, is the amethyst of purple mixed with blue. The wall set above the tiers was of jasper that shone like gleaming glass. I recognized it by the description of the apostle John in the Apocalypse.

As John devysed yet sagh I thare
Thise twelve degres wern brode and stayre;
The cyté stod abof ful sware,
As longe as brode as hyghe ful fayre;
The stretez of golde as glasse al bare,     1025
The wal of jasper that glent as glayre;
The wonez wythinne enurned ware
Wyth alle kynnez perré that moght repayre.
Thenne helde uch sware of this manayre
Twelve forlonge space, er ever hit fon,     1030
Of heght, of brede, of lenthe to cayre,
For meten hit sygh the apostel John.

### XVIII

As John hym wrytez yet more I syghe:
Uch pane of that place had thre yatez;
So twelve in poursent I con asspye,     1035
The portalez pyked of rych platez,
And uch yate of a margyrye,
A parfyt perle that never fatez.
Uchon in scrypture a name con plye
Of Israel barnez, folewande her datez,     1040
That is to say, as her byrth-whatez:
The aldest ay fyrst theron watz done.
Such lyght ther lemed in alle the stratez
Hem nedde nawther sunne ne mone.

As John described it I also saw there that these twelve steps were broad and steep, and above stood the city absolutely square, precisely as long as it was broad as it was high. The streets of gold were like lustrous glass, and the wall of jasper glistened like albumen. The dwellings within were adorned with every kind of jewel that might be assembled. Each square side of this city extended a distance of twelve furlongs from end to end, stretching out in height, width and length, for the apostle John saw it measured.

### XVIII

I saw still more as John describes it: each side of that place had three gates, so that I saw twelve in the surrounding wall, the gateways fitted with magnificent metal plates, and each gate made of a margarite, a perfect pearl that never dims. Each one bore in writing a name of one of the children of Israel, following their dates, that is to say in order of their birth: the eldest was put on first. Such a light shone there in all the streets that there was no need for either sun or moon.

Of sunne ne mone had thay no nede;                    1045
The self God watz her lombe-lyght,
The Lombe her lantyrne, wythouten drede;
Thurgh hym blysned the borgh al bryght.
Thurgh woghe and won my lokyng yede,
For sotyle cler noght lette no lyght.                 1050
The hyghe trone ther moght ye hede
Wyth alle the apparaylmente umbepyghte,
As John the appostel in termez tyghte;
The hyghe Godez self hit set upone.
A rever of the trone ther ran outryghte              1055
Watz bryghter then bothe the sunne and mone.

Sunne ne mone schon never so swete
As that foysoun flode out of that flet;
Swythe hit swange thurgh uch a strete
Wythouten fylthe other galle other glet.             1060
Kyrk therinne watz non yete,
Chapel ne temple that ever watz set;
The Almyghty watz her mynster mete,
The Lombe the sakerfyse ther to refet.
The yatez stoken watz never yet,                     1065
Bot evermore upen at uche a lone;
Ther entrez non to take reset
That berez any spot anunder mone.

They had no need of sun nor moon; God Himself was their lamp-light, the Lamb was indeed their lantern; through Him the city shone brightly. My gaze penetrated wall and house, for their transparent clarity did not obstruct the light. You could see there the high throne with all its trappings arranged round it, as the apostle John set down in writing; the High God Himself was seated on it. Directly from the throne there flowed out a river brighter than both the sun and moon.

Sun and moon never shone as sweetly as did that abundant river flowing out of that floor. Without dirt, impurity or slime, it poured rapidly through every street. There was no church, chapel or temple ever yet built in there; the Almighty was their noble temple, the Lamb was the sacrifice to nourish them there. The gates had never been shut, but were always open at every street. No one at all who carries any blemish enters there to take shelter.

The mone may therof acroche no myghte;
To spotty ho is, of body to grym,                    1070
And also ther ne is never nyght.
What schulde the mone ther compas clym
And to even wyth that worthly lyght
That schynez upon the brokez brym?
The planetez arn in to pouer a plyght,               1075
And the self sunne ful fer to dym.
Aboute that water arn tres ful schym,
That twelve frytez of lyf con bere ful sone;
Twelve sythez on yer thay beren ful frym,
And renowlez nwe in uche a mone.                     1080


Anunder mone so great merwayle
No fleschly hert ne myght endeure,
As quen I blusched upon that baly,
So ferly therof watz the fasure.
I stod as stylle as dased quayle                     1085
For ferly of that frech fygure,
That felde I nawther reste ne travayle,
So watz I ravyste wyth glymme pure.
For I dar say wyth conciens sure,
Hade bodyly burne abiden that bone,                  1090
Thagh alle clerkez hym hade in cure,
His lyf were loste anunder mone.


The moon can derive no radiance from there; she is too blemished and ugly in appearance, and also it is never night there. Why should the moon ascend in her orbit there to compete with that glorious light that shines upon the water's edge? The planets are in too weak a condition, and the sun itself far too dim. Around the water are the bright trees that readily bear twelve fruits of life; twelve times a year they bear abundantly, and renew themselves again every month.

On earth no heart of flesh could stand up to such a great marvel as I saw when I looked on that city, so ravishing was its appearance. I stood as still as a dazed quail, in amazement at that lovely sight, so that I felt neither rest nor exertion, I was so enraptured by pure radiance. I can say with absolute conviction, if a man in the flesh had experienced that favour, his life on earth would have been lost, even though all the wise men had him in their care.

## XIX

Ryght as the maynful mone con rys
Er thenne the day-glem dryve al doun,
So sodanly on a wonder wyse          1095
I watz war of a prosessyoun.
This noble cité of ryche enpryse
Watz sodanly ful wythouten sommoun
Of such vergynez in the same gyse
That watz my blysful anunder croun;          1100
And coronde wern alle of the same fasoun,
Depaynt in perlez and wedez qwyte;
In vchonez breste watz bounden boun
The blysful perle wyth gret delyt.

Wyth gret delyt thay glod in fere          1105
On golden gatez that glent as glasse;
Hundreth thowsandez I wot ther were,
And alle in sute her livrez wasse;
Tor to knaw the gladdest chere.
The Lombe byfore con proudly passe          1110
Wyth hornez seven of red golde cler;
As praysed perlez his wedez wasse.
Towarde the throne thay trone a tras.
Thagh thay wern fele, no pres in plyt,
Bot mylde as maydenez seme at mas,          1115
So drogh thay forth wyth gret delyt.

## XIX

Just as the mighty moon rises before the light of day entirely fades, just so I was suddenly and strangely aware of a procession. This noble city of glorious splendour was suddenly and spontaneously full of virgins dressed in the same clothes as my lovely girl with her crown. And all were crowned in the same fashion, adorned in pearls and white robes; on each one's breast was securely fastened the blessed and delightful pearl.

With great delight they proceeded together on golden streets that shone like glass. I know there were hundreds of thousands, and their garments were all matching; it was hard to tell the happiest face. The Lamb with seven horns of bright red gold proudly went before them; His clothes were like precious pearls. They made their way towards the throne. Though they were many, there was no crowding together, but as gently as decorous maidens at Mass they advanced with great delight.

Delyt that hys come encroched
To much hit were of for to melle.
Thise aldermen quen he aproched,
Grovelyng to his fete thay felle.                          1120
Legyounes of aungelez togeder voched
Ther kesten ensens of swete smelle.
Then glory and gle watz nwe abroched;
Al songe to love that gay juelle.
The steven moght stryke thurgh the urthe to helle      1125
That the vertues of heven of joye endyte.
To love the Lombe his meyny in melle
Iwysse I laght a gret delyt.

Delit the Lombe for to devise
Wyth much mervayle in mynde went.                       1130
Best watz he, blythest, and moste to pryse,
That ever I herde of speche spent;
So worthly whyt wern wedez hys,
His lokez symple, hymself so gent.
Bot a wounde ful wyde and weete con wyse               1135
Anende hys hert, thurgh hyde to-rente.
Of his quyte syde his blod outsprent.
Alas, thoght I, who did that spyt?
Ani breste for bale aght haf forbrent
Er he therto hade had delyt.                            1140

The delight that His coming brought would be too great to describe. When He approached the elders, they fell prostrate at His feet. Legions of angels summoned together scattered sweet-smelling incense there. Then glory and joy were celebrated anew; all sang in worship of that lovely Jewel. The sound that the heavenly angels joyfully sang could have passed through the earth as far as hell. Indeed I felt a great desire to praise the Lamb in the midst of His retinue.

Delight at gazing upon the Lamb filled my mind with great wonder. He was the best, most admirable and most excellent that ever I heard spoken of; His clothes were so wonderfully white, His expression without pride, He Himself so gracious; but a wound open and bleeding was visible near His heart, torn through His skin. His blood gushed out of His white side. Alas, I thought, who inflicted that cruelty? Any heart should have burnt up for sorrow before it delighted in that.

The Lombe delyt non lyste to wene.
Thagh he were hurt and wounde hade,
In his sembelaunt watz never sene,
So wern his glentez gloryous glade.
I loked among his meyny schene                    1145
How thay wyth lyf wern laste and lade;
Then sagh I ther my lyttel quene
That I wende had standen by me in sclade.
Lorde, much of mirthe watz that ho made
Among her ferez that watz so quyt!               1150
That syght me gart to thenk to wade
For luf-longyng in gret delyt.

### xx

Delyt me drof in yghe and ere,
My manez mynde to maddyng malte;
Quen I segh my frely, I wolde be there,          1155
Byyonde the water thagh ho were walte.
I thoght that nothyng myght me dere
To fech me bur and take me halte,
And to start in the strem schulde non me stere,
To swymme the remnaunt, thagh I ther swalte.     1160
Bot of that munt I watz bitalt;
When I schulde start in the strem astraye,
Out of that caste I watz bycalt:
Hit watz not at my Pryncez paye.

No one would have wanted to doubt the Lamb's delight. Though He was hurt and wounded, it was never seen in His expression, so gloriously happy was His countenance. I observed how those among His lovely retinue were brimming with life; then I saw my little queen there that I had thought was standing by me in the valley. Lord, how much she rejoiced among her companions, she who was so white! Such was my longing desire that the sight made me think of wading over in my great delight.

### xx

Delight invaded my eye and ear, and my human mind dissolved into madness; when I saw my lovely one I wanted to be there, though she was across the water. I thought nothing could harm me by striking me a blow and taking hold of me, and no one would restrain me from plunging into the stream and swimming the rest of the way, even if I died there. But I was shaken out of that intention. When I was about to rush misguidedly into the river, I was checked in the attempt: it did not please my Prince.

Hit payed hym not that I so flonc 1165
Over mervelous merez, so mad arayde.
Of raas thagh I were rasch and ronk,
Yet rapely therinne I watz restayed,
For, ryght as I sparred unto the bonc,
That braththe out of my drem me brayde. 1170
Then wakned I in that erber wlonk;
My hede upon that hylle watz layde
Ther as my perle to grounde strayd.
I raxled, and fel in gret affray,
And, sykyng, to myself I sayd, 1175
'Now al be to that Pryncez paye'.


Me payed ful ille to be outfleme
So sodenly of that fayre regioun,
Fro alle tho syghtez so quyke and queme.
A longeyng hevy me strok in swone, 1180
And rewfully thenne I con to reme:
'O perle', quod I, 'of rych renoun,
So watz hit me dere that thou con deme
In thys veray avysyoun!
If hit be veray and soth sermoun 1185
That thou so stykez in garlande gay,
So wel is me in thys doel-doungoun
That thou art to that Prynsez paye.'


It did not please Him that I should fling myself so madly over the marvellous waters. Though I was eager and impetuous to plunge in, I was quickly restrained from that, for as I rushed to the bank, my violence roused me from my dream. Then I awoke in that beautiful garden; my head was laid on that mound where my pearl fell to earth. I stretched, and was seized with dismay, and sighing I said to myself, 'Now may everything be as that Prince pleases.'

It pleased me very little to be banished so suddenly from that lovely country, from all those sights so vivid and delightful. A deep sorrow seized me, and then I sadly cried out: 'O pearl of great glory', I said, 'what you taught in this true vision was very precious to me. If it is really true that you remain like that in your bright crown, then in this dungeon of sorrow I am happy that you are pleasing to that Prince.'

To that Pryncez paye hade I ay bente,
And yerned no more then watz me geven,     1190
And halden me ther in trwe entent,
As the perle me prayed that watz so thryven,
As helde, drawen to Goddez present,
To mo of his mysterys I hade ben dryven;
Bot ay wolde man of happe more hente     1195
Then moghte by ryght upon hem clyven.
Therfore my joye watz sone to-riven,
And I kaste of kythez that lastez aye.
Lorde, mad hit arn that agayn the stryven,
Other proferen the oght agayn thy paye.     1200

To pay the Prince other sete saghte
Hit is ful ethe to the god Krystyin,
For I haf founden hym, bothe day and naghte,
A God, a Lorde, a frende ful fyin.
Over this hyul this lote I laghte,     1205
For pyty of my perle enclyin,
And sythen to God I hit bytaghte
In Krystez dere blessyng and myn,
That in the forme of bred and wyn
The preste uus schewez uch a daye.     1210
He gef uus to be his homly hyne
Ande precious perlez unto his pay.


Amen.    Amen.


If I had always submitted to what was pleasing to that Prince, wanted no more than I was given, and kept myself to that with true resolve, as the pearl that was so lovely had asked me, quite probably, led into God's presence, I should have been admitted to more of His mysteries. But a man always wants to seize more good fortune than belongs to him by right. Therefore my joy was shattered at once, and I was cast out of eternal regions. Lord they are mad who struggle against You or propose anything that is not pleasing to You.

To please the Prince or to be reconciled is very easy for the good Christian, for I have found Him, both day and night, a God, a Lord, an excellent friend. On this mound I had this adventure, bowed down with sorrow for my pearl, which I afterwards entrusted to God, with my blessing and the precious blessings of Christ, whom the priest shows us every day in the form of bread and wine. May He grant us to be servants in His household and precious pearls to please Him. Amen.

# JOHN GOWER: *TEREUS AND PROCNE*

John Gower (1330–1408), a Kentishman and a Londoner, was a friend of Chaucer and a dedicatee of *Troilus and Criseyde*. He wrote three major works, the first in French (*Mirour de l'omme*), the second in Latin (*Vox clamantis*), and the last, the *Confessio Amantis*, in English. The text here is from a manuscript of Gower's final version of 1393, Bodleian MS. Fairfax 3, which is edited by G. C. Macaulay, *The Works of John Gower* (Oxford, 1899–1902). The tale of Tereus and Procne, adapted from Ovid, is related as an example of the sin of 'ravine' (i.e. rapine or rape), a branch of avarice. It is taken from *Confessio Amantis*, Book 5, 5551–6047.

> Ther was a real[1] noble king,
> And riche of alle worldes thing,
> Which of his propre[2] enheritance
> Athenes hadde in governance,
> And who so thenke therupon,　　　　　　　　　　5555
> His name was king Pandion.
> Tuo douhtres hadde he be his wif,
> The whiche he lovede as his lif;
> The ferste douhter Progne hihte[3],
> And the secounde, as sche wel mihte,　　　　　　5560
> Was cleped[4] faire Philomene,
> To whom fell after mochel tene[5].
> The fader of his pourveance[6]
> His doughter Progne wolde avance,
> And yaf[7] hire unto mariage　　　　　　　　　　5565
> A worthi king of hih lignage,
> A noble kniht eke[8] of his hond,
> So was he kid[9] in every lond,
> Of Trace he hihte Tereus;
> The clerk Ovide telleth thus.　　　　　　　　　　5570
> This Tereus his wif hom ladde[10];

1. royal, 2. own, 3. was called, 4. named, 5. much sorrow, 6. The father to provide for the future, 7. gave, 8. also, 9. known, 10. took home.

A lusti lif with hire he hadde;
Til it befell upon a tyde,
This Progne, as sche lay him besyde,
Bethoughte hir hou it mihte be                                 5575
That sche hir soster myhte se,
And to hir lord hir will sche seide,
With goodly wordes and him preide
That sche to hire mihte go:
And if it liked him noght so,                                  5580
That thanne he wolde himselve wende,
Or elles be[1] som other sende,
Which mihte hire diere soster griete,
And schape[2] hou that thei mihten miete.
Hir lord anon to that he herde                                 5585
Yaf his acord[3], and thus ansuerde:
'I wole,' he seide, 'for thi sake
The weie after thi soster take
Miself, and bringe hire, if I may.'
And sche with that, there as he lay,                           5590
Began him in hire armes clippe[4],
And kist him with hir softe lippe,
And seide, 'Sire, grant mercy.'
And he sone after was redy,
And tok his leve for to go;                                    5595
In sori time dede he so.
    This Tereus goth forth to schipe
With him and with his felaschipe;
Be see the rihte cours he nam[5],
Into the contre til he cam,                                    5600
Wher Philomene was duellinge,
And of hir soster the tidinge
He tolde, and tho[6] thei weren glade,
And mochel joie of him thei made.
The fader and the moder bothe                                  5605
To leve here douhter weren lothe,
Bot if[7] thei weren in presence[8];

1. by, 2. arrange, 3. Gave his agreement, 4. embrace, 5. took, 6. then, 7. Unless, 8. attendance.

And natheles at reverence[1]
Of him, that wolde himself travaile[2],
Thei wolden noght he scholde faile                    5610
Of that he preide, and yive hire leve:
And sche, that wolde noght beleve[3],
In alle haste made hire yare[4]
Toward hir soster for to fare,
With Tereus and forth sche wente.                     5615
And he with al his hole entente[5],
Whan sche was fro hir frendes go,
Assoteth[6] of hire love so,
His yhe[7] myhte he noght withholde,
That he ne moste on hir beholde[8];                   5620
And with the sihte he gan desire,
And sette his oghne[9] herte on fyre;
And fyr, whan it to tow aprocheth,
To him anon the strengthe acrocheth[10],
Til with his hete it be devoured,                     5625
The tow ne mai noght be socoured.
And so that tirant raviner[11],
Whan that sche was in his pouer,
And he therto sawh time and place,
As he that lost hath alle grace,                      5630
Foryat[12] he was a wedded man,
And in a rage on hire he ran,
Riht as a wolf which takth his preie.
And sche began to crie and preie,
'O fader, o mi moder diere,                           5635
Nou help!' Bot thei ne mihte it hiere,
And sche was of to litel myht
Defense ayein so ruide a knyht
To make, whanne he was so wod[13]
That he no reson understod,                           5640
Bot hield hire under in such wise,
That sche ne myhte noght arise,

---

1. And nevertheless out of respect, 2. trouble, 3. stay, 4. ready, 5. And he whole-heartedly, 6. Becomes infatuated, 7. eye, 8. To avoid looking at her, 9. own, 10. is drawn, 11. ravisher, 12. Forgot, 13. mad.

Bot lay oppressed and desesed[1],
As if a goshauk hadde sesed
A brid, which dorste noght for fere      5645
Remue[2]: and thus this tirant there
Beraft[3] hire such thing as men sein
Mai neveremor be yolde ayein[4],
And that was the virginité:
Of such ravine[5] it was pité.      5650
    Bot whan sche to hirselven com,
And of hir meschief hiede nom[6],
And knew hou that sche was no maide,
With wofull herte thus sche saide:
'O thou of alle men the worste,      5655
Wher was ther evere man that dorste
Do such a dede as thou hast do?
That dai schal falle, I hope so,
That I schal telle out al mi fille,
And with mi speche I schal fulfille[7]      5660
The wyde world in brede[8] and lengthe.
That thou hast do to me be strengthe,
If I among the poeple duelle,
Unto the poeple I schal it telle;
And if I be withinne wall      5665
Of stones closed, thanne I schal
Unto the stones clepe[9] and crie,
And tellen hem thi felonie;
And if I to the wodes wende,
Ther schal I tellen tale and ende[10],      5670
And crie it to the briddes oute,
That thei schul hiere it al aboute.
For I so loude it schal reherce,
That my vois schal the hevene perce,
That it schal soune in Goddes ere.      5675
Ha, false man, where is thi fere?
O mor cruel than eny beste,

1. molested, 2. Move, 3. Took from, 4. given back, 5. rape, 6. took heed, 7. fill, 8. breadth, 9. call out, 10. the whole story.

Hou hast thou holden thi beheste
Which thou unto my soster madest?
O thou, which alle love ungladest[1],　　　　　　5680
And art ensample of alle untrewe,
Nou wolde God mi soster knewe,
Of thin untrouthe, hou that it stod!'
And he than as a lyon wod
With hise unhappi[2] handes stronge　　　　　　5685
Hire cauhte be the tresses longe,
With whiche he bond ther bothe hire armes,
That was a fieble dede of armes,
And to the grounde anon hire caste,
And out he clippeth also faste　　　　　　5690
Hire tunge with a peire scheres.
So what with blod and what with teres
Out of hire yhe and of hir mouth,
He made hire faire face uncouth[3]:
Sche lay swounende unto the deth[4],　　　　　　5695
Ther was unethes[5] eny breth;
Bot yit whan he hire tunge refte,
A litel part therof belefte[6],
Bot sche withal no word mai soune[7],
Bot chitre and as a brid jargoune[8].　　　　　　5700
And natheles that wode hound
Hir bodi hent[9] up fro the ground,
And sente hir there as be his wille[10]
Sche scholde abyde in prison stille
For everemo; bot nou tak hiede　　　　　　5705
What after fell of this misdede.
　　Whanne al this meschief was befalle,
This Tereus, that foule him falle[11],
Unto his contre hom he tyh[12];
And whan he com his paleis nyh,　　　　　　5710
His wif al redi there him kepte[13].
Whan he hir sih, anon he wepte,

1. makes miserable, 2. bringing disaster, 3. unrecognizable, 4. She lay in a dead swoon,
5. scarcely, 6. remained, 7. utter, 8. Except twitter and warble like a bird, 9. lifted, 10.
where at his command, 11. whom may evil overtake, 12. went, 13. awaited.

And that he dede for deceite,
For sche began to axe[1] him streite,
'Wher is mi soster?' And he seide 5715
That sche was ded; and Progne abreide[2],
As sche that was a wofull wif,
And stod betuen hire deth and lif[3],
Of that sche herde such tidinge;
Bot for sche sih hire lord wepinge, 5720
She wende[4] noght bot alle trouthe,
And hadde wel the more routhe.
The perles weren tho forsake[5]
To hire, and blake clothes take;
As sche that was gentil and kinde, 5725
In worschipe of hir sostres mynde
Sche made a riche enterement,
For sche fond non amendement[6]
To syghen or to sobbe more:
So was ther guile under the gore[7]. 5730
   Nou leve we this king and queene,
And torne ayein to Philomene,
As I began to tellen erst[8].
Whan sche cam into prison ferst,
It thoghte[9] a kinges douhter strange 5735
To maken so soudein a change
Fro welthe unto so grete a wo;
And sche began to thenke tho,
Thogh sche be mouthe nothing preide,
Withinne hir herte thus sche seide: 5740
'O thou, almyhty Jupiter,
That hihe sist[10] and lokest fer,
Thou soffrest[11] many a wrong doinge,
And yit it is noght thi willinge.
To thee ther mai nothing ben hid, 5745
Thou wost hou it is me betid:
I wolde I hadde noght be bore[12],
For thanne I hadde noght forlore[13]

---

1. ask, 2. cried out, 3. And was on the point of death, 4. thought, 5. abandoned, 6. relief, 7. hidden deceit, 8. first, 9. seemed to, 10. sittest, 11. allowest, 12. born, 13. lost.

Mi speche and mi virginite.
Bot, goode lord, al is in thee, 5750
Whan thou therof wolt do vengance
And schape[1] mi deliverance.'
And evere among[2] this ladi wepte,
And thoghte that sche nevere kepte[3]
To ben a worldes womman more, 5755
And that sche wissheth everemore.
Bot ofte unto hir soster diere
Hire herte spekth in this manere,
And seide, 'Ha, soster, if ye knewe
Of myn astat[4], ye wolde rewe[5], 5760
I trowe, and my deliverance
Ye wolde schape, and do vengance
On him that is so fals a man.
And natheles, so as I can,
I wol you sende som tokninge[6], 5765
Wherof ye schul have knowlechinge
Of thing I wot, that schal you lothe[7],
The which you toucheth and me bothe.'
And þho withinne a whyle als tyt[8]
Sche waf[9] a cloth of selk al whyt 5770
With lettres and ymagerie[10],
In which was al the felonie
Which Tereus to hire hath do;
And lappede[11] it togedre tho
And sette hir signet therupon 5775
And sende it unto Progne anon.
The messager which forth it bar,
What it amonteth[12] is noght war;
And natheles to Progne he goth
And prively takth hire the cloth, 5780
And wente ayein riht as he cam,
The court of him non hiede nam[13].
   Whan Progne of Philomene herde,
Sche wolde knowe hou that it ferde,

1. arrange, 2. again and again, 3. wished, 4. condition, 5. be sorry, 6. sign, 7. be hateful to, 8. quickly, 9. wove, 10. pictures, 11. folded, 12. signifies, 13. took no notice.

And opneth that the man hath broght,                     5785
And wot therby what hath be wroght
And what meschief ther is befalle.
In swoune tho sche gan doun falle,
And efte[1] aros and gan to stonde,
And eft sche takth the cloth on honde,                   5790
Behield the lettres and th'ymages[2];
Bot ate laste, 'Of suche oultrages[3],'
Sche seith, 'wepinge is noght the bote[4].'
And swerth[5], if that sche live mote[6],
It schal be venged otherwise.                            5795
And with that sche gan hire avise[7]
Hou ferst sche mihte unto hire winne
Hir soster, that no man withinne,
Bot only thei that were suore[8],
It scholde knowe, and schop[9] therfore                  5800
That Tereus nothing it wiste[10];
And yit riht as hirselven liste[11],
Hir soster was delivered sone[12]
Out of prison, and be the mone
To Progne sche was broght be nyhte.                      5805
      Whan ech of other hadde a sihte,
In chambre ther thei were alone,
Thei maden many a pitous mone;
Bot Progne most of sorwe made,
Which sihe[13] hir soster pale and fade                  5810
And specheles and deshonoured,
Of that sche hadde be defloured;
And ek upon hir lord sche thoghte,
Of that he so untreuly wroghte
And hadde his espousaile broke.                          5815
Sche makth a vou it schal be wroke[14],
And with that word sche kneleth doun
Wepinge in gret devocioun;
Unto Cupide and to Venus

1. next, 2. the pictures, 3. offences, 4. remedy, 5. swears, 6. might, 7. began to consider, 8. sworn to secrecy, 9. arranged, 10. should know of, 11. she wanted, 12. at once, 13. Who saw, 14. avenged.

Sche preide, and seide thanne thus:        5820
'O ye, to whom nothing asterte[1]
Of love mai, for every herte
Ye knowe, as ye that ben above
The god and the goddesse of love;
Ye witen[2] wel that evere yit        5825
With al mi will and al my wit,
Sith[3] ferst ye schopen[4] me to wedde,
That I lay with mi lord abedde,
I have be trewe in mi degre,
And evere thoghte for to be,        5830
And nevere love in other place,
Bot al only the king of Trace,
Which is mi lord and I his wif.
Bot nou allas this wofull strif!
That I him thus ayeinward[5] finde        5835
The most untrewe and most unkinde
That evere in ladi armes lay.
And wel I wot that he ne may
Amende his wrong, it is so gret;
For he to lytel of me let[6],        5840
Whan he myn oughne soster tok,
And me that am his wif forsok.'

   Lo, thus to Venus and Cupide
Sche preide, and furthermor sche cride
Unto Appollo the hiheste,        5845
And seide, 'O myghti god of reste,
Thou do vengance of this debat[7].
Mi soster and al hire astat
Thou wost[8], and hou sche hath forlore
Hir maidenhod, and I therfore        5850
In al the world schal bere a blame
Of that mi soster hath a schame,
That Tereus to hire I sente;
And wel thou wost that myn entente
Was al for worschipe[9] and for goode.        5855

1. escape, 2. know, 3. Since, 4. arranged for, 5. in return, 6. thought, 7. conflict, 8. knowest, 9. honour.

O lord, that yifst the lives fode
To every wyht, I prei thee hiere
Thes wofull sostres that ben hiere,
And let ous noght to the ben lothe;
We ben thin oghne wommen bothe.'              5860
    Thus pleigneth[1] Progne and axeth wreche[2],
And thogh hire soster lacke speche,
To him that alle thinges wot
Hire sorwe is noght the lasse hot;
Bot he that thanne had herd hem tuo,          5865
Him oughte have sorwed everemo
For sorwe which was hem betuene.
With signes pleigneth Philomene,
And Progne seith, 'It schal be wreke[3],
That al the world therof schal speke.'        5870
And Progne tho seknesse feigneth,
Whereof unto hir lord sche pleigneth,
And preith sche moste hire chambres kepe,
And as hir liketh[4] wake and slepe.
And he hire granteth to be so;                5875
And thus togedre ben thei tuo,
That wolde[5] him bot a litel good.
Nou herk hierafter hou it stod
Of wofull auntres[6] that befelle:
Thes sostres, that ben bothe felle[7] –       5880
And that was noght on hem along[8],
Bot onliche on the grete wrong
Which Tereus hem hadde do, –
Thei schopen for to venge hem tho.
    This Tereus be Progne his wif           5885
A sone hath, which as his lif
He loveth, and Ithis he hihte:
His moder wiste wel sche mihte
Do Tereus no more grief
Than sle this child, which was so lief[9].     5890
Thus sche, that was, as who seith[10], mad

1. complains, 2. vengeance, 3. avenged, 4. it suited her, 5. intended towards, 6. deeds, 7. ruthless, 8. attributable to them, 9. dear, 10. so to say.

Of wo, which hath hir overlad[1],
Withoute insihte of moderhede[2]
Foryat pité and loste drede,
And in hir chambre prively                               5895
This child withouten noise or cry
Sche slou, and hieu him al to pieces:
And after with diverse spieces
The fleissh, whan it was so to-heewe[3],
Sche takth, and makth therof a sewe[4],              5900
With which the fader at his mete[5]
Was served, til he hadde him ete;
That he ne wiste hou that it stod,
Bot thus his oughne fleissh and blod
Himself devoureth ayein kinde[6],                       5905
As he that was tofore unkinde[7].
And thanne, er that he were arise[8],
For that he scholde ben agrise[9],
To schewen him the child was ded,
This Philomene tok the hed                             5910
Betwen tuo disshes, and al wrothe
Tho comen forth the sostres bothe,
And setten it upon the bord.
And Progne tho began the word,
And seide, 'O werste of alle wicke[10],               5915
Of conscience whom no pricke
Mai stere[11], lo, what thou hast do!
Lo, hier be nou we sostres tuo;
O raviner, lo hier thi preie,
With whom so falsliche on the weie                    5920
Thou hast thi tirannye wroght.
Lo, nou it is somdel aboght[12],
And bet[13] it schal, for of thi dede
The world schal evere singe and rede
In remenbrance of thi defame[14];                     5925
For thou to love hast do such schame,

---

1. overcome, 2. Without maternal feelings, 3. chopped up, 4. stew, 5. meal, 6. unnaturally, 7. previously wicked, 8. before he had got up, 9. So as to horrify him, 10. evildoers, 11. move, 12. partly expiated, 13. be better, 14. dishonour.

That it schal nevere be foryete.'
With that he sterte up fro the mete,
And schof the bord unto the flor,
And cauhte a swerd anon and suor                    5930
That thei scholde of his handes dye.
And thei unto the goddes crie
Begunne with so loude a stevene[1],
That thei were herd unto the hevene;
And in a twinclinge of an yhe                        5935
The goddes, that the meschief syhe,
Here[2] formes changen alle thre.
Echon of hem in his degre
Was torned into briddes kinde[3];
Diverseliche, as men mai finde,                      5940
After th'astat[4] that thei were inne,
Here formes were set atwinne[5],
And as it telleth in the tale,
The ferst into a nyhtingale
Was schape, and that was Philomene,                  5945
Which in the wynter is noght sene,
For thanne ben the leves falle
And naked ben the buisshes alle.
For after that sche was a brid,
Hir will was evere to ben hid,                       5950
And for to duelle in privé place,
That no man scholde sen hir face
For schame, which mai noght be lassed[6],
Of thing that was tofore passed,
Whan that sche loste hir maidenhiede.                5955
For evere upon hir wommanhiede,
Thogh that the goddes wolde hire change,
Sche thenkth, and is the more strange[7],
And halt hir clos[8] the wyntres day.
Bot whan the wynter goth away,                       5960
And that Nature the goddesse
Wole of hir oughne fre largesse

---

1. voice, 2. Their, 3. bird's form, 4. According to the condition, 5. differentiated, 6. lessened, 7. timid, 8. keeps hidden.

With herbes and with floures bothe
The feldes and the medwes clothe,
And ek the wodes and the greves                       5965
Ben heled[1] al with grene leves,
So that a brid hire hyde mai,
Betwen Averil and March and Maii,
Sche that the wynter hield hir clos[2]
For pure schame, and noght aros,                      5970
Whan that sche seth the bowes thikke,
And that ther is no bare sticke,
Bot al is hid with leves grene,
To wode comth this Philomene
And makth hir ferste yeres flyht;                     5975
Wher as sche singeth day and nyht,
And in hir song al openly
Sche makth hir pleignte and seith, 'O why,
O why ne were I yit a maide?'
For so these olde wise saide,                         5980
Which understoden what sche mente,
Hire notes ben of such entente.
And ek thei seide hou in hir song
Sche makth gret joie and merthe among[3],
And seith, 'Ha, nou I am a brid,                      5985
Ha, nou mi face mai ben hid.
Thogh I have lost mi maidenhede,
Schal no man se my chekes rede.'
Thus medleth[4] sche with joie wo
And with hir sorwe merthe also,                       5990
So that of loves maladie
Sche makth diverse melodie,
And seith love is a wofull blisse,
A wisdom which can no man wisse[5],
A lusti[6] fievere, a wounde softe:                   5995
This note sche reherceth ofte
To hem whiche understonde hir tale.
Nou have I of this nyhtingale,

1. covered, 2. She who kept hidden in winter, 3. at times, 4. intersperses, 5. inform, 6. vigorous.

Which erst was cleped[1] Philomene,
Told al that evere I wolde mene[2],     6000
Bothe of hir forme and of hir note,
Wherof men mai the storie note.

    And of hir soster Progne I finde,
Hou sche was torned out of kinde
Into a swalwe swift of winge,     6005
Which ek in wynter lith swounynge[3],
Ther as[4] sche mai nothing be sene.
Bot whan the world is woxe[5] grene
And comen is the somertide,
Than fleth sche forth and ginth[6] to chide,     6010
And chitreth out in hir langage
What falshod is in mariage,
And telleth in a maner speche
Of Tereus the spousebreche[7].
Sche wol noght in the wodes duelle,     6015
For sche wolde openliche telle;
And ek for that sche was a spouse,
Among the folk sche comth to house,
To do thes wyves understonde
The falshod of here[8] housebonde,     6020
That thei of hem be war also,
For ther ben manye untrewe of tho[9].
Thus ben the sostres briddes bothe,
And ben toward the men so lothe,
That thei ne wole of pure schame     6025
Unto no mannes hand be tame;
For evere it duelleth in here mynde
Of that thei founde a man unkinde[10],
And that was false Tereus.
If such on be amonges ous     6030
I not[11], bot his condicion[12]
Men sein[13] in every region
Withinne toune and ek withoute

---

1. was previously called, 2. wished to stay, 3. asleep (swallows were thought to hibernate), 4. Where, 5. grown, 6. begins, 7. adultery, 8. their, 9. those, 10. evil, 11. do not know, 12. character, 13. say.

Nou regneth comunliche aboute[1].
And natheles in remembrance                         6035
I wol declare what vengance
The goddes hadden him ordeined,
Of that the sostres hadden pleigned:
For anon after he was changed
And from his oghne kinde stranged[2],               6040
A lappewincke mad he was,
And thus he hoppeth on the gras,
And on his hed ther stant upriht
A creste in tokne[3] he was a kniht;
And yit unto this dai men seith,                    6045
The lappewincke hath lore[4] his feith
And is the brid falseste of alle.

1. Now prevails generally, 2. altered, 3. signification, 4. lost.

# THE BLACKSMITHS

This evocative poem was written down before 1450 in B.L. MS. Arundel 292. For a discussion of the text and the background, see Elizabeth Salter's article in *Literature and History* 5 (1979), 194–215.

Swarte-smekyd smethes, smateryd wyth smoke[1],
Dryve me to deth wyth den of here dyntes[2].
Swech[3] noys on nyghtes ne herd men never;
What knavene[4] cry, and clateryng of knockes!
The cammede[5] kongons[6] cryen after 'col, col!'          5
And blowen here bellewys that al here brayn brestis[7].
'Huf, puf!' seyth that on[8]; 'haf, paf!' that other.
Thei spyttyn and spraulyn and spellyn many spelles[9];
Thei gnauen and gnacchen[10], thei gronys togydere
And holdyn hem[11] hote wyth here hard hamers.          10
Of a bole-hyde ben here barm-fellys;
Here schankes ben schakeled for the fere-flunderys[12];
Hevy hamerys thei han[13] that hard ben handled;
Stark[14] strokys thei stryken on a stelyd stokke[15].
'Lus, bus! Las, das!' rowtyn be rowe[16].          15
Swech dolful a dreme the devyl it to-dryve[17]!
The mayster longith a lityl, and lascheth a lesse,
Twyneth hem tweyn, and towchith a treble[18].
'Tik, tak! Hic, hac! Tiket, taket! Tyk, tak!
Lus, bus! Lus, das!' Swych lyf thei ledyn,          20
Alle cloye-merys[19]; Cryst hem gyve sorwe!
May no man for brenwateres[20] on nyght han hys rest.

1. Smoke-blackened smiths begrimed with smoke, 2. noise of their blows, 3. Such, 4. workers', 5. bent (?), 6. deformed men, 7. bursts, 8. one, 9. struggle and tell many tales, 10. grind and gnash their teeth, 11. keep themselves, 12. Their leather-aprons are of bull-hide; their legs are protected from the sparks, 13. have, 14. Strong, 15. steel anvil, 16. crash one after another, 17. May the Devil drive away such a dreadful noise, 18. The master-smith lengthens a little piece, and beats out a smaller one, twists them together, and strikes a treble note, 19. horse-lamers, 20. because of water-burners (i.e. those who dip red-hot iron in water).

# THOMAS HOCCLEVE: THREE ROUNDELS

Thomas Hoccleve (*c.* 1368–1426) was a clerk at the Privy Seal Office in London. His major work is *The Regement of Princes*, in which he praises his friend 'fader Chaucer' and writes of the duties of a prince, but he also wrote a number of shorter poems which are edited by F. J. Furnivall and I. Gollancz for the Early English Text Society (Extra Series, 61 and 73, reprinted 1970).

### 1. COMPLAINT TO LADY MONEY

Wel may I pleyne on[1] yow, Lady Moneye,
That in the prison of your sharp scantnesse
Souffren me bathe[2] in wo and hevynesse,
And deynen nat of socour me purveye[3].

Whan that I baar[4] of your prison the keye,    5
Kepte I yow streite[5]? Nay, God to witnesse!
Well may I (etc.)

I leet yow out; O, now of your noblesse,
Seeth unto[6] me; in your deffaute[7] I deye.
Well may I (etc.)    10

Yee saillen al to fer; retourne I preye,
Conforteth me ageyn this Cristemesse;
Elles I moot in right a feynt gladnesse[8]
Synge of yow thus, and yow accuse and seye:
Well may I (etc.)    15

1. complain about, 2. both, 3. And do not deign to provide me with help, 4. held, 5. confined, 6. Look after, 7. without you, 8. Otherwise I must, with an entirely feigned joy.

## II. THE REPLY

Hoccleve, I wole it to thee knowen be,
I, Lady Moneie, of the world goddesse,
That have al thyng undir my buxumnesse[1],
Nat sette by thy pleynte risshes three[2].

Myn hy might haddest thow in no cheertee[3]          5
Whyle I was in thy slipir sikirnesse[4].
Hoccleve (etc.)

At instance of thyn excessif largesse[5],
Becam I of my body delavee[6].
Hoccleve (etc.)          10

And syn that[7] lordes grete obeien me,
Sholde I me dreede of thy poore symplesse[8]?
My golden heed akith for thy lewdnesse[9].
Go, poore wrecche! Who settith aght by thee?
Hoccleve (etc.)          15

## III. THE PRAISE OF MY LADY

Of my lady wel me rejoise I may!
Hir golden forheed is ful narw and smal,
Hir browes[10] been lyk to dym reed coral,
And as the jeet hir yen[11] glistren ay.

Hir bowgy[12] cheekes been as softe as clay,          5
With large jowes[13] and substancial.
Of my lady (etc.)

Hir nose a pentice[14] is, that it ne shal
Reyne in hir mowth, thogh shee uprightes[15] lay.
Of (my lady, etc.)          10

1. Obedience, 2. Do not give three rushes for your complaint, 3. regard, 4. slippery security, 5. Urged on by your excessive generosity, 6. dissolute, 7. since, 8. foolishness, 9. stupidity, 10. eyebrows, 11. eyes, 12. bulging, 13. jaws, 14. sloping roof, 15. on her back.

Hir mowth is nothyng scant, with lippes gray;
Hir chin unnethe[1] may be seen at al.
Hir comly body shape as a footbal,
And shee syngith ful lyk a papejay[2].
Of (my lady, etc.)

15

1. scarcely, 2. parrot.

The *Second Shepherds' Play*, which comes from the Towneley cycle of plays from Wakefield, was written in the first half of the fifteenth century.

The staging may be visualized as follows: one side of the stage represents the field and also 'the crooked thorn'; on the other side a structure represents first Mak's cottage, and later the stable at Bethlehem. The action alternates between one side of the stage and the other.

The few stage directions in the manuscript have been translated from Latin. Others have been supplied in brackets. The speakers indicated in the manuscript as 1 Pastor, 2 Pastor, 3 Pastor, Uxor, have been assigned (as indicated by the text) to Coll, Gyb, Daw and Gyll respectively. The standard edition of the play is A. C. Cawley, *The Wakefield Pageants in the Towneley Cycle* (Manchester, 1958).

[*A field. Enter* COLL]

COLL. Lord, what these weders ar cold! And I am yll happyd[1].
　　　I am nerehande dold[2], so long have I nappyd.
　　　My legys thay fold, my fyngers ar chappyd.
　　　It is not as I wold[3], for I am al lappyd[4]
　　　In sorow.　　　　　　　　　　　　　　　　　5
　　　In stormes and tempest,
　　　Now in the eest, now in the west,
　　　Wo is hym has never rest
　　　Mydday nor morow!

　　　Bot we sely husbandys[5] that walkys on the moore,　　10
　　　In fayth we ar nerehandys outt of the doore[6].
　　　No wonder, as it standys, if we be poore,
　　　For the tylthe[7] of oure landys lyys falow as the floore,
　　　As ye ken.

1. clothed, 2. nearly dazed, 3. would like, 4. enfolded, 5. wretched farm-workers, 6. destitute, 7. arable part.

We ar so hamyd[1],                                                    15
Fortaxed and ramyd[2],
We ar mayde handtamyd[3]
With thyse gentlery men[4].


Thus thay refe[5] us oure rest, oure Lady theym wary[6]!
These men that ar lord-fest[7], thay cause the ploghe
    tary;                                            20
That men say is for the best, we fynde it contrary.
Thus ar husbandys opprest, in ponte to myscary[8]
On lyfe;
Thus hold thay us under,
Thus thay bryng us in blonder[9];                                      25
It were greatte wonder
And[10] ever shuld we thryfe.


For may he gett a paynt slefe or a broche[11] now-on-dayes,
Wo is hym that hym grefe or onys agane says[12]!
Dar no man hym reprefe, what mastry he mays[13];       30
And yit may no man lefe[14] oone word that he says –
No letter.
He can make purveance[15]
With boste and bragance[16],
And all is thrugh mantenance[17]                                       35
Of men that ar gretter.


Ther shall com a swane[18] as prowde as a po[19],
He must borow my wane[20], my ploghe also;
Then I am full fane[21] to graunt or[22] he go.
Thus lyf we in payne, anger, and wo,                                   40
By nyght and day.
He must have if he langyd[23],
If I shuld forgang it[24];

---

1. crippled, 2. Overtaxed and oppressed, 3. submissive, 4. By these gentry, 5. take away from, 6. curse, 7. retainers, 8. on the point of coming to harm, 9. trouble, 10. If, 11. i.e. livery, 12. ever refuses him, 13. No one dare reprove him, whatever force he uses, 14. believe, 15. He can requisition our property, 16. arrogance, 17. support. (It was a common complaint that lords protected riotous retainers.), 18. retainer, 19. peacock, 20. cart, 21. glad (sarcastic), 22. before, 23. has wanted (it), 24. Even if I must do without it.

I were better be hangyd
Then oones[1] say hym nay.                                    45

It dos me good, as I walk thus by myn oone[2],
Of this warld for to talk in maner of mone[3].
To my shepe wyll I stalk[4], and herkyn anone,
Ther abyde on a balk[5], or sytt on a stone
Full soyne[6];                                               50
For I trowe, perdé,
Trew men if thay be,
We gett more compané
Or it be noyne[7]. [*Enter* GYB, *without seeing* COLL]

GYB.  Bensté[8] and Dominus, what may this bemeyne[9]?       55
Why fares this warld thus? Oft have we not sene[10].
Lord, thyse weders ar spytus[11], and the wyndys full kene,
And the frostys so hydus[12] thay water myn eeyne[13] –
No ly.
Now in dry, now in wete,                                     60
Now in snaw, now in slete,
When my shone[14] freys to my fete
It is not all esy.

Bot as far as I ken, or yit as I go[15],
We sely wedmen dre mekyll wo[16];                            65
We have sorow then and then[17]; it fallys oft so.
Sely[18] Copyle, oure hen, both to and fro
She kakyls;
Bot begyn she to crok[19],
To groyne or to clok[20],                                    70
Wo is hym is oure cok[21],
For he is in the shekyls[22].

1. once, 2. alone, 3. complainingly, 4. go, 5. tussock, 6. Right away, 7. Before noon,
8. Bless me, 9. mean, 10. i.e. seen it this bad, 11. cruel, 12. terrible, 13. eyes, 14. shoes,
15. have experienced, 16. We poor married men suffer great sorrow, 17. again and again,
18. Poor, 19. croak (when laying an egg), 20. To groan or cluck, 21. Our cock is in
trouble, 22. shackles.

These men that ar wed have not all thare wyll,
When they ar full hard sted[1], thay sygh full styll[2].
God wayte[3] thay ar led[4] full hard and full yll;          75
In bowere nor in bed thay say noght thertyll[5].
This tyde[6]
My parte have I fun[7],
I know my lesson:
Wo is hym that is bun[8],          80
For he must abyde.


Bot now late in oure lyfys – a mervell to me,
That I thynk my hart ryfys[9] sich wonders to see,
What that destany dryfys it shuld so be –[10]
Som men wyll have two wyfys[11], and som men thre          85
In store[12];
Som ar wo that has any.
Bot so far can I:
Wo is hym that has many,
For he felys sore.          90


Bot, yong men, of wowyng[13], for God that you boght[14],
Be well war[15] of wedyng, and thynk in youre thoght:
'Had-I-wyst' is a thyng that servys of noght[16].
Mekyll styll mowrnyng has wedyng home broght[17],
And grefys,          95
With many a sharp showre[18];
For thou may cach in an owre[19]
That shall sow the full sowre[20]
As long as thou lyffys.


For, as ever rede I pystyll, I have oone to my fere[21]          100
As sharp as thystyll, as rugh as a brere[22],

1. burdened, 2. all the time, 3. knows, 4. treated, 5. have no say, 6. Now, 7. learned, 8. shackled, 9. bursts, 10. What Fate brings will come to pass, 11. i.e. remarry, 12. abundance, 13. with regard to courting, 14. redeemed, 15. circumspect, 16. doesn't help, 17. Marriage has caused much endless sorrow, 18. flurry of blows, 19. hour, 20. That which will pain you terribly, 21. For I have one as my mate, on my word (literally: as I read the Epistle – a wry anacronism!), 22. briar.

She is browyd lyke a brystyll, with a sowre-loten chere[1];
Had she oones wett hyr whystyll, she couth[2] syng full
  clere
Hyr Paternoster.
She is as greatt as a whall,                 105
She has a galon of gall;
By hym that dyed for us all,
I wald[3] I had ryn to[4] I had lost hir! [COLL *catches his attention*]

COLL.   God looke over the raw[5]! Full defly ye stand.
GYB.    Yee, the dewill in thi maw, so tariand![6]     110
       Sagh thou awre[7] of Daw?
COLL.                 Yee, on a ley-land[8]
       Hard I hym blaw[9]. He commys here at hand,
       Not far.
       Stand styll.
GYB.         Qwhy?
COLL.  For he commys, hope[10] I.              115
GYB.    He wyll make[11] us both a ly
       Bot if[12] we be war. [*Enter* DAW, *without seeing the others*]

DAW.   Crystys crosse me spede[13], and Sant Nycholas!
       Therof had I nede; it is wars then it was.
       Whoso couthe take hede[14] and lett the warld pas,   120
       It is ever in drede[15] and brekyll[16] as glas,
       And slythys[17].
       This warld fowre[18] never so,
       With mervels mo and mo –
       Now in weyll[19], now in wo,            125
       And all thyng wrythys[20].

       Was never syn[21] Noe[22] floode sich floodys seyn,
       Wyndys and ranys so rude[23], and stormes so keyn –

1. She has eyebrows like pig's bristles, and a sour expression, 2. could, 3. wish, 4. run until, 5. May God guard the people (i.e. the audience?), 6. The Devil take you for being so late, 7. anything, 8. pasture, 9. blow his horn, 10. think, 11. tell, 12. Unless, 13. save me, 14. If one observed, 15. danger, 16. fragile, 17. And passes away, 18. fared, 19. happiness, 20. changes, 21. since, 22. Noah's, 23. rough.

Som stamerd[1], som stod in dowte[2], as I weyn.
Now God turne all to good! I say as I mene,                    130
For ponder:
These floodys so thay drowne,
Both in feyldys and in towne,
And berys all downe[3];
And that is a wonder.                                          135

    [*Is momentarily frightened at seeing* COLL *and* GYB]

We that walk on the nyghtys, oure catell[4] to kepe[5],
We se sodan syghtys when othere men slepe.
[*Aside*] Yit me thynk my hart lyghtys[6]: [*to others*] I se
    shrewys pepe[7];
Ye ar two all-wyghtys[8] – I wyll gyf my shepe
A turne.                                                       140
Bot full yll have I ment[9];
As I walk on this bent[10],
I may lyghtly[11] repent,
My toes if I spurne[12].

A, syr, God you save, and master myne!                        145
A drynk fayn wold I have, and somwhat to dyne.
COLL.   Crystys curs, my knave, thou art a ledyr hyne[13]!
GYB.    What, the boy lyst rave! Abyde unto syne;
    We have mayde it[14].
Yll thryft on thy pate[15]!                                    150
Though the shrew cam late,
Yit is he in state[16]
To dyne – if he had it!

DAW.    Sich servandys as I, that swettys and swynkys[17],
    Etys oure brede full dry, and that me forthynkys[18].      155
We ar oft weytt and wery when master-men wynkys[19];
Yit commys full lately both dyners and drynkys[20].

---

1. staggered about, 2. fear, 3. And destroy everything, 4. livestock, 5. guard, 6. is relieved (at recognizing the others), 7. devils appearing, 8. evil spirits, 9. But I've behaved badly (by pretending his friends are devils), 10. field, 11. easily, 12. By stubbing my toes (as penance), 13. lazy servant, 14. Look, the boy is mad! Wait until later; we've already eaten, 15. May evil befall you, 16. ready, 17. labour, 18. displeases, 19. sleep, 20. Yet food and drink take a long time to come.

Bot nately[1]
Both oure dame and oure syre,
When we have ryn in the myre,                    160
Thay can nyp at oure hyre[2],
And pay us full lately[3].

Bot here my trouth[4], master: for the fayr[5] that ye make[6],
I shall do therafter[7] – wyrk as I take.
I shall do a lytyll, syr, and emang ever lake[8],   165
For yit lay my soper never on my stomake
In feyldys.
Wherto shuld I threpe[9]?
With my staf can I lepe;
And men say, 'Lyght chepe                         170
Letherly foryeldys[10].'

COLL.  Thou were an yll lad to ryde on wowyng[11]
       With a man that had bot lytyll of spendyng.
GYB.   Peasse, boy, I bad[12]. No more janglyng[13],
       Or I shall make the full rad[14], by the hevens kyng!  175
       With thy gawdys[15] –
       Where ar oure shepe, boy? – we skorne.
DAW.   Sir, this same day at morne
       I thaym left in the corne,
       When thay rang lawdys[16].                          180

       Thay have pasture good, thay can not go wrong.
COLL.  That is right. By the roode[17], thyse nyghtys ar long!
       Yit I wold, or[18] we yode[19], oone gaf us a song.
GYB.   So I thoght as I stode, to myrth[20] us among[21].
DAW.   I grauntt[22].                                      185
COLL.  Lett me syng the tenory.
GYB.   And I the tryble so hye.
DAW.   Then the meyne[23] fallys to me.

1. But well and truly, 2. cut short our wages, 3. tardily, 4. on my honour, 5. food, 6. provide, 7. accordingly, 8. play at other times, 9. haggle, 10. 'A cheap purchase gives a poor return', 11. You'd be a poor servant to take on a courting trip, 12. said, 13. quarrelling, 14. frightened, 15. tricks, 16. Lauds, 17. cross, 18. before, 19. went, 20. entertain, 21. meanwhile, 22. I agree, 23. middle part (in harmony).

Lett se how ye chauntt. [*They sing*]

MAK *enters, wearing a cloak over his doublet*

MAK. Now, Lord, for thy naymes seven, that made both moyn
    and starnes[1],         190

Well mo then I can neven, thi will, Lorde, of me
    tharnys[2].

I am all uneven[3]; that moves[4] oft my harnes[5].

Now wold God I were in heven, for ther wepe no
    barnes[6]

So styll[7].

COLL. Who is that pypys[8] so poore[9]?     195

MAK. Wold God ye wyst how I foore[10]!

Lo, a man that walkys on the moore,

And has not all his wyll.


GYB. Mak, where has thou gone? Tell us tythyng[11].

DAW. Is he commen? Then ylkon take hede to his thyng[12].   200

*He takes the cloak from him*

MAK. What! ich[13] be a yoman, I tell you, of the kyng,

The self and the some, sond from a greatt lordyng[14],

And sich.

Fy on you! Goyth hence

Out of my presence!     205

I must have reverence.

Why, who be ich?


COLL. Why make ye it so qwaynt[15]? Mak, ye do wrang.

GYB. Bot, Mak, lyst ye saynt[16]? I trow that ye lang[17].

DAW. I trow the shrew can paynt[18], the dewyll myght hym
    hang!     210

MAK. Ich shall make complaynt, and make you all to thwang[19]

At a worde,

1. stars, 2. More than I can express, Lord, I don't know what you want of me, 3. at a loss, 4. disturbs, 5. brain, 6. children, 7. Unceasingly, 8. cries, 9. piteously, 10. fared, 11. news, 12. Has he come? Then everyone guard his possessions, 13. I (In this speech Mak affects a fashionable Southern dialect; see l.215), 14. The very same, envoy of a great lord, 15. speak so affectedly, 16. do you want to play the saint, 17. want to, 18. deceive, 19. be whipped.

And tell evyn how ye doth.

COLL. Bot, Mak, is that sothe?
　　　Now take outt that Sothren tothe[1],　　　　　　215
　　　And sett[2] in a torde!

GYB. Mak, the dewill in youre ee[3]! A stroke wold I leyne[4]
　　　　you.
DAW. Mak, know ye not me? By God, I couthe teyn[5] you.
　　　　　　[MAK *decides to recognize them*]
MAK. God looke[6] you all thre! Me thoght I had sene you!
　　　Ye ar a fare compané.　　　　　　　　　　　220
COLL. 　　　　　　　　　Can ye now mene you[7]?
GYB. Shrew, pepe[8]!
　　　Thus late as thou goys,
　　　What wyll men suppos?
　　　And thou has an yll noys[9]
　　　Of stelyng of shepe.　　　　　　　　　　　　225

MAK. And I am trew as steyll, all men waytt[10];
　　　Bot a sekenes I feyll that haldys me full haytt[11]:
　　　My belly farys not weyll; it is out of astate[12].
DAW. Seldom lyys the dewyll dede by the gate[13].
MAK. Therfor　　　　　　　　　　　　　　　230
　　　Full sore am I and yll,
　　　If I stande stone-styll,
　　　I ete not an nedyll[14]
　　　Thys moneth and more.

COLL. How farys thi wyff? By thi hoode, how farys she?　235
MAK. Lyys walteryng[15] – by the roode – by the fyere, lo!
　　　And a howse full of brude[16]. She drynkys well, to;
　　　Yll spede[17] othere good that she wyll do!
　　　Bot so
　　　Etys as fast as she can,　　　　　　　　　240

1. Southern speech, 2. put, 3. eye, 4. give, 5. hurt, 6. preserve, 7. remember, 8. Devil,
appear!, 9. bad reputation, 10. know, 11. afflicts me terribly, 12. sorts, 13. roadside (i.e.
don't trust a devil when he appears to be down), 14. May I be turned to stone if I have
eaten a scrap, 15. sprawling, 16. children, 17. bad luck to (i.e. there's nothing else she's
capable of).

And ilk yere that commys to man
She bryngys furth a lakan[1] –
And som yeres two.

Bot were I[2] now more gracyus[3] and rychere be far,
I were[4] eten outt of howse and of harbar[5].                    245
Yit is she a fowll dowse[6], if ye com nar[7];
Ther is none that trowse[8] nor knowys a war[9]
Then ken I.
Now wyll ye se what I profer?
To gyf all in my cofer                                           250
To-morne at next to offer
Hyr hed-maspenny[10].

GYB.  I wote so forwakyd[11] is none in this shyre;
       I wold slepe, if I takyd les to my hyere[12].
DAW.  I am cold and nakyd, and wold have a fyere.               255
COLL. I am wery, forrakyd[13], and run in the myre –
       Wake thou[14]!
GYB.  Nay, I wyll lyg[15] downe by,
       For I must slepe, truly.
DAW.  As good a mans son was I                                  260
       As any of you. [*Shepherds lie down*]

       Bot, Mak, com heder! Betwene shall thou lyg downe.
MAK.  Then myght I lett you bedene of that ye wold rowne,
       No drede[16].
       Fro my top to my too,                                    265
       *Manus tuas commendo,*
       *Poncio Pilato*[17];
       Cryst-crosse me spede[18]!

       *Then, when the shepherds are asleep, he gets up and says*
       Now were tyme for a man that lakkys what he wold[19],
       To stalk prevely than unto a fold,                       270

1. Every single year she produces a child, 2. even if I were, 3. fortunate, 4. would be, 5. home, 6. slut, 7. near, 8. can imagine, 9. worse, 10. Tomorrow promptly to offer a requiem mass for her, 11. exhausted, 12. even if I should earn less, 13. footsore, 14. You keep watch, 15. lie, 16. Then I could immediately stop you from whispering (about me), certainly, 17. (Into) your hands I commend (my spirit), Pontius Pilate. (Perversion of Luke 23.46.), 18. The Cross of Christ save me!, 19. wants.

And neemly[1] to wyrk than, and be not to bold,
For he myght aby[2] the bargan, if it were told
At the endyng.
Now were tyme for to reyll[3];
Bot he nedys good counsell                                275
That fayn wold fare weyll,
And has bot lytyll spendyng. [*He casts a spell*]

Bot abowte you a serkyll, as rownde as a moyn,
To[4] I have done that I wyll, tyll that it be noyn,
That ye lyg stone-styll to[5] that I have doyne;          280
And I shall say thertyll of good wordys a foyne[6]:
'On hight,
Over youre heydys, my hand I lyft.
Outt go youre een[7]! Fordo[8] youre syght!'
Bot yit I must make better shyft                          285
And[9] it be[10] right.

Lord, what thay slepe hard! That may ye all here.
Was I never a shepard, bot now wyll I lere[11].
If the flok be skard[12], yit shall I nyp nere.
                    [*Catches sheep*]
How! drawes hederward! Now mendys oure chere[13]          290
From sorow.
A fatt shepe, I dar say,
A good flese, dar I lay.
Eft-whyte[14] when I may,
Bot this will I borow. [*Takes sheep home*]               295

How, Gyll, art thou in? Gett us som lyght.
GYLL.  Who makys sich dyn this tyme of the nyght?
I am sett for to spyn. I hope[15] not I myght
Ryse a penny to wyn, I shrew them on hight[16]!
So farys                                                  300
A huswyff that has bene,

---

1. nimbly, 2. pay a penalty for, 3. make haste, 4,5. till, 6. few, 7. eyes, 8. Lose, 9. If,
10. shall be, 11. learn, 12. frightened, 13. Hey! Come here! Now my mood improves,
14. (I shall) pay back, 15. think, 16. Earn a penny by getting up. I curse them aloud!

To be rasyd thus betwene[1].
Here may no note[2] be sene
For sich small charys[3].

MAK.   Good wyff, open the hek[4]! Seys thou not what I
      bryng?               305

GYLL.   I may thole the dray the snek[5]. A, com in, my swetyng!

MAK.   Yee, thou thar not rek of my long standyng[6]!

GYLL.   By the nakyd nek art thou lyke for to hyng[7].

MAK.   Do way!
      I am worthy my mete,        310
      For in a strate[8] can I gett
      More then thay that swynke and swette
      All the long day.

      Thus it fell to my lott, Gyll; I had sich grace.

GYLL.   It were a fowll blott to be hanged for the case.   315

MAK.   I have skapyd, Jelott[9], oft as hard a glase[10].

GYLL.   'Bot so long goys the pott to the water,' men says,
      'At last
      Comys it home broken.'

MAK.   Well knowe I the token[11],      320
      Bot let it never be spoken!
      Bot com and help fast.

      I wold he were flayn; I lyst well ete.
      This twelmothe[12] was I not so fayn of oone shepe-mete.

GYLL.   Com thay or he be slayn[13], and here the shepe
      blete –      325

MAK.   Then myght I be tane[14]. That were a cold swette!
      Go spar[15]
      The gaytt-doore.

GYLL.                Yis, Mak,

---

1. That's how it goes for anyone who has been a housewife, to be got up in the middle of things, 2. work, 3. chores, 4. door, 5. I'll let you draw the latch (i.e. open it yourself!), 6. You needn't bother about me being kept waiting, 7. likely to hang, 8. time of need, 9. Gyll (pet form), 10. blow, 11. proverb, 12. year, 13. If they (the shepherds) come before he's killed, 14. arrested, 15. bolt.

|        |                                                                           |     |
|--------|---------------------------------------------------------------------------|-----|
|        | For and[1] thay com at thy bak –                                          |     |
| MAK.   | Then myght I by, for all the pak,                                         | 330 |
|        | The dewill of the war[2]!                                                  |     |

|        |                                                                           |     |
|--------|---------------------------------------------------------------------------|-----|
| GYLL.  | A good bowrde[3] have I spied, syn[4] thou can[5] none:                    |     |
|        | Here shall we hym hyde, to[6] thay be gone,                               |     |
|        | In my credyll. Abyde! Lett me alone,                                      |     |
|        | And I shall lyg besyde in chylbed, and grone.                            | 335 |
| MAK.   | Thou red[7],                                                              |     |
|        | And I shall say thou was lyght[8]                                          |     |
|        | Of a knave[9]-childe this nyght.                                          |     |
| GYLL.  | Now well is me day bright                                                 |     |
|        | That ever was I bred[10]!                                                 | 340 |

|        |                                                                           |     |
|--------|---------------------------------------------------------------------------|-----|
|        | This is a good gyse[11] and a far cast[12];                              |     |
|        | Yit a woman avyse[13] helpys at the last.                                 |     |
|        | I wote never who spyse[14]; agane[15] go thou fast.                      |     |
| MAK.   | Bot[16] I com or[17] thay ryse, els blawes a cold blast!                  |     |
|        | I wyll go slepe. [*Returns to shepherds*]                                 | 345 |
|        | Yit slepys all this meneye[18];                                           |     |
|        | And I shall go stalk prevely,                                             |     |
|        | As it had never bene I                                                    |     |
|        | That caryed thare shepe. [*Lies down*]                                    |     |

|        |                                                                           |     |
|--------|---------------------------------------------------------------------------|-----|
| COLL.  | *Resurrex a mortruus*[19]! Have hold my hand!                             | 350 |
|        | *Judas carnas dominus*[20]! I may not well stand,                         |     |
|        | My foytt slepys, by Jesus, and I water fastand[21].                      |     |
|        | I thoght that we layd us full nere Yngland.                               |     |
| GYB.   | A, ye?                                                                    |     |
|        | Lord, what I have slept weyll!                                            | 355 |
|        | As fresh as an eyll,                                                      |     |
|        | As lyght I me feyll                                                       |     |
|        | As leyfe on a tre.                                                        |     |

1. if, 2. Then I might suffer, from the lot of them, a devil of a time, 3. trick, 4. since, 5. know, 6. until, 7. get ready, 8. delivered, 9. boy, 10. born, 11. contrivance, 12. clever trick, 13. woman's advice, 14. is watching, 15. back, 16. Unless, 17. before, 18. company, 19. He rose from the dead. (Misquote from Creed.), 20. Sing Judas to the Lord. (*Judas* misquoted for *Laudes*, 'praises'), 21. am faint with hunger.

DAW. Bensté[1] be herein! So me qwakys,
My hart is outt of skyn, whatso it makys[2].                    360
Who makys all this dyn? So my browes blakys[3],
To the dowore[4] wyll I wyn[5]. Harke, felows, wakys!
We were fowre –
Se ye awre[6] of Mak now?

COLL. We were up or[7] thou.                                    365

GYB. Man, I gyf God avowe,
Yit yede he nawre[8].

DAW. Me thoght[9] he was lapt in a wolfe-skyn.

COLL. So ar many hapt[10] now, namely[11] within.

DAW. When we had long napt, me thoght with a gyn[12]          370
A fatt shepe he trapt; bot he mayde no dyn.

GYB. Be styll!
Thi dreme makys the woode[13];
It is bot fantom, by the roode.

COLL. Now God turne all to good,                               375
If it be his wyll.

GYB. Ryse, Mak, for shame! Thou lygys right lang.

MAK. Now Crystys holy name be us emang!
What is this? For Sant Jame, I may not well gang[14]!
I trow I be the same. A! my nek has lygen wrang[15].           380

[*They straighten it*]

Enoghe!
Mekill thank! Syn yister-even[16],
Now by Sant Stevyn,
I was flayd with a swevyn,
My hart out of sloghe[17]!                                     385

I thoght Gyll began to crok and travell full sad[18],
Wel-ner at the fyrst cok, of a yong lad
For to mend oure flok[19]. Then be I never glad;

1. Blessings. 2. My heart is 'out of its skin' (i.e. in my mouth), whatever causes it. (He has had a nightmare). 3. darken. 4. door. 5. run. 6. anything. 7. before. 8. Man, I swear to God he didn't leave. 9. i.e. I dreamed. 10. covered. 11. especially. 12. snare. 13. mad. 14. walk. 15. I hope I shall recover. Ah, my neck has been lying crooked. 16. Many thanks! Since last night. 17. I was harrowed by a dream, my heart (jumped) out of its skin (cf. l.360). 18. groan and go into heavy labour. 19. To add to our family.

I have tow on my rok¹ more then ever I had.     390
A, my heede²!
A house full of yong tharmes³,
The dewill knok outt thare harnes⁴!
Wo is hym has many barnes⁵,
And therto lytyll brede.

I must go home, by youre lefe, to Gyll, as I thoght.     395
I pray you looke⁶ my slefe, that I steyll noght;
I am loth you to grefe, or from you take oght. [*Exit*]

DAW.  Go furth, yll myght thou chefe⁷! Now wold I we soght,
This morne,
That we had all oure store⁸.     400

COLL.  Bot I will go before;
Let us mete.

GYB.          Whore?

DAW.  At the crokyd thorne. [*Exeunt*]

[*Outside* MAK's *cottage. Enter* MAK]

MAK.  Undo this doore! Who is here? How long shall I stand?

GYLL.  Who makys sich a bere⁹? Now walk in the
wenyand¹⁰!     405

MAK.  A, Gyll, what chere? It is I, Mak, youre husbande.

GYLL.  Then may we se here the dewill in a bande¹¹,
Syr Gyle¹²!
Lo, he commys with a lote¹³
As he were holden in¹⁴ the throte.     410
I may not syt at my note¹⁵
A handlang while¹⁶.

MAK.  Wyll ye here what fare¹⁷ she makys to gett hir a glose¹⁸?
And dos noght bot lakys, and clowse hir toose¹⁹.

---

1. business to attend to (lit. 'flax on my distaff'), 2. head, 3. bellies, 4. brains, 5. children, 6. examine, 7. bad luck to you, 8. animals, 9. noise, 10. damn you (lit. 'walk in the time of the waning moon'), 11. i.e. Mak under arrest, 12. Sir Guile (i.e. Mak), 13. sound, 14. held by, 15. work, 16. Any time at all, 17. fuss, 18. excuse, 19. play and scratch her toes.

GYLL.   Why, who wanders[1], who wakys[2]? Who commys, who                        
        gose?                                                               415

        Who brewys, who bakys? What makys me thus hose[3]?

        And than

        It is rewthe to beholde –

        Now in hote, now in colde[4],

        Full wofull is the householde                               420

        That wantys[5] a woman.


        Bot what ende[6] has thou mayde with the hyrdys[7], Mak?

MAK.   The last worde that thay sayde when I turnyd my bak,

        Thay wold looke that thay hade thare shepe, all the pak.

        I hope[8] thay wyll nott be well payde[9] when thay thare

           shepe lak[10],                                             425

        Perdé[11]!

        Bot howso the gam gose,

        To me thay wyll suppose[12],

        And make a fowll noyse,

        And cry outt apon me.                                     430


        Bot thou must do as thou hyght[13].

GYLL.                                       I accorde me thertyll;

        I shall swedyll[14] hym right in my credyll.

          *[Wraps up sheep and puts it in the cradle]*

        If it were a gretter slyght, yit couthe I help tyll[15].

        I wyll lyg downe stright[16]. Com hap[17] me.

MAK.                                         I wyll.

GYLL.   Behynde!                                             435

        Com Coll and his maroo[18],

        Thay will nyp us full naroo[19].

MAK.   Bot I may cry 'out, haroo[20]!'

        The shepe if thay fynde.


      1. never rests, 2. stays vigilant, 3. hoarse, 4. i.e. in all circumstances, 5. is without, 6. conclusion, 7. shepherds, 8. think, 9. pleased, 10. miss, 11. By God, 12. But whatever happens, they'll suspect me, 13. arranged, 14. swaddle, 15. Even if it were a more complex trick, I could help with it, 16. at once, 17. cover, 18. partner, 19. They'll seize us firmly, 20. help!

GYLL.  Harken ay when thay call; thay will com onone.    440
        Com and make redy all, and syng by thyn oone[1];
        Syng 'lullay'[2] thou shall, for I must grone
        And cry outt by the wall on Mary and John,
        For sore[3].
        Syng 'lullay' on fast[4]    445
        When thou heris at the last,
        And bot I play a fals cast[5],
        Trust me no more.

*[At the crooked thorn. Enter shepherds]*

DAW.  A, Coll, goode morne! Why slepys thou nott?

COLL.  Alas, that ever was I borne! We have a fowll blott[6] –    450
        A fat wedir[7] have we lorne[8].

DAW.                      Mary, Godys forbott[9]!

GYB.  Who shuld do us that skorne[10]? That were a fowll spott[11].

COLL.  Som shrewe.
        I have soght with my dogys
        All Horbery shrogys[12],    455
        And of[13] fyftene hogys[14]
        Fond I bot oone ewe[15].

DAW.  Now trow me, if ye will – by Sant Thomas of Kent,
        Ayther Mak or Gyll was at that assent[16].

COLL.  Peasse, man, be still! I sagh when he went.    460
        Thou sklanders hym yll; thou aght to repent
        Goode spede[17].

GYB.  Now as ever myght I the[18],
        If I shuld evyn here de[19],
        I wold say it were he    465
        That dyd that same dede.

DAW.  Go we theder, I rede[20], and ryn on oure feete.
        Shall I never ete brede, the sothe to I wytt[21].

---

1. alone, 2. a lullaby, 3. pain, 4. quickly, 5. When you finally hear (them), and if I don't play a trick, 6. disgrace, 7. ram, 8. lost, 9. God forbid!, 10. insult, 11. shame, 12. All the bushes of Horbury (near Wakefield), 13. among, 14. young sheep, 15. i.e. the ram was gone, 16. involved in that, 17. Quickly, 18. as I wish to thrive. (An oath), 19. die, 20. advise, 21. till I know the truth.

COLL. Nor drynk in my heede[1], with hym tyll I mete.

GYB. I wyll rest in no stede[2] tyll that I hym grete, 470
My brothere.
Oone I will hight[3]:
Tyll I se hym in sight,
Shall I never slepe one nyght
Ther[4] I do anothere. [*They go to* MAK's *cottage*] 475

DAW. Will ye here how thay hak[5]? Oure syre lyst croyne[6].

COLL. Hard I never none crak[7] so clere out of toyne[8].
Call on hym.

GYB.                    Mak, undo youre doore soyne[9]!

MAK. Who is that spak, as[10] it were noyne[11],
On loft[12]? 480
Who is that, I say?

DAW. Goode felowse, were it[13] day.

MAK. As far as ye may,
Good[14], spekys soft,

Over a seke womans heede that is at maylleasse[15]. 485
I had lever[16] be dede or she had any dyseasse.

GYLL. Go to anothere stede! I may not well qweasse[17].
Ich fote that ye trede goys thorow my nese[18]
So hee[19].

COLL. Tell us, Mak, if ye may, 490
How fare ye, I say?

MAK. Bot ar ye in this towne today?
Now how fare ye?

Ye have ryn in the myre, and ar weytt yit[20];
I shall make you a fyre, if ye will sytt. 495
A nores[21] wold I hyre. Thynk ye on[22] yit?
Well qwytt is my hyre – my dreme, this is itt –
[*Points to cradle*]

---

1. head, 2. place, 3. One thing I'll promise, 4. In the same place as, 5. trill, 6. Our master (i.e. Mak) likes singing, 7. sing, 8. tune, 9. immediately, 10. as if, 11. midday, 12. Out loud, 13. (as you'd see) if it were, 14. Good people, 15. ill, 16. rather, 17. breathe, 18. nose (i.e. head), 19. loudly, 20. still wet, 21. nurse, 22. Have you caught my hint (that my wife has had a baby).

A seson[1].
I have barnes, if ye knew,
Well mo then enewe[2];     500
Bot we must drynk as we brew,
And that is bot reson.

I wold ye dynyd or ye yode[3]; me thynk that ye swette.

GYB. Nay, nawther mendys oure mode drynke nor mette.

MAK. Why, syr, alys you oght bot goode[4]?

DAW.                 Yee, oure shepe that we gett[5]  505
Ar stollyn as thay yode[6]. Oure los is grette.

MAK. Syrs, drynkys!
Had I bene thore[7]
Som shuld have boght[8] it full sore.

COLL. Mary, som men trowes that ye wore[9],     510
And that us forthynkys[10].

GYB. Mak, som men trowys that it shuld be ye.

DAW. Ayther ye or youre spouse, so say we.

MAK. Now if ye have suspowse[11] to Gill or to me,
Com and rype[12] oure howse, and then may ye se   515
Who had hir.
If I any shepe fott[13],
Ayther cow or stott[14] –
And Gyll, my wyfe, rose nott
Here syn she lade hir[15] –     520

As I am true and lele[16], to God here I pray,
That this be the fyrst mele that I shall ete this day.

COLL. Mak, as have I ceyll[17], avyse the[18], I say:
He lernyd tymely[19] to steyll that couth not say nay.

[*Shepherds search about*]

GYLL. I swelt[20]!     525

1. I've been fully paid, for the time being. My dream (about the baby, l.387), here it is, 2. enough, 3. I'd like you to eat before you go, 4. i.e. is there anything wrong, 5. tend, 6. walked about, 7. there, 8. suffered for, 9. were (there), 10. upsets, 11. suspicion of, 12. search, 13. took, 14. heifer, 15. lay down, 16. honest, 17. bliss, 18. reflect, 19. early, 20. I'm dying.

Outt, thefys, fro my wonys[1]!
Ye com to rob us for the nonys.

MAK.  Here ye not how she gronys?
Youre hartys shuld melt.


GYLL.  Outt, thefys, fro my barne[2]! Negh[3] hym not
     thor[4]!                                        530

MAK.  Wyst ye how she had farne[5], youre hartys wold be sore.
Ye do wrang, I you warne, that thus commys before
To a woman that has farne – bot I say no more.

GYLL.  A, my medyll!
I pray to God so mylde,                     535
If ever I you begyld[6],
That I ete this chylde
That lygys[7] in this credyll.


MAK.  Peasse, woman, for Godys payn, and cry not so!
Thou spyllys[8] thy brane, and makys me full wo.     540

GYB.  I trow oure shepe be slayn. What fynde ye two?

DAW.  All wyrk we in vayn; as well may we go.
Bot hatters[9]!
I can fynde no flesh,
Hard nor nesh[10],                           545
Salt nor fresh,
Bot two tome[11] platers.


Whik catell bot this[12], tame nor wylde,
None, as have I blys, as lowde[13] as he smylde[14].

GYLL.  No, so God me blys, and gyf me joy of my chylde!   550

COLL.  We have merkyd amys; I hold us begyld[15].

GYB.  Syr, don[16].
Syr – oure Lady hym save! –
Is youre chyld a knave[17]?

MAK.  Any lord myght hym have               555

---

1. house, 2. child, 3. Approach, 4. there, 5. suffered, 6. tricked, 7. lies, 8. You are injuring, 9. Damn it!, 10. soft, 11. empty, 12. Livestock apart from this (baby), 13. strongly, 14. smelled, 15. We've made a mistake. I believe we've been tricked, 16. entirely, 17. boy.

This chyld to his son.

When he wakyns he kyppys[1], that joy is to se.

DAW. In good tyme to hys hyppys, and in celé[2]!
Bot who was his gossyppys[3] so sone redé[4]?

MAK. So fare fall thare lyppys[5]!                                    560

COLL.                          [*To* DAW] Hark now, a le[6].

MAK. So God thaym thank,
Parkyn, and Gybon Waller, I say,
And gentill John Horne, in good fay[7] –
He made all the garray[8] –
With the greatt shank[9].                                            565

GYB. Mak, freyndys will we be, for we ar all oone[10].

MAK. We? Now I hald for me, for mendys gett I none[11].
Fare well all thre! All glad were ye[12] gone.

DAW. Fare wordys may ther be, bot luf is ther none
This yere. [*Shepherds go outside cottage*]                         570

COLL. Gaf ye the chyld any thyng?

GYB. I trow not oone farthyng.

DAW. Fast agane[13] will I flyng[14];
Abyde ye me there. [*Returns*]

Mak, take it to no grefe[15] if I come to thi barne.              575

MAK. Nay, thou dos me greatt reprefe[16], and fowll has thou
farne[17].

DAW. The child will it not grefe[18], that lytyll day-starne[19].
Mak, with youre leyfe[20], let me gyf youre barne
Bot six pence.

MAK. Nay, do way! He slepys.                                        580

DAW. Me thynk he pepys.

MAK. When he wakyns he wepys.

---

1. grabs, 2. A good and happy (*celé*) fortune to him (lit. to his hips), 3. godparents, 4. prepared, 5. Good luck to them (lit. to their lips), 6. lie, 7. faith, 8. commotion, i.e. music(?), 9. long legs, 10. at one, 11. We? I'll look after myself now, since I'll get nothing out of you, 12. (I'd be) very glad if you were, 13. back, 14. hurry, 15. don't be upset, 16. harm, 17. behaved, 18. disturb, 19. star, 20. permission.

[COLL *and* GYB *return*]

I pray you go hence!

DAW. Gyf me lefe hym to kys, and lyft up the clowtt[1].
What the dewill is this? He has a long snowte! 585

COLL. He is merkyd amys. We wate ill abowte[2].

GYB. Ill-spon weft, iwys, ay commys foull owte[3].
Ay, so!
He is lyke to oure shepe!

DAW. How, Gyb, may I pepe! 590

COLL. I trow kynde will crepe
Where it may not go[4].

GYB. This was a qwantt gawde[5] and a far cast[6]:
It was a hee[7] frawde.

DAW.                Yee, syrs, wast[8].
Lett bren this bawde[9] and bynd hir fast. 595
A fals skawde[10] hang[11] at the last;
So shall thou.
Wyll ye se how thay swedyll
His foure feytt in the medyll?
Sagh I never in a credyll 600
A hornyd lad or[12] now.

MAK. Peasse, byd I. What, lett be youre fare[13]!
I am he that hym gatt[14], and yond woman hym bare.

COLL. What dewill shall he hatt[15], Mak? Lo, God, Makys ayre[16]!

GYB. Lett be all that! Now God gyf hym care[17], 605
I sagh[18].

GYLL. A pratty child is he
As syttys on a wamans kne;
A dyllydowne[19], perdé,
To gar[20] a man laghe. 610

---

1. clothes, 2. He's deformed. We shouldn't pry about, 3. Badly-spun weft (i.e. poor heredity), indeed, always turns out wrong, 4. I suppose nature will creep where it can't walk (i.e. will emerge somehow), 5. clever device, 6. smart trick, 7. high, 8. it was, 9. Let's have this slut burned, 10. scold, 11. will hang, 12. before, 13. noise, 14. begot, 15. be named, 16. heir, 17. misery, 18. I saw (the sheep), 19. darling, 20. make.

DAW. I know hym by the eere-marke; that is a good tokyn[1].

MAK. I tell you, syrs, hark! – hys noyse was brokyn.
Sythen[2] told me a clerk that he was forspokyn[3].

COLL. This is a fals wark; I wold fayn be wrokyn[4].
Gett wepyn!                                                    615

GYLL. He was takyn with an elfe,
I saw it myself;
When the clok stroke twelf
Was he forshapyn[5].

GYB. Ye two ar well feft sam in a stede[6].                    620

COLL. Syn thay manteyn thare theft, let do thaym to dede[7].

MAK. If I trespas eft[8], gyrd of[9] my heede.
With you[10] will be left.

DAW.                          Syrs, do my reede[11]:
For this trespas
We will nawther ban[12] ne flyte[13],                         625
Fyght nor chyte[14],
Bot have done as tyte[15],
And cast hym in canvas.

[MAK *is tossed in a sheet. Then shepherds return to fields*]

COLL. Lord, what I am sore, in poynt for to bryst[16]!
In fayth, I may no more; therfor wyll I ryst[17].            630

GYB. As a shepe of seven skore[18] he weyd in my fyst.
For to slepe aywhore[19] me thynk that I lyst.

DAW. Now I pray you
Lyg downe on this grene.

COLL. On these thefys yit I mene[20].                          635

DAW. Wherto shuld ye tene[21]?
Do as I say you. [*They lie down. Enter* ANGEL *above*]

*The* ANGEL *sings 'Gloria in Excelsis', and then says*

ANGEL. Ryse, hyrd-men heynd[22], for now is he borne

---

1. bit of evidence. 2. Later. 3. bewitched. 4. revenged. 5. He was disfigured. 6. You are two of a kind. 7. Since they persist in their theft, have them put to death. 8. again. 9. strike off. 10. In your mercy. 11. what I advise. 12. curse. 13. quarrel. 14. chide. 15. But get it over at once. 16. nearly bursting. 17. rest. 18. 140 lbs. 19. anywhere. 20. I'm still thinking about these thieves. 21. Why be angry. 22. noble shepherds.

That shall take fro the feynd that Adam had lorne[1];
That warloo to sheynd[2], this nyght is he borne.                   640
God is made youre freynd now at this morne,
He behestys[3].
At Bedlem[4] go se
Ther lygys that fre[5]
In a cryb full poorely,                                             645
Betwyx two bestys. [*Exit*]


COLL.   This was a qwant stevyn[6] that ever yit I hard.
        It is a mervell to nevyn[7], thus to be skard[8].
GYB.    Of Godys son of hevyn he spak upward[9].
        All the wod on a levyn[10] me thoght that he gard[11]       650
        Appere.
DAW.    He spake of a barne
        In Bedlem, I you warne[12].
COLL.   That betokyns yond starne[13];
        Let us seke hym there.                                      655


GYB.    Say, what was his song? Hard ye not how he crakyd[14] it,
        Thre brefes to a long?
DAW.                          Yee, Mary, he hakt[15] it:
        Was no crochett wrong, nor nothyng that lakt it[16].
COLL.   For to syng us emong, right as he knakt[17] it,
        I can.                                                      660
GYB.    Let se how ye croyne[18]!
        Can ye bark at the mone?
DAW.    Hold youre tonges! Have done!
COLL.   Hark after, than. [*They sing*]


GYB.    To Bedlem he bad that we shuld gang[19];                    665
        I am full fard[20] that we tary to lang.
DAW.    Be mery and not sad – of myrth is oure sang!


1. what Adam lost, 2. So as to destroy the Devil, 3. He promises, 4. Bethlehem, 5. Where that noble one lies, 6. (most) excellent sound, 7. relate, 8. frightened, 9. from above, 10. in a bright light, 11. caused to, 12. tell, 13. Yonder star signifies that, 14. sang, 15. trilled, 16. was missing, 17. trilled, 18. sing, 19. go, 20. afraid.

Everlastyng glad to mede[1] may we fang[2],
Withoutt noyse.

COLL. Hy we theder, forthy[3],           670
If[4] we be wete and wery,
To that chyld and that lady.
We have it not to lose[5].

GYB. We fynde by the prophecy — let be youre dyn! —
Of David and Isay[6] and mo then I myn[7],      675
Thay prophecyed by clergy[8], that in a vyrgyn
Shuld he lyght and ly, to slokyn[9] oure syn,
And slake[10] it,
Oure kynde[11], from wo;
For Isay sayd so:      680
*Ecce virgo*
*Concipiet*[12] a chylde that is nakyd.

DAW. Full glad may we be, and abyde that day
That lufly to se that all myghtys may[13].
Lord, well were me for ones and for ay,      685
Myght I knele on my kne, som word for to say
To that chylde.
Bot the angell sayd
In a cryb was he layde;
He was poorly arayd,      690
Both mener[14] and mylde.

COLL. Patryarkes that has bene, and prophetys beforne,
Thay desyryd to have sene this chylde that is borne.
Thay ar gone full clene; that have thay lorne[15].
We shall se hym, I weyn, or it be morne,      695
To tokyn[16].
When I se hym and fele,
Then wote I full weyll
It is true as steyll

1. joy as a reward. 2. get, 3. therefore, 4. Even though, 5. We must not fail, 6. Isaiah, 7. more (others) than I remember, 8. learning, 9. get rid of, 10. release, 11. Mankind, 12. (Lat.) Behold a Virgin shall conceive, 13. To see that dear one who is almighty, 14. very lowly, 15. They have all died, and have missed that (sight), 16. As a sign.

That prophetys have spokyn:                                        700

To so poore as we ar that he wold appere,
Fyrst fynd[1], and declare[2] by his messyngere.

GYB.   Go we now, let us fare; the place is us nere.

DAW.   I am redy and yare[3]; go we in fere[4]
To that bright.                                                    705
Lord, if thi wylles be –
We ar lewde[5] all thre –
Thou grauntt us somkyns gle[6]
To comfort thi wight. [*They enter the stable*]

COLL.   Hayll, comly and clene! Hayll, yong child!        710
Hayll, maker, as I meyne[7], of[8] a madyn so mylde!
Thou has waryd[9], I weyne, the warlo[10] so wylde:
The fals gyler of teyn, now goys he begylde[11].
Lo, he merys[12]!
Lo, he laghys, my swetyng!                                         715
A wel fare[13] metyng!
I have holden my hetyng[14]:
Have a bob of cherys[15].

GYB.   Hayll, sufferan[16] savyoure, for thou has us soght!
Hayll, frely foyde[17] and floure, that all thyng has
   wroght!                                              720
Hayll, full of favoure[18], that made all of noght!
Hayll! I kneyll and I cowre. A byrd have I broght[19]
To my barne.
Hayll, lytyll tyné mop[20]!
Of oure crede[21] thou art crop[22];                              725
I wold drynk on thy cop[23],
Lytyll day-starne.

---

1. find (us), 2. make known (his birth), 3. eager, 4. together, 5. ignorant, 6. some joyful thing, 7. believe, 8. (born) of, 9. condemned, 10. Devil, 11. The false and harmful deceiver is now himself deceived, 12. is happy, 13. wonderful, 14. I've kept my promise, 15. (Cherries are a traditional miracle of Christmas), 16. sovereign, 17. lovely child, 18. grace, 19. (A bird symbolises the Holy Spirit), 20. baby, 21. faith, 22. head, 23. chalice.

DAW.  Hayll, derlyng dere, full of godhede[1]!
      I pray the be nere when that I have nede.
      Hayll, swete is thy chere[2]! My hart wold blede     730
      To se the sytt here in so poore wede,
      With no pennys.
      Hayll! Put furth thy dall[3]!
      I bryng the bot a ball[4]:
      Have and play the withall,     735
      And go to the tenys.

MARY.  The fader of heven, God omnypotent,
      That sett all on seven[5], his son has he sent.
      My name couth he neven, and lyght or he went[6].
      I conceyvyd hym full even thrugh myght, as he ment[7];   740
      And now is he borne.
      He kepe you fro wo!
      I shall pray hym so.
      Tell furth[8] as ye go,
      And myn on[9] this morne.     745

COLL.  Fare well, lady, so fare to beholde,
      With thy childe on thi kne.
GYB.                          Bot he lygys full cold.
      Lord, well is me! Now we go, thou behold.
DAW.  Forsothe, allredy it semys to be told
      Full oft.     750
COLL.  What grace we have fun[10]!
GYB.  Com furth; now ar we won[11]!
DAW.  To syng ar we bun[12] –
      Let take on loft[13]! [*Exeunt shepherds singing*]

1. divinity, 2. appearance, 3. hand, 4. (A ball is an emblem of sovereignty and of God the Father), 5. created everything in seven days, 6. He called my name and became incarnate before He departed, 7. entirely through His power as He intended, 8. Spread the news, 9. remember, 10. received, 11. redeemed, 12. obliged, 13. Begin to sing aloud.

There are forty-eight plays in the York Cycle, preserved in B.L. Additional MS. 35290, dated 1430–40. The play of the Crucifixion was performed, fittingly enough, by the pinners' guild. There are no stage directions in the manuscript. The whole cycle was edited by L. Toulmin Smith, *The York Plays* (Oxford, 1885).

> [*Calvary. The Cross lies on the ground*]

|                  |                                                            |    |
|------------------|------------------------------------------------------------|----|
| 1ST SOLDIER.     | Sir knyghtis, take heede hydir in hye[1]!                  |    |
|                  | This dede on dergh we may noght drawe[2].                   |    |
|                  | Yee wootte[3] youre selffe als wele as I                    |    |
|                  | Howe lordis and leders of owre lawe                        |    |
|                  | Has geven dome that this doote[4] schall dye.               | 5  |
| 2ND SOLDIER.     | Sir, alle thare counsaile wele we knawe.                    |    |
|                  | Sen[5] we are comen to Calvarie,                            |    |
|                  | Latte ilke[6] man helpe nowe as hym awe[7].                 |    |
| 3RD SOLDIER.     | We are alle redy, loo,                                      |    |
|                  | That forward[8] to fullfille.                               | 10 |
| 4TH SOLDIER.     | Late[9] here howe we schall doo,                            |    |
|                  | And go we tyte thertille[10].                               |    |

|                  |                                                            |    |
|------------------|------------------------------------------------------------|----|
| 1ST SOLDIER.     | It may noght helpe her for to hone[11],                     |    |
|                  | If we schall any worshippe[12] wynne.                        |    |
| 2ND SOLDIER.     | He muste be dede nedelyngis[13] by none.                    | 15 |
| 3RD SOLDIER.     | Thanne is goode tyme that we begynne.                       |    |
| 4TH SOLDIER.     | Late dynge[14] hym doune, than is he done;                  |    |
|                  | He schall nought dere[15] us with his dynne.                |    |
| 1ST SOLDIER.     | He schall be sette and lerned[16] sone,                     |    |
|                  | With care[17] to hym and all his kynne.                      | 20 |
| 2ND SOLDIER.     | The foulest dede[18] of all                                 |    |
|                  | Shalle he dye for his dedis.                                |    |
| 3RD SOLDIER.     | That menes crosse[19] hym we schall.                        |    |

---

1. quickly, 2. We may not postpone this deed, 3. know, 4. fool, 5. Since, 6. Let each, 7. he ought, 8. agreed business, 9. Let us, 10. quickly to it, 11. to delay here, 12. praise, 13. necessarily, 14. beat, 15. harm, 16. taught a lesson, 17. sorrow, 18. death, 19. crucify.

4TH SOLDIER.   Behalde so right he redis[1]!

1ST SOLDIER.   Thanne to this werke us muste take heede,                    25
      So that oure wirkyng be noght wronge.

2ND SOLDIER.   None othir noote to neven is nede[2],
      But latte us haste hym for to hange.

3RD SOLDIER.   And I have gone for gere, goode speede,
      Bothe hammeres and nayles large and lange.         30

4TH SOLDIER.   Thanne may we boldely do this dede;
      Commes on, late[3] kille this traitoure strange[4].

1ST SOLDIER.   Faire myght ye falle in feere[5],
      That has wrought on this wise[6]!

2ND SOLDIER.   Us nedis nought for to lere[7]                               35
      Suche faitoures[8] to chastise.

3RD SOLDIER.   Sen ilke a[9] thyng es right arrayed,
      The wiselier nowe wirke may we.

4TH SOLDIER.   The crosse on grounde is goodely graied[10],
      And boorede even as it awith[11] to be.            40

1ST SOLDIER.   Lokis that the ladde on lengthe be layde,
      And made me thane unto this tree[12].

2ND SOLDIER.   For[13] alle his fare[14] he schalle be flaied,
      That one assaie[15] sone schalle ye see.

3RD SOLDIER.   [*To* JESUS] Come forthe, thou cursed knave!          45
      Thy comforte sone schall kele[16].

4TH SOLDIER.   Thyne hyre[17] here schall thou have.

1ST SOLDIER.   Walkes oon[18]! now wirke we wele.

JESUS.            Almyghty God, my Fadir free,
      Late this materes be made in mynde[19];             50
      Thou badde that I schulde buxsome[20] be,
      For Adam plyght for to be pyned[21].
      Here to dede I obblisshe me[22],

1. says, 2. There's no need to mention any other business, 3. let us, 4. strong, 5. Good luck to you all, 6. manner, 7. We don't need to learn how, 8. impostors, 9. Since every, 10. well prepared, 11. ought, 12. See that this fellow is laid flat, and fastened then on this cross, 13. Despite, 14. complaints, 15. on trial (i.e. in the event), 16. be lessened, 17. payment, 18. Carry on, 19. considered, 20. obedient, 21. To be tortured for Adam's sin, 22. Here I commit myself to death.

Fro that synne for to save mankynde,
And soveraynely[1] beseke I the,                     55
That thai for me may favoure fynde,
And fro the Fende[2] thame fende[3],
So that ther saules be saffe,
In welthe[4] withouten ende;
I kepe nought ellis to crave[5].                     60

1ST SOLDIER.    We[6]! herke, sir knyghtis, for Mahoundis[7]
                bloode!
                Of Adam kynde is all his thoght.

2ND SOLDIER.    The warlowe waxis werre than woode[8];
                This doulfull dede[9] ne dredith he noght.

3RD SOLDIER.    Thou schulde have mynde, with mayne and
                moode[10],                           65
                Of wikkid werkis that thou haste wrought.

4TH SOLDIER.    I hope that he hadde bene as goode
                Have sesed of sawes that he uppe sought[11].

1ST SOLDIER.    Thoo sawes schall rewe hym sore,
                For[12] all his saunteryng[13] sone.  70

2ND SOLDIER.    Ille spede[14] thame that hym spare
                Tille he to dede be done!

3RD SOLDIER.    Have done belyve[15], boy[16], and make the
                boune[17],
                And bende thi bakke unto this tree.
                [JESUS lies on the cross]

4TH SOLDIER.    Byhalde, hymselffe has laide hym doune,   75
                In lenghe and breede[18] as he schulde bee.

1ST SOLDIER.    This traitoure here teynted[19] of treasoune,
                Gose[20] faste and fette[21] hym than, ye thre,
                And sen he claymeth kyngdome with croune,
                Even as a kyng here have schall hee.       80

---

1. especially, 2. Devil, 3. protect, 4. bliss, 5. I wish to ask for nothing else, 6. Oh, 7. Mohammed's, 8. The scoundrel grows worse than mad, 9. terrible death, 10. all your strength, 11. I think that he should rather have stopped telling the stories he made up, 12. Despite, 13. opinions(?), 14. Bad luck to, 15. quickly, 16. villain, 17. ready, 18. breadth, 19. convicted, 20. Go, 21. fetch.

2ND SOLDIER. Nowe, certis[1], I schall noght feyne[2]
Or[3] his right hande be feste[4].

3RD SOLDIER. The lefte hande thanne is myne,
Late see who beres hym[5] beste.

4TH SOLDIER. Hys lymmys on lenghe[6] than schalle I lede[7],  85
And even unto the bore[8] thame bringe.

1ST SOLDIER. Unto his heede I schall take hede,
And with myne hande helpe hym to hyng[9].

2ND SOLDIER. Nowe sen we foure schall do this dede,
And medill with this unthrifty[10] thyng,  90
Late no man spare for speciall speede[11],
Tille that we have made endyng.

3RD SOLDIER. This forward[12] may[13] not faile,
Nowe are we right arraiede.

4TH SOLDIER. This boy[14] here in oure baile[15]  95
Shall bide full bittir brayde[16].

1ST SOLDIER. Sir knyghtis, saie, nowe wirke we ought[17]?

2ND SOLDIER. Yis, certis, I hope[18] I holde this hande.

3RD SOLDIER. And to the boore I have it brought
Full boxumly[19] withouten bande[20].  100

1ST SOLDIER. Strike on than harde, for hym the boght[21]!

2ND SOLDIER. Yis, here is a stubbe[22] will stiffely stande;
Thurgh bones and senous[23] it schall be soght.
This werke is well, I will warande.

1ST SOLDIER. Saie, sir, howe do we thore[24]?  105
This bargayne may not blynne[25].

3RD SOLDIER. It failis a foote and more,
The senous are so gone ynne[26].

4TH SOLDIER. I hope[27] that marke amisse be bored.

2ND SOLDIER. Than muste he bide in bittir bale[28].  110

1. indeed, 2. stop, 3. Until, 4. fastened, 5. manages, 6. to full extent, 7. draw, 8. bore-hole, 9. hang, 10. thankless, 11. Let no one restrain himself from extra speed, 12. agreed business, 13. must, 14. villain, 15. charge, 16. Must endure a bitter attack, 17. at all, 18. think, 19. obediently, 20. rope, 21. who redeemed you. (A savage anachronism), 22. nail, 23. sinews, 24. there, 25. This business must not stop, 26. contracted, 27. think, 28. torment.

3RD SOLDIER.   In faith, it was overe-skantely scored[1];
                That makis it fouly for to faile.

1ST SOLDIER.   Why carpe[2] ye so? Faste[3] on a corde
                And tugge hym to, by toppe and taile.

3RD SOLDIER.   Ya, thou comaundis lightly as a lorde.       115
                Come helpe to haale[4], with ille haile[5]!

1ST SOLDIER.   Nowe certis that schall I doo
                Full snelly[6] as a snayle.

3RD SOLDIER.   And I schall tacche[7] hym too,
                Full nemely[8] with a nayle.       120


                This werke will holde, that dar I heete[9],
                For nowe are feste[10] faste both his handis.

4TH SOLDIER.   Go we all foure thanne to his feete;
                So schall oure space[11] be spedely[12] spende.

2ND SOLDIER.   Latte see, what bourde his bale myght
                   beete[13];       125
                Tharto my bakke nowe wolde I bende.

4TH SOLDIER.   Owe! This werke is all unmeete[14].
                This boring muste all be amende.

1ST SOLDIER.   A! Pees, man, for Mahounde,
                Latte no man wotte[15] that wondir[16].       130
                A roope schall rugge[17] hym doune,
                Yf all his synnous go asoundre.


2ND SOLDIER.   That corde full kyndely[18] can I knytte[19],
                The comforte of this karle[20] to kele[21].

1ST SOLDIER.   Feste on thanne faste, that all be fytte;       135
                It is no force howe felle he feele[22].

2ND SOLDIER.   Lugge[23] on ye both a litill yitt.

3RD SOLDIER.   I schalle nought sese, as I have seele[24].

4TH SOLDIER.   And I schall fonde[25] hym for to hitte.

2ND SOLDIER.   Owe, haylle[26]!


1. inadequately measured, 2. talk, 3. Fasten, 4. pull, 5. bad luck (to you), 6. quickly,
7. fasten, 8. nimbly, 9. promise, 10. fixed, 11. time, 12. profitably, 13. Let's see what trick
can soothe his pain. (Ironic; cf. l. 134.), 14. wrong, 15. know, 16. strange thing, 17. tug,
18. properly, 19. tie, 20. fellow, 21. lessen, 22. It doesn't matter how painfully he feels
it, 23. Tug, 24. I shan't stop, as I hope to have bliss, 25. try, 26. Oh, pull!

| 4TH SOLDIER. | Hoo nowe! I halde it wele[1]. | 140 |

1ST SOLDIER. Have done, dryve in that nayle,
So that no faute be foune[2].

4TH SOLDIER. This wirkyng wolde noght faile
Yf foure bullis here were boune[3].

1ST SOLDIER. Ther[4] cordis have evill[5] encressed his
paynes, 145
Or[6] he wer tille the booryngis brought.

2ND SOLDIER. Yaa, assoundir are both synnous and veynis
On ilke a[7] side, so have we soughte[8].

3RD SOLDIER. Nowe all his gaudis[9] nothyng hym gaynes;
His sauntering[10] schall with bale[11] be bought. 150

4TH SOLDIER. I wille goo saie to oure soveraynes[12]
Of all this werkis howe we have wrought.

1ST SOLDIER. Nay, sirs, anothir thyng
Fallis firste to you and me.
I badde we schulde hym hyng 155
On heghte that men myght see.

2ND SOLDIER. We woote wele so ther wordes wore[13];
But, sir, that dede will do us dere[14].

1ST SOLDIER. It may not mende for to moote more[15],
This harlotte[16] muste be hanged here. 160

2ND SOLDIER. The mortaise[17] is made fitte therfore.

3RD SOLDIER. Feste on youre fyngeres than in feere[18].

4TH SOLDIER. I wene[19] it wolle nevere come thore[20].
We foure rayse it noght right to-yere[21].

1ST SOLDIER. Say, man, whi carpis thou soo? 165
Thy liftyng was but light.

2ND SOLDIER. He menes ther muste be moo[22]
To heve hym uppe on hight.

3RD SOLDIER. Now certis, I hope it schall noght nede

1. Stop now, I think that's fine, 2. found, 3. tied (to it), 4. These, 5. severely, 6. By the time, 7. every, 8. inflicted pain, 9. tricks, 10. opinions (?), 11. suffering, 12. superiors, 13. were, 14. harm, 15. It won't help to argue any more, 16. villain, 17. mortice, 18. together, 19. think, 20. there, 21. We four won't lift it straight in a year, 22. more.

|               |                                                      |     |
|---------------|------------------------------------------------------|-----|
|               | To calle to us more companye.                        | 170 |
|               | Me thynke we foure schulde do this dede,             |     |
|               | And bere hym to yone hille on high.                  |     |
| 1ST SOLDIER.  | It muste be done, withouten drede[1].                |     |
|               | No more, but loke ye be redy,                        |     |
|               | And this parte schalle I lifte and leede;            | 175 |
|               | On lenghe[2] he schalle no lenger lie.               |     |
|               | Therfore nowe makis you boune[3].                    |     |
|               | Late bere hym to yone hill.                          |     |
| 4TH SOLDIER.  | Thanne will I bere here doune[4]                     |     |
|               | And tente his tase untill[5].                        | 180 |

| 2ND SOLDIER. | We twoo schall see tille aythir side,            |     |
|--------------|--------------------------------------------------|-----|
|              | For ellis this werke wille wrie[6] all wrang.    |     |
| 3RD SOLDIER. | We are redy, in Gode. Sirs, abide,               |     |
|              | And late me first his fete up fang[7].           |     |
| 2ND SOLDIER. | Why tente[8] ye so to tales this tyde[9]?        | 185 |
| 1ST SOLDIER. | Lifte uppe!                                      |     |
| 4TH SOLDIER. | Latte see!                                       |     |
| 2ND SOLDIER. | Owe! Lifte alang.                                |     |
| 3RD SOLDIER. | Fro all this harme he schulde hym hyde[10]       |     |
|              | And[11] he war God.                              |     |
| 4TH SOLDIER. | The devill hym hang!                             |     |
| 1ST SOLDIER. | For grete harme have I hente[12];                |     |
|              | My schuldir is in soundre.                       | 190 |
| 2ND SOLDIER. | And sertis I am nere schente[13];                |     |
|              | So lange have I borne undir.                     |     |

| 3RD SOLDIER. | This crosse and I in twoo muste twynne[14],       |     |
|--------------|---------------------------------------------------|-----|
|              | Ellis brekis my bakke in sondre sone.             |     |
| 4TH SOLDIER. | Laye downe agayne and leve youre dynne,           | 195 |
|              | This dede for us will nevere be done.             |     |
| 1ST SOLDIER. | Assaie, sirs, latte se yf any gynne[15]           |     |
|              | May helpe hym uppe, withouten hone[16];           |     |
|              | For here schulde wight[17] men worschippe wynne,  |     |

---

1. doubt, 2. On his back, 3. ready, 4. i.e. carry at the foot, 5. And attend to his toes, 6. go, 7. take, 8. listen, 9. now, 10. protect himself, 11. If, 12. received, 13. destroyed, 14. separate, 15. Try, sirs, and let's see if any device, 16. delay, 17. strong.

|                | And noght with gaudis alday to gone[1]. | 200 |

2ND SOLDIER. More wighter men than we
Full fewe I hope[2] ye fynde.

3RD SOLDIER. This bargayne[3] will noght bee,
For certis me wantis wynde[4].

4TH SOLDIER. So wille of[5] werke nevere we wore[6];          205
I hope this carle some cautellis caste[7].

2ND SOLDIER. My bourdeyne satte me wondir soore[8];
Unto the hill I myght noght laste.

1ST SOLDIER. Lifte uppe, and sone he schall be thore[9],
Therfore feste on youre fyngeres faste.          210

3RD SOLDIER. Owe, lifte!

1ST SOLDIER.          We, loo!

4TH SOLDIER.                    A litill more.

2ND SOLDIER. Holde thanne!

1ST SOLDIER.               Howe nowe!

2ND SOLDIER.                         The werste is paste.

3RD SOLDIER. He weyes a wikkid weght.

2ND SOLDIER. So may we all foure saie,
Or[10] he was heved on heght,          215
And raysed in this array[11].

4TH SOLDIER. He made us stande as any stones,
So boustous[12] was he for to bere.

1ST SOLDIER. Nowe raise hym nemely for the nonys[13],
And sette hym be this mortas[14] heere,          220
And latte hym falle in alle at ones,
For certis that payne schall have no pere.

3RD SOLDIER. Heve uppe!

4TH SOLDIER.          Latte doune, so all his bones
Are asoundre nowe on sides seere[15].

1ST SOLDIER. This fallyng was more felle[16]          225
Than all the harmes he hadde,
Nowe may a man wele telle

1. And not go playing the fool all day, 2. think, 3. business, 4. I'm short of breath, 5. unsuccessful in, 6. were, 7. I think this fellow played some tricks, 8. My burden weighed very heavily on me, 9. there, 10. By the time that, 11. manner, 12. massive, 13. quickly now, 14. mortice, 15. every side, 16. painful.

The leste lith[1] of this ladde.

| | |
|---|---|
| 3RD SOLDIER. | Me thynkith this crosse will noght abide[2], |
| | Ne stande stille in this morteyse yitt. |

230

| | |
|---|---|
| 4TH SOLDIER. | Att the firste tyme was it made overe wyde; |
| | That makis it wave, thou may wele witte. |
| 1ST SOLDIER. | Itt schall be sette[3] on ilke a side, |
| | So that it schall no forther flitte[4]; |
| | Goode wegges[5] schall we take this tyde[6], |
| | And feste the foote, thanne is all fitte. |

235

| | |
|---|---|
| 2ND SOLDIER. | Here are wegges arraied |
| | For that, both grete and smale. |
| 3RD SOLDIER. | Where are oure hameres laide |
| | That we schulde wirke withall[7]? |

240

| | |
|---|---|
| 4TH SOLDIER. | We have them here even atte oure hande. |
| 2ND SOLDIER. | Gyffe me this wegge; I schall it in dryve. |
| 4TH SOLDIER. | Here is anodir yitt ordande[8]. |
| 3RD SOLDIER. | Do take[9] it me hidir belyve. |
| 1ST SOLDIER. | Laye on thanne faste. |
| 3RD SOLDIER. | Yis, I warrande! |

245

| | |
|---|---|
| | I thryng thame same, so motte I thryve[10]. |
| | Nowe will this crosse full stabely stande; |
| | All yf[11] he rave thei will noght ryve[12]. |
| 1ST SOLDIER. | [*To* JESUS] Say, sir, howe likis thou nowe |
| | This werke that we have wrought? |

250

| | |
|---|---|
| 4TH SOLDIER. | We praye youe sais us howe |
| | Ye fele, or faynte ye ought[13]. |

| | |
|---|---|
| JESUS. | Al men that walkis by waye or strete, |
| | Takes tente ye schalle no travayle tyne[14], |
| | Byholdes myn heede, myn handis and my |
| | feete, |
| | And fully feele nowe, or[15] ye fyne[16], |
| | Yf any mournyng may be meete[17] |

255

---

1. smallest limb, 2. remain steady, 3. fixed, 4. move, 5. wedges, 6. time, 7. with, 8. ready, 9. Bring, 10. I shall ram them down together, as I hope to thrive, 11. Even though, 12. tear apart, 13. at all, 14. Take heed you do not fail to observe any of my suffering, 15. before, 16. stop, 17. equal.

Or myscheve[1] mesured unto myne.
My Fadir, that alle bales[2] may bete[3],
Forgiffis thes men that dois[4] me pyne[5].          260
What thei wirke wotte thai noght[6];
Therfore, my Fadir, I crave,
Latte nevere ther synnys be sought[7],
But see ther saules to save.

1ST SOLDIER.  We! Harke! He jangelis[8] like a jay.          265
2ND SOLDIER.  Me thynke he patris[9] like a py[10].
3RD SOLDIER.  He has ben doand all this day,
              And made grete mevyng of[11] mercy.
4TH SOLDIER.  Es this the same that gune us say[12]
              That he was Goddis sone almyghty?          270
1ST SOLDIER.  Therfore he felis full felle affraye[13],
              And demyd[14] this day for to dye.
2ND SOLDIER.  *Vah! Qui destruis templum*[15].
3RD SOLDIER.  His sawes[16] wer so, certayne.
4TH SOLDIER.  And, sirs, he saide to some          275
              He myght rayse it agayne.

1ST SOLDIER.  To mustir[17] that he hadde no myght,
              For all the kautelles that he couthe kaste[18];
              All yf he wer in worde so wight[19],
              For all his force nowe is he feste.          280
              Als Pilate demed[20] is done and dight[21],
              Therfore I rede[22] that we go reste.
2ND SOLDIER.  This race mon be rehersed right[23],
              Thurgh the worlde both este and weste.
3RD SOLDIER.  Yaa, late hym hynge here stille,          285
              And make mowes on[24] the mone.
4TH SOLDIER.  Thanne may we wende at wille.
1ST SOLDIER.  Nay, goode sirs, noght so sone.

1. injury, 2. sorrows, 3. remedy, 4. cause, 5. pain, 6. They do not know what they are doing (Luke 23.34), 7. examined, 8. chatters, 9. prattles, 10. magpie, 11. appeal (to God) for, 12. said to us, 13. very severe terror, 14. was condemned, 15. Oh, you who would destroy the temple (Matt. 27.40), 16. words, 17. make a show of, 18. Despite all the tricks he could play, 19. Although he was so strong in words, 20. decreed, 21. carried out, 22. suggest, 23. This course of events must be accurately described, 24. faces at.

|                | For certis us nedis anodir note[1]: |     |
|                | This kirtill wolde I of you crave. | 290 |
| 2ND SOLDIER. | Nay, nay, sir, we will loke be lotte[2] | |
|                | Whilke[3] of us foure fallis it to have. | |
| 3RD SOLDIER. | I rede[4] we drawe cutte[5] for this coote[6], | |
|                | Loo, se howe sone, alle sidis to save[7]. | |
| 4TH SOLDIER. | The schorte cutte schall wynne, that wele ye woote, | 295 |
|                | Whedir itt falle to knyght or knave. | |
| 1ST SOLDIER. | Felowes, ye thar[8] noght flyte[9] | |
|                | For this mantell is myné. | |
| 2ND SOLDIER. | Goo we thanne hense tyte[10], | |
|                | This travayle here we tyne[11]. | 300 |

*[Exeunt soldiers]*

---

1. For indeed there's another matter we need to do, 2. draw lots, 3. Which, 4. suggest, 5. lot (by cut straws), 6. coat, 7. to protect all our interests, 8. need, 9. argue, 10. at once, 11. We're wasting our effort here.

# NINE SLOANE LYRICS

These short poems are all taken from a fifteenth-century manuscript, B.L. MS. Sloane 2593. The contents are both secular and religious, and the tone ranges from the reverent (no. 1) to the satiric (no. 7), and from the reflective (no. 6) to the obscene (no. 9). Four of the poems printed here are carols (nos 6–9), a term which refers not to their subject matter but to their form, in that they are songs which have a refrain to be repeated after each stanza. The carols are edited by R. L. Greene, *The Early English Carols* (2nd edn, Oxford, 1977). For the complete collection of Sloane lyrics see T. Wright, *Songs and Carols* (London, 1856).

### 1. I SING OF A MAIDEN

I syng of a mayden
That is makeles[1],
Kyng of alle kynges
To here sone che ches[2].

He cam also stylle[3]                              5
Ther[4] his moder was,
As dew in Aprylle
That fallyt on the gras.

He cam also stylle
To his moderes bowr,                              10
As dew in Aprille
That fallyt on the flour.

He cam also stylle
Ther his moder lay,
As dew in Aprille                                 15
That fallyt on the spray.

---

1. matchless (with play on 'mateless'), 2. She chose as her son, 3. just as quietly, 4. Where.

Moder and maydyn
Was never non but che;
Wel may swych[1] a lady
Godes moder be!                                    20


## II. I HAVE A GENTLE COCK

I have a gentil[1] cook,
Crowyt me day;
He doth[2] me rysyn erly,
My matyins for to say.


I have a gentil cook,                                5
Comyn he is of gret[3];
His comb is of reed corel,
His tayil is of get[4].


I have a gentyl cook,
Comyn he is of kynde[5];                            10
His comb is of red corel,
His tayl is of inde[6].


His legges ben of asor[7],
So geintil and so smale[8];
His spores[9] arn of sylver qwyt[10],               15
Into the wortewale[11].


His eynyn[12] arn of cristal,
Lokyn[13] al in aumbyr,
And every nyght he perchit hym[14]
In myn ladyis chaumbyr.                             20


1. such

1. well-bred, 2. makes, 3. distinguished lineage, 4. jet, 5. high birth, 6. blue, 7. azure,
8. slender, 9. spurs, 10. white, 11. root, (i.e. from top to bottom), 12. eyes, 13. Set, 14.
perches.

### III. GIVE US A DRINK

'Omnes gentes plaudite[1]',
I saw myny bryddis setyn on a tre;
He[2] tokyn here[3] fleyght and flowyn away,
With 'ego dixi[4]', have good day!

Many qwyte federes haght[5] the pye[6];        5
I may noon more syngyn, my lyppis arn so drye!
Many qwyte federis haght the swan;
The more that I drynke, the lesse good I can!

Ley stykkys on the fer; wyl mot it brenne[7];
Yeve us onys drynkyn er we gon henne[8]!        10

### IV. ADAM

Adam lay ibowndyn[1],
Bowndyn in a bond,
Fowre thowsand wynter
Thowt[2] he not to long.

And al was for an appil,        5
An appil that he tok,
As clerkes fyndyn wretyn
In here[3] book.

Ne hadde the appil take ben[4],
The appil take ben,        10
Ne hadde never our Lady
A[5] ben hevene qwen.

1. All nations clap your hands (Psalm 46), 2. They, 3. their, 4. I said (Isa. 38.10), 5. has, 6. magpie, 7. well may it burn, 8. Give us a drink before we leave here.

1. imprisoned, 2. Thought, 3. their, 4. If the apple had not been taken, 5. Have.

Blyssid be the tyme
That appil take was,
Therfore we mown[1] syngyn                                    15
'Deo gracias[2]!'


### V. I HAVE A YOUNG SISTER

I have a yong suster
Fer beyondyn the se,
Many be the drowryis[1]
That che[2] sente me.

Che sente me the cherye                                       5
Withoutyn ony ston,
And so che dede the dowe[3]
Withoutyn ony bon.

Sche sente me the brere[4]
Withoutyn ony rynde[5];                                       10
Sche bad me love my lemman[6]
Withoute longgyng.

How shuld ony cherye
Be withoute ston?
And how shuld ony dowe                                        15
Ben withoute bon?

How shuld ony brere
Ben withoute rynde?
How shuld I love myn lemman
Without longyng?                                              20

1. may, 2. Thanks be to God.

1. keepsakes, 2. she, 3. dove, 4. briar, 5. bark, 6. dear one.

Quan[1] the cherye was a flour,
Than hadde it non ston;
Quan the dowe was an ey[2],
Than hadde it non bon.

Quan the brere was onbred[3],                              25
Than hadde it non rynd;
Quan the maydyn haght that che lovit[4],
Che is without longing.


## VI. THE SUN OF GRACE

Al the meryere is that place
The sunne of grace hym schynit in[1].

The sunne of grace hym schynit in
In on[2] day quan[3] it was morwe[4],
Quan our Lord God born was                                 5
Withoute wem[5] or sorwe.

The sunne of grace hym schynit in
On a day quan it was pryme[6],
Quan our Lord God born was,
So wel he knew his tyme.                                   10

The sunne of grace hym schynit in
On a day quan it was non[7],
Quan our Lord God born was
And on the rode[8] don[9].

The sunne of grace hym schynit in                         15
On a day quan it was undyrn[10],
Quan our Lord God born was
And to the herte stongyn[11].

---

1. When, 2. egg, 3. in the seed, 4. has what she loves.

1. That the sun of grace shone in, 2. one, 3. when, 4. morning, 5. stain, 6. dawn, 7. mid afternoon, 8. cross, 9. put, 10. evening, 11. pierced.

## VII. YOUNG MEN I WARN YOU

How! Hey! It is non les[1];
I dar not seyn quan che seygh 'Pes![2]'

Ying men, I warne you everychon[3],
Elde wywys take ye non[4],
For I myself have on[5] at hom;                               5
I dar not seyn quan che seyght 'Pes!'

Quan I cum fro the plow at non,
In a reven dych[6] myn mete is don[7];
I dar not àskyn our dame a spon[8];
I dar not (etc.)                                              10

If I aske our dame bred,
Che takyt a staf and brekit myn hed,
And doth[9] me rennyn[10] under the led[11];
I dar not (etc.)

If I aske our dame fleych[12],                                15
Che brekit myn hed with a dych:
'Boy, thou art not worght a reych[13]!'
I dar (etc.)

If I aske our dame chese,
'Boy', che seyght, al at ese[14],                            20
'Thou art not worght half a pese[15].'
I dar not sey quan che seyght 'Pes!'

1. lie, 2. I dare not speak when she says 'Quiet!', 3. every one, 4. Don't marry old wives, 5. one, 6. broken dish, 7. put, 8. spoon, 9. makes, 10. run, 11. cauldron, 12. flesh, 13. worth a rush, 14. coolly, 15. pea.

### VIII. SIR PENNY

Go bet[1], Peny, go bet, go,
For thou mat[2] makyn bothe frynd and fo.


Peny is an hardy knyght,
Peny is mekyl[3] of myght,
Peny of wrong he makyt ryght,     5
In every cuntré qwer[4] he goo.


Thow[5] I have a man islawe[6]
And forfetyd[7] the kynges lawe,
I shal fyndyn a man of lawe
Wyl takyn myn peny and let me goo.    10


And if I have to don[8] fer or ner,
And[9] Peny be myn massanger,
Thann am I non thing in dwer[10];
My cause shal be wel idoo[11].


And if I have pens bothe good and fyn,   15
Men wyl byddyn[12] me to the wyn;
'That[13] I have shal be thine';
Sekyrly[14] thei wil seyn[15] so.


And quan[16] I have non in myn purs,
Peny bet[17] ne peny wers,      20
Of me thei holdyn but lytil fors[18]:
'He was a man; let hym goo.'


1. Hurry, 2. can, 3. great, 4. wherever, 5. Even if, 6. slain, 7. broken, 8. i.e. have business, 9. If, 10. doubt, 11. done, 12. invite, 13. Whatever, 14. Certainly, 15. say, 16. when, 17. better, 18. They have little regard for me.

## IX. CHAPMEN

We ben chapmen[1] lyght of fote,
The fowle weyis for to fle.

We bern[2] abowtyn non cattes skynnys,
Pursis, perlis, sylver pynnis,
Smale wympeles for ladyis chynnys;                    5.
Damsele, bey[3] sum ware[4] of me.

I have a poket for the nonys[5],
Therine ben tweyne[6] precyous stonys;
Damsele, hadde ye asayid hem onys[7],
Ye shuld the rathere[8] gon with me.                   10

I have a jelyf[9] of Godes sonde[10],
Withoutyn fyt[11] it can stonde,
It can smytyn[12] and haght[13] non honde;
Ryd[14] yourself quat it may be.

I have a powder for to selle,                          15
Quat it is can I not telle;
It makit maydenys wombys to swelle;
Therof I have a quantyté.

1. pedlars, 2. carry, 3. buy, 4. goods, 5. purpose, 6. two, 7. once tried them, 8. sooner, 9. jelly, 10. a gift of God, 11. feet, 12. strike, 13. has, 14. Guess.

# ROBERT HENRYSON: *THE FABLE OF THE LION AND THE MOUSE*

Robert Henryson (d. *c.* 1500) wrote thirteen fables, many of which, like this one, are based on medieval Latin and French versions of *Aesop's Fables*. The text printed here is from the Bannatyne MS. (N. L. S. MS. Advocates 1.1.6), which was edited by W. Tod Ritchie for the Scottish Text Society, New Series 26 (1930). The standard edition of the complete poems is that of D. Fox (Oxford, 1981). Note that the spelling *quh-* represents modern *wh-*, e.g. *quha*, 'who', *quhilk*, 'which'.

### THE PROLOGUE

In myddis of June, that joly sueit sessoun,
Quhen that fair Phebus with his bemis brycht
Had dryit up the dew fra daill and doun,
And all the land maid with his lemys[1] lycht,
In a mornyng, betuix midday and nycht,                      5
I rais, and put all slewth and sleip on syd;
Ontill a wod I went allone but gyd[2].

Sueit wes the smell of flouris quhyt and reid,
The noyis of birdis rycht delicius;
The bewis bred blumyt abone my heid,                       10
The grund growand with gres gratius[3];
Off all plesans that place wes plenteus,
With sueit odour and birdis armony,
The mornyng myld; my mirth wes mair forthy[4].

The roisis reid arreyit rone[5] and rys[6],                 15
The prumros and the purpour viola;
To heir it was a poynt of paradys,
Sic myrth the mavis and the merle cowth ma[7];
The blosummis blyth[8] brak[9] upon bank and bra[10],

---

1. rays, 2. without a guide, 3. The broad boughs flowered above my head, the earth growing with lovely grass, 4. as a result, 5. thicket, 6. branch, 7. Such joyful sounds did the thrush and the blackbird make, 8. lovely, 9. opened, 10. hill.

The smell of herbis and of fowlis cry,                                    20
Contending quha suld[1] haif the victory.

Me to conserf[2] than fra the sonis heit,
Undir the schaddow of an awthorne grene
I lenyt doun, amangis the flouris sueit,
Syne maid a cors[3], and closit baith[4] myne ene[5].          25
On sleip I fell amang the bewis bene[6],
And in my dreme me thocht come throw the schaw
The fairest man befoir that evir I saw.

His goun wes of a claith[7] als quhyt as mylk,
His chymmeris[8] wer of chamelet[9] purpour broun,             30
His hude of skarlet, bordowrit[10] with silk,
In hekle wys[11] untill his girdill doun.
His bonat round wes of the auld fassoun,
His heid was quhyt, his ene wes grene and gray,
With lokar[12] hair quhilk[13] our[14] his schulderis lay.     35

A roll of paper in his hand he bair,
A swannis pen stickand undir his eir,
Ane ynkhorne with a pretty gilt pennair[15],
A bag of silk all at his belt he weir.
Thus wes he gudly grathit[16] in his geir,                     40
Of stature lerge, and with a feirfull[17] face;
Evin quhair I lay he come a sturdy pace.

And said, 'God speid, my sone!' And I wes fane[18]
Off that cowth[19] word and of his cumpany.
With reverence I salust[20] him agane[21],                     45
'Welcum, fader!' and he sat doun me by.
'Displeis yow nocht, my gud maister, thocht[22] I
Demand your birth, your faculty[23] and name,
Quhy ye come heir, or quhair ye dwell at hame.'

1. who should, 2. To protect myself, 3. sign of the cross, 4. both, 5. eyes, 6. lovely boughs, 7. cloth, 8. robes, 9. fine woven material, 10. bordered, 11. With a fringe, 12. curly, 13. which, 14. over, 15. pen-case, 16. equipped, 17. awe-inspiring, 18. glad, 19. courteous, 20. greeted, 21. in return, 22. if, 23. profession.

'My sone,' said he, 'I am of gentill blude;              50
My natall[1] land is Rome, withowttin nay[2],
And in that toun first to the scoullis yude[3],
And science[4] studeit full mony a day.
And now my winnyng[5] is in hevin for ay.
Isope[6] I hecht[7]; my wrytin and my werk              55
Is cowth and kend to mony cunnand clerk[8].'

'O maistir Ysop, poet lawreat,
God wait[9] ye ar full deir welcum to me.
Ar ye nocht he that all thir[10] fabillis wrate,
Quhilk in effect, suppois thay fenyeit be[11],          60
Ar full of prowdens[12] and moralité?'
'Fair sone,' said he, 'I am that samyne[13] man.'
God wait gif that[14] my hairt wes mirry than!

I said, 'Isop, my maistir venerable,
I yow beseik hairtly, for cherité[15],                   65
Ye wald dedene[16] to tell a pretty feble[17],
Concludand with a gud moralitie.'
Schakand his heid, he said, 'my sone, lat be.
For quhat is worth to tell a fenyeit[18] taill,
Quhen haill[19] preiching may nothing now availl?'      70

'Now in this warld me think rycht few or nane
Till[20] Godis word that hes devotioun.
The eir is deiff, the hairt is hard as stane,
Now oppin syn without correctioun,
the e[21] inclynand to the erd[22] ay doun.             75
Sua rowstit[23] is the warld with kanker blak,
That my taillis may littill succour mak.'

---

1. native, 2. indeed, 3. went, 4. learning, 5. dwelling-place, 6. Aesop, 7. am called, 8. Are well known to many learned men, 9. knows, 10. these, 11. Which actually, even though they are fictional, 12. wisdom, 13. same, 14. if, 15. I urgently beseech you that, 16. deign, 17. fable, 18. fictional, 19. lit. whole, i.e. straightforward, 20. To, 21. eye, 22. ground, 23. corrupted.

'Yit, gentill ser,' said I, 'for my requeist
Nocht till[1] displeis your fadirheid[2], I pray,
Undir the figure[3] of sum brutall beist,        80
A morall fable ye wald dedene[4] to say.
Quha wate nor[5] I may leir[6] and beir away
Sum thing thairby heireftir may availl?'
'I grant,' quod he, and thus begowth[7] a taill.

### THE FABLE

'A lyone at his pray wery for-ron[8],        85
To recreat[9] his lymis and to rest,
Bekand[10] his breist and belly at the son,
Undir a tre lay in the fair forrest.
Sua[11] come a trip[12] of mys out of thair nest,
Rycht tait[13] and trig[14], all dansand in a gys[15],        90
And our[16] the lyone lansit[17] twys or thrys.

He lay so still, the mys wes nocht afferd,
Bot to and fra attour[18] him tuke thair trais[19];
Sum tirlyt[20] at the campis[21] of his berd,
Sum sparit nocht to claw him on the fais.        95
Myrry and glaid thus dansit thay a spais[22],
Quhill[23] at the last the noble lyoun wouk[24],
And with his pow[25] the maister mows he tuke.

Scho gaif a cry, and all the laif[26] agast
Thair dansing left, and hid thame heir and thair.        100
Scho that wes tane[27] cryit and weipit fast,
And said, "allais! for now and evir mair,
Now am I tane a wofull presonair,
And for my gilt trestis incontinent[28]
Of lyfe and deth to thoill[29] the jugement."        105

1. That it may not, 2. dignity, 3. representation, 4. deign, 5. Who knows but that, 6. learn, 7. began, 8. quite exhausted with running, 9. revive, 10. Basking, 11. Then, 12. group, 13. nimble, 14. sprightly, 15. dance, 16. over, 17. jumped, 18. about, 19. dance, 20. tugged, 21. hairs, 22. while, 23. Until, 24. woke, 25. paw, 26. others, 27. caught, 28. And because of my guilt I expect at once, 29. suffer.

Thane spak the lyone to that cairfull[1] mous:
"Thow catyve[2] wreche, and vyle unworthy thing!
Our-malapart[3] and our-presumpteous
Thow was to mak our me thyne tripping.
Knew thow nocht weill I wes baith lord and king          110
Of all beistis?" "Yis," quod the mous, "I knaw;
Bot I misknew[4] becaus ye lay so law.

"Lord, I beseik thy kingly ryalté,
Heir quhat I say, and tak in patience.
Considdir first my semple poverté,                       115
And syne[5] thy michty he[6] magnificens;
Se als how thingis done by negligence,
Nocht of malys nor of presumptioun,
Erer[7] suld haif grace and remissioun.

"We wer repleit and had grit haboundance                 120
Off alkyn fude sic as till us affeird[8];
The sueit sessoun provokit us to dans,
And mak sic[9] mirth as nature to us leird[10].
Ye lay so still and law upone the erd[11]
That, be my saule, we wend[12] ye had bene deid,          125
Ellis wald we nocht have dansit our your heid."

"Thy fals excus," the lyoun said agane[13],
"Sall nocht availl a myt, I undirta[14]!
I put the cais[15], I had bene deid or slane,
And syne[16] my skin bene stoppit[17] full of stra;       130
Thocht[18] thow had fund my figour lyand swa[19],
Becaus it bair the prent[20] of my persoun,
Thow suld for dreid on kneis haif fallin doun.

"For thy trespas thow can mak na defens,
My noble persoun thus to vilipend[21];                   135

---

1. sorrowful, 2. miserable, 3. Over-impudent, 4. failed to recognize (you), 5. next, 6. high, 7. Sooner, 8. Of every sort of food that suited us, 9. such, 10. taught, 11. ground, 12. thought, 13. in reply, 14. assure (you), 15. Supposing, 16. then, 17. stuffed, 18. Even though, 19. lying thus, 20. imprint, 21. dishonour.

Of thy fers[1] nor thyne awin negligens
For till excus thow can no caus pretend[2].
Thairfoir thow suffer sall a schamefull end
And deid[3], sic as to tressoun is decryit[4] –
Onto the gallows hangit be the feit."                    140

"A! Mercy, lord, at thy gentrice[5] I as[6]!
As thow art king of beistis corronat[7],
Sobir[8] thy wreth, and lat thi yre ourpas[9],
And mak thy mynd to mercy inclinat.
I grant offens is done to thyne estait;                   145
Thairfoir I wirdy[10] am to suffer deid
Bot gife[11] thy kingly mercy reik remeid[12].

"In every juge mercy and rewth suld be,
As assessouris and collaterall[13].
Without mercy, justice is crewelté,                       150
As said is in the lawis spirituall.
Quhen rigour sittis in the tribunall,
The equety of law quha may sustene?
Rycht few or nane, bot[14] mercy go betuene.

"Also ye knaw the honor triumphall                        155
Off all[15] victor upone the strenth dependis
Of his compeir[16], quhilk manly in battell
Throw juperdy[17] of armes lang defendis.
Quhat price[18] or loving[19] quhen the battell endis
Is said of him that ourcumis a man                        160
Him to defend that nowdir may nor can[20]?

"A thowsand mys to keill and eik[21] devoir
Is littill manheid untill a strong lyoun;
Full littill wirschep haif ye won thairfoir,
To quhois strenth is no comparesoun.                      165

1. companions, 2. You can put forward no case to excuse, 3. death, 4. decreed, 5. clemency, 6. ask, 7. crowned, 8. Assuage, 9. anger pass away, 10. fit, 11. Unless, 12. should grant clemency, 13. As advisors and assistants. (Legal terminology), 14. unless, 15. every, 16. rival, 17. hazard, 18. honour, 19. fame, 20. Who is unable to defend himself, 21. also.

It will degraid sum pairte of your renoun
Till[1] slay a mows, quhilk may mak no defens
Bot askand[2] mercy at your excellens.

"Also it semys[3] nocht your celcitud[4],
Quhilk[5] usis daylie meitis delicius,                                    170
To fyle[6] your teith or lippis with my blude,
Quhilk to your stomok is contagius[7].
Unhelsum meit is of a sary mous[8],
And namely[9] till a noble strang lyoun
Wont to be fed with gentill venysoun.                                    175

"My lyfe is littill, and my deid[10] far les,
Yit and[11] I leif[12], I may, peraventour,
Supplé your hienes beand in distres[13];
For oft is sene a small man of stature
Reskewit hes a lord of hie honour,                                       180
Keipit that was in poynt to be ourthrawin[14]
Throw misfortoun; sic[15] cais may be your awin[16]."

Quhen this wes said, the lyone his langege
Pasit[17], and thocht accordand till ressoun,
And gart[18] mercy his crewell yre assuege,                              185
And to the mous grantit remissioun,
Oppynnit his pow, and scho on kneis fell doun,
And baith hir handis unto the hevin upheld,
Cryand, "Almychty God mot yow foryeld[19]!"

Quhen scho wes gone, the lyone yeid[20] to hunt,                         190
For he had nocht, bot levit on his pray,
And slew baith tame and wyld as he wes wunt,
And in the cuntré maid a grit dirray[21];
Till at the last the peple fand the way

---

1. To, 2. Apart from asking, 3. befits, 4. high status, 5. Who, 6. defile, 7. harmful, 8.
The meat of a wretched mouse is unwholesome, 9. especially, 10. death, 11. if, 12. live,
13. Help your Highness in distress, 14. Preserved one who was on the point of being
overthrown, 15. such, 16. own, 17. Moderated, 18. caused, 19. reward, 20. went, 21.
disturbance.

This crewall lyone how that thay micht him tak;                    195
Off hempin coirdis strang nettis cowth[1] thay mak.


And in a rod[2] quhair he wes wont to rin,
With rapis rude[3] fra tre to tre it band[4],
Syne kest a raing on raw the wod within[5],
With hornis blast and canettis[6] fast calland.                    200
The lyone fled, and throw the rone[7] rynnand,
Fell in the net and hankit[8] fute and heid;
For all his strenth he cowth mak no remeid[9].


Volvand[10] about, with hiddous rowmissing[11],
Quhyle[12] to, quhyle fro, gif[13] he mycht succour get;           205
Bot all in vane, that velyeit[14] him nothing,
The moir he flang[15] the fastir wes he knet[16].
The rapis rude was so about him plet[17]
On every syd, that succour saw he non,
Bot still lyand, thus murnand maid his mone:                       210


"O lamit lyoun, liggand[18] heir so law,
Quhair is the mycht of thy magnificens
Off quhome all brutall beist in erd stud aw[19],
And dred to luke unto thy excellens?
But howp[20] or help, but succour or defens,                       215
In bandis strong heir mone[21] I byd[22], allace,
Till I be slane; I se non uthir grace.


"Thair is no wy[23] that will my harmis wraik[24],
Nor creatur do confort to my croun.
Quhay[25] sall me bute[26]? Quhay sall thir bandis breik?          220
Quha sall me put fra pane of this presoun?"
Be[27] he had maid his lamentatioun,
Throw avintur[28] the littill mows come neir,

---

1. did, 2. path, 3. crude, 4. tied, 5. Then they placed a band of men in a line within the wood, 6. dogs, 7. thicket, 8. was snared, 9. redress, 10. Turning, 11. roaring, 12. Now, 13. if, 14. availed, 15. flailed about, 16. tied, 17. twisted, 18. lying, 19. stood in awe, 20. Without hope, 21. must, 22. remain, 23. man, 24. avenge, 25. Who, 26. help, 27. When, 28. By chance.

And of the lyone hard the petows beir[1].

And suddanly it come intill hir mynd                              225
That it suld be the lyone did[2] hir grace,
And said, "Now wer I fals and rycht unkynd
Bot gife I quit sumpairte thy gentilnes[3]
Thow did to me." And on with that scho gais
Till hir fallowis, and on thame fast can[4] cry,               230
"Cum help! Cum help!" and thay come on in hy[5].

"Lo!" quod the mous, "this is the same lyone
Quhilk gaif me grace quhen that I wes tane,
And now is fast heir bundin[6] in presone,
Wrekand[7] his hurt with sair murnyng and mane.          235
Bot we him help, of supplé wait he nane[8].
Cum help to quyt[9] a gud turne for anothir!
Go lows[10] him sone[11]!" And thay said, "Ye, gud bruthir!"

Thay tuke no knyfe, thair teith wes scherp ennuch[12];
To se that sicht, forsuth, it wes grit wondir                    240
How that thay ran amangis the raipis tuche[13],
Befoir, behind, sum yeid abone[14], sum undir,
And schure the raipis of the mastis in schundir[15],
Syne[16] bad him rys, and he stert up annone
And thankit thame; syne on his wayis is gone.              245

Now is the lyone fre of all dengeir,
Lows and deliverit till his libertie
Be[17] littill beistis of ane small poweir,
As ye haif hard, becaus he had peté.'
Quod I, 'Maister, is thair a moralité                              250
In this fable?' 'Ya, sone,' said he, 'rycht gude.'
'I pray yow, ser,' quod I, 'ye wald conclud.'

---

1. heard the piteous noise, 2. was the lion that did, 3. If I did not repay a part of your kindness, 4. did, 5. haste, 6. bound, 7. Expressing, 8. Unless we help him he will find no aid, 9. repay, 10. release, 11. at once, 12. enough, 13. tough, 14. went above, 15. And cut the ropes of the nets asunder, 16. Then, 17. By.

## MORALITAS

'As I suppois, this mychty gay lyoun
May signify a prince or empriour,
A potestat, or yit a king with croun,                    255
Quhilk suld be walkryfe gyd[1] and govirnour
Of his peple, and takis no lawbour
To rewll nor steir the land, nor justice keip,
Bot lyis still in lustis, slewth[2] and sleip.

'The fair forrest with levis loun and le[3],              260
With fowlis song and flouris ferly[4] sueit,
Is bot the warld and his prosperité,
As fals plesandis myngit with cair repleit[5].
Rycht as the ros, with frost and wintir weit,
Faidis, so dois the warld, and thame dissavis[6]         265
Quhilk in thair lustis maist confidens havis.

'Thir littill mys ar bot the commonté[7],
Wantone, unwys, without correctioun.
Thir lordis and princis quhen that thay se
Of justice makis non executioun[8],                      270
Thay dreid nothing to mak rebellioun
And disobey, for quhy thay stand none aw;
That garis[9] thame thair soveranis to misknaw[10].

'Be this fable, ye lordis of prudens
May conciddir the vertew of peté,                         275
And to remyt sumtyme a grit offens,
And metigat with mercy crewelty.
Ofttyme is sene a man of small degre
Hes quyt a commoun[11], baith for gude and ill,
As lord has done rigour or grace him till[12].           280

---

1. an alert guide, 2. sloth, 3. quiet and still, 4. wonderfully, 5. Like false pleasures mingled with great sorrow, 6. deceives, 7. common people, 8. When they see that these lords and princes do not execute justice, 9. causes, 10. disregard, 11. Has repayed an obligation, 12. As a lord has acted towards him with harshness or with kindness.

'Quha wait[1] how sone a lord of greit renoun,
Rolland in warldly lust and vane plesandis,
May be ourthrawin, distroyit or put doun
Throw fals Fortoun, quhilk of all varians
Is haill maistres[2] and leder of the dans          285
Till lusty men, and bindis thame so soir
That they no perrell can provyd befoir[3].

'Thir crewall men that stentit[4] hes the nett,
In quhilk the lyone suddanely wes tane[5],
Waitit alway amendis for till get[6] –          290
For hurte, men wrytis in the marble stane[7].
Moir till expone as now[8] I latt allane,
Bot king and lord may weill wit[9] quhat I mene;
Fegour[10] heirof oftymis hes bene sene.'

Quhen this was sayid, quod Isope, 'My fair chyld,          295
Perswaid the kirkmen[11] ythandly[12] to pray
That tressone of this cuntré be exyld,
And justice ring[13], and lordis keip thair fey[14]
Unto thair soverane lord both nycht and day.'
And with that word he vaneist, and I woik;          300
Syne throw the schaw my jurney hamewart tuke.

---

1. knows, 2. complete mistress, 3. foresee, 4. stretched, 5. captured, 6. Anticipated getting recompense (for the lion's depredations), 7. i.e. people never forget an injury, 8. interpret at present, 9. know, 10. Example, 11. clergy, 12. assiduously, 13. reign, 14. faith.

# TEXTUAL NOTES

All substantive alterations to the manuscript readings, except those noted in the introduction, are listed here. The reading of the text is followed after the bracket by the reading of the manuscript. *Om.* means the word is omitted.

### Three Harley Lyrics

I. ALISON   30. hendi] hend, II. LENTEN IS COME   11. wynne] wynter, 22. doth] doh.

### Winner and Waster

14. no] *om*, 15. tham] hir, 25. three] thies, 58. holte] hate, 64. ther] thre, 144. bulles] bibulles, 157. galegs] galeys, 164. balle] balke, 166. mayne] maye, 176 *and*, 186. *transposed in ms.*, 189. wittnesse] of wittnesse, 201. wy] wyes; demeth] doeth, 215. sowede] sowrede, 264. thou (2)] tho, 270. rychely] ryhely, 288. tynen] tymen, 300. freres] it freres, 353–60. *ms. damaged*, 353. Caudles] ... ls, 354. Dariels] ... ls, 355. Mawmene] ... nene, 356. Aye a] *lost*, 357. Thoughe] ... e, 358. Me tenyth] ... nyth, 359. That iche] *lost*, 360. Than] *lost*, 364. ones] one, 366. forther] forthe, 370. pure] poure, 372. that it] and, 411. sleghe] elde, 420. wedes] werdes, 454. hert] *om*, 468–73. *ms. damaged*, 468. come] co ..., 469. take] *lost*, 470. beryinge-day] ber ..., 471. to passe] *lost*, 472. wonne ther ever] won ..., 473. wynge theruntill] wyng ... ntill, 485. spred] spre ..., 500. silver] si ..., 502. kayren] layren.

### Piers Plowman

The scribe's *oe* and *ae* have been simplified to *o* and *a* where appropriate (e.g. *olde* for *oelde*, *one* for *oen*, etc.). His spellings of *he* for *she* and *ho* for *who* have also been altered. The emendations listed below take account of the readings of other manuscripts of the text, in particular those of B.L. MS. Add. 35157.

*Passus V* 21. therby] the by, 35. yong] yong yong, 43a. in qua] quia, 47. psalmes] phalmes, 58. fanne-] famne-, 62. knaves] knave, 76. mendenants] mendenant, 81. or] *om*, 84. discret] desirede, 90. begge] bygge, 95. and (2)] an, 96. He boughte] Aboute, 98. wyrdes] wordes, 98a. que] qui.

*Passus XX* 24. *and* 32. Pers *and* Plouhman] *erased in ms*, 25. dount] doiunt, 33. bringe] beynge, 74. Two] Tho, 76. cam and] of tho theves cam a, 87. trinen] turnen, 104. recreaunt] creaunt, 106. lordeyns] lordeyne, 152. Job] Jop, 159. be] *om*, 184a. matutinum] matitinum, 198. dwellen] down, 230. was] *om*, 239. was] wast, 242. ther blased] that blased as, 260. it] lihte, 268. bileve] bilewe, 284. blente] brente, 285. chine] shine, 288. catel] car, 297. ne] ne do, 299. by] of, 323. ne] no, 338. be] *om*, 342. gret] *om*, 347–8. ther ... lesynge] *om*, 353. her] hem, 359. and ... answeride] *om*, 382. be *and* in] *om*, 386. lete] lede; anyented] anended, 392. be] *om*, 419. bretherene] brethene,

425. yeve] yove, 431. I] Or, 434. in] and, 445. bonde] boynde, 450a. post
... Phebus] etc, 456. ne] *om*, 473. the (1)] th.

## Sir Launfal

The scribe's *d* has been altered to *th*, where appropriate, and vice versa.
58. ylyche] ylyke, 140. tresour] tosour, 142. fre] fr, 272. they] the, 450.
knyghtes] kyghtes, 500. Launfales] Launfal, 503. her] he, 509, That] That
that, 554. knave] kna, 575. Launfales] Launfal, 624. he] *om*, 656. sche] sch,
669 unryght] unrryght, 675, manere] marnere, 700. wroghth] wroght, 721.
wroth] worth, 800. schuld] schild, 823. upon] upan, 828. tydynge] tydynde,
913. supposed] suppose, 918. thou] *om*, 997. nyme] myne, 999. lemman]
lemmam, 1036. this] thus.

## Pearl

In a few cases the scribe's *v* has been altered to *w*.
25. mot] ... t, 26. runne] runnen, 35. spryngande] sprygande, 54. fyrce] fyrte,
60. precios] precos, 72. adubbemente] adubmente, 95. gracios] gracos, 115.
As] A, 138. over] other, 142. hoped] hope, 144. ay] a, 185. hoped] hope,
192. precios] precos, 197. biys] viys, 286. broght] brogh, 302. levez] lovez,
303. uncortayse] uncortoyse, 308. levez] lovez, 323. man] ma, 335. perle]
perlez, 342 in] and, 353. Stynt] Stynst, 363 I] *om*, 369. kythez] lythez, 382.
manerez] marerez, 433. sayde] syde, 460. tryste] tyste, 479. he] ho, 524. pay]
pray, 529. date] day; day] date, 532. hem] hen, 538. and] and and, 558.
waning] wanig, 572. called] calle, 596. pretermynable] pertermynable, 616.
fere] lere, 649. out] out out, 672. As] At, 673. thus] thus thus, 675. face]
fate, 678, hylle] hyllez, 690. Koyntise onoure] kyntly oure, 691. ho] he, 700.
For] Sor, 714. touch] toucth, 739. ryghtwys] ryghtywys, 752. carped] carpe,
802. nem] men, 817. In] *om*, 829. swete] swatte, 836. sagh] saytz, 848. nouther]
non other, 856. that] tha, 861. Lombe] Lonbe, 892. that swe] thay swe, 911.
bose] blose, 932. I] And I, 934, gracious] gracous, 958. flesch] fresch, 977. I]
*om*, 997. John] *om*, 1012. hew] how, 1014. jacynght] jacyngh, 1058. As] A,
1063. mynster] mynyster, 1064. refet] reget, 1068. anunder] annundez, 1086.
frech] freuch, 1097. enpryse] enpresse, 1104. gret] outen, 1111. golde] glode,
1179. quyke] quykez, 1196. moghte] moghten.

## Tereus and Procne

5769. tyt] tyd, 5962. largesse] larchesse.

## The Second Shepherds' Play

10. husbandys] shepardes, 24. under] hunder, 57. wyndys] weders, 71. oure]
or oure, 93. that] it, 193. ther] the, 218. teyne] teyle, 244. now] not, 291.
From] Fron, 359. me] my, 370, 372. *Speakers' names transposed*, 375. God]
t god, 383. Stevyn] Strevyn, 407. se] be, 421. That] A that, 428. suppose]

si suppose, 617. myself] myfelf, 621, 623. *Speakers' names transposed*, 629. *Speaker's name om*, 673 lose] s lose.

## The York Crucifixion Play

97. nowe] howe; ought] nowe, 101. 1 Sold] 2 Sold, 118. snelly] snerly, 154. you and] youe, 230. morteyse] moteyse, 273. Vah] Vath; destruis] destruit.

## Nine Sloane Lyrics

The letter *x* has been printed as *sh* (e.g. *shuld*).
I. I SING OF A MAIDEN  1. syng] syng a; mayden] myden.
II. I HAVE A GENTLE COCK  11. corel] scorel.
III. GIVE US A DRINK  9. it] is.
V. I HAVE A YOUNG SISTER  7. the] om.
VI. THE SUN OF GRACE  4. morwe] mor. 16. undyrn] undy.
VIII. SIR PENNY  17. thine] thi.
IX. CHAPMEN  5. wympeles] wympele.

## The Fable of the Lion and the Mouse

Where appropriate, the scribe's *w* is represented by *u* or *v*, and his final *-ss* by *-s*. The emendations are based on the readings of the Bassandyne print of 1571. 15. roisis] roiss, 53. full] om, 117. how] fow, 118. presumptioun] promissioun, 126. have] om, 136. fers] fors, 161. nor] no, 169. nocht] to, 180. hie] his, 184. accordand] accordit, 189. foryeld] yeld, 214. thy] thy grit, 218. wy] joy, 233. that] that at, 248. ane] om, 266. lustis maist] lust, 272. disobey] discobey, 277. with mercy] mercy with, 280. lord] lordis.

# PART V

# APPENDIX

## COMPILED BY BARRY WINDEATT

# PART FIVE

## LIST OF ABBREVIATIONS

| | |
|---|---|
| Ch.R. | *Chaucer Review* |
| E.E.T.S | Publication of the Early English Text Society (E.S., Extra Series) |
| E.&S. | *Essays and Studies* |
| M.A. | *Medium Aevum* |
| M.L.R. | *Modern Language Review* |
| M.S. | *Mediaeval Studies* |
| P.B.A. | *Proceedings of the British Academy* |
| P.M.L.A. | *Publications of the Modern Language Association of America* |
| R.E.S. | *Review of English Studies* |
| S.T.S. | Publication of the Scottish Text Society |
| abr. | abridged |
| ed. | edited |
| edn | edition |
| mod. | modernized |
| repr. | reprinted |
| rev. | revised |
| transl. | translated |
| b. | born |
| fl. | flourishing |
| d. | died |
| *c.* | circa |

# FOR FURTHER READING AND REFERENCE

*In the 'Authors and Works' section, under each author or work there appears first a standard biography (if any), second the standard edition(s), and third a selection of books and articles (listed in alphabetical order of authors).*

## General Background

### I. GENERAL HISTORY

Barber, R. *Edward, Prince of Wales and Aquitaine: A Biography of the Black Prince* (London, 1978)

Barnie, J. *War in Medieval Society: Social Values and the Hundred Years War 1337–99* (London, 1974)

Bindoff, S. T. *Tudor England* (Penguin, 1950)

Boulay, F. R. H. Du *An Age of Ambition* (London, 1970)

Boulay, F. R. H. Du and Barron, C. (eds), *The Reign of Richard II* (London, 1971)

Dobson, R. B. *The Peasants' Revolt of 1381* (London, 1970)

Froissart *Chronicles*, transl. G. Brereton (Penguin, 1968)

Harriss, G. L. *King, Parliament, and Public Finance in Medieval England* (Oxford, 1975)

Harvey, J. *The Black Prince and His Age* (London, 1976)

Heer, F. *The Medieval World: Europe 1100–1350* (London, 1962)

Hewitt, H. J. *The Organization of War under Edward III 1338–62* (Manchester, 1966)

Holmes, G. *The Later Middle Ages 1272–1485* (London, 1970)

Huizinga, J. *The Waning of the Middle Ages* (London, 1924; Penguin, 1965)

Jacob, E. F. *The Fifteenth Century 1399–1485* (Oxford, 1961)

Jones, R. H. *The Royal Policy of Richard II* (Oxford, 1968)

Keen, M. H. *The Laws of War in the Late Middle Ages* (London, 1965)

Keen, M. H. *England in the Later Middle Ages* (London, 1973)

Kendall, P. M. *The Yorkist Age* (London, 1962)

Kirby, J. L. *Henry IV of England* (London, 1970)

McFarlane, K. B. *Lancastrian Kings and Lollard Knights* (Oxford, 1972)

McKisack, M. *The Fourteenth Century 1307–1399* (Oxford, 1959)

Myers, A. R. *England in the Late Middle Ages* (Penguin, 1953)

Power, E. *Medieval People* (London, 1924; repr. 1966)

Powicke, F. M. *The Thirteenth Century 1216–1307* (Oxford, 1953)

Rickert, E. *Chaucer's World* (New York, 1948)

Southern, R. W. *The Making of the Middle Ages* (London, 1953)

Steel, A. B. *Richard II* (Cambridge, 1962)

Stenton, D. M. *English Society in the Early Middle Ages* (Penguin, 1951)

Tuchman, B. W. *A Distant Mirror: The Calamitous 14th Century* (Penguin, 1979)

Tuck, J. A. *Richard II and the English Nobility* (London, 1973)

## II. SOCIAL AND ECONOMIC HISTORY

Bennett, H. S. *Life on the English Manor, 1100–1400* (Cambridge, 1937)

Denholm-Young, N. *The Country Gentry in the Fourteenth Century* (Oxford, 1969)

Hatcher, J. *Plague, Population and the English Economy 1348–1530* (London, 1977)

Hilton, R. H. *Bond Men Made Free* (London, 1973)

Hilton, R. H. *The English Peasantry in the Later Middle Ages* (Oxford, 1975)

Homans, G. C. *English Villagers of the Thirteenth Century* (New York, 1960)

Jusserand, J. J. *Wayfaring Life in the Middle Ages* (London, 1889; 1950)

Keen, M. *The Outlaws of Medieval Legend* (London, 1961)

Mathew, G. *The Court of Richard II* (London, 1968)

McFarlane, K. B. *The Nobility of Later Medieval England* (Oxford, 1973)

Mead, W. E. *The English Medieval Feast* (London, 1931; 1967)

Murray, A. *Reason and Society in the Middle Ages* (Oxford, 1978)

Newton, S. M. *Fashion in the Age of the Black Prince* (Cambridge, 1980)

Orme, N. *English Schools in the Middle Ages* (London, 1973)

Platt, C. *English Medieval Towns* (London, 1976)

Platt, C. *Medieval England: A Social History and Archaeology* (London, 1978)

Power, E. *The Wool Trade in English Medieval History* (London, 1941)

Reynolds, S. *An Introduction to the History of English Medieval Towns* (Oxford, 1977)

Richards, P. *The Medieval Leper and his Northern Heirs* (Cambridge, 1977)

Robertson, D. W. *Chaucer's London* (New York, 1968)

Sumption, J. *Pilgrimage* (London, 1975)

Thrupp, S. L. *The Merchant Class of Medieval London* (Chicago, 1948)

Ziegler, P. *The Black Death* (London, 1967)


## III. THE CHURCH

Blench, J. W. *Preaching in England in the late Fifteenth and Sixteenth Centuries* (Oxford, 1964)

Bloomfield, M. W. *The Seven Deadly Sins* (Michigan, 1952)

Edwards, K. *The English Secular Cathedrals in the Middle Ages* (Manchester, 1967)

Finucane, R. C. *Miracles and Pilgrims: Popular Beliefs in Medieval England* (London, 1977)

Gasquet, F. A. *Parish Life in Medieval England* (London, 1936)

Gilson, E. *The Spirit of Medieval Philosophy* (London, 1936)

Knowles, D. *The Religious Orders in England* (Cambridge, 1948–59; 3 vols)

Knowles, D. *The Evolution of Medieval Thought* (Cambridge, 1962)

Knowles, D. *Saints and Scholars* (Cambridge, 1962)

Leclercq, J. *The Love of Learning and the Desire for God* (transl. New York, 1974)

Leclercq, J. *Monks and Love in Twelfth-Century France* (Oxford, 1979)

Leff, G. *Medieval Thought* (Penguin, 1958)

McDonnell, E. W. *The Beguines and Beghards in Medieval Culture* (Rutgers, 1954)

Moorman, J. R. H. *Church Life in England in the Thirteenth Century* (Cambridge, 1946)

Moorman, J. R. H. *A History of the Franciscan Order* (Oxford, 1968)

Oberman, H. and Trunkhaus, C. (eds) *The Pursuit of Holiness in Late Medieval and Renaissance Religion* (Leiden, 1974)

Owst, G. R. *Preaching in Medieval England* (Cambridge, 1926)

Pantin, W. A. *The English Church in the Fourteenth Century* (Cambridge, 1955)

Power, E. *Medieval English Nunneries* (Cambridge, 1922)

Powicke, F. M. *The Christian Life in the Middle Ages* (London, 1935)

Smalley, B. *The Study of the Bible in the Middle Ages* (Oxford, 1952)

Smalley, B. *English Friars and Antiquity in the Early 14th Century* (Oxford, 1960)

Southern, R. W. *Western Society and the Church in the Middle Ages* (Penguin, 1970)

Thomson, J. A. F. *The Later Lollards 1414–1520* (Oxford, 1965)

Thompson, A. H. *The English Clergy and Their Organization in the Later Middle Ages* (Oxford, 1947)

Thomas, K. *Religion and the Decline of Magic* (London, 1971)

Trevelyan, G. M. *England in the Age of Wycliffe* (London, 1929)

### IV. THE ARTS AND SCIENCES

#### The Visual Arts

Anderson, M. D. *Misericords: Medieval Life in English Woodcarving* (London, 1956)

Brieger, P. *English Art 1216–1307* (Oxford, 1957)

Cave, J. P. *Roof Bosses in Medieval Churches* (Cambridge, 1948)

Bruyne, E. De *Esthetics of the Middle Ages* (New York, 1969)

Evans, J. *English Art 1307–1461* (Oxford, 1949)

Frankl, P. *Gothic Architecture* (Penguin, 1967)

Harvey, J. H. *Gothic England* (London, 1948)

Harvey, J. H. *The Gothic World* (London, 1950)

Henderson, G. *Gothic* (Penguin, 1967)

Henderson, G. *Early Medieval* (Penguin, 1972)

Jordan, R. M. *Chaucer and the Shape of Creation* (Cambridge, Mass., 1967)

Kolve, V. A. in *Geoffrey Chaucer*, ed. D. Brewer (London, 1974)

Mâle, E. *The Gothic Image* (transl. London, 1913)

Marks, R. and Morgan, N. *The Golden Age of English Manuscript Painting 1200–1500* (London, 1981)

Meiss, M. *French Painting in the Time of Jean de Berry: The Late 14th Century and the Patronage of the Duke* (London, 1967)

Meiss, M. *French Painting in the Time of Jean de Berry: The Limbourgs and their Contemporaries* (London, 1974)

Meiss, M. *French Painting in the Time of Jean de Berry: The Boucicaut Master* (London, 1968)

Meiss, M. and Longnon, J. *Les Très Riches Heures de Jean de Berry* (London, 1969)

Panofsky, E. *Early Netherlandish Painting* (Cambridge, Mass., 1955)

Panofsky, E. *Gothic Architecture and Scholasticism* (New York, 1957)

Pearsall, D. and Salter, E. *Landscapes and Seasons of the Medieval World* (London, 1973)

Pickering, F. P. *Literature and Art in the Middle Ages* (London, 1970)

Rickert, M. *Painting in Britain: The Middle Ages* (Penguin, 1954)

Stone, L. *Sculpture in Britain: The Middle Ages* (Penguin, 1955)

Varty, K. *Reynard the Fox* (Leicester, 1967)

Wood, M. *The English Mediaeval House* (London, 1965)

## Science

Curry, W. C. *Chaucer and the Medieval Sciences* (London, 1926; rev. edn 1960)

Gimpel, J. *The Medieval Machine* (London, 1977)

Hookyas, R. *Religion and the Rise of Modern Science* (Edinburgh, 1972)

White, L. Jr, *Medieval Technology and Social Change* (Oxford, 1962)

## Music

Harman, R. A. *Medieval and Early Renaissance Music* (London, 1958)

Harrison, F. L. *Music in Medieval Britain* (London, 1958)

Hughes, A. and Abraham, G. *Ars Nova and the Renaissance 1300–1540* (New Oxford History of Music, 1960)

Stevens, J. *Music and Poetry in the Early Tudor Court* (London, 1961; Cambridge, 1979)

Wilkins, N. *Music in the Age of Chaucer* (Cambridge, 1979).

## *Medieval English Literature*

### V. BIBLIOGRAPHY

Brown, C. and Robbins, R. H. *Index of Middle English Verse* (New York, 1943)

Pickford, C. E. and Last, R. W. *The Arthurian Bibliography* (Cambridge, 1981–)

Stratman, C. J. *Bibliography of Medieval Drama* (New York, 1972)

Watson, G. *New Cambridge Bibliography of English Literature*, vol. I (Cambridge, 1974)

*A Manual of the Writings in Middle English 1050–1500* (1967–)

### VI. MEDIEVAL LITERARY HISTORY AND GENERAL CRITICISM

Aers, D. *Chaucer, Langland, and the Creative Imagination* (London, 1980)

Auerbach, E. *Mimesis* (Princeton, 1953)

Auerbach, E. *Literary Language and Its Public* (London, 1965)

Benson, C. D. *The History of Troy in Middle English Literature* (Cambridge, 1980)

Blake, N. *The English Language in Medieval Literature* (London, 1977)

Bennett, H. S. *Chaucer and the Fifteenth Century* (Oxford, 1947)

Bennett, H. S. *English Books and Readers 1475–1557* (Cambridge, 1952)

Bethurum, D. (ed.) *Critical Approaches to Medieval Literature* (New York, 1960)

Bolgar, R. R. *The Classical Heritage and its Beneficiaries* (Cambridge, 1954)

Bolton, W. (ed.) *A History of Literature in the English Language*, vol. I, *The Middle Ages* (London, 1970)

Burrow, J. A. *Ricardian Poetry* (London, 1971)

Chambers, E. K. *English Literature at the Close of the Middle Ages* (Oxford History of English Literature, II, 2, 1945)

Chaytor, H. J. *From Script to Print* (Cambridge, 1945; 1967)

Clanchy, M. T. *From Memory to Written Record: England 1066–1307* (London, 1979)

Coleman, J. *English Literature in History 1350–1400: Medieval Readers and Writers* (London, 1981)

Cooper, H. *Pastoral: Medieval into Renaissance* (Cambridge, 1977)

Curtius, E. R. *European Literature and the Latin Middle Ages* (London, 1953)

Daiches, D. and Thorlby, A. (eds) *The Medieval World* (London, 1973)

Doob, P. B. R. *Nebuchadnezzar's Children: Conventions of Madness in Middle English Literature* (New Haven, 1974)

Everett, D. *Essays on Middle English Literature* (Oxford, 1955)

Farnham, W. *The Medieval Heritage of Elizabethan Tragedy* (Berkeley, 1936)

Fowler, D. C. *The Bible in Early English Literature* (London, 1977)

Gradon, P. *Form and Style in Early English Literature* (London, 1971)

Green, R. F. *Poets and Princepleasers: Literature and the English Court in the late Middle Ages* (Toronto, 1980)

Kane, G. *Middle English Literature* (London, 1951; rev. 1971)

Kelly, H. A. *Love and Marriage in the Age of Chaucer* (Cornell, 1975)

Ker, W. P. *Medieval English Literature* (London, 1912; Oxford, 1969)

Lanham, R. A. *The Motives of Eloquence: Literary Rhetoric in the Renaissance* (New Haven, 1976)

Lawlor, J. (ed.) *Patterns of Love and Courtesy* (London, 1967)

Legge, M. D. *Anglo-Norman Literature and its Background* (Oxford, 1963)

Lewis, C. S. *The Allegory of Love* (Oxford, 1936)

Lewis, C. S. *English Literature in the Sixteenth Century (excluding Drama)* (Oxford History of English Literature, III, 1954)

Lewis, C. S. *The Discarded Image* (Cambridge, 1964)

Lewis, C. S. *Studies in Medieval and Renaissance Literature* (Cambridge, 1966)

Mason, H. A. *Humanism and Poetry in the Early Tudor Period* (London, 1959)

McGinn, B. *Visions of the End: Apocalyptic Traditions in the Middle Ages* (New York, 1979)

Metzlitzki, D. *The Matter of Araby in Medieval England* (New Haven, 1977)

Murphy, J. J. *Rhetoric in the Middle Ages* (Berkeley, 1974)

Murphy, J. J. (ed.) *Medieval Eloquence* (Berkeley, 1978)

Muscatine, C. *Poetry and Crisis in the Age of Chaucer* (Notre Dame, 1972)

Nolan, B. *The Gothic Visionary Perspective* (Princeton, 1977)

Owst, G. R. *Literature and Pulpit in Medieval England* (Oxford, 1962)

Pearsall, D. *Old English and Middle English Poetry* (London, 1977)

Peter, J. *Complaint and Satire in Early English Literature* (Oxford, 1956)

Pichler, P. *The Visionary Landscape: A Study in Medieval Allegory* (London, 1971)

Scattergood, V. J. *Politics and Poetry in the Fifteenth Century* (London, 1971)

Schlauch, M. *English Medieval Literature and its Social Foundations* (Warsaw, 1956)

Shepherd, G. T. 'The Nature of Alliterative Poetry in Late Medieval England', P.B.A. 56 (1970)

Spearing, A. C. *Criticism and Medieval Poetry* (2nd edn; London, 1972)

Spearing, A. C. *Medieval Dream-Poetry* (Cambridge, 1976)

Speirs, J. *Medieval English Poetry: The Non-Chaucerian Tradition* (London; rev. edn, 1962)

Speirs, J. *The Scots Literary Tradition* (London, 1940; 1962)

Tristram, P. *Figures of Life and Death in Medieval English Literature* (London, 1976)

Turville-Petre, T. *The Alliterative Revival* (Cambridge, 1977)

Tuve, R. *Allegorical Imagery: Some Mediaeval Books and Their Posterity* (Princeton, 1966)

Ullmann, W. *Medieval Foundations of Renaissance Humanism* (London, 1977)

Vasta, E. (ed.) *Middle English Survey: Critical Essays* (Notre Dame, 1965)

Weiss, R. *Humanism in England during the Fifteenth Century* (New York, 1941)

Wilson, R. M. *Early Middle English Literature* (London, 1939; 1968)

Wilson, R. M. *The Lost Literature of Medieval England* (London, 1952)

Zacher, C. K. *Curiosity and Pilgrimage: The Literature of Discovery in Fourteenth-Century England* (Baltimore, 1976)

Zumthor, P. *Essai de poétique médiévale* (Paris, 1972)

### VII. MEDIEVAL ROMANCE

#### Collections of Medieval Romance

French, W. H. and Hale, C. B. (eds) *Middle English Metrical Romances* (New York, 1930)

Mills, M. (ed.) *Six Middle English Romances* (London, 1973)

Rumble, T. C. (ed.) *The Breton Lays in Middle English* (Detroit, 1965)

Sands, D. B. (ed.) *Middle English Verse Romances* (New York, 1966)

Schmidt, A. V. C. and Jacobs, N. (eds) *Medieval English Romances* (2 vols; London, 1980)

#### Some Medieval Romances

*Amis and Amiloun*, ed. M. Leach (E.E.T.S., 1937)

*The Awntyrs off Arthure*, ed. R. Hanna (Manchester, 1974)

*Athelston* (in Sands, and Schmidt and Jacobs, above)

*Le Bone Florence of Rome*, ed. C. F. Heffernan (Manchester, 1976)

*Emaré* (in Mills, above)

*The Erle of Tolous* (in Rumble, above)
*Floris and Blancheflour* (in Sands)
*Gamelyn* (in Sands)
*Havelok the Dane* (in Sands, and Schmidt and Jacobs)
*King Horn* (in Sands, and Schmidt and Jacobs)
*Ipomadoun* (extracts in Schmidt and Jacobs)
*Lai le Fresne* (in Sands)
*Le Morte Arthur*, ed. L. D. Benson, in *King Arthur's Death* (New York, 1976)
*Morte Arthure*, ed. L. D. Benson, in *King Arthur's Death*; selections, ed. J. Finlayson (London, 1967)
*Octavian* (in Mills)
*Sir Amadace* (in Mills)
*Sir Degaré* (in Schmidt and Jacobs)
*Sir Gowther* (in Mills)
*Sir Isumbras* (in Mills)
*Sir Launfal*, ed. A. J. Bliss (London, 1960); (in Sands)
*Sir Orfeo*, ed. A. J. Bliss (Oxford, 1954; 1966); (in Sands)
*Ywain and Gawain* (extracts in Schmidt and Jacobs)

Medieval Romance: Some Studies

Barber, R. *Arthur of Albion: Arthurian Literature and Legends of England* (London, 1961)
Barber, R. *The Figure of Arthur* (London, 1972)
Barber, R. *The Knight and Chivalry* (London, 1970)
Beer, G. *Romance* (London, 1970)
Bezzola, R. R. *Le sens de l'aventure et de l'amour* (Paris, 1947)
Everett, D. *Essays on Middle English Literature* (Oxford, 1955)
Frye, N. *The Secular Scripture: A Study of the Structure of Romance* (Cambridge, Mass., 1976)
Gradon, P. *Form and Style in Early English Literature* (London, 1971), ch. 4 ('The Romance Mode')
Green, D. H. *Irony in the Medieval Romance* (Cambridge, 1979)
Hanning, R. W. *The Individual in Twelfth Century Romance* (New Haven, 1977)
Kane, G. *Middle English Literature* (London, 1951; rev. 1971)
Ker, W. P. *Epic and Romance* (London, 1908; New York, 1957)
Loomis, L. H. *Mediaeval Romance in England* (New York, 1924)
Loomis, R. S. *The Development of Arthurian Romance* (London, 1963)
Loomis, R. S. (ed.) *Arthurian Literature in the Middle Ages* (Oxford, 1959)
Luttrell, C. *The Creation of the First Arthurian Romance* (London, 1974)
Mehl, D. *The Middle English Romances of the Thirteenth and Fourteenth Centuries* (London, 1968)
Mills, M. *Six Middle English Romances* (London, 1973), 'Introduction'
Pearsall, D. 'The Development of Middle English Romance', M.S. 27 (1965)
Pearsall, D. 'The English Romance in the Fifteenth Century', E. & S., 29 (1976)

Southern, R. W. *The Making of the Middle Ages* (London, 1953), ch. 5 ('From Epic to Romance')

Stevens, J. *Medieval Romance* (London, 1973)

Vinaver, E. *The Rise of Romance* (Oxford, 1971)

Weston, J. L. *From Ritual to Romance* (Cambridge, 1920; New York, 1957)

Wittig, S. *Stylistic and Narrative Structures in the Middle English Romances* (Austin, 1978)

## VIII. MEDIEVAL DRAMA

Anderson, M. D. *Drama and Imagery in Medieval English Churches* (Cambridge, 1963)

Axton, R. *European Drama of the Early Middle Ages* (London, 1974)

Bevington, D. M. *From Mankind to Marlowe* (Cambridge, Mass., 1962)

Brody, A. *The English Mummers and their Plays: Traces of Ancient Mystery* (London, 1970)

Chambers, E. K. *The Medieval Stage* (Oxford, 1903)

Craig, H. *English Religious Drama of the Middle Ages* (Oxford, 1955)

Craik, T. W. *The Tudor Interlude: Stage, Costume and Acting* (Leicester, 1958)

Denny, N. (ed.) *Medieval Drama* (Stratford-on-Avon Studies, 16, 1973)

Gardiner, H. C. *Mysteries End: An Investigation of the Last Days of the Medieval Religious Stage* (London, 1946; 1967)

Hardison, O. B. *Christian Rite and Christian Drama in the Middle Ages* (Baltimore, 1965)

Harris, Markham (transl.) *The Cornish Ordinalia* (Washington, D. C., 1969)

Kahrl, S. J. *Traditions of Medieval English Drama* (London, 1974)

Kinghorn, A. M. *Medieval Drama* (London, 1968)

Kolve, V. A. *The Play Called Corpus Christi* (London, 1967)

Nelson, A. H. *The Medieval English Stage* (Chicago, 1974)

Potter, R. *The English Morality Play* (London, 1975)

Rossiter, A. P. *English Drama from Early Times to the Elizabethans* (London, 1950)

Southern, R. *The Medieval Theatre in the Round* (London, 1957; 1975)

Southern, R. *The Staging of Plays before Shakespeare* (London, 1973)

Speirs, J. (in his) *Medieval English Poetry: The Non-Chaucerian Tradition* (London, 1957)

Taylor, J. and Nelson, A. H. (eds) *Medieval English Drama: Essays Critical and Contextual* (Chicago and London, 1972)

Tydeman, W. *The Theatre in the Middle Ages* (Cambridge, 1978)

Welsford, E. *The Court Masque* (Cambridge, 1927; New York, 1962), chs I, II

Wickham, G. *Early English Stages, 1300–1660* (2 vols; London, 1957–72)

Wickham, G. *The Medieval Theatre* (London, 1974)

Williams, A. *The Drama of Medieval England* (East Lansing, Michigan, 1961)

Wilson, F. P. *The English Drama 1485–1585*, ed. G. K. Hunter (Oxford, 1969)

Woolf, R. *The English Mystery Plays* (London, 1972)

Young, K. *The Drama of the Medieval Church*, 2 vols (Oxford, 1933)

## IX. LYRIC AND BALLAD

Collections: *Medieval English Lyrics: a Critical Anthology*, ed. R. T. Davies (London, 1963)

*English Lyrics of the XIIIth Century*, ed. Carleton Brown (Oxford, 1932)

Religious: *Religious Lyrics of the XIV Century*, ed. Carleton Brown (Oxford, 1924; rev. edn G. V. Smithers, 1952)

*Religious Lyrics of the XVth Century*, ed. Carleton Brown (Oxford, 1939)

*A Selection of Religious Lyrics*, ed. D. Gray (Oxford, 1975)

Secular: *The Harley Lyrics*, ed. G. L. Brook (Manchester, 1948; 1964)

*Secular Lyrics of the Fourteenth and Fifteenth Centuries*, ed. R. H. Robbins (Oxford, 1956)

Carols: *The Early English Carols*, ed. R. L. Greene (Oxford, 1935; 2nd edn, 1977)

*A Selection of English Carols*, ed. R. L. Greene (Oxford, 1962)

Songs with music: *Medieval English Songs*, ed. E. J. Dobson and F. Ll. Harrison (London, 1979)

*Music, Cantelenas, Songs etc.*, ed. L. S. Myers (London, 1906)

*Medieval Carols*, ed. J. Stevens [*Musica Britannica*, vol. IV (London, 1952; 1958)]

*Music at the Court of Henry VIII*, ed. J. Stevens [*Musica Britannica*, vol. XVIII (London, 1961)]

*Early Tudor Songs and Carols*, ed. J. Stevens [*Musica Britannica*, vol. XXXVI (London, 1975)]

Ballads: *The English and Scottish Popular Ballads*, ed. F. J. Child (London, 1882–98; repr. New York, 1965), abr. edn G. L. Kittredge (Cambridge, Mass., 1904)

*The Oxford Book of Ballads*, ed. J. Kinsley (Oxford, 1969)

*Faber Book of Ballads*, ed. M. Hodgart (London, 1965)

See B. H. Bronson, *The Ballad as Song* (Berkeley, 1970)

D. Buchan, *The Ballad and the Folk* (London, 1972)

P. Dronke, *Mediaeval Latin and the Rise of the European Love Lyric* (2 vols; Oxford, 1965–6)

P. Dronke, *The Medieval Lyric* (London, 1968)

D. Gray, *Themes and Images in the Medieval English Religious Lyric* (London, 1972)

M. J. C. Hodgart, *The Ballads* (London, 1950)

G. Kane, *Middle English Literature* (London, 1951)

S. Manning, *Wisdom and Number* (Lincoln, Nebraska, 1962)

A. K. Moore, *The Secular Lyric in Middle English* (Lexington, 1951)

R. Oliver, *Poems without Names: The English Lyric 1200–1500* (Berkeley, 1970)

J. Speirs, *Medieval English Poetry: The Non-Chaucerian Tradition* (London, 1957; rev. edn, 1962)

J. Stevens, *Music and Poetry in the Early Tudor Court* (London, 1961; Cambridge, 1979)

H. Waddell, *Mediaeval Latin Lyrics* (London, 1929; Penguin, 1952)

S. A. Webber, *Theology and Poetry in the Middle English Lyric* (Columbus, 1969)

R. Woolf, *The English Religious Lyric in the Middle Ages* (Oxford, 1968)

L. C. Wimberley, *Folklore in the English and Scottish Ballads* (Cambridge, 1928; repr. New York, 1965)

## X. PROSE

Bennett, H. S. 'Fifteenth Century Secular Prose', R.E.S. 21 (1945)

Blake, N. F. 'Late Medieval Prose', in *The Middle Ages*, ed. W. F. Bolton (London, 1970)

Chambers, R. W. *On the Continuity of English Prose* E.E.T.S., 1932)

Gordon, I. A. *The Movement of English Prose* (London, 1966)

Hodgson, P. *Three 14th-Century English Mystics* (London, 1967)

Riehle, W. *The Middle English Mystics* (London, 1981)

Schlauch, M. 'The Art of Chaucer's Prose', in *Chaucer and Chaucerians*, ed. D. S. Brewer (London, 1966)

Stone, R. K. *Middle English Prose Style: Margery Kempe and Julian of Norwich* (The Hague, 1970)

Wilson, R. M. 'Three Middle English Mystics', E.&S. n.s. 9 (1956)

## XI. ANTHOLOGIES

*Early Middle English Verse and Prose*, ed. J. A. W. Bennett and G. V. Smithers (2nd edn; Oxford, 1968)

*Middle English Religious Prose*, ed. N. F. Blake (London, 1972)

*English Verse 1300–1500*, ed. J. Burrow (London, 1977)

*English Verse between Chaucer and Surrey*, ed. E. P. Hammond (Durham, N. C., 1927; New York, 1965)

*Historical Poems of the XIVth and XVth Centuries*, ed. R. H. Robbins (New York, 1959)

*Late Medieval Scots Poetry*, ed. T. Scott (London, 1967)

*Fourteenth Century Verse and Prose*, ed. K. Sisam (Oxford, 1921; rev. 1955)

*Oxford Book of Medieval English Verse*, ed. K. Sisam and C. Sisam (Oxford, 1970)

*Medieval English Literature*, ed. J. B. Trapp (New York, 1973)

# AUTHORS AND WORKS

ANCRENE RIWLE (*c.* 1200?): most important prose work of Earlier Middle English Period; devotional manual, originally composed for guidance of three young gentlewomen who had withdrawn from the world to live as anchoresses.

> *English Text of the Ancrene Riwle*, B. M. Cotton MS. Nero A. XIV, ed. M. Day (E.E.T.S., 1952; 1957)
> *Ancrene Wisse, Corpus Christi College Cambridge*, MS. 402, ed. J. R. R. Tolkien (E.E.T.S., 1962)
> *The Ancrene Riwle*, mod. edn, M. B. Salu (London, 1955)
> *Ancrene Wisse*, pts 6 and 7, ed. G. Shepherd (London, 1959)
> See R. W. Chambers, *On the Continuity of English Prose* (E.E.T.S., 1932)
>     E. J. Dobson, *The Origins of Ancrene Wisse* (Oxford, 1976)
>     L. Georgianna, *The Solitary Self* (Cambridge, Mass., 1981)
>     R. M. Wilson, *Early Middle English Literature* (London, 1939; 1968)

ASCHAM, ROGER (1516–68): humanist: b. Yorkshire (?); St John's College, Cambridge; prominent Greek scholar; *Toxophilus*, on archery and education, published 1545; tutor to Princess Elizabeth 1548; secretary to English ambassador to Charles V, 1550–53; Latin secretary to Mary I, 1553; private tutor and secretary to Elizabeth I, 1558; reputed to have lived and died in poverty owing to addiction to dicing and cock-fighting; chief work on education, *The Schoolmaster*, published 1570.

> *English Works*, ed. W. A. Wright (Cambridge, 1904; 1970)
> See L. V. Ryan, *Roger Ascham* (Stanford, 1963)

CAXTON, WILLIAM (*c.* 1422–91): printer and translator: b. Kent; received good education; apprenticed to cloth merchant; successful commercial career; learned art of printing in Cologne, 1471; set up his own printing press, Westminster, 1476; printed works of Chaucer, Malory, Gower, Lydgate, and other books shrewdly chosen for his clientele.

> *Prologues and Epilogues*, ed. W. J. B. Crotch (E.E.T.S., 1928; 1956)
> *Selections from William Caxton*, ed. N. F. Blake (Oxford, 1973)
> See N. F. Blake, *Caxton and his world* (London, 1969)
>     N. F. Blake, *Caxton's Own Prose* (London, 1973)
>     C. F. Bühler, *William Caxton and his Critics* (Syracuse, 1960)

CHARLES D'ORLEANS (1394–1465): nephew of Charles VI of France; married in 1406 to Isabella (d. 1409), child-widow of Richard II; captured at Agincourt, remained prisoner in England until 1440; apparently wrote poems in both English and French, like his friend and gaoler, the Duke of Suffolk.

> *The English Poems of Charles of Orleans*, ed. R. Steele (E.E.T.S., 215, 220, 1941–6; repr. 1970)
> *Charles d'Orléans*, ed. J. Charpier (Paris, 1958)
> See J. Choffel, *Le Duc Charles d'Orléans (1394–1465)* (Paris, 1968)
>     N. L. Goodrich, *Charles of Orleans: A Study of Themes in his French and in his English Poetry* (Geneva, 1967)

J. Fox, *The Lyric Poetry of Charles d'Orléans* (Oxford, 1969)

E. McLeod, *Charles of Orleans, prince and poet* (London, 1969)

D. Poirion, *Le poète et le prince: L'evolution du lyrisme courtois de Guillaume de Machaut à Charles d'Orléans* (Paris, 1965)

CHAUCER, GEOFFREY (*c.* 1340–1400): poet, diplomat, civil servant; b. London, son of John Chaucer, vintner; page to Countess of Ulster 1357; taken prisoner and ransomed in French wars 1359–60; annuity from Edward III 1367; lifelong association with court circles; *c.* 1366 married Philippa Roet, sister of Katherine Swynford (third wife of John of Gaunt, Chaucer's patron); after 1368 various visits to France on diplomatic missions; *Book of the Duchess*; visits to Italy 1372–3 and 1378; possibly also visited Spain; from 1374 active in public affairs; Controller of Customs for Wool 1374–86; (before 1380 *House of Fame*; 1380–86, *Parliament of Fowls, Palamon, Boece, Troilus, Legend of Good Women*); 1386 M.P. for Kent; *c.* 1387 onwards worked on *Canterbury Tales*; 1389–91 Clerk of King's Works; additional pension from Richard II 1394; sued for debts 1398; additional pension from Henry IV 1399; leased house in Westminster Abbey garden December 1399; died following year.

D. S. Brewer, *Chaucer* (3rd edn; London, 1973)

D. S. Brewer, *Chaucer and His World* (London, 1978)

M. M. Crow and C. C. Olson, *Chaucer Life-Records* (Oxford, 1966)

*The Works of Geoffrey Chaucer*, ed. F. N. Robinson (2nd edn; London, 1957)

*The Complete Works of Geoffrey Chaucer*, ed. W. W. Skeat (6 vols; Oxford, 1894)

*Chaucer's Poetry: An Anthology for the Modern Reader*, ed. E. T. Donaldson (New York, 1958)

See J. A. W. Bennett, *The Parlement of Foules* (Oxford, 1957)

J. A. W. Bennett, *Chaucer's Book of Fame* (Oxford, 1968)

I. Bishop, *Chaucer's 'Troilus and Criseyde': A Critical Study* (Bristol, 1981)

M. Bowden, *A Reader's Guide to Geoffrey Chaucer* (New York, 1964)

D. S. Brewer, *Chaucer in his Time* (London, 1963; 1973)

D. S. Brewer (ed.), *Chaucer and Chaucerians* (London, 1966)

D. S. Brewer (ed.), *Geoffrey Chaucer* (London, 1974)

D. S. Brewer (ed.), *Chaucer: The Critical Heritage* (2 vols; London, 1978)

R. B. Burlin, *Chaucerian Fiction* (Princeton, 1977)

J. D. Burnley, *Chaucer's Language and the Philosophers' Tradition* (Cambridge, 1979)

J. A. Burrow (ed.), *Geoffrey Chaucer: A Critical Anthology* (Penguin, 1969)

W. Clemen, *Chaucer's Early Poetry* (London, 1963)

T. D. Cooke, *The Old French and Chaucerian Fabliaux* (Columbia, 1978)

T. W. Craik, *The Comic Tales of Chaucer* (London, 1964)

G. R. Crampton, *The Condition of Creatures* (New Haven, 1974)

W. C. Curry, *Chaucer and the Mediaeval Sciences* (London, 1960)

N. Davis et al., *A Chaucer Glossary* (Oxford, 1979)

E. T. Donaldson, *Speaking of Chaucer* (London, 1970)

R. W. V. Elliott, *Chaucer's English* (London, 1974)

D. Everett, *Essays on Middle English Literature* (Oxford, 1955)

I. L. Gordon, *The Double Sorrow of Troilus* (Oxford, 1970)

D. R. Howard, *The Idea of the Canterbury Tales* (London, 1976)

T. Jones, *Chaucer's Knight* (London, 1980)

R. M. Jordan, *Chaucer and the Shape of Creation* (Cambridge, Mass., 1967)

P. M. Kean, *Chaucer and the Making of English Poetry* (2 vols; London, 1972)

G. L. Kittredge, *Chaucer and his Poetry* (Cambridge, Mass., 1915)

J. L. Lowes, *Geoffrey Chaucer* (Boston, 1934)

J. Mann, *Chaucer and Medieval Estates Satire* (Cambridge, 1973)

R. P. Miller (ed.), *Chaucer: Sources and Backgrounds* (New York, 1977)

A. Miskimin, *The Renaissance Chaucer* (New Haven, 1975)

C. Muscatine, *Chaucer and the French Tradition* (Berkeley, 1957; 1964)

C. Muscatine, *Poetry and Crisis in the Age of Chaucer* (Notre Dame, 1972)

J. Norton-Smith, *Geoffrey Chaucer* (London, 1974)

R. O. Payne, *The Key of Remembrance* (New Haven, 1963)

D. W. Robertson, Jr, *A Preface to Chaucer* (Princeton, 1962)

T. W. Ross, *Chaucer's Bawdy* (New York, 1972)

B. Rowland (ed.), *Companion to Chaucer Studies* (2nd edn; Oxford, 1980)

P. G. Ruggiers, *The Art of the Canterbury Tales* (Madison, 1965)

E. Salter, *The Knight's Tale and The Clerk's Tale* (London, 1962)

M. Salu (ed.), *Essays on Troilus and Criseyde* (Cambridge, 1979)

K. Schaar, *The Golden Mirror* (Lund, 1955; 1967)

*Sources and Analogues of Chaucer's Canterbury Tales*, ed. W. F. Bryan and G. Dempster (Chicago, 1941; New York, 1958)

A. C. Spearing, *Medieval Dream-Poetry* (Cambridge, 1976)

A. C. Spearing, *Chaucer: Troilus and Criseyde* (London, 1976)

J. Spiers, *Chaucer the Maker* (London, 1951; rev. edn, 1962)

C. F. E. Spurgeon (ed.), *Five Hundred Years of Chaucer Criticism and Allusion 1357–1900* (3 vols; Cambridge, 1925)

J. M. Steadman, *Disembodied Laughter* (Berkeley, 1972)

A. Thompson, *Shakespeare's Chaucer* (Liverpool, 1978)

J. Wimsatt, *Chaucer and the French Love Poets* (Chapel Hill, N. C., 1968)

B. A. Windeatt (transl.), *Chaucer's Dream Poetry: Sources and Analogues* (Cambridge, 1982)

C. Wood, *Chaucer and the Country of the Stars: Poetic Uses of Astrological Imagery* (Princeton, 1970)

Collected criticism: *Chaucer Criticism*, ed. R. J. Schoeck and J. Taylor, 2 vols, *I The Canterbury Tales, II Troilus and Criseyde and the Minor Poems* (Notre Dame, 1960–61); *Chaucer: Modern Essays in criticism*, ed. E. Wagenknecht (Oxford, 1959)

CLANVOWE, SIR JOHN (*c.* 1341–91): soldier, diplomat, administrator, and writer; fought bravely in French wars; associated with the 'Lollard Knights', apparently a group of earnest, secular, intellectual knights, known to Chaucer. Died on pilgrimage near Constantinople.

*The Works of Sir John Clanvowe*, ed. V. J. Scattergood (Cambridge, 1975)

'THE CLOUD-AUTHOR': anonymous priest and author of *The Cloud of Unknowing*; also assumed author of six other spiritual treatises, all written in latter half of fourteenth century, probably in East Midlands (*The Epistle of Privy Counselling; Deonise Hid Divinite; Benjamin; Epistle of Prayer; Epistle of Discretion of Stirrings; Treatise of Discretion of Spirits*).

*Thr Cloud of Unknowing and The Book of Privy Counselling*, ed. P. Hodgson (E.E.T.S. 1944; repr. 1973)

*Deonise Hid Diuinite and other Treatises on Contemplative Prayer related to The Cloud of Unknowing*, ed. P. Hodgson (E.E.T.S. 1958)

Mod. Eds by J. McCann (London, 1952) and by C. Wolters (Penguin, 1978).
See also J. E. G. Gardner, *The Cell of Self-Knowledge* (London, 1910)
See J. A. Burrow, 'Fantasy and Language in *The Cloud of Unknowing*', *Essays in Criticism* 27 (1977)
  H. L. Gardner, 'Walter Hilton and the authorship of the *Cloud*', R.E.S. 9 (1933)
  P. Hodgson, *Three 14th-Century English Mystics* (London, 1967)
  W. Johnston, *The Mysticism of the Cloud of Unknowing* (New York, 1967)
  D. Knowles, *The English Mystical Tradition* (London, 1961)
  C. S. Nieva, *This Transcending God* (London, 1971)
  C. Pepler, in his *English Religious Heritage* (London, 1958)
  G. Sitwell, in *English Spiritual Writers*, ed. C. Davis (London, 1961)
  M. Thornton, *English Spirituality* (London, 1963)
  J. Walsh (ed.), *Pre-Reformation English Spirituality* (London, 1965)


DOUGLAS, GAVIN (*c.* 1475–1522): Scottish poet and bishop: aristocratic background, much involved in secular and ecclesiastical politics; M.A. St Andrews, 1494; Bishop of Dunkeld, 1515; died in disfavour, an exile in England. His poem *The Palace of Honour* (*c.* 1501) is an allegorical dream-poem, partly modelled on Chaucer's *House of Fame*. Greatest work is his translation of the *Aeneid* into Scottish verse (called better than the original by Ezra Pound).

*Works*, ed. J. Small (4 vols; Edinburgh, 1874)
*Aeneid*, ed. D. F. C. Caldwell (4 vols; S.T.S. 1957–64)
*The Shorter Poems*, ed. P. Bawcutt (Edinburgh, 1967)
*Selections*, ed. D. F. C. Caldwell (Oxford, 1964)
See P. Bawcutt, *Gavin Douglas: A Critical Study* (Edinburgh, 1976)
  D. Fox, 'The Scottish Chaucerians', in *Chaucer and Chaucerians*, ed. D. S. Brewer (London, 1966)
  J. Kinsley, *Scottish Poetry: A Critical Survey* (London, 1955)
  G. Kratzmann, *Anglo-Scottish Literary Relations 1430–1550* (Cambridge, 1980)
  C. S. Lewis, 'The Close of the Middle Ages in Scotland', in *English Literature in the Sixteenth Century (Excluding Drama)*, (Oxford History of English Literature, III, 1954)
  J. Speirs, *The Scots Literary Tradition* (London, 1940; rev. edn, 1962)


DUNBAR, WILLIAM (*c.* 1460–*c.* 1520): poet: little known of his life; probably aristocratic background; B.A. St Andrews 1477; employed at Scottish court, received pension from James IV in 1500; in London 1501 with mission to negotiate marriage between James IV and Margaret Tudor; priest's orders by 1504. Great range of writing: divine poems, courtly love-poems, moralities, comic visions, allegories, satires.

J. W. Baxter, *William Dunbar: A Biographical Study* (Edinburgh, 1952)
*Works*, ed. W. Mackay Mackenzie (Edinburgh, 1932)
*Poems* (selections), ed. J. Kinsley (Oxford, 1958)
*Poems*, ed. J. Kinsley (Oxford, 1979)
See T. Scott, *Dunbar: A Critical Exposition* (Edinburgh, 1966)
  H. Harvey Wood, *Two Scots Chaucerians: Robert Henryson, William Dunbar* (London, 1967)
See also Fox, Kratzmann, Lewis, Speirs (cited under Douglas)

'THE GAWAIN-POET': anonymous author of *Sir Gawain and the Green Knight*, and also frequently supposed author of the other three poems in the *Gawain* MS. (British Library MS. Cotton Nero A.x, Art. 3): *Pearl, Patience, Cleanness* (*Purity*). Probable date: latter half of fourteenth century; MS. language points to N.W. Midlands origin.

*The Poems of the Pearl Manuscript*, ed. M. Andrew and R. Waldron (London, 1978)

*Pearl, Cleanness, Patience and Sir Gawain and the Green Knight*, ed. A. C. Cawley and J. J. Anderson (London and New York, 1976)

*Pearl*, ed. E. V. Gordon (Oxford, 1953)

*The Pearl*, ed. and transl. Sr Mary V. Hillmann (Notre Dame, 1967)

*Cleanness*, ed. Sir I. Gollancz; repr. with transl. by D. S. Brewer (Cambridge, 1974)

*Cleanness*, ed. J. J. Anderson (Manchester, 1977)

*Patience*, ed. J. J. Anderson (Manchester, 1969)

*Sir Gawain and the Green Knight*, ed. J. R. R. Tolkien and E. V. Gordon, 2nd edn, rev. N. Davis (Oxford, 1967)

*Sir Gawain and the Green Knight*, ed. R. A. Waldron (London, 1970)

*Sir Gawain and the Green Knight*, ed. J. A. Burrow (Penguin, 1972)

*Sir Gawain and the Green Knight*, ed. and transl. W. R. J. Barron (Manchester, 1974)

### General

R. J. Blanch (ed.), *Sir Gawain and Pearl: Critical Essays* (Bloomington, 1966).

D. S. Brewer, 'Courtesy and the *Gawain*-Poet', in *Patterns of Love and Courtesy*, ed. J. Lawlor (London, 1966)

W. A. Davenport, *The Art of the Gawain-Poet* (London, 1978).

D. Everett, 'The Alliterative Revival', in *Essays on Middle English Literature*, ed. P. Kean (Oxford, 1955)

A. C. Spearing, *The Gawain-Poet: A Critical Study* (Cambridge, 1970)

J. Speirs, *Medieval English Poetry: The Non-Chaucerian Tradition* (London: rev. edn, 1962)

E. Wilson, *The Gawain-Poet* (Leiden, 1976)

### Pearl

I. Bishop, *Pearl in its Setting* (Oxford, 1968)

J. Conley (ed.), *The Middle English 'Pearl': Critical Essays* (Notre Dame, 1970)

P. M. Kean, *The Pearl: An Interpretation* (London, 1967)

P. Piehler, 'Pearl', in *The Visionary Landscape* (London, 1971)

A. C. Spearing, 'The Alliterative Tradition: *Pearl*', *Medieval Dream-Poetry* (Cambridge, 1976

### Cleanness

P. B. R. Doob, *Nebuchadnezzar's Children: Conventions of Madness in Middle English Literature* (New Haven, 1974)

M. M. Foley, 'A Bibliography of *Purity* (*Cleanness*), 1864–1972', *ChR* 8 (1973–4), 324–34

A. C. Spearing, '*Purity* and Danger', *Essays in Criticism* 30 (1980)

### Sir Gawain and the Green Knight

W. R. J. Barron, *Trawthe and treason* (Manchester, 1980).

L. D. Benson, *Art and Tradition in Sir Gawain and the Green Knight* (New Brunswick, 1965).

M. Borroff, *Sir Gawain and the Green Knight: A Stylistic and Metrical Study* (New Haven, 1962)

E. Brewer, *From Cuchulainn to Gawain* (Cambridge, 1973)

J. A. Burrow, *A Reading of Sir Gawain and the Green Knight* (London, 1965)

D. Fox (ed.), *Twentieth Century Interpretations of Sir Gawain and the Green Knight* (Englewood Cliffs, N. J., 1968)

D. R. Howard and C. K. Zacher (eds), *Critical Studies of Sir Gawain and the Green Knight* (Notre Dame, 1968)

A. C. Spearing, *Criticism and Medieval Poetry*, 2nd edn (London, 1972), ch. 2

A. C. Spearing, *The Gawain-Poet* (Cambridge, 1970), ch. 5

GOWER, JOHN (*c.* 1330–1408): poet in three languages; friend of Chaucer; probably London-based, connected with the law, owning land in Kent. Wrote didactic poem in French, *Mirour de l'omme* (29,444 lines); also Latin poem *Vox Clamantis* (10,265 lines) on state of England. Major work, English poem *Confessio Amantis* (33,444 lines), first dedicated to Richard II, but after 1393 to Henry of Lancaster, later Henry IV. Buried in Priory of St Mary Overy (now Southwark Cathedral), where his tomb can still be seen.

*Complete Works*, ed. G. C. Macaulay (4 vols, Oxford, 1899–1902)

*English Works*, ed. G. C. Macaulay (2 vols, E.E.T.S., 1900–1901; repr. 1957)

*Confessio Amantis* (selections), ed. R. A. Peck (New York, 1968)

*The Major Latin Works*, transl. E. W. Stockton (Seattle, 1962).

*Selections*, ed. J. A. W. Bennett (Oxford, 1968).

See J. A. W. Bennett, 'Gower's *Honeste Love*', and J. Lawlor, 'On Romanticism in the *Confessio Amantis*', in *Patterns of Love and Courtesy*, ed. J. Lawlor (London, 1966)

W. G. Dodd, *Courtly Love in Gower and Chaucer* (Boston, 1913)

A. B. Ferguson, *The Articulate Citizen and the English Renaissance* (Durham, North Carolina, 1965)

J. H. Fisher, *John Gower, Moral Philosopher and Friend of Chaucer* (New York, 1964)

P. J. Gallacher, *Love, the Word and Mercury* (Albuquerque, 1975)

C. S. Lewis, *The Allegory of Love* (Oxford, 1936), ch. V

D. Pearsall, 'Gower's narrative art', *PMLA* 81 (1966), 475–84.

R. A. Peck, *Kingship and Common Profit in Gower's Confessio Amantis* (Carbondale, 1978)

HENRYSON, ROBERT (*c.* 1425–*c.* 1500?): poet and schoolmaster; possibly studied at continental university and Glasgow; probably master at Benedictine Abbey grammar school, Dunfermline.

M. W. Stearns, *Robert Henryson* (New York, 1949)

*Poems and Fables*, ed. H. Harvey Wood (Edinburgh, 1933; rev. 1958)

*Poems* (selections), ed. C. Elliott (Oxford, 1963; 2nd edn, 1974)

*Testament of Cresseid*, ed. D. Fox (London, 1968)

*The Poems of Robert Henryson*, ed. D. Fox (Oxford, 1980)

See D. Gray, *Robert Henryson* (Leiden, 1980)

J. MacQueen, *Robert Henryson: A Study of the Major Narrative Poems* (Oxford, 1967)

H. Harvey Wood, *Two Scottish Chaucerians: Robert Henryson, William Dunbar* (London, 1967)

R. L. Kindrick, *Robert Henryson* (Boston, 1979)

A. C. Spearing, *Criticism and Medieval Poetry* (2nd edn, London, 1972)
See also Fox, Kratzmann, Lewis, Speirs (cited under Douglas)

HEYWOOD, JOHN (*c.* 1497–*c.* 1580): playwright, musician, professional entertainer; entered royal service at early age; friend of More; in great favour under Mary I but, because of Catholicism, lost favour on accession of Elizabeth I; fled to Low Countries.

> *The Foure P's*; *Johan Johan*; *The Play of the Wether* (in) *The Chief Pre-Shakespearean Dramas*, ed. J. Q. Adams (Boston, 1924)
> See R. de la Bere, *John Heywood Entertainer* (London, 1937)
> R. C. Johnson, *John Heywood* (New York, 1970)

HILTON, WALTER (d. 1396): mystical writer; Augustinian canon of Thurgarton, nr Southwell, Notts; probably had degree in Canon Law; number of MSS of *Scale of Perfection* suggests one of most widely read English mystical works; first printed 1494 by Wynkyn de Worde at command of mother of Henry VII; four subsequent editions by 1533; very influential spiritual writer in late medieval England; shows knowledge of Rolle and of *Cloud of Unknowing*.

> *The Scale of Perfection*, mod. ed. E. Underhill (London, 1923); transl. G. Sitwell (London, 1955); excerpts in *The Mediaeval Mystics of England*, ed. E. Colledge (London, 1962)
> *The Goad of Love*, mod. ed. C. Kirchberger (London, 1952)
> *Minor Works*, ed. D. Jones (London, 1929)
> *Eight Chapters on Perfection*, ed. F. Kuriyagawa (Tokyo, 1967)
> See R. W. Chambers, *On the Continuity of English Prose* (E.E.T.S., 1932)
> P. J. Croft, in his *Lady Margaret Beaufort* (London, 1958)
> T. W. Coleman, *English Mystics of the Fourteenth Century* (London, 1938)
> M. Deanesly, 'Vernacular Books in England in the Fourteenth and Fifteenth Centuries', M.L.R. 15 (1920)
> H. L. Gardner, 'Hilton and the Mystical Tradition in England', E. & S. 22 (1936)
> P. Hodgson, *Three 14th-Century English Mystics* (London, 1967)
> A. C. Hughes, *Hilton's Directions to Contemplatives* (Rome, 1962)
> D. Knowles, *The English Mystical Tradition* (London, 1961)
> J. E. Milosh, *The Scale of Perfection and the English Mystical Tradition* (Madison, 1966)
> W. Riehle, *The Middle English Mystics* (London, 1981)
> J. Russell-Smith, 'Walter Hilton', in *Pre-Reformation English Spirituality*, ed. J. Walsh (London, 1965)
> G. Sitwell, 'Contemplation in *The Scale of Perfection*', *Downside Review*, 67–8 (1949–50)
> M. Thornton, *English Spirituality* (London, 1963)
> E. Underhill, *Mixed Pasture* (London, 1933)

HOCCLEVE, THOMAS (*c.* 1368–*c.* 1430): civil servant and poet; worked some thirty-five years in Office of Privy Seal; wrote poetry in spare time; problems of money and poor health figure in poetry; passages of apparent self-revelation, lively, direct.

> *Works*, ed. in E.E.T.S. (ed. F. J. Furnivall, 1892; ed. I. Gollancz, 1925; repr. 1970)
> *Selections from Hoccleve*, ed. M. C. Seymour (Oxford, 1981)

See H. S. Bennett, *Six Medieval Men and Women* (Cambridge, 1955)
P. B. R. Doob, *Nebuchadnezzar's Children* (New Haven, 1974)
J. Mitchell, *Thomas Hoccleve: A Study in Early Fifteenth Century English Poetic* (Urbana, 1968)

INTERLUDES (sixteenth century): term loosely applied to describe plays in first half of the sixteenth century which were not limited to abstract figures but also employed secular characters for secular diversions; though some interludes were anonymous, many were by known authors.

*Medieval Drama*, ed. D. Bevington (Boston, 1975)
*English Miracle Plays, Moralities and Interludes; Specimens of Pre-Elizabethan Drama*, ed. A. W. Pollard (repr. Oxford, 1972)
*Tudor Interludes*, ed. P. Happé (Penguin, 1972)
*English Moral Interludes*, ed. G. Wickham (London, 1976)
*Youth and Hickscorner*, ed. I. Lancashire (Manchester, 1980)
*John Skelton: Magnyfycence*, ed. P. Neuss (Manchester, 1979)
*Three Rastell Plays*, ed. R. Axton (Cambridge, 1979)
*The Plays of Henry Medwall*, ed. A. H. Nelson (Cambridge, 1980)

KING JAMES I of Scotland (1394–1437): detained in England from 1406; married Joan Beaufort, February 1424, and returned to Scotland; poem *The Kingis Quair* possibly written as St Valentine's Day poem, 1424. After struggling to impose order on his kingdom, James I was eventually murdered.

E. W. M. Balfour-Melville, *James I, King of Scots* (London, 1936)
*The Kingis Quair*, ed. J. Norton-Smith (Oxford, 1971)
*The Kingis Quair of James Stewart*, ed. M. P. McDiarmid (London, 1973)
See also Kratzmann (cited under Douglas)

JULIAN OF NORWICH (b. c. 1343; d. after 1413): mystical writer; recluse in cell attached to St Julian's Church, Norwich; during illness in May 1373 at age thirty, experienced revelations; twenty years later experienced further revelations illuminating earlier ones; two written versions of revelations; shorter version records original visions; fuller, later version embodies understanding of initial revelations gained over many subsequent years of contemplation.

*A Book of Showings to the Anchoress Julian of Norwich*, ed. E. Colledge and J. Walsh, 2 vols (Toronto, 1978)
*Julian of Norwich: A Revelation of Love*, ed. M. Glasscoe (Exeter, 1976)
*Julian of Norwich's Revelations of Divine Love, The Shorter Version*, ed. F. Beer (Heidelberg, 1978)
*Revelations of Divine Love* (longer version) tr. J. Walsh (London, 1973)
*A Shewing of Divine Love* (shorter version) tr. Sister A. M. Reynolds (London, 1958)
See C. Davis (ed.), *English Spiritual Writers* (London, 1961)
    D. Knowles, *The English Mystical Tradition* (London, 1961)
    P. Molinari, *Julian of Norwich: the Teaching of a Fourteenth Century English Mystic* (London, 1958)
    C. Pepler, *The English Religious Heritage* (London, 1958)
    A. M. Reynolds, in *Pre-Reformation English Spirituality*, ed. J. Walsh (London, 1965)
    W. Riehle, *The Middle English Mystics* (London, 1981)

R. K. Stone, *Middle English Prose Style: Margery Kempe and Julian of Norwich* (The Hague, 1970)

M. Thornton, *English Spirituality* (London, 1963)

E. I. Watkin, *Poets and Mystics* (London, 1953)

R. M. Wilson, 'Three Middle English Mystics', E. & S. 9 (1956)

B. A. Windeatt, 'Julian of Norwich and her Audience', R.E.S. n.s. 28 (1977)

B. A. Windeatt, 'The Art of Mystical Loving: Julian of Norwich', in *The Medieval Mystical Tradition in England*, ed. M. Glasscoe (Exeter, 1980)

KEMPE, MARGERY (*c.* 1373–*c.* 1439): mystic; autobiography gives vivid account of her tumultuous life; daughter of leading citizen of King's Lynn; married to another worthy *bourgeois*; underwent spiritual conversion after Christ appeared to her, restoring her reason during fit of insanity after birth of first child; has frequent visions and raptures; makes pilgrimages to Jerusalem, Rome, Compostela; travelled widely in England visiting churchmen and holy places; also visited Julian of Norwich; autobiography remarkable as human document and in suggesting late medieval life and religious feeling.

*The Book of Margery Kempe*, ed. H. E. Allen and S. B. Meech (E.E.T.S., 1940; 1961)

*The Book of Margery Kempe*, mod. ed. W. Butler-Bowdon (World's Classics, 1954)

See E. Colledge, in *Pre-Reformation English Spirituality*, ed. J. Walsh (London, 1965)

L. Collis, *The Apprentice Saint* (London, 1964)

J. C. Hirsh, 'Author and Scribe in *The Book of Margery Kempe*', M.A. 44 (1975), 145–50

D. Knowles, *The English Mystical Tradition* (London, 1961)

R. K. Stone, *Middle English Prose Style: Margery Kempe and Julian of Norwich* (The Hague, 1970)

M. Thornton, *Margery Kempe, An Example in the English Pastoral Tradition* (London, 1960)

E. I. Watkin, *Poets and Mystics* (London, 1953)

R. M. Wilson, 'Three Middle English Mystics', E. & S. 9 (1956)

LANGLAND, WILLIAM (b. *c.* 1330): poet; biography surmised from manuscript ascriptions and allusions within the poem *Piers Plowman*: the son (illegitimate?) of Stacy de Rokayle, a man of gentle birth holding land under the Despensers at Shipton-under-Wychwood, Oxon. Probably educated in monastery at Great Malvern, taking only Minor Orders, because of death of his patrons, and prevented from advancing in church. Perhaps led wandering life; knew London well, describes living with wife and daughter in cottage on Cornhill, making poor living by singing Office of Dead for wealthy patrons. Now accepted that one man wrote all three successive versions of *Piers*, the A, B, and C Texts.

*Piers Plowman in Three Parallel Texts*, ed. W. W. Skeat, 2 vols (Oxford, 1886; repr. 1954)

*Piers Plowman: The A Version*, ed. G. Kane (London, 1960)

*Piers Plowman: The B Version*, ed. G. Kane and E. T. Donaldson (London, 1975)

*Piers Plowman: An Edition of the C-text*, ed. D. Pearsall (London, 1978)

*The Vision of Piers Plowman: A Complete Edition of the B-Text*, ed. A. V. C. Schmidt (London, 1978)

*Piers Plowman* (selections from the C-text), ed. E. Salter and D. Pearsall (London, 1967)

*Piers Plowman, The Prologue and Passus I–VII of the B text*, ed. J. A. W. Bennett (Oxford, 1972)

*Piers the Ploughman*, transl. J. F. Goodridge (Penguin, 1959)

See D. Aers, *Piers Plowman and Christian Allegory* (London, 1975)

R. M. Ames, *The Fulfilment of the Scriptures: Abraham, Moses, and Piers* (Evanston, 1970)

A. Baldwin, *The Theme of Government in Piers Plowman* (Cambridge, 1981)

M. W. Bloomfield, *Piers Plowman as a Fourteenth-Century Apocalypse* (New Brunswick, 1962)

P. Cali, *Allegory and Vision in Dante and Langland* (Cork, 1971)

R. W. Chambers, *Man's Unconquerable Mind* (London, 1939), 88–171

E. T. Donaldson, *Piers Plowman: The C-Text and its Poet* (New Haven, 1949)

T. P. Dunning, *Piers Plowman: An Interpretation of the A-Text*, 2nd edn, rev. T. P. Dolan (Oxford, 1980)

R. W. Frank, *Piers Plowman and the Scheme of Salvation* (New Haven, 1957)

G. Kane, *Piers Plowman: The Evidence for Authorship* (London, 1965)

E. D. Kirk, *The Dream Thought of Piers Plowman* (New Haven, 1972)

J. Lawlor, *Piers Plowman. An Essay in Criticism* (London, 1962)

P. Martin, *The Field and the Tower* (London, 1979)

D. W. Robertson and B. F. Huppé, *Piers Plowman and Scriptural Tradition* (Princeton, 1951)

E. Salter, *Piers Plowman: An Introduction* (Oxford, 1962)

B. H. Smith, *Traditional Imagery of Charity in Piers Plowman* (The Hague and Paris, 1966)

A. C. Spearing, 'The Art of Preaching and *Piers Plowman*', in *Criticism and Medieval Poetry* (2nd edn, London, 1972)

E. Vasta, *The Spiritual Basis of Piers Plowman* (The Hague, 1965)

J. A. Yunck, *The Lineage of Lady Meed: The Development of Medieval Venality Satire* (Notre Dame, 1963)

*Collections of Critical Essays*

R. J. Blanch (ed.), *Style and Symbolism in Piers Plowman* (Knoxville, 1969)

S. S. Hussey (ed.), *Piers Plowman: Critical Approaches* (London, 1969)

E. Vasta (ed.), *Interpretations of Piers Plowman* (Notre Dame, 1968)

LAYAMON: Poet and priest who describes himself living on the banks of the Severn at King's Areley, Worcs., at start of his *Brut*, a history of Britain from its legendary founder Brutus; written in forceful semi-alliterative verse, with a relish for the heroic, martial, patriotic, and archaic; composed late twelfth or early thirteenth century, drawing on *Roman de Brut* by Anglo-Norman poet Wace; the first telling of Arthurian story – and of Lear story – in English.

*Brut*, ed. G. L. Brook and R. F. Leslie (E.E.T.S., 2 vols, 1963, 1978)

*Selections from Layamon's Brut*, ed. G. L. Brook (Oxford, 1963)

*Wace and Layamon: Arthurian Chronicles*, transl. selections (London, 1912; repr. 1977)

See D. Everett, *Essays on Middle English Literature* (Oxford, 1955)

R. S. Loomis (ed.), *Arthurian Literature in The Middle Ages* (Oxford, 1959)

J. S. P. Tatlock, *The Legendary History of Britain* (Berkeley, 1950)

LYDGATE, JOHN (*c.* 1370–*c.* 1450): poet; born Suffolk, admitted to Bury St Edmund's Abbey, *c.* 1385. Studied at Oxford; enjoyed patronage of Henry V and Humphrey, Duke of Gloucester; much of life passed outside cloister, retiring to Bury, *c.* 1434. Vast, uneven output of verse, reflecting range of fifteenth-century tastes and interests, includes: imitations of Chaucer, 'mummings', saint's lives (e.g. *Life of Our Lady*), translations and compilations (the *Troy Book*, *Fall of Princes*, *Pilgrimage of Life of Man*). Much interested in style, especially the polysyllabic 'aureate' diction.

*Poems* (selections), ed. J. Norton-Smith (Oxford, 1966)

*Minor Poems*, ed. H. N. MacCracken (E.E.T.S., 1910–33; repr. 1961)

E. P. Hammond, *English Verse between Chaucer and Surrey* (Durham, N.C., 1927; repr. New York, 1965)

See W. F. Schirmer, *John Lydgate: A Study in the Culture of the XVth Century* (1952: transl. London, 1961)

    A. Renoir, *The Poetry of John Lydgate* (London, 1967)

    D. Pearsall. *John Lydgate* (London, 1970)

LYNDSAY, SIR DAVID (*c.* 1485–*c.* 1555): poet; courtier of James IV of Scotland; supervised early education of James V (b. 1512), whom he later served as herald and ambassador; his work springs from court life (*Ane Satyre of the Thrie Estatis* developed from a royal entertainment) but draws on wider popular traditions of humour and satire.

W. Murison, *Sir David Lyndsay, Poet and Satirist of the Old Church of Scotland* (Cambridge, 1938)

*Works*, ed. D. Hamer (4 vols, S.T.S., 1931–6)

*Ane Satyre of the Thrie Estatis*, ed. J. Kinsley (London, 1954)

*Squyer Meldrum*, ed. J. Kinsley (London, 1959)

See J. S. Kantrowitz, *Dramatic Allegory: Lindsay's Ane Satyre of the Thrie Estatis* (U. of Nebraska Press, 1975)

See also Kratzmann, Lewis, Speirs (cited under Douglas)

MALORY, SIR THOMAS (d. 1471): author of *Le Morte D'Arthur*, which he finished March 1470; precise identity unclear, but probably son of John Malory who owned land at Newbold Revel, Warwickshire; in service of Earl of Warwick in French wars after 1414; by 1440 settled as country gentleman; knighted before 1442; M.P. 1445; after 1450 led lawless and desperate life; charged with various crimes of violence, rape, theft, extortion; much of life largely in prison, but escaped or released several times; *Morte* written during imprisonment; buried in Greyfriars' church, Newgate.

W. Matthews, *The Ill-framed Knight* (Berkeley, 1966)

*Works*, ed. E. Vinaver (3 vols, 2nd edn; Oxford, 1967); (1 vol. Oxford Standard Authors, 1971)

*Morte Darthur Parts Seven and Eight*, ed. D. S. Brewer (London, 1968)

*King Arthur and his Knights*, ed. R. T. Davies (London, 1967)

*Le Morte Darthur: The Seventh and Eighth Tales*, ed. P. J. C. Field (London, 1978)

See J. A. W. Bennett (ed.), *Essays on Malory* Oxford, 1963)

    L. D. Benson, *Malory's Morte Darthur* (Cambridge, Mass., 1976)

    R. T. Davies, 'The Worshipful Way in Malory', in *Patterns of Love and Courtesy*, ed. J. Lawlor (London, 1966)

    A. B. Ferguson, *The Indian Summer of English Chivalry* (Durham, N.C., 1960)

    P. J. C. Field, *Romance and Chronicle* (London, 1970)

S. Knight, *The Structure of Sir Thomas Malory's Arthuriad* (Sydney, 1968)

M. Lambert, *Malory: Style and Vision in Le Morte Darthur* (New Haven, 1975)

R. M. Lumiansky (ed.), *Malory's Originality* (Baltimore, 1964)

S. T. Miko, 'Malory and the chivalric order', M.A. 35 (1966), 211–30

T. Takamiya and D. Brewer (eds.), *Aspects of Malory* (Cambridge, 1981)

E. Vinaver, *Malory*, 2nd edn (Oxford, 1970)

MANDEVILLE'S TRAVELS (fourteenth century): guide-book for pilgrims travelling to Holy Land, and description of marvels of the Orient; unique mixture of information and entertainment; although presented as by 'Sir John Mandeville of St Albans' (a fictitious person), in fact a compilation first made in French (*c.* 1357); translated into English in later fourteenth century; vastly popular, translated into many languages.

Ed. P. Hamelius (E.E.T.S., 1919, 1923, repr. 1960–61)

Ed. M. C. Seymour (Oxford, 1967)

See J. W. Bennett, *The Rediscovery of Sir John Mandeville* (New York, 1954)

M. Letts, *Sir John Mandeville* (London, 1949)

C. K. Zacher, *Curiosity and Pilgrimage* (Baltimore, 1976)

ROBERT MANNYNG OF BRUNNE (fl. 1288–1338): poet; native of Bourne, Lincs.; probably spent some time at Cambridge where met Robert Bruce; belonged to Gilbertine priories, first at Sempringham, later at Sixhill, Lincs.; *Handlyng Synne* is a confessional manual for laymen interspersed with lively, realistic narrative *exempla*. Finished verse *Chronicle of England* 1338.

*Handlyng Synne*, ed. F. J. Furnivall (E.E.T.S., 119, 123, 1901–3)

See Ruth Crosby, 'Robert Mannyng of Brunne: A new Biography', *PMLA* 57 (1942)

D. W. Robertson, 'The cultural tradition of *Handlyng Synne*', *Speculum* 22 (1947)

MIRACLE OR MYSTERY PLAYS (in fifteenth-century MSS.): cycles existed in perhaps twelve towns; performance usually on Corpus Christi day; two plays survive from Coventry cycle, one from Norwich, one from Newcastle; several plays of *Abraham and Isaac* have not been localized; York, Chester, *N-town*, and Wakefield (Towneley) cycles almost completely preserved.

*English Mystery Plays*, ed. P. Happé (Penguin, 1975)

*Everyman and Mediaeval Plays*, ed. A. C. Cawley (London, 1953)

*Medieval Drama*, ed. D. Bevington (Boston and London, 1975)

*Ten Miracle Plays*, ed. R. G. Thomas (London, 1966)

*Non-Cycle Plays and Fragments*, ed. N. Davis (E.E.T.S., 1970)

*Chester Cycle:* twenty-four plays preserved; possibly derived from French originals; Whitsuntide not Corpus Christi plays; performed occasionally as late as 1575; more homogeneous than other cycles – possibly work of a single author who may have been the chronicler, Ranulph Higden.

Ed. R. M. Lumiansky and D. Mills (E.E.T.S., 1976)

See F. M. Salter, *Medieval Drama in Chester* (London, 1956)

*N-town* (probably East Anglian) *Cycle:* often called *Ludus Coventriae* because of mistaken seventeenth-century identification with Coventry plays;

plays given in instalments; cycle has forty-two sections; contains particularly full instructions for staging and performance; emphasis on Life of Mary.

    Ed. K. S. Block (E.E.T.S, 1922; 1960)
    Ed. R. T. Davies in *The Corpus Christi Play of the Middle Ages* (London, 1972)

*Towneley (Wakefield) Cycle:* thirty-two plays preserved; some plays in common with York Cycle; contains also five plays of much higher quality, including Noah and the Two Shepherds' plays.

    Ed. G. England and A. Pollard (E.E.T.S, E.S., 1897; 1952)
    *The Wakefield Pageants in the Towneley Cycle,* ed. A. C. Cawley (Manchester, 1958)
    *The Wakefield Mystery Plays,* transl. M. Rose (London, 1961)
    J. Gardner, *The Construction of the Wakefield Cycle* (Carbondale, 1974)

*York Cycle:* forty-eight plays preserved; performed as early as 1378 and as late as 1580; themes cover whole of Biblical history. Often considered, with Wakefield, the most dramatic in quality of the Mysteries.

    Ed. L. T. Smith (Oxford, 1885; repr. New York, 1960)
    Mod. edn J. S. Purvis (London, 1957)

MORALITIES (fourteenth–sixteenth-century): plays in which characters represent abstract qualities (e.g. Gluttony, Wisdom) or generalized types (e.g. Everyman); allegorical treatment of themes expounding religious or ethical lessons; abstract figures are given human and contemporary characteristics.

*Castle of Perseverance* (early fifteenth century): longest of English Moralities; describes man's life from birth to appearance at Seat of Judgement; played outdoors.

    Ed. M. Eccles, *The Macro Plays* (E.E.T.S., 1969)
    Ed. P. Happé, *Four Morality Plays* (Penguin, 1979)

*Mankynd* (late fifteenth century): written for popular stage; Mankind attacked by three rascals, Nowte, Newgyse and Nowadays who provide horse-play and low comedy; only morality motive in character of Mercy; performed in halls.

    Ed. M. Eccles (*Macro Plays,* above)
    Ed. G. A. Lester, *Three Late Medieval Morality Plays* (London, 1981)

*Wisdom* (c. 1460): describes how Wisdom, representing Christ, rescues Mind, Will and Understanding from enticement of Devil; possibly directed to a monastic audience.

    Ed. M. Eccles (*Macro Plays,* above)
    *Everyman* (c. 1500): ed. A. C. Cawley (Manchester, 1961)
    *The Pride of Life* (c. 1350?): ed. N. Davis, *Non-Cycle Plays and Fragments* (E.E.T.S., 1970)

MORE, SIR THOMAS (1478–1535): author, scholar, statesman; son of famous London lawyer; brought up in household of Archbishop Morton; Oxford; became lawyer; friend of Erasmus; M.P. 1503–4; from 1516 prominent at court; present at Field of Cloth of Gold 1520; undertook many diplomatic missions; Lord Chancellor 1529; refused to take oath accepting royal supremacy over the church; confined in Tower and executed.

*Lives of St Thomas More by William Roper and Nicholas Harpsfield*, ed. E. E. Reynolds (London, 1963)

*English Works*, ed. W. E. Campbell and A. W. Reed (2 vols., London, 1931; repr. Menston, 1978)

*Works* (The Yale Edition): vol. 2, *The History of King Richard III*, ed. R. S. Sylvester (New Haven, 1964); vol. 3, *Translations of Lucian*, ed. C. R. Thompson (New Haven, 1974); vol. 4, *Utopia*, ed. E. Surtz and J. Hexter (New Haven, 1965); vol. 12, *A Dialogue of Comfort*, ed. L. L. Martz and F. Manley (New Haven, 1976).

*Selected Letters*, ed. E. F. Rogers (New Haven, 1976). *Utopia*, transl. P. Turner (Penguin, 1965)

See R. W. Chambers, *Thomas More* (London, 1935)

    J. C. Davis, *Utopia and the Ideal Society: English Utopian Writing 1516–1700* (Cambridge, 1981)

    J. Guy, *The Public Career of Sir Thomas More* (Brighton, 1980)

    J. H. Hexter, *More's Utopia: The Biography of an Idea* (Princeton, 1952)

    R. S. Johnson, *More's Utopia: Ideal and Illusion* (New Haven, 1972)

    C. S. Lewis, *English Literature in the Sixteenth Century* (*Excluding Drama*), (Oxford, 1954)

    H. A. Mason, *Humanism and Poetry in the Early Tudor Period* (London, 1959)

    R. J. Schoeck, *The Achievement of Thomas More* (Victoria, 1976)

    E. Surtz, *The Praise of Pleasure: Philosophy – Education – Communism in More's Utopia* (Harvard, 1957).

    E. Surtz, *The Praise of Wisdom: A Commentary on the Religious and Moral Backgrounds of St Thomas More's Utopia* (Chicago, 1957)

    R. S. Sylvester (ed.), *St Thomas More: Contemplation and Action* (New Haven, 1972)

    R. S. Sylvester and G. Marc'hadour, *Essential Articles: Thomas More* (Hamden, Conn., 1977)

THE OWL AND THE NIGHTINGALE (*c.* 1189–1216): vigorous, poised, witty debate-poem of the Earlier Middle English period; learned in allusion, sophisticatedly graceful in literary technique; references in poem suggest written after death of Henry II (1189), by Master Nicholas of Guildford; poem possibly a plea for ecclesiastical preferment.

    Ed. both texts and transl., J. W. H. Atkins (Cambridge, 1932)

    Ed. J. H. Grattan and G. F. Sykes (E.E.T.S., 1935)

    Ed. E. G. Stanley (London, 1960)

    Mod. trans. Brian Stone (Penguin, 1971)

    See J. W. H. Atkins, *English Literary Criticism: The Medieval Phase* (Cambridge, 1943; repr. New York, 1967)

    K. Hume, *The Owl and the Nightingale: The Poem and its Critics* (Toronto, 1975)

    R. M. Wilson, *Early Middle English Literature* (London, 1939; 1968)

PASTONS (*c.* 1420–*c.* 1500): remarkable letter-writers; well-to-do Norfolk family; their letters to each other on practical and pressing matters give detailed picture of lives of three generations; description of middle-class society, preoccupied with money-matters, leases, management of property and lawsuits in fifteenth century provincial life; much information too on domestic life and issues. Male writers usually write themselves; the women dictate.

*Paston Letters*, ed. J. Gairdner (6 vols, London, 1904; New York, 1967)

*Paston Letters and Papers of the Fifteenth Century*, ed. N. Davis (2 vols; Oxford, 1971, 1976)

*Paston Letters* (selections), ed. N. Davis (Oxford, 1958)

See H. S. Bennett, *The Pastons and their England* (Cambridge, 1922; 1968)

    N. Davis, 'The Language of the Pastons', P.B.A. (1954)

    Virginia Woolf, 'The Pastons and Chaucer', in *The Common Reader* (1925)

RICHARD ROLLE OF HAMPOLE (*c.* 1300–49); mystical writer and hermit; b. Thornton-le-Dale, Yorks.; studied at Oxford but left at nineteen for spiritual reasons; ran away from home to become hermit, in makeshift habit cut from father's rainhood and sisters' frocks; settled as hermit under protection of Dalton family and composed early works; later moved cell to become spiritual director of Cistercian nuns at Hampole, who after his death (probably of plague) compiled an office in hope of his canonization, recording many of his miracles; although never canonized he was regarded as a saint till Reformation. Author of influential diversity of writing in Latin and English, prose and verse, often alliterative.

*Writings Ascribed to Richard Rolle, Hermit of Hampole, and Materials for his Biography*, H. E. Allen (New York, 1927)

*English Writings of Richard Rolle*, ed. H. E. Allen (Oxford, 1931)

*Yorkshire Writers: Richard Rolle of Hampole and His Followers*, ed. C. Horstmann (2 vols; London, 1895; repr. Cambridge, 1979).

*Incendium Amoris*, ed. M. Deanesly (Manchester, 1915); transl. as *The Fire of Love*, by C. Wolters (Penguin, 1972)

*Melos Amoris*, ed. E. J. F. Arnould (Oxford, 1957)

See T. W. Coleman, *English Mystics of the Fourteenth Century* (London, 1938)

    F. M. M. Comper, *The Life and Lyrics of Richard Rolle* (London, 1927)

    C. Davis (ed.), *English Spiritual Writers* (London, 1961)

    D. Knowles, *The English Mystical Tradition* (London, 1961)

    C. Pepler, *The English Religious Heritage* (London, 1958)

    W. Riehle, *the Middle English Mystics* (London, 1981)

    M. Thornton, *English Spirituality* (London, 1963)

    R. M. Wilson, 'Three Middle English Mystics', E. & S. 9 (1956)

    R. Woolf, *The English Religious Lyric in the Middle Ages* (Oxford, 1968)

SKELTON, JOHN (*c.* 1460–1529): poet, scholar, priest; Cambridge; poet laureate 1489; took holy orders; tutor to young Prince Henry, later Henry VIII; described by Caxton as humanist scholar; verse-structure characteristic of fifteenth century but satiric quality anticipates Reformation period.

H. L. R. Edwards, *Skelton; The life and times of an early Tudor poet* (London, 1949)

*Poems*, ed. V. J. Scattergood (Penguin, 1983)

*Poems* (selections), ed. R. S. Kinsman (Oxford, 1969)

*Complete Poems* (mod. edn), ed. P. Henderson (London, 1931; 4th edn, 1964)

See S. E. Fish, *John Skelton's Poetry* (New Haven, 1965)

    W. O. Harris, *Skelton's Magnyfycence and the Cardinal Virtue Tradition* (Chapel Hill, 1965)

    A. R. Heiserman, *Skelton and Satire* (Chicago, 1961)

    W. Nelson, *John Skelton, Laureate* (London, 1939; New York, 1964)

    M. Pollett, *John Skelton* (Paris, 1962; transl. London, 1971)

SURREY, HENRY HOWARD, EARL OF (1518–47): brilliant, tumultuous career as poet, scholar, soldier, courtier; much of childhood spent at Windsor with Duke of Richmond, natural son of Henry VIII; several times imprisoned, once for striking, once for challenging another courtier. Imprisoned 1543 for riotous behaviour in London streets. Yet also saw military action. Beheaded on trumped up charges of treason. Much of his important poetic work was translation or adaptation; his important inventions were in metre, syntax, and diction, with use of sonnet, blank verse, poulter's measure.

> E. Casady, *Henry Howard, Earl of Surrey* (New York, 1938)
>
> H. W. Chapman, *Two Tudor Portraits* (London, 1960)
>
> *Poems*, ed. F. M. Padelford (rev. edn, Seattle, 1928)
>
> *Poems*, ed. E. Jones (Oxford, 1964)
>
> *Aeneid*, ed. F. H. Ridley (Berkeley, 1963)
>
> See C. S. Lewis, *English Literature in the Sixteenth Century (Excluding Drama)* (Oxford, 1954)
>
> See also Mason (cited under Wyatt)

TREVISA, JOHN (d. 1402): translator, scholar, priest; b. Cornwall; contemporary of Wycliffe at Oxford; expelled 1379 probably because of Wycliffite leanings; most subsequent life as vicar of Berkeley, Gloucs.; important translations made at command of Thomas, Lord Berkeley.

> Life in *John Trevisa Dialogus etc.*, ed. A. J. Perry (E.E.T.S., 1925)
>
> *On the Properties of Things*, ed. M. C. Seymour *et al.* (Oxford, 1975)
>
> *Polychronicon* (transl. from R. Higden), ed. C. Babington and J. R. Lumby (9 vols, Rolls Series, London, 1865–86)

WYATT, SIR THOMAS (1503–42): poet and diplomat: son of Sir Henry Wyatt; distinguished but precarious career at court; on diplomatic missions to France, Italy and Spain; introduced Petrarchan sonnet into English verse; imprisoned 1536 at time of Anne Boleyn's downfall, and again in 1541 after his patron, Thomas Cromwell, was executed; the satires, expressing disillusionment with the courtier's life, and the translation of the Penitential Psalms probably belong to the periods when he was out of favour; it was not long on either occasion before he was re-employed by the King, and he died of a fever at Sherborne on his way to welcome a Spanish envoy.

> *Sir Thomas Wyatt: The Complete Poems*, ed. R. A. Rebholz (Penguin, 1978)
>
> *Sir Thomas Wyatt: Collected Poems*, ed. J. Daalder (Oxford Standard Authors, 1975)
>
> *Collected Poems of Sir Thomas Wyatt*, ed. K. Muir and P. Thomson (Liverpool, 1969)
>
> *The Poems of Sir Thomas Wiat*, ed. A. K. Foxwell 2 vols, (London, 1913; repr. New York, 1964)
>
> K. Muir, *Life and Letters of Sir Thomas Wyatt* (Liverpool, 1963)
>
> See P. Thomson, *Sir Thomas Wyatt and his Background* (London, 1964)
>
> H. A. Mason, *Humanism and Poetry in the Early Tudor Period* (London, 1959)
>
> R. Southall, *The Courtly Maker* (Oxford, 1964)
>
> J. Stevens, *Music and Poetry in the Early Tudor Court* (Cambridge, 1961)

WYCLIFFE, JOHN (*c.* 1328–84): priest, ecclesiastical reformer and writer: b. Yorkshire; Oxford *c.* 1345; Master of Balliol, 1360; rector of Fillingham, 1361; rector of Ludgershall, 1368; Doctor of Theology, 1372; rector of Lutterworth,

Leicestershire, from 1374; inspired initiation of English version of Bible; attacked church endowments and denied right of Church to interfere with secular matters; attacked doctrine of transubstantiation *c.* 1379 and was publicly condemned in Oxford, 1380; spent rest of life in Lutterworth and spread doctrines among people through 'poor preachers'.

*English Works*, ed. F. D. Matthew (E.E.T.S., 1880)

*Select English Works*, ed. H. E. Winn (London, 1929)

*The Wycliffite Bible*, ed. J. Forshall and F. Madden (4 vols, Oxford, 1850)

*Selections from English Wycliffite Writings*, ed. A. Hudson (Cambridge, 1978)

*Jack Upland, Friar Daw's Reply and Upland's Rejoinder*, ed. P. L. Heyworth (Oxford, 1968)

See M. Deanesly, *The Lollard Bible* (Cambridge, 1920)

    D. C. Fowler, *The Bible in Early English Literature* (London, 1977), ch. 4

    S. L. Fristedt, *The Wycliffe Bible* (Stockholm, 1953)

    P. A. Knapp, *The Style of John Wycliffe's English Bible* (Hague, 1977)

    K. B. MacFarlane, *Wycliffe and the Beginnings of English Nonconformity* (London, 1952; 1972)

    J. A. Robson, *Wyclif and the Oxford Schools* (Oxford, 1961)

# NOTES ON CONTRIBUTORS

RICHARD AXTON Fellow of Christ's College and Lecturer in English, in the University of Cambridge. A Director of The Medieval Players, Ltd. Author of *European Drama of the Early Middle Ages* (1974), translator (with John Stevens) of *Medieval French Plays* (1971), editor of *Three Rastell Plays* (1979) and General Editor (with Marie Axton) of a new *Tudor Interludes* series of play texts.

DOMINIC BAKER-SMITH Professor of English Literature at the University of Amsterdam. Formerly Professor of English at University College, Cardiff. Has served as Chairman of the Society for Renaissance Studies.

IAN BISHOP Senior Lecturer in English, University of Bristol. Author of *'Pearl' in its Setting* (1968) and *Chaucer's 'Troilus and Criseyde': A Critical Study* (1981).

DEREK BREWER Master of Emmanuel College and Reader in Medieval English, in the University of Cambridge. Author of *Chaucer* (3rd edn, 1974), *Chaucer and his World* (1978), *Symbolic Stories* (1980), etc.

J. A. BURROW Winterstoke Professor of English, University of Bristol. Author of *A Reading of 'Sir Gawain and the Green Knight'* (1965); *Ricardian Poetry: Chaucer, Gower, Langland and the Gawain Poet* (1971), *English Verse 1300–1500* (1977). Forthcoming: *Middle English Literature: An Introduction*.

PATRICK CRUTTWELL Emeritus Professor of English, Carleton University, Ottawa. Author of *The English Sonnet* (1966) and *The Shakespearian Moment and its Place in Poetry in the 17th Century* (1970).

T. P. DOLAN Lecturer, Department of Old and Middle English, University College, Dublin. Co-editor of Poole's *Glossary of the Old Dialect of the English Colony in the Baronies of Forth and Bargy, County of Wexford* (1979); revised and edited *Piers Plowman: An Interpretation of the A Text*, by T. P. Dunning (2nd edn, 1980).

D. W. HARDING Emeritus Professor of Psychology in the University of London. Author of *Experience into Words: Essays on Poetry* (1963), *Words into Rhythm: English speech rhythms in verse and prose* (1976), etc.

DAVID HOLBROOK Fellow and Director of English Studies at Downing College, in the University of Cambridge. His recent works include *Lost Bearings in English Poetry* (1977); *English for Meaning* (1980), and *Selected Poems* (1980).

JILL MANN Fellow of Girton College and Lecturer in English, in the University of Cambridge. Author of *Chaucer and Medieval Estates Satire* (1973), and 'Taking the Adventure: Malory and the *Suite du Merlin*', in *Aspects of Malory* (1981).

DEREK PEARSALL Professor of English at the University of York, and Co-Director of the Centre for Medieval Studies; author of *John Lydgate* (1970) and (with Elizabeth Salter) of *Landscapes and Seasons of the Medieval World* (1973); editor of the C Text of *Piers Plowman* (1978).

IAN ROBINSON Senior Lecturer in English Language and Literature, University College of Swansea, and Director of The Brynmill Press Ltd. Best-known publications *The Survival of English* (1973) and *The New Grammarians' Funeral* (1975).

V. J. SCATTERGOOD Professor of Medieval and Renaissance English at Trinity College, Dublin. Author of *Politics and Poetry in the Fifteenth Century* (1971) and *The Works of Sir John Clanvowe* (1975); editor of *The English Poems of John Skelton* (1982).

A. C. SPEARING Fellow of Queens' College and Lecturer in English, in the University of Cambridge. Author of *Criticism and Medieval Poetry* (1972), *The Gawain-Poet* (1971) and *Medieval Dream-Poetry* (1976).

JOHN SPEIRS Died 1979. Was Reader in English, University of Exeter: the University conferred a Litt. D. (not officially received owing to his death). Author of *The Scots Literary Tradition* (1940), *Chaucer the Maker* (1951), *Medieval English Poetry, the Non-Chaucerian Tradition* (1957), and *Poetry towards Novel* (1971).

JOHN STEVENS Professor of Medieval and Renaissance English in the University of Cambridge. His publications include *Music and Poetry in the Early Tudor Court* (1979) and three editions of medieval and early Tudor songs in the series *Musica Britannica*. In 1980 he was appointed C.B.E. 'for services to musicology'.

DEREK TRAVERSI Professor Emeritus, Swarthmore College, Pennsylvania, U.S.A. Successively British Council Representative in Uruguay, Chile, Iran, Spain and Italy (1948–70). Author of *An Approach to Shakespeare* (1938, 1956, 1968), *T. S. Eliot: the Longer Poems* (1976), and *The Literary Imagination: Studies in Dante, Chaucer, and Shakespeare* (in the press).

THORLAC TURVILLE-PETRE Lecturer in English Studies at the University of Nottingham. Author of *The Alliterative Revival* (1977), and articles on fourteenth-century poetry.

BARRY WINDEATT Fellow and Director of Studies in English at Emmanuel College, in the University of Cambridge. Author of articles on Chaucer and other mediaeval literature.

# INDEX

## MORE ABOUT PENGUINS
## AND PELICANS

For further information about books available from Penguins please write to Dept EP, Penguin Books Ltd, Harmondsworth, Middlesex UB7 ODA.

*In the U.S.A.:* For a complete list of books available from Penguins in the United States write to Dept CS, Penguin Books, 625 Madison Avenue, New York, New York 10022.

*In Canada:* For a complete list of books available from Penguins in Canada write to Penguin Books Canada Ltd, 2801 John Street, Markham, Ontario L3R 1B4.

*In Australia:* For a complete list of books available from Penguins in Australia write to the Marketing Department, Penguin Books Australia Ltd, P.O. Box 257, Ringwood, Victoria 3134.

*In New Zealand:* For a complete list of books available from Penguins in New Zealand write to the Marketing Department, Penguin Books (N.Z.) Ltd, P.O. Box 4019, Auckland 10.

## THE NEW PELICAN GUIDE TO
## ENGLISH LITERATURE
### EDITED BY BORIS FORD

Authoritative, stimulating and accessible, the original seven-volume *Pelican Guide to English Literature* has earned itself a distinguished reputation. Now enlarged to nine titles this popular series has been wholly revised and updated.

What this work sets out to offer is a guide to the history and traditions of English literature, a contour-map of the literary scene. Each volume includes these standard features:

  (i) An account of the social context of literature in each period.
 (ii) A general survey of the literature itself.
(iii) A series of critical essays on individual writers and their works – each written by an authority in their field.
(iv) Full appendices including short author biographies, listings of standard editions of authors' works, critical commentaries and titles for further study and reference.

The *Guide* consists of the following volumes:

  1. Medieval Literature:
     Part One: Chaucer and the Alliterative Tradition
     Part Two: The European Inheritance
  2. The Age of Shakespeare
  3. From Donne to Marvell
  4. From Dryden to Johnson
  5. From Blake to Byron
  6. From Dickens to Hardy
  7. From James to Eliot
  8. The Present

# PENGUIN CLASSICS

## THE EARLIEST ENGLISH POEMS

*Translated by Michael Alexander*

As a literary language Anglo-Saxon seemingly died after the Norman Conquest; in the mouths of ordinary people, however, it survived to become the tap-root of the language we speak.

Preserving the original metre and alliteration Michael Alexander has translated the best Anglo-Saxon poetry into modern English. In addition to passages from *Beowulf*, this anthology includes, amongst other poems, *Widsith, Deor, The Wanderer, The Seafarer*, and *The Battle of Maldon*. Together these fairly represent a body of alliterative poetry which, at its best, moves with a sad and stately nobility of its own.

## BEOWULF

*Translated by Michael Alexander*

*Beowulf* is the most important Old English poem and perhaps the most significant single survival from the Anglo-Saxon period. Though its composition was completed in England in the eighth century, the poem is set in the heroic societies of a fifth-century Scandinavia.

We have here something more than merely a heroic poem of historical interest: *Beowulf* has a truly epic quality and scope, and this new verse translation successfully communicates this poem's artistry and eloquence.

# PENGUIN CLASSICS

### THE EXETER BOOK RIDDLES

*Translated by Kevin Crossley-Holland*

When Leofric, first Bishop of Exeter, died in 1072, he bequeathed to the Cathedral library the *Codex Exoniensis*, or *Exeter Book*. Only four great miscellanies of Old English poetry now survive, and this is one of them.

As well as being poems of great charm, zest, and often subtlety, the ninety-six riddles in the *Exeter Book* constitute a delightful and informative introduction to the Anglo-Saxon world. On topics ranging from natural phenomena to animal and bird life, from the Christian concept of the creation to prosaic domestic objects, from weaponry to the peaceful pursuits of music and writing, the riddles are full of sharp observation, earthy humour, and, above all, a sense of wonder.

The main text of this volume contains seventy-five riddles – all those that are not very badly damaged or impenetrably obscure – and a further sixteen are translated in the notes. Possible solutions are given for all of them.

### THE QUEST OF THE HOLY GRAIL

*Translated by P. M. Matarasso*

The bright and colourful world of Arthurian Romance lends itself to medieval allegory in *The Quest of the Holy Grail*. The varied and often dangerous peregrinations and encounters of Arthur's knights in their search for the Holy Grail symbolize man's equally perilous search for the Grace of God. These chivalrous adventures sweeten the author's didactic pill, and the fusion of Christian symbolism and Celtic legend gives a mystical aura and tragic grandeur to the whole. The *Quest* is in fact a renunciation of the courtly ideals of the Romances sung by the early troubadours.

# PENGUIN CLASSICS

## CHAUCER

*Translated by Nevill Coghill*

### TROILUS AND CRISEYDE

During the great siege of Troy, quizzing the girls in the temple, Troilus sees Criseyde and falls in love with her. Later, with the help of Pandarus, the first great comic character of English literature, Troilus wins Criseyde's love and this is the beginning of his real joy, just as later it is to cause his sorrow and death.

*Troilus and Criseyde* (c. 1380–85) is both comedy and tragedy. Nevill Coghill counts himself among those who believe it to be the most beautiful long poem in the English language. In it Chaucer 'meditates on the nature of love as it enraptures and afflicts us in this sublunary world'.

### THE CANTERBURY TALES

*The Canterbury Tales* stands conspicuous among the great literary achievements of the Middle Ages. Told by a jovial procession of pilgrims – knight, priest, yeoman, miller, or cook – as they ride towards the shrine of Thomas à Becket, they present a picture of a nation taking shape. The tone of this never-resting comedy is, by turns, learned, fantastic, lewd, pious, and ludicrous. 'Here', as John Dryden said, 'is God's plenty!'

Geoffrey Chaucer began his great task in about 1386. This version in modern English, by Nevill Coghill, preserves the freshness and racy vitality of Chaucer's narrative.

# PENGUIN CLASSICS

## LANGLAND

### PIERS THE PLOUGHMAN

*Translated by J. F. Goodridge*

*Piers the Ploughman*, the work of an unknown minor cleric of the late fourteenth century, was perhaps the most widely read work of its day and is now recognized as the great representative English poem of the late Middle Ages. While it offers a vivid picture of fourteenth-century life and is placed firmly in the world of every day, its theme is the pilgrimage of man's soul in search of ultimate truth. Alone among English poets, Langland combines satirical comedy with a rare power of prophecy and vision.

### SIR GAWAIN AND THE GREEN KNIGHT

*Translated by Brian Stone*

*Sir Gawain and the Green Knight* is the masterpiece of medieval alliterative poetry. The unknown fourteenth-century author (a contemporary of Chaucer) has imbued his work with the heroic atmosphere of a saga, with the spirit of French romance, and with a Christian consciousness. It is a poem in which the virtues of a knight, Sir Gawain, triumphant in almost insuperable ordeals, are celebrated to the glory of the House of Arthur. The impact made on the reader is both magical and human, full of drama and descriptive beauty.

# PENGUIN CLASSICS

## MEDIEVAL ENGLISH VERSE

*Translated by Brian Stone*

This is an anthology of modern verse translations of English poetry of the thirteenth and fourteenth centuries. In a very full selection about half the space is devoted to short poems, including religious and secular lyrics as well as moral, political, polemical, and comic verse. The other half contains short narrative poems, and of these 'Pearl', the longest and most important, ranks among the finest elegies in English. In addition to 'Patience', a minor epic, and 'Sir Orfeo', defined as a Breton lay, the collection includes a rollicking example of medieval bawdry, 'Dame Siriz and the Weeping Bitch'.

## THE OWL AND THE NIGHTINGALE
## CLEANNESS
## ST ERKENWALD

*Translated by Brian Stone*

The Middle English poems in this book exemplify three major genres in medieval religious writing: saint's legend, Bible epic and religious debate. *St Erkenwald*, perhaps the best saint's legend in English poetry, tells how a bishop of London raised a pagan judge from the dead and sent his soul to heaven. In *Cleanness* (often known as *Purity*) such events as the Flood, the destruction of Sodom and Gomorrah and Belshazzar's feast are recounted with the descriptive eloquence of the poet who wrote *Sir Gawain and the Green Knight*. *The Owl and the Nightingale* is a charming, if occasionally virulent, contest between two birds who debate, owl-wise and nightingale-wise, the traditional morals of the church and the ideals of courtly love.